The Long War Series

PERSIA RISING

By

Mark Langford

I0653280

Published by Mark Langford

ISBN   978-0-615-52031-5

Join the discussion at www.persiarising.com and on Facebook.

This book is dedicated to all the brave and selfless men and women of the American armed forces and law enforcement. To those vigilant few who bar the gates against the wolf and protect our loved ones at home, and those courageous young who crawl through hell to seek out and slay the dragon in its very lair.

May God bless you and keep you safe until you return to your loved ones safe and whole.

To Melissa, my wife, mi corazón. You have my deepest love and respect. You keep me true and sane (mostly). Thank you for your guidance, wisdom, and love. This story would be nothing but for you.

Acknowledgements

Although *Persia Rising* uses many true historical references, the story is entirely a work of fiction. However, everything within the story could happen tomorrow. I would like to thank a few people in my life and career who taught me much and made this novel possible.

James Casias – An honest heart and compassion go a long way.
Jess Gibson – You were a hard-ass and I was an asshole. Good times.
Greg Feinman – Friends are hard to find.
Clint Smith – One of the wisest men I ever met.
Dave Grossman – Thanks for everything you do, brother. Hunt the wolf!

Father – I am the man I am by your guidance, thank you.

PREFACE

THE REASON I write this story is buried deep inside the emotion of fear. My fear drove me to ask myself: What story would future investigators piece together if my worst suspicions are realized by the United States being attacked and destroyed? I then went to my police training and began to answer the six basic questions with this story. Who? When? What? Where? Why? How?

My fear started on September 11, 2001. I was working graveyard shift at the police department and had gotten off at 3:00 a.m. I woke up midmorning, started the coffee and began flipping channels on television. I didn't know it at the time but the first tower had just fallen. Seconds later I was catapulted into the reality everyone else was already in, 9/11. I have never returned to the person I was before that day. I changed inside forever and I think America did as well.

I don't think you and I are very different. The shock and horror of what happened was devastating – so much so that I still feel it fresh every time I think about it and most people I speak with feel the same. I know the whole post-9/11 thing has buried much of the intensity of that day under the last ten years of societal controversy and wrangling. Time passes and the emotional distance increases between that day and the 'now' of our personal lives and its daily minutiae. The poignant memory of the catastrophe seems to get clouded and obscured by the political pros and cons that have followed, bringing us the War on Terror.

But when stirred, I find that the emotional depth and psychological impact of that day is not just raw, but persistent inside us, every day. I think it's analogous to the static left from the Big Bang. It will be with us forever. I know it is with me.

I lost my father in 2008 after a long physical deterioration due to COPD (Chronic Obstructive Pulmonary Disease). COPD describes several different types of symptoms that affect a person's body but it always ends the same – with the lungs slowly but inevitably losing the ability to transfer oxygen into the blood stream. He wasted away, his body being ever-so-slowly suffocated to death by his failing lungs. The various organs of his body just started to die from lack of oxygen and they eventually shut down, one by one. His loss is tragic to me and my family, but death is a natural thing that we know comes to each of us in our own way none-the-less. Like it's been said: no one gets out of this alive.

The pain of losing the most important man I have ever known has been very harsh. But in a way it is less hurtful to me than the pain of 9/11.

After a great deal of thought and introspection I think I know why I feel that way. My father's death happened and now it's over, a natural part of life, a singular natural event in history that is gone, never to be experienced by me or my family again. Whereas 9/11, a mass slaughter of American civilians, is not a singular event to history, and we all know it. It has happened before on smaller scales and I believe it is going to happen again, and again, and again, and…. it's just a matter of when and how bad it is going to be, when more Americans are murdered in massive numbers.

I have watched myself and my countrymen over the past decade go through their own 'stages of grief' while recovering from 9/11, but when you go just a tiny bit deeper under the emotional surface a bitter anger still smolders, along with a real fear of a repeat attack on the same scale. The seething collective fury of millions of Americans watching those jumpers on 9/11 plummeting to the concrete, seeing the fireballs of the planes filled with innocent passengers impacting the Twin Towers, the sinking dark clouds of dust, pylons, girders; a moment when we understood that our fellow Americans were dying by being ground into dust as the buildings came crumbling down onto the streets of Manhattan.

Universally, a very human primal scream went through the minds of most Americans that said: "We will make those responsible pay for this! This cannot be allowed to happen again!"

As I complete this novel UBL (Usama bin Laden) has been eliminated by our military, found inside an expensive and large compound a stone's throw from the Pakistani version of West Point. Things that make you go, hmm?

I ask myself, is the Egyptian, Zawahiri, alive and loose? Yes. Does Al Qaida, the Taliban, and the Haqqani network still exist, intact, dangerous, capable, and growing? Yes. Yes. Yes! Has the threat of global terrorism increased or decreased? It's increased. Has placation of the Islamic world gotten us more love or respect in the region? No. Did removing Saddam stop the possibility of weapons of mass-destruction from being used by terrorists against America? No. Is our enemy poking and prodding at our defenses practically every day, plotting, scheming, planning, formulating, recruiting, and actually acting out more terrorist attacks on United States soil? Yes. Is Iran going to be allowed by us and the United Nations to get nuclear capability? Yes. Is America safer? No.

So, have we made ourselves a world that will never allow another 9/11? No. Under these conditions, and using these tactics, are we going to repeatedly suffer through one major attack after another here on our soil? Yes. Is it going to be bad? Yes. Has a decade of our efforts in time, treasure, blood, sweat, and political will made the situation better for us or made our country safer?

No and no.

I am not offering a discussion. I am just saying how I feel. If you honestly see different answers to the questions I pose, I truly do not understand you, and to a certain extent I fear you. I'm not brilliant nor am I particularly clever, but my vision and mind are clear. I believe that understanding human relations and human nature, even on a global scale, boils down to very simple things. I also believe that finding answers to problems arising from human relations are not difficult, either. It is the will to act in the solving of those problems that poses the difficulty.

What experience has taught me is that most people will very often avoid implementing the answers to their human-relation problems because of a lack of moral, emotional, or intellectual courage to act, not because they truly do not see the solution to the issue. It is very often a form of risk-conflict aversion that motivates their actions. With regards to 9/11, I believe that as a country and a culture, we have refused to act upon the answers that would give us security because of our human desire to avoid living with the hard but simple choices that will gain us actual security. That is a jagged emotional pill we still refuse to swallow.

I'm a simple man, a retired cop who had a fairly uneventful career, said 'to hell with it' when I had enough and walked away after seventeen years. I no longer try, with futility, to babysit grown people, to prevent them from doing stupid things, or try to make the system do what is right when all it wants to do is nothing or even what's blatantly wrong. I'm a pretty average guy who is pissed off about 9/11 and flabbergasted that we are in this position of weakness and vulnerability, almost a decade later.

We have the most powerful, best-equipped, most motivated, most professional, best-trained, outstanding military to ever exist on this planet. It is manned by volunteers who are the greatest men and women this country has ever produced; the smartest, bravest, healthiest, and most patriotic group of people to ever to put on the uniforms of this nation. I say categorically: I believe these military volunteers are equal to or even surpass those volunteers of the Revolution, Civil War, and even our 'greatest generation' of WWII with love of country and patriotism! They are our future and we are blessed for that. I am in awe of their sacrifice and the sacrifice of their loved ones. These warriors are the ones who walk the dust, dirt, and blood of every shithole place on this planet with the courage to engage our enemies in deadly combat and win. While they battle this deadly foe their families try to sleep at night and carry on through multiple deployments, knowing their loved ones are out there walking the line and facing down the dragon. God bless them all.

But after all their sacrifice and loss in the ten-plus years of the War on Terror – What has all of that really achieved for our nation's safety and security against another 9/11, or something far worse? Sadly, it had achieved nothing at all. Not one damn thing. And really, deep inside, every single one of us knows it. If it has really achieved anything at all, I personally believe it has shown our enemies that the supposed 'Great Satan' can shoot our wad uselessly, and when spent, lick our wounds in denial and self-effacing rhetoric until our enemies can kick us in the nuts once again.

With our nation's technical and tactical expertise and military capability unsurpassed, why is our nation still so vulnerable to attack and harm? No legitimate answer exists to this question.

I have heard since day-one after 9/11 that this war can never have a victory like the surrender we got out of Hitler's Germany or the Japanese on the deck of the USS Missouri. The paradigm is too different. It just isn't possible. People say our victory in the War on Terror will be a 'matter of perspective' and difficult to quantify. Well, for their part, our enemies don't believe that bullshit for one goddamn second, and, for my part, I know it's bullshit too.

Like most Americans, I really didn't know that much about Islam before 9/11, other than it was a major religion and a lot of people in the Middle East practiced it. After watching endless hours of the Disney movie, Aladdin, with my step-son I knew far more about Jafar, Jasmine, Apu, and Aladdin than I did Muslims themselves. Forget about details like Sunni, Shia, Sufi, Pashtu, Tajik, Muhammad, Mecca, Medina, the hadith and so on.

I'm no expert and I never will be, nor do I purport to be. But I am now no longer completely ignorant and I have learned quite a bit more about Muslims and our jihadist enemies, and one of those things I have learned is that Muslim, and enemy, are not synonymous.

Until April 2008, when the Report of the Commission to Assess the Threat to the United States from Electromagnetic Pulse (EMP) Attack was published, my concerns were limited to another 9/11 scale event. But after that report, my concerns changed and expanded. What I now know scares the holy hell out of me. I believe it should terrify you, too!

9

This novel is my attempt to give a realistic portrayal; grounded in science, fact, and human nature that is based upon my personal knowledge and experience; of what I am deeply fearful of happening to us in the future. Let me be clear about that danger – I believe it's real and coming, and will happen in some form, it's unavoidable. It's practically foretold by history, and is an imminent threat to our personal safety and national survival.

There is no amount of 'turn the other cheek,' wishful thinking, coexist bumper-sticker, 'give peace a chance' hippie bullshit that is going to stop it. We simply must protect ourselves from this threat, immediately.

Aside from the protection of my nation, there is more than fear that motivates me to write this story. There is a piece of 9/11 that resides within me that never leaves my mind or soul. A personal issue I have that leaves me staring at the dark ceiling at night. We know stories of the survivors, the rescuers, the victim's families, a great deal about the hijackers, and we know about the lives of the victims before they died. But only in a very few examples do we know anything but short snippets about what was happening to those who died while the attacks were actually occurring.

In the South Tower 618 people struggled to live for over fifty-six minutes above the impact of United 175, before that tower fell. While the fire in the North Tower raged for one hundred-two minutes, over 1,366 people fought to survive above the impact of American 11. The people in the North Tower were the first to be trapped and many of them watched in horror as the South Tower fell first, surely knowing they must soon follow. Inside the maelstrom of horror during that day, roughly 200 people made the conscious choice to jump to their deaths instead of burning alive or being crushed to death, and roughly 2,000 more chose not to.

What would your choice be? What choice would you want your dearest loved one to make? Your son? Your daughter? Your mother? Those innocent Americans – before the eyes of the world – faced the choice of burning alive, being crushed to death, or willfully, intentionally, desperately choosing to step out and plummet to the concrete. As each grappled their fate in a death struggle, fighting to survive until the bitter end – we will never know those stories, those sacrifices, the want to live, the battle to save themselves, the struggle to help others, the hope for rescue, and the bitter desolation of no hope. Did they make their own choice of death or did fate choose it for them? We know nothing of their ordeal and never will, not until the day we stand with them before God and ask our missing countrymen and women to share those stories with us.

In some small way, through this story, my story, I hope to give whatever personal homage I can to those brave Americans who faced the worst and fought to the end against all odds, yet still died. May God bless them, care for them, and bring peace to their souls and those of their families.

This novel is not their story. This story is about those people who will live and who will die alone or together, never telling us their stories of what they will do when the entire United States is brought down, just like the Twin Towers in Manhattan, under those clear blue skies.

Do not be fooled, our blood is in the water and the predators are hungry. This story can happen any day. This fictional account is set in the real world that you and I live in – there are no aliens, no super villains, no super flu, no gods, no monsters – just real politics and plain human beings. If you think the great and powerful United States of America cannot be militarily defeated by our terrorist enemies in a single day – you are sadly mistaken.

PROLOGUE

"You have the rest of your life to solve your problems.
How long you live depends on how well you do it."
Clint Smith-Thunder Ranch

*****

FRED KNEELS in the mud amid a thick patch of red-sally weeds; their bright lavender petals are now fading along with their aroma. He examines the tracks in the dark red dirt, tracing the outline of the shoeprint with his fingers. It is the same, he knows it. He's become very familiar with this track now; the Adidas symbol in the tread being worn and nicked enough here and there to be instantly recognizable, proving that he still follows the same three murderers he has been hunting for a day and a half.

He reaches into the thigh-high weeds and, picking up the discarded Coke can, turns it upside down, letting the last few dribbles of soda pour onto the shoe print. He watches the small bubbles of leftover carbonation foam and float on the tiny puddle of dark liquid. He is getting very close now.

Setting the can down, he grips the stock of his rifle in his right hand while holding the reins of his lead horse in his left. Gazing up into the dense grove of maple trees towering before him, he knows they're up there somewhere, and if he is going to stop them he'll have to go in there and find them.

As he scratches the curly stubble of his salt-n-pepper beard, something catches his attention. He sniffs at the air and his eyes dart around, trying to see where the smell comes from. *Wood smoke! A campfire?* It is very faint but it is there. It could be residual smoke from another burning house in the valley, but it smells fresher – it smells closer.

The lead horse, Saul, senses the tension in Fred's muscles and twitches nervously. The spritely filly that follows behind flicks her tail and gives a snort of dissatisfaction at waiting so long. Fred cringes and grits his teeth at the noise the horse makes and knows he can't risk taking the horses with him into those trees. He needs silence and stealth to succeed in stopping these bastards.

So far, he has only discovered four bodies along the roads leading to Hudson, NY; if there are more he doesn't know. He is positive that all four were killed by these same three murderers. Somehow, it just doesn't seem possible that people can become serial killers just two days after the whole modern world has come to a screeching halt. Maybe these three evil men came together when the event happened, and feeding upon the evil within each other, they began taking out their hatred of life on the poor souls who got stranded in their sadistic path. Now, they could do whatever they wanted. Anyone they came across who didn't have the ability to fight back was at their mercy – and these three have no mercy.

Nothing exists to stop them – no law enforcement, no CSI, no posse, no accountability at all – nothing but Fred. Everything is in free-fall and will be that way for weeks before anything resembling law and order takes hold again. The people these bastards will come across between now and then will be helpless if Fred doesn't stop them now. If he doesn't take up the task or if he fails, only God knows how many innocents will die before they are stopped.

Fred's mind still recoils at the memory of what he saw when he found the first two victims. The similarity in their faces spoke to them being father and son. He prays neither was forced to watch what happened to the other; the ghoulish sight of their eviscerated bodies hanging like bloody scarecrows was the single most horrific sight Fred had ever witnessed.

The last two victims he found staked out this morning on the shoulder of Claversack Road about a mile back. According to the driver's licenses he found in their belongings, they were Georgia Plum, age 71, and her husband Richard, age 74. They were from Portland, Maine and would never make it home again. Georgia had obviously been brutally raped and beaten and Richard's angular face was smashed into an unrecognizable mass of silver hair, dried blood, and brain matter. Their corpses were left splayed on the ground, outstretched arms tied to the bottom of delineator posts. Proud of their terrible acts the killers had intentionally posed the bodies to shock the next passersby.

They succeeded in their intent. Fred was shocked. Soon, he would deliver a message back to the murders.

Pulling the horses, Fred backs away from the tree line and soon has them tied up out of sight in a stand of scrub brush. Fred moves to leave but Saul doesn't like being left behind and nudges Fred hard on the shoulder as he passes by. Fred turns to the majestic horse and runs his big black hand along the horse's face. They have become attached to one another even though they met only four days ago. The animal is smart and talented, and Fred must rely heavily on him to get across the long and dangerous roads ahead, to reach his daughter.

He frees the reins from the brush. "I very well may die up there, my faithful friend," he says to the large dark eyes of the horse. "I can't leave you tied up here to starve if I don't make it back. Keep

13

these other two close by for me while I'm gone, okay? I'll try and be back soon."

Fred stares at the steep hillside with deep reservations about his intended mission. His personal considerations can easily take priority over dispensing justice. Not the least of which is a certain amount of trepidation in placing his own safety in jeopardy. He doesn't know the people who've been murdered, and developing an excuse to avoid this confrontation with evil men would not be hard. *How easy it would be to just walk away.* He thinks back to a warm afternoon in the sun-filled living room in his childhood home in Macon, Georgia. A line from the novel he read so long ago flashes before his eyes.

The lessons of yesterday had been that retribution was a laggard and blind.

The character, Henry Fleming, contemplates the ease with which he escaped exposing his cowardice during the previous day's Civil War battle in the great American novel by Stephen Crane – *The Red Badge of Courage*. Henry found that through chance and choice, cowardice could easily remain hidden, buried deep in the unknown, where only your soul and the Lord God knew the truth.

Fred's memory shows him again the horrific sights of the dead that these killers have left in their wake. *If not me, then who? If not now, When?* Steeling his mind and heart against many dreaded possibilities he begins taking slow steps forward.

"Retribution is not blind today," he mutters stoically while scanning the hillside.

Golden rays of sun break over the horizon as Fred begins his hunt. Trying to make little noise, he slowly and methodically plants his feet on the crackling dried leaves that litter the ground. Soon he is far up the slope and pauses for a few moments to catch his breath. He no longer sees the horses below, obscured by the thick stand of trees he has just climbed through. He sniffs at the air and the smell of wood smoke is stronger now. He rests his thumb on the safety of his AR10 rifle, takes a deep breath, and starts moving up the slope again.

*****

HER BABY sister's little feet wriggle and shove into the small of her back, waking her. A sense of disassociation swims around her head as she tries to remember where she is. The ground is hard and small rocks poke into her ribcage, quickly reminding her. She thought she had cleared the ground before laying their bed of two thin blankets out in this spot. Now, though, the aching in her back and ribs tells her

14

she still needs improvement in bed-making at future camp sites. She stretches out, rolling onto her back. Her feet slip out from under the covers and she immediately feels the cold air chilling her toes. She quickly pulls them back under the covers, bumping her little sister and causing the two-year old to give a sleepy moan. Aneeta smiles as she looks at the smooth palm of her sister's tiny hand lying just before her nose. She can see in the dim light under the blanket the little puffs of steam her baby sister's breathing makes in the cold morning air.

Aneeta doesn't want to poke her head out yet. As hard as the ground is, plus her desperate need to urinate; they are still not incentives enough for her to brave the cold air. She was forced to get up several hours ago during the night to pee and that excursion had been a quick, stumbling sprint into the blackness to a nearby bush. She remembers, while she was trying to relax enough to release her burden, she saw an odd orange glow from far over the horizon. Her heart skipped for joy for a brief moment when she thought that maybe the electricity at some city in that direction had come back on. Her joy quickly sank to gloom as she realized that the color of the light was not from electrical lights but from a great fire of some sort. She had briefly wondered what kind of fire could cause such a glow from such an obviously great distance away. *Maybe it's a forest fire or something?* The cold night air ended that mental quandary, and finishing her task, she quickly sprinted back to the warmth of the blankets. She decides that she will ask her father about that fire later, but first she has to brave leaving her warm bed. She takes a deep breath, and with wide eyes pulls the blanket down exposing her face to the sunlit morning.

The scene is idyllic in its beauty. The crisp, cool September morning is beginning to warm. The smell of newly fallen maple leaves blend with the rich aroma from the freshly disturbed dark soil, reminding her of her mother's freshly baked almond spice cookies. The dappled sunlight dances lightly through the brilliant ambers, reds, tans, and browns of the leaves. It is a picture-perfect setting that is tailor-made for a fairytale, where any moment a tall and muscled knight will appear, riding upon some magnificent steed, his beautiful hair blowing in the morning breeze. Her eyes watch the scene and she relishes the crisp air.

Then, letting go of her thoughts of heroes and horses Aneeta Singh suddenly feels lonely as she ponders whether such natural beauty as this actually requires a person to appreciate it. She wonders, would the magnificence of this place be lost if no human eyes ever saw it? Does it take a soul to recognize the splendor of nature's places or does the weight of its worth exist on its own? Without her appreciating eye does beauty still exist? How important are people to the traits of the world? All nature and existence was here before she was born and will be here after she is dead, but what value did it actually have without participation, interaction, and appreciation from a human like her? Her young mind had never considered such questions before her literature class teacher posed a question a few weeks ago.

"When a tree falls in the forest and no one is around to hear it, does it make any sound?"

At that time, sitting in the classroom, she considered the question to be silly. Of course the tree makes sounds as it crashes to the ground. That's physics; that's math; that's reality and you can't argue with reality and science. Hard facts don't need human interaction to be valid. They exist just fine without the human mind grasping their worth or value. The rotation of the solar system around the sun was a scientific fact that existed just fine for over four-and-a-half billion years without the mind of any human perceiving it. When molecules collide a sound will be made – so, of course, the falling tree will make sound. It's a mathematical certainty.

Mr. Walters' gorgeous grey eyes looked at her warmly as she stood and said so in front of the class, proud of her ability to make her point so logically against an adult. She looked forward to admiring his handsome features throughout the school year. For being so old, a man in his forties, he's really cute, she thought. He gave a gentle smile before asking her something that made her stop her self-admiration and think twice.

"Well, Aneeta," he had said. "If all you need are molecules rubbing against one another to make sound, then why won't the vacuum of space allow that sound to exist there? Is the vacuum of your science's space so jealous of sound that it keeps itself segregated? Isolated from the joy that sound can bring?"

Aneeta stared, perplexed, at the man at the front of the classroom who very rapidly lost the handsome features she had admired moments earlier. "Uh, well, that question doesn't make any sense," she stammered. "Sound is a vibration through the air, and space is a vacuum that lacks air so sound can't exist there and joy – and uh, jealousy is emotion – uh, right?"

The deep grey pools that made up the heart of Mr. Walters' eyes sparkled as Aneeta sat back in her chair, wanting to quickly be forgotten for the rest of the day. His white teeth showed as he replied with enthusiastic passion.

"My goodness! I think we're all going to have a marvelous year! Such intelligence, such thoughtfulness, ladies and gentlemen, this will help make our time together a wonderful partnership. We are going to take a marvelous journey into the world of literature, which, we must always remember, is a trip of the human spirit as much as it is a trip of the mind."

He looked back at Aneeta and gave a wink. "So, as you all go away for the weekend, think about this and we'll talk about it next week. What is the mathematics of romance? Can an equation tell us the value of pride? Does joy exist in a vacuum?"

Mr. Walters' handsomeness returned in spades as Aneeta watched him adoringly as he chatted with other students after the class bell rang. He posed those questions three weeks ago last Friday, and she has been considering them off and on ever since.

Her mind drifts away from thinking of the aged, but cute, Mr. Walters and back to pondering the cold morning. The thin blankets do little to keep her warm and she sees the small fire her father, Ramesh, has started, enticing her out from under the covers. Her stomach growls as she quickly dashes from the blankets to the edge of the fire, soaking up its heat. Her quick movement has finally awoken her sister, who now sits up dumbfounded, wrapped in blankets, looking around at the unfamiliar surroundings of the camp. Aneeta goes over and lifts her up and holds her against her hip as they both enjoy the fire. The little girl, Mishti, sucks her thumb and turns her head this way and that at the encircling woods.

Now, this morning, the third day after the strange event that had caused this whole mess, Aneeta doubts she will ever see Mr. Walters again. Ramesh had taken her and Mishti to Albany on a quick two-day trip to see the fall foliage along the Hudson River Valley. Her mother had stayed behind to work weekend shifts at the hospital, and to postpone the trip might mean missing the brash display of color. They headed home from Albany only a few hours before the disastrous episode happened.

Driving among the hills, they had just passed through the small town of Brainard. She and her father missed much of the natural beauty that morning, as they listened earnestly to the breaking news of the terrorist attacks in California, when, suddenly, absolutely everything just quit working for them.

Their 2009 Dodge Caravan died and Ramesh was barely able to coax it to a safe stop. The steering wheel locked up and they veered off the road into a horse pasture. The van's radio stopped along with the engine, and it wasn't long before they realized her Ipod and laptop had also stopped working. Their cell phones, watches, camera, and every other electronic device they possessed no longer functioned. What began as a quick weekend trip through the Catskills and an overnight visit to her uncle had turned into this horrible, long trek to get back home to Philadelphia.

The first day they had tried to get help in Brainard but no one there knew anything about what had happened and there was no one who could get the van going. Aneeta heard all kinds of weird talk there about how this was the end of the world and that nothing electronic would ever work again. One guy even said that terrorists had intentionally brought on the return of the Stone Age, while others said it was punishment from God for sin. But when Ramesh heard people calling him and his daughters Muslims and that they were a part of why this whole thing had occurred, he rapidly gathered up their belongings and a couple of blankets that a nice lady gave them and they began their long walk.

The next two days were endless walking, after more endless walking, as mile after mile she pushed her sister's stroller while they marched by the never-ending rows of stalled vehicles abandoned on the roads. They saw several vehicles moving, and a group of ten people passed right by them, riding crammed atop of a big green tractor. Everyone they came into contact with had the same stories as they did and no one knew what was going on or why all the cars and electronic devices no longer operated. People they met were kind enough the first couple of hours, but later on they all seemed to look at them with a bit of fear that harbored a hidden want, or maybe desperation, that made her father nervous.

Yesterday there was quite a bit of smoke floating through the Hudson Valley from burning stores and houses. Some are accidental, she is sure, but her father thinks some may have been started by arsonists and that it is best if they stay away from the towns. She hopes they will never meet anyone so horrible as a person who would set fires for no reason. She knows from the road atlas they collected from an abandoned gas station, they still have over two hundred miles to go to get back to their home and her mother. She can clearly picture the sight of her distraught mother standing at their apartment window, staring out onto the city streets, worrying about them every minute. They made their camp in a small grove of maple trees on a hill above the highway.

She leaves the fire to urinate and then quickly returns to the warmth of the flames. As the warming rays of the morning sun slowly filter into her blood, she cannot help but look and listen to her surroundings and ponder the beauty. Squirrels chattering, birds fluttering as they lift into the sky, the warm crackling of twigs burning in the little fire all catch her attention. They all seem to be brand-new things, as if no human ear had ever heard anything like them. She feels like she is the first human being to ever experience the warmth of living and the enjoyment of touch, sounds, smells, and sight. Her most acute sensation at the moment, though, is hunger, as the growling of her empty belly gives testimony. The sisters wait patiently for their father to return from searching some nearby vehicles for food.

It's not long before he does and she is delighted to see that he's been successful. He comes up the hill, panting from the exertion of the climb, with two small lunch-sized bags of chips, one, Doritos, and the other, Fritos. Neither are Aneeta's favorites, but she is very hungry and looks forward to getting some sustenance in her empty belly. Her father opens the tiny bags and takes two chips. Placing one in each hand, they bow their heads together and say their prayer of Grace.

"The act of offering is God, the oblation is God," Ramesh says as he tosses the two tiny chips into the flames. "By God it is offered into the fire of God, God is that which is to be attained by him who sees God in all." As they complete their prayer, he hands one chip each to his daughters. When they finish eating them he hands them each another and in this way they eat slower to hopefully stave off the future pangs of hunger a little bit longer.

Ramesh had become a naturalized citizen two years before, shortly after the birth of his second daughter. He had come to work in America during the 1990s for a job as a pediatrician at the Children's Hospital of Philadelphia and decided to stay and earn his citizenship. When asked why he no longer wanted to live in India he would say. "I wish to live in a country where even the poor people are fat."

He smiles watching his Mishti use her tiny fingers to quickly fork the meager breakfast into her mouth and gobble it down. Grinning in amusement he holds his hands to the low flames to warm his cold fingers. A born and bred city boy from Calcutta, he has no experience as a camper, but he learned quickly how to make a fire. The heat feels good as he observes his intelligent-eyed Aneeta watching cardinals flitter among the branches above her.

Then, instantly, spawn of the devil brings hell itself to his family's morning meal.

Twenty-feet away a large black man stands whooping and hollering like a berserker, and charges toward the fire. Ramesh stands, eyes wide with surprise and fear. He moves to confront the attacker, yelling to his daughters to get down. Aneeta screams and grabs for her little sister. The charging black man proves a successful diversion as two white men, one fat and one skinny, come running silently up behind Ramesh.

19

Fixated on the bellowing black man Aneeta's father never even knows the other two men exist. He only hears the high-pitched scream coming from Aneeta a mere moment before the machete welded by the fat man slices into his neck, severing his spinal cord, nearly decapitating him. His limp body crashes to the ground, sounding like a bag of cement hitting the earth. The machete stays stuck in his neck muscle and bone; the weight of the falling body tearing the machete from the fat man's hand. The murderer quickly lurches forward to retrieve his lost weapon and curses as he finds it difficult to work the blade free.

The next few seconds blur in Aneeta's shocked and disorientated mind as the black man slaps her hard across the face and violently jerks her yelping sister from her arms and flings the toddler into the bushes.

Bright little glittering stars fill Aneeta's fuzzy vision as her mind losses all track of Mishti. A panicked fear sweeps through her mind as her attacker uses his terrible frenzied strength to rip off her jeans, leaving her half naked on the dirt. Frozen from shock and fear, she stares up at the beast-like figure as he tears at his own clothes.

The hard rock's in the dirt bite hard into her bare buttocks as the giant dark-skinned man climbs on top of her and she feels the putrid stink of his humid breath blow over her face. The animal's weight crushes down upon her like a suffocating mountain and she worries that she will be unable to breath. From between her legs comes an unbelievably excruciating pain that sears her mind with agony as he plunges violently into her body. She rears her head back and gives a piercing scream to the universe directly into his ear.

"Fuck!" he yells.

Wincing at her scream, he angrily shoves his right elbow violently into her chin pinning her face against the musty soil with all of his weight as he continues raping her.

"Now, scream, you little fuck'n cunt! Scream like the rag-head cunt you are!"

The weight on her throat makes it hard to breath and impossible to scream. Her mind slips in and out of consciousness. Whenever her mind clears enough to be considered conscious, the rapist beast has her head pinned to the ground in such a way that she is forced to see her father's contorted body lying nearby. His familiar and handsome face lies at a very unnatural angle to his body, puzzling her foggy mind. She did not see the fat man yank the machete out of her father's neck, and does not know that her father's head stayed attached to his body by only a few tendons and a flap of skin.

20

The pain in her belly is extreme and she knows something is very wrong inside her. She was still a virgin but is very familiar with her menstrual periods. She knows she is bleeding and guesses that something inside her has been torn.

The brutal attack seems to last forever and she is not sure when it finally ends. Her foggy brain realizes the huge man's weight has lifted and the pain in her belly is less sharp, but a sickening and throbbing hurt stays behind his evil work. She tries to see her sister but her blurry vision and swimming head make it hard to focus. Suddenly, she smells the stale stink of some unknown alcoholic beverage being breathed on her face as the murky sight of the skinny white man's face hovers above hers. Her vision clears somewhat and she see his unshaven face grinning down, examining her naked body. His cruel grin vanishes as he looks down with disgust at her genitals.

"Gawd damit, Charlie," he giggles, "that fucking horse cock of yours has done ripped this fucking chick apart! Dude, come on, what the fuck, huh?"

Several feet away Charlie wipes blood and semen from his genitals with the thin blanket Aneeta and Mishti had shared not long ago.

"Too fucking bad, pencil dick! You want some tight shit? Fuck her in the ass, then, and shut the fuck up!"

Shrugging, the skinny man grabs Aneeta by her long, matted hair and rolls her onto her stomach. As he mounts her she can feel his breath blowing across her cheek and his slimy tongue licking at her ear as a horrible new pain erupts below her waist. Her face is shoved into the ground forcing dirt into her mouth. As her teeth chew the gritty soil it losses any hint of smelling like her mother's cookies. Her mind drowns in a sea of sickening disorientation at what is happening. She coughs and gags as she inhales the gritty dirt down her throat, and her stomach revolts at the worm-like taste. The man's panting is mixed with giggles as he repeatedly pushes into her.

His sniggering and thrusting stop abruptly when she thinks she hears a loud cracking noise. That same moment she feels his entire weight crash down on top of her, pinning her to the ground. His body does not move nor does the man even breathe as she tries to clear her mind to understand what is happening. A flood of very warm fluid gushes across her face and pools on the ground. Even in the haze of her tortured mind she recognizes it as blood. A lot of blood.

A desperate vision of her sister comes to her mind, which is now cleared enough for her to think coherently. With a sudden burst of power and strength flowing into her arms she pushes up against the weight of the man on top of her. As she twists her body he falls limply to her side and as she looks over her shoulder it becomes obvious why the skinny man stopped raping her; the left side of his skull is gone and the majority of brain matter has been blown out onto the grass. Where once his left ear had been, there is now a gaping hole, giving a clear view of the crisp white inner lining of his brain pan. A sharp squeal comes from her sister several feet away.

Thoroughly bewildered, Aneeta has no idea how or why the skinny man has been killed. She hears the very loud cracking noise again, and it doesn't happen just once but is repeated three times in rapid succession. This time her mind is able to identify the sound immediately as gunshots. A hollow grunt follows the echo of the shots and she sees the large black man's body collapse in a heap on the ground, his pants still down around his knees while still holding the bloody blanket at his genitals. Aneeta stares at his corpse and feels grim satisfaction as his lifeless eyes stare at the dirt.

Suddenly, another squeaky cry from her sister catches her attention and she turns to look over her other shoulder. There she sees the fat white man holding Mishti up in front of him with his arm wrapped tightly around her tiny throat. His other holds the blood-covered machete up against Mishti's chest as he stumbles backward, yelling at someone approaching through the trees.

"You fuck'n back off or I'll gut this little rag-head bitch," he screams in a fear-laden voice. "Back off, I say!"

She watches the fuzzy shape of a tall man approaching through the trees solidify and clear. He has a slow, steady crouching walk, pointing a black rifle at the fat man. Even after the panicked threat is made the approaching figure doesn't hesitate and advances. Her clearing vision shows her savior to be a fiftyish black man wearing a cowboy hat, speaking with a calm baritone voice filled with deliberate authority as he continues taking small steps forward.

"Let the child go," the voice says.

"What? Fuck you!" he yells. "You fuck'n kill'd Charlie and Jim. I let this thing go and you'll shoot me, too." Sweat beads on his forehead and Dorito crumbs cling to his lips as he staggers backward.

Again, the cold baritone voice.

"Let her go."

The fat man looks frantically in all directions for a way to escape.

"What the fuck, man? What the fuck are you doing? After what these fuck'n rag-heads have done to America? Why let'em live?"

The deep voice replies, "You *are* going to die. Die fast or die slow, your choice. You hurt that child and I'll carve on you all day

22

before I let you die. You let her go and I'll kill you quick. That is all that I'm willing to offer your worthless soul, you sick fuck."

The fat man's eyes bulge in his sockets, protruding in fear as he now knows his fate. He quickly ducks his fat and swollen head behind Mishti's body, which he holds forward as if the small wriggling form were a crucifix and the man bearing the rifle was a hungry vampire.

"Back off! I'll gut 'er if you don't *back-the-fuck-ooffff*," he screams.

He presses the gore-covered point of the blade harder against Mishti's shirt as she wails.

Aneeta watches the older man slowly place one steady foot in front of the other. It reminds her of the way ninjas moved in the karate movies her father loved to watch. The stock of his rifle is pressed solidly against his cheek and his eyes are locked on the fat man. He has closed the distance between them to little more than fifteen feet; Aneeta can almost feel the fear exuding from the fat man's pores and his desperation is palpable. She sees his eyes dancing wildly as he searches for a way out. Mishti bawls and squirms as Aneeta's heart has pangs of stark fear for her sibling. The fat creature keeps stepping backward, left foot leading, right foot following. He takes one more desperate step backward as the man with the rifle acts.

The movement is so fast and sure that it is obvious, even to the young Aneeta, that it has been preplanned. The barrel of the rifle lowers slightly, aimed at the fat man's leg. The loud report of the shot reverberates boldly through the woods as the bullet tears into the meat of his thigh. The damage to the fat man's leg is immense as blood, meat, and bits of bone blast from the back of the shattered leg and onto the brush behind him. The fat man screams, loses his balance and pitches backward in shock and pain.

Immediately after the shot rings out the man with the rifle rushes forward; rapidly closing the distance, he is on top of the fat man as he and Mishti hit the ground. Before the injured man can react or hurt the girl in any way the man shoves his rifle into the fat man's belly and fires off four quick shots. The fat man's t-shirt barely contains the expanding swell of his belly as the muzzle blast from the four bullets is injected into his torso. He tries to scream but can only stare open-mouthed and silent at the man with the rifle.

Aneeta's savior grabs Mishti's blouse with his free hand, lifting her up and away from the dying fat man. He retreats with the little girl and sets her gently down next to the trunk of a tall maple tree. He returns to the fat man with his rifle up and at the ready, but any threat in using the machete again is long gone. The devastating

23

attack has left the man lying in shock and paralyzed. He pulls his shirt up and stares at his destroyed and exposed bowels. The muzzle blast into his belly has pulverized the skin, fat, and bowel contents into a mass of gore. His trembling fingers open, letting the machete fall and make a clinking sound as it lands on rocks next to his head.

The savior stands above the disemboweled fat man. The dying man's eyes display equal amounts of fear and shock as he looks up. The savior places the barrel of his rifle on the center the fat man's chest.

"I pray that God may have the worst places of hell reserved for you and your pals."

The rifle barks loudly, sending a 180-Gr. JHP .308 bullet plunging through the chest, obliterating the monster's heart.

The echo of the rifle shot dissipates into the distance. With tears flowing down her dusty and mud-covered face, Aneeta drags herself across the ground toward her sister, who sits sobbing in shock. Aneeta's body leaves a trail of blood on the soil behind her as she digs her bloodied elbows into the ground, forcing her body forward. She doesn't register his approach, and the soft touch of Fred's large hand on her shoulder makes her flinch. The whites of his big brown eyes have a hint of yellow as he looks down at her with deep sadness and compassion.

"Let me help you, lil' girl," he says softly.

Aneeta physically and emotionally collapses. Fred cradles her limp body and carries her like an infant and lays her next to her sobbing sister. The little girl instantly puts her hands on Aneeta's chest and sobs as her older sister wipes weakly at her tears. Fred retrieves the one clean blanket and wraps them in it.

"I've killed the three who hurt you. You're safe now. I'll be back very soon. Take care of this baby until I get back, okay?"

With tear-filled eyes she asks weakly, "My father?"

Fred gives a terse shake of his head while staring at her with soft eyes. Aneeta clamps her eyes shut and cries as he disappears into the trees.

True to his word he soon returns with three horses in tow behind him. Panting and sweating from his climb up the hillside Fred quickly takes his sleeping bag from one horse and unrolls it on the ground next to Aneeta. She moans as he lifts her onto it as easily as he can. She winces but soon begins to feel the warmth of the bag after he places her inside. A deep sense of gratitude sweeps through her as she hugs her weeping sister under the covers of the bag. Fred goes about busily retrieving medical supplies out of a backpack.

She reaches out touching his arm, making him pause. She gives his arm a squeeze and silently mouths the words, "thank you." He nods and gently moves her hand back and wraps her arm around her sister again while he works with his supplies.

He gently holds her head up, offering her sips of bottled water. The cool liquid tastes wonderful in her parched mouth as it washes away the mud from her tongue. She coughs several times and is only able to get half the bottle down. He gives the rest to Mishti, who gulps eagerly from the bottle.

He grabs another and opens it.

"Girl, I need to lift this cover up and wash you off so I can see how you're hurt. Do you understand?"

Aneeta nods, holding onto her sister tightly. She bites her lower lip remembering the brutal attack as he begins his examination. She feels his soft touch and can feel the cool water rinsing away the grime and blood. His grim expression doesn't soften as she jerks and winces at the sting of the cleansing waters being poured over her terrible wounds.

Fred sees a large flow of fresh blood escaping from her genitals. The blood loss is terrible and he knows she will soon experience hemorrhagic shock and die, and there is absolutely nothing he can do for her. She needs an emergency operation and transfusions to survive this and neither of those things is available now, not for her nor anybody else in this part of America, for the past three days now. Even though his touch is as soft as silk during his examination, pain shoots through Aneeta's body and becomes blinding sheets of agony that overwhelm her. Unable to take anymore she reaches down and pushes his hands away from her body, making him stop.

Her young face grimaces in pain. She sees in Fred's eyes what she already feels deep inside of her body. There is no way to get her help and she is going to die.

She clutches her sister and asks in a weak voice, "Please, my father?"

"I'm sorry. I would bring him close to you but I don't want this child to see him."

The horror of what he says flows across her features.

"I'm so sorry," he says meekly.

Tears fall as she bites her lip.

"My mother, Shashi, is in Philadelphia. Will you take my sister to her? Please?"

"I am searching for my own daughter. I cannot guarantee I can get this child to her mother. I will take her with me and I will see that she is safe and protected. I swear to you she will be safe. I'll try and get her to her home. I'm sorry – I can't promise you more."

She nods and whispers, "Please bury me next to my father."

"I will."

She reaches into the air and he grabs her hand. She winces from a jab of sharp pain shooting through her body. Weakness rapidly seeps into her cold limbs. What little warmth that came from being in the sleeping bag is now gone and her chin shakes as though she is freezing cold. Spasms and convulsions violently rack her body as hemorrhagic shock fully sets in. Fred does his best to hold her, to keep her from further harming herself or accidently hurting the terrified child next to her. The spasms finally subside and he looks down and sees a small, but expanding, dark circle appearing on the surface of the sleeping bag as it becomes saturated with her blood. Her eyes suddenly open; they show she is lucid and her mind has momentarily cleared.

"Has America been destroyed? Is it gone?"

The man looks sadly around at the forest surrounding him before answering, staring her in the eye.

"I don't know."

"H – How could this ha – happen?"

Her fingers feel icy cold and he can barely discern her pulse through his thickly callused hands. He gently strokes her thin wrist as he watches her shallow breathing become more labored. Her eyes seem to search the air above her face for some dancing ethereal thing that moves and flits to and fro until slowly it stops and her gaze locks on a single point above.

An ashen hue spreads through her cheeks and her last breath is expelled gently by the meager weight of her falling chest. Silence reigns over the surrounding voices of nature as a single tear leaves a wet path over Fred's cheek as the only requiem to mark the girl's passing.

"I don't know, sweetheart. I'm sorry," he says impotently to her last inquiry.

He bows his face into his hands, cradling the dead girl's fingers near his lips. *I wasn't fast enough.* He speaks a quiet prayer that her soul finds its way to God, and then he lays his other hand over her empty eyes, closing them for her eternal rest.

He looks at the small child sitting, staring stupidly up at him with uncomprehending, teary eyes. He wonders if he will be able to find her name somewhere in the belongings that lay strewn around the small campsite. He has a lot to do and burying the bodies will take a while and he wants to be moving again as quickly as he can. His daughter might need him as much as this little child did and he has so very far to go to get to her. Time is not on his side.

Book One – AMERICAN JIHADI

Throughout his life a man has more of these four things than he knows: Sins, Debts, Years, Foes.
Persian Proverb

*****

October 29, 1947 22:33pm UTC+5:30
Wular Lake,
Jammu and Kashmir, India

THE DARK night was moonless, without a hint of breeze. The bearded men were gathered in a tight circle as they quietly conversed by the small fire. They squatted inside a walled courtyard that encircled the modest dwelling of the clan's patriarch. Most of the two dozen men held their single shot Martini-Enfield rifles in their hands while the others laid theirs across their knees. Loud screams of pain echoed around the dwellings and spoke clearly of the agony being suffered by the patriarch's youngest wife, who was in the throes of childbirth. The wailing would occasionally intensify and then subside. Occasionally the muttering of the midwife would be heard coming from the two-story house, tucked into the steep flanks of the imposing Mount Rajkain.

The wailing and muttering of women blended with the solemn discussions of men, but neither drowned out the sound of sporadic gunfire coming up from the valley. Below them, some distance from the swollen Wular Lake the city lights of Sopore twinkled. Sounds of a vicious battle there came clearly through the thin mountain air.

Tonight the water of the lake was a dark canvas but under a full moon, the glow off Wular Lake made the valley floor appear as if it were filled with pure silver. The reflected light would brighten the valley until all of the majestic mountain ranges that flanked it were visible. Their dark hulking shapes would appear to be like giant slumbering dragons that disappeared into horizon.

Tonight the beauty of the three great Himalayan mountain ranges of the Karakoram and Zanskar to the north and west, and majestic Pir Panjal to the south, were hidden by the dark gloom surrounding the Majumbar clan's encampment. The patriarch, Abdulla Khan, a well-built and still quite robust and hale man of sixty-three, stood as motionless as a statue. His richly carved face, lined from

28

many cares and much hard work, still showed the firm appearance of a man well within the prime of his life.

His steel-grey eyes stared out into the dark night, far beyond the little fire, where he could see the distant lights of numerous villages. The wide land stretching out below was where many famous and powerful men fought throughout history believing it to be the most beautiful valley in the entire world, the Vale of Kashmir. Abdulla had lived upon these slopes above that valley all his life and his mind's eye could see every God-made and man-made feature below him as if it were broad daylight.

He smelled the lush pine and sacred deodar trees that forested the hillsides of the mountain around him. Toward the valley floor the trees opened up onto grassy slopes and grazing meadows full of sheep and cattle, and then closer to the great brawling Jhelum River there were water-filled paddies of rice and saffron that framed the naturally formed Wular Lake. A surrounding sea of reeds marks seasonal highs and lows that fluctuated greatly as the spring floods later became a trickle in the fall. The Jhelum River wound off into a distance filled with glades and orchards of walnut, almond and huge apple trees until, splitting the valley it joined the powerful and famous Indus River. Together, with turbulent and raging waters, they emptied the deep mountain snows from the northern flanks of the Karakoram and Zanskar mountain ranges, into the Arabian Sea far to the south. Abdulla agreed with those great men of history; this place was indeed a paradise on earth, blessed by the merciful Allah.

Many centuries before Christ preached in Palestine, the Buddhist Emperor Ashoka claimed this territory, only to have Hindu kings take control for centuries after his reign was forgotten. The Muslims installed the Sultan Dynasty that brought in the arts and craft makers from as far away as Samarkand and Persia, who were such skilled craftsmen they still rivaled any Persian rug-maker for the highest quality tapestry made. Later, the Mughal Emperor Akbar conquered the region and cultivated many of the beautiful gardens that populated the rich and fertile plains of the valley. Later still, the Mughals fell before the marauding Afghans who came rampaging out of the north. Their empire, in fullness of time, was also destroyed and the people living here were subjugated by Maharaja Ranjit Singh who installed the Sikh Empire over Kashmir.

But even the great Sikh kings could not rule this land forever. They were replaced by the last great empire to subjugate this land, the reviled British. Abdulla had been told that the sun never sat upon the Empire of Queen Victoria while she sat upon some throne in England, but he did not believe such nonsense. There was no power but Allah's that circumnavigated the globe. The British had come to this land many generations before Abdulla and conquered everyone on the subcontinent. Now, the great British Empire was dissolving away like a river slug after salt is poured on it, but as they shrunk and wilted away they were still trying to leave their lackeys in charge behind them.

Even in the dark, Abdulla turned and looked directly at the soft faint light emitted from Sharikot Hill, where a spiral roadway twisted its way up to the Shrine of the pious Sufi saint, Hazrat Baba Shirkir-u-din-Wali. One week ago Abdulla made a pilgrimage to that shrine to pray for advice and guidance in handling the evils that afflicted his life and his clan.

Allah had only allowed him to produce two healthy boys who had survived the illnesses and accidents of life. Tonight, if his thirteen-year-old wife managed to produce another male heir, he would be very pleased and give prayers of thanks to the Sufi mystic, din-Wali. Unlike his past wives that had given him his young surviving sons, this adolescent woman had won over Abdulla's heart with her kind eyes and gentle ways. He was anxious to see her give birth to another son and to survive herself. But he betrayed no signs of weakness or emotion for her to his clan, who warmed themselves by the nearby fire.

As leader of the clan he could not show weakness and look in on the young woman whom he deeply loved. Right now all he could display for his clansman was concern for their plight and their future. His duty was to provide leadership in this time of battle for the clan's rights and privileges. The very future of the clan's status in this ancient and complex society was at stake with the recent troubles. Together they must secure their rights and land after the division of Pakistan from India, or they could lose everything. The fledgling nation state of Pakistan and its revered leader Quaid-e-Azam had called on them to rise up in jihad against the British and Hindus, and the Majumbar clan had rallied to the call for holy war.

The lands his clan lived on and worked from would soon be on the wrong side of the new division of Kashmir and place the clan and their land under the control of the Indian government and away from the new Muslim state of Pakistan. The evil Brittan, Lord Mountbatten, had advanced the cause of the powerful and clever Indian Prime Minister Nehru by expanding his control over this district. These new annexations in Gurdaspur were nothing less than a giant power grab before the plebiscite. If Mountbatten proved successful in his greed, it would guarantee that the Majumbar clan and many other Muslim clans from here would never be free of the

Hindus. This land grab by the British would inevitably force the clan to flee down to the lower Punjab plains, to be servants and untouchables in the caste system of the subcontinent, nothing more than disgusting dom or shilpkar, to be forever laughed at and ridiculed by the Hindus.

In the caste system, the loss of one's place as an esteemed Brahman and property owner would be far more than just loss of money or prestige. It would mean possible starvation, assured ridicule, no chance of betterment, and endless debasement of his entire clan. But with the help of Almighty Allah, these proud Pahari tribesmen were going to stop that from happening.

So far their skirmishes with the hated British and their sycophant coolie Hindus had been brief but bitter. Sadly, his brother Ashok was wounded by a grazing bullet to his skull and his uncle Raheem had died yesterday from a rifle's bullet striking him in the lower abdomen. Abdulla was contemplating what he hoped was an effective plan of action that would allow success in their upcoming battles and allow for them to retain control of their Gujjar pasture land overlooking his beloved Vale of Kashmir.

The screams continued from his home as he hovered over the worn map and debated with the other clan elders on whether or not another assault on the morning's supply train would achieve any success, or whether it would just invite the British to lay a trap for them.

Abdulla finally decided that he would risk another attack on the morning supply trains, and as he told those assembled around him that they would indeed attack again, the screams coming from the dwelling abruptly stopped. Abdulla fell silent as well, and every man's face craned around and stared across the dirt courtyard, the fire light accentuating their facial features. As the moments slowly passed and no more cries came from the house Abdulla started to walk slowly to the structure. Suddenly the vibrating wail of a baby's cry rose from the windows, filling the sky with its shrill bellow of life.

Abdulla approached the front door just as two small women exited. The first bent with age, opened the door and addressed him. "Your new son breathes the air of the Zanskar Mountains, sayyid, but your wife has lost her battle for life. There was nothing I could do for her – please forgive me," the midwife said in a timid voice that trailed off weakly as she meekly bowed her head before Abdulla.

Abdulla's steel-grey eyes were set in a pool of anguish; tears tried to appear but he fought to keep them from falling upon his face. He raised his eyes to the quietly sobbing servant girl who stood behind the old crone. Rocking in her cradling arms was the crying baby that now was all the patriarch had of his lost love. A single tear forced itself through Abdulla's iron will and left a trail through the thin dust that covered his cheek. He looked down at the wrinkled ancient face of the old midwife and said heavily, "He will be called Pushkar Abdul."

The old woman lifted her head and saw the faint trail the single tear left upon her master's face. She reached out and softly held his hand saying, "Yes, sayyid, *Allah yu'tiik al-aafiya.*"

Abdulla abruptly turned and walked with a stiff stride back to the gathering of clansmen at the fire and immediately began directing them in the tasks they would have in the forthcoming attack on the British. His heart beat slowly in his chest, as cold as the barren stones of the Himalayas that surrounded him.

*****

October 31, 1947 17:45pm UTC +5:30
Sheikh-ul-Alam Airport
Srinagar, India

THE OIL lamp's docile flame slowly danced in the mild breeze. The light was kept low on purpose; with enemy sharpshooters outside the airport fencing, too much light could prove very deadly for those inside. The dark-skinned Hindu orderly squinted under his thick eyebrows while writing out the dispatch his commander was dictating. Field Marshall Sir Claude Auchinleck had spent the day settling into his new headquarters at the airport and collecting his subordinate's reports. Now he paced slowly back and forth in his glossy black boots, the heels making a dull thud as he walked between the small desk and the window, reciting his message to the Indian Prime Minister.

"Your Excellency Nehru, I am pleased to report that yesterday morning the proud and loyal servants of the Indian State, your Indian Army, have again successfully stopped two more raids upon the military supply train bound for Sopore and territories north of the Jhelum River. The count of tribal militants killed in these two sorties number forty-seven with an additional fourteen collected as prisoners. Interrogations are presently ongoing and have proven successful in the divulging of pertinent information regarding enemy actions. These hostiles are also being questioned about Governor General Jinnah's involvements in these attacks, which I am positive will be confirmed.

"The military resistance may continue, as previously discussed, for some period in the more heavily Muslim districts of the rural pastures and valleys. But, the political conversion to the new order of things continues to move along in an orderly manner. As I relayed in my post to you this morning I do not foresee any more difficulties with the local magistrate, Hari Singh, who appears to be willing to acquiesce to your over-lordship and..."

*****

DAWN CREPT over the mountain peaks slowly and the sun had just placed its first ethereal tendrils of honey-colored light on their crowns as the fajr prayers were being ritually sung from the small minaret. The roar of the mighty Jhelum River was deafening as it bashed against the large boulders in the valley. The spring runoff was just beginning and was quickly filling Wular Lake. The river's torrent of muddy water would soon swell to even greater amounts as the warmth of the spring melted the thick snowpack with increasing speed.

An old farmer adjusted his turban as his donkey slowly trotted through the narrow streets of the village. They both exhaled small white clouds into the cold morning air as the man gently swatted a small stick against the animal's flanks to keep the stubborn animal going. The beast unhappily obeyed the prodding without enthusiasm. The animal and rider negotiated their way around the corner of a mud-walled courtyard as they headed toward a group of small mud-brick buildings. In the road several chickens scratched and pecked in the dust for food. Suddenly, the birds squawked and fluttered into the air in panic, with one heading directly for the donkey's muzzle. Badly startled, the beast reared and snorted as the rider almost fell off the donkey's slender back. Out of the rising dust three boys came running down the dirt street, laughing.

"Miscreants!" the farmer yelled while shaking his fist in the air at the boys as they continued running while giggling over their shoulders at the irate farmer.

Pushkar Abdul Majumbar's bare feet pounded the dusty road as he ran. The third surviving son of the now-dead Abdulla gasped for breath as he tried to keep up with his two older brothers' longer-legged pace. The oldest of the three, Mayur, ran with the fluid and sophisticated stride of early manhood. A year younger than Mayur came Subhash, whose timid mind loved poetry much more than tests of physical skill. But his ability to outrun the youngest was still present and he looked back at Pushkar with a smile, urging him on.

33

They approached the small adobe madrasah that was also used by the small community as a masjid. The elderly imam stood smiling near the door, waving one arm encouraging them to hurry to prayer. They arrived in the order of their ages, as usual, with Mayur breathlessly pulling up to the doors first and Subhash getting to them just a second behind while Pushkar, as always, came in last. But he did not mind being last, as his naturally sunny and happy personality never held any envy for the feats and abilities of his brothers.

They quickly moved to the water fountain and set about washing their callused feet. Pushkar, not realizing the imam had followed them in, mischievously splashed his brothers with water and giggled as they threatened to splash him back. All the playing from the two older brothers ended quickly as they saw the now stern and critical looking imam hobbling in behind Pushkar. Thinking he would succeed in splashing his brothers again Pushkar readied himself to swing another handful of water at his siblings when the imam raised his cane and, with a sharp jab, poked its end into the small of Pushkar's back, causing him to yelp from surprise and pain as he received the rude lesson of discipline in the house of worship and learning.

"I didn't lose this leg to the British, fighting with your father, to see you commit sacrilege in the house of God's learning, boy! What would your father say to such frivolity in my school?" the elderly man asked with raised eyebrows and a mocking halfhearted sneer.

"My apologies, teacher, please forgive me." Pushkar replied wincing at the pain in his back and rubbing his new injury vigorously with the back of his hand. Glancing sideways at his brothers he saw them smirking at his punishment, and happy at how they had escaped their teacher's early morning lesson.

The imam quickly sized up the spectacle of the three boys with a scowl and then his stern face softened.

"Enough, inside with you," he said, motioning them inside the place of learning with his cane as though he would jab them all with it.

It was Pushkar's positive outlook and influence that kept the brothers together since their father was killed down in the Punjab while looking for better work after the loss of their lands and cattle herds. The leadership influence that Pushkar had with his brothers was maintained by his strong personality, which was highly unusual since he was the youngest. The imam, among others, claimed Pushkar received a spirit from Allah that was closest to his father's and that had helped him to become the leader of the two older boys.

Pushkar would have his work cut out for him soon, since the long winter was now retreating toward the days of summer and the three brothers would soon leave their home village and head to the city of Leh, far to the north. There they will be seeking out work as coolies and porters for supply wagons or maybe, God willing, they will be able to get in with some foreigners doing expeditions up into the Ladakh or Himalaya ranges where they would be able to make far better wages as guides. Pushkar was positive about their chances for success; his outgoing manner endeared him to strangers quickly. Only their hard work, time, and the good will of Allah would say how things would play out.

*****

July 8, 1965 10:55am UTC+5:30
Salloro Ridge above Siachen Glacier,
Jammu and Kashmir

EVEN IN the middle of summer the temperatures remained cold in the upper elevations of the Karakoram mountain range. Above 20,000 feet they stayed locked in perpetual ice, snow, and bitter winds that blew with hurricane force between the serrated peaks and rough shoulders of the jagged spires that touched the floor of heaven. This inhospitable place was the home to a majestic and regal animal that was the top predator of its territory. It moved through the rocky snow-capped landscape like some reigning lord of a kingdom who had no rivals and no peers. There was no contender that would ever dare compete against the Snow Leopard's perfect fit in these mountains.

Most local tribesmen and mountain peoples of the subcontinent lived out their lives never having seen one, and those who did stood a good chance of never seeing anything again. A hapless lone traveler would, very occasionally, become a good meal for the great cat. Being one of the most nimble, wary, sublime, and reclusive animals on the planet, the leopard blended its talents perfectly to survive, and even thrive, at elevations few animals could even live in. Along with these natural skills, the mighty cat also displayed great beauty, nobility, and regal bearing that was both highly admired and prized by big game hunters around the globe.

Some hunters killed for food, some for sport and some evil few for malice. But all hunters recognized the challenge of the hunt itself as a large part of the hunt's worth. To hunt for a creature like the leopard at the heights of the Himalayas was an epic event. The challenge combined the greatness of the animal with the expense, effort and difficulty to reach these remote, hostile, rugged, and deadly mountains. It made the trip equal parts dream and nightmare.

For the Texas millionaire oilman and part-time cattleman, Sam Ferguson, it would be his greatest hunt. If he could actually kill such an animal in this place, it would solidify his status as a great hunter at the pinnacle of sport hunting for all time. In Sam's mind, he was sure it measured up against the greatest hunting stories of the ages! And certainly none of the others at the San Antonio Hunting Club would ever be able to top his achievement. Match it? Maybe, but never beat it. His place as best hunter-of-the-best hunters in the Texas millionaire hunting and social club societies would be assured. It would help him and his partner Bill 'Red' Walker obtain the financial support for an association to help preserve these creatures in a healthy population so that hunts like this would be available into the foreseeable future.

This strong young man who had been his guide for this hunt, Pushkar, had done a spectacular job of trailing the big cat. They had gotten two good views of the magnificent creature the day before, even though its grey and black camouflage coat blended so well into the hard crags and precipices around it. Unfortunately, both of those opportunities were at distances of almost three quarters of a mile and there was no way Sam was willing to try and take that shot. The boy had assured Sam, though, that he would have a better chance if the animal continued westward to another ridgeline. Sam agreed to try and so they carefully followed the animal throughout the day until the weather turned bad. After fighting a howling snow storm through the night they left the porters, Pushkar's brothers, at a hastily set up camp while Sam and the boy had gone ahead to scout out the giant feline.

Before first light they rose from their camp and moved up the mountain where they had come upon a small herd of Ibex goats on a ridge, right where the boy-guide said they should be. There they hunkered down, waiting out the tail end of the storm in a small stone hide that had been built long before by people unknown. When morning dawned clear and cold the boy led Sam to this small overlook that the boy was obviously familiar with. The spot was a perfect place to look down upon the little bench below the saddle of the ridge, where a small stand of gnarled old pine trees provided a sanctuary for the goat herd, and created a hunting ground for the leopard.

After the last frigid night and eight days of eating frozen canned hash and enduring the discomfort of defecating over frozen stones would have ended with Sam giving up and leaving had Pushkar not encouraged him to stay and wait. As dawn came and lit up the snow in brilliant sunlight they used binoculars to glass the craggy bench below the trees. A half hour later, Pushkar nudged Sam lightly and pointed out the slow, tentative movement below them where the great male cat silently stalked an ibex.

The thrill of watching the graceful beast made Sam's heart race as it moved so slowly and methodically, hunting its own prey. The predator moved with the stealth of an assassin across the rocks as the goat blindly went about its own daily routine. Sam delighted as he watched the balance of nature's never-ending struggle to survive play out in real time below him. He worked to record the images in his mind so that it would be a moment-by-moment memory he could relish for the rest of his living days.

Without warning, the coiled energy inside the large cat let loose like a dam bursting as the ibex herd scattered, trying to escape the explosive attack. The muscular body of the feline pounced lightly from one rocky ledge to the next jutting pinnacle as it closed the gap between itself and the fleeing goat it had targeted, and which was desperately trying to evade the claws of the pursuing predator. Small rocks and some larger boulders were knocked loose and were sent careening down into the valley below as the animals ran above the abyss. The ibex tried its best to escape and live, but failed, and the leopard's teeth and claws finally punctured its flesh. In seconds the tension of the hunt and chase ended with the snapping of the goat's neck.

The cat lay next to the ibex panting and relishing its successful hunt, licking the fur of its dead prey as Sam, with the boy's help, marked the range for the shot that would bag the cat. They quietly made their calculations and determined the cat was 530 yards away on a 35 degree downward slope. The shot was made all the more complicated by an uneven cross wind that gusted between 15 to 30 mph. It would be a very challenging shot for any rifleman but doable if Sam put all his skill into pulling it off. Sam rested his Weatherby Mark V rifle across cold stones and watched through his 6x Redfield scope as the beautiful cat's mature and noble face licked at the fur of the ibex.

Sam hesitated from taking his shot while watching with appreciation the beast's noble bearing. Sam tried several times to slowly apply pressure to the trigger and dispatch the glorious creature but a pang of unrighteousness crept into his heart at the thought of ending the life of such an awe-inspiring animal. A strange thought entered his mind: that all of his investment of money, time, and hardship to reach this point, where the collection of his prize was mere seconds away, now seemed to be a very unjust act.

Pushkar, astutely measured Sam's wavering mind, gently placed his mitten covered hand on Sam's shoulder while whispering,

"Sayyid, he is our prey and Allah has given us this chance. Don't falter. You have earned the right to succeed in your hunt, just as he succeeded in his hunt."

Sam saw the boy's maturity shine as he spoke with equal parts assurance and conviction, giving Sam a deep tone of wisdom that far exceeded the young man's years. Sam could also feel a deeply buried current flowing inside of the boy's words that said he, Pushkar, had also worked for this moment of success just as hard as Sam. The guide had experienced the privation of the hunt and wanted to experience the triumph of the hunt as well. He wanted to have the exhilaration of success course through his veins almost as much, or maybe even more than Sam did.

Sam rested his cheek on the rifle's stock while leaning his face toward the freezing steel surrounding the scope's eyepiece. The vast expanse of frozen slopes of the Himalayas stretched out for miles around in the gleaming sun as Sam centered the crosshairs on his point of aim and waited for the wind to calm. He thought about what both he and the young guide had gone through to be here and that gave him some comfort and solace in his choice to end the life of the marvelous predator.

He relaxed his muscles and took long, steady breathes while watching the fine crosshair inside his scope dancing back and forth over the ideal shot placement on the cat. His concentration focused and the crosshair movement subsided into a rhythmic and repetitive motion that coincided with his breathing. As he took in a deep breath and let it slowly and smoothly escape through his frost-covered beard, the crosshairs settled motionless above the cat's neck. Just as the bottom of his exhale reached the optimum point where his lungs were completely empty, and yet before they started to cry for more air, he had a rock solid platform that lacked any movement other than the gentle beat of his heart.

Smoothly applying the remaining amount of pressure needed on the trigger, the moment of completion came and went with the quickness of a bullet travelling at over 2,300 feet per second through the cold air. The shot was perfect in its placement and the great leopard jerked under the impact of the 120-Gr. bullet striking at the rear of the skull, separating the spinal cord from the brain and immediately dispatching the animal's soul to whatever paradise God grants to these animals of his creation.

The celebration and exultations between Sam and his guide lasted for several minutes and only subsided after Sam bonked his head hard against the low stone roof of their rocky perch. *A good, hard knock of reality always brings things back to Earth.* Sam rubbed at his smarting head. A short time later they carefully made their way down the rocky slope to the carcass and admired the fine specimen that they collected.

Sam thought the coat of the animal was special from a distance, but now, as he ran his fingers through the silky fine hair he was truly impressed with the magnificent fur. Pride-filled visions of this beast, finely mounted and displayed in the main hall above the great stone fireplace at the hunting club went through his head. The luxuriously thick tail and huge paws rested on the cold stones as Sam draped one of the muscular forearms of the cat over his shoulder and posing with a smile as Pushkar took several pictures. The posing and picture taking went on for some time and Sam used this time to spring an idea on Pushkar that Sam has been contemplating for the past couple of days.

"Push, you've been a great guide and have shown a lot of talent that I really admire. I got a question for you to consider, son," Sam said with a grin.

Pushkar lowered the camera and smiled back at the American he had come to like very much. The man eagerly sought Pushkar's advice and followed it without question. His tales of places in America and of the cowboys of the 'old West' were favorites of Subhash and himself. Their growing friendship has become a connection he had never made before with one of these foreigners. Of all the groups he and his brothers have guided into the high Himalayas he liked this American the best. The British were difficult to cope with because of what their country had done in destroying his clan, and at times Pushkar needed to keep a close eye on Mayur who wanted very much to slit their throats in the night.

"Yes, sayyid Sam, please ask."

"Well, Push, you told me that your family used to be in cattle and you've proven to me to be an intelligent and resourceful man who can handle most anything that comes your way." Sam scratched at his three-week-old growth of natty beard.

"Son, I got a fair-sized spread of a ranch back in Texas, and I was wondering what you'd think of working for me back in the good ol' USA – you and your brothers up to becoming Texans?"

Pushkar paused for several seconds, taking in the enormity of what the American said, trying to understand just exactly what this man was asking him. The realization of the opportunity he was being offered sank into his mind. The long, hard years he and his brothers had put into surviving had finally paid off and a feeling of elation and joy flooded into his chest as a wide grin of happiness swept across his face. The rich American returned his smile as they stood together at the top of the world.

*****

A HOT Texas breeze sent occasional gusts across the tall pasture grass below the farmhouse. The temperature was well over a hundred degrees and even the shade offered scant relief from the heat. Pushkar had just finished his dhuhr prayers and began packing the clothes he would take with him on his journey back to his Muslim homelands. His faithful brother, Subhash, had committed to the jihad along with Pushkar and would be accompanying him into the certain dangers that lay ahead.

Subhash had not assimilated into the Muslim community around San Antonio like Pushkar had. But his cheerful nature and devotion to his brother kept him in Texas over the years. Now that devotion would bring him back to the lands he loved so much. He happily quoted chapter and verse his favorite poems of the Sufi's Chishti order of saints as he packed his clothes in his nearby bedroom.

The last seventeen years had passed pleasantly for Pushkar since that day high in the Himalayas when Sam Ferguson invited him to immigrate to the United States. Subhash had followed, but Mayur had refused to leave the mountains of his birth in the Pir Panjal. He had become obsessed with reclaiming the Majumbar clan's ancestral pastures above the Vale of Kashmir. He worked toward gaining the independence of their homeland from both the Indians and the Pakistanis who each wanted it annexed into their countries. Pushkar thought it was a hopeless struggle but he still prayed daily for his brother's safety and success in achieving a free and independent Kashmir.

Pushkar's time in America had been doubly blessed with him finding love in this foreign place. In the decent-sized Muslim community around San Antonio he had pursued and captured the love of a beautiful woman from another Rajput Parhari family that had immigrated here a decade before he had. Asha was her name and she radiated the light of heaven from her eyes. He loved her more than his life and devoted himself to making a success of working for Mr. Ferguson and building a happy life for her. She bore him a strong-willed son he named Ajay. The name was a strong and proud Kashmiri name that Pushkar liked but was pronounced much like the names of

40

other Texan children, and he felt that would help his son become part of that culture.

Sam Ferguson's wife had died in 1974 and through the years Sam and Pushkar had become close friends as the wealthy man grew into old age. The oilman had always regretted killing the great cat on the Sallorro ridgeline and would sit for hours staring at the animal's stuffed body, wishing he had not killed the beast. He grew to hate big-game hunting and had spent much of his elder years working toward building a conservancy movement to protect the Snow Leopard and ending the hunts of the great cats. Pushkar and his brothers acted as his guides on several more trips back to the Himalayas where the man would shoot camera film instead of bullets at the regal animals.

Pushkar and Subhash mainly worked as ranch hands and were pleased with their work. Sam allowed them to also follow their Sufi rituals and prayers without hindrance. But, unlike the benevolence of their Christian employer, the brothers found they were not so warmly welcomed into the rest of the Muslim community. The old Sunni prejudices against their Sufi mystics and poets were still strong here, and had even caused division inside Pushkar's own household.

As Ajay had grown older Pushkar had pointedly noticed that the differences between the Sufi and Sunni branches of Islam were starting to become a point of stress for his son, who wanted to attend the madrasah in the city, but Pushkar refused, wanting him to follow in his beliefs.

As the boy reached his teenage years and became ever more challenging to both his father and his mother, Pushkar had been forced to resort to beating the boy on occasion in order to gain the proper respect due from the child. His insolence and arrogance would have been removed at an early age back in the old country, where there were less frivolous freedoms and more hours of hard work to instill more piety and obedience in the boy. But here, in this lavishly wealthy society of America, Ajay did not have the pressures necessary to sculpt him into respectable manhood so directly. Pushkar worried that he could lose the boy's soul to the vast opportunities and influences of such an unrestricted society.

Over the years in his new country Pushkar admired how this nation housed people of every faith and nationality in peaceful coexistence. Such a level of tolerance was a thing he feared that his homeland would never learn. He marveled at how the wealth of economic prosperity, and relatively consistent legal justice in America had produced such a peaceful civilization. He saw how this nation of self-determination and rational laws had brought reliable jurisprudence to a vast and diverse populace and kept the meaner spirits of man's soul somewhat suppressed. But, he had also watched with deep disgust as the free-loving hippies had turned into cocaine-snorting businessmen, and he noted how the daily decadences of this nation allowed for far too much over-indulgence in heathen acts by the weaker souls. He knew that no matter what goodness came from this nation's stated principles; its great weakness was a lack of moral clarity and discipline, which he saw gnawing evilly at its majesty.

Pushkar, being raised in a tribal caste society, had seen a far darker form of society growing up than his son would ever know. A society where stratification of status happened at birth and discrimination was institutionalized by the brutal. A culture where the wicked and cruel had free reign over the daily acts and wishes of men and would never allow for the opportunities that was so abundant here. Such hard lessons as Pushkar had learned in his youth were wholly unknown to the helpful, cheerful, spoiled and pampered Texans around him. America rolled in her prosperity like a pig happily splashing around in its own soiled mud hole and its people knew virtually nothing of the privations of life or the desperation of the human spirit that so many others in the world lived within.

Pushkar watched the Americans work diligently at pushing back against the human misery on the planet, attempting to replace it with the hope of their enlightenment, as if appointed by the Almighty to lead the future of all mankind. Yet, he saw with great disappointment, that they refused to give the thanks due to the Almighty for his divine sanction of their peace and prosperity.

Rather than acknowledging the grace of God, their secularist minds were forever searching the myriad paths of life for literal human justice while ignoring divine justice. They endlessly dissolved their intellect into the minutia of legal providence and yet forgot that providence was what created their intellect. They acted as if the logic of their courts could finally divest the very presence of God from the hearts and minds of men, like an infection was worked out of a festering wound.

This was foreign to him and contrary to the wisdom of his own faith that used the hadith to sanction all of God's Law into the cultures and futures of all mankind.

Time had shown Pushkar that this was America's great failing and he knew they were fools for indulging in it. Pushkar also knew Allah was forever and would claim his creation on the day of his choosing. The arrogance with which these too-free peoples sought oneness within their secularist thought, where only man was the creator and moderator of all law. *Twice fools!* All true oneness with providence was in the mind of Allah and could only be achieved through his law – sharia, not the laws of mere men. And Pushkar understood that by its very nature, sharia was wholly incompatible with the nature of this country's secularist principles.

He deeply feared for the good people of this welcoming land and the divine punishments from Allah that they must surely someday pay; and yet he and Asha had stayed and he became a citizen and was immensely thankful for all the blessings bestowed upon him.

And now he had been given a great opportunity to fulfill an oath of service and patriotism to his new country! The American government had sent FBI agents to speak with Pushkar and Subhash, pleading for their assistance in Afghanistan. The agents had requested their help with propagating the influence of the United States with the various mujahedeen warlords who were in a brutal war of independence against the godless-Soviet communists. Pushkar relished the opportunity to help his new homeland as well as relishing in the chance to resist the enemies of Allah so close to the sacred home of his own Sufi beliefs. Allah had blessed him with so many joys and now he would be able to repay a portion of his debt. Soon he and Subhash would be in Herat, Afghanistan, very near the place where their Sufi Chisthi order was founded and its mystical beliefs were first preached at the Abu Ishaq Shami shrine.

He and Subhash would be leaving in a few short weeks and as the time approached Pushkar was becoming more concerned about his son, and about how the boy would change and grow in the absence. If it was Allah's will that Pushkar never return to his family it would be hard on both his wife and son, but his heart compelled him to fulfill his heartfelt responsibilities. If he never returned it would simply be up to his wife to raise the boy. Asha was a good woman but she indulged the boy greatly. Unfortunately, they were never able to have any more children and that was a hard blow for them both to come to peace with.

So, he hoped that his son would grow stronger and more resilient in his absence and not lose his heart to vanity or idleness. *Either way, he will prosper or fail in his own choices. It is in the hands of the Almighty.*

*****

THE BLISTERING sun beat down on the green fields surrounding the ranch where cattle grazed among the sparsely scattered pinion and mesquite trees. Alfalfa fields, with their bouquets

43

of small purple flowers, created a thick and heady sweet aroma that attracted bees by the thousands.

The insects buzzed hurriedly in the air above Ajay Khan Majumbar's head as he sullenly walked along the weed-covered bank, setting irrigation tubes in the muddy water. One after another, he cupped his hand over one end, swung the tube several times back and forth in the water to create suction inside, and then quickly rested the tube over the bank letting the suction start the flow of water down the row to irrigate the crop of beans.

He had already set over one-hundred fifty tubes and had another two-hundred more to set in this field before he could move on to the four neighboring fields, to set thousands more tubes there. Then there were still two more fields of alfalfa to do after that. It was a long and drearily day of monotonous work ahead and he was already very hot, tired, and extremely bored. But more than anything else, he was furious that he was even forced to do this work at all.

Manual labor was something Ajay detested enough as it was, but what infuriated him was that the endless monotony of the work his father and uncle did on the ranch that he felt was below them, and especially him. These menial tasks were meant for lower caste people, not the duties that should be given to someone of such grand lineage, and the fact that he was still only thirteen-years old meant that he would be doing these tedious chores at the ranch forever! It seemed like it would be an eternity before he was old enough to walk away from this miserable existence.

His friend and chore partner Miguel was also moping lethargically farther down the ditch, punching his shovel into its banks, thinning out the weeds and grass that threatened to choke off the flow of water. Miguel was two-years older than Ajay but they were always together in chores and mischief. Miguel's father was serving time in a Mexican prison for murdering a man during a drug deal and his mother was a prostitute in San Antonio. So he was being raised by his older brother, Juan, who rarely stayed outside of the local jailhouse for more than a couple weeks at a time. Miguel and Ajay were both misfit outsiders at school and were regularly picked on by the white rednecks there; Ajay for his Muslim heritage (everyone called him *Hadji* after the cartoon character on Johnny Qwest) and Miguel for just being a poor Mexican.

Ajay hated boredom and craved excitement like what his father and uncle Subhash were experiencing now in their Islamic homelands, taking jihad to the godless kafir Soviets. Ajay did not want to be here doing these useless chores on the ranch for the 'old cripple' Ferguson. Even before the old man had the stroke that left him

44

drooling in his wheelchair, he had never been what Ajay considered a good man. Always calling his father disrespectful things like 'son' and even shortening his proper name to 'Push' all the time, treating his father like he was some kind of pet.

Ajay could not comprehend how his father could allow such disrespect. But his father, a man born to the Brahman caste, would just wave off Ajay's indignation by smiling and telling him how thankful he should be for the generosity the man had, and that he would not be here in America with a family without that benevolence. But Ajay did not see it that way at all. As a descendent of the strong Majumbar clan of the Pahari people, who were descended from the divine Lord Shiva; Ajay deserved more than to be the servant to some kafir unbeliever. He wished to be walking the peaks of the great Himalayas and not here stomping in the cow shit and mud of this despicable bean field.

He wished his father would be more like his brave Uncle Mayur, and stand up for himself and his rightful place in the community.

Compared to Mayur, Ajay felt his father was a weakling, too tolerant of the indignities given him by the old cripple and the community elders. Mayur was the kind of strong leader that Ajay would someday be. Ajay listened with rapt attention to Mayur's many stories; like of the night of his father's birth or of his brave grandfather, Abdulla, struggling against the British and Hindus to free their ancestral lands. Mayur spoke bitterly of the hardships, indignities, and disgraces that the clan has faced after the loss of their lands, herds, and, most importantly, prestige in the caste culture. When their Brahman status was taken from them by the despised Hindus and imperialist British, and how they took a hatchet to the old property boundaries in Kashmir, forcing the clan to become shilpkar just to survive.

Ajay proudly listened as Mayur addressed the Muslim elders in San Antonio in an attempt to raise more money for the jihad in Kashmir, regaling them with tales of the exploits of brave mujahedeen there. But unlike Mayur, his father and mother refused to join the struggle. They willingly rebuffed Mayur's leadership in the clan and rejected participating in the struggles in Kashmir. They said their future was here in America and not back there on the subcontinent. The weak and despicable imam, as well as the other elders in the community agreed, and refused to become involved. They were all too soft and feeble, and Ajay hated them for that. He hated them all. He wanted more. He deserved more. He swore that one day he would have more and that they would pay for their failings and cowardice.

45

Then, four weeks ago, everything in Ajay's life changed when the government men in suits came, flaunting their FBI badges and spoke with his parents and uncle Subhash. After the agents left, his parents called him out and explained that the government was asking for help in supporting the mujahedeen battling against the Soviets in Afghanistan. That was the first time his parents told him that Mayur was already assisting the American CIA there. Ajay was shocked that he had not been told anything by Mayur the last time he visited. He only knew of Mayur's fighting for the independence of Kashmir – and his father's refusal to participate there – but now he discovered they had all been lying to him.

His father told him how the CIA promised Mayur that America would help in Kashmir's struggles for independence if they would help in America's efforts against the Soviets. They wanted to use the Majumbar clan's connections within Kashmir and Pakistan to make contacts in the region, and help in moving resources, materials, and funds into Afghanistan.

His father spoke of a 'domino effect' and how he and Subhash were being called upon to help America in a righteous and pious fight that he could support, since it was a jihad against an invasion of atheist Russians into Muslim lands. His father told him that he must become a man early and take up the responsibility for providing for his mother and doing the necessary ranch work.

The thought of being stuck with his father's work on the ranch infuriated Ajay. He suddenly realized that he would be alone, doing menial things, treated like he was some migrant worker. He was also enraged with being lied to. Ajay spoke bitterly of his resentment, demanding to know how his father could leave at the request of the Zionist American government, yet refuse to join the jihad for Kashmir.

At first his father had just smiled and placed his hand on Ajay's head as he spoke, "My son, I am proud that you wish to see the beauty of Kashmir free. Your uncles and I wish for the same thing, but that fight cannot be won without many things being discussed between great nations. The Americans, British, Indian, and Pakistanis all must come to that table and agree over great topics for us to see our homeland free. You are young and willful, you just do not understand."

Bitterness at his father's words swelled in Ajay's heart and he could not stop himself from blurting out what he thought and felt. He swiped at his father's hand in frustration.

"You don't care about what I want! You treat me like a child and tell *me* to obey! You are leaving and I'm forced to stay and work the fields – I deserve better!

46

Pushkar's eyes widened rapidly in surprise and then changed to anger, as if Ajay had slapped him across the face. His explosive response was shocking to everyone in the room as he recoiled from Ajay's words as if Ajay had suddenly turned into a snake. With a beet-red face he punched Ajay square in the face with a closed fist, sending him flailing backward with blood gushing from a cut lip and shattered nose.

Ajay remembered lying in shame and bawling while his throbbing nose bled into his hands. Little sparks of light danced in the air before his eyes as his father towered menacingly above him with clenched fists and was roughly held back by Subhash to restrain him from pummeling Ajay further. His sobbing mother held Ajay in her arms demanding for Pushkar to control himself.

Pushkar stared coldly down at Ajay.

"You know nothing of hardship! You know nothing of struggle! You only know the luxuries possible here in this country. You are indulgent and weak! You know nothing and yet you demand things that cannot be given. My honor and sacrifices will be respected! *Haadi*! You will not dishonor me. You will never speak to me like that again or I will kill you!"

Asha gave a sharp gasp and the room went very quiet as Subhash eyed Pushkar closely and Ajay cried. The tension between everyone was thick as Pushkar repeatedly clenched his hands until finally his body noticeably relaxed and his face softened.

"You will respect and obey your mother while I am gone. Honor my choice in this, I am your father." Pushkar then turned and left the room without saying another word.

Ajay cried while filled with humiliation and hurt as he tossed and turned in his bed all that night. He knew the teachings of the Quran demanded that he obey and honor his parents, but he refused to let those words extinguish a seed of anger that burned inside his heart over the injustice done to him. His father avoided him for several days, never even looking at him. Both Subhash and his mother increased this indignity by following his father's lead, as they also avoided any contact with him. His mother spoke with him briefly at meal times but otherwise she became far more distant than usual and seemed cold when she spoke to him.

Over the next week his father and Subhash had met many times with elders at the masjid and then he and Subhash had just left for Pakistan, with Ajay never talking to his father again, except to say goodbye at the airport in Houston. He knew what was expected of him – to show deference and humility to his father and pledge obedience in his absence. As the airport farewells were said, over the hum of idling

47

jet engines, Ajay felt like he was groveling as he gave platitudes to the man he no longer viewed worthy of his devotion.

Ajay remembered the sight of the large white and blue Pan Am plane lifting off the runway, and the feeling of relief and release that came with its leaving. He knew he need not fear his father's wrath anymore and he just needed to figure out how to take advantage of the situation. His mother would be easily to manipulate. But he needed to escape if he was going to get all of the things he wanted in life.

He mulled those thoughts as he methodically continued down the ditch, placing one irrigation tube after another and contemplating how rotten and unacceptable his situation was. He wished to be older. He wished to be powerful.

Then he heard the faint sound of approaching music and looking up he saw a yellow El Camino bouncing in the dust of the county road, mariachi music blaring from the car's sound system. Ajay immediately brightened; the car was driven by Miguel's brother, Juan, and the loud accordion and guitar-laced music screaming out of the stolen Kenwood speakers made perfect time with the car bouncing down the road. Ajay threw down the tube in his hands and took off running down the ditch to join Miguel, who now stood at the barbed wire fence waiting for his brother.

Ajay watched as Miguel disappeared into the cloud of dust kicked up as the El Camino as it skidded to a stop. He ran up to the fence, panting hard, and saw Miguel dancing next to the grill of the car, looking adoringly up at his older brother, while the sound of accordions, guitars, and trumpets blended with a high-pitched troubadour singing a mariachi tune. The music was so loud that the line of dingle-ball skirting that hung from the four windows vibrated in time with the rhythm of the music. Miguel spun and danced in the road.

Ajay stared at the beautiful brown-eyed Latina, her complexion the color of dark mocha and skin as smooth as rose petals. She climbed out of the car with her breasts bouncing and sat on a fender with her swinging feet kicking the tire below her as she laughed, watching Miguel dance. Her long legs were covered with skin-tight bellbottom jeans, the ends of which slapped each other as she kicked. Large gold-colored hoops dangled from her ears and costume jewelry rings were on each of her fingers.

Juan pulled two long neck bottles of beer from the car and joined his younger brother in gyrating to the rhythm of the mariachi. Then handing one beer to the girl he snuggled up close, standing between her legs and bounced his hips off her inner thighs. Ajay watched in juvenile lust as her thick supple lips encapsulated the open

48

head to the bottle and her throat chugged as she gulped down the cold beer.

Juan enjoyed the same show just inches from her face as his hips tapped her thighs. His black three-inch-high platform loafers had lost their shine due to the dust, and with his brown polyester bellbottom pants, matching vest, high-collared yellow button shirt, open to his navel, he looked very much like John Travolta in the disco movie *Saturday Night Fever*. He wore shiny gold-colored jewelry: a watch, several rings, two necklaces, and a chain bracelet with the letters CCRM engraved on it. Looking over his shoulder at Ajay, Juan smiled as he pulled a thick joint from his inner vest pocket. After lighting it he took a deep drag off the marijuana cigarette, and handed it to the Latina who did the same and coughed hard.

"Que' esta' sucediendo, amigo?" Juan asked while coughing.

"Muy bien, hermano," Ajay replied, smiling.

"Ayee! Way to go – Miguel is teaching you well, hombre," Juan exclaimed, taking the cigarette from the girl and handing it to his little brother.

"I hear your papa is gone back to the old country for a while, man. That right?" Juan asked eyeing Ajay's reaction.

"Yah, so what?" Ajay asked as he took the marijuana cigarette from Miguel and inhaled.

"Miguel was telling me that he doesn't want to be out here doing this crap for that pinche cabron gringo, Ferguson. He also tells me that you may want to come with us Chicanos and party?"

Ajay looked back over his shoulder at the large fields needing irrigation. The first tingle of a buzz started to crawl through his brain, followed by the departure of any sense of responsibility he had left.

"Fuck'n-A, amigo! Where are we going?"

"All right! You and Miguel jump in man, we're headed to a party in San Marcos of the *Movimiento Estudiantil Chicano Aztlán*. We're gonna dance, and drink, and smoke some good shit. Ain't that right baby," Juan said as he grabbed and squeezed the Latina's rump, causing her to giggle.

"I gotta bro at the meeting who says he can pay me to go down to Monterrey – they got a ranch up in the Sierra Madra that grows some great Mexican Gold. Your papa is gone for a while, eh? Well, listen here, little hermano – let me bring some of that Mexican Gold and keep the shit here at the ranch – maybe down at the corrals, eh? And I'll pay you some good bread, my man. What you say?"

Ajay felt his head swim from the effects of his long drag on the marijuana cigarette and he enjoyed it. He had not considered until now just how much it could work to his advantage having his father

49

gone. There would be no way for him to hide anything like this from him, but his mother – so trusting, gullible, and, well, a woman. Ajay was the man in the house now. It would be her place to not challenge him and he should have no problems hiding anything from her. A large smile spread across his face as he thought of everything he could do with only the 'old cripple' Ferguson's son, Marshall, to worry about.

"You're on, bro, but I want to go."

"Woohoo! Yeah?" Juan said punching at the air in front of him.

New horizons and ideas flooded into Ajay's mind.

"Yeah, I want to see Monterrey, too."

"You and me, we're going to make good amigos, dude! We're gonna make some big-time bread and then we'll become the Man! We're going to take this all back and send the pinche gringo back to fucking Europe, my man!" Juan yelled while they crammed onto the bench seat of the vehicle.

Ajay's mind floated in a wild haze as he squished in next to the beautiful Latina. Her plump breast pressed softly into his shoulder and her perfume was intoxicating. His stiff erection pressed uncomfortably against his pants as he laughed at how great life was going to be now that his father was out of his way.

"This is what I should have – and much, much more," he said quietly to himself.

The tires spun and gravel flew as the vehicle fishtailed down the road, music still blaring out the windows. The Latina held onto a drag from the joint as long as she could and then coughed it out hard, making her eyes water as mascara started running down her cheek. She downed half the bottle of beer, bobbing her head in time to the music.

"*Aztlán!*" she yelled.

*****

September 25, 1998 16:10pm CST UTC -6:00
Texas State Penitentiary
Huntsville, TX

AFTER THREE long years of sitting in his dank prison cell, hearing its near constant cacophony of mechanical sounds, human activity, and endless drone of voices – it had almost achieved the emotional quality of home-life for Ajay. It gave the feeling of security and familiarity but heavily mixed with sadness, boredom, hatred, depression, and desperation.

Every day made him feel like a fetus in the womb, waiting to be aborted – floating in an endlessly constraining vacuum, imprisoned in eternal tedium, locked unwillingly into unrelenting dreariness that would only end in a brutal awakening, naked, bloody; to be tossed onto the putrid pile with more aborted fetuses and then to be hauled to the dump, forgotten. The prison, like the womb, was a hell. Created for his misery and the last place in the world he should have ever been. His pain was deep and his hatred grew daily.

He hated the noise even more than the ceaseless monotony. The prison noises made a maddening loop that played out in his head, like a cracked record bouncing on a turntable, endlessly repeating itself. The clanking steel-barred gates constantly being opened and shut; the ceaseless buzz of electrical motors and the warning horns and beeps that went off before an automated door was unlocked via remote control centers. Wintertime brought the popping of the heated steel pipes as their scalding steam moved throughout the old red-bricked building to all the hundreds of radiators spread throughout. The near-constant shuffling of incarcerated men wearing flip-flops, moving to and fro along the catwalk, some wore rattling leg chains and some not. The solid thump of the guard's boots escorting them or just making their rounds along the tier, keeping an eye on everything the inmates did and still not seeing anything the inmates wanted to remain hidden. The tinkling of keys and the rap from the batons being knocked against cell bars. Then there was the annoying sound of the high squeak of the bad wheel on the magazine cart. It was pushed along the tier everyday by the retard, Forndike. Forndike – a mental incompetent who only knew how to rape little boys outside the walls. And all he knew inside the walls was how to get raped in turn, and, of course, how to irritate the shit out of Ajay.

But the most pervasive and repulsive sounds were the thousands of voices that never shut up. Ajay was forced to constantly hear the mumbled conversations from hundreds of two-legged vermin that rudely invaded his poor ears with their chatter on a daily basis.

The inevitable yelling of some inmate-guard confrontation, the faint mewing and crying of a weak man-pet or some prison-bitch after he was raped by a predator. The nervous laughter of newbie's hanging close to the older inmates or stronger leaders on the cell block, trying desperately to keep from becoming one of the raped. The voices of guards as they constantly yelled out roll calls and daily head counts, or issued their mindless orders as they bullied the weak and bowed to the strong. The hated prattle never ended, filling Ajay's mind with their gibberish.

At twenty-eight, there were no sounds Ajay could not identify inside a prison anymore. Since his father had left for jihad, Ajay had racked up a long list of incarcerations. Spending over a year serving time in juvi-hall up in Bexar, doing a couple of days at a time for the various petty, and sometimes not so petty crimes during his teenage years. At eighteen he graduated to doing harder time in the county jails in Hays and Travis counties, where he served a couple of thirty-day stints for theft and drug possession, and almost a full year after he cut up a Mexican kid in San Marcos. Ever since the eighth grade the punk-kid loved to call Ajay, the Ayatollah. Now-a-days the bastard said nothing at all with his slit vocal cords.

For the past three years Ajay has been serving out a five-year sentence in this hell hole. The oldest piece-of-crap prison in the whole Texas Department of Criminal Justice, the Walls, they called it inside, but outside everyone knew it as the Huntsville Unit, and it had been around in one form or another since the mid-1800s.

Ajay's reckless juvenile thoughts of unrestricted fun and pushing his rebellious attitude to the limit had maintained his irresponsible path as a teenager, all the while running around causing hate and discontent with Miguel. Even being sent to juvenile hall meant nothing to him back then. His mother followed him around making her pathetic excuses for his behavior.

All that changed after his father had returned after three years away, fighting the Soviets in his precious jihad. Pushkar had returned disfigured, crippled, and emotionally defeated. His uncle, Subhash, had been killed by the communists in the same attack that had crippled his father, and Mayur had fled back to Kashmir vowing to never get involved with the CIA again. His father was sullen, angry, and disconnected and with Subhash dead it left Ajay almost as unsupervised as he had ever been. By the time he became an adult Ajay graduated from having juvenile fun to seeking power and money.

Upon Pushkar's return Asha was forced to attend to the needs of the old cripple, Ferguson, and also her wounded husband, who suffered with having only one leg and a broken spirit. Pushkar was much colder and seethed with an anger that could come to the surface quickly and with very little provocation. Deeply ashamed at what Ajay had done in his absence, he and Ajay argued regularly whenever Ajay was not incarcerated. Things had come to blows one night when he had grabbed Ajay by the arm to keep him from leaving after an argument. No longer a child, Ajay refused to submit to any heavy-handed treatment and simply swept his leg under his father's prosthesis, sending Pushkar crashing to the floor. That night their roles

52

had fully reversed as Asha cradled her husband, who lay humiliated on the floor, while Ajay glared down at them.

Ajay had not returned home once in the seven years since that night and had not spoken to his father at all, while only speaking occasionally to his mother. He morphed over the ensuing years, from the punk kid who smoked dope, snorted coke, and committed petty thefts and burglaries, into a robber and smuggler. He worked with Miguel and Juan in bringing dope and illegal immigrants across the border, and for fun, he and Miguel would often rob Mexicans around Monterey and Nuevo Laredo like bandits. They had not killed anyone yet but Ajay knew that was a matter of time as the itch to kill one of the filthy spic's only increased with each robbery.

He hated being a coyote and being forced to put up with the sight and smell of the weak, filthy, and pathetic migrants that he smuggled across the border. He preferred the money made from bringing in loads of dope. The migrants stank and were grimy, making his truck stink for days after the haul. Occasionally he would have some fun beating the crap out of one when they refused to cough up some piso before the crossing. But he refused to mess with the likes of the ex-Sandinistas and their enemies, the ex-Contras from Nicaragua. Those bastards were not like the dirt farmer Mexicans; they were real bad-asses! The real surprise to him, though, was the small dark-skinned Guatemalans – every once in a while there would be an ex-member of the URNG-MAIZ in a group of those midgets. After Ajay had watched one of those tiny bastards slice up a Mexican Federale in a mesquite field, he made sure to be very careful around them, as well. They were awfully small, but after thirty-six years of civil war, some of them knew how to gut a person real quick.

Smuggling dope with Juan and Miguel proved very lucrative compared to the robbery gig. Robbing Mexican shops could be fun but there just was not any money in it and the kidnapping thing was dominated by local bandits. A few bales of marijuana and a handful of migrants were no big deal with the green-shirted INS or the DEA. They were after the coke, and it was not until Ajay started making big money by bringing in the 'white gold' that he had gained their attention. The DEA caught up with him in Austin with two kilos and now he was serving hard time for it. The only luck he had in the whole rotten deal was getting to serve out his time in the state prison system instead of in a federal lock-up somewhere.

His personal drug use through the years had graduated from alcohol and marijuana to cocaine and even heroin by the time he got busted by the DEA. After first arriving at 'the Walls' he went through the agony of withdrawal and it almost killed him, but he survived and came out of it clean, but far more pissed off than before.

His father refused to come to any of the court proceedings and he only allowed Asha the occasional visit at the prison. Ajay was alone and isolated inside the penal system, but luckily his connection with Miguel and Juan served him well. They worked for Osiel Cardenas and his Gulf cartel in the Matamoros to Monterrey smuggling corridor. Juan used the cartel's partnership with La Familia Michoacana to give Ajay ample protection inside the system. The American La Familia saw that he stayed safe and unmolested.

Not being Latino or Christian cut off much of the other protections and services available to other inmates. Then one day his old life shifted dramatically when he was assigned another Muslim, Ali Hussein, as a cell partner. The man quickly became his instructor and guide back to Islam, teaching Ajay things he never was taught as a child.

For the first time since he was a small child Ajay had someone close to him every day that refused to allow him indulgences. Ali became the leader of the cell the very first day he arrived, giving out his rules for the cell: 1) Remove your shoes upon entering the cell, 2) Clean the floor every time you leave the cell and, 3) Never make any noise during prayers. In a very short time he began to instruct Ajay in the teachings of Imam Sayyid Qtub and the ways of Salafist Islam.

Ajay had paid little attention to Sufi Islam or the deep mysticism of the Dervish that his father and uncles practiced. As a child Pushkar refused to allow him to attend the Sunni madrasah in San Antonio like he wished. His only teachings about the Prophet and saints came from his father and Subhash and their personal introspection and constant recitation of the mystic's poetry was nothing he cared for.

With Hussein he found a mentor who taught him the true meaning of the dáwah of the Prophet. He learned that his father's weak beliefs were heretical teachings that led Ajay into a time-of-weakness, ultimately resulting in him sitting in this prison cell, just as Muhammad's Jamáah had experienced their hardships in Mecca. Hussein instructed Ajay in first cleansing himself of the jahili stench that his father had forced upon him, living a life of drugs and debauchery in America. Hussein made Ajay commit to a hijra and then the jihad.

Ajay quickly learned everything Hussein was able to teach and soon realized that not only was he gaining focus and clarity about his life and how he had wasted so much of it in juvenile thoughts and petty criminal activity, he also learned just how evil and corrupt his father's practices were to the true teachings of Islam. Hussein opened his eyes to the corruption of the Sufi and the immorality of the Zionist-controlled jahili America were the causes of all of his problems.

Hussein explained how Zionists Jews used mujahedeen, like his father, as pawns in plots with the atheist Soviets to supplant the rightful Taliban from ruling Afghanistan, and fed the righteous Muslim warriors into a meat grinder of war. He spoke of how America's drug addiction was just a way for the Zionists to control the poor and uneducated masses.

Ajay learned of the struggles and deprivations of the Palestinians under the long occupation by the Zionists and their British thugs of Jerusalem, the third holiest city of Islam, and how it mirrored the deprivations of the occupation by the British and their Hindu allies in Kashmir. He learned the histories of the Muslim expansion during the Arabic conquests and the establishment of the Rashidun Dynasty.

Suddenly, Islam became more than just vague, spiritual stories his parents told in childhood; it was now real, concrete, and clear. He learned more about sharia, and how it must be applied to the lives of peoples all over the world. Hussein spoke of how the jihad for sharia was tied to everything, from the mujahedeen in Chechnya battling against the Russians, to the bombing of the World Trade Center in 1993 by Ramsi Yousef and his teacher, Sheik Omar Abdel Rahman. And he showed Ajay how it was tied to every struggle for Muslim freedom from the oppressive regimes in Egypt, Jordan, Syria, and all of Arabia.

Hussein taught Ajay how Sayyid Qtub's vision of a pan-Islamic state, a great Caliphate, would someday supplant the hated and reviled House of Saud that ruled with an iron fist. One day the Holy Cities of Mecca and Medina would be the center of that global Islamic Empire.

Ajay finally understood how all of these seemingly divergent commentaries were directly related to his own suffering. He saw how the Salafist path could achieve things that he had sought his entire life - power and glory. From before he was even born, the world of the kafir had worked against Ajay in every way possible by destroying his chances and diverting his mind to frivolous pursuits. Now, seeing how it all fit together with his suffering, Ajay vowed to make the world pay.

His foolish father and uncles had been nothing but lackeys for the infidels in Washington, DC, and all weak-hearted Muslims like them brought nothing but shame to Salafist Islam. It would take a cleansing of the Muslim heart, mind, and body for Islam to regain its rightful dominance on the Earth. Ajay could now be a major part of the struggle to bring the sharia to the masses and exact violent revenge against the kafir pigs that infested the globe.

Before he could begin to accomplish any of those things he needed to find a way to make all his new dreams of revenge and greatness possible. He needed a plan. It would take time, effort, study, and above all else, it would take patience. He had never showed much talent for these qualities, but he must now develop these skills if he wanted to succeed. He picked Hussein's brain for every bit of information on the pious Salafi and any personal contacts he could obtain before he was to be released.

Ajay knew to be careful with what he said, what he did, who he was seen with, and what kind of trail he left behind him. There would be false allies along the way, weaklings he would meet who would snitch him out in a second. People often cracked from the slightest pressure applied by the cops, the FBI, or the CIA. Patience was the key. Planning was imperative. Nothing impetuous or reckless could achieve the glory he craved or the status he demanded. The weak would learn to submit to him; and if he so chose that death should be their only reward for obedience, then they would learn to happily accept that as their fate. He was going to make sure that they would all learn the hard way. It was his right. It was his destiny. His parents, America, the whole world would learn of his greatness in a very hard way.

But he needed to commit a grand act that would match his desire for the immortality of glory, and also overwhelm the hearts of people. The devastation after the destruction wrought by McVeigh in the 1995 Oklahoma City bombing would pale in comparison to his act. The first inklings of an idea sparked into his mind and he chuckled. He would light a match to burn his name into the future of the Earth and that would place him on a pedestal next to Allah. Yes, the Prophet would sit at the left hand of God and Ajay would sit at the right.

Ajay tumbled the idea in his mind as he started penning a letter to his mother and father. Unfortunately, he would still need their help at the beginning – there was simply no way of avoiding that. He was destitute and needed a public and legal makeover if he was going to fit into the community again. He needed to get the DEA and cops off his tail so he could move and plan freely. What he needed was legitimacy, and his parents could help give him that. He would use them and then discard them into the cesspool of the world that he would eventually burn. The wording in the letter must be just right to pass his father's scrutiny. Ajay must perform perfectly in his acts of humility and bring a subtle mind to conversations with the cripple. The

56

old man was no fool and no glimpse of what was in Ajay's heart could be shown, not in the slightest, or he would lose everything.

So he wrote a story of his religious resurrection, and a new-found devotion to Islam. He begged for his father's encouragement and forgiveness, praying that if his father would but open his heart to believe in his son once again, Ajay would forever change into the good son he should have always been. The letter was long and tedious for Ajay to write but it brought fruition quickly. A reply letter showed up from his mother in less than three weeks. As he read her reply he smiled broadly.

*****

January 5, 1999 08:23am CST UTC -6:00
Easy Creek Ranch
Sattler, TX

AS ASHA Majumbar picked up the dishes from the small table the cowl of her hijab fell from her shoulder, forcing her to adjust it so that it would not fall across her eyes again. She watched her husband closely as she placed the dishes into the sink for washing. His once muscular and robust arms appeared thin as they rested limply on the table while he stared quietly out the window at the cold morning. Neither spoke; both keeping their thoughts inside and the only noise was the faint ticking of snowflakes landing against the kitchen window.

This morning Asha recited the prayer of salat-al-istikhara, asking for guidance; she felt that Allah had pointed her heart in the right direction. Since Ajay and Pushkar no longer spoke to each other, she offered to broker Ajay's idea to her husband on her son's behalf. She looked out at the rare Texas blizzard and saw the hunched-over form of her son, sitting patiently inside a little Nissan, its windows heavily fogged, waiting to hear his father's decision. Physically, she was warmer and more comfortable here inside her home but emotionally, she felt as vulnerable as her son waiting for her husband to make his choice.

Thin wisps of windblown snow crossed over the yard on stiff gusts of wind. The frigid winter landscape around the ranch house was all that remained of the once large ranch owned by the late Sam Ferguson. His son, Marshall, found him dead last August, sprawled on the hardwood floor in front of the stuffed leopard he had killed so many years before.

After his death, Marshall quickly sold off sections of the ranch, until the only thing left was the ten acres around the old ranch

57

house and barn. He fulfilled a wish his father had decided upon many years earlier but had not put into his will before he had his stroke. Per Sam's wishes, Marshall offered to sell the property at the old ranch house to Pushkar and Asha at one third its value. They were immensely grateful for his gesture of kindness and friendship, and readily accepted the offer, securing a home for them with what was left of their settlement from the Federal government for Pushkar's service to the United States in Afghanistan.

While Asha continued cleaning the morning dishes Pushkar sat quietly, considering his life's path and the generosity of the Ferguson family over the years. They had given him the opportunity to come to America and meet his beautiful wife. This ranch gave him good employment for many years and the graciousness of Marshall allowed them to survive financially while Pushkar was gone to the jihad. Upon his return he kept Pushkar employed throughout the years and even made allowances in his duties for the handicap of his missing leg.

Pushkar had made the poor choice to leave his strong-willed son in the care of his mother. He cursed himself repeatedly for that mistake and knew that if he had just taken more time to work with the Muslim community, to establish a surrogate father figure for his son at the madrasah; to receive proper guidance, Ajay might not have followed the path of self-destruction that he had.

Pushkar never imagined his efforts in Afghanistan would take him away for so long – three long years. By the time he had returned his son had already drifted too far down the path of corruption and arrogance. They were now so far apart in their feelings that he did not know how to repair it. The anger inside both of them created a chasm that was far too deep and wide to ever be filled by cheap words.

Pushkar shifted the stump of his left thigh wincing slightly as the small pieces of shrapnel inside jabbed into what was left of his atrophied leg muscles. He sometimes moved the wrong way and his tendons jumped from small electrical pulses that shot through them.

He laid his palm on the point of pain and gingerly massaged the ache. He looked up at the finely mounted leopard above the fireplace that Marshall gave him as a gift after Sam's death. He kept it now as a memory of his longtime friend and the times that he and the Texas cowboy had together. The cat was forever set in a dignified pose of power and majesty.

Thinking back to that frigid day on a mountain top on the other side of the world, Pushkar wondered if his choice to accept the offer to come here had been a mistake. He wondered if he could have found a good wife as precious as his Asha back in Pakistan or

Kashmir. Would a life there, in his homeland, give him more healthy children, and would those children have been loyal and good children? Would they dishonor him and the Muslim community in which they lived? He did not know, and those wistful thoughts did not matter anyway.

"He has money of his own to do this?" Pushkar asked, breaking the silence of the room.

"He says he has friends who will loan him a truck to start the business, but he doesn't want hawala, he does not trust it. He says these people will actually provide him with a legitimate business loan," Asha replied.

"These new friends of his aren't just more drug smuggler types, are they?"

Asha looked coolly at her husband as Pushkar returned her gaze evenly, displaying no emotion. She turned away slowly and looked out the bay window above the kitchen sink, staring out on the frozen windblown world. The snow flew across the driveway and was beginning to pile against the tires of her son's car. She could no longer see Ajay's face, only a hulking shape sitting there; the fog on the windows had become too thick. The old heater inside the car did not work well enough to keep up with his breath.

"I don't believe smugglers co-sign bank notes, my husband, but, Allah knows, I could be wrong," she said finally. "He has started doing the prayers every day and appears to have become closer to his faith. He tells me that he found a teacher while he was being held in that prison. That imam helped him to cleanse his soul and has inspired him to follow a path to God. I believe he is sincere, Husband, but only time will show if he can calm his spirit. He has a sincerity and maturity that I haven't seen in him before."

She finished, still not saying who was actually loaning the funds to their son. She could feel Pushkar's eyes staring at the back of her head while he waited patiently for the information she wanted to conceal. As the silence continued she knew he would wait until hell itself froze over, so she finally relented and said what he wanted to know.

"The funding is to be provided by the Arabic outreach as part of an employment program for ex-convicts."

"Aww, the Saudis! I should have guessed. Does he realize they'll have strings attached to their friendship, and their money?"

Asha's eyes flashed as she snapped a reply.

"Would their strings be any worse than the strings he has now, of being a petty criminal with no future, my husband?"

"No. But you know they are much like mafioso. They will expect payment back at a high price."

After considering the thought of strings being attached to the success of his son's endeavor, Pushkar thought that it could also be a great motivator for his son to stay out of trouble.

"Maybe with their financing being connected to this business it will help keep him focused and committed, instead of snorting up more drugs," he offered aloud, saying it as much for himself to hear as for Asha.

Asha continued to stare out upon the bitterly cold winter day, watching as the fog from Ajay's breath continued to condense on the windows inside the sputtering car. A gloved hand pushed against the windshield, circling several times to create a hole in the condensation. She could see her son's face again and pangs of love and compassion went out to him.

"He is cold out there. Can he not come in while you consider his ideas, Husband? Can your heart not let your son come and enjoy the warmth and love of this house?"

"A drowning man is not troubled by the rain," Pushkar replied coldly, as he stared up at the stuffed leopard.

Asha bit at her lip in anger and frustration at her husband's cryptic, cold response. He had changed so much, no longer the man with a ready smile or the person able to bring levity to a room with his charm. His demeanor was cold and stern and she detected that a deep bitterness, often times hidden to others but visible to her, had crept into his soul after his brother's death and his own infirmity. She could no longer achieve the closeness of spirit they once shared between them, and her attempts to help bring a healing and grace back to his mind and spirit were often rebuffed.

"Your son is cold – you are warm. Will you sit in that chair and watch him shiver for hours before you decide? I want our son to have a chance to regain himself and his dignity. I want you to support his effort to better himself – I will say nothing else."

Pushkar glanced sideways at his wife after her unusually biting comment. He always considered her an exceptionally strong and intelligent Pahari woman. Her body was outlined against the light of the window and he admired her fine profile as she stood rigid and proud, simmering in frustration with him.

He was so proud of her and yet he had never really told her so. He regretted that – as he regretted so many other things in his life. She was a far better woman than the burqa-wearing slaves back in Pakistan and Afghanistan. That type of slavery was what the Talib and Pashtu wanted from their women, but it was not what he wanted in his.

She was far stronger than Ajay gave her credit for. He confused her love for weakness. She was strong but could not be the father that Pushkar should have been. She did well to keep herself and Ajay together while Pushkar was gone so long, and she had done so without complaint. Since the day he had approached her father, broaching the possibility of a courtship, he had seen that inner strength of hers. To this day he knew that of all the choices in his life, she was the best.

On the other hand, his worst choice turned out to be his decision to fight in the jihad for Afghanistan. Pushkar and Subhash had proved very good at marching the mujahedeen, Stinger missiles, food, medicine, and other supplies through the jagged mountain peaks of the Hindu Kush that divided the Balistan regions of the Northwest Territories from the Kafiristan homelands of northern Afghanistan.

He and Subhash had guided the fighters and their supplies from the Chitral Airport to the staging bases around Singur. After the fighters acclimated for several days to the elevation they marched them above the Gorem-Chassma Road into the high passes above twenty thousand feet. Many of the fighters failed the passage across the mountains and had frozen to death or dropped dead from exhaustion and lack of oxygen during those hard treks near the roof of the world. Once through the passes the caravan would make their way down into the Togab-e Monjan valley where they would be turned over to either the Jamiat-i-Islami commander, Ahmad Shah Massoud, or the Maktab-al-Khidamat (Afghan Service Bureau-ASB) commander Abdullah Azzam and the warlord, Jalaluddin Haqqani.

Mayur worked as their facilitator between Azzam's ASB and the CIA's agents that were in-country. With the ample funding being supplied by both the CIA and Azzam's wealthy Saudi partner in the bin Laden family, Mayur never ran into any difficulty getting the items Pushkar and Subhash needed for those long, terrible marches. Those three years were the most physically difficult and challenging of Pushkar's life, and he left behind much of his soul while trekking across those hard, cold rocks of the Hindu Kush.

The snow whipping across the frigid landscape outside the ranch house reminded him of the day Subhash was killed during an attack by the Soviet helicopters. That terrible morning the caravan had begun descending toward the valley floor when a vicious wind sent a similar snowstorm down upon the caravan of men and donkeys.

Typically, blizzards were a blessing and a curse. The blessing was the protection from Soviet eyes and helicopters that they afforded, but the curse was the bitter cold and harsh bite as they dug icy tendrils into every gap of their clothing, freezing the skin underneath. Pushkar was positive that the storm over the slopes of Kohe Khrebek that day was doubly cursed. As quickly and ferociously as it had hit the caravan, freezing each man down to the bone, it seemed to dissipate in seconds, leaving the group of young men shivering and exposed on the flanks of the mighty mountain. The unnaturally still air was ominous in its silence as Subhash tried to get the men moving faster down the hillside. Suddenly, the roar of the four Mi-24 Hind helicopters came from over the ridge top as they swept down upon them like falcons hunting rabbits.

Pushkar clearly remembered his brother, running ahead, seeking the protection of a pile of boulders as snow and bits of rock were kicked up by hundreds of 23mm bullets striking nearby. Subhash reached the boulders at the same time an 88mm rocket hit, instantly obliterating his body. To this day, so many years later, Pushkar still vividly remembered, with horror, as the mass of meat and gore that was once his brother flew through the air along with large chunks of rock that exploded off of the shattered boulders.

His mind's eye, in slow motion, recorded in minute detail, as a skull-sized chunk of granite shot directly for him. His body moved far too slowly, unable to evade the projectile. It smashed into his right thigh spinning him through the air like some broken doll. He landed hard and lay sprawled and contorted on the ground, bleeding out onto the cold, hard stones as the fighters who were still alive tended to his wounds. The excruciating trip off those mountain ridges, with no morphine or medicine, was horrible, but the thoughts of his brother's body left in pieces, scattered across the barren and cold mountainside was the cruelest misery by far.

That day cost Pushkar his brother and his leg. Mayur watched over him in Peshawar for two months while he convalesced. The privations of the work, the loss of his leg, and above all the loss of Subhash had ended both Mayur and Pushkar's commitment to the struggle in Afghanistan.

It had also become extremely clear to them that both their CIA and Saudi benefactors were not interested or concerned in the least with the liberty of their Kashmiri homeland and would forever refuse to help them against the British and Hindus.

Today, Pushkar faced another choice. His troubled son was now a man who had thrown away much of his life. He was coming to them for help in establishing a business here on the ranch property, wanting to become a legitimate part of the community. He and Asha needed any extra money and this business might bring those finances in. Their funds were low after purchasing the land from Marshall. There was also the possibility, that maybe, just maybe this trucking business idea would be the thing that could give his son the direction and incentive to settle his spirit and keep him from falling back into drugs and criminal activity. Perhaps this time, just maybe this time, Pushkar would make a better choice, the right choice. Maybe he could resurrect his relationship with his son and start to make amends by rebuilding closeness within his family. Maybe Allah would give him the happiness he had before he left for jihad. He closed his eyes and made a silent prayer to Allah. Then he spoke.

"My answer is yes," Pushkar said quietly, "but he must work very hard and never bring any dishonorable activity here. Please ask him to come inside where it is warm and we will talk."

Asha's heart jumped with happiness. Turning with a broad smile she beamed with joy.

"He will be thankful and I believe that you will not be disappointed in your son this time. Thank you, my husband."

*****

September 12, 2001 11:30am CST UTC -6:00
AJ Trucking Inc. @ Easy Creek Ranch
Sattler, TX

THE SMALL television screen showed massive bent beams around a jagged opening in the side of the smooth shining metal and glass surface. Perpendicular lines of façade siding were bracketed by pale windows, many of which had distraught faces jutting as far out as possible and gasping at fresher air. Dark smoke billowed as arms waved and mouths uttered unknown words as thousands of sheets of paper fluttering down like snow. The size of the scene was small and shot at great distance, but had been zoomed in to show maybe fifty or more desperate people languishing and pleading for help. Ajay grinned.

Ajay thought the irony was supreme. It was just three days ago that he and his father had gotten into another of their many arguments. As Ajay's confidence grew with the success of the trucking business he found it easier to challenge his father and he spoke often about the Salafi and how Muslims could only find true freedom by following the orthodoxy of that pious religious view.

Pushkar argued that the rigid doctrine of the Salafi was not only incompatible with a modern pluralistic society, but was a corrupt view of the Prophet's teachings. Ajay argued that Salafist Islam was the final revelation of Allah and that it would one day sweep across the globe through jihad to form a paradise on Earth that would be wholly obedient to sharia and that it should begin in Kashmir.

Pushkar had tried to make his counterpoint.

63

"You must understand that Allah favors no man's purpose – if the weight of reality favors the enemy of that purpose, my son. The British are now long gone from Kashmir and as these Americans are fond of saying, 'all politics are local,' and that is the current state of Kashmir. You are a product of America and know little of the land of my birth or its politics."

"Maybe, Father, but the imam calls for the jihad, and what am I if I fail to fight in the sight of Allah?"

"Allah, Alsalam and the all-knowing, sees into the souls of each man and knows the true value of your heart. Be not taken from the path of God by the bigoted beliefs of soulless men. Salafi-Jihad is not spoken with Allah's voice but by the voice of men. Men who haven't set foot on the ground that my father's shadow crossed. Our ancestral land is not their concern; their only concern is the power that their words give to themselves."

"Do the calls of the imams for jihad hold no validity in our lives today?"

Pushkar breathed deeply and gave a weary sigh.

"The Imam al-Madhi has already come at the time appointed by Allah's wisdom. Many men in the past and others now in the present want, for very earthly reasons, to claim connection to the Madhi. Their claims of authority are as false as that of Hurqus ibn Zuhair before he received divine justice and was sent to the rewards of hell's afterlife." Pushkar could tell that Ajay's mind was frozen but he still tried to reach further. "My life has shown me, my son, that all men are weak and only Allah is strong. What does an imam from Saudi Arabia, Egypt or Yemen know of the struggle of my homeland? I have fought with the mujahedeen and watched as they were recruited with talk of this or that."

Ajay was stone-faced and Pushkar stopped and bowed his head to keep from raising his voice in frustration at his son.

"Allah's path to paradise doesn't go through the words of proud men sending children with bombs to martyr themselves against the innocent. That is the wicked path of Shaitan – and it leads straight to the gates of Hell."

"But, Father, Kashmir is but one front in the worldwide struggle for the mujahedeen in restoring the peace of Islam and preserving the honor of sharia – Bosnia, Tajikistan, Somalia, Burma, Palestine..." as Ajay recited the names he counted them one after another with his fingers. "Father, the Prophet Muhammad, peace be upon him, spoke of the duties of all Muslims to strike against the infidel...."

Pushkar cut him off angrily.

"I need not be lectured about the Prophet! I know my faith well and also the validity of jihad. You know nothing of the politics involved in Kashmir! These conflicts you speak of – they – they are not about religion; they are about regional politics and age-old blood feuds between tribes and ethnicities! If you were to go to Kashmir to fight in jihad you would quickly find that Pakistan's puppet, Amanullah Khan, and the Haqqani network will use you and spit you out anywhere their masters in the ISI want your blood spilled. They do this for their own political purposes and not in the interests of Allah or the Prophet, or even the independence of Kashmir. It would be the same with any other Fedayeen commander in the places you name so readily. You aren't a young boy anymore. You are a large, grown man. Think of becoming a leader in your own beliefs, not a follower of other men's wasteful causes."

"Father, Mayur continues the struggle and Subhash …."

Pushkar recoiled at the mention of his dead brother, whipping his head toward Ajay with a cold and steely gaze.

"Subhash is dead and I do not want pieces of my son rotting on barren stone like him! And Mayur is no longer lost to the jihad as if he were some slave to violence! Even he believes jihad is a useless effort in Kashmir. He now works within what system there is to free Kashmir and tries to make the plight of our people less severe by more peaceful means now. He knows co-existence with the other peoples of the subcontinent is necessary and he has laid down his sword of violence. – I, I will speak no more of this right now; you need to go to work. Let us speak of these things another time. I grow tired."

Ajay forced his body to obey as he extended his arm, gently placed his hand on his father's shoulder and gave a squeeze as he walked out the door. Days like that were hard for Ajay to tolerate.

Chastened, Ajay was forced to swallow his anger deeply so that he could walk out of the house that day, frustrated, forced to stay calm and not act out in violence against the old man. He knew the door that was open between them could also slam shut quickly if he pushed too far with his thoughts. Now, he sat in his office watching the footage of the attacks in New York City, and he smiled at how he had once again been proven right in his arguments against his father.

Ajay was overwhelmed at the success the jihadists had with these attacks. He could hardly believe that he was watching something real. The television showed an aerial shot of the smoky haze that had settled into the orderly man-made canyons of buildings in Manhattan. The sight of the smoke lying among the spires of steel reminded him of a thick fog resting above the river on a cold morning, with the tops of trees poking into the air through the canopy of mist.

CNN anchor Aaron Brown was dutifully describing the carnage and death at the site. No real, solid figures of the number of dead and injured were confirmed yet as they searched the rubble for survivors the day after the towers fell. Estimates said that the total dead might exceed ten thousand, depending on how many people had gotten out of the buildings before they collapsed. *I wish none had gotten out!* Heat and smoke from the fires still hampered the rescue efforts. The ghostly silhouettes of firemen crawling through the rubble with respirators covering their faces reminded him of old World War I footage of soldiers with gasmasks wandering through the mustard gas on the battlefields of Flanders and the Somme.

Occasionally, they would cut away from New York City and show scenes of the destruction at the Pentagon. The deep gouge in the green grass and dark soil created by the third airplane's death plunge into that building looked to Ajay like a huge spear jutting from the side of some bloated beast that now lay motionless and dead. *Ahab finally got you, didn't he, Moby Dick!* The jagged blackened wound in the Pentagon looked as if it could have been made by the monstrous tooth of some mythical creature. The newness of the gouge in the dirt showed the dampness of freshly turned soil, and Ajay greatly desired to smell the odor of that the freshly turned soil mixed with jet fuel; a smell he knew that the rescuers fighting the flames were breathing. The body count continued to rise as they found one charred and mangled body after another.

The CNN film crew zoomed in on some medical personnel pushing a stretcher across the lawn with a body bag containing someone's loved one inside. Ajay hoped it was some army major or even better, a general. They quickly shoved it inside of a waiting ambulance and the film crew went back to shooting film of the billowing smoke and raging fire.

Like everyone else, Ajay could not pull himself away from the carnage as the media showed it from every conceivable angle and vantage. There was no way he could allow his emotions to show as they did not mirror those of his employees as they sat with him, watching. They cried at what they were witnessing, while next to them Ajay swelled with pride and joy at what he saw. *The jihad wins!* Innocent people stumbling amid the destruction, or unjust murder committed against civilians? Those things were not what he saw at all. No, Ajay watched something far different – he saw justice being delivered to a jahili society of kafirs that needed to be gutted to the bone! He was witnessing a victory by the Salafi against the mongrel unbelievers! Above all else, it was payback for America's evils, decadence, and arrogance.

Yesterday, his parents had watched the attacks unfold live and Pushkar realized very quickly that the men who flew the planes into the World Trade Center buildings, the Pentagon, and the plane that crashed in the field in Pennsylvania were Muslim jihadists. He called Ajay's cell phone advising of the attacks and warned him that some people might seek reprisals against uninvolved Muslims or people they thought were Muslim. He warned Ajay to be very quiet and to keep his last name unspoken unless absolutely necessary until the immediate fallout from the attacks was over. He did not want Ajay to be the victim of some mob and end up like the white truck driver who had been brutally beaten by the mob during the Los Angeles riots after the Rodney King verdict. Ajay agreed, and saw the logic of the old fool's advice and grudgingly thanked his father for the call and then listened intently, in rapture, throughout the rest of the day to the attacks on his semi truck's radio.

Ajay remembered how Pushkar's voice broke as he described the attacks saying he was ashamed and horrified that Muslims could be responsible for attacks such as these. Pushkar used words like 'tragedy' and 'an offense before God' and 'innocent people.' He claimed that true jihad, even violent jihad, was fought soldier-to-soldier, even during the time of the prophet and that these attacks on America were disgraces that would sentence the terrorist's; these modern kharijites he had called them, to hell for eternity. *I can't believe the pathetic old cripple actually cried!*

His father would simply never understand these jihadists. Ajay scoffed silently at his father's words. *He's such a weakling. A cowardly misguided old fool!* Ajay loved what he saw. The only thing that upset him about the attacks was that their glory dwarfed his own future plans. Ajay's plans must be improved if he was to achieve more.

Ajay concentrated on the scenes coming from the television as they rotated between scenes of the smoldering Pentagon, the smoky haze over New York City, and a blackened pit in a pasture in Pennsylvania where the scattered pieces of United 93 lay. His mind was transfixed by the bloodbath wrought by such a small group of committed mujahedeen. He realized that he must give up his plans of acting alone and that he obviously needed to procure this kind of assistance in order to achieve the devastation he wanted. *My atrocity will be a thousand-fold worse!*

The ideas he came up with sitting inside his cell in Huntsville now seemed puny. After watching this; what greatness, what glory, and what immortality could Ajay obtain for himself by working alone?

The bar for greatness was now set to a high marker and he needed to surpass these attacks if he was to gain his immortality.

So far his plans had moved apace with the business expanding to seven drivers that hauled daily cargo and freight in box-van trailers along I-35 between Austin and San Antonio. They would then cross the border at Laredo and make hauls on down to Monterrey. It was lucrative enough hauling produce and cattle down to Mexico with return trips of cars, furniture, and auto parts back to Austin and Dallas. His drivers also did regional shipments to discount stores and supermarkets, while Ajay exclusively ran loads across the border, becoming an almost daily sight for the INS staff at the Laredo crossing.

He had those guards eating out of his hand now and had no problems making selective shipments of both illegal migrants and dope for Miguel and Juan. He was so successful that the brother's wanted him to do more for them but he knew that would only make him a target for the DEA again. This was not about money – it was about his immortality.

One of his drivers, Eduardo Reyes, sat inches away on the edge of Ajay's desk, staring at the small television. The front of the desk butted up against the desk of his secretary/truck dispatcher, Carol Rogers. She quietly sobbed as they watched CNN anchor Aaron Brown gravely warning viewers that the next scenes were very disturbing, and if there were children at home, he recommended that they leave the room.

The next scene showed the Twin Towers still piercing the clear blue sky, the grievous injuries in their flat sides emitting dark clouds of smoke and spitting orange flames from the jagged impact holes. Thousands of pedestrians gawked with faces tilted upward displaying similar states of horror and shock. It reminded Ajay of scene from a hidden camera inside of a theater that watched the reactions on the faces of people at a scary movie, these cameraman stayed glued to the faces of the Manhattanites while they watched a real-life horror movie play out before their eyes.

Then, they jumped, pointed skyward, squealed and squirmed as they were jolted into an even greater state of shock; eyebrows raised, eyes widened, mouths agape, and then screams and groans follow the sight of another jumper.

The television showed split-screen the jumper falling on the right side and the crowd's reaction playing out on the left. Sometimes the jumper was a man, other times a woman; falling, their arms, dresses, skirts, jackets, and pants trailed behind them as they plummeted. Other times it was a couple in a death-pact jumping and holding hands as they twirled to their doom, clutching tightly to one another in a partnership of death.

Unlike a skydiver, with nothing but air and the horizon behind him, there were now large burning buildings where pieces of paper fluttered all around, acting as reference points to the tremendous speed of their descent. Some plummeted with their faces pushed into the onrushing air while others turned their backs to the imminent cold concrete and asphalt of Twelfth Avenue. Like the jumpers who refused to watch their own fate, some gawking pedestrians turned away from watching the inevitable collision, burying their faces in their hands or the shoulder of a stranger next to them. Others stared on in horror, covering only their mouths as they held their grisly vigil over a fellow human being dying in such a gruesome way.

The people on the streets were unnoticed strangers just a short time before. But now they held side by side communion on the well-kept avenues of the Big Apple as they held vigil. By extension, the television coverage brought emotionally together fellow humans from across the country and around the globe, to collectively share an intensely intimate, personal, and yet global moment to their collective psyche that was filled with such horror and grief. It was unlike the unifying emotion of pride that filled human hearts when Neal Armstrong put the first human foot prints in the soil of the Moon, or the global sigh of relief that was exhaled when Apollo 13 safely landed in the Pacific Ocean. This day was shared grief, death, and horror.

But around the world and even in America there were those who did not share those feelings.

Ajay could tell they had edited the scenes; one thing missing was the loud 'slap' of the body striking the concrete. Or maybe even the scream of the plummeting jumper had been caught on tape, but would never be aired. They would cut away just before the body struck, but Ajay's mind saw what it must be like as the bodies landed; the kinetic force must have looked just like the disintegration of a water balloon thrown at a wall.

A whimper escaped Carol's throat as she buried her face into her hands, sobbing.

"No, oh, dear God, no."

Ajay glanced down with contempt at the woman. He then looked out the corner of his eye at Eduardo and saw in profile a wet cheek with a stream of tears flowing down it. The muscles in the trucker's jaw were clamped down tight and bulged under the flowing tears. His fists slowly clenched and unclenched in a spasmodic

69

fashion. A swollen vein in his forehead kept rhythmic time with his heart.

Ajay was cold to such feelings and was incapable of conjuring up similar emotions, and he knew why. He may have been born in America, but it was not his home, neither was Kashmir. Nowhere was his home and Ajay's soul was the king of the land of nowhere, and he wanted everyone to be in his kingdom, filling up the emptiness inside and feeling the same cold vastness that he did. If he could not make them feel the same, then they just needed to be dead like the people plunging from those buildings.

He grimaced at the mewing and sobbing coming from the two people who sat with him. It was an irksome noise that took away from his enjoyment. The blithering CNN fools were now showing video of people in the streets of Gaza, Egypt, Syria, and other nations of the Muslim world that were jumping, cheering, and dancing in praise of the attacks.

The anchor complained about their joyous reactions to the deaths of so many people. *Fool, the slaughtered sheep doesn't understand the joy of the family cheering it being cooked for dinner, either.* Someday Ajay would make these fools understand. He wished to be on those streets right now – dancing, cheering and able to enjoy this moment like them.

The last place Ajay wanted to be right now was stuck here with this foolish woman with snot running down her face, and this stupid dull Mexican. The brown bastard did not even believe in the Chicano movement. *What an idiot!* He probably knew nothing of Aztlán or any of the things Juan and Miguel preached to Ajay in his youth. *Weaklings! Just pathetic weak infidels, ready to be slaughtered.* Ajay almost laughed out loud at the irony that existed in the room. He watched the enthusiastically cheering crowds and imagined the wild cheers that his future attacks would receive, dwarfing these.

Eduardo leaned forward, holding Carol's shoulders and giving them a gentle squeeze.

"There, there, girl, you got to try and buck-up, darlin'. It'll work out somehow."

"I…I just can't belie…believe what I'm seeing."

"It hurts, girl. It's like someone just keeps punching me in the gut and doesn't stop. But you got to pull yourself together now, okay, hon?"

Carol's composure broke and she sank into another crying fit that violently shook her shoulders. Eduardo looked over his shoulder at Ajay to say something and stopped with his mouth open, staring. Ajay turned and saw Eduardo looking at him with a puzzled, maybe even shocked look. He had caught a glimpse of Ajay exhibiting too clearly something from inside, and Ajay worked quickly to hide away any trace of his inner self as fast as he could. He felt the veneer of an emotional mask once again camouflage his face. But Eduardo had saw something and judging from the reaction on his face it was definitely something Ajay had not wanted the stupid Mexican to see.

A few seconds passed as the two men assessed each other. Eduardo tensed and ever so slightly moved his body away from Ajay while Ajay attempted to produce a tight smile and also attempted to reach over and touch the man in a reassuring manner. Eduardo recoiled, shooting Ajay a distrustful look.

Ajay bit the inside of his cheek as he worked to keep the 'tender' smile on his face, but it looked more like a contorted grimace to Eduardo. Ajay ended up resting his hand on Carol's shoulder. Her tear-stained face looked up as he gave her arm a small pat.

"Why don't you both go on home?" he said, looking up at Eduardo. "Eddie, take Carol home, will ya? We'll be doing nothing here for a few days, I think, and she can't drive home like this."

Eduardo gauged his boss a moment longer until he dismissed acting on whatever he saw. He leaned over and gently lifted the grief stricken woman from her chair and guided her for the office door.

"Come on, hon, let's get you home to Bill and the girls. Come on, let's go now."

Ajay held the door as they left and watched as they made their way to Eduardo's truck. Before they drove away he said, "You two don't worry about this, I'll pay you for today and tomorrow. It'll be okay, and Eddie, you don't worry about your Friday delivery. It can wait until Monday. I'll call if I need you two before next week, okay?"

"Uh, okay," Eduardo said without enthusiasm, as he avoided bringing his eyes up to look at Ajay. His body language said he wanted to be very far from Ajay, as fast as he could get there.

Moments later the dust cloud kicked up from Eduardo's truck was settling in the driveway as Ajay stood at the door looking after the vanished vehicle. Relieved that they were gone, his mind raced to think of what he had done to make such a negative impression on the dull Mexican. He looked a moment longer, then shrugged with indifference and reentered the office. He stood behind his desk watching as Aaron Brown advised that they had received more disturbing scenes from the Arab world. The screen showed hundreds, if not thousands, of men and women in the streets of various cities of Muslim nations. The people had joyous smiles, and glowed with elation and happiness as they jumped, and danced while chanting "Allahlu akbar!"

71

Ajay raised his arms above his head and started to dance.

*****

February 7, 2005 10:11am UTC+5:30
Watlab village
Jammu and Kashmir

AJAY NEVER had camaraderie with the other Muslims inside the closely knit communities around San Antonio, San Marcos, and Austin. To greater or lesser degrees they knew of him but they never warmed to him and most still shunned him for his criminal past. Nonetheless, he expected a far better reaction to the success of the 9/11 Attacks, and he was deeply disappointed in their response. To a large degree they publically and even privately condemned the attacks as unjustified. He argued that support should be extended to others who might try to accomplish similar attacks but he was rudely rebuffed as a radical who was stirring up trouble and who had done little for their community over the years.

After he had a loud shouting match with the imam at the masjid, that prompted the elders to approach Pushkar where they expressed their concerns that Ajay could bring harm to the community and that he must be silenced. And of course, Pushkar had come trotting to Ajay like their obedient dog, rebuking him and demanding that he must not bring any embarrassment or trouble to the family or the local community again. *Groveling old bastard!*

But what jolted him into complete silence was when FBI agents appeared, asking questions of the elders regarding the status of members of the community and what their views may be regarding the 9/11 attacks. Ajay suddenly realized he had made a huge mistake and immediately shut up. Pushkar's respected and esteemed place in the community and the help he provided to the CIA and mujahedeen in Afghanistan helped protect Ajay from anything but a cursory interview by the agents. Cleaning up his image over the last several years and becoming a successful small businessman quickly dissipated interest in a more scrutinizing investigation. Anyway, he had actually done nothing yet other than be too vocal.

Two months later, another agent suddenly showed up unannounced at the ranch. This time it was a man of Iranian descent, Special Agent Faraz Hamidi, who asked for assistance from both Pushkar and Ajay in finding out if Mayur would be willing to help the CIA. He was also curious to find out if they were aware of any other contacts back in Kashmir or Pakistan of people who may be willing to assist.

72

Pushkar politely rebuffed the lawman's requests by saying he had long ago gotten out of any business like that, and so had Mayur. Ajay easily deflected interest in his capabilities since he had never been back to the homeland since he was a child. But that contact rattled Ajay deeply once he realized just how much the government knew about him, his family, and what kinds of things they were requesting. He was in a fishbowl and had to stay out from under their microscope.

Ajay carefully studied the fatwas of the imams like al-Zawahiri on the Internet, and he soaked up anything he could find on bin-Laden and Al Qaeda. He waited anxiously for the American military to be humiliated in Afghanistan, and be sent running back home broken, bleeding, and defeated by the Taliban, just like the Soviets had been.

But instead, it was the Taliban who crumbled under a minuscule number of Green Berets and some stealth bombers. This shock rudely brought Ajay back to his senses on the limitations of those boorish rag-heads. *What a waste my life would've been if I had been born in that Stone Age place!*

Ajay was shocked again when President Bush invaded Iraq and quickly defeated Saddam and his sons there as well. All of the people Ajay thought might be able to help him were rapidly being taken out of the picture, forcing him to re-assess just who in the Muslim world was worth his time and efforts. The list of worthy benefactors was quickly diminishing. The Middle East regimes were either too militarily weak or they worked for America. The Muslims he had watched dancing in the streets after 9/11 were too cowardly to commit to the jihad or were simply too weak to be of any use.

He felt stuck, forced to sit at his desk smiling and conducting boring trucking business, all the while idiot-Carol sat next to him, dispatching the trucks and jabbering her mindless prattle. He had a good plan but he had no contacts and no way to find any. Then one afternoon an idea came to him while listening to – of all people – his silly secretary.

"….should be landing about 4 o'clock in the afternoon, Rome time, and we're hoping to check in at the hotel by 5:30. It'll be a terribly long flight and we'll sure be ready for bed, but, God All Mighty, will I be happy to finally be there!" Carol exclaimed.

"I bet you will. That's a hellava long flight, huh. It'd kill my bad back, I tell ya," chimed in a smiling Ben Tucker while making exaggerated rubs of his back as if it was sore.

Skinny Tim Vasquez gave Ben a short jab to the ribs that made the heavyset man grunt and chuckle.

"You ain't got nothing to worry your big butt, over, Bennie, you ain't goin' no how."

"Now, you two just hold off on that rough-housing in AJ's office, right now I say! This is no truck driver's play-pen," Carol scolded with a smile.

"Oh, okay, Carol," Tim said. "I sure wish I could take my Rosy on a big trip like that someday. She'd love to go see the Holy Father like you're a get'n to do."

"I know! Rosella would just love it. Ooh, I'm so excited to see his Holiness!" Carol said, with a squeal of glee in her voice. "Me and my old man have been hoping and saving for a trip to the Vatican all our lives and now we're a going to see the big man himself. Whooee!"

"That sure ought to be sumpin', Carol. I hear tell that the show there is big and beautiful for sure. You should have a swell ol' time," Ben said.

Carol, with pent-up excitement, sat stiff in her chair with her hands on her thighs like she needed to urinate badly.

"It's probably a sin, but I'm so excited..."

Carol had blabbed for weeks about her upcoming trip to Italy to see the Pope and Vatican. But that morning a light bulb suddenly went off in Ajay's head. As a Muslim, he had the perfect way to get to the Middle East and quietly seek out contacts without attracting any suspicion – the Hajj! A religious pilgrimage that should cause no more suspicion than her trip!

But Ajay could not just go off bumbling his way around the secret spy dragnets that were spread all over the Middle East, just waiting to catch dumb schmucks wandering around asking for help in committing terrorist attacks. Ajay would not be so stupid, and his mind churned with ideas that might get him where he wanted to go without alarming anyone, not even his father. He needed some connection that would facilitate an introduction to real jihadists. That evening, at supper, he moved an idea foreword.

"Father, the business is doing very well. I've got all my loans paid off and this housing boom has got the economy cranking. I've been working hard and want to take some time off and I also wish to thank you both for your support and opportunity to use the ranch."

Pushkar looked up from his dinner and smiled at his son.

"Your hard work and staying out of trouble is a great enough reward for me, Ajay. Your mother and I need no further thanks. I am deeply proud of your success."

"You could thank me by finally being interested in finding a wife," Asha chided.

Ajay's face reddened and he ground his teeth hard at her comment. A wave of irritation swept over him like a blast of heat from a furnace; he suppressed it with a look of embarrassment and gave his mother a sheepish smile.

"He is not a child, Asha. We're not to say when he will bring us grandchildren," Pushkar said gently rebuking his wife. "Our son is strong and in due time will bring many grandchildren into our home for your happiness. Remember, my father did not have me until he was in his sixties."

Disappointed, Asha looked down at the meal on her plate and said quietly, "I don't want to be so old I cannot enjoy my grandchildren."

Ignoring her, Ajay swallowed some iced-tea and cleared his throat so he could speak, causing his father to pause before he continued on with the unwanted conversation.

"Maybe soon, Mother, but I have things to do first, and one of those things is – I wish to take the Hajj and I also wish to take the two of you along with me on the trip."

He blurted out the sentence so quickly that he cringed inside at how silly he must have sounded.

Pushkar and Asha sat in stunned silence, eyes wide, completely dumbfounded at the unexpected announcement from their son. On their income they never expected to be able to take the Hajj. Even though it was one of the Five Pillars of the Islamic faith, they had resigned themselves to never journeying to Mecca and reciting the shahada as they circled the Káaba. Ajay knew very well they dearly wanted to go and he believed that it was important enough for them that they would never question his motives.

"I am honored and extremely pleased, my son," Pushkar said, with the slightest tremble in his voice. Asha sought out Pushkar's hand and held it tightly. "I don't know what else to say to you. This is very unexpected," he finished with wet eyes.

Ajay knew he had scored a homerun by his father's reaction and he reached across the table and squeezed his hand. Watching his parents closely he said, "It is something I have wanted to give you as thanks for quite some time now. With the company on its feet and doing so well I want us to take this opportunity, as a family, and experience this together."

They held hands with tears coming down Asha's cheek. Both of them radiated pride as Asha looked down at Pushkar.

"Can we, Husband?"

Pushkar turned and rested his hand on her forearm.

"Yes, my love, if Ajay can afford it without hurting the business, I will not turn down his generous offering." Turning back to Ajay, he asked, "Are you sure you can afford to send all of us? If you do not have enough finances I will stay and you may take your mother with you."

"You need not fear about me affording this trip. You may see the books if you doubt it, Father. We are blessed, praise Allah."

"Yes, yes, praise Allah. I am very happy, and thanks to America for making this possible for us," Pushkar said, and with a carefree smile he hugged his wife.

Ajay sucked hard on his lip to hide his reaction to his father's last statement.

"Yes, I suppose so," he finally volunteered.

After several seconds of watching them celebrate he pushed forward with the next idea.

"I also wish for another to join us, Father – and I'm sorry, Mother, it's not a soon-to-be wife," he said, with a forced smile and wink.

"Another?"

"Yes, Father, I want to bring all the Majumbar family together with the blessing I have received. I wish us to invite Uncle Mayur to come and join us on the Hajj."

His second surprise bomb had now been dropped but the reaction was not as bad as he expected. Asha tensed and stood motionless as Pushkar stared intensely at his son, studying him closely before he finally spoke.

"Mayur is a hard man and not made for family outings, Ajay. You haven't seen him since you were a teenager and I have not spoken to him in years. I don't even know if he would consider it."

Ready for this, Ajay calmly replied, "This is more than a family jaunt, Father, and I want the surviving sons of Abdulla Majumbar to experience the pilgrimage together. If it is possible for you and me to find our common ground and be father and son again, I do not think it is too much to ask that you two can stand to be with one another before Allah."

Ajay knew his challenge would press hard on his father's heart and he saw that he was close to landing him like a fish – hook, line, and sinker.

Pushkar considered his thoughts carefully for several minutes and Ajay began to think he may have misjudged and overreached with his brash challenge. Asha sat quietly looking hard at Ajay; and he suddenly became aware that he was not sure what she was thinking for possibly the first time in his life.

"I love my brother and I believe he loves me. I will not hold my pride up against a pillar of our faith to begrudge my brother anything," Pushkar said solemnly. "If he will consent to be our guest I would take the Hajj with him and my heart would burst at the joy of it."

Ajay felt exhilaration course through his body. He knew the devil was in the details and he just took care of a huge detail.

*****

OVER THE next several months Ajay relaxed and let his father and mother make most of the arrangements for the trip. Asha became a beehive of activity spending day-after-day getting the smallest details of their trip organized and planned. But it was Pushkar who made the final choices on the important matters. The only thing Ajay stayed deeply involved in was the completion of the message to his uncle. Everything rested on Mayur's assistance later on, so Ajay made certain he was front and center in all dealings between Mayur and his father. When they finally heard back that Mayur had indeed accepted the invitation to join them on the Hajj, Ajay was ecstatic.

Mayur could afford his own trip to the Saudi Kingdom but Asha and Pushkar made all the arrangements for the hotels, meals, and the return trip. They planned to meet at the King Khalid International Airport in Riyadh and then make their way to Medina and then Mecca. In the meantime Ajay made arrangements for Carol and his lead driver, Tom Runyon, to run the day-to-day operations of the business until he returned. Finally, in January 2005 they left on the long flight to Saudi Arabia.

Shortly after arriving, Ajay's immediate impressions of the Saudis was both encouraging, and yet very disappointing. The fabulous buildings and opulence of the Kingdom were impressive but he quickly saw the underlying current of how the Saudis used the Hajj as a complex mechanism to not only control Muslim pilgrims but the rest of the Muslim world as well. The mutawas were everywhere, and they were more than just the government's morality police; they also acted as overseers who managed the ebb and flow of the large mobs of people, enforcing the rules that kept the huge mass of travelers in line with the Saudi vision of Islam.

There were many shysters in every crowd that worked the angles to get every penny out of the sucker pilgrims. Ajay often found himself chuckling at the way the gawking, poor, and smelly pilgrim-tourists ran around getting used by the locals, much like watching a hillbilly-hayseed back in Texas, getting suckered by a carnie at a county fair. The Hajj was purportedly the greatest journey a Muslim would ever make but for Ajay it quickly turned out to be a lousy tourist trip to an Arabian theme park.

The reunion between Pushkar and Mayur went as stiffly as expected but no arguments ensued. As family tensions receded they all became immersed within the Hajj rituals. Their ability to speak their native Dardic-Kashmiri, as well as speaking Farsi made conversing easy enough and they completed the rites of the Hajj with little difficulty. Pushkar's physical handicap even became an advantage as people became aware that he suffered the injury during the struggles in the jihad against the Soviets. He and Mayur were both given deference by the other pilgrims for their involvements the jihads of Afghanistan and Kashmir, while Ajay stewed in jealousy.

The only excitement during the trip came while they did the Tawaf az-Ziyareh; as they made their way to throw the ritual rocks at the jamarat in Mina a stampede of people started not far ahead of them. Luckily they were able to get out of the panicked mass of people that trampled forty-four other pilgrims to death. Everyday Ajay was physically miserable, hot and sweaty, with sand stuck in places on his body that he did not like at all, but he still could not help but snort at the stupidity of the spectacle of the crushed and injured that day.

The rest of the Hajj went without incident and was a deeply moving experience for everyone except Ajay, who found the whole thing far less interesting than he ever imagined possible. All the Islamic preaching's of his father and even the Salafist, Hussein, were all turning out to be the same sort of crap. It left him with an even larger feeling of hollowness and deep coldness. No new spiritual revelations came to him, on the contrary, instead of finding oneness with a God or a common spirituality with the strange, ugly people that surrounded him, the entire Hajj experience became an extremely tiring, boring, and sickeningly repetitive scam. The huge crowds of worshippers marching mindlessly around the Kaába reminded him of large herds of bleating and mewing sheep that covered the plains of central Texas. He was rapidly losing his connection with Islam and Allah. The Hajj may have been one of the Five Pillars of the faith, but to Ajay it turned out to be nothing but a tourist trap. To Ajay, Islam, like any other religion, was turning out to be nothing relevant to his view of the world at all. It was becoming just another tool for him to use to get what he wanted.

He finally decided that all these people should one day bow and worship at his feet. It turned out he had nothing more in common with these Muslim cockroaches than he did with the jahili infidels.

Ajay Kahn Majumbar was meant for bigger and better things than these scurrying bugs surrounding him.

So he forced his mind and body to go along but toward the end of the trip his mother started observing his lagging sense of enthusiasm and became concerned enough to make comments. Her nosy questions forced him to claim that the local foods did not agree with him. That was enough to hide his emotional doldrums for the remainder of the trip and Asha spent much of her time after that picking foods for him, keeping her busy and out of his way.

As it turned out, Ajay was very successful in endearing himself to Mayur by simply continuing to put forward an affable and subservient manner with constant questions about Kashmir and everything Mayur had done in the cause of freeing that nation from its bondage. Once he felt at ease, his uncle proved very talkative about Kashmir and his work with the fighters and politicians there. Ajay eventually broached the question he had spent this entire trip waiting for: to get Mayur's permission to travel with him back to Kashmir when the Hajj was over and it was received well by his uncle. *Success!*

Ajay then gave his parents an impassioned speech on how he wished to see the Vale of Kashmir and experience the lands of his heritage before returning home. His parents expressed their concerns about the workings of the trucking business in his absence. He alleviated their concerns and assured them he would keep the company going by maintaining the contracted routes he had. He claimed that he would supervise the company via email and telephone until he returned in a couple of weeks. Satisfied, they were soon headed back to Texas while he left with Mayur for Kashmir.

A week later, he stared out the passenger window of an old Toyota truck winding along a muddy road skirting the icy Jhelum River. His view was flanked on three sides by the mighty Himalayan Mountain ranges capped in their perpetual snow, while ahead sat the valley where his father and uncles were raised. The winter beauty escaped him as his mind raced with the unending possibilities that now lay ahead of him. He was out of his element and must be very careful and yet his heart pounded enthusiastically as he was now much closer to bringing his plans to fruition.

December 23, 2009 09:02am UTC+5
ISI J+K Wings Regional HQ
Mardan, Pakistan

AJAY'S LAST four years had been challenging and yet very productive. After attending numerous terrorist training camps Ajay was now finally on his way to meet with the Iranians for the first time and he was excited. The road to Mardan had been long, bumpy, and uncomfortable trip while riding alongside the silt-laden waters of the Kalpani River to today's meeting place northwest of Peshawar.

Unpleasant as the trip had been, there was no use in complaining, especially since he had experienced far worse roaming through the mountain camps of Waziristan while being beat to crap in the bed of old trucks. The ISI driver turned the plush Toyota Land Cruiser onto the Hoti Bridge leading into the provincial city's downtown bazaar. People quickly parted before the obviously important government VIP vehicle. Ajay stared out at the flood of dirt-poor humanity that choked the streets around the vehicle in a hive of noise and activity. It was a far different place than the paved roads and motorized lives of Texas. The paths he had travelled between the two had been long, crooked, and dangerous.

In October 2005, shortly after arriving in Kashmir after the Hajj, Ajay had nearly been buried under tons of debris as he dashed out of his uncle's adobe house as the massive 7.6 earthquake that erupted along the Eurasion and Indian tectonic plates that year. That earthquake would eventually kill over 80,000 people throughout Kashmir and Pakistan. Ajay took his survival as a sign from God that he was meant to succeed in his plans. It was not long after the earthquake that Mayur had facilitated, at Ajay's request, contact with the Lashkar-e-Tayyba (LeT), a Kashmiri separatists group.

Although Mayur was at first reticent to fulfill the unexpected request, it did not take Ajay very long to explain how much difficulty he had with Pushkar's reluctance to allow Ajay to become involved in jihad over the years. Quickly Mayur understood why Ajay had been forced to use the ruse he had to gain access to the jihad he wished to participate in. Mayur acquiesced to Ajay's request even though he knew it would destroy his relationship with his brother. In a short time Ajay found himself being taught bomb making and attending small weapons training at the LeT training camps in the North-West Frontier Provence. He chuckled at how it was similar to attending a vocational school back in America.

He spoke more freely now but he still wisely kept his main plots and plans a closely guarded secret. He also had to work hard at keeping secret his rapidly growing contempt for the Islamic propaganda that was used to recruit men to the jihadist cause. He quickly, but grudgingly came to the realization that his father had been correct about the motivations of the jihadist commanders who overwhelmingly used religious propaganda as a motivational tool on the idealistic fools that came to be cannon-fodder for the jihad. But regardless of motivations, Ajay's experience in the camps was a mental rehabilitation for his pent-up anger as he relished in finally being headed down a path to the fulfillment of his destiny. Mayur lacked his enthusiasm, was too old, and was no longer interested in jihad so he and Ajay had quickly parted ways.

The group's leader, Maulana Fazlullah, took great interest in the Kashmiri-American from Texas. But Ajay was disappointed that Fazlullah's jihadist interests were strictly local to Kashmir and he had no interest in expanding his influence outside of South Asia. Yet their relationship blossomed and he took Ajay as a protégé as Ajay delighted in his new environment. Meanwhile Fazlullah promised to make inquiries through his own benefactors in the Pakistani ISI and the Haqqani network to see if any other powerful groups would be willing to give Ajay the patronage he sought.

As time passed Ajay found that he held a celebrity status with the other jihadists at the camps and had to work at keeping a low profile. The others spoke of grand attacks and gave sweeping gestures of pious faith and worship to Allah that Ajay considered infantile, but he humored their talk nonetheless. They urged him to join their efforts in fighting the U.S. military in Iraq and Afghanistan. They said that, being an American, he was a great asset, but their plans were far too small for his consideration. As an American jihadist he could easily see himself being blown to bits in some canyon from a Predator drone missile strike if he rose to any public prominence, so he waved off their requests.

Ajay's made few trips back to Texas and operating the trucking company ended shortly after the beginning of 2006 with him handing it to his distraught parents, whom he now actively ignored. Tensions were again bitter between them as the business began to fall apart and his priorities, while back in the States, went to working solely with Juan and Miguel in Monterrey to build up his cash reserves. The rest of his time was spent travelling back to Kashmir and the various training camps. The trucking company's business contracts were eventually lost and without Ajay's help his parents were unable to carry on with the business. He let the business wither and die on the vine just like his relationship with his parents.

Upon arriving back at the LeT headquarters at Markaz-e-Taiba north of Lahore last fall, a man came unannounced to meet with him. Fazlullah said the man was a Pakistani ISI Captain named Massoud. The wary ISI agent claimed he was interested in Ajay's plans and could possible help him with logistics and manpower for a major operation.

Ajay had watched first hand as ISI Pakistani Naval officers trained the Munbai attackers that were so successful the previous year. He had always been curious about the ISI as a patron but considered their interests too centered in Kashmir. He wanted to make a worldwide impact and the only place he could achieve what he wanted was in the United States. Feeling safe at the camp Ajay decided to divulge some limited parts of his plan and Massoud quickly became intrigued with the opportunities possible but it was a plan that was beyond his capabilities.

The Pakistani said he knew people who were seeking somebody just like him and that he could arrange a meeting with them if Ajay was interested. Ajay's heart leapt with excitement but he tried to stay cagy and expressed concerns about the ISI helping the American military and that Massoud could just be an agent who was 'feeling out' a jihadist. He also pointed out that even if Massoud was a legitimate agent, the ISI still had numerous moles and snitches in their midst that could undermine Ajay's plans. Massoud then surprised Ajay with his response.

Notwithstanding Fazlullah's long and committed service to the ISI and the Afghan Taliban, Massoud made it clear that even with Fazlullah vouching for Ajay, their meeting only occurred after a year of the ISI, and their partner, investigating and observing Ajay at the camps and also when he was back inside America. Their intentions were to find a way to carry out a major successful attack on America and they had become very good at sniffing out moles and would have assassinated him at the very first signs of any suspicious activity. He assured Ajay they knew every infiltrator in their ranks and that when the moment was right they would purge them all.

Massoud then pointedly asked if Ajay would be interested with further meetings with his associates in Hezbollah and their masters in the Iranian IRGC. Immediately, Ajay knew two things; first, if he refused the meeting he would be killed right then and there, and secondly, if the offer were true the Iranian support could provide all the logistical and financial support necessary to make everything he wanted to happen, happen.

He remained quiet for several minutes watching the ISI agent and trying to contain his emotions until finally replying that he was indeed very eager to discuss his plans with them.

Now, a few months later, at the ISI's Mardan headquarters, Ajay sat bare-footed on silken cushions, waiting for Capt. Massoud to come in. He stretched out his legs, letting them relax after the tiring trip. He sipped on a cup of black tea and ate date cookies that he had developed quite an affinity for.

He watched out the window as several bearded trainees did calisthenics in the courtyard. He smirked quietly at how he would never be caught dead doing such mindless crap as he munched on another cookie. Watching them jump up and down he realized that one of them was oddly familiar but he could not place him. With so many different jihadists at the various camps he had been in, remembering where he had seen this one would be difficult. But the longer he stared at the man the more sure he was that they had met before. He was still working through his memory when Massoud and a thin uniformed Pakistani soldier came in.

"Welcome, I hope you are recouping well from your long journey. Are there more refreshments I can have brought in for you before we sit and talk, my friend?" Massoud asked.

"No, thank you, I'm fine."

"Excellent. Then if you are prepared, I will take you inside to meet with my friend. He is very eager to meet you and become your friend as well."

Ajay stood dusting cookie crumbs that clung to the front of his thobe. "I'm even more eager to meet with him. I've been waiting a long time for this day."

Massoud took two steps forward but stopped once he noticed that Ajay was not following. He turned and saw Ajay staring out the window at the men in the courtyard. After several seconds of silence he reached a tentative arm out toward Ajay.

"Is there a problem, my friend?" he asked, with a questioning tension in his voice. "Are you having second thoughts?"

The captain's muscles tensed and his bodyguard companion cast a tense glare at Ajay who still looked out upon the courtyard, ignoring them. Just as Massoud began to withdraw his extended hand Ajay smiled happily and turned from the window. He gave Massoud an enthusiastic wink while reaching up and squeezing the ISI agent's arm.

"No, no. There is nothing wrong, Captain," Ajay said grinning. "I have no reservations whatsoever. What I do have – shall we say – will be interesting news for you and our Iranian friend that should be very welcome and beneficial. Please, let us go inside and I'll be happy to share with you what I now know."

Massoud noticeably relaxed and nodded to the soldier to lead the way. As they began moving forward he gave Ajay a quizzical look that caused Ajay to smile broadly.

Ajay glanced once again over his shoulder toward the window but he could no longer see the men outside. "You know, Captain? I believe today is going to be the beginning of a very good relationship, a very good relationship indeed!" he said, slapping Massoud on the back.

*****

THE BRIGHTLY colored boats of local fishermen bobbed on the foam-capped Persian Gulf waters. Lazy waves migrated ashore where they lapped easily against the beach sands and breaker stones that bordered the seaside of the Khalij-e-Fars highway. Inland, across the busy roadway, stood tall palm trees and vibrantly painted stucco buildings of the 'Old City'. Speeding between the two vistas, the shiny mocha Mercedes Benz E63 swerved through the busy traffic. The driver's face displayed a hungry and enthusiastic grin as the vehicle's V8 engine rumbled, which caused the dual exhaust to emit a throaty baritone roar.

Every day IRGC Major Faruk Amir Sabiri used this road for his enjoyment, treating it like it was his personal Grand Prix race track. Being the son of the IRGC Air Force commander Brigadier General Hossein Sabiri had its perks, of which the car was one; a benefit of his position and his familial connections within the Iranian military.

He missed the liveliness of cosmopolitan Tehran but he gladly took advantage of what benefits he had to help cope with being in this dull port city. With the scope of this project being of the utmost importance and secrecy, it gave the major the latitude to use the entire city as his personal playground.

His valuable and irreplaceable passenger (and, for all intents and purposes, prisoner, in the insanely driven vehicle) was a graduate of the prestigious Massachusetts Institute of Technology with a PhD in Nuclear Physics. The scientist was employed by the Ministry of Science, Research, and Technology and had a Professorship of Civil Engineering at the Persian Gulf University here in Bushehr.

84

Professor Aram Hormoz Zanjani hated these daily maniacal trips through the bustling traffic of the hectic city with the arrogant man who was his chauffer, his escort, his watchdog, and his very deadly bodyguard. Notwithstanding his respect for the major's considerable driving skills, which were very impressive, the professor viewed the IRGC commando and his actions as pure stupidity and recklessness on the part of the young military officer. A man who milked his father's position for everything it was worth. His arrogance put the entire *Asman-Rayan* project and the future of the Islamic State at risk.

Zanjani knew that if he were to be seriously injured or killed by the major's need to express his childishness the whole project would end abruptly, and after seven years of planning, manpower, and money that the government had invested in *Asman-Rayan*, the professor acutely doubted that the power and prestige of Brigadier General Sabiri would be enough to save his foolish son from a miserable end.

Rigid in the passenger seat, Zanjani did the same things every morning: his left hand gripped his laptop computer and briefcase lying across his legs, while his right hand held a white-knuckled grip on the door's armrest. Even with his seatbelt cinched-down and his legs straining to press his feet hard against the floorboard, his torso still bounced back and forth as the major dodged around the slower-moving traffic. Zanjani often worried that he would actually vomit his guts all over the interior of the luxury car when the traffic was really terrible, but he learned to eat light in the morning for fear of doing that very thing.

They completed a sweeping right, dodging several trucks and cars as they passed the Ghadam Gaah-e-Emam Ali shrine, and the professor calmed somewhat as the ride neared its end. *Allah be praised!* The vehicle slowed slightly just before the major deftly cut between two large delivery trucks, and sped down a non-descript industrial alleyway at the port facilities. Traffic horns blew from the two shocked truck drivers as the gleaming car continued between the massive metal buildings at the IRISL shipyards. Dozens of unassuming men milled around the area ahead, moving quickly to get out of the driver's way.

The men dodging the car appeared, by design, to be nothing more than dock workers, mechanics, welders and the like but they were in fact very stone-faced and observant IRGC Quds Force and Secret Unit members who were tasked with providing security for this top-secret military facility. They were few in number but were far more effective than any fences or cameras could ever be. They drew no attention to the terminal or dock facilities, but anyone even remotely suspected of being curious about the area was quickly taken into custody, thoroughly interrogated and was then typically dead within a few hours.

The major pulled his car up to a small garage door at a massive hangar, waiting for admittance. A burly face appeared in a small window, and abruptly the garage door lifted, the man waving them inside.

Zanjani's heart rate was once again normal as the car stopped near a large metal shipping container painted bright blue with the word MEARSK in large white letters on the side. The exquisitely air conditioned interior of the vehicle was rudely replaced with a furnace-like 102 degree heat as he opened the door and stepped out into the broiling conditions inside the large building.

Even though he was well-rested he could not help but feel energy being rapidly sucked from his body by the hot and humid air. He and the major donned overcoats and hardhats, then quickly walked across a large bay to the center of the hangar. Once there, they climbed a catwalk running the length of the building to complete their morning inspection of the facility.

The interior of the quarter-mile long hangar was hectic with sweating men, going about their tasks in the sweltering conditions. Glowing orange sparks bounced on the cement floor from blow torches cutting metal below them. Ahead the iridescent sparks from grinders smoothing welds made great sweeping arcs of yellowish-colored bits of molten metal into the air. A sulfuric odor and black smoke mixed with the heavy humidity causing Zanjani's eyes to sting and water from the acrid air. The gigantic hangar below them was segregated into four large sections of end-to-end industrial work areas that filled the south side of the hangar. Meanwhile, the entire north side of the building housed a closed office area.

The two men took long strides along the metal catwalk while below them electricians checked voltage readings on wires, circuit boards, and computers while other technicians checked hydraulic and fuel hoses for leaks.

Each of the innocuous-looking shipping containers in the first construction area below them housed lengths of pipes, wires, and large oval fuel tanks secured with thick welds inside precut holes. A strange welded contraption sat inside each container with a mass of thick electrical wires and hydraulic hoses underneath it. The object was recognizable as a chopped-down medium-range ballistic missile launcher that was missing its trailer and wheels. Atop the hydraulic lift of the launcher were several technicians in grey coveralls with the insignia SBIG emblazoned on their backs, sitting in the concave harness where very soon a nuclear warhead-armed Shahab-4 missile would rest.

The two production areas further along the catwalk were also a beehive of activity where long rolls of cables and lengths of pipe were hauled by cranes above their heads. The last MRBM scud launcher was just beginning to be dismantled and readied for installation into the final set of containers.

Two men sat on the floor, working at disconnecting one of the last hydraulic lift cables from the system's trailer as Major Sabiri and Professor Zanjani came striding up to inspect their work. The workers paused and looked nervously up at the two project supervisors, waiting for orders until the major gave them a dismissive wave of his fingers, indicating they could continue. They quickly returned to their work and purposefully avoided any further eye contact.

Zanjani looked down at his wristwatch, shaking his head in frustration at the amount of work still left to be done.

"We are getting very close to our deadline for completion for this last module. We must work faster."

Major Sabiri looked at the skinny scientist out of the corner of his eye as he folded his arms over his chest and responded to the concerns of the nuclear physicist sarcastically.

"I can prod them to work faster, Professor, but you've been telling me all along that this process must be done methodically. Which is it – methodical or quick?"

The tension between the two existed since the first day they met, before the project began, and had worsened over time. All of the men working on the project were familiar with the two verbally sparring with each other, and worked hard at ignoring them.

Zanjani tapped his foot against the grating as he bit his tongue to keep from saying exactly how he felt.

"Your thuggish treatment of people is of no use in this part of the project. I would sooner get in there and turn wrenches myself than allow you to interfere," he said, while softly beating his palm against his chest in time to his words. "*This system must not fail at the moment of deployment*! They all must fire correctly – there are no second chances! You know this as well as I. If we don't achieve complete coverage of the continent with this strike, the Americans and Europeans will annihilate us. Not to mention the Zionists!"

The major rolled his eyes at the scientist's melodramatics.

"Yes, yes. We are all doomed if we don't destroy the kafirs and Jews in the first strike. I have heard this many times before,

Professor. You always forget the Russians and Chinese. We have our blanket of protection."

This time it was the professor's opportunity to sneer at the younger man.

"I think you rely far too much on one type of infidel to protect us from another type, Sabiri! I don't believe your father would approve of that strategy alone to save us if these three systems do not operate as they must."

The military officer visually flinched at the mention of his father by the pointy-nosed elitist standing next to him.

Zanjani continued without fear.

"Your job is to make these men work faster, not to jeopardize this project with your brutish thuggery!"

Pushed farther than usual, Major Sabiri turned and glared at the little man who stood so defiantly next to him. He longed for the day when he would listen to the educated man scream while Sabiri pressed his thumbs into his eye sockets and watched the bloody mush from his ruptured eyes squish out the sides. *Someday, little man, someday.*

"My methods will meet with your approval and the approval of my father – as always – I'm quite sure, Professor," he replied, keeping a steady glare at the scientist.

"Yes, well, that will be fine," Zanjani said, sensing the venom coming from the major's eyes, "I simply want this to be done quickly, but it must be done right as well. Please see it is done."

"I assure you that it will."

Zanjani knew there was no further use talking with the major. He had pushed a button on the man that he rarely used and it had triggered a response this morning that he did not like. But it was done and nothing could ever bring it back. He glanced back at his watch.

"They are waiting. Is your presentation ready?"Zanjani asked, looking up into the cold-eyed major. He was not sure if the man's eyes had blinked once in several minutes as he stared back at the scientist.

"Yes, I am ready, Professor."

"Very well."

Zanjani turned and quickly headed to the steps leading to the offices along the north wall, the whole time trying to shake off the chills that ran down his back as the major's eyes drilled holes into him. His pace quickened even more as he sought to escape the blistering heat of the hangar and return to air-conditioned space.

The need for secrecy inside the building was non-existent due to everyone inside being a necessary and active part of the project.

They were all vetted true believers to the cause: expanding the Islamic Republic of Iran into the Islamic Persian Caliphate.

The military had achieved success in keeping the project secret under the ever watchful eyes of satellites, local spies, and the military intelligence networks of America and NATO. Even with the puppet United Nations IAEA Director General Elbaradei being replaced with the stern Yukiya Amano, they still had managed to maintain blanket security. While their enemies and spies kept their focus on the far-flung nuclear sites around the country, the IRGC had used this non-descript warehouse to construct the very means for destroying their enemies in total.

Everything had gone smoothly throughout the conception, design, and production phases. They were now just one module away from completing the construction phase. Final testing should be completed by February and then the operational phases would begin. Zanjani knew the project was moving toward success and he did not really fear that they would fall short of their completion date, but he enjoyed tweaking the major anyway. With great satisfaction plastered across his face, the scientist led the major inside the cool environment of the meeting room where the other participants for the meeting were waiting.

"Father, it is good to see you," Sabiri said, sauntering toward the far end of the large metal table in the middle of the room. "Is your tour complete? Have you any concerns about our progress?"

"Greetings, my son, and greetings, Doctor Zanjani," General Sabiri replied, smiling and hugging his son while kissing his cheeks. "Yes, our tour is complete but as always I have many questions for the two of you, as do the others here. I hope you both have the answers we are looking for."

IRGC Navy commander Rear Admiral Morteza Razmara, sat to one side of the table with several blueprints, forms, and documents placed in neatly separated groups on the table before him. His plump cheeks were permanently set in a stern and humorless expression. With fingers interlaced over the top of his rotund stomach, his thumbs methodically and slowly tapped each other in a contemplative manner as he nodded silently to both the major and professor. Standing behind him, intently examining schematics of the hyper-modified scud MRBM launchers was his attaché and the naval commander for the mission, Lieutenant Nader-ed-Din.

"Hello, gentlemen, I am pleased to see you all. Please have patience as I prepare here," Zanjani said, working to set up his computer. "We will move forward with your questions shortly. I would like to begin by saying that I am very pleased with the design's stability within the containers and that our previous concerns with the cooling system's connections between the upper and lower sections of the modules have been significantly reduced with the addition of the larger rubber bushings to dampen the vibration concerns. These changes should allow for far less damage during transport and facilitate the reliable transfer of the liquid propellant at time of launch. I assure you that this is the case even if heavy seas are encountered by the vessels during their voyages."

Lt. Din spoke without turning away from the schematics.

"I see from my inspections this morning that Modules One and Two appear to be fully operational with the hydraulics no longer leaking like lanced boils. That is excellent work, Professor, but I'm not convinced that the liquid propellant transfer will be successful yet. This system must survive the open oceans; Module One will be transiting the Mediterranean and Atlantic, while Module Two must survive both the Indian and Pacific. Hurricane and typhoon seasons will be active and the hardware must be prepared to survive those conditions. What exactly have you scientists changed with the rubber gaskets that will ensure that damage is not incurred? You will have to prove to me that you have the systems fully protected."

"I think you will be pleasantly surprised, my young friend," Major Sabiri boasted with unabashed pride and a hint of sarcasm toward his rival.

Turning from the schematics and facing the major with an unimpressed glance Lt. Din replied defiantly, "With deference to your father I hope you're right, Major Sabiri. This is the single greatest military operation in the history of the world and it is imperative that *all* three modules succeed. Failure of one will risk too great a chance of retaliation, as you know well. Our enemy must be broken logistically, militarily, socially. We must use this attack to rip his very heart and soul from him."

The major leaned forward, placing his knuckles face down on the table top.

"As I have been lectured by the good professor here, I am well aware of the necessity of our success. My commitment to that success is as guaranteed as is yours, Lieutenant. The corrections will work as promised."

From a back corner of the room came the silky soft, almost feminine voice belonging to the IRGC Secret Unit Commander Brigadier General Abdol-Ali Nakisa.

"Yes, my two fine warriors. We all know the tactical and strategic necessities involved and we all know that your parts in leading our strikes on air, land, and sea are of the most fundamental importance to our mission's success. Please, Lieutenant, let us hear what the major and professor have to say, shall we?"

Lt. Din nodded quietly his submission to the omnipresent Nakisa, who was the architect of the plan they were all working on. Din moved to his seat next to the admiral and sat with folded arms across his chest.

With the slightest movement of his head, akin to a snake adjusting the location where it intended to sink its fangs, Nakisa transfixed his cold, emotionless eyes upon Major Sabiri, who stood in his tailored Armani suit next to his father.

"Shall we see what you are so proud of, Soldier?"

Nakisa gestured toward the muscular, bearded man wearing gold-rimmed sunglasses, sitting at his side.

"My friend and I will be travelling to Tehran to brief Major General Quashqai and the Supreme Leader tonight. They are both very anxious to learn about our progress. I hope that you will be able to allay all of their curiosities, eh? I also have many questions for you and the professor here about the mission and the progress you are making."

Nakisa looked away from the younger Sabiri and stared at his father, who coolly returned the gaze.

"We are on a tight schedule, General. The little diversion we have planned with the Kashmiri-American jihadist is tenable at this time, but we do not want to rest all our hopes on him, do we, gentlemen?" Nakisa asked while nodding to his companion in the sunglasses.

While he stared at the elder Sabiri, Nakisa spoke, "Your son still has much to accomplish with the infiltration strike teams and the work here seems to be taking far too long. Can we still rely upon your son to positively move all of these efforts forward at the same time or should the efforts be more widely distributed? Perhaps my protégé Major Al-Doleh can assist you?"

Lt. Din barely raised the corners of his mouth in a small smile as he watched the two Sabiris put on the defense by the sinister and powerful leader of IRGC's secret intelligence services.

General Sabiri's look turned very cold as he replied to the hook-nosed master assassin.

"My son is fully capable of seeing to it that all of our projects move forward apace with our needs. You can rest easy, my friend, all will turn out quite fine in the end." General Sabiri moved his eyes to Major Al-Doleh sitting next to Nakisa. "This jihadist plaything that the two of you have hatched up has many possible beneficial uses in our plan, but he is also the single most unsecure avenue to achieving our aims. I trust he is on a short leash?"

"The shortest," Al-Doleh replied without emotion.

Nakisa's thin fingers opened a folder on the table in front of him as he exhibited another emotionless smile to the general.

"I, and all of us present, are pleased to hear that your confidence in your son is no less than mine, my dear friend."

Nakisa's voice trailed off behind the last word, adding an emphasis that chilled the entire room.

"I will surely rest easier tonight with that positive news. Regarding the jihadist, since he has absolutely no information regarding our much broader aims, his involvement will do us great service if it is successful but it is not required for our ultimate ends."

Nakisa paused and visually canvassed the dozen IRGC commanders and religious agents in the room. General Sabiri had quickly turned the tables on him in front of the group and Nakisa did not like that at all.

He held all the cards with the group and having the elder Sabiri try to make this meeting a search for quorum regarding Nakisa's personal investments into the project was very unwelcome. Outwardly, he showed none of this displeasure and rested his thin fingers on his companion's arm as he replied.

"My longtime friend here and his old companions in the SSG brought this jihadist to my attention. He is actively monitoring the Kashmiri to gauge any possible leaks or vulnerability. At the smallest sign of his mission being compromised, the jihadist will be eliminated. But I might add that this little – plaything as you call him – was instrumental in identifying the undercover agent that had infiltrated our ISI partners. As you all know, the Kashmiri is not the only jihadist project I have formulated, and that other operative is ready to go operational immediately."

Nakisa eyed every member of the room as he sized up their emotions, until his eyes stopped their roving and rested back on General Sabiri as he concluded.

"If I may paraphrase – our chickens are not all hatched, but I have laid them with extreme care. Would you care to make a closer inspection of the operation?"

The blatant offer sent a cold spike of reality down the backs of both Sabiris. The general knew well that it was Nakisa who not only first broached the idea of this attack, but he had the better political instincts that had led to the government and the Supreme Leader to endorse the plan. It was he who had moved the project to proceed to this point. There was absolutely no way Nakisa would ever lose in a battle of wills between them. The assassin had always been able to easily outmaneuver the air force general in the past. What goaded Sabiri's emotions the most was Nakisa's supreme arrogance to challenge him so openly in front of so many peers, and in front of his son! Not a single person in the room had any illusions that if he accepted the invitation to such an inspection it would likely result in his quick disappearance.

The general did his best to smother his emotions under grim stoicism but it was obvious to everyone in the room that he had submitted as his physical form diminished ever so slightly away from his usual bombastic confidence.

"I – am quite certain that your efforts are well in hand and – I thank you – for your masterful handling of this delicate matter. I will decline your gracious offer."

The room remained silent as Nakisa basked in his reestablished position as the dominant entity in the room, but he kept his eyes focused on General Sabiri. Seeing the opportunity to squelch the issues surrounding the method of infiltration for the strike teams once and for all, he stated a directive that he knew must be openly disagreed with at this moment or it would be established forever.

"I am so appreciative of your confidence in me and my associate. With that being the case I am appointing Major Al-Doleh here in charge of managing the infiltration of men and supplies into the American infrastructure. That way – uh, your son can remain focused on completing the vast array of tasks necessary here without being weighed down by such a far-flung concern." His eyes roved the room again. "This is agreeable, yes?"

Eyes around the room sank to the floor as the many heads nodded acquiescence to the new order of things. Major Sabiri's face was ashen at the loss of such a prestigious assignment while his father's face blushed red with anger. Both knew it was useless and deadly to fight the matter as they both nodded acceptance with the rest.

Nakisa absorbed the universal agreement in the room as he opened two large manila folders in front of him. One showed a large photograph of Ajay Majumbar stapled to the top of the folder while the other folder showed several smaller photographs of a bearded Middle Eastern man with gapped teeth. Nakisa tapped the photo with his pen and looked back at Major Sabiri.

"Shall we continue, Major?" he asked.

Major Sabiri swallowed with more visible effort that he liked since his mouth was suddenly so very dry.

"Yes, General, of course – uh, Professor?" he said fighting back the desire to cough.

"Uh yes, of course, of course." Zanjani held back a delighted smirk as he watched the arrogant major squirm. "Let me begin by addressing the concerns of the lieutenant, then, shall I?"

The professor began his presentation with projections of schematic blueprints detailing the construction of the covert missile launching systems. He pointed to a section of the drawing where pipes and wires appeared to cross between the various containers, with everyone in the room paying very close attention as he spoke.

*****

AS THE afternoon daylight filtered down into the large room through the grimy skylights, it projected a distorted reflection of blue sky and clouds on the brownish liquid sheen spread across the filthy concrete floor. Ajay watched with great interest the human-on-human butchery that was on full display inside the old warehouse. He closely observed as the eyes of the hapless prisoner fixated upon the reflection of the sky on the floor as if it were some tangible ray of hope that would allow him to believe his future was not actually going to be the same horrible end that his companions had previously suffered. Their mutilated and dismembered body parts littered the floor in a loose pile nearby, along the opposite wall. The terror of what had happened to those bodies radiated from the man's soul, and was clearly displayed in his eyes. *He doesn't know his end will be different and he won't like it!*

Earlier, the fool had begged desperately for his life, but has since become silent and resigned, but no less terrified. Ajay figured he must have finally came to the realization that nothing will ever allow him to escape what was soon to occur, and as the seconds ticked by, the miserable conclusion to his useless life moved closer. It was at these moments of utter defeat that Ajay enjoyed this work the most. He gave a small chuckle every time one of Miguel's men made any noise and the prisoner's eyes would instantly be drawn away from the reflection on the slime, and dart to and fro trying to see where his next tormentor would come from.

Miguel's brother, Juan, had suffered a similar fate at the hands of the Tijuana Cartel two-years ago and Ajay marveled at how efficient and ruthless his boyhood friend had become in doling out

94

death and torture. The obvious enjoyment Miguel got from the experience was nearly as much as Ajay's.

Although Ajay marveled at the changes in Miguel, he was also astonished at the changes that had come to the drug business in Mexico and to the country's very soul. He sensed a level of danger and pathos that pervaded the place and permeated its people that had never existed before. To cross the southern border today was to enter a realm of deceit, fear, and death that was unimaginable just a few years ago. *My, how times do change. And I say they change for the better!*

The Mexico he remembered, a place once known for peasants, banditos, beaches, margaritas, and a basic level of pervasive government corruption, was now strictly a nation built upon a criminal industry that dealt in hard cash and brutal death. The country's mythological romance with petty corruption, siestas, and beautiful women had sold its soul to the capitalism of drugs, murder, and extortion. Even the omnipresent but forlorn hope of poor peasants for their next Zapata to come rescue them had died in the utter ruthlessness that infested the streets today.

The cold brutality of the real Mexico had ground away everything good from the old society, leaving only a cheap façade that could still hide the bodies, but did nothing to cover the smell of their rotting corpses. To Ajay, this nation; once like a beautiful Latina who was gorgeous, seductive, and fun, if not very bright. Was now a sickened and aged whore, contaminated with diseases to its core, and soon to be left putrid and dead in the gutter.

Once upon a time the Mexicans' were only a conduit for the smugglers of Columbian cocaine, Central American marijuana, and Asian heroin. But they had since changed from being mere smuggling bandits to becoming extremely vicious and ruthless murderers who had taken complete control of the entire North American smuggling operation. It was virtually all theirs now, from the point of production all the way through to the end distribution of the many illicit products that the gringos craved so much.

Compared to the days when bringing across a couple kilos in the saddlebags of a motorcycle was an evening jaunt for Ajay, these days it was like an excursion into a minefield where the explosives were moved nightly. In his early days of smuggling the only thing Ajay feared was getting past the Texas Rangers and DEA. Nowadays, getting busted on the U.S. side was the least of worries for any smuggler. Where once singular banditos patrolled the cross-border traffic of migrants and drugs; rival cartels now enforced absolute control and vied for the territory of their rivals.

Even for a very experienced coyote smuggler such as Ajay, getting hijacked by sicarios working for another cartel was a very real possibility with every haul north. *The drug business isn't what it used to be.*

The long-corrupt Mexican government now wanted direct access and control of the revenue stream supplied by the American drug addiction. For mere survival, the government bureaucrats and politicians were now forced to directly compete with the cartels for control of the smuggling routes into North America, and getting nabbed by the Federales was as much a guaranteed death sentence as getting captured by a competitor cartel. Mexico had long lost its soul and if the government did not survive, the country would soon lose all of its societal institutions as well.

As a matter of reality, getting grabbed by anyone was now a guaranteed death sentence throughout Latin America. From the Gulf to the Pacific, the entire northern half of Mexico was in a constant state of civil war between the various cartels and government over who would collect tolls and be in command of everything in the trafficking business. That dangerous situation was now having real effects on Ajay's plans and had forced him to pay very close attention to securing the infiltration route of his Iranian benefactor's strike teams. Luckily, the Monterrey cartel was still strong and dominated in this area.

He looked over his shoulder at the stubby submersible sitting on a trailer near a garage door. It was one of the cartel's latest contraptions for smuggling dope and people across the border. And Miguel had told him that it had proved successful thus far. Useful or not, Ajay still thought the thing looked ridiculous and must be a gimmick that would be doomed to failure once the U.S. Navy and Coast Guard really went searching for things like it. The DEA was already bought and paid for but Ajay doubted the military could be bought off in the same way.

He understood full well that the cartel only concerned itself with moving massive volumes of product. They cared nothing for the welfare or safety of the human coyote's that hauled the products into the States. The cramped interior of the craft looked flat-out dangerous and Ajay knew he would never set foot inside the damned thing. Even with the dangers of rival cartels, he was good enough at doing it the old fashioned way – right through the border checkpoint at Nuevo Laredo.

He had done a lucrative smuggling business for years, mixing his legitimate freight with moderate amounts of cocaine and heroin in the false containers on his rigs, and he was certain the same could be done again for a last haul. Even with the slaughter going on south of the border, the DEA and INS were still as lax and apathetic as ever at actually stopping the flow of immigrants and dope. The ready cash and crooked politics of the cross border smuggling business had only increased.

His running of contraband had financed the trips back to Kashmir but now that the Iranians were footing all the bills and money was no longer a consideration for Ajay to worry about. He could now concentrate solely on getting his route set and ready. He would simply grease the right hands with Persian cash and slip right through with enough weapons and commandos in a single truck to wreak havoc across the entire country.

All it took to successfully smuggle dope or shitbag illegal's was to have patience and minimize the amounts carried, as well as grease the squeaky wheels of the smuggling world. Since he only needed one haul and he had a year to plan it out – he knew it was a guarantee that he would be successful.

But as he considered the little sub, he grasped that keeping his mind open to its possibilities might actually prove to be useful after all. He walked over and examined it more closely. The tiny deck rode above the water line by a couple inches, easily getting swamped by little more than a foot-high wave. But the sub was airtight and would be hard to flood easily. Several short pipes provided air to the diesel engine and occupants. It was barely big enough for five people to cram into but that was all the space that Ajay required for the mission he had in mind for the odd craft.

Yes, after Ajay contemplated it further, this harebrained machine might just be exactly what Ajay needed for a special little task.

Satisfied with his scheme, Ajay's turned his attention to the howling wind that kicked dust up and tapped small grains of dirt against the tin walls of the building and made the roof rattle and vibrate.

He walked over to a filthy window, its blinds covered with aluminum foil taped to the inside; an easy and surefire way to make sure no unwanted eyes could press up against the glass and spy in on the gruesome activities inside. *As if anyone in this neighborhood of Monterrey would be stupid enough to do that.* He shifted the lower corner of the blinds and looked through the grit-covered glass and saw the dark clouds that rolled in from the east as hurricane Alex made its way inland from the Gulf of Mexico.

Below the foreboding clouds, the steep slopes of the Sierra de La Silla rose menacingly, piercing the sky like the spiked back of a slumbering monster. The sharp peaks sat brooding above the hustling traffic that moved back and forth along the Jardines de La Silla highway outside. People scurried down the sidewalks looking for cover from the biting dust grains as they went about gathering provisions before the oncoming storm reached the city and knocked out the electricity. It was only a category-two storm but still created a mess as it blew the trash in from the slums across the entire city.

The attacks were planned for next September, smack dab in the middle of the hurricane season. Ajay once considered praying to Allah for help with the weather but then dismissed the foolish gesture from his mind. His faith in Islam was now as worthless as the Mexican peso since the Hajj. After spending three years in Fedayeen training camps spread throughout the territories of Kashmir, Pakistan, Iran, and Iraq; Ajay was tired of the religious crap all the other moron jihadists preached about. He knew now that all their Salafist ranting was nothing but political cover and idealistic propaganda for the stupid and the uneducated.

It irritated him that he had even bought into those ignorant rants from his prison cellmate, Hussein. Ajay had discovered that the twisting of religion may motivate most jihadists, but their masters and financiers cared less about religion and more about power. For them it was all about dreams of empire for governments and the placing of pure power into the hands of a few. Their ability to control and direct huge masses with cheap propaganda and an authoritarian structure were simply bolstered by the claim that a god endorsed it. Ajay learned that the motivations were the same whether the leaders were Saudi or Iranian.

For Ajay – religion, empire, and even power meant absolutely nothing. For him it was about hate, retribution and his immortality. For Ajay it was all about death.

A croaking scream came from the captive, pulling Ajay back from his musing to again watch the show. He knew Miguel was trying to impress him, knowing that Ajay had just returned from his eighth trip back to the 'lands of jihad,' and Miguel wanted to prove that a Mexican could be as thorough at slaughter as any Arab. Ajay looked on attentively, but Miguel would have to work hard at his show if he was truly going to astound, especially considering what Ajay had seen and done during his travels.

The Iranians had proved very cooperative in teaching him what needed to get done to obtain the full extent of destruction they all craved to achieve with this plan. They had taken him to their battlefields in Afghanistan and Iraq where they showed him how to lay out attacks and plan out the tactics for striking the chosen targets. The

98

weaker and more unprotected the target was, the better. He was even given the opportunity to help plan, deploy, and observe three separate attacks; a bazaar in Kabul, a mosque in Mosul, and a police check point in Baghdad.

He was very impressed with how good they were at what they did, but he knew he could do better. So when he finally proposed the plans that he had been keeping to himself for so many years, he laughed at how they almost fell out of their chairs in reaction to his idea. They enthusiastically endorsed them and soon he was elevated in their eyes to the status he craved. Soon he would die but he did not care. His acts of carnage would give him all that truly mattered to him.

As Ajay watched the captive being pummeled once again by Miguel's fists he considered it remarkable just how similar the bloodshed here in Mexico compared to the violence of the battlefields he had toured over the years.

He had seen many death rooms, the spitting image of this one, which populated so many dark places of the planet. But he always remembered one more fondly than the rest; the one where he had proven his ruthlessness to the Iranians by decapitating a captured Iraqi Kurd. Ajay was told that the man was the brother of a low-level politician in Mosul who had reneged on a construction contract for work on an oil pipeline in his district. The Shiite family that had lost the bid for the contract had very close ties to the IRGC and the man's death was a message to the politician to reconsider his foolish decision before he lost any more members of his household.

Ajay remembered his indoctrination to slaughtering another human being very well. His handler, Major Al-Doleh, was a serious and sour personality that never particularly warmed to Ajay throughout his training. As the politician's brother wept and prayed, bound and beaten kneeling in the center of the room, the major had sat calmly watching as Ajay was instructed on how to do the decapitation. Several Quds Force thugs observed while chanting praises to Allah while one recorded the act on video. Ajay approached the pathetic sobbing man, wondering how it would feel afterward as he waited for the order.

Once the major directed him to begin, all trepidation left him as a sudden flood of enthusiasm flowed into his veins. He violently jerked the man by his hair until he pinned his head to the floor under his knee as the man screamed. The sound quickly turned into high-pitched gurgling as his knife cut through the gristle-like windpipe and arteries. Blood spurted onto his chest and face as he sawed back and forth and twisted the head around and positioned the blade into the joints between the vertebras of the neck. The head popped away from the neck and he stood up holding it as blood dripped from his white-knuckled grip on the dead man's blood-soaked hair. The major looked on satisfied. That was the moment when Ajay realized, completely, for the very first time, that he had finally found his true purpose – ending life.

His training had ended only after many more such experiences which Ajay often indulged in replaying in his mind. But the time for such fun was now gone and Ajay was kept very busy these days pulling together his end of the plans here in Mexico and he would soon shift to the labors of obtaining and then staging the necessary items at the many far-flung places within the United States.

Soon he would make it so that the death chambers of Mexico and the Middle East would be recreated inside dark corners of the United States itself, and the whole jahili society would be destroyed from within by the very access that was made possible by their own weaknesses with their addictions.

The decadent and weak kafir gringos of America still looked to Mexico and their drug habit in innocent terms, like it was some dumbass movie, such as *Easy Rider* where Dennis Hopper and Peter Fonda pulled south of the border to grab some coke for a stupid hippie adventure. *The pinche fucks!* Little did they realize the catastrophic monster they were creating just miles away from their homes across the Rio Grande. The horrors that monster would soon deliver to their homes and lives would be paid for in rivers of blood and pain! *Fucking delicious!*

"Allahlu Akbar, fuck'n-A, mine is the divine justice, sayeth the God Majumbar," Ajay muttered quietly with a smirk.

The 55-gallon drum was about half-full of liquid sodium hydroxide that sloshed around inside the barrel as Miguel's henchman pulled the pallet jack into place in front of the terrified prisoner. The wheels of the device made a repetitive squeaking sound that reminded Ajay of the book cart that drove him crazy back in Huntsville. He was pleased when the henchman pulled it away, receding into the shadows of the warehouse.

Meanwhile the luckless prisoner hung trussed up in a fetal position below the steel hook and cable of a hydraulic port-a-lift. The device was designed to lift engine blocks from vehicles but today it was being used for a very different purpose. The steel wire mesh bound the man in such a tight fetal position that he would fit easily into the open top of the drum. The chicken wire bit into his skin causing several deep cuts that bled significantly.

The metal wiring would not be affected by the acid in the barrel and Miguel joked that he liked to use the chicken wire since it kept the bones together. He told Ajay that he would enjoy seeing the sight of the non-dissolved head sitting atop a pile of bleached bones in a wire sack.

The captive tried to scream but his hoarse throat merely gurgled inside the ball-gag placed over his mouth. After the beating he had received from Miguel, Ajay was certain that his red and swollen face was no longer easily recognizable, even to people who knew him personally. But what was easy enough to recognize was the terror in his eyes as they bulged in their sockets at the sight of the drum sitting in front of him.

His blood-soaked black fatigue uniform with Mexican Army patches hung in tatters from the top of the hydraulic lift behind him. It showed he was not of high rank, just a terribly unlucky foot soldier that had been plucked up with a group of other army conscripts during a small raid by the cartel on a poorly guarded patrol on the outskirts of the city. Ajay watched as Miguel and his men captured the soldiers and he was still astounded at how easily they surrendered when they should have known that it would be far better to die on the streets than inside this dungeon.

Miguel came walking out of the shadows and sat a video camera on a tripod a few feet in front of the terrified man and carefully positioned it to capture the entire vision of cruelty that was about to take place. His knuckles were still swollen from the pitiless beating he had dished out to the miserable soldiers but they still worked well enough for him to activate the camera. He walked up to the man and grasping his hair, violently jerked the face upward so a full view was given to the camera's lens. Miguel faced the camera lowering his face next to the prisoner and smiled as if they were taking a portrait together.

"Calderon! Ver su future, pendejo!" he snapped. He then pushed the port-a-lift forward until the dangling victim was suspended above the waiting vat of acid.

The naked and bleeding body trussed inside the chicken wire swung above the barrel as Miguel activated the hydraulics, slowly lowering the man toward the chemicals. The pathetic wretch tried to scream behind the ball-gag but could not get the sounds out. Ajay admired how Miguel used everything he could to humiliate the poor bastards that he killed. *The Mexicans have definitely gotten good at this shit!*

Miguel had certainly proven to Ajay that he could indeed teach the IRGC a thing or two about pain, humiliation, and pure terror. Ajay's jihadist brothers were definitely good at killing but their use of torture was no worse than here.

He giggled at the thought of this horror show playing-out just a few miles from where all those silly soccer moms, soccer dads, and their impish and spoiled soccer children played-out their own dull lives. Not far from this macabre play they nonchalantly went about doing all of their irrelevant errands; oblivious to the un-caged and bloodthirsty creature that lurked close by and was ready to feed. Those fools had no idea what atrocious hell Ajay was preparing to unleash upon them.

The ill-fated man's gagging screams lasted far longer than Ajay would have imagined possible.

"The wolf is at your door, America, and I'm going to huff – and puff – and blow your whole fucking world down," he muttered with a grin as he watched the show.

*****

November 2, 2010 13:20pm EST UTC -5:00
NCTC-National Counterterrorism Center
McLean, VA

HARRY MCDERMOTT leaned back in his chair and stared at the photograph of his smiling wife and daughter. The little knickknack frame sat on a small shelf above his computer screen and over the past four months he had been drawn to staring at it more and more every day. And every time he did, he contemplated just how nice it would be once he finishes this last year with the FBI and retires with thirty-years of service under his belt. Being a computer analyst instead of a street agent, his career had been long and unremarkable, sitting behind computer screens, sifting through tons of electronic data instead of car chases and shootouts. He longed for the whole monotonous thing to end.

Once he left the bureau he intended to just relax with his family and enjoy the remainder of his years by living out his private dream, painting landscapes on the small deck of their vacation home in the Adirondacks. October 2011 was his actual anniversary date, but by this spring he would have stored up over three-hundred hours of vacation time that he could use to leave the office a couple of months early. *It can't come fast enough.*

In the photo his wife, Sally, and their daughter, Shenandoah, sat hugging with flat, wet hair from a recent swim in the lake. The photo was Harry's favorite since it showed the pure joy of that perfect day they all experienced two-years ago in upstate New York. And his happiness was clearly reflected in the faces of the two people he loved so much. The whole picture oozed bliss and contentment for Harry.

But there was one thing in the picture that Harry wished did not exist, and it was the tiny little sparkle in the photo that, even though it was small it was still easily noticed, just like the first bright star in an early evening sky. The sparkle stood out in the lower corner as a glint of sunlight that was reflected off of Shenandoah's leg braces.

The family actually had a small collection of those braces now; since Shenny was twelve she had gone through several different sizes while growing up with cerebral palsy. The wonderful girl was somewhat lucky in that it was a relatively mild case of the disease compared to some of the other children Harry had seen at the various hospitals and doctor's offices over the years. She could not walk without braces and had some mild dysarthria that caused her to mumble her b's and r's and left spittle on her lips. But the most embarrassing thing for the young teenager was her incontinence, which was really upsetting to her now that she was starting puberty.

Harry longed to be with her and very soon he would be rid of this daily grind at the Bureau and would take his little angel up to the beauty of Schroon Lake where they will have day after day of joy to share and give to each other.

Harry's hatred for the disease was intense as it had robbed his baby girl of the spectacular life she deserved. Her intelligence, wit, charm, and inner-strength were such, that without the disease to hold her back, she could have been destined to be a superstar in whatever she wanted to do. Unfortunately, she was cursed to being one of those innocents' who were fated to be the loving cross that people like herself and her parents had to shoulder with compassion and love until the infirmity eventually took their joy and light from the world. That burdensome cross was something Harry watched his daughter bear uncomplaining, and it was a heavy cross that he bore with equal parts pride and bitter stoicism as he watched over her.

Actually, he blamed himself for Shenny being imprisoned in a body that did not work right. In fact, it was he who had dropped her off at the daycare as a happy, running and bubbly five-year old. Everything she did then was as graceful as a dancer; running, jumping, dancing, laughing, and playing were all a joyous ballet for her. And that was how his mind remembered her as she twirled and hopped away from him that morning.

He sometimes imagined, during his long days in front of the computer screens, what she must have looked like as she ran laughing and yelling around the playground just before the accident happened that changed all of their lives forever. He was later told that little Drake Warner had been chasing her in a game of tag when somehow her feet got twisted (so strange for a girl so perfect, Harry always

103

thought) and she fell with the back of her head striking the base of the jungle gym, knocking her out cold.

The neurological damage done to her brain and nervous system was permanent and the onset of the palsy followed within a year of the accident, robbing her of freedom and a fully functional body. Harry and Sally went to every doctor and specialist and the news was always the same: none of the medical field's horses and none of the medical field's men would ever be able to put his little Shenny back together again.

Harry hated the uselessness of the doctors and their modern medicine nearly as much as he hated the disease.

His rumpled shirt did a poor job of hiding his potbelly and his tie only accentuated his double chin as it rolled over the top of his shirt collar. He felt the numb tingle of a cramp starting in the back of his left leg and he reached down to massage it. He was sure that it was his years of sitting at desks and methodically plodding through the never-ending amounts of data that came through the agency that were the main reasons for his weight gain over the years and also for the varicose veins that now plagued both of his legs. Usually, by this time of day, they started throbbing and became so uncomfortable that he needed to get up and walk around.

Harry, being a creature of habit, followed a routine that rarely varied during the long tedium of his day. Today was no different, so he decided the time was right to take his daily jaunt to the water cooler. He figured he would go down the north hallway first and shoot-the-shit with Sharon outside the director's office for ten minutes or so. After that he would proceed to his workplace man-cave, the toilet, and leave some business behind with the porcelain deity. By the time he made it back his legs should be feeling better and it would only be a short while before he could start his daily close-down routine, then he would head out and face the depressing snarl of traffic and the inevitable long delays that came with his commute home.

As he swung his sport coat over his shoulders and started to push an arm down a sleeve, his computer terminal started making a low beep that notified him that his search through the multijurisdictional intelligence software was complete and had generated the report he had requested. He completed pulling his arms through the sleeves, leaned over his chair and clicked his mouse.

Immediately the computer screen displayed a large file, which Harry scrolled through until he reached a section with dozens of photographs. Passport photos were followed by a myriad of surveillance field shots that were taken at some distance, with a circle highlighting the same person featured in the passport photos.. Some pictures showed the man firing a rifle, but most just showed him standing within a group of similar looking men and talking or praying.

None of the surveillance photos of the terrorist training camps were taken at a close distance, with most being distant snapshots and without highlighting the man within a circle he could easily be overlooked. Harry's eyes returned to the passport photos of Ajay Khan Majumbar and he stared for several seconds at Ajay's eyes before he continued. *You can always tell what's inside a person through their eyes – this bastard is cold.* Finishing up with the photos, he went back to scanning the report summary as he rubbed at the back of his aching leg.

"So you've been doing some travelling around the homeland, eh, asshole? Visiting with long-lost terrorist shit-bag friends?" Harry muttered with annoyance and marginal interest.

Nothing in the report was really jumping out at him with too many red flag warnings. He could see that Ajay's uncle was still loosely affiliated with the Lashkar-e-Tayyiba (LeT) and that Ajay had attended several of their camps, but there were no obvious indications that he or his uncle had ever been involved in anything more than Kashmiri resistance against the Indian administration there. In fact, he read how Ajay's father was injured and his other uncle had been killed supporting American efforts with the mujahedeen in Afghanistan during the 1980s.

It certainly was not unusual for Harry to discover children of older mujahedeen wanting to follow their parents into other jihads. *Carrying on the family traditions, huh?* So far Harry was unimpressed with what he was reading.

Harry had only generated the report after receiving notice from his friend, Parsad Jat Bhachu, who worked for Area-One in the Indian Research and Analysis Wing. As Harry's liaison with the Indian government's security forces, Parsad had advised Harry that their intelligence had observed that Ajay was having some unusually high-level contacts in the ISI's rogue branch, the J+K Wing, who was the top facilitator of the Haqqani Network. But Parsad had still been unable to ascertain exactly why the ultra-hardcore branch of Pakistan's intelligence services was so interested in him.

After giving the report a cursory review, Harry certainly did not see why the ISI would want anything to do with him either; other than to be a useful American agent against Indian interests in that war-torn region. And, with Obama in the White House cozying up to the Indians, that could be a real political thorn, if, as an American, he did a too-big terrorist act somewhere in Kashmir, creating a damn international incident with the Indians. *The White House would get pissed over something like that.*

Harry saw that Ajay's fairly successful trucking business was now shut down and he had spent a considerable amount of time travelling back to Kashmir in recent years. The ISI had always been a lackluster partner in America's war in Afghanistan and had their hands in just about every terrorist act ever committed against the Indian government. Without the U.S. paying them several billion dollars a year in blood money, they could quickly become a direct antagonist, and that could certainly mean that one of that nation's nukes could quickly disappear into the possession of Al Qaeda or the LeT.

Harry still wondered if the leads that the CIA and military intelligence were following up in Abbottobad would actually turn out to be the hiding place for bin-Laden. *Wouldn't that just be something? UBL protected all these years by the ISI? Go figure.*

Parsad was not one for treating every swinging-dick wannabe terrorist as a big deal and said he was just giving Harry a head's-up on the guy. Now, after looking at the report, Harry knew he would have to pay this some closer attention if the ISI actually wanted something to do with this Texan dude, and he decided that he should do some more checking into this Majumbar guy and see where things went. If the guy was involved in some bad stuff over there it should not take too much effort to plug his name into the Watch List and, if necessary, the Big 'bama was not averse to sending a couple of cruise missiles from a Predator right up the ass of a problem child.

But, with this dude being an American citizen, Harry would have to play this carefully with some extra attention to detail and get good documentation to clear a strike on someone like that. *Whacking a citizen could really stir the political crapbag and send shit flying if you're not careful, Harry. That's the last fucking thing you need this close to retirement.*

Harry shrugged his shoulders and closed up the report and buttoned his coat. He would check this guy out, just like he did all the other fuck-heads that came across his desk.

After the commies were defeated and the Cold War ended with a whimper instead of a bang, Harry had little to do until everything had changed after 9/11. When that happened, he had found out that the real long war had begun. A never-ending saga of violence that stretched back centuries and was far more complex than simple clashes over socialism or capitalism; or even culture and religion. It included local, regional, and global politics over water, land, including the big issue of crude oil that the world guzzled daily by millions of barrels. All of that was mixed in a stew pot of tribalism and age-old feuds that needed a constant supply of fresh blood to keep them well-greased and active.

Since 9/11, every day for Harry started another new emergency, some spot-fire that needed tamped out here or there all over the globe. Harry often felt as though he was some giant voyeur looking down on a kicked anthill, searching for the one ant in the frenzied mass that dodged and dashed for the means to bring down the giant who had kicked its nest. Harry was burned out and sick-'n-fucking tired of the constant pile of shit stinking up his life. He desperately longed for retirement so that it would all be taken away and get handed it off to someone else. *Somebody else needs to do this heavy lifting for a change!*

The computer screen went dark and he turned and began his afternoon stroll. Now, one more time, his latest spot-fire was some redneck Muslim from Texas with a hard-on for Kashmir. *Weird, of all the damn places for this asshole to spring from, Texas. Go figure.*

"I'll get on your ass tomorrow, son, and we'll see if you've been up to any crap," he muttered quietly as he walked down the hallway between the cubicles, rubbing hard at the veins in the back of his thigh.

*****

March 13, 2011 18:45pm UTC+3:00
Piazza degli Incendi Taulud Island
Massawa, Eritrea

WALKING QUICKLY, General Nakisa and Major Al-Doleh, came out the doors of the old Red Sea Hotel and climbed into the rear seats of the black high-security model BMW 7 series sedan. Upon the vehicle doors closing the driver pulled swiftly out of the hotel parking lot and headed across the piazza, immediately followed by two Toyota Four Runners filled with heavily armed IRGC Secret Unit personnel.

As they completed the circle of the piazza the short caravan passed the Eritrean War Memory Square, a sad military monument that consisted of three old rusted Russian T-55 tanks that sat in regal display at the center of the piazza, in celebration of the small nation's successful, but long forgotten, war of independence from Ethiopia that had finally ended in 1993.

Evening light was rapidly fading into darkness as the vehicles kicked up thick clouds of dust as they barreled down the old street that was lined with dilapidated stucco Turkish architecture. Many of the buildings still displayed the pockmarked craters in their facades and sides from where the bullets that impacted during the long-ago pitched battles that were fought along these dusty avenues. Such signs as those, of bloody conflict in city streets, were a common acquaintance to Major Al-Doleh's life. As he examined the scarred features that passed by he could easily visualize the splattered blood and mangled bodies that had littered the area during the height of the vicious fighting that had flourished here. It gave him a feeling of more than just familiarity, but also comfort and a real sense of hominess. The brutal killer felt this way often as he spent the last fifteen years deep inside the struggles of jihad throughout Afghanistan, Iraq, Bosnia, and the Balkans.

The customary signs of death, decay, and intimate violence that were evidenced throughout this small port city felt very much like all those other places Al-Doleh had been to across Asia Minor. They were all natural hunting grounds for a predator; a predator that both flourished at, and deeply enjoyed the hunting of men; a predator just like him.

The echo of gunfire had long since disappeared from this dusty city. A ramshackle and desperate city that looked longingly out upon the busy international shipping traffic that floated uncaringly by on the smooth surface of the Red Sea. The captains of those vessels ignored the harbor just like passersby on 5th Avenue did beggars. If any did glance toward the port, it was to assess whether the fishermen coming from there were legitimate or possibly scouts for the Somali pirates farther down the coast.

Al-Doleh's eyes could still make out the last of the dark-skinned fishermen tying their small fishing boats along the Mitsiwas harbor docks while others made repairs to their nets under the dim light of hanging kerosene lanterns. None of these scrawny men were spies, just poor fishermen.

Without turning away he said, "I believe the meeting went well, General. Our friends in the Muslim Brotherhood appear to be set to grab hold of the reins of power in Egypt and are also making some progress with their efforts in the Saudi Kingdom, and especially Yemen. But I am disappointed that Al-Shabaab refuses to assist us in those labors in Arabia."

Nakisa's silky-cold voice replied confidently, "Don't be too unhappy with them, my friend. They are hard pressed to move against the African Union troops in Somalia without the significant assistance given by the Kingdom of Saud. Soon, when they have the majority of their finances coming from us, they will be far more eager to participate in our whims. Right now I am satisfied that they are being

108

cooperative in our destabilizing efforts in North Africa. Tripoli will make another fine jewel for Hezbollah and the caliphate."

"Yes. it will. I must say, your progress in these endeavors has been an inspiration to me, General. The kafirs ally, Mubarak, was the perfect choice of your first exploitation of this tactic. The wild successes that have followed his usurpation are remarkable. I admit to you, your plan to use the strengths of last year's Green Revolution in Tehran as a weapon to destabilize our Muslim rivals was a spark of divine genius, sir. I again bow to your intellect. Your inspired insight will see the destabilization of all of our rivals across the breadth of Asia and Africa. Quite brilliant, sir."

"My thanks, Major, your words are appreciated. But in all truth, I must divulge that I believe it is simply proof that Allah has blessed the Children of Ali with his radiant and imperishable divine inspiration. His will works through them, and me, and will soon bring low our Ahlas Sunnah brothers. They will then be very amenable to the caliphate and they will be in no position to do anything but bend to our will after the kafirs are removed from consideration."

"The boy-lover family will be greatly upset at their Wahab sect falling from the lead role of our faith in Arabia."

"Ah, King Fahd will be lucky if the Supreme Leader allows him to live! Soon he and those in his impish brood, who are still alive when we have rested control, will be relegated back to herding their camels across the sands. On that day, the two Holy Cities and the Kaába shall once again be in the hands of Persia," Nakisa said triumphantly.

Off to their left, Al-Doleh observed the cracked white paint on the bombed-out ruins of the late Emperor Haile Selassie's palace. The once beautiful island citadel glowed orange in the evening light as the driver turned their vehicle right and headed for a narrow causeway that led across a shallow inlet of water and took them into the Old City of Massawa on their way to the port docks.

"I will be glad to be rid of this miserable place. I have much to do in preparation for my mission and have little stomach for these Africans. They make good slaves and servants but little else."

"Never fear, my young commander, we will soon be loaded aboard the Deyanat and headed for Bushehr. You still have plenty of time to complete the training of your men. I must say, I am impressed with the tactics that you and the Kashmiri-jihadist have decided upon. You shall strike a deep blow that will shake the kafirs to their core."

The fast-moving caravan turned left in front of the Hotel Torino with few of its Turkish arched windows showing any lights or any other signs of occupancy. The gloom of the passing alleyways quickly receded into deeper darkness that the vehicle headlights refused to penetrate. Upon seeing the caravan, the few pedestrians that were present, rushed even further into the shadows of those alleys and arched doorways to avoid any semblance that they harbored interest in what had brought so may powerful and deadly people to their tiny, and forgotten port city.

The caravan made its way toward several tall cranes, with many bright lights, that stood bordering the long concrete piers of the main port facilities. The Iranian flagged container ship sat silently moored under those bright incandescent lights, waiting patiently for the two murderous dignitaries to arrive and have their vehicles craned aboard.

Barely noticeable to anyone who was not looking for it, a green laser light flashed several times off in the darkness, well beyond where the Deyanat was moored. Both Nakisa and the major had been searching for the light and immediately after he saw it the general ordered the driver to continue slowly by the ship. The two security escorts obediently stopped and let the sedan move away and disappear into the growing darkness away from the crane lights.

While the ship's crew rapidly worked to hoist the security detail aboard, the sedan moved several hundred yards further until they saw a dark-clad man standing in the road who motioned for the vehicle to pull into a dirt courtyard that sat before the ruins of the old Massawan Bank of Italia.

The once regal two-story masonry and concrete structure was completely encircled by cracked colonnades of Corinthian columns on both the ground floor patio and second floor deck. Its windows had long since been destroyed in massive blasts that left their gouging scars across the exterior, and indeed, throughout the obliterated interior. Makeshift and ramshackle squatter huts, which consisted mainly of any piece of trash and material worthy of making a structure, leaned against the colonnades exterior along the front of the structure but the hapless builders of those squalid dwellings were nowhere to be seen.

The driver stopped the BMW below the center stairs that led to the destroyed vestibule that was directly below a gigantic, but ruined circular window. Several dark figures stood in the shadows, the thin outlines of their rifle barrels protruded from their shadowy profiles.

Nakisa turned to his protégé. "You must wait here for me to return."

"How long should it be before I come for you, General?"

Nakisa shot his underling an incredulous glance.

"If they choose that I not return you will know that when they come here and kill you. Now stay here and remain quiet until I return."

He left the car without looking back at the Quds Force officer, who sat and stewed at his commander for giving such deference to the Asians.

In a lithe, almost feminine stride, Nakisa quickly scrambled up the steps and entered the ruined building. Rubble crunched under his feet as he followed the arm wave of a silent and brooding figure that held a Chinese machine-gun. As the man continued to climb through the ruins of the old structure, the general followed obediently behind, closely watching his steps among the scattered debris. They eventually made their way across the second floor landing where the general noticed the bodies of a family of three Eritreans lying in fresh pools of blood along the wall. They were evidently the residents of the old ruin, until tonight when they were so rudely evicted and sent to Hell.

The man Nakisa followed paid the corpses no attention and continued upward until they reached the roof. Once there his deadly valet stopped and pointed to a lone figure standing at the edge of the rooftop. Nakisa slowly walked toward the backside of the man who was staring off toward the remnants of a faint blushing glow that framed the western horizon above the distant mountains of the Semenawi Bahri National Park.

"It is good to see you again, General Li," Nakisa said.

The tall Chinese spy stared off toward the horizon but spoke warmly to the Iranian master assassin.

"My old friend Abdol, how pleased I am to speak with you. I cannot wait for you to tell me how our operations are proceeding, nicely, I hope?"

"Yes! Yes, things are moving apace toward our goals with a steady tempo. I foresee no issues at this time."

"That is pleasing news. Come, first tell me of the little meeting you just had and then we will move onto other topics shall we? I have news of my choreography with the Russians that I am sure you will find informative."

General Li turned to face the Iranian and gave a thin smile.

"I believe it is about time we get that old Russian bear up and doing some cute tricks for us, don't you?"

June 30, 2011 16:20pm UTC+4:30
IRGC Bahonar Garrison
Karaj, Iran

LIEUTENANT Nader-ed-Din stood impatiently at the window with his arms folded across his chest and drumming his fingers on his sleeve. He greatly wanted to be on his way as quickly as possible and he did not like the wasteful delay that today's inspection by the Supreme Leader was causing to his plans. He had intended for his men to leave the garrison tonight and be in Bushehr by early morning. He needed to conduct his last inspections and his men still needed to become more familiar with the three ships before they set sail for at-sea training. His schedule was very tight and he felt his men required a minimum of thirty days at sea to familiarize themselves with the ship and launching equipment to ensure the flawless execution of attacks.

But, unfortunately, he was stuck for the remainder of today, chaperoning the playboy, Major Sabiri, here at Karaj. At the moment, Din watched as Sabiri took every opportunity to ingratiate himself to the Supreme Leader on yet another tour of the facility. For Din it was exceedingly tiring to do this tawdry assignment that he knew full well would be unnecessary if the elder Sabiri truly had the control over his arrogant son that he should. Babysitting General Sabiri's progeny from his own bombastic ego and even bigger mouth, and quite possibly humiliating his powerful family and his own self before the group of ayatollahs, mujtahid, and mullahs was far beyond frustrating for the naval commander.

Din sighed and glanced over his shoulder marveling at the assembled crowd of sycophants that stood near and heavily lauded every word spoken by the Supreme Leader with praise, and loyal assurances of his deep wisdom. Presently, the Grand Ayatollah was closely watching out the window as the commandos below worked hard in the extreme afternoon heat to display their skills for his approval.

Din quickly covered his mouth to hide a smirk as he observed the endless mewing, placating, and deference given by all the political hacks, military men, and mullahs. It was so extreme that it was blatantly comical to him, but he dared not give an uncontrolled snicker of laughter at the pathetic assembly. Even with his high position in the attack – a loss of decorum like that would result in an immediate death sentence. He turned his back to the group and did his best to ignore Major Sabiri diligent narrating to the Supreme Leader and his entourage. Din's babysitting duties were suddenly becoming dangerous.

Out the window and to his left the forty-two men of the naval security forces and land strike teams conducted live-fire search and destroy operations in a cinderblock four-story building. Each floor had raised catwalks that crisscrossed above the labyrinth of corridors and rooms where Din's and Major Al-Doleh's men searched through and fired at targets as they methodically moved through the structure. Meanwhile instructors observed from the catwalks critiquing the men, pointing out mistakes as well as successes.

The eighteen naval commandos participating were tasked with protecting the nuclear missiles and repulsing any seaborne assault on the ships that could come from U.S. Navy SEALS or possibly British SAS commandos who might try to board any of the three vessels. Din realistically believed that it was a foregone conclusion that his defenses would be breached but if his men could just stop the attackers long enough for the launch to be completed, it was all he needed from them. The twenty-four ground force commandos participating in the attacks were tasked with being able to defeat police SWAT and possibly military units that would be sent against them as they marauded their way through the streets in their ground assaults.

The clamor of guns firing wound its way through the building's warren of passages toward the roof of the building. Occasionally the observers saw the bright burst of an explosion from some hand-grenade lighting up a room a few seconds before the dull thud of the compression wave reached them that accompanied the loud bang of the explosion, causing the window to wobble ever so slightly.

A copious amount of gunfire erupted from the building that drew the attention of the Supreme Leader and his mewing train who all turned their heads in that direction. None of the observers were high enough to see the men actually firing inside the building but they were able to observe their progress by watching the movement of the lead instructor, Major Rashid Al-Doleh, who followed along on the catwalks above the commandos.

The major was a nineteen-year veteran of the IRGC Quds Force who now worked directly under Brigadier General Nakisa in the Secret Unit. Al-Doleh was an equal peer to Lt Din and was co-commander in the operational deployment of the project. He was in charge of all operational ground force commandos while Din commanded the operational naval forces.

Din respected and admired Al-Doleh, a man who had over twenty incursions into Iraq where he had actually engaged U.S. Army and Marine units in multiple firefights and IED ambushes. He was the

113

most skilled and experienced commander inside the Quds Force and had spent the past three-years training Taliban, Al-Shabab, Hezbollah, Chechen and Shiite death squads. And he was the one responsible for finding and bringing into the project the Kashmiri-jihadist who would help facilitate so much of their ground attacks in America. A ruthless, cold-blooded killer, Al-Doleh was perfect for the mission.

The smile of satisfaction from the Supreme Leader and his accompanying ayatollahs gave allowance for the lesser mullahs to gleefully cheer at the demonstration. Din was pleased with the response and soaked up the adulation that his men's performance had achieved. He would pass on the reaction to his team later. They would be pleased.

The city of Karaj was nestled against the low southern flanks of Alborz Mountains, deep in the desert terrain that existed on the southern base of the mountain range. Here, there was very little of the moist air from the Caspian Sea that made the northern flanks so lush and covered in verdant forest. Here, arid winds and small clouds brought little rain and the towering ridges and peaks were mainly a dull brown, dotted here and there with stands of pine and cedar trees and some other hardy plants that were successful in eking out life from the dry soil.

Karaj was now little more than a suburb of the metropolitan sprawl from Tehran but its residents still tried to act as if they were a separate city. The main buildings for the IRGC garrison stretched off to Din's right and as Sabiri directed the Supreme Leader's attention to that area Din followed with his own eyes.

In the busy streets and alleys of Karaj, spreading far out into the distance, lived the citizens who moved around in the fertile playground that was the usual training ground for the truck drivers of the ground strike teams. But for the dignitary's show today, the inside of the fencing was the necessary playground and had a continuous cloud of dust being stirred up by the half dozen tractor-trailer trucks that maneuvered their way among the buildings of the military complex. The trucks did not follow each other in a line, but instead, each followed its own path through the small maze of streets on the base. They often passed in opposite directions or met at intersections where they were forced to maneuver around one another just like they would in the regular traffic they would be forced to encounter in America's busy city streets.

On normal training days the trucks and their drivers made their way around the hectic streets of Karaj, but today they were simply another display item for the Grand Ayatollah's inspection. Din smiled as he took note of the many examples of damage to the trucks and their trailers that had been caused by the many minor wrecks and collisions with the residents of Karaj. The drivers had been selected for their driving skills from Major Sabiri's best commandos but they still had much to learn about the driving of tanker trucks and luckily there had only been eight fatalities among the population of the city, so far.

Glancing at the Supreme Leader, Din doubted if the man ever took notice of such trivial things as the deaths of his people. Sizing up the old man and his sycophant entourage, all dressed in their fantastic robes and clapping with their soft manicured hands, Din believed such details were far below the notice for such men.

The oft rehearsed and well-staged show outside the window was starting to wind down to its conclusion and Din was very much pleased by that. He still needed to complete his personal presentation of the overall attack plan to the dignitaries before he could assemble his men and leave.

The end-game for project *Asman-Rayan* was rapidly approaching. And stress was building on not just him but his men and he strongly objected to such wasted days as this. Tonight they would all be in Bushehr and aboard their vessels, and where Major Al-Doleh would finish up the training of his commandos, and the drivers could start to cruise the streets of that port city in the last weeks before they went operational.

Major Sabiri had done surprisingly well today and Din had not been forced to interject himself. The major's suave playboy good looks and carefree attitude had been hardening into a more calloused and stress-filled maturity over the last couple of months. Hard lines and wrinkles appeared on his face and his once robust physic was now more frail and thin, and for Din, it was much like watching a person slowly succumb to the ravages of a disease like cancer. Sabiri looked old and his penchant for having a standard rotation of debutants had dried up. The steady progression of the operation had obviously worn on the man and Din was certain that the fellow deeply regretted taking on the giant task of moving the project forward from theoretical possibility, planning, and finally the construction and training stages.

There was now just a short space of time before deployment was started. The intense work and commitment leading up to this point had weighed heavily on the man. The boost to Sabiri's career and family had been an opportunity that he and his father could not pass up in the beginning, but it had come at cost.

Failure in this attack would result in the destruction of their government and could potentially result in the deaths of all seventy-four million Iranians in a retaliatory strike from the Western powers. It was an all or nothing gambit and the oppressive stress of that venture was now tearing down the young playboy. Din almost pitied the arrogant fool for taking on the central role of organizing the preparation for the operation.

In comparison, Din's involvement was essential but straight forward and would most likely end in glorious martyrdom. So even if the mission were to fail, Lt Din's place in heaven was assured. The same could not be said for Sabiri who might find a truly bad end at the hands of the Supreme Leader if the mission were not to succeed.

It now seemed a very long time ago when Din had first heard of the project and at the time he was certain it would develop into nothing but wishful thinking inside the strategic mind of General Nakisa.

In 2004, America was lashing out after the damage done to them on 9/11 and Iran was isolated, sandwiched between the Great Satan's soldiers in Iraq and Afghanistan. The cowboy, Bush, had named them one of the Axis of Evil and it was obvious from what had happened in their neighboring countries that the Iranian military stood no chance in a head-on military confrontation with Washington DC.

Then came the day when the Russian's had secretly deployed several tactical nuclear weapons into Iran, on the eventuality that they might need to stop America's rampaging so close to their borders and so close to their own oil interests in the Middle East. Nakisa had just returned from Asia and brought this asymmetric plan to the leadership. It had lukewarm reception at the beginning, but as the war of attrition against the Americans in Iraq continued to wax and wane through their Shia proxies, the plan continued to be mulled and considered.

As 2007 ended and their Shiite and Sunni surrogates in Iraq were eventually defeated by the hated Petraeus Plan, that, along with the betrayal by the Sunnis in the Awakening, it had become obvious to everyone that the traditional way of confronting the West would forever result in Persia's eventual defeat. A different way had to be found and considered if the Islamic State of the Ayatollahs was to survive and outlast the secular West. That was when the leadership had finally embraced Nakisa's plan completely and after the scare brought on by the Green Revolution, the administration under Ahmadinejad had become fully dedicated to the aggressive attacks embodied in *Asman-Rayan*.

For his part, Din was filled with enthusiasm for the operation from day one. Putting aside all geopolitical considerations, he understood that for the Persian people to stay strong and for Shia Islam to take its rightful place at the head of the future Islamic Caliphate, this type of action against the infidels was required.

Not only did Allah, the Great and Merciful, mandate that the infidel be destroyed, Din believed they would receive great reward for their bravery in ultimately destroying the Great Satan. Din fervently believed that the monumental reward that would be bestowed upon him personally, and his fellow martyrs would be greater than any reward of heaven since the time of the Prophet and the Twelfth Imam. Furthermore, his beloved Iran would be rewarded by shaping the future of the Islamic Caliphate with a Persian-centered dynasty that would ultimately control the entire Muslim world and would jump start Islam's divine propagation around the globe.

After that glorious day finally arrived, the Persian's would then begin the cleansing of the kafir Sufi and the proud Sunni would be made to grovel, as they deserved, under the boots of the Followers of Ali. *Soon, very soon.*

The commotion of the dignitaries starting to break up aroused Din from his musing. He moved from the window as they moved to the waiting cushions and chairs. Din's presentation would be starting momentarily so he headed to the front of the room as Major Sabiri ushered the Grand Ayatollah away from the observation window. In a short period of time everyone but Din was all seated in their respective places around the Supreme Leader's place of honor in the center, and who looked relaxed and confident in the preparations made by Sabiri, Din, and Al-Doleh.

Away from the Grand Ayatollah and his sycophants, the Commander-in-Chief of the IRGC, Major General Quashqai, was flanked by Din's boss, Admiral Razmara and General Sabiri, while General Nakisa held his usual spot of somber brooding in a back corner of the room. Orderlies came in and as everyone in the room was given their refreshments, Din lifted the cloth covering from the table and revealed the plastic models of the transport ships that would soon transport the multiple nuclear warhead strikes to their launch points. There were several nautical charts strung up along the wall on each side of his PowerPoint screen.

As the assembled people directed their attention to the front of the room Din moved to the podium and greeted them. "Khosh Amadid! Velayat-e faqih, Rahmah Allah 'Alayh…."

August 8, 2011 21:45pm UTC+8:00
Miyun Reservoir
Beijing, China

FLOATING SHADOWS of passing clouds wavered their way across the water's surface in the moonlight, while darker shadows hugged the shoreline beneath tall willow and magnolia trees that bent slightly in the breeze. The soft gusts licked lightly at the liquid surface of the picturesque Shan shui-like scene, causing the silver sheen of the moon's glowing reflection to break up and bob in a glittering and undulating pattern. The strong sweet smell of roses drifted up to meet the Russian minister's nostrils as he puffed on his Cuban Cohiba cigar. He relaxed in the wooden deck chair, enjoying the idyllic setting and contemplated his situation. He flippantly blew bad smoke rings into air filled with billions of sparkling stars that hovered far above the dark looming shapes of hills on the far side of the pooled water.

The three-story cottage behind him, built to look like an ancient Buddhist pagoda, was one of the many dozens of secret structures that were built during the Great Leap Forward of the Mao years. But like so many of the private retreats that had been commissioned by Mao as 'safe houses', it had never actually been used by the Great Leader.

The Chinese hosts referred to the structure as a cottage but it certainly qualified as a mansion to Yuri. The above ground structure was nothing more than a veneer over the top of a fully functional military command bunker that had two levels of subterranean facilities that were typically used for detention and interrogations of domestic dissidents nowadays. Yuri did not consider the idyllic setting to be at all ironic to the torture and butchery that occurred regularly underground. Over the years he had used such places to perform interrogations and found the opportunity to leave a brutal questioning and quickly get some fresh air in a beautiful place made the work that much easier.

The creator of the People's Republic of China kept the safe house near the capitol city so that in case of an emergency like a coop or an assassination attempt, he could quickly flee here until things were properly controlled and suppressed.

Betrayal, as it was for all dictators, had always been Mao's greatest fear and with good reason. Since his regime was directly responsible for the deaths of over seventy million of his countrymen, the list of his enemies was very long indeed. Whether by government policies that institutionalized wide spread starvation, or the direct murder of millions by guns, bombs, and torture. Those acts done during his tenure as leader of the oldest continuous civilization in history had produced a great number of people throughout the government, military, and society who would gladly have killed him many times over and thus made safe houses, like this one, essential to his long term survival and tenure.

Even today, so many years after Mao's death, very few people knew about them all. Yuri was probably one of the few non-Chinese who knew every one of them and had walked through most of them. He considered Mao's political success and ability to survive his enemies as a unique and remarkable achievement for such a slovenly and uncouth man. Being born to the backwoods of his nation with a weak physical nature, spoiled tastes, and limited capabilities gave Mao little chance for such greatness. Nonetheless, Mao had proven by his cunning intellect and unbridled narcissism one thing in his long life; he was the ultimate survivor and broker in games of power within China.

Yuri remembered clearly the first time he ever laid eyes on this cottage by the lake. He was a young nineteen-year old Spetsnaz lieutenant on his first trip to China. His duty, as a bodyguard for a Soviet delegate, had brought him within a few feet of the Chinese Chairman and he still remembered distinctly, and with revulsion, witnessing the blackened teeth and smelling the vile rotted breath of the elderly dictator.

Yuri had been warned about the man's deplorable hygiene but he was still taken aback upon experiencing it in person. Soon afterward, the dictator had his first stroke and was transformed into an even more toad-like creature, losing much of the aura of fear that surrounded him. Yuri always felt Mao was a case study in just how a devious and conniving murderer who was absolutely ruthless, and who also had more than his fair share of luck, could rise to become one of the most powerful men to ever walk the planet.

Yuri had joked in later years, about the bloated Gollum-esque creature Mao later became as 'the filthy-peasant-who-would-be-chairman'.

In his forty years of working for the Russian Foreign Intelligence Service, Yuri Puliptanski had met virtually every major political leader of the world during his tenure. For the last seven years he had been Deputy Director of Directorate S, Russia's ultra-secret and powerful foreign espionage wing. As such, he was one of the five most powerful and deadly men in the world of terrorism and sabotage, yet he was unknown to 99.99% of all people.

119

Yuri held an iron grip on Directorate S, and kept a secure lock on his lofty position as number two in line to Vladimir Putin's ear. The many years he had faithfully served Putin as a young KGB officer in East Germany, working hand-in-hand with the cold-blooded Stasi, the East German secret police, got Yuri appointed to his position of power and trust in the cold world of Russian spy-craft.

He took another sip of vodka from his signature silver flask as the gentle breeze fluttered cool air across the substantial coat of hair on his arms, chest and stomach that caused goose bumps to dimple his skin. The pagoda tiered-cottage here was Yuri's inspiration for the construction of his own Moscow dacha that was widely regarded as eccentric among his peers. His Chinese friends had made the amenities here very Russian-esque as an overture of good will to him and the work they had accomplished together over the years with Mother Russia. That was the main reason why he used it exclusively on his visits to confer and strategize with his counterpart in the Chinese army's Military Intelligence Directorate.

Their meetings were usually pre-scripted and perfunctory so that there was seldom need for consultation with Moscow to complete most arrangements. This meeting, however, was very different and far more sensitive than usual, but to bring more people would have attracted too much attention from the CIA or MI6. In fact, the whole affair had been rushed due to the quickly developing nature of the Iranian plan. Their eagerness to move at this seemingly opportune time was propelling today's meeting with his counterpart, General Wang Li. And if Li failed to come back with what Yuri expected, he would be forced to leave very rapidly to confer with Putin

But still, Yuri could not help but smirk at the ruffling of feathers that came with his visit and the Iranian's persistence at wanting answers from both the Russians and Chinese so quickly. That had made it easier for Yuri to rattle Li's cage, which was a very rare and enjoyable event. Yuri learned long ago that the wheels of bureaucracy in China moved very slowly and they usually screamed loudly when forced to move faster than their want. Yuri was sure that the pressure he had put on General Li and the Chinese bureaucracy with this trip had gotten them to howling.

The Iranian's long-term commitment to follow their strategist, Nakisa's ideas of direct military and nuclear engagement with the United States, was unexpected and surprising to Yuri over the years. At the beginning, Yuri and other analysts at the SVR had forecast that they would shy away from the plan but for reasons that he did not fully understand, they had stayed persistently focused on the strategy. Yuri was the one who had arranged for Russia to deploy the three nuclear warheads into Iran as a tactical asset for Russia to bulwark her national and strategic interests in Iran and the greater Middle East. Russia would only allow so much activity from the maverick cowboy, Bush, to threaten their future interests in Asia Minor, and then as now, it was always Yuri's job to see to it that the nasty things were done and readied for a worst case scenario with the West. A job he did with great pride and enthusiasm.

But still, neither Yuri nor Moscow had ever expected that Nakisa or the Ayatollah's would get so ambitious with the opportunity the nukes represented, or would stay so committed once they developed their strategy. But that was irrelevant now, since it had turned into the greatest opportunity to ever be presented to Mother Russia in a hundred years!

The Iranian's insistence on confrontation had the Chinese more than a little unnerved and that typically made then very hesitant to endorse such a high-risk scenario. The Chinese were deeply ingrained in their conservative Buddhist and Confucian nature, which often led them to be uncooperative with high-risk ventures like this. Yuri fully appreciated their natural tendencies in matters such as this, especially since it had served them so extremely well over the long centuries of their existence. He could not deny their wisdom, especially since throughout China's long history; except for the Japanese taking advantage of the country's disunity after the British-instigated Opium Wars, China had never been invaded successfully since the time of the Mongols. They were expert strategists and Yuri knew their perspective was to be respected in matters as momentous as this.

But when it was in their interests, they could be extremely aggressive, even if it was couched in great subtlety. The Chinese were prudent to weigh their abilities very hard against the costs of involvement in these scenarios, a classic cost-benefit analysis that they had been practicing successfully for over ten centuries.

But, throughout the Soviet period, Yuri had watched them chafe at their second-fiddle relationship with Russia. And since the end of the Cold War, with Russia's precipitous decline, they were now far less reticent and much more willing to display an aggressive posture as Russia's dominance in their relationship had suffered so greatly after the Soviet empire's collapsed. With Nakisa working through Yuri for Russia's patronage in this plan to attack the Americans it would again make the Russian Bear the dominant partner in the post-America world to follow. Yuri was positive that might help prompt General Li's masters into becoming active collaborators in the plot.

With the calamitous breakup of the Soviet Bloc Yuri was forced to work very hard to keep China fully engaged in the few joint opportunities that had blossomed occasionally over the past decade. He and Putin saw clearly that their little oriental friends to their south certainly felt their time of preeminence was fast approaching and that they were finally to become the great Dragon-of-Asia. It was a very wise thing that Putin had orchestrated with the alliance of the Shanghai Five, which had now progressed into the stabilizing SCO. *Keep your friends close, and your enemies closer. Gotta love that SunTzu.*

If this Iranian attack is successful, China could then easily dominate the smaller and weaker nations around them, unfettered by the western powers in their Asian sphere. But with the SCO, Russia had a strong position against the Chinese in Eurasia that would secure her southern border. And thus, Russia would be free to dominate Europe and China could move into the Pacific. Yuri took in smoke from his cigar and savored the flavor as he imagined the cost China would exact upon Taiwan once the Americans and Brits were neutralized. *Time to pay the bitch her due!*

Yuri admired how successfully China had abandoned their blatant communism and had built a strong model of economic power by placing the strengths of capitalism under the command of their authoritarian state. And while this was accomplished, they still had maintained an effective level of belligerence, independence, and expanding military might that blunted every effort by the Americans and Europeans to halt their extension of influence into the Asian theater.

All the while, Yuri's Russia had watched, with growing envy as the Chinese methodically kicked out the British from Hong Kong and brilliantly transformed themselves into the American's ATM machine. He especially enjoyed how they were now forcing the American taxpayer to pay for the very military expansion and modernization that would play a crucial part in destroying the foolish Americans. Yuri was pleased that he had arranged for the Chinese to only purchase Soviet-era military hardware these last five years. They could be a terrible problem if they had the newer stuff.

Unfortunately, Yuri's beloved Mother Russia had failed to accomplish the same level of success with their sphere of influence across Europe. Histories and hatreds across that continent ran long and deep, forcing the Russian Bear to repeatedly and regularly flex her influence in order to keep the old Eastern Bloc countries and traitorous Baltic States in proper line. They all understood the fine line they walked with Russia controlling their main natural gas supplies, and things were slowly getting back into suitable order since their would-be savior, the incompetent Americans, had failed to take advantage of Russia's weakness and disarray after the USSR broke apart. *So like the Americans to piss away such a golden opportunity. What global amateurs.*

Russia's puissant leader, Putin, had also habitually served notice to the weakling Europeans that the same pipelines that supplied them with power and heat were the same strong nooses around their necks that were also around the necks of the old Eastern Bloc nations. Yuri always had to caution Putin to remember that those same European cowards that whined so loudly when the spigot of oil and gas was shut off still had vague but real memories of their strength during the two World Wars that had raged across their soils. But as the older generations died off the young were ripe for another go 'round. *Soon they will know what their grandparent knew.*

Yuri knew that Europe would not fold as readily as the politically disjointed governments and pathetically small militaries that populated the Asian sphere. China only needed to complete her naval expansion to fully enforce her will and completely dominate that region, and that was progressing apace. Regrettably, it would take more than natural resources and a navy for Russia to dominate Europe and now the Iranians were about to hand the Big Red Bear the entire European continent on a silver platter.

Yuri well-remembered when the smug Europeans had watched as the old Soviet regime had collapsed, it had been a devastating blow for his nation's prestige and confidence to take assistance and charity from them.

Then Yuri had to watch as piece-by-piece the Soviet Bloc had been dismantled and there was nothing he could do but stare on with humiliation coursing through his soul. But time went by and he had watched closely as the meandering minds of the Americans and their NATO allies lost their military and political focus that the now defunct Soviet Bloc had given them. That was when the forward thinking and strategic leaders such as he and Putin had moved to the fore and took the 'loss' of the Cold War and began to actually turn it into a tremendous strategic victory for both Russia and her southern neighbor, China. That brilliant strategy would soon culminate in their combined total victory!

Very soon, through their suicidal proxies in Iran, a Sino-Russian partnership would facilitate the complete military, economic, social, and geopolitical destruction of their American and European antagonists and it would be directly due to the hard work that loyal patriots like Yuri had done in the service of his people. *Life is good.*

Yuri savored another drink of his vodka and smiled happily at the thought of his country's approaching triumph. All he needed now, to make the first domino fall and begin the progression toward the obliteration of Russia's enemies, was for his Chinese compatriots to come out and obediently endorse his plan.

He turned his cigar slowly in his pouched lips while considering the enjoyment entailed in cleansing so many rivals and enemies in a single day.

"The work for the proletariat never ends," he muttered before gulping down more vodka.

He glanced up from his musing to see General Li approaching across an ornate stone bridge with numerous carved dragon heads and squat, plump armored Chinese warriors carved into the grey marble.

Yuri stood and stretched his arms, then jabbing the cigar into his mouth he made his way into the cottage where the meeting would take place. He sauntered confidently through a glass doors and seated himself in a cushioned chair as his counterpart entered the room with a smile of greeting; his young female aid followed close behind in a perfectly pressed army uniform. Yuri absentmindedly wondered if he could actually shave on the creases on her sleeves as they had the vague appearance of armor rather than fabric.

General Li was fluent in Russian and liked to exercise his skills at every opportunity. In his high-pitched sing-song voice he greeted the Russian as they vigorously shook hands.

"Greetings, my good friend, I hope your evening seclusion on our shores has rested your bones from your extensive travels of late? These Persians certainly do seem to have ways of keeping you busy with their ideas. Your labors never seem to come to conclusion."

"As always, Wang, the atmosphere of this place invites me to return at every opportunity, even with my busy schedule. My labors are always in the service of my country – they will never end."

Nodding agreement, Wang released Yuri's hand and sat down in a matching chair facing Yuri as he crossed his legs and accepted a glass of freshly poured bourbon, neat, from his female aid. They sat quietly together as he sipped the drink and enjoyed the heady aromas' coming from the liquor. He held the drink up to the light and slowly swirled the cocktail to examine the amber color better. Yuri watched in silence and waited patiently for the news of the Chinese leadership's decision.

"As you know, I have always enjoyed a good blended whiskey and I have come to learn over the years that Kentucky makes the very best there is. Do you suppose that will still be the case if this endeavor of the Persian's comes to fruition, Yuri?"

"My understanding of the distillation of vodka is better than that of whiskey, my friend, but I believe the process of making the very best whisky is most properly done without the modern machinations of a wired world anyway. So it would stand to reason that your indulgence would be as fine or maybe made even better in a future world without a modern Kentucky."

General Li frowned at Yuri's comments. "Unfortunately, I don't see that there is much of a future for this sweet industry if some friends of ours have their way. This is a very aggressive plan that you have delivered to us."

"Then might I recommend stocking up on the item quickly so that delivery is not impinged. The plan is rather time sensitive."

General Li considered the brusque comments as he studied the color within the last remnants of liquor in his glass. With slow turns of his wrist he watched the warm light play until he finally closed his eyes and took the last pull from the glass into his mouth. Slowly he savored it in his cheeks and rolled it across his tongue, letting the burning liquor seep into every pour before he slowly swallowed the liquid. He then inhaled deeply the last of the aroma paying attention to the nuances as it eventually faded away from his pallet. Opening his eyes after the self-indulgent experience he leveled a set of very cold and serious eyes on Yuri.

"It is better to have loved and lost than to never have loved at all, eh? That is the question of the great poet, is it not? Is a thing of value ever truly appreciated without the knowledge of its loss, my vodka drinking friend? I have a long and good memory, and yearning for what once was can be a reward for the soul as well. I don't believe I have need of adding to my stock, Yuri. What was once shall be again, or it will be lost forever. But I will have my memories until I die."

General Li continued to stare coldly at Yuri.

"The sweeping nature of this attack on the Americans is so broad in scope of consequence that it was very difficult for consensus to be reached. The ramifications will be felt for generations and it is virtually impossible to gauge what response will come from the Americans. There are innumerable variables that come into play when such a strong beast is cornered."

Yuri's mouth went very dry and before he spoke he took another small sip of vodka so his voice did not crack.

"A cornered beast, gravely wounded, will sell its fate dearly with brave struggle and bitter retaliation if pressed too hard at that moment of defeat. But if handled correctly, like an old rutting buck that is vanquished – by the younger, stronger, more virile buck – it goes limping off into the forest to whine and mope over its lost status in the herd, but it never comes back for another taste of the fight. The latter is what Moscow and I believe will be the case with the devastated Yankees. The Europeans? They grovel now; after this attack they will cower, begging for our benevolent guidance and leadership."

Yuri paused, outstretching his arm with a tightly clenched fist.

"If we simply stand firm together and allow them enough space to come to grips with their new future, they will crumble! Unlike the jihadists, they are not suicidal."

General Li's emotionless face gave absolutely no indication of his thoughts as he sat staring, stone-like, while he very slowly tapped the bottom of his empty glass against his knee.

"Such is the wisdom that we too have come to believe. A truly monumental place in history is before us both."

Yuri held his breath in anticipation.

"The cost of failure can be minimized by the use, as proxies of our intent, these supposedly 'suicidal Muslims' as you refer to them. The benefits of their success are also very high. We will endorse this plan as you have offered it. We will sign the addendum to the 2001 Sino-Russian Treaty, Article 9, on the date of the strike – if it is successful."

A broad smile spread across Yuri's face as Li's message sank in. *Success!* Yuri had gotten all that he had come for and he was well pleased with himself.

"Plausible deniability is assured by way of our sequential message on the 20th. Does your leadership agree with the wording?" Yuri asked.

General Li waved at his female aid and she instantly brought a leather binder to him.

"We have added to your original wording only slightly, not liking the tone very much. The severity of the victim's response can still be quite terrible and we thought a less belligerent feel in the message will be received with more amiability by the Americans and their NATO allies as they take in the extent of the damage to their abilities. We also feel that until we have assessed the effectiveness of the strikes it would be ill-advised to be too strident with our mutual demands," General Li said while his aid handed Yuri the sheet of paper.

Yuri examined the paper and even though he did not like the changes he nodded approval and said, "I foresee no issues with this."

"I am glad you can live with our decision – it is not negotiable," Li stated firmly. "We are in agreement that the disjointed Europeans will acquiesce quickly to the new order of things, but we still have reservations about the Jewish question. They are the wildcard that cannot be underestimated. Their reaction to the attacks must be properly assessed before our commitment to hard military action in the Middle East."

Yuri nodded agreement as he spoke, "They will be between the proverbial hammer and anvil, and they have very sharp teeth. We are in agreement that they are unpredictable in this situation but we know their response will be swift. They will acquiesce like the Europeans or their response will be directed away from any of our interests and toward the Persians. Either way, we are certain there will be no direct confrontation for us since their capabilities are strictly limited to a regional conflict," Yuri stated confidently, as he drank another large gulp from his flask.

"Besides, my dear Wang, they were exiled for two-thousand years in antiquity and survived it, they can do so again. They are a practical people who will not be interested in standing alone against the new order. I assure you, they will accept exile and Diaspora over annihilation." Yuri boasted.

"As long as the Jews and Iranian's both understand that whatever the reaction is – the oil fields are not in play."

"That is well understood by the Iranians. I will deliver the Jews that message personally the day of the strike to ensure that they know their position well."

"The Iranian's must also understand that our part in the umbrella of protection from the American retaliation is completely dependent on their success in making a broad and devastating impact on the infrastructure. The brazenness of Nakisa's plan has many nerves dancing here in the Standing Committee and the Secretary General is perfectly willing to let the Iranians be irradiated if their exercise fails in achieving total success. I must make it clear to you Yuri, and to them: we will not stand in the way of their destruction if they fail in this attempt or even have marginal success. It is all or nothing for them."

"We are, again, in complete agreement and barring some unfortunate reaction by someone in the extended American military apparatus we feel that most of the dangers rest with their centralized government's reactions. The Brits may also feel the need to flex some power to assert their place, but like Israel they are isolated, and they are fully aware that their Empire is gone and they are far more the paper tiger than the fierce bulldog they once were. They will obey us – even if they don't like it very much."

"Yes, we agree."

Relaxing, General Li stretched out and crossed his legs and motioned for his aid to get him another whiskey. She quickly went to the Cherry wood dry bar, while Li looked hard at Yuri.

"The strategic consideration we made to support your leadership's secret movement of your three warheads to Iran after the Americans invaded Iraq was done with the understanding that it would be a tactical bulwark against any expansion of their little war getting too near to our interests. We have also been impressed with Ahmadinejad's ability to keep that so well hidden from the IAEA inspectors."

Yuri gave a little snort.

"Come now, Wang, Al Baradei and Annan were good little monkeys. They didn't see anything we told them not to. Ahmadinejad simply follows orders nicely like the monkey he is, just as well or maybe better than those in the IAEA."

Li chafed at the Russian's repeated improper use of his name. The fat man had done this repeatedly over the years since the first day they had met and it grated on Li every time. Notwithstanding his irritation, Li's ability to hide his annoyance until the time for payback was legend.

"Yes, as true as that may be, we are still pleased and it gives us confidence that this current endeavor will be successful. The yield for the three strikes is in the mega-ton range, yes?"

"Of course, all of them are our standard 1,200kg warhead."

"Well, if they are successful at deployment, the effects should meet our desires."

"I assure you, Wang, our technicians are ensuring their launch platforms are fully capable. The operational success is dependent upon the Iranians but the technical ends are covered by us.

"I see. Acceptable," General Li said as he received from his aid the second drink and then motioned her aside. "I am curious, what of this agent-of-mayhem jihadist that they have found? They have vetted him well, I hope?"

"Seldom does such an opportunity come. I have personally vetted his credentials and made his profile. He has been the biggest surprise hasn't he? It appears that mania can motivate even the unschooled to succeed on occasion. His stability is questionable as the deadline approaches but regardless if he is discovered or not, the main thrust of our efforts will not be adversely affected since he is not aware of his connection to them in any way."

"I beg to differ with you, Yuri. The connection is the Iranians. If he is discovered too soon the Americans may place too much unwanted attention upon our surrogates."

"I understand your concerns completely," Yuri reassured. "Listen, the Kashmiri is nothing but a coup d'état on the psychological impact of the attacks. This new American administration is fully aware of the Persian's involvement in obstructing their efforts in Iraq and Afghanistan and still they timidly do nothing. If the jihadist is found out I suspect that this rube in the White House will take hold of that discovery as nothing more than a success story to lord over his domestic opponents in his re-election efforts, just as he has done with the success of the bin-Laden strike."

"The Standing Committee is split on that assessment, but the Secretary General concurs with you. But, nevertheless, I strongly suggest though that you keep a close eye on this loose end. We, by our nature, do not enjoy having unknown variables running amok in our plans."

"I give you my personal assurance that he will be illuminated at the very first sign of any liability."

General Li nodded his approval and raised his glass in toast to Yuri.

"A new day dawns soon. Powers will soon shift dramatically. Being neighbors, we shall need a permanence of cooperation between us. We look forward to this long war with the western powers soon coming to a successful conclusion."

Yuri stood and raised his flask.

"Here is to the future of the Russian and Chinese people and may they rule the world for hundreds of generations!"

Both men drank their toast and sat back down.

"Yuri, this operation will be successful. I do not foresee any events that will stop our achievement this time. You know, this will embolden the Persians and you already have a separatist problem. We will insist on being involved in all negotiations between the two of you regarding the opening of new resources and territories."

"Of course, they have already conceded to our demands to cease all nuisance jihadist operations against our domestic interests in the Caucuses immediately," Yuri said.

"As for me, immediately after the strike by the Iranians is successful, I am to oversee Chechnya being purged to the last man, woman, and child as an example to the other Tartars along our southern borders. I made it clear to Ahmadinejad that with the

Americans out of the way there will be no interference by him or his Grand Ayatollah tolerated throughout the Balkans and Crimea, or we will purge much more thoroughly than the Caucuses. He understood completely," Yuri asserted.

"As the future moves along, Yuri, we are not interested in constantly reminding these Muslims of the consequences of directing their religious efforts the wrong way." Li commented coolly.

Yuri nodded as he pulled his flask from his lips too fast and sent a rivulet of liquor running down his cheek that he was forced to wipe away before he spoke.

"I have personally made it clear that extinction is the only alternative to cooperation and obedience. That religion of theirs may assure them of paradise when they are dead, so be it, and dead they will be if they ever make the mistake of reaching too far with us. As with all things, a religion's true believers never become leaders of nations and the theocracy there well understands our intent and the costs of their disobedience," Yuri said while wagging his finger.

"We foresee no problems from them regarding that issue of jihad. With the incompetent constraints of America and NATO removed from us, they know full well there will no longer be any mechanisms that will mitigate our response or stop us from enforcing our will. This childish playtime with their jihad will end, immediately. With us allowing the creation of this promised Caliphate and the oil dollars that will roll in with it, should eliminate their need to control their masses by way of that ginned-up hyperbole. It will die on the vine or they will pay an extremely heavy price for that kind of miscalculation."

Li carefully gauged Yuri's seriousness and once satisfied with what he had been told he replied, "Then I think we will have an interesting winter ahead of us, my friend."

"Yes, I believe it will be very interesting indeed," Yuri said with genuine pride.

He had worked his entire career and never believed that an opportunity like this would ever materialize. Now that the final hurdle was crossed and the operation would soon to be in the hands of skilled commandoes, he could relax a tiny bit and be like his friend General Li; a curious spectator to one of the most monumental days in man's history on the Earth.

He knew that when this operation succeeded he would quickly become very busy again, starting the next process of consolidating their gains and watching their new 'friends' here in China. General Li and his leadership agreed to their role in this project and that said much about their confidence in their own capabilities, both strategically and tactically. It appeared that the great Asian Dragon was indeed ready to rise and take control of its realm. That placed their motives and intentions for the future in a wholly different scale of aggression for Yuri's future consideration.

Yuri was somewhat taken aback at how that made him feel. It made him feel far more anxious than he would have guessed it would; it actually made him feel very anxious indeed.

*****

September 11, 2011 05:34am PST UTC -8:00
Tracy, California

MANY TIMES over the last three years Hamal had felt like he knew exactly what the Greek god, Atlas, had gone through while holding up the weight of the world on his shoulders. Some days he felt as though he could not take another moment of his life without going completely insane. It was only his dreams of vengeance to come that kept him focused enough to survive each dreadful day. He often prayed that the moment would finally arrive when he could take the terrible weight from his shoulders and crush his enemies with it. At every prayer time throughout the day he would ask Allah for help in bearing the burden of his pain and loss. Now, finally, the great and merciful Allah had answered his prayers!

Hamal stared at his reflection in his small apartment's bathroom mirror and felt a powerful wave of relief and gratitude move through his body that made him shiver. It welled up inside his chest, making his heart pound with anticipation as tears for his emancipation started to dampen his eyes. Then, from deep down inside his bowels the anger welled back up and caused him to gnash his gapped and rotting teeth together until it made his temples ache.

He had sworn a blood oath of vengeance while holding the severed head of his beloved mother, Amira, in his lap. It had been left, displayed prominently in the foyer of his family's house, by the Shiite's death squad, so that it would be the first thing he saw as he entered. It was but the first 'present' left for him to find that day. There were more presents for him to find, many more. But as he screamed and ranted his agony, and while he cradled the ghastly appendage he made a vow: to never cry again until he was reunited with her in heaven. And through the rest of that horrible day, as he found each new grisly present after another, he never shed another tear. Now as tears of gratitude attempted to spring from his eyes he ground them into the dust of his hatred, willing them away as if he was made of stone.

131

His tall gaunt face was framed by jet black hair and a full beard. He had a strong Afghani appearance with his aquiline nose and sharp angular features. The characteristics of his appearance were so pronounced that it had caused him to be mistaken more than once for Tajik or Pashtu instead of the Iraqi Sunni he was. While he was in the insurgency working for al-Zarqawi he was called by his fellow mujahedeen 'The Pashtu' because of his looks. Even though it was intended as an insult he never cared what they said or thought, but it had the benefit of allowing him to never use his real name.

He had always been impressed with Zarqawi's tactical mind for the kind of deadly attacks that were so very hard for the enemy to defend against. He was also impressed with the terrorist leader's ability to organize, by brutality, the Sunni factions vying to control the movement that fought against the coalition forces that had invaded his homeland.

The leader of Al Qaida in Iraq had a vicious single-mindedness of purpose, and that focus gave Hamal the clarity of vision to know that if they pushed just hard enough against the weak-spirited infidels they could actually win the battle. Zarqawi had never wavered in his certainty of their eventual victory and that had always bolstered Hamal's own certainty. Even on the last day Hamal spoke with him, the actual day the infidels had killed him, Zarqawi had helped him focus on using the loss of his family as his pillar of support to complete this mission.

It had been very hard and dangerous work fighting the Americans throughout the Al Anbar province for those three long years that Hamal was in the insurgency, and he had barely survived it, while none of the fighters he had known during that time had. And he would never have survived it either, if his leader had not seen in him the capability to work independently from the group, and still be successful in his missions. This was the quality that got him selected for his current mission. When Hamal first entered the ranks of the insurgency he had eagerly agreed to martyr himself but that glory had passed by him through the years until Zarqawi had chosen him for this task.

Hamal stared longingly at the smiling faces in the family portrait that sat on the counter before him and he fondly remembered them and the many joys of his childhood in Ar Ramadi, Iraq. His favorite memories were of their weekly picnics when they left the stuffy confines of their home and braved the heat of afternoon.

His father drove them south of the city where they stopped across the Euphrates River from the island of Jazirat al Huwayjah. There Hamal ran with his sisters, Sahirah and Zudorah along the banks of the flowing waters and played on shaded sand below the date palm trees, wading in the cool waters and splashing his sisters mercilessly. His father and mother walked slower until they reached their favorite place along the banks. His father would then, with an air of pomp and reverence for his mother, spread the blanket on the sand, where they then talked quietly together while watching their children play.

After hours of games and fun Hamal and his sisters would run back to their parents and eat a home-cooked meal of his mother's Moroccan stew, sun-dried tomatoes, and sweet kirieche treats that had been laid out for them. After they ate and performed their prayers, Hamal and his sisters would run and play until sundown when they drove back home. Hamal held those memories as tightly as he could but they always faded away, to be replaced by his last memories of his family and their dismembered and charred bodies lying in the baking sun, strewn throughout his family home.

When the Americans invaded, they had, in their ignorance, destroyed the balance of power that had existed under Saddam. That balance, maintained by the necessarily brutal acts of Hussein and his sons, was the only guarantee that had safely secured Sunni dominance over the rejectionist Shias and Kurds for almost fifty years.

The loss of that balance had allowed the heathen Shia militias to run amok killing, raping, and terrorizing the Sunnis tribes. Hamal's father had worked for the Báath government in Ar Ramadi, where he doled out construction contracts for the regime to the many tribal sheiks. The arrival of the U.S. Army disrupted that flow of funds to the tribes, and when the Coalition Provisional Authority, under Paul Bremer, mandated CPA control over who his father would give contracts to, the Sheik Amal Muhammad of the Shia Janabi tribe considered this reticence in handing out contracts as an insult. He wanted to send a message that withholding the usual contracts from his tribe would not be tolerated.

His militiamen, dressed in their Iraqi police uniforms, had stormed his family compound and butchered Hamal's entire family in December of 2004 as a way of sending that message to other bureaucrats working for the coalition. Hamal's heart died along with his family that day, and he lived now only on hatred and his need for revenge on the kafir dogs that had invaded Iraq and tore his entire world apart.

The Americans had no idea what damage they had done to the thousands of Sunnis when they took the Hussein government down, releasing the despicable Shia and Kurds from their rightful Sunni masters. Soon the infidels would learn that there would be a severe payment for that act of arrogance in blood.

133

The things Hamal did for the insurgency was brutal but not at all unpleasant for him. He did everything possible to make his homeland the literal Triangle of Death for the infidel soldiers. Sometimes the work was very rewarding, especially when he was able to get a hold of several relatives of Sheik Muhammad. Hamal had spent nearly a week taking revenge out on their bodies and sent the Janabi tribe the pieces. The security forces of the so-called police were nothing more than Shia militia sanctioned by the government to terrorize the Sunnis. It was mainly those supposed security forces who had lost so many of their numbers to Hamal's hands.

The righteous cause against the kafir invader was extremely demanding, but the insurgency had pushed through the difficulties. They lost many Fedayeen in the battle of jihad, most of them Iraqi patriots, but many foreign fighters had flooded to the fight and helped bolster their cause with manpower, enthusiasm, and training. They had so many successes that by 2006, Hamal believed they would finally break the will of the Americans to stay and fight. That year the Army and the Marines had removed themselves from the city and a cleansing of the Shia was well underway.

Zarqawi kept Hamal's presence on missions low so that even other mujahedeen knew nothing of the confidence Zarqawi put in him and assessed him as nothing more than another foot soldier. His knowledge and skills improved steadily as he operated throughout Ramadi, Baghdad, and Khalidiyah. He had kept operations and attacks on schedule and extorted funds from the various tribal sheiks who tried to stay independent of the Awakening.

Those jihadists captured by the Americans or Provisional Iraqi troops were never able to identify him within the insurgency and therefore they never captured him with the intelligence machine that had spelled disaster for so many other Fedayeen.

Those other jihadists were so caught up in their own personal glory and martyrdom, they desperately needed to put their names to each attack so their families would gain respect back home, and most importantly their families would get a generous money payment by the Arab Bank for their sacrifice in the jihad. Hamal had no family, no one to love or that would need cared for after he died, and he had no want for money himself. All he wanted was vengeance.

He made it alive through the many close calls without sustaining any battle injuries to scar his body or impair his skills. Zarqawi took notice of his acts of dedication and moved him into his close circle of auxiliary aids, making Hamal more of a messenger and enforcer for Al Qaida than an actual active fighter against the coalition.

134

They had seemed to be on the verge of an ultimate triumph, just like the North Vietnamese had been when they smashed the will of the American public. The insurgency was just months away from forcing the weak political leaders of America, to order their infidel armies to crawl away on their bellies in defeat and disgrace, just like they had done when fleeing Saigon in 1975. But then the jihadist fighters were betrayed in the end by the treacherous Sunni Sheiks of the Awakening and the cause was lost, stripping Hamal of his vengeance.

The tribal sheiks had refused to kowtow to Zarqawi and Al Qaida. Like corrupt mafioso, the sheiks demanded their ancestral rights and powers in their communities and refused Zarqawi the unity and cooperation he mandated in order to ultimately defeat the Americans.

Soon Hamal had found himself being hunted by the very fighters that had been his allies against the coalition forces just weeks before. The traitorous sheiks now viewed Hamal as a traitor to Iraq and sent squad after squad to search him out and kill him. He had been so absorbed in the battle against the infidels that he had not taken notice of the crumbling support among the sheiks. They detested the foreign mujahedeen that had flooded into Iraq and the success against the Coalition had spurred the sheiks into fearing for their traditional place of dominance in the province. They feared being usurped by Zarqawi and Al Qaida. The sheiks' self-interest forced Hamal to make the choice to stand with Zarqawi and turn his back against the very people he had known all his life.

Whether it was a premonition of his own inevitable death or just his exquisite timing, Zarqawi summoned Hamal to meet him at a safe house in the southern suburbs of Ramadi. Hamal knew that something unusual was happening when he arrived, since Zarqawi rose in his formal bisht dress and dismissed his two bodyguards, which he never did. With an air of informality, akin to that between a father and son, he warmly greeted Hamal with hugs, handshakes and kisses. Together they sat and Zarqawi actually began to serve up a steaming hot cup of black tea for each of them as though he were one of Hamal's servants.

After handing over a small glass cup of very dark and aromatic tea, Zarqawi sat quietly, inhaling the steam from his own cup while holding it under his large nose, his checkered ghutra hiding any hint of the terrorist mastermind's emotions from Hamal. So much time passed that Hamal became nervous and was about to speak when his commander produced from the folds of his thobe, a photograph of Hamal's family and laid it gently on the floor between them. Hamal's trembling hands picked up the picture of his smiling family and he looked earnestly at his leader.

Zarqawi spoke quietly, "My friend, your family was lovely and Allah has taken them to reside with him in heaven. Will you join them by martyrdom?"

Hamal's heart raced as he realized that it was now his time to die for the jihad. Finally, he was going to be allowed to sacrifice his life and would soon give away his pain to seek paradise with his long-missed loved ones.

"Yes! What can I do in your service?" he asked eagerly.

"You have been a valuable asset to me. You can speak the language of the infidel. You hide away your pride. You are intelligent and clever. You are focused. Will you accept the will of Allah and use those talents to strike a death blow to God's enemies?"

"Yes! Please, yes!"

"Before the blasphemous dogs invaded these lands your father had arranged for you to drive trucks in most of the construction contracts he gave out, yes?"

"Yes. For many years. Dozers, tractors…."

"Trucks? Trucks with tanker trailers?"

"Uh, yes. Sometimes I would drive water trucks."

Zarqawi smiled.

"Do you have the strength to focus on a mission that may take a long time to accomplish? Can the memory of your loved ones sustain you through the trials of interrogation? Can you leave this battlefield behind and go to the very home of our enemy and create a battlefield in their very backyard?"

The scope of what his commander was asking made Hamal's head swim with possibilities as much as it swam with confusion. Whatever plan it was, it went far beyond anything they had ever attempted before. Hamal spoke his concerns.

"How can I possibly get there and what could I, one person, do to truly harm them even if I did make it there?"

Zarqawi raised a dismissive hand and continued his questioning.

"There are ways I have found. Now answer me. It will be a long wait to get your revenge. It will be the most difficult mission. Can you hold onto your hatred and make your strike at the best time? Can you hold onto your faith through the time required and then, at the perfect moment, plunge your dagger into the throat of our enemy inside his very home?"

Hamal considered what Zarqawi said while looking down at the photograph of his now long dead family. *Not just dead – butchered!*

He wished to die and join them in paradise. He wanted to be released from his world of death and misery. *An attack against America itself!*

What would that take to accomplish? What would he have to do? What misery would it be if he were captured? What could one man possibly do? He traced his finger across the surface of the photograph, following the outlines of his mother's face, but the smiling and lovely face that stared back from the paper was not what he saw. He envisioned blood-matted hair stuck to swollen cheeks, tendrils of clotted blood dangling from jagged cuts where the savage murderers had severed her head from her shoulders. His nostrils smelled again the metallic odor that rose from the clotted blood that had covered her skull as he stared transfixed at her vacant, dead eyes.

Hamal raised his face with wet eyes filled with seething hatred.

"Yes! Tell me what I can do! I swear that I will see that it is done!"

They sat and spoke for hours as the plan was laid out and Hamal absorbed the idea of what he was volunteering to do. From that day on paradise was postponed and the intervening years had become a special misery that he sometimes doubted he could survive. Zarqawi chose him for this mission, this most important mission. It was a task that took every bit of his cunning, intelligence, patience; a task done openly under the microscope of the West's entire intelligence and law enforcement dragnet. Zarqawi had made sure that he was prepared for all of those things by field testing during the insurgency. Hamal had been selected for this mission, and today, finally, he had received his orders to go operational. His waiting had ended.

Through the years he carried his great burden of loss and followed his orders, remaining quiet and tame. He did so without gaining unwanted attention to himself from law enforcement or intelligence agencies as he gingerly swam around their nets. To get out of Iraq he had received his new identity papers and a passport with the help of the Shu'bat Mukhabarat al-'Askariyya. From there he was able to immigrate to France under the illusionary story of being a fleeing Iraqi who sought asylum from the very insurgency he had fought with.

To obtain a visa to get into the United States he was forced to gain the trust of the foolish and yet ever-so-happy to please US State Department. They questioned him repeatedly over a period of several months, and as Zarqawi instructed him to do, he sacrificed several of the mujahedeen soldiers still fighting in Iraq to secure the trust of the arrogant American interrogators. That was a difficult but necessary step to get him positioned inside America itself.

He had stayed focused on his mission and all personal affronts or insults to his ego were brushed aside like water flowing off a duck's back. He tucked his anger away, keeping it hidden so that he could present the meekness required to convince the placating fools to open the crack wide enough so he could finally worm himself through. In the end, he proved himself to be the wiser and more patient protagonist in the mind-duel with his interrogators as they relented, allowing him to obtain a work visa.

He did not give the slightest hint of conspiracy or subversive behavior, settling quietly into the large Muslim community near San Francisco where he concentrated on working as a short-haul delivery truck driver. He performed his daily rituals of work, prayer, and sleep with no deviation from the norm. He made every effort to become invisible and did nothing to engage in odd or distracting activity of any kind.

He found that the many American whores who populated the area were an excellent cover for him and his activities. The personal ads in the *San Francisco Chronicle* provided an easy way to meet desperate women, all too eager to believe anything he said, especially since he came from an exotic land. Lisa Consuela, a silly woman he met, had become the perfect shield for him. She was naive and submissive in her 'search for the heart of an Arab man.' They never became intimate but she gave Hamal everything he needed: the appearance of stability.

The government dutifully kept him under surveillance, which he was well prepared for. He found himself escorted into the FBI field office in San Francisco three separate times for questioning by his case agent, Gibson. By using his expansive skills in taqiyya it became almost perfunctory for him to answer the questions and pass their little tricks and tests to see if he would make a mistake, he had not.

He maintained steady work by staying out of trouble and succeeded in disappearing into the folds of this so-called sanctuary city. He was irritated and insulted at how the coddling fools who lived here arrogantly thought that by being quisling dhimmi, it would somehow save them. The irony of it had a sweetness Hamal greatly enjoyed since the only asylum these collaborating infidels were going to receive would be in the inferno of hell he would send them to.

The bay area was large, wealthy, and deep into hedonism – a target-rich environment, a perfect place for Hamal's wrath. He went about his daily work and used his talents to ascertain the target location where he would detonate his weapon to achieve the maximum effect. Then he went about ascertaining and identifying the means by which he would burn the city in his holy fire.

The people felt so secure and safe here, thinking they were immune from his world. They dismissed any thoughts of personal danger from jihad. They never used the words towel-head or sand-nigger aloud but he saw it in their eyes. Constantly deluding themselves with their own talks of placation but truly unwilling to make the necessary walk of redemption.

They childishly viewed him with pity, lamenting loudly at how apologetic they were for the acts of their government under their hated monster, Bush. They spoke his name like it was an epithet that could be used to scare children. They railed about his decision to bring his war to Iraq as if they were separate from it, and him. They bitterly exalted their righteousness, as if they held victim status for just having him as their leader. All the while they lived every moment of their hedonistic lives in luxury provided by a world-dominating power that they complained so cynically about. They vehemently used their impotent and hypocritical mewing as a form of absolution that could pardon their souls from the sin of being born American.

Their pathetic cowardice disgusted him. *Apostates!* They swam in milk and honey, growing huge and bloated, leeching off their luxury. Worshipping hedonism for their God, and allowed the most immoral of acts to occur between men and women in their midst every day. They did not even rise to the level of bleating sheep. They were servants of Shaitan. They scurried around like filthy, disgusting insects, just pathetic bugs that infected Allah's creation that deserved obliteration.

The woman he had found, Lisa, had many of those child-like attitudes of her people. He chose her because she lived close to the area where he would obtain the explosive material he would use. She made an excellent tool for his surveillance, so his regular presence never seemed out of place or suspicious. She liked his attentions and attended the mosque obediently, as he demanded. She was the only distraction he had in this alien place where the values of his culture were dismissed so readily. He had briefly considered marrying her for the added cover it could provide but her weaknesses were many and a challenge for him, such as abiding her arrogance in speaking her thoughts too freely. A holdover from her American upbringing that had, on more than one occasion, almost caused him to kill her out of pure frustration with her infidel ways. His life had been too hard for him to long stomach her juvenile prattle that spewed from her childish mind.

His daily heartache remained unquenched as he patiently waited for the command to go operational. He was shocked when he opened the personal ads section in the *San Francisco Chronicle* this morning, as he did on the eleventh day of each month, where he saw the covert message in the paper instructing him to go operational immediately. The attack was set for the 20th, just a week away! Reading the secret message sent a jolt through him and he re-read it over two dozen times to make sure that his eyes were not playing tricks on his mind. With just eight days to prepare Hamal did not have time to waste.

He raised his black martyrdom bandana to his head, tying it into place with the flowing Arabic script centered on his forehead. He adjusted the military ballistic vest he wore, and picked up the SKS rifle propped against the wall as he walked into the small living room where hanging blankets covered the windows.

A video camera sat on a tripod in the center of the room. A large black martyrdom flag was pinned to the drywall. On the floor sat several knives, three loaded ammunition magazines for his rifle, and a snub-nosed revolver. All of these items were easy enough to obtain over time from the many gangs in the city. There was nothing Hamal could not buy from them. But the centerpiece of his display was a creation of his own. Sitting on the floor was a normal looking black and yellow toolbox that he bought at a discount lumber store.

Looking at the view finder screen he adjusted the view of the camera slightly so everything he wanted filmed easily fit within the screen. He pushed the record button and stepped before the flag and began, in his thick Baghdadi dialect, narrating his martyrdom video.

He had longed to do this and now that the day had finally come, his burden became lighter and lighter by the moment. While he described himself and his mission his rotted teeth showed in the first genuine smile he had made in a very long time. He leaned his rifle against the wall and knelt behind the toolbox. As he opened, displaying its contents for the camera his grin widened. The little improvised explosive device he displayed took a considerable amount of time to construct and was the mechanism he would use to deliver his soul to paradise with his family.

Hamal reached in and pulled out a small switch box with long strands of wire and described the workings of his bomb. It was a simple device, of a type that he had deployed dozens of times against American Humvees back in Iraq, but this time it would be used for a very different purpose. This time his small device would destroy an entire city.

Eight days! A sparkle in Hamal's eyes gleamed brightly as he realized his time had come. Only eight days!

*****

LIKE MARCHING columns of ants exiting their hill, the evening rush of commuters moved to and fro and was rapidly picking up its volume and would soon clog the roads. Ajay was amazed that such a marked increase could occur in just the single hour since his arrival.

The day of his long-awaited attack was getting very close and the preparations made his life busier by the day, as he worked at the multitude of tasks that required completion. Once upon a time, he thought this moment would never arrive as the long years went slowly by, but now it seemed like he did not have enough time in a day to get everything done that was necessary. He was doing the work of ten men and he was hard pressed to get everything accomplished.

He felt under the gun and was stressed out for a time table set for the 20th that was not flexible. He still had so many things to get staged at so many different places, and the driving back and forth across the country was taking its toll. He still had many miles to cover tonight before he could even think of resting. He walked across the flattened grass and grabbed the door handle of the Hyundai rental car, but before he jumped in he turned to survey his last accomplishment.

Along the far side of the property sat a long row of tall cottonwood trees that shaded the ground along the back fence line. Along that fence the bottom slope of the outlying hillside relaxed into a rolling six-acre parcel of scrub sage and tall grass. The vacant land was enclosed by a barbed wire fence that he hoped would keep most inquisitive people out of his business here.

Instead of using his own name Ajay had used his defunct trucking company's name to lease the land from a local realtor. The property was zoned for residential use and the line of tanker trucks with their gasoline filled trailers, parked against the back fence were in clear violation of the lease but Ajay could not care less about that. Those trucks would be here for little more than a week and he was certain that they would not gain the attention of anyone worrisome in that short time. When he wrote the check to the real-estate agent for a first twelve-month lease, and it had cleared, the agent was so ecstatic to get the business that Ajay knew she would do anything he wanted if by some unlucky chance any county official began asking questions.

The three Volvo 435 day-cab tractors with their crammed-full tankers sat uniformly alongside one another under the trees. Their white paint and chrome stacks shined in the evening sun, looking like they could be put in a military parade. Ajay had backed them as far out of sight as possible so that a casual observer might not even notice them. Each truck had a gleaming stainless-steel fuel tanker with over 9,600 gallons of fuel stuffed inside.

Parked between each of the rigs was a leased passenger van painted bright red. He liked the color combination that had been chosen for the strike teams. The uniformity of white trucks and red vans made identification easy for the IRGC Quds Force commandos.

He could imagine seeing the procession of vans and rigs rolling into the city in military-like formation. He longed to see the fires and smoke that would rise from the metropolis, and hear the brazen sounds of gunfire echoing through the streets. But he would never witness the flowering of his destructive creation here since his murderous efforts were going to be occurring at a city far from this place.

Pleased with the progress he has made in his preparations for the mayhem to come, he had parked the last tanker for the California attack at this staging point earlier today. All of the weapons and ammunition the commandos would use was now waiting, stored and ready at Miguel's warehouse in Monterrey, awaiting the arrival of the strike teams that were currently on their way via many separate international flights that would be converging at Monterrey in just two days.

Ajay quickly rechecked his pockets to make sure he had all of the keys to the trucks and vans with him. *Six sets!* Shortly after his arrival this afternoon he had climbed into each vehicle and started up their engines. They all fired up just fine and were ready to go, but he still left portable battery jumpers in the cab of each one just in case they were needed the morning of the attack. Absolutely nothing could be left to chance. He shoved the bundle of keys back into his pocket.

The American security apparatus was designed to prevent such attacks domestically by acting as a world-wide spider web. Their intricate intelligence webs trapping wannabe insurgents if they were foolish, unstable, or too talkative; just like the twitching of a trapped insect alerted the spider to prey. Once they were alerted, the security 'spiders' would then pounce upon the hapless fool who blundered in. Meanwhile, the American spies in the NSA and CIA used computers that searched through billions of bits of data per second in tandem with their field officers to create far-flung tendrils to bag would-be attackers. But, for all that effort and expense, they had failed to stop Ajay from reaching this point.

He swiveled his head looking for anything; any indication at all that showed he was under surveillance, but he saw nothing. He searched first here and then there but there were no tweedledee and tweedledum agents wearing cheap suits sitting in cheap sedans, wearing dark sunglasses and looking through binoculars at him. All he saw was windblown grass and hundreds of vehicles rushing by on Hwy-680. He smiled as he sat down in the small car.

Ajay carefully drove the car over the crushed grass until he got outside the fence and then closed the gate behind him before turning onto Sunol Road, heading for the interstate.

Reaching the interchange, he took the onramp and punched the accelerator to get as much power from the puny vehicle as he could. Entering the busy traffic heading west toward the setting sun, he squinted and lowered the sun visor as he began calculating how far he could get tonight before needing to stop and sleep. His own rig and weapons were already staged and ready for his attack on Denver, so all he needed now was to get back to Texas as fast as possible.

*****

September 16, 2011 20:20pm CST UTC -6:00
AJ Trucking
Sattler, TX

MAJOR AL-DOLEH stood pensively at the entrance to the kitchen, watching Ajay clean his hands and face of the blood splatter covering them. A steady flow of reddish tinted water and suds spiraled down the drain with a hollow echo as it disappeared down the pipes, leaving behind a faint pinkish residue along the sides of the sink.

The major had never been overly impressed with Ajay's intellectual capabilities, but he believed that he was the best option for providing the means by which the major's mission could move forward, and allow him to get his men inside the United States undetected.

Today, the Texan-jihadist had successfully accomplished that task, with the American intelligence networks none the wiser, which made for any possible liabilities that Ajay could now bring far less bothersome to the terrorist commander.

With his men, weapons, explosives, radios, and other equipment safely inside the country, ready to be deployed, the jihadist-psychopath became almost irrelevant. Al-Doleh just needed to decide whether to allow him to stay alive and complete his own personal dreams of mayhem, or whether the major and the broader mission would be better served if he was illuminated now.

For Al-Doleh, the most disturbing aspect about Ajay's psychological profile had always been that his emotional stability was so directly tied to his megalomaniacal aspirations. His very tenuous hold on sanity made it problematic as to whether the would-be jihadist might crack under the pressure before ensuring the success of the mission. Far more was required of him than being just another suicide bomber. This jihadist was responsible for many logistical necessities that were critical in making the ground operations a success. Al-Doleh hated to be so dependent on that, but having his personnel in-country doing those same tasks was simply impossible.

Al-Doleh continued watching as the man cleaned himself in the sink and the major could clearly see that the emotional stresses of the recent weeks had not broken the murderous psychopath at all. On the contrary, the major perceived that Ajay's maniacal state was emboldened by the approaching opportunities to exercise his blood lust. But the deep layers of pure insanity inside the Kashmiri were boiling very close to the surface. As the major took stock to determine the status of Ajay's grip on reality, he rested his scarred and muscular hands on his hips, mere inches from the Glock pistol jammed into the back of his pants.

Ajay lifted his face out of the sink as pinkish suds dripped from his chin. He reached toward the side of the cabinet, where his mother always dutifully kept a full roll of paper towels hanging. He jerked out a long streamer with much left hanging off the edge of the counter.

As he dried his face he observed the major through folds in the towels, regarding him carefully. Ajay knew that after his little rampage the commander was shrewdly judging him and that made Ajay feel very uncomfortable. He had done everything asked of him by the Iranians, and now, just three days from his glorious spree of murder, he may have just sentenced himself to death with his latest outburst.

Assessing the situation that he found himself confronted with, he admitted to himself that his predicament was not an enviable place to be, but he did not regret his actions that had made this current mess. He had so much more death and mayhem to deliver, and tonight was only the beginning of what he wanted to accomplish.

Thinking quickly for something to say that might allow the major to let him survive their little forthcoming chat, he took a deep breath, balled up the soaked paper towels and slowly turned to face the scene that had the major so concerned.

144

Pushkar's body sat on the far side of the small kitchen table in his usual chair, with a partially eaten meal of curry lamb and rice on his plate. The corpse was kept in the chair by the left armrest; his upper torso was bent over it with his left arm awkwardly propping him up, keeping the body from falling to the linoleum floor. His blank, dead eyes stared forward as his cheek and chin rested against his shoulder. An unidentifiable glob of chewed food and drool hung from the corner of his mouth, while his right hand lay across his lap, still clutching the fork he was using when Ajay had come in.

Ajay then looked down at his mother's body, which was sprawled on the floor between the table and refrigerator. Asha lay on her left side with her head bent unnaturally around to face directly behind her. Her once-beautiful features were now masked by blood splatter, numerous cuts, and crushing blunt-force damage done to her facial bones; all of that done while Ajay had wildly hacked away with the meat clever. In fact, its large flat blade was still embedded in her forehead. Her lifeless eyes were not open, as such, but bulged out her mangled sockets in opposite directions from her head, which was nearly decapitated from her shoulders, attached only by the bones of her spine.

During the attack, blood had splattered across virtually every surface of the room; furniture, ceiling, floors and appliances. Ajay could not remember how many times he had struck in his all-consuming rage. His memory had several strangely blacked-out parts that made him lose any concept of time during the episode. It might have been ten seconds or ten minutes of hacking at her, he simply did not know and did not care.

Looking at his handiwork he judged that his actions could be considered overkill by the major. But by his estimation, his outburst was more than understandable given the circumstances. If his parents were going to be so blatantly unsupportive and challenge him so haughtily, then just what could anyone expect when he vented his anger? Overkill? Overkill was exactly what the entire world could expect from him from this day onward, and very soon he would show the world a whole new definition of overkill.

*****

BARELY TWENTY minutes earlier Pushkar was halfway through his evening meal; he sat indignantly with his back rigidly set, fuming. He slowly chewed at his food as Ajay came walking in the door to the kitchen.

145

He and Asha had been patiently watching through the kitchen window as Ajay had driven a semi-truck and box trailer into the yard, parking it alongside the other three gasoline tanker rigs that sat next to the building that was once the busy offices of the thriving trucking business. The business was long ago shut down by Ajay without the smallest explanation to his parents. The weeds had grown shoulder-high around the building during the ensuing years, but they were now trampled flat by the tires of the other heavy trucks and vans parked there.

When they spoke at all over the last few years, Ajay had refused to give little more than a few brash and heated words to his parents. Pushkar was never able to figure out what had caused his son to change so drastically after the Hajj, but their relationship was now worse than ever. He also did not know if these new trucks and strange activity meant that Ajay was starting the company up again or not, but tonight he was set on finding out. He had his fill of his son's erratic behavior and wanted answers.

After parking, Ajay had opened the box trailer's rear doors and climbed inside. Moments later there came the muted sound of hammer blows and, in a few seconds, both Pushkar and Asha were stunned to see Ajay jump out of the trailer, followed by a couple dozen people who milled about the trucks in the dim light.

Asha stood next to her husband, shaking her head as she watched the group of strangers.

"Smuggling, is that what he does now, smuggling?" she muttered indignantly.

Ajay's shadowy shape quickly approached the house and ended with him walking through the doorway and stopping on the opposite side of the kitchen table. His bloodshot eyes and tired expression showed Pushkar that whatever his son was doing, he was bone-tired. Believing Ajay had fallen back into smuggling, with evident plans to use the ranch as a staging point in the operation, Pushkar knew he could never allow that to continue.

The three stared coolly at one another for several seconds until Ajay's raspy voice broke the silence.

"I've many guests outside who are tired and hungry," Ajay grunted rudely to his mother. "When can you have a large meal prepared?"

Asha's eyes widened with indignation and she lost her composure and with anger coating her voice she blurted, "When? When? When will you explain yourself to us about what you are doing? What is going on with you? We have not seen much of you over the last months and even when we do you hardly speak to us."

146

Her arms flailed and pumped at the air as she ranted.

"Now you show up with all of these illegals here at your father's house and you demand food? Are you a master and I a slave? My son, what has become of you? Have you no respect, at all, for me and your father anymore?"

Ajay's shoulders tightened and his fists clenched.

"I didn't come here to be questioned by you, or to explain myself. The responsibilities I carry are so much greater than you can even imagine! I say again – how long before you have meals made?"

Trembling with hurt and anger, Asha pleaded with her son.

"We do not see you for months at a time. We are forced to live off your father's disability, which barely covers the bills. You come and go as you please. How can you do this to us, Ajay?"

Ajay's tired eyes flashed with more than irritation; there was venom in them.

"Woman, do as I instruct you to do! You will maintain your place in silence! I have too much at stake right now to waste my time arguing with you."

"What do you have at stake with those men out there, Ajay?" Asha demanded, pointing out the window. "You closed the business years ago and, out of the blue, over the past two weeks you start showing up here with trucks again, without so much as a single word to us? What are you up to? What is going on? Are you smuggling more than people? Maybe drugs? Please, tell me that you are not using drugs again?"

"Shut up! Do as…."

"*Haadi*!" Pushkar yelled, as his fist slammed down onto the table, causing plates to clatter and bounce. His glass of tea overturned and fell to the floor, shattering.

Pushkar had sat silent while his wife and son sparred with each other. His slender jaw jutted out further and further as he listened with growing fury at Ajay for speaking so disrespectfully to his wife. He had reached the end of his tolerance, and as his long-building anger welled to the surface, his fury exploded as he yelled at his son.

"You will remove yourself from my home! I have lost you again! You have gone back to that world that I once thought you had escaped from. Your heart has blackened, and turned hard and cold! Your mind is lost to foolishness! Allah has set you adrift and you are aimlessly wandering upon this hard Earth. I will not allow you to insult me or your mother anymore. *Be gone from my sight*!"

Pushkar watched as a glint of something very wrong and unexpected moved across Ajay's face. A layer of vile hatred and personal enmity flowed into view, just under the surface, more like the

147

shimmer of a ghost than movement of skin and muscle. A deep vein of fear crept into Pushkar's blood as he looked upon his son. A chilling thought, not completely formulated in his soul, began to creep into his conscious mind: maybe he had never known his son at all. A dawning of knowledge that Ajay was a stranger, and was finally being unmasked. Pushkar suddenly felt like he was looking upon a creature that he had never met before, and that strangely unfamiliar animal now stood mere feet away, with the vicious, hungry eyes of a rabid wolf.

Silently, almost reflexively, Ajay widened his feet slightly while his arms went from hanging loosely at his sides to being crossed over his chest. Swelling his chest with a large breath, he stared down the ridge of his nose as he replied.

"I am lost to you, old man? You never saw me as your son, even when I was a child and you went off to your glorious crusade in Afghanistan! I am lost to you? I was never found by you! I am a *Brahman*, not some silly Texas farmer! I am not a mover of dirt clods and cow shit like these ignorant rednecks around here," he asserted as he pumped a fist against his chest.

Ajay continued to scream as he gestured wildly.

"I am a man of destiny and greatness! You took on the cause of a nation of godless *infidels* over the rightful placement of your own blood, *me*, *your son*!"

One of Asha's hands fell to her husband's shoulder while her other covered her mouth, and she took a small step backward in shock. Pushkar, frozen in alarm, stared at the screaming man he did not know while Ajay continued his whining and lie-filled rant.

"You left me to wander in the wilderness of this heathen-land of backward rednecks, to suffer the pains of temptation and decadence that permeate this sewer! I fell low, and in the manner of a beggar at the door, I came – I came begging you for the chance to start a life of redemption."

He then jabbed a rigid finger toward his father and squinted while whispering more contemptuous lies, "And like a great lord, *you*, barely bestowed upon me the favor to do it! The money I made with that company bought and paid for this land! This home! And that makes it *mine*! Not yours, you old cripple."

Ajay panted heavily in his rage.

"You never asked where that money came from then, or what I did to get it before now. Smuggler? *Ha!* You have no idea the many drugs and illegals I've brought to this place. Mexicans, Guatemalans, Hondurans, Nicaraguans – every kind of bastard Latino you can name, came across that border over the years, in my trucks!"

Staring at them with a mocking sneer he continued, "Cocaine, heroin, and pot came to this ranch by the ton! I am very good at what I do and never got caught, not once. You demand that I leave *my house*, old man? I don't think so, I have found my destiny! I have Allah on my side!"

"You have not found Allah, my son," Pushkar replied quietly.

"No?"

"You may have been to the holy cities, and walked around the Káaba at the Masjid al-Haram. But you have never found God. What perversion you have in your heart is of Shaitan – not Allah."

Ajay sneered at his father's assertion.

"Don't lecture me about God, old man. I saw the sick and poor that crowded around that black box in the desert, mewing like sheep. They don't go there for salvation. They seek out something that doesn't reside inside a big, black rock! Devils don't live in stone pillars. Devils reside in the hearts of men and if Shaitan resides in mine then so be it! If Allah won't serve me – let Shaitan bring forth my greatness!"

Deeply depressed and shocked, Pushkar shook his head sadly at his son.

"Nothing but the arrogance of childish human pride fills your soul. The vain weakness of that pride shall be your downfall. You have no greatness in you! You rant at your mother and me as though we did not matter to this world? I do not know you. How could your weakness be hidden from me for so long?" Pushkar lamented.

"I have sacrificed much in the service of Allah, and I will never shirk from his path. But I will not abide your sickness in my presence. You defile the memory of your family name and the warmth and beauty of your mother. I have failed you as a father, but you have failed me as a son as well. The blackness in your heart is far darker than I ever knew and I set here aghast at its manifestation. Take the men you smuggled here and leave, I beg you," Pushkar pleaded.

Ajay smirked at the sight of his helpless father issuing out meaningless requests.

"You sit there humbled and defeated, slumping in that little metal chair like a beaten down old street beggar. I marvel at how you; nothing but a pathetic old bastard! It is impossible my blood line could come from such a weak fool as you. Maybe, Uncle Mayur bedded this woman who gave birth to me, eh?" Ajay raised an eyebrow to his mother. "There is no possible way someone as great as I could ever come from the loins of some feeble mongrel such as you."

Asha was trembling in rage and forcibly bit into her tongue to keep from screaming at her son; a son she had always defended and spoke up for to her husband and helped through his difficult years of adolescence; a son who now stood before her, a grown man, blatantly mocking and insulting her and his father with an arrogant ease that shocked and humiliated her.

She clenched her teeth and accidently bit her tongue, tasting blood in her mouth. She would not have been able to keep silent if not for the calm and gentle hand of her beloved Pushkar, slowly stroking and caressing her hand on his shoulder. His gentle nature showed through more at this moment than she had ever known in their forty-two years of marriage.

Pushkar calmly replied to his son's inflammatory words. "Your tongue is sharp in your mouth and your heart is black in your chest. You only show your weakness with your insults."

Pushkar sighed as he assessed Ajay. "Mayur is a good man, a devoted and beloved brother who never wronged our family name. You sprouted from my loins, and now I regret that more than anything I have been responsible for in my entire life. Tell me, my son, have you been insane your entire life or did the drugs do this to you?"

Pushkar looked upon Ajay with pity. "The evils of my life may be many but are you my greatest evil? You will never be the great man you claim. I'm afraid, my son, your fate is a small one. You will be remembered for nothing more than a brutally insulting and wicked tongue. Shaitan now leads you to a small purpose – leave here."

Ajay chafed at his father's words as he spoke through closed teeth. "I once lay on this very floor bleeding and weeping. Your fury that day was brought on by far less provocation from me, old man. Either you control your anger better now, or perhaps your fear of me keeps your little self pinned to your chair, yes? Running off to your Holy War and losing your brother and a leg has evidently softened your outbursts."

Pushkar looked down at the stump of his leg as he remembered that day, long ago, when he had struck out at his son, and the vision of Subhash's body being torn apart in the explosion played out for his mind again as well.

"Yes, I reacted far more quickly to provocation when I was younger. The loss of Subhash was a quenching of that blaze in my soul; a quenching that left in its wake dust and ash. The taste in my mouth grows more bitter with the passage of time. It was a regretful mistake to leave my family and enter the jihad; a mistake that may have influenced your imbalanced mind and soul."

Pushkar raised his eyes to level on his son. "But it is not fear that stays my anger with you now, my son – just sadness and contempt. For whatever mistakes I have made in my life, they are mine. You have grown to be a fool, and your failings and your evil are your own."

Ajay's lower lip quivered in anger. "You should think more of fear if you wish to continue to push me like that, old man! You say my greatness will never come. Bah! You have no idea what I've become and what I will do! You think I am a mere criminal who runs a smuggling operation? You know nothing, old fool."

"Just leave, my son."

"*Quit saying that*!" Ajay screamed, his chest heaved with large breaths.

"You think I spent this night bringing in fucking Mexicans? You're sadly mistaken! Those aren't fucking illegal Mexicans out there…."

Ajay paused as a crooked grin blended grotesquely with his hate-filled eyes.

"You think you have an idea of what Holy War is? Huh? You don't. I have brought to this country that you love so dearly, my own version of Holy War and very soon it will burn this whole place to cinders!"

Pushkar's eyes squinted to thin slits as he considered what his son just said.

"What do you mean – holy war?"

"Ha, ha!" Ajay's head rocked back and a cackling sick laughter roared out of his lungs. He finally saw the reaction he wanted on his father's face.

Egging himself on, he gleefully yelled, "You're paying attention now? You have no idea *how fucking hard I've worked* for the coming days! Ever since I was locked in that hellhole at Huntsville, I've dreamt of the next few days!"

Sarcasm dripped from his voice. "I used the two of you time and time again, without you ever becoming the wiser. One slow step after another, methodically, systematically, I've stalked my prey like a lion and now I'm about to deliver the death blow! I am about to slit the throat of this godforsaken kafir-land."

He finished and leaned on the back the chair opposite of his father with a hard, triumphant grin on his face.

Pushkar looked out the window at the dark figures walking around in the weeds by the tankers. His mind swam with terrible thoughts and suddenly he realized that his son had given very dangerous weapons to some very dangerous people.

Looking up at Ajay he said, "Whatever you are planning to do Ajay – you must stop this. I beg you. This place is our country now

151

and it is a good place, with good people. The horrors of the old country must not be brought here."

The three-day old growth of whiskers coating Ajay's face bent and twisted as his grin broadened. His voice came in a whisper.

"You cannot fathom the horror I'm going to unleash on these insects. I have made many new friends since the Hajj. Your heart has forgotten those lands of your youth as you bask in the excesses of these heathen-lands and you have forgotten about me. At least one Majumbar still fights for my dignity and my rightful place!"

Alarmed, Pushkar stared open-mouthed at his son. Asha still stood at his side with tears streaming down her cheeks.

"Ajay – please – what have you done, my son?" she begged.

Ajay relished the fear he saw in their faces.

"Asha, bring me the phone, my wife," Pushkar said without taking his eyes off his son.

She made a small step toward the wall phone that hung no more than five feet away, but stopped when she heard Ajay say in a sarcastic tone, "You think I would allow that? You think I would ever possibly allow you to interfere with my plans?"

He let go of the back of the chair and produced, from the small of his back, a Glock pistol.

Pushkar's eyes widened with shocked surprise as his face flushed red with anger and fear.

"You dare threaten us? How could you ev…."

Ajay quickly raised the pistol and fired two quick rounds into his father's chest, silencing him forever. Asha screamed as Pushkar grimaced and clutched at his chest. Asha's long-wail ended as she reached for him.

His body went limp in her arms and she wailed for several moments before lifting her face above her husband's shoulder, glaring in fear and anger at her son. Horror filled her soul when she saw him grinning back at her.

Ajay suddenly felt a lightness of spirit and a freedom in his mind now that his father was finally gone. Exhilarated over what he did, his tired limbs had a burst of fresh new energy, just like when he had beheaded the Kurdish prisoner back in Iraq.

He stared back, unabashed, at the fear-filled eyes of his mother and contemplated whether he would feel the same relief with her death. He decided he would, and slowly raised his weapon until it was pointed at her face, with his finger resting lightly on the trigger.

The blunt realization of her own cold-blooded murder at the hands of her son dawned on Asha's overwhelmed mind. Quicker than a cat she burst away from her husband's corpse as the bullet fired from

Ajay's pistol missed her face by inches. She bolted to the counter, grabbing at the knife handles jutting out of the top of the butcher's block, while her other hand hurled a salt shaker directly at Ajay's face.

To keep from being hit squarely on the nose by the salt-filled glass projectile, Ajay was forced to duck. A faint chuckle escaped his throat as he considered the audacity of his mother's meager attempt to fight back.

Then, while still bent over from his duck, Ajay looked at her with a big grin as she pulled a butcher knife from the block and faced him at less than ten feet. He raised himself up to full height but left his pistol hanging down along his thigh.

"You were always stronger than that old bastard, Mother," he said.

Like a caged animal with nowhere to run, she bent forward with the knife held in both hands. Misery-filled tears ran down her face as she looked at the vile creature that leered at her and had so flippantly murdered her husband. That familiar thing, jovial at her misery, looked like her son but it was clear now that she had never seen it for what it was before tonight. Desperation swelled in her as she raised the knife above her head and gave a high-pitched scream and charged forward.

Ajay dropped the pistol to the floor as he stepped toward her charge, easily grasping her arms in one hand, and clasping his other hand around her slender throat. He shoved her back into the refrigerator, tilting it backward onto its rear legs and slamming it against the kitchen wall.

He twisted her wrist, and with a cry of pain she let the knife clatter to the floor. Releasing her wrists he placed both hands on her throat and began to squeeze. She desperately tried to pull at his arms but he was far too strong. As her lungs screamed for air she reacted by crashing her knee into his groin.

Grunting in pain, he released her neck and reached for his testicles as he stumbled backward, almost collapsing to his knees. Asha, in her momentary freedom, tried rushing for the door, but as she moved by him his arm curved around her waist and he threw her back.

Moaning and leaning against the counter, Ajay's left hand blindly searched the countertop for anything it might find. Finally, gripping the handle of something, he raised it above his head as Asha screamed. He brought the object down and her scream abruptly ended as Ajay watched the meat clever he had grabbed sink deep into the side of her neck.

Blood gushed upward onto his face. Frenzied, he violently jerked his arm back and forth as he repeatedly struck out as she crumpled to the floor.

He continued until he was exhausted and covered in dripping gore.

*****

AL-DOLEH had closely watched Ajay's confrontation with his parents after following Ajay to the house, and stood on the porch, just outside the kitchen door, listening. After the bloodshed was done he saw Ajay get off his knees, and then step carefully across the bloody floor toward the sink as if he were walking across slippery ice. Now, as Ajay stood with his back against the counter, looking at his mother's corpse for several minutes, Al-Doleh could see that Ajay was re-living the experience though his haze.

Finally, Ajay shook his head as if waking up, and looked around the room before he turned to face the major.

"I believe that your men should not come in here and see this little mess of mine, Major. I can bring them their food myself, and they can stay in the garage below to eat and sleep. Do you agree?"

Ajay's compartmentalization amazed Al-Doleh. The major had been involved in many missions that required him to commit acts of severe brutality; throughout them all he never wavered in his resoluteness or shirked away from any of his responsibilities.

He had seen men crack, and fail to do what they were supposed to out of weakness, fear, and many other pressures that a deep covert operation could put upon a man's mind. But this was the first time he actually observed such exquisitely compartmentalized insanity. He was not sure if he could trust that Ajay would remain focused enough, over the next few days, to not jeopardize the rest of the mission.

He certainly felt that the psychological release of murdering his parents might have affects that could not be properly assessed in the field. Tomorrow he would leave with his teams for California while his second-in-command, Lieutenant Jafar ud-Daulah, would remain here to complete the strikes in Texas.

With his thick Farsi accent Al-Doleh addressed his concerns directly.

"You are an unpredictable force on this mission and I don't think you share my commitment to this endeavor. Why should I let you live?"

154

Ajay replied to the major's question with surprising confidence, even to himself.

"I am concerned with nothing but our mutual success in this operation."

Waving his hand at the two bodies, he continued, "They were nothing but a liability to our cause, and they would have laid all of our efforts to waste if I had not stopped them. You saw this and therefore know this. Furthermore, my father would have been devastated by what I am going to do. Now, he can seek heaven with Allah's grace, unfettered by concerns with me. I have more to do here regarding the mission and I can still be of invaluable assistance to you and your men. That is why I should live."

The major's hand itched and he almost reached for his weapon, to rid himself of such an unknown factor immediately, but something made him pause. He had never encountered anyone like this before. He stared hard at Ajay for many heartbeats before finally making his decision. Then, finally, noticeably relaxing, he allowed his shoulders to lower as he smiled at Ajay, who returned the smile as if he were meeting an old friend on the street.

The major pointed to the Glock lying on the floor and said, "You should retrieve that and then bring any food you can that will be easy and quick to make. My men and I are famished after the past two days being stuck inside that terrible box of yours. I will go make sure none of my men ever come up here – they would never understand. Are there toilets in that building down there?"

"Sure is. I'll have food down after a while and I'll bring bedding down after that," Ajay said as he picked up his pistol from the blood-covered floor.

*****

September 17, 2011 11:23am CST UTC -6:00
Amistad National Recreation Area
Comstock, TX

THE FADED royal-blue 1991 Saturn S-series sputtered as the worn-out 4-cylinder engine complained by ejecting oily-black smoke out the tailpipe. Its balding tires travelled north on US 90 toward a small cluster of buildings that appeared like a huddled-up football team a half mile down the road. Those two dozen or so structures in Comstock were what passed for a town in this part of south Texas.

Even with the windows down the three occupants of the old car sweated heavily, as the oppressive and unrelenting heat of over

112 degrees, mixed with 100% humidity, stewed under the blazing Texan sun. Yesterday's soaking rain had drenched the landscape, leaving behind mud and large stagnant pools of water in the weed-filled ditches. The humidity hung so condensed in the air that the weak but thick breeze caressing their faces felt like steamy fabric and did nothing for their sweltering discomfort.

The myriad of paths the three bronze-skinned men had travelled over the last eight months had indeed been arduous and many times they thought they would be stopped, caught like mice in traps, but their luck had held. They were now inside the belly of the beast.

The nighttime storm had been intense with lightening, rain, and a hard wind that blew with such fury that they all felt punch-drunk. The raging storm had almost made their border crossing from Mexico impossible as the deep blackness was periodically illuminated by bright flashes of Zeus's anger. But through it all, the human-coyote smuggler, Miguel, had remained calm and had successfully led them through the gauntlet of wind, waves, and federal agents easily enough. The storm kept the border agents, on both sides, out of their way, hunkered inside their offices rather than patrolling with their infrared and night vision. Even so, Miguel boasted he had done the crossing a thousand times and that the border guards throughout this area were all very well paid to not interfere, regardless of the weather.

The angry, swollen waters of the Amistad Reservoir had made for a difficult crossing during the storm. And the little man driving the sputtering car, Aziz, had almost drowned in the dark and muddy waters after he stepped off the wet deck of the tiny submarine into the reeds and willows along the shoreline. But where he thought there was land, he found only deep water, immediately disappearing under the choppy surface. He had never learned to swim, and without the help of his compatriots who dove in and fished him out of the water, he would never have made it out and up the steep bank covered with thorny mesquite brush.

Standing bedraggled atop the bank, covered in mud and panting from dragging the half-drowned Aziz out of the water, the three highly trained murderers watched as the odd smuggling vessel disappeared into the driving rain. Together, they then walked warily for several miles down the gravel road to a small, vacant campground and found the blue car waiting for them, just as Miguel had said.

As instructed, they searched a portable shitter that sat near the car and found the vehicle's keys and three handguns and ample supplies of ammunition taped inside zip-loc bags that were submerged in the pool of filth under the seat. Exhausted, they pulled their grubby and soaked forms into the car and, using a map hidden with the guns, headed north from the border. Their enthusiasm grew as they absorbed their success and realized they would soon be meeting with the leader of their strike team outside of Denver. Once outfitted and equipped, they would quietly leave Colorado and go on to complete their mission to attack the Mall of America in Bloomington, Minnesota.

As the sputtering vehicle reached the group of houses, its brakes whined as Aziz slowed the car. A sign instructed that Hwy-163 headed north, and with a smiling nod to his two passengers, Aziz turned the car up the narrow two lane road as they followed the directions outlined on the map. The gutless little car backfired several times as it slowly cleared the small community and started across the sun-baked grassland of the infidel nation that they had come to devastate.

*****

September 19, 2011 05:30am MST UTC -6:30
Campo Cemetery
Campo, Colorado

THE MANY scattered thunderstorms had come one after another out of the southwest as the three men continued making their way across Texas. They had slept in shifts inside the tiny car they had quickly come to despise. During a fuel stop in Amarillo, Faraz thought that they would never get the sad worn-out engine going again. He was sure the lousy piece-of-shit car would force the end of his investigation then and there. He was preparing to signal his FBI support team, in the two close-by surveillance vans, to come swooping in and execute the arrests of his two murderous travelling companions. But then, at the last moment, just before he gave the signal, Aziz had finally gotten the misfiring motor running again and they were able to continue on their way to the rendezvous with this terrorist cell's leader; the final target of this multi-year operation.

The mysterious leader of this terrorist cell was known only to be some anonymous American traitor, who was the in-country contact and facilitator for this planned terrorist attack. The FBI and CIA had never gotten this close to the unidentified traitor before and Faraz was pleased that they were still on track to bust the bastard when they arrived for the meeting in Denver. He was fixated on capturing or killing the traitor before the sun set on this last day of his undercover operation.

Faraz was the first, and only, FBI agent to have successfully infiltrated the international global terrorist networks of financiers, facilitators, recruiters, and trainers of the Haqqani and Al-Qaida

157

terrorist organizations. The two terrorists he had trained and now travelled with could have been targeted and killed a long time ago, along with the mujahedeen in the numerous training camps that were identified during his undercover operation. But CIA, NSA, and military intelligence had identified that these two men were being assisted by an unidentified American collaborator who would be the mechanism for their infiltration into America, and indeed, that person had now become the main focus and target for the end of this multi-year investigation that was a successful offshoot of Operation Cannonball.

Nearing the end of his involvement, Faraz looked back with pride at successfully identifying the intricate and very dangerous subversive routes that the terrorists had constructed to get them to America. Now that he had travelled the winding paths, he was certain that nothing but an undercover operation could have identified the very complex system they were using. And now his long assignment was about to end and he was infinitely grateful to Allah. But, nonetheless, he was absolutely drained, both mentally and physically. His mental and physical health had been relentlessly tested. But still he was happy being back here, at home on American soil. It was much like a glorious religious experience that buoyed his soul. *I'm home!*

The autumn rains had come in heavy waves last night, creating thick sheets that were difficult to drive through, and nobody in the car was able to get any real sleep. Through the night his companions had even taken small doses of amphetamines to help them stay alert as the dreary and soaking miles ticked by.

Faraz had begun to notice that the closer they got to their mission objective, the more paranoid and on edge the other two men were becoming. Some of that tension was getting directed toward him, and after almost two years of being around these men, he was getting nervous. He was positive they still had no idea that he was an enemy to their cause, and he was sure he knew them well enough to be able to tell if they suspected him. But this last day could not end quickly enough since he surmised that his companions were approaching a mental tipping point.

Kneeling, he stretched his arms high into the air while inhaling the cool but clammy morning air that drifted on the mild breeze. Dawn's first hazy amber light crept into the sky above the wind-blown grass of the high plains of eastern Colorado. The mild sweetness from the nearby blooming alfalfa fields, in their last cutting of the season, mixed with the odor coming from the small apple orchid.

It appeared to Faraz that the little orchard may very well have been planted there over a hundred-years ago, standing in a row of gnarled shapes along the rusted barbed-wire fence that bordered the tiny cemetery. The graves sat a short distance off the old two-lane highway; and were the place that Aziz had decided to make their camp for the night. They had huddled together, trying to rest in the miserable car for the past three hours during the blinding, wind-driven rainstorm. Now that the dark clouds had left and were heading to Kansas, the wind had died and the sun was rising. As tired as he was, Faraz appreciated how the mixture of aromas created a wholesome, fresh feeling in his muscles as he greeted his final day in this intense and exhausting role he had been playing for so long.

Successfully infiltrating an FBI agent into the dangerous world of global terrorist cells had been the most ambitious, and to date, most successful operation the agency had ever conducted since 9/11. The United States had never before got one of their own this deep inside these networks, exposing a vast array of targets that had been systematically eliminated by Predator drone strikes over the past three years. The intelligence that Faraz had gained during this mission was instrumental in connecting the various dots his fellow interrogators had gotten out of KSM that helped lead to the elimination of UBL in May - the single proudest accomplishment of Faraz's life!

Now, deep inside Al Qaida's last great attempt to penetrate into America and cause heartache and death, he was poised to put the last nail in the coffin of a network that had caused so much misery around the globe. Faraz felt himself to be the literal personification of the extreme tip of America's spear in the War on Terror, which was primed to cripple a significant part of state-sponsored global terrorism.

Unexpectedly though, his companions had insisted on stopping during the storm, ending up here at the cemetery. And Faraz was now stopped in this small, isolated place where his FBI Swat cover team was forced to stay well away since there was no way his support teams could risk exposing themselves to either his companions or the American traitor.

Taking these rural roads always worried Faraz due to the possibility of running into some small-town cop or sheriff's deputy out here with the two well-trained murderers. It was a certain death sentence for any cop who contacted them for if he pulled a gun to help the officer he would just as likely be shot for the cop as his companions. Aziz and Faruk were both well-trained on how to eliminate local law enforcement threats to this mission. But there was a secondary worry in taking these pre-designated roads on the map;

the traitor could be anywhere and might be looking for any cover teams and that could blow the entire operation.

No other agent in the history of the Bureau had ever been required or authorized to do what Faraz had done during this investigation. The secret Executive Order signed by Bush and then re-issued by Obama, authorizing him to 'take any and all action necessary for the successful completion of the investigation' was the first blanket kill-as-necessary order issued since the Cold War.

Faraz was not only willing to die, but to kill for his country; even the cold-blooded murder of innocent people held no power of persuasion to stop him in completing his mission, if it meant that he would infiltrate the global terrorist networks. And to prove his loyalty to the Iranian, Haqqani, Al Qaida, and Pakistani handlers, he had been ordered to immediately kill on demand several times. *Thank God none of them had been American soldiers!* The first had been a young Somali man who had only been at the Peshawar camp for about two weeks. The poor kid was both illiterate and idealistic, but not suicidal. Volunteering to battle in the global jihad, Faraz was certain the boy had never even considered that he would end up being randomly slaughtered as a sacrificial animal.

Murdering that weeping kid by blowing his brains across the gravel of that courtyard had been the single hardest thing Faraz had ever done up to that time. He thought the look in that boy's eyes would haunt him every night for the rest of his life, and he was right. The other two kills had been easier but made for no less vivid nightmares. Faraz had stayed alive with those acts of murder and he justified the killing by telling himself that he had saved untold numbers of innocents that would have been killed by those same boys, in some series of unknown attacks somewhere.

That, however, was cold consolation for his soul and mind. But, in order to guarantee the safety of his fellow Americans, there was nothing he could not do, period!

Faraz knelt on his prayer rug and noticed an old white-marble headstone glistening with moisture. The words chiseled into the stone tablet read:

Benjamin F. Lincoln
1st SERG
Company C
9 US CAV
June 2, 1854
February 10, 1882
Buffalo Soldier

Faraz prostrated himself and began reciting the fajr prayers, and could not help but ponder what kind of life that soldier had lived. Being a buffalo soldier meant he was a black man, maybe born and raised in slavery, but died free – a soldier, after that abysmal practice was destroyed in the cataclysm of the Civil War.

What had that man seen in a life that spanned from being a slave to serving as a U.S. Cavalry NCO. What trails did he travel to be buried in this lonely place, forgotten, isolated, and unheralded? How did he die; illness, accident, battle, or something else? What did the initial 'F' stand for – Faraz or Franklin? Was he a good man and a good soldier? Did he die right? Did he die poorly? Faraz wanted the answers to those questions of the life of Benjamin F. Lincoln.

Introspection and soul-searching into the depths of his own heart had become a constant in the life of FBI Special Agent Faraz Sarfraz Hamidi. It kept him focused through the many hardships of his life. He slowly moved his dark-skinned hands ritually before his face while reciting his prayers. *The same hands that have committed murder. Necessary – it had been necessary.*

The prayers that he had memorized since childhood helped clear his mind of any troubling thoughts as he concentrated upon Allah. He then felt rejuvenated as solace and peace came back to his spirit, helping his mind to become whole again. As he repeatedly prostrated his body before the Almighty he felt the grit of the earth brush his bare toes and felt, deep inside his soul, the connection between the energy of all God's creation being channeled through his spirit. The divine spirit of Allah supported his soul the same as the Earth supported his body.

The freshness of the morning air helped calm his wandering mind, until he could again focus. As his Muslim companions prayed next to him, he felt again the contradiction of his brotherhood with them. He listened to them recite the same words he did, and he could feel the zeal and conviction held in their beliefs. A belief in the same God he worshiped; yet they had such differing views of the world and how their proper relationship should be with the other children of the Almighty that populated the planet.

Faraz wished to preserve the great flowering of the human spirit that was found in America, while they wished to destroy it, utterly. In his heart and soul Faraz feared that one day the conflict in those competing visions would tear the religion of Islam itself apart, forever, and all of its believers with it.

For Faraz, it was only his faith in the infinite wisdom of Allah that brought him the mental comfort and spiritual calmness to truly understand the basic truth within the disparity of belief between him and the men kneeling next to him. That truth was that Islam and the path to Allah was for redemption and grace for Faraz. But for his companions, and their kind, Islam was used as a convenient excuse, and tool, to exercise hatred and bigotry, instead of confronting the huge political and social hardships of their people.

Faraz had come to know the jihadist mind set very well, yet it was still difficult for him to see how their shared religion brought out such thoughts of blind-hatred and bitterness of spirit that motivated both Aziz and Faruk. For Faraz, the well-spring of Allah brought justice, not bitterness; joy, not sorrow; love, not hate.

But Aziz al-Hassan and Faruk al-Hussien were totally committed to strapping to their bodies vests filled with RDX explosive, metal nuts and bolts, and then detonating themselves, using them to kill hundreds of innocent people in a murderous, pathetic and wasteful attack against those who neither harmed them nor their religion. The very thought of the beauty of Islam being continually bloodied by such willing and brutal men disgusted Faraz.

For over ten centuries, the old pagan tribalism of the Middle East had bent the religious purity of Islam, making it into a political machine for power and control. The search for the true and pious divinity of Allah was slowly being lost. Faraz knew Islam had absolutely nothing whatsoever to do with the socio-political grievances of the modern Middle East and Asia. His saw his religion was being brutally hijacked by an evil and suicidal death-cult, which germinated out of the misrepresentations in the teachings of Salafist Islam that had corrupted the hearts, minds, and souls of his Muslim brethren around the world. This terrible perversion of pious Islam was, like all corruption of good, the act of the ultimate deceiver – Shaitan. The evil creature his Christian friends called the Devil.

Shaitan, the fallen one, infected the modern Salafi followers into becoming a death-cult that hid behind the words of the sacred jihad in the ranting of a multitude of political hacks, corrupt imams, and the despotic merchants-of-death who happily whipped and twisted the heartfelt passions of pious worshippers, into the evil passions of hatred and intolerance.

Through evil murder and brutal intimidation, Shaitan's whispered influences had infected the great faith of Islam and Faraz feared it would keep spreading, like a cancer, created by the evil Shaitan and intended to destroy his faith. God's rebel angel, and the great deceiver of men's souls, was seeking a momentous victory against Allah.

Through constant war and struggle against the will of Allah – Shaitan had used his many agents like; ibn Abd-al-Wahhab and Sayyid Qtub, to corrupt the teachings of the Prophet and steal the memory of the pious Salafi by distorting their virtuous memory into a domineering political force that was bent on the destruction of God's Law and the very faith of Islam. Faraz, like all Muslims, believed in the holiness of jihad and, indeed, Faraz waged his own personal jihad: to succor his faith from the terrible influences of the vile liar, the wicked Iblis Shaitan.

That struggle, for the future of his faith, became interwoven with his work as a government agent securing the safety of America. Allah's teachings showed Faraz that his very existence was part of the eternal struggle between good and evil. Once this death-cult, that tainted Islam, was defeated, the softening of men's souls could begin to reshape the petty bitterness and hatreds of Middle Eastern life flourish into ideas of more goodwill and common purpose with all peoples. Coexistence between Muslim and non-Muslim was his true purpose and goal for his patriotic jihad to protect America.

If, through his efforts, he could expand access to personal and political freedoms throughout the oppressive regimes of the Middle East and Asia he would have, in some small way, helped bring about the restoration of his faith and faithfully served Allah.

He believed, with all of his heart, that the liberties, freedoms, and economic opportunity that were represented psychologically, and embodied physically in America, were the correct path by which those same freedoms and opportunities could eventually spread to his Muslim brothers and sisters around the globe. But for that to happen, America's good must survive the terror that Shaitan yearned to inflict upon it and all men's souls. That pure evil was the horror that Faraz fought against every day of this taxing mission

His father, Aban, as part of the Jadgal tribe growing up in the Makran region of Iran, had been a devout Muslim and had supported the Ayatollah's return to Iran. But with the passage of time, the oppressive rule of the mullahs showed his father how the opportunities he thought would come with the religious purity of the Islamic Revolution against the Shah, had, in fact, failed. And he saw that failure was directly due to the evil in the hearts of corrupt men who hid inside the black silken robes and long cloaks of the ayatollahs.

Aban had watched in dismay as the revolution was blatantly hijacked by the narrow-minded interests of the politically motivated mullahs, for self-empowerment – not religious fidelity with the purity of Allah. The institutions of politicized religion created a corrupt political hydra apparatus within the government that replaced a single despotic Shah, with an entire cadre of despotic mullahs led by their equally despotic Grand Ayatollah. His father had fled the perversion of the revolution and had immigrated with his family, and a young four-year old Faraz, to the United States in 1980. Aban eventually tenured his services to the CIA and FBI as a translator and when Faraz grew up he attended the FBI Academy.

Faraz followed his father in service to the United States as a wide-eyed and eager agent of the FBI, filled with optimism about the future. But just a few days after graduation from the academy his heart was broken by a double tragedy on 9/11. His idealism evaporated and his future turned very dark as he watched, along with his other Quantico classmates, as the towers collapsed. It was only minutes later when his supervisor came in and informed him that his family in Detroit had an emergency and needed him to call. Faraz phoned his brother, Suhrab, who told him how his father, while watching the second plane hit the south tower, had suffered a stroke and died in their living room.

After the funeral, his whirlwind career began. First he was liaison to the Department of Defense at the Signals Intelligence Directorate (SID) at the National Security Agency (NSA) at Fort George Meade, MD. There he did background investigations on the 9/11 terrorists and their facilitators. That work got him assigned back to field operations where he assisted the NSA at the Texas Cryptology Center (TCC) in San Antonio, TX with translation and eavesdropping. As he became evermore immersed in the intelligence aspects he transferred to the FBI's National Security Branch (NSB) helping NATO forces in Operation Enduring Freedom during the first two years of the Afghanistan War where he developed military contacts and worked with ex-Taliban and ex-Al Qaeda members while closely assisting the CIA.

In the lead -up to the invasion of Iraq he was assigned to the Terrorist Threat Integration Center. Then, after the fall of Saddam's regime he was liaison with the newly formed Iraqi National Intelligence Service that replaced Saddam's old Mukabarat intelligence agency. There, in the alleys of Sadr City and the streets of Ar Ramadi, he saw the horrors of Shaitan's work manifest in the deadly fight against Al Qaeda in Iraq's leader, Abu Musab al-Zarqawi. The evil of Shaitan sowed disunion among his Muslim brethren to a horrifying degree. Sickened and infuriated to his core, he quickly realized that if this evil was not stopped it would one day make its way to America and, once there, bleed her dry.

All those long roads eventually brought him to the doorstep of Operation Cannonball and his infiltration of the jihadist global network that began just weeks after the death of Zarqawi.

Presently, Faraz was shaken from his memories as his ears picked up the sound of an approaching vehicle, rolling across the gravel of the road that led to the cemetery.

Stirred from his daydreaming, he started to turn his head to look at the approaching vehicle when he was savagely struck along the side of his head, and he pitched forward onto his face.

Barely conscious, his body was racked by convulsions caused by the devastating shock from the blow to his skull. Uncontrollably, he vomited liquid bile onto the ground under his face. His mind reeled as he tried to regain some form of a cogent thought. His brain throbbed and began to swell inside his skull and he could see nothing out his right eye.

He was roughly grabbed and lifted to his knees, as his arms were mercilessly pinned behind his back. His left eye saw the glint of sun off a shiny pair of nickel-plated handcuffs as they landed with a small clink on the rocks before his knees. A strange male voice with a Texas drawl focused his swirling mind on the new threat.

"Put those on him, quickly," the voice said in a slow east-Texas drawl.

Faraz tried to raise his head and focus on the blurry shape of the man standing before him. His right eye was swollen shut and his mouth hung loosely with bile and vomit-soaked mud clinging to his face. Along with the intense throbbing in his skull, Faraz could feel warm liquid running down the side of his head and neck that he figured must be his blood flowing from his ruptured ear canal. He felt the violent clamp of the handcuffs being applied to his wrists and he winced at the pain as they dug into the thin flesh on his wrists.

"As-salamu alaykum," the smiling man said, as he gave a light touch to his forehead with his right hand.

He squatted inches from Faraz, and with his hands grabbed hair and beard as he jerked Faraz around, appraising the blow to his head and gave a long whistle.

"Damn, you really look like shit. I imagine that hurts like a real son of a bitch in that noggin' of yours. It sure looks mighty painful to me."

Unforgiving hands jerked Faraz upright by his shoulders as a new spasm of nausea swept through him and he involuntarily heaved, but only thick saliva poured off his lower lip as the kneeling man grimaced in disgust and leaned back to keep from being touched by the substance.

165

"Well, we meet again my little FBI agent friend. You remember me at all?" Ajay asked.

Faraz tried to collect his muddled thoughts. He could tell the damage caused by Aziz's attack was very bad. He figured Aziz must have struck him with a rock to hurt him so badly. But at the moment he was more concerned with the Texan. *This is the traitor! How? When was my cover blown?*

He sensed something familiar about the man who looked as if he was from the Middle East, not Texas, but there was no mistaking that his voice was native Texan. His heart raced in his chest at the realization at his monumental failure. Furious and frustrated tears welled up in his one working eye.

The traitor he had been after for so long was now mere inches from him and he could do nothing. He was trapped, alone, with no back-up or assistance anywhere near. How long had this trap been set? Months? Years? Faraz desperately worked through the faces of all the people this man could possibly be, but the myriad of faces just blended together and he could not place where they had met. Despair flooded into his heart.

Ajay gave Aziz a disgruntled look as he saw that this conversation was not going to be a two-way opportunity for smug banter like he had hoped.

"You don't look up to the task of remembering me, FBI-boy. My good friend here has put a world of hurt on your ass! So let me try and help you figure out who I am."

Faraz tried to focus as he listened intently to what Ajay was saying but it was getting increasingly difficult.

"You and I met some years ago at my family's ranch down in Sattler, Texas. You asked for my father's help in your country's little war over in Iraq; just like he'd foolishly done against the Soviets before. You even asked for my help then, too. It was shortly after 9/11. You do remember any of that?"

Ajay smiled as he saw the dawning recognition enter into the agent's one working eye.

"Oh yes, you do remember me now don't you? I certainly remembered you, too when I just happened to see you, by chance, back in Pakistan once, but you didn't see me. That is too bad for you eh? After that day I had the inside track with these Iranian hombres, here," he said, glancing up at Faruk and Aziz.

"They appreciated me blowing your cover and all. From that day on, they had your butt square in their sights and I've often wondered why they just didn't waste your ass a long time ago. I guess they had their own fun with you."

166

"There was even talk of ransoming your carcass back to the old US-of-A in a big media circus to thoroughly embarrass the CIA. I told them that it would've been fun but they got real edgy about being too public. I can't really fault them I guess, especially since secrecy worked out so good in the end."

Faraz's head rolled back and forth as he tried to stay conscious.

"They did decide to test you. To see what kind of guy the U.S. had finally sent so deep into their business. I guess they had fun watching you kill that first nigger. I know I sure did. Oh yeah, I was there watching! Hee hee, you put on a good fucking show that day!"

Ajay leaned in closer.

"Personally, to tell you the God-honest truth – I didn't think you had it in you to do in that nigger. I thought they had you in a tight spot where you'd blow your own cover before killing that kid. Imagine my shock! You up and blew that dumb bastard's head clean off his shoulders. I almost shit myself, you know! Shit! Damn! But that was pretty good coldhearted shit there."

Ajay savored watching as his words sink in.

"I never thought some goodie-two-shoes FBI agent could do that. You really did impress me! The feds finally found a mongrel who could do what's needed in this fight, and make no mistake, asshole, that sure caught their attention back in Iran, boy, did it!"

"They sure know what the situation is now. It's shit or get off the pot time with the old USA! I think it made them pretty nervous to see you all finally getting serious. I guess they never figured you'd get down in the mud with'em."

Ajay stretched his arms out wide, gesturing.

"But you see this thing is big, and man I ain't joking, its real big, a hell of a lot bigger than you know! And them folks over there are pretty serious themselves, you know. They're clever and pretty good at playing you fuckers for a bunch of dhimmi fools, especially with this dumb-fuck nigger we got in the Whitehouse. Lordy! He's just soft putty in their hands. That stupid fucker has no idea what's about to come cramming up his scrawny ass, that's for sure."

Ajay chuckled and reached into the back of his waistband and pulled out his pistol. He lightly slapped the side of Faraz's face with the barrel of the gun. Faraz's eye opened but could not focus well as Ajay held his head up by the chin. Ajay looked up at Aziz in disappointment.

"You sure wanted this guy dead a long time, huh? You damn near busted the whole side of his head open. This isn't fun."

Aziz shrugged and said with cold voice that was full of malice, "There is no time for this. This is no game. End it."

Ajay shrugged and looked back at Faraz.

"I'm a very busy man these days, mister FBI agent-boy, and you know these fellas and I would just love to stay and chat up a storm with you and have a good ol' time. Maybe we would play some games from back in the old country. I think that maybe you wouldn't like that. Maybe, you'd do a little dancing and singing for us, huh? No?"

Frowning at the lack of response, Ajay shrugged.

"Yeah, well your luck is done gone now. We've got to go before your friends come back around here checking on you. So, bye-bye sucker."

He stood and placed the barrel against Faraz's head. As the cold steel pressed into his skin, deep down in his dazed mind, Faraz considered again the buffalo soldier in the nearby grave. He prayed to Allah that they would soon meet to discuss their lives, their fates, and maybe how opportunities are won and lost.

"Ma shaa' Allah," were the last words uttered by Faraz Hamidi before the bullet careened through his skull and deposited the majority of his brain matter on the ankle-high wheatgrass behind him.

Moments later the settling dust from the gravel road still hung in the slowly moving air, glowing with rays of sunlight through the gaps in the leaves of the little orchard where a few squat prairie cedar trees fought for space and moisture with the apple trees. A Western meadowlark landed lightly on a branch inches above Agent Hamidi's body.

It tilted its tiny head from side to side, watching as the black flies gathered around to feast on the bounty of blood and matter spread upon the grass. The bird ruffled its black feathers and began to sing its melodious but piercing morning song. The bird's sharp rolling call played across the dawn silence like a bugler sounding taps.

Night yielded to day as the sweet and wholesome aroma of nature's dawning hour blended with the high-low pitch of the bird's song. A few moments later the bird's song ceased and quiet peace settled once more across the deserted cemetery. The bird lifted into the sky, leaving behind the silence of dead men's souls as the lonely prairie took back ownership of the hallowed ground that was now home to another American hero.

September 19, 2011 17:20pm MST UTC -7:00
Trinidad, CO

THE AFTERNOON thunderclouds had gathered above the distant Sangre de Cristo Mountains. Often dry lightning appeared as thin silver lines that would streak out from below the brooding dark formations that lied in their promise of rain. The thin, deadly shafts pierced into the vast forests lying along the mountain flanks, making many local hearts tremble at the possibility of raging fire.

Ajay steered his way down the busy street, looking forward to getting back to the campsite outside the little town. Now that his own terrorist cell strike team was fully assembled and the undercover agent had been eliminated, he did not want either of his terrorist compatriots left alone for any extended time in this unfamiliar place. He and Aziz had gone into the town to exchange the worn-out Saturn for Ajay's company van, and had left Faruk alone. It would be very bad luck indeed if some nosey local cop checked into the Iranian man waiting alone along the railroad tracks.

The FBI cover teams had surely found the dead agent's body by now and assuredly had sent out a massive alert that would be issued country-wide for them. Ajay just did not need to deal with problems like that right now, especially since he was just one night away from completing his masterpiece.

In the morning, after fajr prayers, they will head for Denver to complete his own attack against the unsuspecting city while the feds would be searching for them, supposedly heading to Bloomington. On the way north to Denver, Ajay was certain that they would already be hearing over the radio the first news being aired from the other attacks occurring across the country.

Ever since the days when he sat stewing in his prison cell down in Huntsville, he knew this day would eventually come. Major Al-Doleh was to lead the massive strike aimed against San Francisco, while his lieutenant would lead another massive strike against Houston. Meanwhile, Ajay Khan Majumbar would fulfill his destiny by burning a large portion of the Mile High City to the ground.

Ajay literally trembled with excitement. *Finally!*

*****

September 19, 2011 20:27pm MST UTC -7:00
San Isidro Creek
Trinidad, Colorado

THOUSANDS OF years ago, the first Athabasca Indian tribes had migrated their way down the mighty Colorado Rockies, with some ending up settled along the lower eastern slopes of that great mountain range. On the high plains and in the deep canyons along the banks of what was now called the Purgatory River, located in southern Colorado, they prospered and diversified into many different tribes, with some continuing to spread south throughout the New Mexico and Texas regions of the American southwest.

Time slowly passed and they were eventually encountered by the Europeans when Spanish conquistadors, led by Francisco Vasquez de Coronado, searched for the mythical Seven Cities of Gold in the 1540s. Coronado was never able to plunder any golden cities, but he did give the Indians living there their first European name, Querechos. Later, other Spanish explorers came to the region, calling them Vaquero Indians.

One tribe from that great migration of human beings has since become known to the world as the fierce Jicarilla Apache, a name that was first documented in records at a Spanish mission near Taos, New Mexico in 1733, describing those Indians that settled along the Purgatory River near the future town-site of Trinidad, Colorado. A small but vibrant city, with the languid Purgatory River cutting through its middle as it continued its ancient serpentine course eastward.

The conquistadors left with their dreams of Golden Cities having turned to dust, but they left behind a prized commodity that would forever change the landscape and lifestyle of the western American Indian – the horse. Arguably, the Indian tribe that took the most advantage of what the horse could do was an offshoot of the Shoshone tribe that lived near the Platte River, in present day Wyoming. It was by their hands that the full tactical advantage the horse gave was realized for both transportation and warfare. They went on a bloody spree of violent expansion that achieved lordship over all neighboring tribes. This band of warriors and the people they subjugated were to eventually become a single tribe, the most feared and violently domineering tribe known to the entire American west, the Comanche.

Over the following century, the Comanche and Jicarilla Apache vied for supremacy on the southern plains, mountains, valleys,

170

and river canyons of Colorado, where they fought many pitched and bloody battles that were never named and are no longer remembered. While those tribes fought their blood feud, the white European and Mexican peoples quickly expanded into the territory to wrest control over the land, and to eventually dominate both warrior tribes.

This influx of non-Indians resulted in many huge land grabs by those Mexicans and white Europeans that followed close behind the first explorers. The clamor for control of the vast lands reached its peak when Cornelio Vigil and Ceran St. Vrain attempted to become the largest landowners in the entire history of the young and expanding United States of America.

They petitioned the Mexican Governor Armijo in 1843 for a large portion of the Maxwell Land Grant that the Mexican Government was then doling out, to expand settlement into the wild and savage lands of the southwest. The request they submitted was for an amazing four-million acres of land. They were eventually successful in getting a massive section on the map allotted to them, which then brought them into direct contention and violent confrontation with the Jicarilla Apache who had not yet been pacified. Already that tribe had been on numerous war paths against the Spaniards and Mexicans for much of the past two-hundred years. Now they bravely battled the newly arriving American settlers.

During the rebellion of the Jicarilla Apache, which occurred during the Taos Pueblo Uprising of 1847, following the land grant acquisition, a young and brave Spaniard by the name of Juan Diego Trujillo made a name for himself with acts of surpassing bravery in the service of Cornelio Vigil. But even with his heroics in the defense of his benefactor's interests, he was unable to stop the Indians from killing and savagely mutilating Vigil's body. But Juan's bravery did gain him high-status in the Vigil family and opened many opportunities in the growing settlements sprouting up on the Vigil and St. Vrain land grant.

With hard work and good business insight his efforts truly paid off when he was able to purchase from Vigil's son a significant 4,164 acre homestead parcel that ran along the northern slopes of Raton Mesa (later to be named Fisher's Peak). There he befriended two of the founders and promoters of the future town of Trinidad, Eugene Leitensdorfer and Felipe Baca, and with them he later became a patriarch of the town.

That was the beginning of the Trujillo Ranch, and as Juan built up his cattle business he found a beautiful and bright young bride in the local Jicarilla Apache village along the eastern flanks of Raton Mesa, and wedded her in a happy Catholic ceremony in the fledgling dirt streets of Trinidad. That was how the founder of the Trujillo clan began his family that eventually numbered fifteen children, of which only twelve survived to adulthood.

The land was hard and so were many of the times during that period when he and his wife carved out their future from the tired hills and meadows of the ancient countryside. One of their surviving children was named Joaquin whose oldest grandson was named Richard, the modern day patriarch of the Trujillo Ranch.

Richard Trujillo was tremendously proud of his ancestry and the history of the entire area. He was very well known to recite facts, dates, and other little known (and just maybe unverifiable) historical minutiae every chance he got. Those chances usually coincided with every time he opened his mouth. The folks around Trinidad would probably say Richard was more obsessed with Richard than his family history, or the history of the area, but they loved him and his many stories nonetheless. His oratory was legendary at the Holy Trinity Catholic Church, where every Sunday school he basked in the rapt attention of all the children, boys and girls.

His deep rancher drawl resonated within the thick sandstone and adobe walls, much like the deep voice of the late actor Roscoe Lee Browne; manly, sophisticated, and intimately personal. His voice, seemingly touched by the Almighty, carried the dreams and fantasies of children high into the world of their imaginations. It was a rare Sunday school class they did not beg and plead for him to give another amazing word-for-word recitation of Browne's character, Jebediah Nightlinger, making his final prayer as he was about to be lynched in the John Wayne movie, The Cowboys. The kids went crazy every time he did it and he loved it almost as much as they did.

Richard liked his name, too, but unfortunately for him the only person who called him Richard was his lovely wife, Constance. Everybody else just called him Dick, and he hated that to no end, but it was useless to try and get them to stop. It was the never-ending-joke for them to get under his skin by calling him by that name. After sixty-eight years he just gave up on it, learning to live in stoic companionship with the name he disliked so much.

But, his beautiful Constance called him by his proper name since the very first day they had met at the county fair, where he got up on the stage in front of everyone in town and sang to her the Jim Reeves song 'He'll Have To Go.' The entire audience at the dance hall went wild at his wooing of her away from her date that night, Jimmy Page. And even though it had gotten Jimmy so mad that he and Richard had fought out in the parking lot where they both ended up with broken noses, Richard never swayed from his devotion and love for Constance. He won her heart that night, beginning a love affair that had lasted to the present day. She let her long, beautiful jet-black hair grow until it hung below her waist, and if it did not weigh so much, she would gladly let it grow longer for him. Their love was one for the ages that made the term soul-mates an understatement for the trust, love, respect, and caring they had for each other.

This morning she had sent him off to work, accompanied by their youngest son, Jake, with a supper of cold fried chicken. The two men both loved her chicken but Richard could only eat it occasionally since he had to watch his cholesterol so closely. They dared not mess around with that after his mild heart attack last year. The chicken was a rarity and she knew it made him feel special when she allowed him to have some. Jake loved it, too, but he would also eat just about anything that could even be mistaken for food, if it came within arm's reach of his mouth.

Jake was skinny as a rail but could put away half a horse a day in his belly, and Richard always lets him have most of their meals. He did the same today, just for the pleasure of watching the boy eat. Richard loved all his children and with the six oldest off to college or serving in the military, it was getting a little quiet around the ranch with only Jake running around now. Just having the opportunity to enjoy his son's company was something Richard did not pass up these days.

At twenty-three, Jake had pretty much given up on attending college, and leaving the ranch was not anything he wanted to do. He took after his dad in loving the way of life the ranch gave to the family and he seemed like he just might be getting serious with that cute Salazar girl from 'over the mountain' in Raton, New Mexico. Jake went to see her every chance he got. Richard and Constance had already decided that they would start turning more of the bookkeeping work over to him this winter to see if he took that up with the same interest in the business end of the ranch as he did the ranch work. They needed to know the boy could handle all aspects of the ranch before they gave him the reigns and let him run with it.

Even with an early start and the help of their two herder dogs, Toby and Sam, they still had a long, hard day of chasing cattle. It was time for winter inoculations and they were very busy getting them rounded up in the corrals. By the time they finally quit for the day, they were able to get two-hundred-thirteen penned in the upper corrals by sundown. Richard figured that by the weekend they should have the other four-hundred-thirty head corralled as well.

Then they would vaccinate the entire herd of Venezuelan Nelore cattle by the end of the month. That would ensure that this new breed Richard had bought would not have any risks of getting Trypanosomiasis Peste-boba disease, a nasty illness particular to this breed. He did not want to take any chance that it could spread to any of his beloved Angus. He was positive that the mixing of these two breeds could make an excellent new beef strain that would sell in the burgeoning specialty meat markets and bring in some needed cash to the ranch.

"I'll sure be happy when these cattle are done with their shots. Whooee, it's been an awful long day but it was a good day. By God almighty, I'm ready for the sack tonight," Richard said as dust flew up from the dually tires of the flatbed truck, bouncing down the county road.

"I hear that, Pop, my ass is drag'n a little, too," Jake replied as he managed the truck along the winding dirt road with ease. "You think mama will be back from town and done visiting with Aunt Sally by the time we get home?"

Richard leaned back in the bucket seat and used his callused right hand to take his well-worn and crumpled black Stetson off his head, then set it down on his knee. Then with both hands he rubbed his face vigorously before running all ten fingers through his matted and sweaty hair, scratching at his itchy scalp with gusto.

"That sister of your mother's is a hen that can cluck nonstop from sun up to sun down, Jake, no doubt. But if there is anyone on this blessed earth that can extricate their person from Sally's chattering presence – it's your mother. I'll betcha she'll have a couple of cold brews waiting on us! Whatcha think?" he replied with a smile.

"That sure would be great! I could use a cold one, Pa," Jake exclaimed at the suggestion. But he was not mollified by his father's words about his aunt and he continued with his complaints, "It's just that Sally's been living up that attention since her surgery on her gallstones last month. It seems like mama is down there every day. That thing's been healed now for three weeks or better, and she still can't do nothing but complain! Keeps everything focused on her. I just don't see why mama has to be down there and be her maid."

"Well, now, son, you're not all wrong there, I have to admit. But I know your mother is worried about her sister and you have to admit, too, Sally's been in a pretty sorry state since your uncle Wilber passed on last year. Heck, no one thought he'd go so young and he was the horse and wagon that carried the load in that house."

"You're right, Pop, and I don't want to sound hateful – you know I don't. It's just that my ma ain't a maid for no one. Not Sally, not anyone." Jake asserted firmly.

174

"That's a fact, son, and your statement includes me and you in that, you know. Your ma is just doing the Christian thing for her sister who's still hurting. So why don't we just let her do what she thinks is best. She knows how to handle this all better than you or me, anyhow."

"You're right as always, Pops. I'll let it go."

"Anyhow, we still got a lot of work to do in the morning and we won't have Jose and Bill back to help us until the day after tomorrow. We did a real good piece of work today, but we still have a lot of cattle to move. Let's get home and stretch out for a bit. We'll be get'n up mighty early."

"Your wish is my command, Pop," Jake said with a glancing smile at his father.

But instead of maintaining its speed the truck started to slow. Jake used the steering wheel to pull himself forward, looking past his father out the corner of the windshield as he said, "Who the hell is out there?"

Curious, Richard turned his head to look where his son was staring. His tired eyes squinted and tried focusing in the dark. It took him a couple seconds of scanning back and forth in the gloom before he saw, out in the distance, some light that should not have been there. It looked like headlights, somewhat hidden in a stand of pinion trees, about four-hundred yards off the road. Jake slowed the truck to a stop in the road as Richard reached behind his seat and felt around on the floorboard. A moment later he produced a pair of binoculars, bringing them up to his face, and he focused the lenses.

Fiddling with the knob for a couple of seconds of frustration, he finally muttered sheepishly, "Well, hell, Dick, take the doggone lens caps off, why don't you." He did so and then went back to focusing on the distant lights up the arroyo.

"What do you see, Dad?"

Richard brought the binoculars down.

"Looks like we got some campers. I see a truck and a small fire."

"Fire! It's as dry as a popcorn fart with no rain here in over a month! We've already had some roasting-big fires around the county this year. With all the rain either going north or south of us this summer the last thing we need is some fool starting a fire that could get out of hand and burn half the ranch. Assholes!" Jake said angrily.

"Watch your mouth, son," Richard stated calmly. "It's probably just some of hikers wanting to climb up Fisher's Peak, like those others we found last May over on the west side of Sandoval gulch. We'll just go out there, let them know we don't allow trespassing or camping, and send them packing into town, to stay at a hotel somewhere."

Jake's head moved back and forth as he examined the terrain.

"I think for us to get up there, where they're at – we'll have to go down the road here and look for their tracks on the far side of the creek. I don't think we can get there from this side." Jake said, and then began pulling the truck forward.

"You sure you don't want to call the sheriff's out here for this, Dad?"

"Naw, I believe we can handle some kids. You weren't around yet when the hippies were running around here in the 60s and 70s, Jake. We had the occasionally naked pot-smoker roaming around the ranch every once in a while. Your granddaddy and I would have to chase them off every now and then. I think me and you can do the same," Richard said confidently.

Seeing campers on his private property was not a great shock to Richard. Strangers to the modern west often saw open space without any fencing up and thought it must be public land, and then they would just take off where they wanted to go without any consideration for finding out if it might be private. Richard had not been forced to deal with it much over the years since he was blessed with his ranch being several miles away from both I-25 and US 350/160. But, when he did find them, it was usually only people who wanted to get closer to Fisher's Peak.

They made their way slowly along the dirt road for about a half mile until they saw the fresh tire tracks in the loose soil of the bar ditch. Jake turned off the roadway and followed the trail through the dry grass as it went deeper onto the ranch. They bounced their way around the point of a small hill and saw the campfire through the trees, much closer now.

Jake wound the Dodge through the pinions until they got close enough for Richard to see that what he thought was a simple hiker's camp did not look quite right. No tents, RV, or towed camper of any kind. There was a newer model Ford F250 Econoline van with a company logo on the side: AJ Trucking. It was parked next to an old ratty Chevy U-haul truck with a scratched up silver and orange box van that was probably sold at some auction after having a million or more miles of wear and tear put on it. The camp fire sat in a shallow pit in front of the van; behind stood a dark-skinned man leaning against the van's grill. He had a beard, wore a strange cap stretched over the top of his head, and had some sort of robe on that looked like a woman's night shirt. He watched them closely as they pulled up to the camp but he did not move.

The dogs, Toby and Sam, paced restlessly on the flatbed after they saw the fire, whining and snorting in anticipation of something new. Jake pulled the truck up and stopped about twenty feet from the fire with their headlights on the man standing there.

"That's a pretty weird looking hiker, Pop. You and Papa ever see any hippies like this?"

"Nope, I sure haven't, son," Richard replied, while surveying the man who stared back at them evenly. "I'm not sure what to make of this one. But there is more than just this one fella. He didn't get both of these vehicles up here by himself. So play this easy and grab the .30-30 out of the back and keep an eye out, alright?"

"Okay, Pops," Jake said, while he brought up the lever-action rifle from the floor gun rack.

Richard stepped out and the two dogs immediately jumped down and joined their master. The strange man did not react or utter a sound, but just eyed them closely as Richard moved to the front of the Dodge and snapped his fingers, making Toby and Sam halt and sit quietly on each side of his legs.

Jake came up and stood close to his father while holding the rifle in the crook of his left elbow. They both displayed surprise when the man they stared at spoke in an easy Texas drawl.

"Howdy, gentlemen, what can I do for you?" he asked nonchalantly. "Am I trespassing on your land or something?"

Richard was taken aback by more than the stranger's voice, but also by the straightforwardness of his questions. He saw there was more to this guy than what his eyes told him, and so he did not reply right away while he tried to size up the odd stranger. Finally he said, "Well, yes, mister. You are trespassing, but I'm most concerned about the fire there. It's been awful dry around here this year and I don't need you start'n a blaze on my land."

"I'm very sorry, old timer; I didn't mean to cause you any trouble with that small fire. I was only planning on being here for the night and thought I'd start up a little one to keep my feet warm. I'll put it out for you," Ajay said, lying, as he stepped up to the fire, lightly kicking at the dirt next to the flames but not getting any in the fire itself.

Tilting his face up from the fire Ajay gave the rancher a contemptuous stare from under his eyebrows. "Quite frankly, Old-timer, I didn't think I'd be seen by anyone back here, away from the road this far. And, you know, there've been quite a few thunderstorms down our way in Texas. I thought they would've made their way up here and you'd be wetter 'round here."

177

Richard did not like the challenging tone or country-side sarcasm that came from the trespasser from Texas. It was fast becoming apparent that there was nothing good about the man.

"Well, you'd be wrong," Richard said. "Where are your friends?"

"Friends?" Ajay asked, cocking an eyebrow at the old rancher.

Richard frowned with displeasure at the lie.

"You didn't drive both those vehicles up here by yourself, mister. Now, I want you to get your friends out here so we can see all of you, okay?"

"Why, sure, Old-timer," Ajay said as he looked at the old rancher with disappointment.

None of Ajay's banter had worked today. Not with the FBI agent, nor with this old rancher and his shit-kicker kid with the rifle. He needed to kill these two before they could cause any real problems. He gave Richard an evil smirk.

"You're not as dense as the rednecks down in Texas, you old cuss."

Both dogs at Richard's feet squirmed and Toby whined as Richard dug his hands into his pocket, giving Ajay a stern look.

"Do as I say, mister, and be right quick about it."

In a blasé fashion Ajay tilted his head back. Then he suddenly tensed and yelled over his shoulder.

"*Now!*"

Jake was too slow to react like he should have, being focused on watching for someone to come from behind the van. He never would have had a chance in hell if not for the dogs, Sam and Toby, reacting as fast as they did. When Ajay yelled, Sam's sharp canine ears picked up movement out in the darkness of the trees and he barked wildly in that direction. Toby's ears perked up and he tensed like a coiled spring as his head shifted from Ajay to the direction Sam was barking, but they both stayed obediently next to their master.

As Richard saw an evil grin spread across Ajay's face, he knew he did not have much time to act and he yelled, "Go, Sam!" and dog charged like a shot into the dark.

As Jake turned to watch Sam run, a sudden burst of gunfire erupted from where the dog had disappeared, and bullets smashed into the Dodge directly where Jake had just been standing. Although shocked, Jake did not freeze and quickly backpedaled; he was still hit by two slugs in his stomach, which caused him to fold over as he collapsed to his knees.

178

Meanwhile, Richard's hair had been standing on end when Sam took off barking. He had been slightly more ready than his son for something bad to happen, and acted quicker by pulling from his pocket a small pistol he kept there. As the gunfire started from the trees he moved swiftly forward toward Ajay, to close the distance as rapidly as he could. The pistol he pulled out was a small Berretta .25 that he had never gotten a permit to carry, but still hauled around religiously for over thirty years, a handy tool for killing snakes around the ranch. ("It's for both the slithering kind and walking-on-two-legs kind," he always said to those few who knew he kept it.)

Toby had stayed close to his master, even when Sam was ordered to charge, but as Richard moved he yelled, "Toby, go!" and dirt flew as the dog rushed at Ajay, snarling and biting.

Behind them the blast of Jake's .30-.30 rifle told Richard that his son was alive and fighting. He knew that whoever was shooting from the trees had waited in ambush for the order from this Texan, and that hopefully meant that the shooter would stop if Richard closed the distance and got hold of him.

Standing smug seconds before, Ajay was caught completely by surprise at how fast the old man reacted and he was knocked backward by the dog slamming into him. Its sharp white teeth viciously bit into his flesh, and like a furious and furry buzz-saw the animal tore off chunks of his skin and muscle. His mind barely registered the sounds of the boy-rancher's .30-30 rifle rounds that snapped return fire as Jake engaged in a gun battle with Faruk and Aziz, hidden in the pinions.

Ajay blindly backpedaled and his bare feet came out of his sandals as he frantically tried to get away from the frenzied dog. Toby's teeth gripped and tore at anything he could bite, which forced Ajay to try and protect everything from his toes to his face from the ferociously attacking dog. He backed into sagebrush and tripped ass-over-tea-kettle backward into a large batch of prickly-pear cactus.

The pain was excruciating and he screamed as the dog continued rending his flesh, totally oblivious to the cacti. Ajay rolled back and forth in the thorny plants as he fought for his life, with the snarling and biting dog trying to rip out his throat. His repeated high-pitched screams for Aziz and Faruk to help him were useless as the terrible ball of fur and teeth slashed and ripped at his arms and face.

All the while he felt hundreds of two-inch long barbs of cacti become embedded all over. Waves of agony assailed his body and mind as the dog's attack seemed to last an eternity while he recklessly flipped, turned, pulled, and rolled in every direction to escape the large patch of cactus but he still failed to find its edge.

179

Meanwhile, Richard stood close-by, flummoxed, as he watched the writhing mass of the man and dog battling on the ground at his feet. He simply did not know what to do now that Toby and the man were locked together in a death struggle in the cactus patch. The two violently struggled as the dog kept trying for get to the man's throat. Richard could not help the dog, or get any closer to just shoot the man. They were both covered in the barbs from the plants and the barbs only seemed to enrage the dog further, sending Toby into an even more vicious and frenzied attack. There was no way for Richard to get them separated and at his age there was no way he would dare try and muscle either of them.

Suddenly the rat-a-tat volley of gunfire from the trees stopped and he heard Sam's barking. Frantic and startled voices of the men up in the trees began to yell and howl. Faithful Sam had finally found the others and Richard pumped his fist in the air, yelling, "Get'm, boy! Rip them fuckers into a million pieces! Get'm, get'm!"

Richard turned to see where his son was. His eyes fell upon his son, lying in the dirt, clutching at his belly while trying, feebly, to rack the lever on the rifle and load another round into the chamber.

"Jake?" Richard said weakly as he made a step toward his son.

Jake tilted his head, and with a pained expression, looked up from the rifle and met his father's eyes, and groaned in a trembling voice, "Dad, I…."

Richard took another step as a blast of bullets came from off in the darkness, toward the young man and truck behind him. Jake recoiled as a dozen high-powered rounds struck his chest and he fell forward onto his face, dead.

Dust from the powdery dirt was ejected up into the air as Jake's body landed beside the truck, his face hidden under his hat but a growing puddle of dark blood oozed from under the brim, moistening the dry soil. Bubbling blood seeped from the numerous holes in the back of his shirt as his final breath escaped into the night air.

Richard stared in shock at his dead son. He made slow, stumbling steps toward the body while barely holding the small, and now useless, pistol in his hand. He stumbled forward as the sounds of Toby and Sam's vicious life and death fights no longer registered in his ears.

Off in the dark came the sound of more gunfire mixed with Sam's sickening yelp, cut abruptly short. A moment later, Aziz, carrying an AK47 rifle, limped out of the trees and stood at the edge of the light from the Dodge's headlights, leveling his rifle at an unsuspecting Richard who now stood at his son's side.

Sobbing, Richard began to kneel as a half dozen 7.62mm slugs tore into the side of his head and torso, sending him crashing into the side of the truck, where he then fell, lifeless, to the ground.

Faruk came running out of the darkness to where Ajay and Toby were still rolling in cacti. Faruk hesitated to shoot for fear of hitting Ajay, and refused to try to grab the cactus-covered dog. A high-pitched scream pierced the air as Toby bit into Ajay's hand, tearing it to shreds. Ajay yanked at the animal's maw, trying to dislodge his hand while Faruk raised his rifle but could not get an angle for a shot.

Aziz finally reached them, bleeding and limping from his own wounds from Sam. He and Faruk began to pummel Toby with the butt stocks of their rifles, trying to disable the animal that was now fanatically fighting against three enemies. Aziz cursed as he dodged Toby's snapping jaws but was finally able to deliver a solid blow to Toby's skull, hard enough to cause the animal to stumble back a step. The blood-covered dog squared itself to leap, giving a deep growl just before Faruk fired a burst of bullets into him, ending the brave animal's battle.

Faruk panted hard as he gawked at the dead dog. "Are there any more of the devil hounds?" he blurted.

"No, I don't think so," Aziz exclaimed.

He spun in a circle pointing his weapon into the dark, looking for any more demon-dogs that might come and attack their flesh like Sam and Toby had.

"Help me, dammit! Help me!" Ajay yelled, his outstretched arms raised and shaking.

The two men reached out but recoiled after being stuck by the numerous barbs poking out from Ajay's hands.

"Damn you, help me up! I'm covered with them!" Ajay screamed.

With loud cursing and grunts they were finally able to get him standing, and moved into the light from the Dodge's headlights. There they stepped away in shock at the miserable sight of Ajay, who stood rigid, his legs spread wide and his arms held away from his torso, as if he were a ghastly over-the-top imitation of Yosemite Sam, preparing to draw his guns. His face had turned into a perfect mask of explosive rage that was only held in check by excruciating pain.

His teeth were mashed together, his face grossly contorted, covered with sweat and blood-soaked dust turned to mud. The gloppy substance covered everything but his eyes and mouth like some dark and appalling face paint. His upper lip and left cheek quivered with dozens of cactus barbs stuck into his face. A large gash in his neck testified to just how closely Toby had come to ripping out his throat.

His thobe was torn to shreds and hung in tatters from his shoulders. Both his forearms had strips of torn flesh hanging, with rivulets of blood dripping from his fingertips. A mass of hundreds of individual cactus barbs, along with dozens of palm-sized pieces of cactus were stuck into virtually every portion of his body, from his head to his scratched and battered bare feet.

Aziz apprehensively approached Ajay and gingerly raised the front tatters of the thobe.

A trembling Ajay watched both Aziz and Faruk grimace in disgust as they saw large chunks of cactus and hundreds of barbs now embedded into Ajay's inner thighs and genitals. Aziz looked over his shoulder at the dead dog and seethed with fury.

Ajay imagined the dreadful sight between his legs from the excruciating pain that he felt there, and he grunted in a bitter tone. "Get some pliers. Now, quickly!"

Faruk ran to the other side of the van to retrieve the tool and in a short time Aziz was busily plucking each one of the barbs out of the wounded and humiliated Texan-jihadist. All the while Ajay stood quivering, tears of pain and fury streaming down his scarred face as he stared at the corpses of the two dead men and their vicious dogs, who just might have destroyed his perfect plans and dreams.

*****

September 19, 2011 11:46pm MST UTC -7:00
Trinchera Road
Trinidad, Colorado

CONSTANCE TRUJILLO stood with her hands clasped, staring out her kitchen window into the night. The darkness outside seemed to stretch to infinity past the edge of glow given from the yard lights of the ranch house. The driveway leading down from the house bent its way past the horse corrals and pointed due north, toward the vast high-plains of eastern Colorado. Even though the darkness hid from her the familiar landscape, the view down the road extended into the valley for many miles and nowhere did she see lights from an approaching truck or activity of any kind.

As the hours had passed she became ever more worried about Richard and her youngest son being out so late, without a single word as to what may have delayed them.

Did they have trouble with the truck? Are they stuck? Were they still getting cows rounded up in the arroyo after dark? Had Richard's heart acted up and caused another arrhythmia?

182

Jake was a good son and watched over his dad well since the heart attack, and Constance knew that was a full-time job since Richard could be as stubborn as a mule about doing his fair share of the work, and refusing to hire any new hands to help with the ranch until he was 'too old to walk, ma.'

If it were serious trouble they were in tonight, she was sure that Jake would have gotten word to her by now if he could. The ranch only had two hired hands, Will Turney and Jose Baca, and they were up in Pueblo picking up feed and hay and would not be back for another two days. Nonetheless, she had still called and asked them if they had heard anything from Richard or Jake, but they had not.

Jose offered to head down tonight and go out looking for them but she told him to stay and get their work done before heading home. But she had decided that she would call the sheriff if they did not show up soon.

She worked at her rosary nervously, kneading the beads between her fingers as she recited a prayer. Richard had never done this before but she still desperately held onto the belief that something simple had occurred. The truck might have broken down, or they might have gotten it stuck somewhere back in the 'toolies' where they loved to go four-wheeling. She was sure they would be just fine and soon she would watch them driving up the road, to then come walking through the door to tell her some tall tale of their heroics against some great trouble. Then the two would laugh and snort good-naturedly at how she had worried, pacing up and down while waiting nervously for them to get home safe. Then, she would chuckle herself and her sweet Richard would be there for her to hold onto.

But something felt different and secretly nagged at her. No, not different, the whole thing just felt wrong. Her fingers were colder and her spirit lower than they should have been. She tried to lift her hopes but felt the troublesome weight of angst pull against them, which threatened to send her into a pool of despair.

A deep fear had settled over her heart and she heard every bone of her seventy-year old body creak when she moved. She felt very old. Weakness seeped into her limbs and she was more alone than she could ever remember being in her life. She was very deeply afraid.

The house cat, Tally, paced back and forth, rubbing against her legs as it meowed for attention. The fat old cat could feel her worry and sought to comfort her, or maybe, because of what it sensed, it wanted to be comforted by her.

The old frontier house, built over a hundred years ago by Juan Trujillo and his Apache bride, sat in a brooding silence that was so complete that she heard clearly the faint movements of tiny metal

183

gears as the wall clock gave a count to the slow minutes that passed by. Tally gave a questioning meow and hum as he rubbed her calf repeatedly. Constance stared into the dark night air and decided that she would give them until 1:00 a.m., and then she would call for a deputy.

Book Two – THE PERFECT DAY
Tuesday, September 20, 2011

"He is one of those people who would be enormously improved by death."
H.H. Munro – *Saki*

*****

02:07am MST UTC -7:00
Bon Carbo, Colorado

JIM LIKED the old days. The good old days when he was younger, when his life, the community, and the whole county was simpler and easier to understand. In the old days, before the county population grew with so many new people who were making the exodus from the big cities in California, New York, and points elsewhere. Before the suburbanites from around the nation grew tired of the great American rat-race and came here to escape that lifestyle and buy up their own 30-acre patch of 'God's Country' in the Rocky Mountains.

In the old days Jim never would have been forced to deal with a scrawny asshole like Pervis Walker. Jim had known his share of toughs, jerks, and assholes during his career, before the diasporas from America's cities brought in elitist people like Mr. Walker. In the old days, the people that Jim and his father had known were all born and bred from local stock or came from the same kind of towns and communities as were here in rural southern Colorado. These new people were too needy and they all had a different view of life, with nothing ever being simple and straightforward. Jim and his father had come from very different backgrounds than the likes of pinheads like Pervis Walker. The clash of those cultures was something Deputy "Big Jim" Griego had to deal with on a regular basis nowadays, whereas he figured that his father had not had such problems in the past when he worked the streets and country roads of Las Animas County.

Right now that had Jim in a bit of a tight spot and he was not at all happy about it. As his partner bounced the police cruiser down the rippled county road of Riley Canyon, adding one wonderful mile after another to the distance between Jim and Mr. Walker, Jim felt better but not happier. And his headache did not soften as he remembered the recent sound of the shrill, pansy-ass voice of Pervis

185

Walker, as Jim collected information for his report at the Walker household a few minutes ago.

"Goddamnit, Deputy! I want that dangerous bastard behind bars now!" Walker screamed, as a vein in his balding head pulsed noticeably.

"He almost ran my daughter down like road-kill! Then, then he shoots a damn gun at me, too! This isn't New York City, and it isn't fucking Somalia, either! Are you telling me that all my taxes get nothing more from you and your redneck department than this?"

The disdain in Walker's expression could not have conveyed higher indignation than it did right then, with glossy wide-eyes and a deep frown, as he pointed his bony finger at Jim's face.

Jim smelled the whiskey on Walker's breath and knew the guy was three-sheets-to-the-wind, drunk, standing there yelling. Normally, Jim would not take this crap from some uppity little guy like Walker, but this guy had a wad of cash and that meant one simple thing. He had money for lawyers, a bunch of them, well-paid and good at being obedient shitheads. Jim could bully most folks with his badge and large size but lawyers did not get bullied easily by small town sheriff deputies.

"Listen, Mr. Walker, all I'm saying is that Lonnie Garcia is known for being a drunk and bar fighter but he ain't known for starting problems like this," Jim said politely.

"Well, I don't give one rat's ass what he's known for, Deputy. All I know is that he shot at me a couple dozen times before I barely got out of there with my life! And -- and my daughter – my poor daughter is sitting right there, bleeding, *bleeding* from the wreck that *old drunk caused*! So, it seems to *me*, that you have plenty of *evv-eee-dence* to go and arrest him and haul his ass to jail," Walker screamed with dripping sarcasm.

Jim looked down at Walker's fifteen-year old daughter, Jennifer, who sat next to her mother Renee on the custom leather sofa, cupping her left arm in a towel with two Ziploc bags filled with ice and crying quietly. She dabbed her eyes with a wad of scrunched up tissue and was obviously hurting from several good scrapes on her elbow. But Jim still knew it was a minor wreck, because if a person wrecked an ATV like she said she had, and only came away with a couple of scratches, it was a minor wreck. Broken, mangled, and possibly DOA were the usual adjectives used in ATV wrecks of any substance. So he figured her little run off the road was not nearly as big of a deal as her father was trying to make it out to be.

Not that Jim necessarily doubted anything she had said earlier about what happened out on the road, but people always related their

186

side of things from their personal perspective on what they did or saw, or at least what they thought they did and saw. She was obviously scared and he was positive that she had not lied about how Garcia had grabbed her right arm. Those deep red bruises on her upper arm's bicep outlined the form of fingers perfectly, which pretty much proved that part of her story. Jim only saw those kinds of bruises on battered women who had either gotten thumped on or thrown around by a man.

He was very interested to hear what lame excuses old Lonnie Garcia would give for having put marks like that on her arm. As far as the shooting went, Jim was fairly certain that the little prick Walker had been as much at fault as Garcia for what happened between the two of them. When Jennifer came in crying after her run-in with Garcia, Walker drove down the road in a huff and challenged the cantankerous old Vietnam-era marine. Walker had apparently gotten a lot more than he had bargained for with his ill-considered idea.

Jim looked out the large living-room windows of the expansive, custom-built log home, and saw his partner, Deputy Billy Lucas, returning from locating and investigating the scene out on the road where the whole mess had occurred. Jim waited quietly as his partner parked their police 2004 Ford Expedition next to Walker's shiny 2011 Cadillac Escalade and came sauntering toward the front door, adjusting his sheriff's cowboy hat on his head.

Billy entered as Jim asked, "Well, Billy, what did it look like?"

Billy gave a curt nod.

"It matches up with her story just fine, Big Jim," he replied. "It looks like it all happened about a half-mile down the road at that last switchback before you drop down into the canyon. There were some skids goin' both ways from the girl's ATV and Garcia's old truck."

He paused and scratched at the back of his neck.

"Looks like there'll be some new damage to that old Dodge of Garcia's. He hit a big pine tree down there and it busted up a headlight. There were glass shards and what looks like a vehicle's turn signal covering lying on the ground there."

Billy paused, looking down at Walker's daughter, who looked sullenly straight-ahead and not at Billy.

"Is there something else, Billy? Jim asked.

"Well, by the way I read the skids, Big Jim, it seems that the girl mighta cut that blind curve pretty tight and that she was in the oncoming lane. It looks to me, anyhow, that if Garcia hadn't swerved real hard, she might've ended up implanted in the grill of that old Dodge. Her swerve sent her into the ditch on her side, off into the

187

brush. It all seems pretty clear to me, that the girl cut'n the corner is what started the whole incident."

He still watched Jennifer as he finished, and she was now staring quietly at her toes, her mother staring at her.

"Now you hold on, Deputy, my daughter didn't cause this! I…."

Jim cut him off.

"Listen up, Mr. Walker. It doesn't matter much to me right now whether she was out of her travel lane or not. There aren't any lanes painted out there on that gravel, anyhow. But I'll point out a fact to you. By YOU letting her drive on the county road on that ATV automatically puts her driving illegally on the road from the very get-go! So just calm yourself down there, mister. What I'm concerned with is Jennifer getting hurt and Garcia shooting at you tonight."

"That's just fine, *Dep-u-tee* Griego. That's why I want you to arrest that man tonight!" Walker stepped closer to Jim, inflating himself with as much bravado as his little body could muster and jutted his finger at Jim's face.

"The sooner you get to do your job – the better off you and *your* job will be!"

That was enough for Jim. He was filled to the top with irritation and could not control himself any longer. He took two large strides forward and lowered his face to within inches of Walker's, so that their noses were almost touching, and backed the man into the table at the edge of the sofa. Walker's pointed finger shriveled up as his arm fell loosely to his side.

Jim spoke in a low voice, "Mr. Walker, I've had just about enough of your shithead attitude tonight. You want in one hand and crap in the other and see which one fills up first. Now, how about I hook your little ass up in cuffs right now, take you along when I pick up Garcia, and shove the both of you into a cell at the jail and let the two of you work out your issues face-to-face? What do you think of that idea?"

Walker understood that the deputy was not making an idle threat. He clearly saw in the big man's eyes that he meant what he said and even Walker's internal anger was not enough to overcome his common sense in dealing with such a large man. He quickly decided to back down for the moment, but he knew that someday soon he was going to teach this big dumb Mexican SOB the lesson to never mess with Pervis Walker.

Finally Walker said awkwardly, "Fine. Okay, you make the decisions, Deputy Griego. But, I've made my wishes clear to you and your subordinate here. As a taxpayer of this county I expect you to do your job."

Jim held all the cards in a physical confrontation with the little man and imagined how pleasing it would be to pinch off this guy's air supply and watch his eyes bulge in their sockets. He could only push so far and if he pushed too hard on a guy like this, it would soon be Pervis Walker who would be holding all the cards on Big Jim. Even having your dad the elected sheriff of the county was no guarantee that Jim would not pay a high price for being too stupid here tonight. He saw the bitterness barely concealed behind the man's eyes, and could tell that this guy would just love to have Jim in that position, too.

Next to them Jennifer desperately pleaded, "Please don't hurt my daddy, sir. It is MY fault that this happened and I'm sorry. I was in a hurry to get home and I cut the turn and caused that man to crash. He just scared me so much when he yelled at me. I thought he was going to hit me. Please don't hurt my daddy because of me."

Jim softened immediately looking down at the child. He stepped back, giving her dad a little space so he could at least stand up straight and get some dignity back. He wanted to let the girl feel better but he still wanted her father to feel his very close and looming presence. He thought of his own daughter, Maggie, and how she also looked so vulnerable when she cried.

"Relax, girl, I'm not hurting anyone, your pa and I are just trying to get an understanding between us," Jim said. "And you don't worry about fault. I'll check this whole thing out and we'll go from there. But you have to understand – no man has any business grabbing you like that, ever," he said pointing to her arm.

He looked over at Billy and indicated they were leaving.

"My partner and I are going to go pick Mr. Garcia up and have a chat with him at the jail about all this."

He turned to follow Billy out the door but stopped and spoke to the girl's mother.

"Ma'am, I'll need you to email me those photos of your daughter's arms and also her statement tonight, okay? I'll need them for the judge to see first thing in the morning."

"Yes, Deputy. I'll send them to you at the address on your business card." Renee Walker gave a sideways glance at her husband and then reached forward and touched the deputy's arm. "I want to thank you for your help, officer, please be careful."

"Thank you, ma'am. I'll call you later if we don't locate Mr. Garcia. But I'm sure he'll be at his family's old house. Good night," Jim said. *Easier said than done, Jimbo!*

189

Billy and Jim climbed into the cruiser and Billy looked over at Jim. "Big Jim, there's one thing I didn't want to say inside."

"Yeah? What is it, Billy?"

"Well, I just figured that if I mentioned blood it'd just get the fur on that mangy asshole in there even more ruffled up than it already was, you know."

"Yeah, I know, I appreciate that. Now you say there's blood? What blood?"

"I saw them tiny scratches on that girl before I headed down there to the crash site and I knew they didn't bleed hardly enough to even cause a scab. So when I got down there and got to looking around I saw quite a bit of blood on the ground with several fresh beer cans tossed in the grass. My guess is that old Lonnie got himself cut up on something during the accident and bled out a bit."

"Interesting, I think you were right not to mention it to pinion-nuts in there. He'd have made some BS claim, I bet. Good job, Billy."

They drove down the winding canyon road, watching for Lonnie's truck pulled over somewhere along the way. They stopped briefly at the scene of the accident so Jim could see for himself everything Billy had described earlier. It also seemed clear to Jim from the tracks in the dirt that the girl had indeed cut Garcia off going around the corner and they had both swerved hard to miss one another.

Cutting corners short was a normal manner of driving out here on the rural county roads and did not surprise Jim, especially since a person could drive all day on these interconnecting mountain roads and rarely see more than two or three vehicles every half hour or so at any given point. Most of the residents who lived up here, and who could afford it, let their kids run around on ATVs to see one another since they usually lived miles apart and the ATVs were more fun to scoot around on and were cheaper on fuel than taking a bigger vehicle.

As they surveyed the accident scene they kept an eye out for spent gun shells but did not see any. Jim was certain old Lonnie would not pick them up so he figured the old man had probably used a revolver. The idea of the good ol' boy having a handgun in his vehicle did not surprise Jim either, considering he knew Lonnie carried at least one rifle up in the window rack of that old Dodge pickup truck he drove around in, and he surely had more. But they did find the busted turn light, and also six fresh Tecate beer cans scattered around the area where Lonnie's blood had sprinkled on the grass.

"I'll bet my virginity that he's pretty soused after downing those beers and bleeding out like that," Billy commented as he looked around at the beer cans.

"Humppft! You've got no virginity to bet, Billy, and I wouldn't want it anyhow."

"Hey, I didn't have any when I bet it with Sally before we got married. But she was at least willing to take on the bet," Billy said, grinning.

"Yeah, well, Sally is a good girl, Billy, but I have to say that she is the only girl I know that would've taken that bet! So I'd count you blessed," Jim said, smiling back. "But I bet you're right about Garcia being drunk. You know, I think that may just be the advantage we need to safely hook his ass up tonight. Are you up for it?"

"I'm right with ya, partner."

Minutes later the gravel rumbled as the road passed under their tires, marking their passage through the pitch-black night with nothing to see other than the view provided by the headlights. Occasionally they saw yard lights at various farms and residences along the way down the canyon but as they neared Lonnie's house there were no lights. Billy slowed as they went by the driveway entrance and all Jim saw through the gloom was that shape of Lonnie's truck parked at the top.

"Did you see the truck up there, Billy?"

"I did," Billy replied. "Are we still going to go up there tonight, Big Jim? You don't think we should wait for daylight?"

"I think tonight will be best. I know I sure don't want to be going up against a sober ornery cuss like him in the day light. I think it'll be better to do it in the dark. We can just park down around the bend, out of sight, and like ninjas, walk our butts back up and catch him sleeping off his drunk and avoid going head-on with that old marine when he has his wits about'im."

"Okay. If that's what you think is best, let's do it."

They eased down the road a half mile until they were out of sight of Lonnie's house. Parking, Billy grabbed the shotgun from its rack while Jim only brought his Colt .45, since he would be the one putting the handcuffs on and Billy would cover with the scattergun. They walked slowly back up the road, making crunching noises as they plodded through the gravel. The time it took to get to the house allowed their eyes to get fully adjusted to the darkness.

As faint shapes against the shadowy background of the hillside passed, he heard coyotes yipping and yapping in chorus in the far distance up the canyon. Once at the driveway they slowly approached the house. The hair on Jim's neck was up and he cringed

191

at every noise they made, as it seemed magnified, reverberating through the quiet night air. They eventually reached Lonnie's truck, parked behind a couple of other beater vehicles closer to the house. Jim felt for heat from the engine as he ran the back of his hand along the truck's grill and he computed that it must have been parked for at least an hour or more. The smell of oil on the crankcase was strong; he briefly tried to inspect the broken headlight but it was too dark to see anything useful.

Fear is a cold sensation that Jim felt deeply inside his guts, staring at the hulking shape of the old house. Even now, nearing 3:00am, it was a comfortable night, only in the low seventies, but his body still gave a shiver as a thin icy-vein of fear crept up and down his spine while he waited motionless and listening to his surroundings. He tried unsuccessfully to shake off the feeling of being watched and that every sound he made was being heard by the entire world. The tingle of trepidation he felt was like the cold, thin edge of a sharp knife being drawn slowly down the skin of his back. It felt bad, real bad. Jim was more nervous and fearful now than he had been in a very long time. His idea had turned out to be a bad one, he knew it, and it was too late to correct it.

A small bead of sweat started near Jim's hairline and slowly zigged and zagged a trail along the ridges of his forehead. He thought it strange to feel like he was freezing inside, yet outside he was sweating like a sun-baked tourist on a Jamaican beach. For a second, it seemed like the bead of sweat would stop, but instead it bounced off his eyebrow onto the ridge of his nose and did a quick dodge back into the corner of his eye, burning and stinging. He abruptly raised his hand to wipe his eye and hit himself square on the nose with his flashlight.

"Shit!" he angrily whispered through clenched teeth, as little bright stars of pain sparkled and then faded before his eyes.

His exclamation was immediately followed by a hushed croak from Billy who stood a few steps behind him with his shotgun held at the low ready. "What? You okay, Big Jim?"

"Yeah, yeah," Jim whispered embarrassed. "Now hold on and be quiet, Billy."

Jim's nose throbbed and he wondered briefly if he was bleeding from it. He was not prone to getting bloody noses easily, like his baby girl, but he had knocked his nose good and it hurt like hell. The salty sweat in his eye stung as well. With much more care this time, he brought up his hand and wiped at his eye.

Blinking out the sting, Jim scanned ahead but could not discern much detail as a few feeble stars were the only light. Jim did make out the dim outlines of several junk cars parked next to one another before the looming shape of the house. He craned his neck around and saw scattered car parts, lumber and other assorted trash all around him. Lonnie's yard had evidently avoided any spring cleaning for several decades. He thought he could also make out a fenced area toward the back but it was hard to count on anything being what he thought it might be without practically touching it to be sure. He even lifted his feet higher than normal just to make sure he did not trip on something.

From memory, Jim knew the dilapidated old adobe house had gone without repairs or upkeep for years. The old house had probably been sitting since the 1800s and would be cold in the winter and hot in the summer. Jim seriously considered turning and leaving but he hesitated, thinking that if he and Billy could just walk up there, nice and easy, and slip the cuffs on his drunken-ass right now, it would be safer than trying it in broad daylight.

To get to the steps leading to the front door they were forced between the junk cars. Once through, they still needed to climb the seven or eight steps to the door. He kept scanning the house windows for any sign of life inside but saw and heard nothing. The windows appeared covered with old sheets or blankets which had not moved. The whole place was as silent and still as a graveyard.

Jim focused on the house but cocked his head to the side and whispered, "Billy, you follow me up, and once we get to the bottom of those steps, you park your butt down at the corner there at the bottom. I'll go on up to the door. You got that?"

"You got it, Big Jim. You just watch your ass going up to that door."

"I hear that."

Jim tightened his grip on the pistol in his right hand, making sure his thumb was resting on the safety, ready to put the gun into action at a moment's notice. The heavy weapon usually was a comfort but the sweat on his palm made it feel squishy and wet. His flashlight gripped tightly in his left, he took a breath, exhaled, and began to move slowly forward.

Jim's 6'5", 265lb frame fit snugly between the two cars, barely able to get through without rubbing or scraping his duty gear along the metal. There was plenty of reason why he was called Big Jim and he needed to get that large muscular mass up to the door without making any noise. He inched his way forward and was just about halfway past the vehicle when his ears picked up the faint sounds of shuffling movement that came from the back of the house.

In the next second several things seemed to happen all at once, and, like an avalanche of rocks coming down a mountainside, there was no stopping the bad coming down on Jim as things went from bad to worse. Instantly that cold knife-edge of fear that had been stroking his spine now suddenly plunged deep into his guts.

The first thing that happened was that both deputies were completely blinded by stunning white light emitted by two extremely bright exterior floodlights attached to the old house. The next thing was the loud barking and snarling of several dogs barely twenty feet away in the backyard.

Jim quickly swung himself in the direction of the animals, pointing his pistol toward what he fully expected to see; a frenzied pack of dogs with biting teeth charging at him. He pushed down the safety on the Colt and activated his flashlight, ready to kill the first dog he saw. But to his surprise, and overwhelming relief, he indeed saw a frenzied pack of dogs but they were safely contained behind a chain-link fence that bulged and strained as they jumped at it.

Just as Jim's brain registered this threat as contained, he heard Billy's squealing whisper, "The door, the fucking door!"

Jim swung his bulk back toward the steps and was once again blinded by the dazzling light as everything seemed to go into slow motion. While this visceral effect hit his vision, his stressed mind caused another strange effect to occur: the sounds of the barking and snarling dogs were tuned down to a barely noticeable background noise. And although he still clearly heard Billy's voice off to his left, it had oddly slowed and sounded like it came from down a long tunnel. Jim also noticed that Billy's normally masculine voice had changed to that of a high-pitched girl, yelling undecipherable gibberish about a gun.

His heart pounded at a seemingly thousand-beats-a-minute, causing his blood to thump loudly in his ears. Jim's eyes focused on what little they could see in the bright light; he found himself looking straight down the barrel of a shotgun, pointed directly at his head, not more than ten feet from the front of his nose. The barrel of the shotgun appeared more like a naval cannon barrel from a battleship than the 12-gauge it was. Jim squinted against the bright light and made out the shape of a large man who stood less than halfway out the front door of the house. He immediately recognized the man as Lonnie Garcia, even with his scruffy face and scraggly hair.

"Don't you move, you sons-a-bitches or I'll blow your asses straight to hell!" Lonnie yelled.

Both Jim and Billy simultaneously yelled back at him, "Drop your gun, drop your gun!"

Jim detected an odd high-toned pitch to his own voice that he did not like as he tried to find some part of Lonnie to aim his pistol at.

But Lonnie only showed a small portion of his body outside the frame of the door and the glare from the lights made him a very hard target to see.

"Fuck if I'll drop this gun, you sumbitches. I never hurt yer little girl none, you asshole! So just clear out now or I'll kill your fuck'n ass like I could'a done earlier, ya prick," was Lonnie's slurred reply.

"He said, drop the fucking gun, you fucker! Do it now or I'll shoot!" Billy yelled, crouching behind one old car and trying to move around to the left to get a better angle on Lonnie.

Lonnie swung the barrel of the shotgun toward Billy, causing him to duck behind the car while Lonnie barked, "You little prick. You come up from behind that old Dodge again and I'll scalp your fuck'n head with my twelve-gauge!"

Billy moved one way and then another as he tried to raise high enough to see Lonnie, and each time he moved the barrel of the shotgun followed him.

"You keep squirm'n around down there and you'll make me nervous, now raise yer hands where I can see'em!" Lonnie ordered.

Jim's finger pressed harder against the trigger of his pistol but he had absolutely nothing but the barrel of the shotgun and a little of Lonnie's nose to shoot at. If he missed and Lonnie opened up with that scattergun, Jim was sure that someone down on the ground was going to die.

"Don't shoot! Put your gun down, dammit!" he screamed.

Lonnie swung the barrel of the shotgun back at Jim, saying, "You couldn't come at me like a man by yourself, huh? Well, that's just fine by me, you fucker! You wanna leave that girl an orphan tonight, that's your fuck'n choice."

Jim was puzzled at Lonnie's words, but he was not puzzled about one thing; he found himself square in the middle of a well-laid trap. He thought he was being clever by sneaking up to the house but all he had actually accomplished was walk with eyes wide-open into beautifully planned fatal-funnel.

His law enforcement academy teachers warned about it repeatedly, his father had stressed it again and again as he taught him over the years to watch out for them everywhere he went in this job. Even his granddad had warned of it when he described how easily he had mowed down Germans in the trenches of Flanders in World War I with his 'trench broom' – a Thompson sub-machine gun.

Lonnie had great cover and concealment in the adobe frame of the front door, and with ten feet of elevation it was easy for him to survey everything in the yard below. The lights were perfectly positioned to flood light down upon anyone coming up and also effectively blocked their view of him. The short distance from the door to the two junk cars funneled the only access to the house through a narrow gap, making it virtually impossible for him to miss hitting someone with a blast from his shotgun. The dogs had obviously been well trained, to keep silent until a person reached the house before they finally made for a noisy and scary distraction. Jim figured the two junk cars were probably planted here for many years with just barely enough room between them to let a person fit through without his hips rubbing against the fenders.

Jim was trapped with no way to retreat, advance, or move side to side without making an even better target. The old Vietnam vet standing over him had thought hard and set up his home defense very well many years before tonight. *I'll bet that SOB had this trap set up before I was out of diapers! You are one fucking cooked goose standing here, Jim, old boy!*

Jim prayed that he could talk his way out of the bad spot he was in. Jim lowered his voice from a yell and spoke as evenly as possible.

"Lonnie Garcia. I am with the sheriff's department. Now drop your gun. I don't want to have to shoot you."

Lonnie squinted and jutted his head out an inch or so to try and get a better look.

"Sheriffs? Shnneaking up here in the dark like some VC bashturd? That ain't like no sheriffs I know, you lying sumbitch! Now, your girl ain't hurt, so you get your ass pack'n back up the road to that fancy-shmancy digs of yours or I'm going to plant your ass and make you fertilizer for my flowers, asshole!"

Jim's irritation started to override his fear.

"This *is* the sheriff's department and I'm Sergeant Griego. Now drop your gun or I'm going to kill your ass!"

Jim's voice had lost the squeak it had a few seconds earlier as frustration crept into it now. That change caught Lonnie's attention and the marine said in a calm, cold voice that chilled Jim's veins.

"Oh? You're gonna kill me?"

He paused as he increased the pressure on the shotgun's trigger.

"If you really are Sheriff Griego's boy – well, mister, you're a helleva lot dumber that I woulda ever guessed one o' his sons could be. The only ones who might be dying tonight is your dumb ass and whoever this other fart'n-da-wind you brought with you is."

Over the years, Jim was called a lot of things by people he arrested but one thing no one had ever called him before tonight was 'kid.' Lonnie had suddenly turned cold in his delivery and Jim sensed that Lonnie's decision to kill him or would be decided by what Jim said next.

In a calm, slow tone Jim spoke, "Now, Lonnie, I *am* Sheriff Griego's son. My name is Jim and I've seen you around my whole life," he hesitated, letting the words sink into the man's drunken mind. "Lonnie, I'm here to arrest you for what happened up the road earlier with the girl on the ATV. So I'm asking you to put that shotgun down. If you don't – I swear, either my partner or I will be forced kill you."

Jim squinted against the intense light in his eyes and did his best to get an accurate bead on Lonnie as he nervously waited for some response from the old man that did not include Jim's head being blown off his shoulders. The next few seconds of waiting felt like months and the reply was not at all what he expected.

The meanness in Lonnie's tone melted away and morphed into surprised indignation. With a sneer of complete contempt Lonnie said, "Kill me, huh? Hmmpft, whatever you say, kid. Anybody as dumb as you must be a fuck'n cop."

The barrel of his shotgun lowered to point at the ground.

"All I can see of you is your little pop guns and the damn light from your flashlights in my eyes. Let me see your badges, if you are who you say you are."

Jim comprehended just how badly he had screwed up in the making of his little plan, now a total fiasco. Chagrined and utterly humiliated he sighed, "Okay."

"Big Jim, what the hell are you doing?" Billy whispered.

"Easy, Billy, easy, you just keep your gun on him."

Jim turned his flashlight off and lowered his pistol so his uniform and badge were fully exposed for Lonnie to see unobstructed.

"Okay, Lonnie, you believe me now?" he sheepishly asked, feeling every bit the proverbial fish in the barrel.

Lonnie gave out a long shrill whistle.

"Damn, boy! You *are* one dumb sumbitch, son! I almost done kill'd you for sneak'n up here on me. Just what in the hell were you a think'n in that pigeon-brain, boy?" he declared.

"Well, evidently, my brain wasn't thinking very well tonight, sir. Now will you please put that gun of yours away so we can talk?" Jim asked.

Lonnie stepped out onto the stairs, his eyes darted to Jim, then Billy, and his chin began to tremble. Lonnie's squared shoulders slumped as he let go of the shotgun, letting it hang limply from his left hand, the tip of the barrel touching the wooden step. His whole body appeared to shrink, and Jim thought he was just about to start crying.

197

Jim also noticed that Lonnie had put a bandage on his forearm which had fresh blood soaked through it.

"There've been way too many heart attacks in one night for this old man," Lonnie croaked in a low voice.

"Lonnie, please put the gun down."

Lonnie looked up at the stars, back down at Jim and then leaned the shotgun against the door frame, saying, "I take it you want me down there, huh?"

"Yes, sir, come on down to me easy and we can talk, okay?"

Lonnie walked down the steps and yelled for his dogs to stop barking.

"Quiet, dogs. Jesus, Chico, Banta, be quiet! It's alright, boys," he said firmly but affectionately.

With that simple command the dogs immediately stopped barking and calmed considerably, but still continued to whine and pace as they kept a suspicious watch on Jim and Billy. Those dogs were trained but Jim thought he saw, for just a moment, something more in Lonnie's bearing, something more akin to nobility than Jim could have imagined possible, considering Lonnie's intoxication and scruffy appearance. *This guy is a strange one to read.* Lonnie reached the bottom of the stairs and stared Jim in the eye.

Lonnie was a big man in his own right and stood eye-to-eye with the cop, which was a rarity with Jim. Lonnie glanced over Jim's shoulder at Billy who was busy grunting and cussing as he untangled himself from some scrub oak he had gotten into while trying to position himself to get a clearer shot at Lonnie. Lonnie grinned at the deputy's discomfort and then looked back at Jim, waiting for some direction.

Jim sized him up for a few more seconds before he said, "I'm going to take you to jail for what happened with the girl up the road earlier tonight, Mr. Garcia. She's got bruising from where you grabbed her arm. You had no business layin' a hand on her like that. You scared the crap outta that kid."

"Scared? Yeah, I suppose she would be scared considering she damn near got herself killed tonight," Lonnie asserted.

"Goddammit! You saying you'd a killed that child for you running into that tree? Why, you worthless drunk! What the fuck is a matter with you?" Billy exclaimed indignantly.

Exasperation covered Billy's face as he dusted oak leaves from his now disheveled uniform shirt, having somehow been pulled up and out of his waistband in his fight with the brush. Billy looked every bit a man who had lost his fight with the tree while trying to get

198

untangled. Jim wanted to snicker at the sight but he kept a straight face.

"That's not what I said, peckerwood," Lonnie responded, addressing Billy in a calm matter-of-fact tone. "She damn near killed herself by her piss-poor driving! Cut'n me off 'round that corner and all. If I hadn't ta ran off the road into that tree she'd be plant'd into the grill o' my truck!"

"Well, I understand that Mr. Garcia, and I agree. But that doesn't give you any right to grab her so hard she's now got bruises on her arms. Hell, I can damn near read your fingerprint pattern in those marks you left, grabbed her so hard," Jim interjected.

Lonnie's face softened slightly and he looked at the ground.

"I, I guess I don't have anything to say to that. I was just so scared that she coulda been kill'd running off into that ditch. When I ran over there, expect'n to see her all chewed up – and then I saw she was up and walk'n! I just saw red and blew my top."

He paused and shrugged.

"My heart was jump'n in my chest and I just boiled o'er and started yell'n." He looked up at Jim and asked, "In all honesty, I don't even remember grab'n her too hard. Is she alright?"

"I think she'll be okay and maybe she can chalk up a good life lesson from the whole thing, but tonight you got to come with us. So I need to put you in cuffs now, but first I need to take a look at that arm. How'd you get cut?"

Lonnie absentmindedly looked down at his arm.

"Oh, that? Oh hell – the knob on the window crank has been long gone. I scraped up my arm a little on it when I hit that tree. It'll be fine."

"Well, it looks worse than that to me and it'll need to be looked at by a doctor before we get to the jail," Jim said as he holstered his weapon. "Hang your arms out here in front. I'm not having you pressing against that arm behind you while we drive to town."

Lonnie slowly raised his arms with his hands close together and Jim put on his handcuffs and then started a pat search. As he made his way around the big man's body he asked, "Lonnie, just who'd you think we were when we first came up here?"

"The way you came sneak'n up here – I sure didn't think you were sheriffs, that's for sure. I thought you mighta been that girl's prick-father com'n up here for payback or something."

He looked over his shoulder at Jim as the deputy patted around his groin area.

"You be careful down in that territory, boy – there's a snake down there, so don't get bit," he said with a smirk.

"Ha, ha – I never heard that one before. I'll try and keep that in mind, old-timer."

"Just what was your dumbass think'n a com'n up here like you're VC, boy?"

"Uh, I'll admit that turned out to be a pretty stupid idea on my part. I apologize for that. I wasn't sure how to get up here and arrest you safely so I figured I'd catch you napping drunk and it backfired on me."

"Listen up, boy, anytime you want to talk to me – you just pull up in your sheriff's car and hit those red-'n-blues. That way I know who you are and then we can sit and talk over coffee. I ain't afraid a pay'n for my mistakes and I'd never hurt you for doing your job. But you can sure get y'rself hurt quick by being a dumbass 'round me, and I ain't joke'n 'bout that," Lonnie slurred.

"I'll remember that for next time, mister." Jim turned to Billy, saying, "Billy, go get the cruiser, okay?"

"Sure, Jim, I'll be right back." Billy quickly disappeared into the dark.

While Billy was gone Jim started getting information for the report. He quickly found out that Lonnie had pulled a small .22 revolver he kept under the truck seat for 'emergencies' on Walker. He said he did it to get him to back off after he showed up, screaming and hollering, with a baseball bat in his hands. Lonnie said after the gun got pulled, the guy took off running and Lonnie just could not help but pop off a couple of rounds into the air to see just how fast he could get the guy to run. Jim chuckled as Lonnie told the story and had no problem telling the ex-marine that he wished he could have seen it.

Lonnie chuckled. "Yeah, it probably wasn't the smartest thing, but I didn't like his attitude none and I ended up pop'n off those couple o' rounds over his head for fun. That little shit sure picked his feet up right quick and got to move'n his uptight ass real good. Hell, I thought he might shit himself, the way he ducked around and went dive'n for the door of that fancy rig of his. After he left I downed a few beers to calm my nerves and headed home."

"Then I was just a sit'n here, chase'n down a last cold one to calm my rattled nerves some more when I looked out and see headlights a pass'n by down there real slow. I thought that maybe that little prick wanted some more o' me. So I hunkered down in there and the pups soon let me know someone was a com'n up the drive. Next thing ya know I got you at the end of that ol' scattergun, screaming at me to give myself up."

"Is the revolver in the truck still? I'll need to collect that."

"Go ahead and grab it, son, it's under the front seat." Lonnie eyed Jim closely. "But I want it back after this is done, understand?"

"I'll have to let the judge decide that one but I'll see what I can do. You popping those rounds off at that fella is the main reason I tried to sneak up here like I did," Jim lamented. "It seemed out of character for what I knew of you and I thought maybe you'd fell off your rocker."

With no humor Lonnie said calmly, "Boy, I'll be responsible for my mistakes but I ain't take'n no blame for your piss-poor ideas. I ain't talked to you since you were a little kid but I figured your pa could raise you smarter. He's a good man and has made a good sheriff, and he wouldn't be that dumb."

"I suppose not," Jim replied, annoyed, while he looked around in the cab of Lonnie's truck for the gun.

"When Chico and the boys let me know you were out here and I almost came out blast'n. You can say yer prayers of thanks tonight that I showed restraint like I did."

Jim picked up the revolver and checked the cylinders to see how many rounds were still in it.

"I'll keep that in mind when I get home and get a kiss from my baby girl, mister. Quite frankly, it sounds more than a bit paranoid to me that you'd think that Walker would come all the way down here after you," shot back Jim, with irritation at being critiqued so harshly by the drunk old man.

"Well, then, you don't know what another human is capable of, boy. I do. I've seen more than my share of shit, kid, and if you ever get VC hunt'n your butt you'll know what I mean."

"VC – you mean Vietcong? You don't think there are Vietcong out here, do you?"

"The *Vee-at-cong* is a group of black pajama-wearing gooks back in Vietnam! Tough, mean sumbitchs, too! The *Vee-Cee* is what I call the mindset of the 'cong and something far worse," Lonnie said angrily. "A mindset that would o' blown your empty pea-brain all over this driveway if I woulda been VC! That Walker, he's a small guy and lives soft off all his money, but make no mistake, he's bad inside. He's VC to his core. Mark my words."

Lonnie glowered at Jim for a couple seconds until his steam cooled, then he lowered his head and sat quietly, ignoring any further attempts by Jim to talk.

Jim finally gave up and shook his head at what Lonnie had said. The lonely old hermit boozed it up on a regular basis and Jim was sure the cantankerous old cuss was a hard personality to work with, but there was no need to argue with the man anymore tonight.

Soon the headlights of the cruiser came bouncing up the road as Billy pulled up and announced out the open driver door window, "Big Jim, I let dispatch know what was going on. I told them to let the jail know we're going to be headed that way as soon we get a medical clearance on his arm."

Jim nodded acknowledgement while escorting Lonnie to the car. "Let's go, Mr. Garcia."

Moments later Billy had the vehicle headed down the dusty canyon road with Jim talking on the radio with the night dispatcher, Noreen.

"Copy, Jim, you're headed to the hospital for a clearance. I'll call the ER and let them know you're on your way. Hey, I got another call pending. I need to know what you want me to do about it."

Jim glanced at the dash clock that read 4:23 a.m.; the last thing Jim wanted was another call.

"Go ahead, Noreen, what you got?"

"Well, it's from the Trujillo Ranch. I was talking with Constance Trujillo and it turns out that old Dick and their boy, Jake, aren't home yet from working cattle up San Isidro Creek. Poor Constance is awful worried. She expected them back by seven yesterday."

Jim had worked for Dick Trujillo a couple years in a row when he was a teenager. He helped with the roundup and knew the only thing that would keep Dick and Jake out this late was something bad happening.

"I copy that, Noreen. Let Constance know I'll get a hold of our day-shift crew and get them up and headed out there as soon as they get dressed. I've got an ETA to the hospital of about thirty minutes."

"I copy that, Jim, I'll let her know. She'll be happy to know someone is on the way."

Jim rubbed his tired eyes as he watched the headlights cast moving arcs of light, illuminating the trees and brush along the valley road. Bone tired, he and Billy exchanged looks of understanding. They knew they would not be heading home anytime soon.

Lonnie spoke from the back seat.

"That old Dick. He's a tough cuss. I hope you find him and his boy okay. I'm sorry for hold'n ya up from go'n and look'n for him."

"My dad or the day crew will head out there to look soon. We really couldn't get there any sooner from here. It is what it is, old timer."

He looked out the windshield over the glow of the dashboard lights and saw the faint outline of the hills as daylight began to slowly creep into the sky.

"Let's pick it up, Billy, but don't hit anything on the way, okay?" Jim said glumly.

"You got it, boss." Billy pushed harder on the gas pedal and the cruiser picked up speed rapidly.

Lonnie sat looking at the same skyline as he mumbled to himself, "It is what is."

*****

05:47am MST UTC -7:00
Starkeville, Colorado

THE FAINT amber glow emanating from the Winnie the Pooh nightlight cast a meek radiance against the pale pink walls of Maggie Griego's bedroom. The colors created a placid hue that quickly faded into the shadows along the far wall. The only sounds in the tiny room were those made by Maggie's shallow breaths of deep sleep and the steady droning hum of the three evaporative humidifiers as they diligently converted liquid water into vapor. The thick humidity they created in the small room kept the dry mountain air comfortably moist so that Maggie's nose did not dry out and crack. In the past, without the humidifiers, the low humidity of the mountain air had caused her to have life-threatening nose bleeds.

The humidifiers had become a fixture in her bedroom after the last time her nose had bled so terribly. It was on the occasion of her eighth birthday party, last winter, after her friends had gone home and she was happily playing with her new My Little Pony action figures that she had received as presents. Her father had just left for work after the last of the party cake had been consumed and she was alone, singing and prancing in her living-room. When she absentmindedly wiped at some wetness on her nose she saw a bright-red bloody smear spread across the back of her hand.

Scared, she ran straight to her mother in the kitchen and tugged on her dress. Kathy Griego turned to her daughter and her pale-green eyes changed from loving curiosity to wide-eyed alarm at the sight of her little baby, a river of blood streaming down her little face. She ran with her daughter into the bathroom where she put a towel over her nose to help stem the flow but it only made the situation

203

worse. It did indeed stop the heavy flow of blood from running out of her nose but did nothing to stop the bleed itself. It just forced it to run down the back of her throat, causing Maggie to choke and gag.

Maggie squirmed to get out from under the towel so she could breath and as her face came free she coughed violently and saw the most horrible and scary thing her child-mind could possibly comprehend. Her cough sent the spray of blood square onto her mother's face, coating it in a red mist. This horrible sight sent the child into a screaming, coughing, and gagging fit, as Kathy, now also dripping blood, ran with her to the minivan. Mortality was a word Maggie did not know and until that day her limited concept of life and death had come from innocuous and guilt-free references of cartoons. But at that singular moment, as her own blood painted her mother's face, she implicitly understood the thought of not only her own mortality, but also her mother's. As Kathy accelerated down the road Maggie passed out and remembered nothing more about that terrible day as her desperate mother rushed the minivan into the parking lot of Mount San Rafeal Hospital.

The emergency room doctor, Dwayne Lovato, rushed Maggie into surgery where he cauterized the ruptured veins to finally stop the massive bleed.

The episode was bad enough that Maggie had lost over three pints of blood and then lapsed into a three-day coma. But by the time she awoke Big Jim had bought up every humidifier in the entire county. Since then the Griego household felt more akin to the Amazon rain forest than it did the Colorado Rockies. The night after Maggie came home from the hospital Jim read her a bedtime story about Pooh, Tigger, and her favorite, Eeyore. Before he tucked her in she asked about the whirring machines making their white noise. He told her that they were part of an army that purred as they watched over her, doing their sentinel duty of protecting her each and every night, so that she would never have another scary day of blood loss.

She took little notice of the noise anymore as her sentinel's purred away, as she lay tightly wrapped in her Dora the Explorer blanket. The legion of other dolls, ponies, and stuffed animals that inhabited every nook and cranny of her room watched her silently as she slept. She always imagined a glowing halo force-field encircling her entire house that was created by the humidifiers. And that all of her stuffed friends made up a great army that would rush to her and her mother's defense, and save them from the mortality that lurked outside in the cold, dry air.

Many times she had dreamt of that horrible day and saw again the blood spray across her mother's face – each little red droplet would transform into thousands of tiny red insects that would crawl and eat away her mother's beautiful face, until it dissolved into a skull covered with a shimmering mass of bugs, coating her face as if they were her new skin. The nightmare vision gave her mother's face a liquid consistency that terrified and disgusted Maggie. She usually woke up at that point in the nightmare, but tonight, the terrible dream kept going.

A thin sheen of sweat dampened Maggie's forehead as her eyelids bounced and rolled, her eyes flittering beneath. She gave a small moan and pressed her face into her pillow as she pawed at her blanket, as if pushing away at an unseen thing. The next moment she was pulling the covers back tightly held, as if the blanket were a comfort and salvation. Her mind sank further down into its horrific dreamscape, destroying the security offered by the sentinel humidifiers and her multitude of stuffed comrades. Happiness faded and hope was forgotten as the world of her nightmare clamped down on her spirit.

Inside her dream, the sound of a rushing mountain stream roared loudly in her ears as Maggie knelt in a thick stand of willows along the bank of the torrent. Her panting and sweating body shivered as her trembling little fingers dug into the moist mud at her feet. She could hardly breathe and was very tired from running and running. The cold dry air caused the back of her throat to ache and itch as she fought for air. She had been running from a massive wave of the small red insects that now covered the ground nearby, following behind, searching for her. Their elongated centipede bodies had a bloated head with a distorted visage stretched across its surface, like some magic-marker face drawn by a child, on the surface of a swollen balloon that was then inflated almost to bursting. The sharp, pointy features of the face moved as their mouths chomped and ghashed, biting at trees, houses, and anything else that the insects came across as they searched her out. They roamed like an undulating carpet as their teeth made a cold metallic *tink-tink* sound as the creatures devoured the dreamscape world.

It seemed as if she had been running through the tall grass and willows along the stream forever. As she paused to catch her breath, in desperation to move again, her eyes darted wildly this way and that as she looked for a way out. The bugs closed in and covered the nearby trees like a moving bark. The dark, leafless branches of the dead trees poked into the starless night sky like sharp needles. The horrid *tinking* sound grew closer and louder. Maggie dug her fingers further into the wet mud and tensed in preparation for yet another dash through the brush. But just before she burst from her hiding place she noticed a spreading glow that rose up over the mountains of the distant horizon which made her pause.

At first she thought that the sun may be rising and that perhaps it would scare away all the terrifying bugs. But this was not the type of bright yellow light that came from the morning sun. It was a much deeper red with a tint in the color that had a thickness and depth that resembled distant light coming through fog. The radiance quickly grew until it filled the far-off skyline, where now little sprouts of yellow flame rose here and there along the horizon. A molten wave of yellow fire suddenly came crashing over the distant horizon, flowing like lava toward her. The entire world was being consumed in a gigantic conflagration that filled every valley with scorching flames as it bore down toward her. The *tinking* noise grew into a crescendo that completely drowned out the sound of the flowing water behind her and caused her ears to hurt.

Staring horrified at the approaching inferno she saw a strange dark shape rise above the far-off skyline. Its monumental size was like watching a mountain lift itself from the depths, to build a towering framework into the sky. The gargantuan shape became fully formed and took the character of a walking man, taller than mountains. His head touched the clouds, and his giant strides were measured in miles as he emerged through the flames and cast a long shadow across the blazing landscape. Maggie could not see his face, as shadow hovered there like a cloak that hid his features, but the massive head first turned right then left as if it searching for something. The writhing mass of insects cowered down every time the shadowy face turned their way, and Maggie knew that the towering man was their creator and he hunted for her, same as the bugs.

Thousands of long and skinny black insects with dragonfly wings burst from behind the monstrous man and flew in large, horrible squadrons. They swooped and buzzed along the ground, joining in the search and feast as the world was consumed by fiery hate and their gluttony. Out of the flaming dust that was kicked up by the colossal monster's feet, Maggie saw the spires of a great but distant city jut up from the inferno. It was a massive burning city where large buildings were ablaze like logs in a campfire.

Within the ghastly vision she saw an immense collection of people that walked calmly toward the flaming city. They did not attempt to escape or divert their path, but marched headlong into the flames as if motivated by a single-mined purpose of self-destruction. Without deviation, the long columns of people wept and sobbed as they were flanked by ranks of the little red centipedes that nibbled at their ankles and feet. The bugs engorged their bodies on the feast, until when bloated; they burst open sending repulsive swill pouring out of their putrid erupted corpses along the path. The lines of people bleated in dismay as they moved forward until the massive throng reached the inferno where they then passed into the flames and ignited into screaming figures that burned brightly until they crumbled into ash and embers.

Maggie blinked through her tears and saw three familiar shapes among a long line of sad figures that marched into the flames. Her mother and father appeared as despondent shapes dressed in ragged clothing, sitting astride a horse-sized Eeyore doll. The large toy animal's fabric-legs marched in step with the other people being shepherded into the flames by the biting insects. In desperate panic Maggie stood up in the willows and waved her arms, frantically trying to get their attention. She screamed loudly for them to stop. *Don't enter the flaming city!* Her cries died out quickly, but finally she must have been heard as her mother slowly turned her blood-smeared face to look back at her daughter. Her mother's broken spirit wept as her lips moved, mouthing silent words as tears cut channels in the smeared blood on her face, until she entered into the engulfing flames and was consumed to ash.

Horrified and aghast at the terrible vision, Maggie cried out. Her sobbing outburst caught the attention of the bugs nearby and they rushed out of the grass toward the willows, charging rapidly at their prey with terrible speed. She remained frozen, unable to move. The torrent of water that once ran so boldly behind her was now a barren and dusty channel. She looked up at the towering figure of the man who now stared directly at her. His prey had been discovered and he roared a sickening laugh. His form rose up even higher into the red sky and she now saw his face for the first time. It was the same stretched and distorted face that all the bugs had, but far larger. But his face also appeared to be crying dark rivers of blood that dripped from his chin. His huge and grotesque form bent with gnashing teeth toward her and she screamed.

Kathy Griego awoke, startled from a deep sleep, to the sound of her baby girl's screams from down the hall. Frantically working to get untangled from her blanket, she finally burst out of her bed and rushed for her daughter. She stumbled and slammed into the dresser, knocking it backward against the wall, sending pictures falling to the floor. She cursed loudly as she worked the door open and banged her toes, and then went charging down the hall to crash through the door into her daughter's bedroom where she scooped Maggie into her arms, cradling her head as they embraced together in tears.

06:12am PST UTC -8:00
I-5 approaching exit 441
Patterson, California

THE NORTHBOUND traffic headed to the Bay Area was not too bad as yet for a Tuesday morning. Sam Thompson had started early and was making good time with his first run of the day. While he kept his left hand on the wheel, his right worked the touch screen of the company's little handheld computer. He took brief glances down to examine the electronic manifest that was displayed on the small screen, trying to get an idea of where he will be delivering product today.

The propane delivery business was currently in full swing for the Sacramento and San Joaquin valleys, which meant Sam had a full day ahead of him. The large farmer co-ops spread throughout the valley's delta region had started to use their huge aerators and dryers on this year's crops of rice, grains, and beans to stop unnecessary spoilage at the warehouses. This extensive use of propane was an annual event in California and also across the entire nation during the massive harvest of crops that took place each September. It was second only to the winter heating season in the consumption of propane for the United States. The millions of BTU per hour that was used in each of the dryers meant thousands of gallons of propane a day were burned to keep the bread-basket of America from rotting before it fed the world.

Sam always liked this time of year since it kept him very busy with several runs a day. With so little boredom he actually got home after a long day feeling much better than when he sat bored, doing little during the slow season. But today he needed to rush more than usual through his work since he really needed to get off on time. He and his wife had planned for their thirty-fifth year anniversary dinner date for tonight and there was no way he was going to be late, so today he would be hustling through his deliveries. But as he drove in the morning rush-hour traffic with a computer on his thigh, his attempt at multitasking was dumb in the extreme.

"Beeeeeeep!"

The desperate horn wailed outside his driver door and jolted Sam's attention from the tiny computer screen as his hands bolted to a death grip on the steering wheel, sending the computer flying. He spun his head and saw that he had drifted his large semi-tractor, pulling 11,000 gallons of liquid propane into the fast lane, and pinned a yellow Toyota Prius onto the shoulder edge of the highway.

The little car missed the delineator post by only inches, and with the driver's eyes bulging in a mixed expression of anger and fear, the driver of the Prius pushed hard on his horn, yelled profanity, and gave Sam the finger, all at the same time as he tried to keep from careening off into the median of the interstate.

"Oh, shit!" Sam exclaimed, as he turned the steering wheel as sharply as he dared in order to bring the big Kenworth back into his own lane.

The computer bounced across the floor of the cab and slammed against the passenger door with a loud thud. His heart raced as he chewed on his lower lip and worked to straighten out the seesawing truck. The powerful slosh and surge of the liquid propane swayed uncontrolled inside the barrel of the trailer, wanting to send the behemoth rig into a jackknife.

As Sam fought to regain control of the rig he cursed himself for the bonehead stunt that could have killed him and others if the rig were to tumble onto its side. Eventually, each tug and surge of the jostling propane got a little less wild as the liquid found its equilibrium, and Sam watched his mirror for any sign that the trailer would give way. After several more seconds it finally died down and the threat of rollover evaporated, and Sam began to loosen his desperate grip on the wheel to let blood circulate once again into his knuckles.

He took a deep breath and chastised himself.

"You're damn lucky you didn't drop this baby on its side, you old fart!"

The horn still blared from the Prius as it accelerated past him with as much gusto as its small engine could muster. Sam watched the car pass and saw a blue and white COEXIST bumper sticker plastered in the rear window, right next to another sticker with the word PEACE and a dove on it. Between the two stickers, in the middle of the rear window, he also saw the driver's fist as it pumped up and down, the middle finger jammed upward in a rude parting shot to Sam.

"Sorry, dude, can't we all just coexist?" Sam muttered sheepishly.

These rigs were big and scary and Sam knew it. He felt bad about scaring the guy, and himself, the way he had. He quickly glanced in his mirrors to see if his actions had affected anyone else but saw that the closest vehicles to him were still far enough behind him to probably not have been involved, or had backed off enough to appear that way. But he figured there were probably several people back there whom had seen everything and Sam guessed that more than one could be calling in his bad driving to the highway patrol right now; Sam sure did not want any tickets or to have his delivery schedule delayed by a stop from the smokies today.

With the economy in the tank, DOT was out in full force with mobile weight check-stations and 'random' safety-check stops, all so they could write every ticket they could to bolster their sagging coffers. If he got stopped for this stunt today he would be on the receiving end of a whopper ticket and that would be very hard to explain to Margaret at dinner tonight. So when he looked ahead and saw the welcoming sign indicating the next off-ramp was, in fact, the exit for his daily morning coffee break at the ABC Truck Stop, he was greatly relieved. He figured it would be smart if he just got off the road for a bit, letting the folks who watched him almost wreck move on down the road and forget about the incident. He would also have a chance to say hi to Sally, the cute clerk inside.

Slowing the rig he took the exit from the interstate and made his way onto McCracken Road, pulling up to the truck stop where he scanned the other big rigs parked around the diesel pumps and large gravel parking area. He smiled when he saw that his usual parking slot was open. As he pulled around the backside of the pumps and slipped his rig into the parking space he unhappily noticed that the same Rockridge Transport rig that he had seen the past month or so was once more parked in the space next to his.

The last several times he had seen that driver, sitting in the cab doing paperwork, and on each occasion the guy stared at him while he pumped fuel or just walked around the place. Sam did not know what the guy found so interesting in him but it gave him the creeps because the guy's eyes were cold and reminded him of the Night Stalker serial killer, Richard Ramirez, with the way he always glared at Sam. The guy looked plain mean and Sam got the willies every time he was around, and had even considered confronting the weirdo about it. But with the freaks out there in the world he had decided to just let it go. Today though, it looked to Sam like he might catch a break. The guy was bent over his toolbox and appeared to be repairing something near his truck's rear axles.

Sam pulled to a stop, settings the brakes and scrounged around the floor looking for the computer that had gone flying. He finally found it, pinned between the passenger door and seat, and examined it for damage. After pressing on the touch screen several times and finding that it worked fine he smiled.

"I guess Toughbook is the right name for you, after all," he muttered with relief.

Setting it on the passenger seat, he reached down and picked up his mug from the holder as he pushed open his door to step out.

Suddenly the door was jerked out of his grasp and, as he quickly turned, he found himself looking into the evil eyes of the Rockridge Transport truck driver, who was pulling himself up the steps of Sam's rig.

Sam was able to get his arm up and tried to shove the man. The weirdo attacker grimaced as Sam's fingers dug into his face. At the same moment Sam felt a sharp pain as the man repeatedly punched him in his side. Bewildered, shocked, and frightened Sam fought for breath as he grappled with the man, and was confused why the punches in his side hurt so badly.

The attacker grabbed the steering wheel in an attempt to pull himself deeper into the cab of the rig while he kept punching Sam in the ribs with repeated quick jabs, each one hurting far worse than the last. Sam finally gave up trying to shove at the man's face and reached down to try to block the punches, and was shocked and terrified to feel the sharp point of a wet and slimy blade slicing-and-dicing his guts with every bitter jab from his attacker. Now gripped by stark terror, Sam tried to scream but was only able to give a croak before he got head-butted in the face and was knocked backward. Frantic and desperate Sam tried to gain some control over the attacker's greasy knife-wielding arm as it darted back and forth, sticking the blade into his guts over and over.

Sam's eyes darted madly around for someone, anyone, who could help but all he saw was an empty and quiet parking lot. His eyes locked with his attacker's evil eyes and he smelled the man's putrid breath as he bore in close to his face, while he stabbed and shoved Sam farther back into the rig.

Grabbing at the slippery hand Sam was finally able to get a good hold on the man's clothing and tried to twist the knife, but his strength was quickly fading and weakness flowed fast into his fingers, arms, and spirit. The attack had lasted for less than ten seconds but a huge wave of exhaustion and helpless bore down mentally and physically on Sam as he fought for control of the slimy arm.

Locked in a close embrace they fell into the tight gap between the two large bucket seats of the cab, with the attacker's full weight pressing down on him. Sam looked down at the blade and saw that everything was covered with his blood and the fear of death banged on the walls of his mind.

Along with the shock of the attack, all thoughts were erased but those of stark, blind fright as he tried again to scream. The merciless attacker grabbed his throat and choked off the scream before it became much more than a squeal; he blew horrid breath into Sam's face and pressed down hard on his throat, trying to extinguish the last resistance from the dying man. Sam recoiled at the stench and used his legs to kick and shove against the dash of the cab as he tried to push their bodies from between the seats where he was jammed and could not move.

Adrenaline forced his heart to race and gave his muscles power again, and with that new-found strength he began to lift the murderer off his chest. With a desperate shove Sam was able to snatch a bit of desperately needed air, which rushed down his throat, into his aching lungs. Surprise flashed into his attacker's eyes as he realized there was still considerable fight in his struggling opponent. The murderer redoubled his efforts and bore down hard with his weight, grimacing with exertion.

Sam strained and pushed against his attacker with everything he had but a wretched feeling akin to numbness began to invade the tiny muscles of his fingers and hands, so that try as he might to grip anything with them, there was no force being created. He felt the attacker's hand rip free from his grip as a seeping coldness rose through his arms and flowed down his legs; the calmness of surrender entered into the back of Sam's mind. Strangely, the thought of never seeing his wife again and that death was about to claim his soul no longer filled him with terror. All that he felt was a despondent sadness from loss and failure. He tried to speak but all that came out of his mouth was a gurgling sigh as blood overflowed his lips and flowed down his cheeks. The killer bent in close and smiled a large mouth full of rotted teeth, smelling of rancid decay. He plunged the knife for a last time deep into Sam's neck until the point severed the spinal cord and all resistance ceased.

Hamal sat straddled over the fat body of the dead kafir as it quivered for several seconds and the last involuntary twitches tapered off. He glared with satisfaction as the light of life dimmed and went out of Sam's eyes. Hamal was surprised at how hard the fat old man had fought and he used these moments of rest to get his breathing under control. He reached over and brought the driver door closed, glancing back and forth to see if anyone nearby saw his attack. There were several truckers fueling at the diesel pumps and one old man who scrubbed busily at bugs on his RV's windshield, but no one else was visible. He sat and watched for a few more seconds until he was certain there was no unusual activity going on outside and that his killing of the man had gone completely unnoticed by everyone.

His breathing calmed and he stared at the dead man with grim contentment, knowing that he was but the first kafir he would have the joy of killing today. Sam's dead eyes stared upward as rivulets of thick blood ran down his pudgy cheeks. His body gave a final small shudder as Hamal pulled his knife out. He reached into the sleeper compartment and pulled out a blanket and wiped at the large amounts of blood covering the knife, his clothing, arms and face. He tried to mop the blood from the floor but finally gave up as blood continued to pour of the numerous wounds to the corpse.

He stood on the slippery surface and tried moving the blood-covered, and rotund, limp body around inside the confined space. With considerable effort and many curses he was finally able to get it pulled onto the small bed in the sleeper. He did a quick search and found the keys to the rig in the man's pants pocket and threw the saturated blanket over the body, covering it from view, closing the canvas flap between the sleeper and the front of the cab. He quickly stepped out of the cab, retrieved the black and yellow toolbox he left on the ground below the door and quickly got back into the cab. He strapped the box securely into the passenger seat, then looked around; seeing no signs of unusual activity he climbed back out of the rig and scampered back to his Rockridge truck. There he pulled out an old green military duffle bag that held his guns and rapidly hauled it back to the propane rig.

Hamal had kept surveillance on several possible trucks to hijack and this one was the most reliable in its routine at this truck stop every day. It was Hamal's safest bet to obtain what he wanted – a propane filled trailer. He had two other trucks that were fall-back options if this one had not turned up, but he was being blessed with success. With luck he would soon make it to his intended target before he could be confronted with any law enforcement interference.

He started the truck's massive diesel engine and while it rumbled he studied the gear-diagram. He let the air brakes out and attempted to pull the truck away but his unfamiliarity with it caused him to let the clutch out too quickly and the massive rig lurched forward several feet with a jerking bounce as the engine sputtered and quit.

Hamal cursed and punched the steering wheel in embarrassment and frustration. He glanced around and saw several truckers had turned and guffawed at the mistake. Hamal ignored them and turned the big diesel over until it came back to life. This time he released the clutch much slower and the truck pulled away smoothly from the lot. The sway from the loaded trailer and the strain the heavy load put on the engine were totally new to him and he marveled at the amount of difference there was in driving this rig compared to his regular delivery truck. He turned onto the on-ramp as he built up speed, heading north on I-5.

BEHIND THE busy sales counter at the ABC truck-stop, Sally rang up one sale after another for customers purchasing their diesel, gasoline, mugs of coffee, Snickers bars, and lottery tickets. As busy as she was she still took notice of Sam's rig pulling around the pumps on its way to park at its usual place. Then, just a few minutes later she saw it lurch and bounce to an embarrassing stop out in the gravel, raising a cloud of dust. A couple of the truckers in the lobby sneered and chuckled at the rookie driving mistake and she felt sad for Sam, who she was sure had been deeply embarrassed by the act. Then his rig had just up and left without Sam ever coming in to stare at her butt and get his coffee. She shrugged and figured he must really be in a hurry today to not come in and visit like usual. She went on with her day and never stopped to wonder anything more about it until much later in the afternoon.

*****

07:45am MST UTC -7:00
San Isidro Creek
Trinidad, Colorado

ANY SMALL movement in the dry soil caused chalky dust to float up into the still air of the dry arroyo, making Ajay cough and hack. Aziz sweated profusely as he worked laboriously with a pair of pliers, plucking out the cactus barbs stuck into Ajay's body in the light cast from the headlights of the dead rancher's truck.

Richard and Jake's corpses were just feet away, a macabre audience to Ajay's suffering. Slowly the growing rose-colored blush of dawn lit up the eastern sky and made the work easier. At first it was simple to remove the large flat pear-shaped chunks of cacti that clung to his body. But later on Aziz had trouble getting hold of or even locating the hundreds of smaller barbs, removing all but the tiniest. Unfortunately for Ajay many of the barbs were broken off at the surface of his skin and they were impossible for the pliers to grip, requiring surgery to get them out. But the most painful, by far, were those barbs impaled in the soft, tender flesh of Ajay's groin and genitals. Aziz refused to even try to remove them and that had forced Ajay to do the excruciating work himself. Aziz and Faruk tried to ignore Ajay's screams and whimpers that came with each completed pull, and it was impossible for them not to be unnerved by the experience.

During those long painful hours, a smoldering inferno of anger built up inside Ajay as he began to realize that his dreams were in ruins. His fury burned like the scorched and blackened juices inside a pot being consumed over a hot burner. *I am being robbed of my glory!*

The pesky rancher had poked his nose where it never should have been and now Ajay's plans were in tatters. *I should never have played games with them! I should have just killed them all on sight!*

He leaned, trembling, against the hood of the truck and stared down at the corpses at his feet; his whole body felt covered in fire, throbbing in pain, and was swelling rapidly. He brooded over his misfortune and considered what he and his accomplices were to do now. His intended attack in Denver was no longer possible, not in his condition. He could barely move and there was no way he could wait for another day. The whole country would soon erupt, so today was his only opportunity – he had to use or lose it. He glanced over at the two Iranian killers who stood on the far side of his van. They talked quietly with each other, watching him. They were also discussing what their options were, for all practical purposes, with him being a crippled and useless appendage that needed to be disposed of. *Is that what they're planning for me?*

He hardly knew them, and they had never actually trained together since they had been assigned to watch over the undercover FBI agent. He knew that they were selected as his 'assistants' due to his having identified the agent. With them being assigned to his part of the attacks today meant they were excluded from all the glory attached to the strikes that their compatriots were involved with. They may be well-trained, and had been submissive to his orders so far, but he suspected that they could quickly become disenchanted with his now-crippled abilities. With him being injured so severely, would they abandon him, or submit to him? He needed to come up with a new plan quickly, since the other attacks would be occurring very soon and the entire country would go on high-alert a short time after that.

For Ajay, nothing for today meant anything if he did not get what he wanted. What he needed: something brutal and big.

The talcum-like dust that covered his face had turned to mud with his sweat, which then poured into his eyes, causing them to burn. He rubbed at his eyes as he limped slowly to the side mirror of the truck. He crouched to see his reflection and what he saw snapped the remaining tendrils of sanity he possessed.

His macabre reflection showed an evil clown mask, made of blood and sweat-soaked muddy makeup spread over his face. His tears had darkened the mud around his eyes and then had run down his

215

cheeks, deepening the visual of his eye sockets. Now his eyes appeared sunken farther into his head, where they glinted with hate while set deep inside a muddy tunnel of misery. His fingers scratched at his cheeks, now elongated and stretched so badly that his face had turned into a distorted and unrecognizable sight, even to him. A wave of nausea erupted out of him as he bent forward and retched down the side of the truck door. His shredded hand bumped the door handle and changed the agonizing ache in it to intense shooting pain.

"Fuck!" he screamed as he stumbled back from the truck, long tendrils of vomit-infused saliva swung below his mouth and chin.

His heel caught on a branch of sagebrush and again he fell over backward. Faruk and Aziz moved forward to help; to their shock he sprang to his feet like a cat and stood, hunched over, holding his injured arm as he swayed back and forth as if drunk. The two Iranians halted a few feet away and stared with amazement at how fast he had moved after he fell.

Ajay slowly raised his head and glared at the two assassins. Their wary expressions caused him to grin broadly. The two stepped farther backward as it became clear to them that whatever sanity Ajay had before was now long gone. Now, physically and mentally he appeared every bit a hunchbacked monster from a children's tale that had disastrously came to life, to grotesquely stand before them, ready to devour anything that strayed too close. Adrenalin and madness pumped through Ajay's veins, eradicating his pain. He reared back and burst out with a loud, cackling laugh. The surreal sound of the inhuman and hysterical laughter made the Iranians step backward again. Ajay stumbled toward them with a wide-eyed maniacal expression and grabbed an AK47 rifle leaning against his van. Aziz and Faruk continued backing away; Ajay stopped and stared at them with the rifle held at his waist, the barrel leveled at them.

"You are going to die today – yes?" Ajay asked with a sneer.

They did not answer and only stared back at him.

Ajay thumbed the safety lever and laid his finger across the trigger. "You, fedayeen! You are going to die today?"

They both slowly nodded their heads.

"Then break out your rugs and say your prayers! Then prepare. I *will* make this kafir pay for interfering with *me*! Right here – do you understand me?" He then spit on the bodies of Richard and his son.

Aziz and Faruk looked at one another and then back at Ajay. They had been ordered to die in the company of this Kashmiri today. It was the mission they had committed many years of training to, and today was the day their nation would take its place as a leader on the world stage, for the first time since the Persian Empire. It mattered little to them whether they did it at some place pre-chosen by this insane maniac, or right here in this place.

"So be it. We will die with you here," Aziz said calmly.

*****

BIG JIM had worried about Richard and Jake Trujillo since he first received the news of them being missing. It grew on his mind until he eventually called his father. Being good friends with the Trujillo's, his father was just as concerned, and immediately got dressed and headed out to the ranch to help Constance with the search. Jim figured they must have had some major trouble since they both had not made it home. Dick Trujillo was a fairly hale man for his age, but if it was Jake who had gotten hurt so that he could not be moved, Dick would be hard-pressed to leave his son alone. Jim just hoped that they were waiting for some help to be sent out to them this morning, not something worse.

Jim looked up as the nurse was coming back into the little examining room where he and Lonnie waited. Nurse Tory Nelson walked with the hurried stride of a person who had an awful lot of things to do and not much time to get it all done. Lonnie sat waiting on the hospital bed, his cut arm resting on the small table where she had earlier sutured up the nasty gash.

Lonnie's drunk had quickly faded and his body was now aching all over from the vehicle crash, while his head throbbed from having too much to drink. Neither stopped him from admiring the shape of the nurse's curves inside her hospital scrubs, nor did they stop him from trying to carry on a conversation with the young lady as she examined her work on his arm.

"You've done a real good job a sewin' me up, honey. I sure appreciate that. I've been a watch'n you running around here, busy all night. That baby ain't crying anymore o'er in da other room – is it doing okay now?"

"Oh, the poor thing's got colic, but between me and her mama we got her to settle down with some TLC. That baby's had a heck of a time. I think it's been here three times this week! If that baby doesn't get over it soon, I think the poor woman might lose all of her hair," she asserted as she finished with his bandage.

"I know! The little hon has one major set a lungs on 'er. Why, I think she could wake a dead mule, I bet."

"Yes, well, Mr. Garcia, that should go a long way to showing you men what these poor young moms have to put up with while

217

you're out enjoying your drink. You would think that baby's father would be here with them, instead of out at the bar, huh? But no."

She raised her eyebrows and placed her hands on her hips as she gave him a pointed look.

Lonnie's big brown eyes sparkled while staring back into hers, and with a soft voice and smile he said, "Now, hon I can't speak fer that tot's papa or why he ain't see'n to business at home, but – if I didn't go out for a drink now an' den – well, then it'd be me right back home, a bawl'n and wail'n like that toddler. You'd ask my poor dogs to take that o'er the smell of a little gin? That sounds a little harsh on my pups, if you ask me."

The big man's eyes danced with hers as a blush came rising to the surface of her skin. She unlocked her glance from his deep brown eyes and went back to patting and fiddling with his bandage.

"No woman wants a wailing and bawling Mr. Garcia at home – terrorizing his poor pets with his crying for his drink! Goodness, no. But they don't need him coming into the hospital all cut up, neither."

"Now there you got me. But if I'd not got'n myself cut up like this, I'd a never been able to meet such a fine woman like y'rself. I count that as the only piece o' good luck I had all night long, sugar," Lonnie said with a wink.

"An old-fart like me may be short on smarts but I know a winner when I see one, and darlin' you take the gold."

Nurse Nelson looked him and up and down before she replied. "Charm is not wasted on me, Mr. Garcia, and it's easy for a woman to see that, even in your condition, you have quite a bit to offer a lady. But ladies like gentlemen and you look like you play a little rougher than that."

Lonnie's shoulders sunk slightly as he ran fingers through his hair before shooting her a mischievous grin.

"I'm wounded deep! Yes, you're right 'bout that, too, darl'n. Foolish games tonight caused this ol' cuss to end up at yer door a bleedin'. But as yer say, play'n gentlemen games ain't my style, sorry. This ol' cowboy can still ride a buck'n bronc for a full eight, though. You ever been to a good rodeo, darling?"

He winked at her a last time before she turned with a smile and left the room. Lonnie watched with devout interest as her backside swung nicely as she made her way back down the hallway of the hospital.

"My, my," Lonnie said quietly, shaking his head.

Jim leaned against a cabinet in the tiny room with his arms folded across his chest, watching the banter. "You can be quite the charmer, Lonnie. I'm surprised you're still single after all these years, with lines like that. I thought you were about to get kissed – or slapped."

Lonnie ignored the chiding as he looked wistfully down the hall. "From a gal like that I would be happy with either."

"I just love the ladies, there, sheriff-man. They're special, you know, and I don't back away from play'n just 'cause I'm old." Lonnie looked at his arm. "I've had a couple o' close calls but none ever decided to stay on. Can't blame 'em, really. I'm a little too ornery for anyone that special ta stay 'round a cuss like me."

"They are indeed special. I'm married to one of the best there is."

"Yeah? Well, you're a lucky bast'rd. A dumb cowboy like me could never get a hold of one o' those and keep 'er."

"Not from lack of trying, by the looks of your playing with the nurse."

"Is she a Mrs., Miss, or Ms.?"

Jim chuckled. "I'm sorry, partner. It's the married kind of Mrs. with Tory, there. She's been married for over a year now."

"Damn! See what I mean, son? No luck at all for schlubs like me."

Jim looked at the big man and wondered why such a good man had chosen to live at the bottom of a bottle. Lonnie was a lifelong fixture in the county even though Jim had never really had anything more than passing contact with him. Lonnie was well known for being a hard drinker and Jim figured that whatever the old man found at the bottom of his liquor bottle had a lot to do with him not being married, with children of his own by now. Jim felt it was a shame, for he believed the man would have made a good husband and father if he had controlled his drinking. Jim finally decided to take the moment alone with him and get something off his chest that had eaten at him ever since they had headed to the hospital.

"Lonnie? I'd like to say something to you before we leave and before Billy gets back from the john."

Lonnie rubbed at his temple, feeling his pounding hangover, but managed to look over his shoulder at the deputy.

"Yeah?"

Jim looked down at his shoes and then back up at Lonnie.

"Mister, you had me dead to rights up there at your place tonight. You could've blown me to hell several times over but you didn't. I've been thinking that the way I came up there tonight damn near caused that confrontation almost as much as anything you did tonight."

219

Jim paused and scuffed at the polished floor with the heel of his boot before he continued.

"We cops are taught to be tactical, cautious, and – well – basically just downright paranoid of everyone we meet. That way, if we run into some real or even a wannabe cop-killer unexpectedly – we are supposed to be as ready as we can to fight and survive."

He looked up at Lonnie.

"My dad's been a sheriff in these parts now for almost forty years. He's been shot at a couple of times and actually been hit twice. He had to kill them two Zamora brothers back in '81, when I was little. That scared the hell out of my entire family. He has seen more than his share of hard times, trouble and bad people, but he's always told me to try and see through to the real person. Not to just treat people like they're a number that I got to get around on my way to retirement. He doesn't see the newer style of law enforcement tactics as being advantageous to a cop's safety. He stresses that treating whoever I run into out there with respect and dignity can get me more personal safety than those tactics."

Jim stopped as Nurse Nelson walked passed their room and continued down the hall toward the colicky baby. Once she was gone he continued, "Well, anyway, I screwed up tonight and used poor tactics, under any circumstance. I endangered my life, my partner's, and yours. I knew better than to try and sneak up there on you – and you were right – we were sneaking. I would've been a lot better off just pulling up to your place or just waiting for daybreak. Well, what I want to tell you is that I really thank you for not teaching me how bad I messed up by killing me tonight with that shotgun."

Jim's large muscular frame was not hidden by the ballistic vest he wore which stretched his uniform tight. But his bulk now appeared smaller as he stared at Lonnie, chagrined.

Lonnie gave a long, steady look with sober eyes before finally saying, "Ain't no shame in liv'n through a mistake. I understand what it is you're say'n to me and I take it with thanks. It takes a man to say what ya did," he said with a nod of respect to Jim, and then turned to stare at the wall.

"I've known yer daddy for many years and he's a good ol' cuss. He's been a sheriff 'round these parts a long time and has done his duty without complaint. I like 'im and respect 'im, too. But you do me a personal favor and think 'bout someth'n when you get home and see yer baby girl and then lay down with your woman t'night, boy."

Lonnie gave a cold hard look over his shoulder at Jim that was so intense it startled him, and caused him to straighten up and drop his arms from across his chest. The man's demeanor had changed so rapidly that Jim was not sure whether Lonnie was going to say something or if Jim would suddenly have to fight with the man.

Lonnie kept the steely gaze but the tone of his voice was soft.

"Your pa is right 'bout know'n the people you serve and work'n within the boundaries of that knowledge, boy. No doubt 'bout that. But your pa – he damn well knows there is evil out there in the world and it takes no time at all for evil to rear its head and strike."

Lonnie turned away.

"Them Zamora boys were that way. Murderers. Rapists of girls! Bad men. Pure VC. Evil to their core. Your daddy planted them bastr'ds in the ground and did the world a big favor when he did."

He slowly nodded his head.

"Yes, he did, and if your pa had been smart'r when he kill'd them two murderous pieces o' shit he might not've been shot himself, but he waited too long to plant'em."

Jim was about to protest but Lonnie just waved a hand dismissively before Jim spoke.

"Listen, your pa is a good and wise sheriff. He's giv'n you good advice. Take it. But you just be careful out there." He turned and leveled another hard gaze at Jim. "The reason you're alive right now ain't cause I'm a good man. It's because I was drunk and foolish enough in think'n I could walk out on my porch, say my peace to that *gringo* peckerwood from up the canyon and still have the drop on the fucker if he wanted more! If I'd a thought it was VC instead o' that wimpy little shit – I'd a blown your fuck'n ass straight to hell right along with that nervous sidekick of yours, and then found out my mistake later."

Jim and Lonnie stared silently at one another.

"I'd a regretted kill'n your ass. But make no mistake: I'd never have lost a second o' sleep o'er it. Nobody takes ol' Lonnie down without a fight! And I've got no apologies to anyone for put'n down dumbasses like you 'cause ya made a stupid fuck'n mistake! Men live and men die by mistakes, boy, and I ain't responsible for your dumb ass."

Jim knew Lonnie was serious in trying to impart some wisdom, and as awkward as it felt to Jim, he also understood that the old marine had his best interests at heart.

"Lonnie, I hear you. No more speeches from me, just a thank you," Jim said, extending his hand.

Lonnie looked at the open hand and then grasped it in his own, and shook it slowly as he looked at Jim's name plate on his uniform shirt.

"Fair enough, Jim. Hope we can keep from any runs-ins like this in the future."

His demeanor was warm and friendly and the fact that he used Jim's name instead of calling him 'son' or 'boy' was a sign of respect that at once gave Jim a deep sense of pride for getting such consideration from the grizzled old hard-ass, but it also told him that Lonnie was extending to him about the closest thing to friendship he probably ever would.

Jim saw that there was an older breed of man deep inside this ex-marine that did not fit well with the modern world or the changes that had come to the countryside. There was too much politeness, too much political correctness in this age of man for a person like Lonnie. Unlike the hyper-critical and hyper-sensitive people in the world around him, this man's self-worth was measured by his own standards and needed no weight of approval from others. It was not arrogance or even rudeness that came out of Lonnie's words and tone – that would require intent, malice, or ignorance to accomplish such a negative connotation. The feeling Jim got from Lonnie was of pure independence; you could take it or leave it as you saw fit, but judging him for it was a waste of time. The man lived by his own rules alone and no others, except maybe God's, and Jim was not even sure about that one.

"You've got hard bark on you, Garcia. You're honest with me – I'll be honest with you. One minute you're a stumbling drunk and the next you're a cold killer. Then, the next moment, you're happily flirting with a nurse and then flip on a dime and you follow that up with a thorough critique of my dad. You're one ornery S-O-B, mister. Where'd you come by seeing things the way you do?"

Lonnie eyes softened a little.

"My pa's rough hand had a part, but I suppose most came during '67, and my first tour with the Corps o'er in 'Nam. Me and the 3/5 spent a couple o' days in and around the small village of Binh Son. Good marines, bad times, and a damned hot jungle. You grow up quick in a place like that. You also learn a lot about good, evil, and the hearts of men, Jim."

Jim nodded.

"I bet you do, partner, I bet you do. Well, anyway, thanks again for not killing my ass tonight. My wife and baby appreciate it as well."

He finished with a smile.

Lonnie perked up with a large grin of his own.

"I like you, kid. I might o' regretted kill'n you more than I realized. Yer ought to come up to the Gulnare Bar and share a drink with me and old Sammy Wilson. He was in the 101st and had some fun back the 'Nam himself, at a real shithole place called Firebase Ripcord o'er in the A Shau. A damn good man I tell ya – like me! He might like you, too, and I think I owe yer a beer or two for shov'n that scattergun in yer face tonight."

"That sounds like a real good time, but I'll be doing the driving, got it?"

"Ah, hell, that sounds righteous to me!" Lonnie roared with gusto and a grin.

Jim looked at his watch.

"I'm afraid we can't stay here much longer and let you play with Tory anymore. We still need to get ourselves down to the jail so you can get bonded out – unless, of course, you feel like sleeping it off in one of my dad's cells."

"I've slept in worse places."

"Yeah, well, I'm sure."

Jim stepped out to the hallway looking both ways.

"I don't know what Billy is doing. He's either pinch'n a big loaf or he fell asleep. You wait here while I go see what he's up to?"

"Sure, I ain't goin' nowhere but to your jail, son. I'll stay here."

Jim glanced back and then started off down the hall. He knew every instructor he ever had at the police academy would freak out if they knew he walked off and left an arrested felon unsupervised and un-handcuffed. But he also knew that once Lonnie gave his word, he would sooner die than ever break it.

It had been one hell of a night and Jim was looking forward to getting home and hugging his wife.

*****

07:46am MST UTC -7:00
EL Moro School
Trinidad, Colorado

WAY BACK in the year 1991, Judy Spencer-Hargrove was still only known as Judy Spencer, a bright-eyed believer in her future success in the nation's education system. Her only other interest, beside teaching, had been in joining the Peace Corps, but that ended after she watched a video at indoctrination which showed just how dirty, smelly, and truly nasty the places were that she could be sent to. That was when her noble idea of helping foreign rugrats was overruled by the effort she would have to invest and the filth she would have to deal with. Bugs, rats, dirt, odors, and hard physical labor were things

223

Judy did not stomach well, and so she stayed with teaching and planned on making her mark by forming the minds of domestic rugrats instead.

Aside from staying a lot cleaner and dealing with far fewer bugs, she envisioned that her future as a teacher to be one grand adventure after another. Her mission would be to touch and properly shape the minds and lives of the children. And by making their stars' shine, hers would shine brightly as well. Through indoctrinating those minds she would be front and center in molding the future of the entire country. Her work would make it a better place that would finally become the fair and equitable place that her free-love parents had dreamt about. It would become a place where the distribution of nature's bounty and life's riches would be doled out with parity by the properly guided; a country where enlightenment was disseminated effectively to both nature and the herds of humanity populating it.

During college she grew to understand that her teaching would also create a new America where the inequality of the country's culture would be eliminated, and the objectionable natures of racism and bigotry would finally be mitigated. And our diverse society could come together in harmony and equality instead of in conflict and disparity. America would finally become the nation where the proper regulation of people's thoughts and actions would meld society into a state of justice and fairness embodied in the words preached by her heroes: Eugene Debs, Karl Marx, and Howard Zinn.

Today, she still felt those dreams had a glorious future and that her molding of young minds would be her part in eventually bringing about the changes to the core ideology of this country to a better, a more humanistic, and conforming system; the improvement of station and status for every living creature on the planet.

Every class which passed before her, bursting with open and empty minds of mush that she could instruct with correct ideology, meant that her vision and those of her heroes became another step closer to reality with every new school year.

Judy was idealistic but not naïve, and she understood that the majority of students were just average and therefore meant for the more menial and mundane places in the future society. But her work with a select few kids showed promise of carrying on the grand evolution toward the progressive utopia. And it is they who would eventually bring down the establishment hegemony that ruled an unjust America.

She felt she had found that perfect place to do her part in establishing the everlasting legacy of her hero's ideals. She liked to think of it as her quaint little 'hobbit hole' community in the rural

224

Colorado Rockies, where for the past five years she had worked with the eighth and ninth grade literature and English classes of El Moro K-12 School. It had become her beautiful little incubator of the nescient minds that went on undisturbed and unfettered.

To say Judy loved her life was a huge understatement. In addition to her teaching career she had a man whom she considered to be what the perfect husband should be: Greg Hargrove. He was a busy man who brought in the cash as a personal injury lawyer by day, and who charged the ramparts of ignorance as a legal activist for progressive environmental causes at night. He worked at securing animal rights everywhere he could when he was not tied down with boring work at the local firm. Very often he did work on pro bono jobs, including his work last year with an environmentalist group in Kansas City that had successfully closed the Cherry Creek Minx Inc., a horrid fur factory. That case had garnered enough attention to get the Sierra Club itself to take notice of Greg, and now things were really taking off. This week he was at a job interview with them in Washington, DC that could catapult his career onto the national stage. Then, who knows, maybe eventually he would move into politics, serving in public office someday. *Halleluiah, baby!*

Judy's world was bright and just getting brighter. But until they reached those heights she dreamed of, she would keep plugging into the brains of these rug rats. She loved how this community was still so small that the whole school complex served all five-hundred students from kindergarten through high school graduation in the same facility; a thing almost unheard of in America anymore. The school year was just beginning and the students she had received this year looked very promising.

Judy pushed her chair back from her desk with a big smile of satisfaction and stretched out. She took in a deep breath and wiggled the her toes in her flip-flops as her outstretched feet poked out from under the desk, and she cracked the knuckles of her boney fingers while reaching high above her head. She stood with a bounce and turned to look out her classroom window onto the main school parking lot on the west-side of the little campus to watch the arriving mush heads.

Since that parking lot was the closest to the school's administration building, it had become, in the small world of school politics, the most prestigious parking lot for the campus. It was reserved for the faculty and school seniors, but was not big enough to handle even that volume of vehicles. The remainder of the daily overflow was then forced into the less-esteemed parking lot across the street. The faculty had reserved spaces and that left the last prime parking spots for the seniors to divvy-up according to the two arcane but time-tested rules of all school-dom. Rule #1: First come, first serve. Rule #2: The cool elite and jocks got everything before the un-cool, the average, and the weak got anything.

So Judy watched as the small-town elites of the little school made their daily ritual procession of cars into the same parking spaces they used every morning. She thought how ironic it was that the same class envy that forced the least cool and unpopular kids to park across the street and walk farther to get to their classes was the same class envy that separated the haves and the have-not's in society. *My work never ends!*

While she scanned the lot she observed as the El Hefe of all student elites at the El Moro School, pulled in driving his mud-covered GMC truck in a slow motion circuit of the entire lot. His slow cock-of-the-walk cruise was done in a truck that looked as if it came right off the cover of some magazine called the Shit Kicker Times. The big, fat mug-grip tires had mud-flaps with chromed naked women in silhouette, a jacked-up suspension so high it was amazing that the truck stayed upright in a turn and a tall shiny chrome roll-bar with seven KC lights across the its top. The rear window was covered with a sun-shade liner that pictured a flowing American flag with a soaring bald eagle screaming across it, with its wings wide and talons sharp. The rear chrome bumper had a large sticker of a hand giving the world the bird and another sticker that read: Vegetarian – Ancient Indian for Bad hunter.

The truck continued around the lot as the blaring speakers, pumping a heavy base rhythm, made sure every student within earshot knew he had arrived as he coasted the truck into his predestined slot.

It was just the kind of arrogant, redneck crap that Judy had come to expect on a daily basis from the school's egotistical jock, Tony Aragon. The school's prized athlete and virtual master of all sports basked in the glory that came with being the best at every sport that the small 3-A school could even consider participating in. Being one of those rare students; that by his natural physical abilities and skill, had been elevated to a legend-like status in both the school and the community. He was given the daily latitudes and deference's that usually only came to the very wealthy or extremely beautiful at this age. He was the all-star linebacker of the football team; a 0.428 batter and great center-fielder for the baseball team; and the 2009 State 3A Middleweight Wrestling Champion. Those successes had made Tony a Greek god-like figure for the school and town.

Judy bristled as the school's 'chosen one' made his grand entrance and immediately became the center of attention for every student and faculty member in the parking lot who dutifully lauded him with their morning platitudes.

"Typical testosterone filled show off," Judy quietly scoffed to the empty room, with a mixture of contempt and admiration in her voice.

She enviously watched as Tony stood by the truck smiling and readily accepted salutations from passerby's with a palm-slap here, a high-five there, and a couple of fist-bumps from his admiring morning attendees. His constant sidekick, and numero uno sycophant, Johnny Grimes, quickly left his spot in the passenger seat of the shit-kicker truck and moved into his devoted position next to his mentor and hero. There he basked in the fringes of his leader's glow and got his daily dose of self-esteem.

The scene outside the window was at once foreign and yet deeply familiar to Judy; a quiet, shy bookworm in her school days, she never received any adoration nor did she participate in doling it out to the more popular kids. She was a cellophane student; transparent, invisible, and uninteresting to her classmates, teachers, and self. She watched Tony closely and wondered what that adoration must feel like for him now and what he would feel like if it vanished overnight. *Could he handle it?*

Meanwhile, Tony hopped into the back of his truck and with the confident ease of a popular politician and began to boisterously explain, with demonstrative gestures to the assembled group, how his truck had gotten so thickly covered in mud during his thrilling early morning four-wheeling expedition into the Purgatory River. His bravado was most eagerly received by a giggling and jiggling set of girls, Stephanie Cordova and Rachel Smith, who both wore far less on this cool-autumn morning than Judy considered appropriate for either the temperature or their age. To Judy, their fifteen-year old bare midriffs and skin tight hip-hugger jeans appeared far more appropriate for the LA bar scene than a small town high school. Judy's mind tried to keep from acknowledging that her plain-n-tall looks were also a sour comparison to the shapely twits that adoringly listened to the school jock.

"My mother would never have allowed me to go to school looking like a slut," Judy huffed as she folded her arms tightly below her breasts.

A woman can always size up another woman and Judy quickly sized up the psychology of the two little girls and their worship of the jock-Adonis who proudly flexed for them. There was a clear nuance of want in their eyes and a stand-just-a-little-closer move to their bodies that said a lot more than simple adulation for his sport's

227

talent. It was also more than just the cool air causing their nipples to push out the front of their tank top shirts. There was a deep need to their body language that all women could see in other women when men were involved. Judy figured that these teenage trollops thought of themselves as being much closer to women than Judy would ever give them credit for.

Yet, Judy's eyes could not help but also be drawn to where the two girl's point-of-focus was and she assessed the young jock for herself. His tall body was tanned and toned into a pleasing athletic form that stood relaxed and confident in his own skin-tight cowboy jeans, where an obligatory circular wear pattern on the back pocket, caused from a chewing tobacco-can, helped bring attention to the firmness of his butt.

Judy liked the way his cowboy boots made his back straighter, his stance firmer, and his butt jut out a little more. His thin waist, flat stomach, and broad muscular shoulders supported a perfect V-shape inside his un-tucked flannel shirt. The shirt also did nothing to hide his wide, burly chest as it slowly drew in and out effortlessly as he laughed. His solid jaw and youthful handsome features were not hidden but were actually enhanced by the hard curve in the bill of his ball cap. Judy slowly let her eyes follow his form down to his jeans where she wondered just how accurate the noticeable bulge in the front of his pants was. Judy prided herself for typically only noticing the intellectual qualities and not the Neanderthal masculinity of men around her, but she knew there was no doubt that her body liked what she saw at the moment.

With cat-like grace Tony spun on the heel of his boot and started striding for the school entrance, in step with Stephanie and Rachel, giggling the whole time. Like a groupie, Johnny devotedly followed his hero while carrying both of their books. Judy's eyes followed the twitch of Tony's ass as he walked up the stairs.

"Shake it, baby, shake it like a Polaroid picture," she murmured quietly, in rhythm with the side-to-side bobbing of her head. She felt the swelling of her own rigid nipples under the fabric of her flowered print dress as a very noticeable heat and dampness grew between her thighs.

"Yeah, he's a definite hottie, isn't he?" came the voice of Kim Thompson, who now stood next to Judy at the window.

Startled, Judy's hands jumped up to her mouth as she gave a squeal at suddenly becoming aware of Kim's presence.

"Kim! Where did you come from?" she asked with an edge of real anger in her voice.

Kim worked hard to keep from snickering at Judy's embarrassment, and felt honestly apologetic for startling the woman so badly. She reached out in consolation, touching Judy's shoulder to offer assurance.

"I'm sorry. I came in just a few seconds ago. I thought you heard me. I didn't mean to make you jump like that."

Judy was hardly mollified by Kim's excuse. Her embarrassment at being caught ogling the boy's butt quickly turned into growing annoyance toward the perfectly proportioned black woman. She had never liked Kim from the first day they had met last year and she disliked her far more than usual right now. She gave Kim an expressive 'fuck you' roll of her eyes and with a terse spin she turned away from the woman's face.

"Yeah, well, you did a lousy job of that, sweetheart. Is there something that you need here?" she asked brusquely.

She dug her knuckles into her biceps as she tightly crossed her arms and glared defiantly at Kim over her shoulder.

"Hey, listen, again I'm sorry for catching you off guard that way. I don't want you to be upset at me for that."

"Whatever."

"*Okay!* I see that we aren't going anywhere good today. Listen, Judy, all I came by for was to see if you were still using the projector today. I saw you had it against the wall and if you aren't going to use it, I'd like to take it. I've got a cute little presentation I found this weekend that I'd like to show my kids. You think I can take it off your hands for the day?"

Emotionally Judy immediately felt better, as a sense of control returned to her world; since the unwanted intruder in her classroom now required her acquiescence it would be easy to gain a little revenge. She flashed a hollow smile at Kim that had all the warmth of crushed ice.

"Oh, I put it over there so I could move some desks around, but I'm afraid I will be using it all day today. Sorry about that. You know I've been thinking of doing a bit on Mark Twain that I just happened to finish last night. Funny that, huh?"

Kim saw the bitter smile and knew what the answer was before she even heard it. She would blame herself for the rebuff if it were not coming from Judy. The snide and snarky, I-wish-I-had-been-born-black liberal never withheld her all-consuming condescension toward anyone who disagreed with her or who did anything she imagined to be a snub. Kim briefly considered challenging her assertion that she would be using the projector by feigning interest and asking to see what presentation on Mark Twain she would show, but then she thought better of it and let it go.

"Okay. Just thought I'd ask. You have a great day, honey," Kim said, turning in her high-heels and sauntering out of the room, feeling every dagger thrown at her back by Judy's eyes as she left.

Judy did indeed watch her leave with as toxic a stare as she could muster and was very glad when Kim finally cleared the door so she could coldly mutter, "Bitch."

*****

09:20am MST UTC -7
Trinidad, CO

THROUGHOUT Faruk's entire life his experiences were encompassed by Shiite tribal culture that was dominated by the secret police of the mullahs, and the restrictions of a military state. He had joined the IRGC, the great Army of the Guardians of the Islamic Revolution, as a sure way for advancement and personal security within his nation's tribal culture. It was more than religious devotion that made the IRGC a good fit, the money and the prestige it gave him and his family within the tribe and community meant even more.

It had been almost a week since he arrived in America and he was more flabbergasted than ever at how easy it was to have unrestricted, and more importantly, unsupervised and unknown movement everywhere he went. In this supposedly most-powerful-nation-in-the-world, there were no checkpoints, no secret police, and no internal security structure whatsoever to stop or hinder him. *How contemptible these kafirs are!*

He was cramped as he squeezed into the driver seat after donning his explosive vest, battle gear, and ammunition. But he still found it easy enough to steer the Ford van down the main street of the sleepy little American town, following closely behind Aziz in the rancher's truck. The corpses of the rancher, his son, and the two dogs lay covered by a blanket on the flatbed of the truck, so they drove slowly to keep the blanket from flying off the bodies. He laughed every time he saw people raise their hand to wave at Aziz in the truck they all recognized, only to lower their arms when they saw a man they did not know driving it. *That won't be your last surprise today!*

Ajay squirmed, miserable in the passenger seat. His adrenalin and madness only did so much to deaden the pain and discomfort he was experiencing. Before they left the campsite he took a large snort of cocaine and rubbed the rest of the white powder over his groin, thereby slightly deadening the pain from the cactus and bite wounds. The meager results did little to lessen the pain around his genitals.

They eventually turned off the main street into the entrance to a grocery store parking lot – their first target. Ajay gave Aziz directions via a little handheld radio-set he purchased over a year ago, as they coasted down a little slope into the main parking area at the front of the store. Aziz drove to the far side of the lot and parked as Faruk followed and then parked alongside so Ajay could talk to Aziz out his window.

Earlier, Faruk had stayed at the campsite while Aziz and Ajay drove through the town, surveying for targets. They located their main target, a school just north of town, and they chose their diversionary attack to occur here at this store. Mere moments away from putting their plan into effect, Ajay sat in the van, racked with pain, sick to his stomach, with waves of nausea and a burning fever. Sweat poured down his swollen, red face. He mumbled his orders to Aziz and then instructed Faruk to drive to a neighboring parking lot. There they parked and watched Aziz pull the truck up to the front of the grocery store where he stopped, as instructed, near a large metal cage of BBQ grill propane bottles that sat under a 'no parking' sign.

Aziz quickly went to the back of the truck, pulled the blanket from the dead bodies and left it lying on the pavement. He limped to the passenger door and pulled from the floorboard a black and yellow toolbox that he placed between the cage of propane bottles and the cinderblock wall of the store. He then started limping rapidly across the parking lot toward Faruk and Ajay, glancing over his shoulder to see if he had gained any attention from the dozen or so people in the lot. But all was quiet and he saw no reaction, and with an evil grin he continued toward his companions.

Meanwhile, Ajay lifted the lid to the center console between the bucket seats and pulled out a small bag. Opening it on his lap he pulled out two cell phones, a digital recorder, and three syringes. He placed the syringes and one phone down while he dialed 911 on the other phone. Placing the phone to his ear he waited two rings and a woman dispatcher spoke.

"911. What is your emergency?"

"My name is Ajay Khan Majumbar. Are you recording this conversation?"

"Uh, yes, all 911 calls are recorded. What is your emergency? You said your name is AJ? Where are…."

"Shut up, woman! I am in charge. I am advising you that I have killed two people and left their bodies in front of the grocery store behind the police department."

231

"Uh, uh, you killed two people?"

"Yes, I did, kafir! And I am going to kill many more unless you stop me. Can you stop me?"

"Uh, wait a moment, please." The line went quiet for several seconds before he heard an older male voice calmly asking, "Hello? Sir?"

Ajay said nothing as Aziz climbed in the back doors of the van.

The voice asked again, "Hello? Who is this? Are you still there?"

"I'm here," Ajay said coldly.

The man's voice was heavily-laden with annoyance as he asked again, "Who are you? Are you trying to be funny? That'll get you in a lotta...."

"I repeat. I have killed two infidel bastards in your town and I am going to kill all of you unless you stop me."

Ajay's eyes followed a woman with a little girl who appeared to be about five-years old, walking across the store parking lot, hand-in-hand toward the truck. The woman smiled and said something to the skipping child that made the child laugh. Suddenly the woman stopped several feet from Richard's truck, jerking the child to her side. The child lost her balance and stumbled into her mother's legs, then fell to her butt on the pavement. The woman screamed, roughly yanked the bewildered child by her arm and ran rapidly away from the dead bodies, cradling the child in her arms.

The three murderers burst out laughing at what they had seen as the annoyed voice came across the phone again.

"Listen, bud, this is no day for calling in pranks to dispatch. You'll find yourself charged with a felony for misuse of the 911 system if you keep this crap up."

Before Ajay replied, he saw the rear door to the police department open and a uniformed policeman came walking out, headed toward the grocery store. After a couple of steps the policeman heard the screams and yells of several people who were now gathering around Richard Trujillo's truck. The officer immediately started running toward the gathering crowd as he lifted a handheld radio to his mouth. Seconds later, a man in slacks and sports jacket burst out the back door and ran toward the store as a growing crowd of horrified people gathered at the store front.

Ajay spoke into the phone.

"Starting to believe me?"

"Hello? Hey, are you still there?"

The annoyance was gone from the voice, replaced by a desperate urgency.

"I am here."

"Who are you? Where are you?"

Ajay ignored the stupid questions.

"I asked that stupid woman who answered the phone if you were recording this call. Are you recording this, kafir?"

"Of course, we are, and it will be used…."

"*Shut up, you fucking idiot*! I am going to give you my manifesto now. Record it!"

Ajay sat the cell phone and digital recorder on the dash and began the recorder. Immediately, Ajay's recorded voice started reciting his manifesto.

His recorded voice droned on while the three killers watched the gathering people in front of the store. A growing number of uniformed policeman directed people while the man in the cheap business suit talked rapidly into a cell phone. The bystanders were herded behind an invisible perimeter that a uniformed cop had established about twenty feet from the truck.

The sounds of sirens echoed from several different directions in the small metropolis. In moments two more marked police cars pulled up, tires screeching, at either end of the store's parking lot, blocking people from entering or leaving. In minutes a large fire engine, followed by an ambulance, arrived and got flagged into the lot by the cops. Soon three more cop cars arrived on scene; two were state police and the third was a truck with the emblem of the Colorado Division of Wildlife on the door. Ajay grimaced in discomfort but managed a meager smile. *A little bit of everything.*

A young female officer started stretching lengths of yellow crime scene tape between the doors to the store and around a large section of the parking lot. Other officers began separating individual witnesses, away from the main group of bystanders and started their questioning while another snapped scene photos.

Ajay picked up the syringes and gave one to Faruk and one to Aziz. They stared at one another for several seconds until Aziz said.

"Allahlu Akbar!"

In unison Ajay and Faruk repeated the chant as they jabbed the syringes, filled with amphetamines, into their veins. Their eyes bulged and they exhaled forcefully as their faces quickly reddened. Aziz threw down his syringe and picked up his AK47 rifle and Faruk pumped his fist against the steering wheel as the drugs started blasting through their systems.

Ajay's heart raced like the wings of a flying hummingbird as he panted feverishly and a thin string of drool poured out the corner of his mouth. He picked up the other cell phone from the console and began to punch in numbers.

*****

SECOND-YEAR Trinidad Police Officer Colby Owens stared despondently at his two dead friends' decapitated bodies lying on the truck bed. The mutilated corpses of the two dogs lay sprawled next to their masters in a disgusting sexual pose.

Colby was shocked to his core and his mind reeled at the sickening sight, and he felt close to vomiting his breakfast. The extreme violence used against the four bodies was horrific; he could see a mix of terror, horror, and revulsion in the faces around him as he walked slowly around the truck and snapped photographs of the appalling scene, which he knew was purposefully staged for the devastating emotional impact it would have on anyone who witnessed it. The evil effect was the ultimate expression of cruelty to both the victims and the witnesses by the evil people who had done this terrible act.

Colby knew the two men and their pets, and he could not fathom how these good men came to such a dreadful fate. Being raised a Catholic, he went to the same church they did and he had graduated from high school with Jake in 2005. They had shared many beers over the years while chasing girls, before the two went in different directions after graduation. Colby had enlisted in the Marines while Jake stayed to work the ranch with his father. They seldom spoke and spent only a little time together upon Colby's return from serving two tours in Iraq, but they were still friends. Now Jake and his father lay inches away from the lens of Colby's police camera, dismembered and starting to swell and bloat in the hot sun as the last of the autumn flies gathered to lay their eggs in the feast of dead flesh.

A sad, empty feeling sank into the pit of Colby's stomach as he collected the grotesque photographs that would record the scene for posterity. Each new click of his camera represented the creation of another sight, frozen for eternity, which would hopefully someday be brought out of a box to shock and educate some jury, sitting in judgment of the heinous monster that had committed this evil deed. Colby volunteered for the terrible duty so the memory of his dead friend's mutilated corpses would be his cross to carry and would not belong to another.

234

Colby saw many bodies very similar to this as he fought with his brother 3/1 Marines in the deadly streets, alleys, buildings, and tunnels of Fallujah, Iraq. There he had been involved in the heaviest urban combat that the Marines had seen since the Battle of Hue in '68. It was hell on earth for those few weeks and he felt lucky to have survived it. The dead bodies of insurgents, civilians, and fellow soldiers were a daily spectacle for him in that wretched city of death. Now he stared at a mirror image of that horror in his own home town. *How the fuck does this shit happen here?*

His mind answered its own question with a sudden flash of insight that hit Colby like a slap across the face. He knew exactly who and what type of people did this sort of terrible thing. They infested every burned-out building and mouse-hole throughout Fallujah. A cold bite of terror enveloped Colby's heart as he lowered the camera, and he looked at the horrific scene around him with new understanding. Colby started running for his closest supervisor.

*****

LONNIE SCRAWLED his name to the hospital's release paperwork for Nurse Nelson, giving her a wink as he did so.

"I sure appreciate your attentions, ma'am. If there is ev'r anything I can do for you in turn, please let me know."

Tory gave him a warm smile that brightened up the room.

"You've been a real treat for me, Mr. Garcia."

She leaned forward and sniffed near his collar.

"But if you ever help me out in the future – you need to have a bath first," she said and returned his wink and then reached up and gave his salt-and-pepper beard a light yank. She then gave a sassy spin and walked out of the room.

"Rough and ready is my middle name, hon'. Yah 'member that now, ya hear," Lonnie said to her swaying backside with a wide grin.

Lonnie turned his grin to Jim who was slowly shaking his head.

"I like that girl. If that boy she married doesn't treat her good I'll havta kick his ass and move right in."

"Keep dreaming," Jim declared, as he stepped forward and examined Lonnie's arm. "She stitched you up pretty good. Are you finally ready to go to the pokey?"

"If yer not will'n to do the time, don't do the crime! That's my motto. Let's get yer partner and…."

The sound of boots thumping down the polished tile floor of the hallway came rapidly closer until Billy slid to a stop at the door to the room, panting hard. His face a ghostly white as sweat ran down his face, he steadied himself with the door frame, holding his portable radio out in front of him as if it was something he did not want to touch.

"Big Jim! Oh, gawd, Jim!"

"Billy! What the hell is the matter with you? You just…."

Billy raised his hand, cutting Jim off.

"Jim, we got to go – right now! I'll tell you in the car."

Both Jim and Lonnie realized something very bad had happened as they both rushed after Billy, who was already headed down the hallway. Lonnie offered up his wrists to Jim.

"No need for cuffs – I won't give you no problem."

"Alright, let's go."

They made their way swiftly out of the hospital as the nurses and doctors looked on, startled and curious.

Crossing the parking lot they piled into the cruiser as Jim demanded, "Billy, what the hell is going on?"

"Oh, gawd, Jim! They found Dick Trujillo and Jake! Oh, gawd!"

"What? They get themselves hurt up on the mountain? Is Dick dead? What the hell, Billy?"

"No, Big Jim! Uh – I guess I don't know. Oh, gawd! They're not up somewhere on the ranch, Jim. The PD has the bodies downtown! They got the cut-up bodies downtown!"

Billy quickly pulled the cruiser out of the lot, squealing tires as he accelerated down sloping St. Vincent Avenue toward Main Street.

Jim could hardly follow what Billy was saying, since it just did not make any sense.

"What the hell are you talk'n about, Billy?" he demanded.

The information being processed through Billy's brain caused a blank expression to cross his face.

"Dispatch says that some bastard called in, say'n that he'd killed Jake and Dick and left their bodies down at the grocery store parking lot – gawd! Can ya believe that shit? So they sent Colby Owens to check things out and, good Lord, he up and finds Jake and Dick lying on the flatbed of their own truck – dead! And not just dead, Big Jim, they tell me that they've been all cut up and that their heads have been lopped off like they were chickens being slaughtered for dinner! Their heads had been cut off, gawd almighty, Jim!"

"What? My God, no!"

236

The cruiser's red and blue lights flashed as the vehicle skidded onto Main Street, headed downtown. All three men stared forward in shock, trying to grasp that information, when a strange grumbling sound was both heard and felt inside the moving vehicle. The very ground under the vehicle had moved.

"What the hell?" Jim gasped.

"Lower my window," Lonnie barked loudly, as bone-deep memories of Vietnam flooded back into his mind; he was certain he knew what must have caused the strange noise and vibration.

Billy mashed the window buttons on his door's control panel and all windows lowered.

Lonnie stuck his head out the window and as the wind blew through his white hair his ears heard several booming thuds echo through the sky. He ducked back inside and yelled, "Dammit! I swear those are damn explosions, boys. What the hell's hap'nin?"

"Are you sure, Lonnie?" Jim asked.

"I've heard plenty of'em o'er the years, Jim! That was an explosion!"

The cruiser continued barreling down Main Street as they all looked with wide-eyed disbelief at a billowing black cloud that began rising above the buildings of historic downtown.

"What the fuck, Big Jim! What the fuck is going on?" Billy yelled.

Lonnie leaned forward with his fingers gripping the metal cage divider between himself in the rear seat and the two lawmen in the front. He shook his head and said grimly, "That there, boys, is VC. That's VC for sure."

*****

08:21am PST UTC -8
Oakland, CA

AS THE I-880 off-ramp descended at the Broadway exit, the picturesque views of the Bay Bridge, Treasure Island and the distant skyline of San Francisco were rapidly lost. The sun glinted off the glossy burgundy paint of the big Kenworth truck as it slowed its approach to the busy intersection. Hamal eased the truck into the right turn lane, precisely following the route that he had practiced so many times before.

The truck crawled as he yielded to passing vehicles, on their way to whatever destination the typical metropolitan driver went to on a Tuesday morning. A dozen vehicles passed by before he had enough space to maneuver the truck forward, into the flow of traffic headed west toward the city center. But before he could continue a red light at 7th Street forced him to stop behind a green Nissan truck and he cursed. This spot was the last place he wanted to stop since it sat directly in front of the Oakland Police Department headquarters building.

He nervously waited for the light to change and tried to keep from looking over his shoulder at the law enforcement building, but he found it was impossible to resist the pull and he glanced over. He immediately became eye-to-eye with a uniformed cop who stood on the curb next to a marked squad car, not more than forty-feet away. The young Asian cop was staring quizzically at the highly unusual sight of the propane tanker in downtown Oakland. Hamal and the cop locked eyes for several seconds until Hamal broke contact and quickly looked away. This route had risks and this was one of them.

Staring impatiently, the seconds ticked by like cold molasses; the light continued to refuse to bend to his will and change. Sweat beads quickly exploded across the surface of Hamal's forehead and he felt the steady trickle as they began pouring down his face. He tapped the steering wheel nervously with his thumbs. Impulsively, unstoppably, and against his will, his body slowly turned, his eyes irresistibly drawn to look back toward the cop. The cop was now talking with another, older, cop at the doors to the station while pointing at Hamal's truck. The black cop was bigger, older, and had stripes on his sleeves. *A supervisor? No! Not now, not when he was so close!*

Hamal abruptly turned back and saw the same red light. *Change! Turn green!* He started to calculate how deep into the city he could get if he just accelerated and rammed through the vehicles ahead of him. How many blocks closer would he get to his target? Two? Four? His hand found the gear-shift knob and just as he started to change the pressure on the floor pedals the light changed to green. Relief rushed through his body as he raised his trembling foot off the brake to begin accelerating behind the Nissan truck. But once again he proved his unfamiliarity with the truck by letting out the clutch too fast.

A grinding pop of metal inside the gearbox made a loud grating snap as the truck violently lurched. Hamal bucked in his seat as if he had been kicked in the ass by a humungous boot. The whole rig bounced rudely on the air-suspension as the engine died, leaving the truck stalled in the middle of the intersection. The body of the dead truck driver fell from the sleeper with a thump onto the floor of the cab; Sam's lifeless eyes stared at Hamal as if laughing at the murderous but incompetent driver. Time seemed to stand still and

Hamal's ears heard nothing but his own inner ridicule and scorn as he gripped the large steering wheel tightly with both hands and cursed aloud his shame. Gritting his teeth he glanced over and saw the two policemen staring intently at him. The large man started walking toward the police car while motioning for the younger man to get in. *No!*

An irritate commuter, stuck behind the stalled rig, blared his horn as Hamal cursed again and quickly reached down and turned the key. The engine cranked over several times before it fired up, sending large clouds of black smoke billowing from the smoke stacks. He nervously eased out the clutch and a grating noise came up from the transmission, but the large rig pulled itself across the intersection and began to accelerate.

He glanced in his rearview mirror but no longer saw the two cops as he drove away under the manicured trees that grew from the center median of Broadway.

The rig approached the next intersection and he crowded into a gap in the left lane for a turn north onto 8th. More irate and inconvenienced drivers expressed their displeasure with the rude truck driver by hitting their horns as they were forced to brake hard.

The light at 8th was green and there was a large opening in the oncoming traffic. He reached the intersection and shot for the gap as he turned his front tires, hard. The turn he cut too short and the rear tires of the trailer ran across the median, causing the heavy trailer to lurch and heave as its mass jumped the four inch curb, making the tanker sway wildly as the liquid inside surged. Dozens of startled pedestrians around the intersection stared and pointed fingers at the poorly driven semi-truck. It eventually straightened out but the engine was bogged down due to Hamal having it in too high of a gear. He fought through the gears to keep the rig from stalling out again and slowly gained speed, cursing loudly the whole time.

Until he had entered the city, driving the heavy rig had been easy, but now he was completely flustered and growing more frustrated and angry by the second. He had no experience with driving a massive liquid load and long trailer in the confined spaces of city streets and it was quickly overwhelming his abilities. *Too close now!*

He looked down at the black and yellow toolbox strapped in the passenger seat and saw that it was still secured and upright. Everything depended on that box. Sweat made his hands wet and slippery and he anxiously wiped them on his pants as he tried to concentrate on the road and traffic ahead. He grabbed his shirt and used it to swipe at the sweat on his brow that flooded into his eyes and blurred his vision.

Everything seemed to accelerate, moving far too quickly for his mind to properly evaluate. Like an over-taxed computer, locked in a loop, his mind fought to deal with all of the rapidly developing input. Small details on the faces of people who walked along the street started to blend with blurry memories of burning buildings, destroyed vehicles, and the mangled and dismembered bodies of his family back in Ramadi. He looked into the rear-view mirror and his vision imagined hundreds of police cars racing up behind him to stop him from completing his mission. Then, suddenly, his mind cleared and the army of cops disappeared. Vertigo assailed his brain and his stomach suddenly retched, spewing vomit all over the steering wheel and dash.

Spindles of drool swung below his chin as his bloodshot eyes looked vacantly ahead and his mind suddenly realized that he had travelled much farther than he thought; his next turn, onto Clay Street, was only a few car lengths ahead. He knew he was moving too fast to make the turn and panicked by slamming hard on the brakes and making all eighteen tires of the tractor and trailer lock up. The angrily complaining tires left long black streaks of melted rubber on the asphalt as the weight of the load continued shoving the rig further down the street.

The tanker started to jackknife and swung out wide to the left of the tractor as Hamal pulled madly, hand-over-hand at the steering wheel, to turn the skidding truck into line with the new street. The swinging trailer continued out until it slammed broadside into the side of a pickup truck moving alongside. The overpowering weight of the trailer ejected the truck from its lane, sending it smashing into vehicles parked along the curb as other motorist behind slammed on their brakes to keep from rear-ending the whole mess.

Pedestrians scattered in panic as many yells punctuated the air, the large rig continuing to attempt the turn with screeching tires with Hamal fighting to pull it into line with Clay Street. Suddenly, like some raging dragon had come charging out of the depths of the netherworld, the normally placid workday morphed into stark terror. Some people backpedaled blindly while others tried ducking behind parked cars, and yet others ran screaming forward, toward the rig and intersection, seemingly oblivious to the laws of physics as blind terror over-stimulated their brains and turned thoughtful human beings into an alarmed herd of animals, charging recklessly in all directions.

A large woman sitting in a Subaru Outback, stopped at the westbound stop sign on Clay Street, screamed as the front corner of the Kenworth smashed into her car, thrusting it violently backward toward the sidewalk as if it were a twig being kicked by a giant. The Subaru was smashed into parked cars, catapulting them up onto the sidewalk where they in turn slammed into a standing man, frozen in shock. The crumpled vehicle tossed the man's body into the air where it sailed under a window awning and crashed against the concrete façade of the building. The car followed close behind the man's body, crashing into the face of the building before it came to rest upside down on the sidewalk. The woman driver moaned for help as she poked her bloodied arm out the side of her demolished car.

The Kenworth rocked from the collision but was otherwise unaffected as Hamal pressed down hard on the accelerator, causing the heavy trailer to whip back into line behind the tractor with a tremendous backward jerk. A sharp sound of metal under immense strain was unmistakable as the contents sloshed aggressively around inside the trailer. As Hamal fought to straighten out the rig he looked over to see that the toolbox was still safely held in the passenger seat but he never looked back to see the destruction he left in his wake, intending to do far worse.

The screams and yells at the scene of the collisions faded away as the distance grew. Ahead he could now see his target location several blocks away. He gave a broad grin as he accelerated down Clay toward the heart of the city he would soon kill. He imagined the frantic 911 calls his actions had precipitated and how they would rapidly be broadcast, to get law enforcement to respond to the accidents he left behind him. The numerous reports being made of a maniac in a tanker truck, smashing through the downtown area, would begin a massive response that would mean his time to set up for detonation was going to be compressed. *Hurry!*

Branches of the handsome trees lining the sidewalks swirled in the wind, stirred as the speeding bomb-tanker passed. The rig swiftly approached the next intersection loaded with heavy cross traffic. Undeterred, and beginning to feel desperate, Hamal maintained his speed, ready to smash his way through.

The rig came into view of the commuters crossing on 9th Street, who upon seeing the charging rig slammed on their brakes, trying to avoid being rammed as the truck burst toward the intersection. The few pedestrians halted in mid-stride, staring, pointing fingers as many searched for their cell phones. The rig blasted through the intersection with inches to spare between screeching vehicles as witness's cringed, waiting for the gigantic impact.

Hamal's heart hammered and perspiration ran down his face. He maneuvered the rig to pass a slower moving red car, a grinning Garfield doll plastered in the rear window.

The front bumper of the rig hung loosely, grating along the asphalt as the truck straddled the yellow center lines. The rear wheels

241

of the trailer clipped the car, sending it careening onto the sidewalk, scattering pedestrians and bashing into a store front. Hamal repeatedly pulled on the air-horn, letting its deep howl clear people and vehicles out of his way. His stomach roiled and he would vomit again had he not already vacated the contents of his stomach. The bitter taste of bile filled his mouth and burned his nostrils. He lowered the windows, allowing fresh air to flow in, stirring up the smells of drying blood, death, vomit, and sweat.

He now heard the yells of alarm from pedestrians; in the distance he discerned the faint noise of sirens. He approached the intersection at 10th Street at over fifty-miles an hour and braced for more collisions with the heavy cross-traffic.

Like a monster suddenly charging out from the flaming gates of hell, the damaged rig erupted into view of the crisscrossing traffic in the intersection. A skinny elderly gray-haired man driving an old brown Datsun truck slammed hard on his brakes, trying to keep from being hit by the rig, but his reaction was too slow and his brakes too old. His effort only succeeded in sending the vehicle sideways into the path of the speeding truck.

The cacophony which followed created a terrible symphony of screams, yells, skidding tires, crunching metal, and shattering glass. The rig's large tires struck the little pickup, spinning it violently, partially ejecting the old man out the driver's window. The metal latch holding the little door shut failed and the door flung open, sending his body tumbling across the street until it stopped in a broken, twisted, unmoving heap. The pickup was lifted forward and slammed into a parked car, somersaulting over it, through the air, to come smashing down onto several pedestrians on the sidewalk. People scrambled to help the hapless victims of Hamal's brutal obsession as he continued charging up Clay Street.

The loud and unusual noises of the crashes at 9th and 10th attracted the attention of dozens of people who began to line the street like spectators at a parade. Some squawked excitedly into cell phones while others used the devices to take pictures and video of the sudden mayhem, for later posting on YouTube and Facebook.

At 11th the rig blasted across the intersection with only a minor collision with a city street sweeper. Several blocks back spectators saw the blue and red strobes of a speeding police squad car, screeching into line with Clay in pursuit of the rig. Two chatting women became aware of the unexpected danger and quickly scampered away. Others stayed glued to where they were. Hamal glanced back, saw the speeding police car, and noticed the ogling spectators; he could not help but laugh. He knew something they did not – they were all about to die.

The light had just changed to green and more traffic started across his last intersection at 12th Street. A short distance beyond sat his target, the federal building. As his speed topped sixty-five miles an hour, he gripped the steering wheel tightly, preparing for the collision to come. A mail-delivery bicyclist, IPod ear-buds in his ears, was oblivious to the danger barreling toward him as he moved with the traffic in front of the rig. Witnesses watched with horror, with many quickly turning their eyes away, as the helpless man was struck broadside by the massive truck's grill.

The bicycle was immediately sucked under the front of the truck as the rider's body was propelled through the air like a ragdoll rocket. All of the mail he carried was ejected into the air. The crushed body struck the front fender of a car two lanes over and cart-wheeled wildly; blood was flung from the shattered skull in sweeping arcs into the air; where it then rained down on the surrounding cars and people.

The rampaging rig followed behind and smashed into the side of a crossing car. An explosion of plastic, metal, and glass sent pieces flying as the car was shoved into the air by the unstoppable machine. Many vehicles were knocked violently sideways while others skidded and swerved in frantic attempts to keep from colliding with the homicidal truck.

Blood from the spinning body of the bicyclist now painted a thick swath of crimson across the rig's windshield, blocking Hamal's view. Unable to see ahead, he poked his head out the door window. He immediately saw the federal building to his left. He kept the gas pedal pressed to the floor as he pulled the wheel and crashed into a line of cars parked between himself and his target.

The rig crashed through and jumped the curb as it plowed forward. Though slowed by the collisions, it still continued stubbornly onward, striking several large concrete planters along the sidewalk. The building landscaping was obliterated and chunks of concrete, dirt, and shrubs were sent flying. The truck crawled slowly through the blocky obstructions while the surging liquid weight in the trailer forced it to jackknife sideways. The grinding of broken axles, bent rims, and shattered gears exhausted itself as the crumpled rig finally stopped pitched at an awkward angle atop the last planter. The groaning tires of the skidding trailer stopped in the middle of the street, blocking the roadway. Steam lifted skyward from radiator fluid pouring from ruptured hoses onto the overheated diesel engine.

A small woman, arms extended straight in a death grip on her steering wheel, sat in a blue Toyota Corolla several feet from the back

243

of the rocking trailer. She looked to see just how close she had come to being killed. Meanwhile Hamal looked up through the shattered and blood-covered windshield to see the skyway bridge between the two towers of the federal building. He grinned evilly. *I made it!*

He quickly worked to release his seatbelt and saw that the toolbox still sat secured in the passenger seat along with his canvas bag, lying on the floor below. His sweaty, slippery hands worked feverishly at the seatbelt as the wailing of fast approaching sirens got closer. The harness finally gave way, spilling him out of the seat and sending him flailing across the leaning cab. He gracelessly clambered as he slipped and slid on the still-moist blood-covered floor as he grabbed for his bag. He hastily freed a Chinese SKS rifle from the bag; outside the rig he heard the screeching of tires and loud, blaring sirens on the street. He climbed across the wet floor mats to look out the driver door window; he saw a police car was now stopped in the middle of the street, fifty feet behind the trailer.

The squad car lurched as the driver shoved the gearshift into park, before the vehicle was even completely stopped. The driver, twenty-nine year veteran of the Oakland Police Department Sergeant James Conrad, jumped out of the driver seat and immediately pulled his service revolver, leveling it at the tractor which he believed was driven by a crazy-man.

Why do I always get these bastards on my shift? Now I have some crazy-ass fucker trying to ram a tanker truck into the federal building – what the fuck's next?

Conrad yelled at the truck, "Driver! Driver! Put your hands out the window where I can see them!"

Meanwhile, Conrad's rookie-trainee, Peter Osaka, exited the patrol car, his Glock pistol drawn, and ran around the back of the large propane trailer to the passenger side of the rig, just as his sergeant had directed him to do. He got to where he could see the other side of the cab and hunkered down behind one of the few parked cars that had not been hit by the skidding tanker.

Peter knew when he first saw the tanker pull off the interstate that there was something wrong with it. He and his training officer had followed it but were still far too slow, and he was amazed and horrified at how much damage the insane driver of the truck had already done. The mangled cars and people Peter had seen while catching up to this rig were the most terrible things he had ever witnessed in his life.

Conrad waited for something to happen as he scanned the truck for movement. He was positive that the driver was still inside the cab since they had gotten here right after it wrecked. But as he saw and heard nothing from the truck he decided to make a quick dash to the nearest wrecked car in order to get that much closer to the rig.

He sprinted in a crouching run toward a smashed car halfway to the rig's cab. Once there he yelled at the unseen driver again, "Driver! Driver, let's see your hands!"

Peter nervously watched the passenger side of the rig for any sign of activity but saw nothing but rising smoke and settling dust. Down the street a large crowd of shaken citizens stared at him. Much closer, across only a single traffic lane from him, Peter observed a woman sitting in the stalled Corolla, just a few short feet of the trailer. She was busily trying to get the old car's engine running again. Peter motioned frantically to the woman to get out and leave, but she purposefully ignored him and kept cranking the ignition in an attempt to get it started.

"Leave the car! Get out of here!" he yelled.

Meanwhile, on the far side of the rig, Conrad finally saw something; a head popped up for just a second in the driver window and then disappeared. *Gotcha, motherfucker-nowhere to go, you bastard!* The comforting sounds of multiple approaching sirens reverberated between the walls of the surrounding buildings and Conrad started to mentally go through the procedures to follow.

"Driver! Let me see your hands! I see you, driver, now show me your hands" he demanded.

Peter heard his sergeant yelling as clearly as he heard the woman in the stalled Corolla cuss, as she slapped the steering wheel in frustration after another failed attempt to get the car started. Even two car lengths away from the rusted vehicle he still smelled the excess gasoline from the old Corolla's flooded carburetor. He figured the fifty-something woman, with graying hair and a vinegar-sour expression, had no idea that the car had no chance of starting anytime soon in such a condition. She once again slapped the steering wheel in her growing frustration, cursed, and went back to pumping the gas pedal and cranking on the starter. Peter glanced up at the rig, saw nothing had changed or moved, and decided to once again try reasoning with the irate woman.

"Listen, ma'am, the car's flooded. It's not going to start. I need you to get out of it and leave."

He pleaded this as he failed to see Hamal's head pop up in the passenger window of the truck.

"Hey, lady, give it up, will ya?"

The woman stopped and let out a heavy sigh of irritation as she contemptuously looked over her shoulder at Peter.

245

"Will you leave me alone? Go be useful and arrest the dumb asshole in that truck," she said, angrily waving her hand toward the wrecked tanker. "That bastard almost hit me! I'm not leaving my car here in this damn mess. I need to get to work!"

"Lady, this is police business and I need you to leave for your own safety. You can't stay here."

"Oh, go find some Jews to roast, you Nazi! Leave me alone, *I am the victim here!*" she yelled at Peter and then went back to trying to start her car.

"Ma'am, you don't understand. You must...."

Conrad heard his rookie yelling at someone, but strangely enough it did not sound like the perp. *Doggone rookie, what's he doing?* Thankfully sirens were getting much closer and he would be very happy when he had more than just Peter with himself trying to contain this scene. Meanwhile he kept his attention focused on the driver door of the truck.

"Driver! Talk to me! Driver! Let me see...."

Hamal recognized the stupid young cop outside, paying attention to the equally stupid woman. He also heard the fast approaching sirens and knew he must act. He undid the seatbelt holding the toolbox and gripped his rifle tightly. He yelled, "Allahlu Akbar!" and pulled the door handle.

Peter's peripheral vision caught the passenger door of the canted truck falling open, and he began to swing his Glock upward as a large duffle bag came out the door and landed on the crushed cement planter. His eyes followed the bag as the woman cranked away at trying to start the car. Hamal leaned out the open door with his rifle in his hands. Peter saw the movement of a man but did not hear anymore sounds; he only saw little bright sparks coming from something in the man's hands, as bits of paint and metal from the car he was crouching behind flew strangely upward.

Hamal had followed the bag he tossed out by leveling his rifle at the young cop who had turned back toward him far too slowly to save himself. The SKS rifle jumped in Hamal's hands as he fired.

Bullets tore a stitched trail across the hood of the parked car as Peter's little Glock fired pathetically back in the general direction of the rig. Peter's blue shirt was ripped and torn as bullets struck against the Kevlar cloth of his ballistic vest. The overmatched fabric vainly tried to shelter his torso from the 123-Gr. FMJ 2,400 f.p.s. projectile attack. The first rounds mushroomed, stopped, but the subsequent rounds were less fazed by the weakened fabric, and they successfully made their way through. As the protective threads disintegrated the bullets found Peter's soft flesh underneath and gored his body

246

repeatedly. More holes appeared in his throat as the Glock flew out of his hands to clatter onto the hood, while his body pitched backward, blood spraying skyward.

The woman in the Corolla let go of her keys and screamed.

"Shit!" Conrad exclaimed.

As he heard the shots and ducked down behind the car, over his shoulder came the sound of screeching tires as two more squad cars stopped behind his. Conrad yelled into his radio mike clipped to his shoulder.

"Shots fired! Clay Street and 13th, shots fired! I repeat, shots fired!"

After he realized there were no incoming rounds headed his way, he rose up and leveled his revolver at the smoldering rig and scanned for any sign of the shooter, but saw nothing. *Dammit, Peter are you okay?*

Hamal watched the wounded officer grasp at his throat while writhing on the sidewalk. The woman in the car screamed like a banshee as he jumped out of the rig with his rifle pointed at her head. Then, deciding to ignore her, he grabbed the toolbox and knelt close to the rig. He then began to crawl toward the rear tires. He moved with haste as he had heard more police cars skid to a stop on the far side of the trailer. Many more sirens in the distance signaled the approach of even more trouble if he did not act quickly. He reached the back tires of the truck and poked his head out. With a quick scan he saw the heads of several more cops who were all kneeling behind a wrecked car along with the older black cop. He laid the rifle down by his leg and turned to his toolbox.

He flipped brackets and lifted the lid, exposing the interior, which he quickly scanned for damage. The box was separated into right and left compartments. The left section had a large diameter steel pipe that sat vertically about ten inches high with a depressed concave metal lid on the top. The pipe was securely held by clamps and was well-cushioned. In the right side compartment sat a small switch-box attached to a long coil of wires whose other ends were connected to two motorcycle batteries.

Hamal grabbed the switch-box and uncoiled the wire. He rose and looked through the gap between the top of the tires and the bottom of the trailer and saw the heads of the four cops. A black female officer with a shotgun in her hands stared excitedly at the rig. She spotted his head in the shadows; they momentarily stared at one another until her face contorted as she yelled at him, swinging the barrel of her gun toward him. Immediately two other cops, a white woman and an older white man broke from behind the car and began

247

running as fast as their legs could move, along the far sidewalk, behind the large concrete planter pots and parked cars, as they went out of sight behind the trailer.

Hamal shoved the toolbox behind the rig's tires and under the trailer with his leg. The female cop continued to scream at him as he worked to position the vertical pipe under the center of the trailer. He fully expected somebody to start shooting at him, but no bullets came. *Fools!*

Conrad knelt next to Officer Mary Long as she barked orders at the suspect. He continued relaying information into his radio, directing responding police units in establishing an effective perimeter around the scene. With the maniac driver now turned into an armed shooter, he had a bad mess. He knew that containment of the area must be created rapidly in order to mitigate the incident to as small an area of downtown as possible.

Suicidal nutcase fucker! Why does he have to pick my city to pull this shit in? Conrad had already ordered the California Highway Patrol's hazardous material units to get en route to handle any leaks from the gas truck. From his radio he heard the dispatcher trying to contact his rookie trainee but they received no return transmissions. *Peter, answer up on the radio, kid. God dammit, I hate this crazy shit!*

Conrad cared nothing for what had motivated this psychopath truck driver to lose it and start some wacko rampage today. All of his focus was on stopping this guy before he hurt any more people in the city that he loved.

"Hey, you! Hey, driver! Let me see your hands," he yelled along with Officer Long. "Hey, you! Look at me, you bastard! Let me see your fucking hands!"

Hamal finished positioning the toolbox and looked up at the cop and screamed back, "Neek hallak, kafir!"

Hamal then backed out of sight behind the tires and, retrieving his rifle, looked up, trying to locate the two cops he saw running around the back of the trailer. They were not visible to him and all he saw was the woman sitting inside the Corolla who stared back at him, wide-eyed, as he gave her an ugly wink, and then backed away toward the front tires of the rig, uncoiling more wire as he went. The smell of hot radiator fluid and leaking oil spilling from the truck's engine was pungent as he sat next to the front tire, the switchbox held tightly in his hands. He closed his eyes and began to pray.

A wise veteran, Conrad had seen and dealt with just about everything a big-city cop could ever be confronted with throughout his almost thirty years on the beat in Oakland. But now he stared, puzzling over the simple yellow and black toolbox and the guy who had just

248

shoved it under the trailer. The cheap thing could be picked up at any discount store and his mind raced to discover what it meant and it boiled down to only one possibility.

Bomb!

His mouth went dry and every beat of his heart exploded inside his ears, like a gong being hit. His skin felt ice cold and for the first time in his entire career he was frozen, unable to move. He had dealt with every drunk, vagrant, doper, hooligan, gang member, rapist, murderer, and wingnut that Oakland and the surrounding Bay Area could produce. He had thought he had run onto his first rampage-shooter today. Practically every strange occurrence that could come to the human imagination had crossed before his weary eyes over the endless graveyard shifts of the inner city, where he had spent a good portion of the last century serving his neighbors, friends, and family with devotion and honor.

And yet, during all those long years, the thousands of people and all the crazy and dangerous incidents he had experienced in his storied career, he had never come anywhere close to feeling what he felt at this second. *I'm about to die.*

Fear made his bowels turn and he felt a sudden urge to defecate. Years of training, discipline, and experience flew out of his head as he knew there was only one thing he could possibly do. *Stop the bomber!* He reacted by lurching to his feet and running toward the back of the trailer as he yelled into his radio mike, waving away nearby civilians.

"*Bomb!* Evacuate the area! *Bomb! Evacuate!*"

Officer Long watched in confused terror as her sergeant ran around the trailer, yelling, and her eyes darted back to the toolbox sitting under the trailer. Realization slapped her brain like a brutal physical force. She immediately stood, turned, and witnessed in horror as hundreds of civilians gathered together down Clay Street and throughout the huge pedestrian mall of Oakland City Center.

The angels of terror kicked her in the ass, making the mild Pacific breeze suddenly feel like frigid arctic air as she sprinted toward the crowds, wildly waving her hands above her head, screaming.

"Get back! Bomb!"

As Conrad cut around the back of the propane trailer his eyes absorbed in slow motion what he saw. A phrase he had religiously preached to every rookie he had trained over the last twenty-six years ran through his brain: expect the unexpected. Those words echoed weak and hollow in his brain as his eyes fixated upon one unexpected sight after another.

249

Ten-year veteran officer Betty Jones knelt over the body of rookie Peter Osaka with her hands mired in his blood, and she tried to apply pressure to the wounds in his neck. She was yelling updates as to his medical condition into her radio mike for responding medical personnel as his pale face grimaced and coughed blood into the air.

Her partner, Ross Benson, a retired teacher who had joined the force to help inner-city kids, covered her by pointing his shotgun toward the front of the tanker. As he heard Conrad scream something about a bomb he broke from cover and started running forward, pointing at the rig's tractor.

"There! He's there!" he yelled as he joined Conrad running forward.

With all the crushed cars shoved high onto the sidewalk, effectively blocking his view of the maniac, Conrad could not see the bomber at first. But his eyes did see the small woman sitting in her Corolla with her eyes and jaw wide-open, looking back at him in bewilderment.

He yelled at her, "Get the fuck out of here!"

Conrad dropped his radio mike as both of his hands brought his trusted revolver up to eye level as he neared the mangled vehicles. Meanwhile Benson ran behind the stalled Corolla with his shotgun at the high-ready. As Conrad neared the vehicles his eyes finally located and focused on the bomber, sitting with his back against the rubble pile of a shattered concrete retaining wall. *What's that in the fucker's hands?*

Stirred from his thoughts, Hamal heard someone yelling close by and opened his eyes. The older black cop, with all the stripes on his sleeves, now pointed a gun at him a few short feet away and yelled silly orders at him. *Drop the box? No. Are you crazy? It is the whole reason I am here.* His eyes turned to another cop, an older white guy with a shotgun who stood behind the stupid woman in the car. *Where did you come from, kafir? You don't know it's too late, do you?*

Conrad watched Hamal's thumb flip up the red cover from the switchbox and moved to press down on the uncovered button. Even though Conrad's reaction was humanly instantaneous, as he began firing his revolver, it was still far too slow.

The instructors at his academy had drummed it into the heads of every recruit: action is faster than reaction. The illustration used for this point was that a policeman who had a weapon pointed at a suspect with his finger ready to press the trigger had a very poor chance of being able to fire his weapon before a prepared suspect could reach, grab, draw, and fire a weapon blindly that was tucked into his waist band. The reasons for this were simple. No matter how much the policeman had 'the drop' on the suspect, in order for the officer to fire his first bullet he must do many things; visually perceive the motion, mentally resolve the intent of the motion, decide a course of response to the action to either fight or flee, send the muscles the necessary commands to carry out the response, and finally, the muscles must then operate the decided-upon action.

Therefore, in the hypothetical scenario, the reason for the suspect's 'action' being able to beat the 'reaction' of the officer was due to the fact that the suspect was already at the final stage of his own thought-action process and his muscles were already in the stages of carrying out the planned deed; the officer was still at the beginning stages of perception.

This explained how Conrad's 125-Gr. JHP bullets were just leaving the short six-inch barrel of his .357 Magnum Smith and Wesson revolver, travelling at 1,230 f.p.s. while at the same time, the electrical signal from Hamal's switchbox was already travelling at the speed of light, 186,282 f.p.s., along the small wires attached to a solid-fuel engine of a toy rocket. That toy igniter was imbedded inside a football-sized plastic bag filled with an explosive mixture of nitrate, oxidizer, and diesel fuel. This small bag sat inside the vertical metal pipe with the concave metal lid which sat within the left side of the toolbox.

The compressed explosion within the pipe instantly melted the concave metal top, inverting its shape into a molten bullet that was forced irresistibly upward until it struck the hull of the trailer filled with eleven-thousand gallons of liquid propane. The projectile easily punched a volleyball-sized hole through the thick steel and then rapidly cooled in the liquid propane, which did not even ignite due to the absence of oxygen. And the now re-hardened metal projectiles began to sink to the bottom of the trailer as the first bullet from Conrad's gun punched into Hamal's belly, rapidly followed by two more bullets from Conrad. Those hits were immediately followed by several .30 caliber pellets of buckshot from Benson's shotgun.

The murderer's body rocked as the well placed rounds pierced his flesh and muscle. He slumped forward as both Conrad and Benson cringed, staring frozen and terrified, at the ball of smoke from the small toolbox explosion, neither quite sure how they were still alive after the bomb exploded. *A dud? The tanker is empty?*

The small smoke cloud that was produced by the explosion was swiftly displaced by a dense white vapor cloud which rose from below the trailer as Conrad gave a small sigh of relief. *I'm going to live.* He conducted a speed reload of his revolver and turned from the rising white cloud to look back at the perp who slumped amid the chunks of broken concrete.

Hamal held his bleeding belly as waves of nausea undulated through his body, and a choking sensation flooded his chest as blood moved from his perforated veins into his equally perforated lungs. He coughed blood and raised his wobbly head. He witnessed the billowing white cloud and smelled the odorant-infused gas as a frigidly cold blast of air hit his face. *Success!* Hamal smiled as he fell face-forward, dead.

Conrad observed the sickening, rotten-toothed grin as the bomber's head fell with a bounce against the concrete sidewalk; at the same instant the smell of the odorant hit his nostrils. Deep fear swelled in his belly as he glanced back at the mortally wounded tanker and watched, through the dense fog of vapor, a gushing torrent of clear liquid splashing down onto the sidewalk. A thick coat of frost formed on every surface the liquid splashed onto. He could barely see the large hole punched into the bottom of the trailer through the dense vapor cloud. *Shit, so that's how those bastards in Iraq can destroy a tank with an IED.*

Hundreds of gallons of propane cascaded out onto the asphalt where it boiled and spat like water thrown into a scalding hot pan. Each gallon then instantaneously vaporized into 272-cubic gallons of gas that blended with the oxygen-rich air. The gas cloud grew immense by its own expansion, but was immediately dispersed into the surrounding city by the constant breeze that rolled in from the Pacific. *Shit! Fuck me.*

Conrad was engulfed inside the cold mist and his eyes followed the lead edge of the already-gigantic cloud as it moved off toward City Hall. He turned and saw a crowd of people had begun rushing out of the federal building. In their midst were two FBI agents whom he had known for years, running toward him, their weapons drawn. *Too late!* He then turned to Benson who returned his helpless and forlorn expression. *It happened too damn fast. We weren't prepared for this!*

The strange coldness of the mist perplexed him as an oddly deep chill sank into his flesh, causing goose bumps to flourish across his skin. The irony of it feeling so wintry on a mild California morning was something he could not reconcile. Then, strangely familiar sounds invaded his conscious thought; there was a foot pumping a gas pedal madly, a palm thumping against a steering wheel, angry cursing, and the distinctive grind of an old starter cranking against all hope.

He spun, extending his arm, palm facing out to the woman in the old Corolla and yelled.

"*Stop!*"

At that moment the gasoline-flooded carburetor in the car sucked in just enough air to allow the tiny ember of a spark from the worn-out sparkplugs to ignite the fuel, causing combustion. The small car jumped as the engine farted and sputtered to life. The woman sat back as her expression widened into relief, while the pressure within the combustion chamber went beyond containment. The remaining fuel was forced out of the ignition chamber and into the exhaust pipe, where it burst out the end of the tailpipe with a loud flaming backfire.

Conrad's ears delivered the sound of the backfire to his mind and his shoulders slumped. *Oh, fuck me, whatta way to go.* The small flame from the tailpipe ignited the propane-oxygen mixture and the last thing Conrad's eyes saw before he was incinerated was a multitude of people running madly away in the distance. *Too damn late.*

The resulting thermobaric explosion reached an internal overpressure surpassing 30-bars in atmospheric pressure that radiated outward at over 3 miles per second. The blast's lateral and vertical force struck the eighteen floors of the Ronald V. Dellums Federal Building North. The disintegrating structure and its obliterated components were lifted northward toward Preservation Park and the Bay Bridge.

The explosion's blast wave instantaneously propagated throughout Oakland, straight away flattening most of City Center, Chinatown, Old Town, and Uptown. As the confined spaces between the buildings amplified the local effects of the blast, the general force of the pressure wave lifted and shoved entire city blocks of material into the air to rain down throughout Oakland, Alameda, and Berkley. Including much debris that soon came crashing down throughout the Bay and east shore of San Francisco.

Over 22,000 people were instantly atomized by the initial blast in the downtown core. The ambient temperature within that blast exceeded 5,200 degrees Fahrenheit, which incinerated all that was left of the city's downtown area. Simultaneously it started countless fires that raged throughout the neighborhoods of Piedmont, Glenview, and along the gentle slopes of the Glen Highlands into Montclair and down to Fruitvale.

(three minutes earlier)
08:39am PST UTC -8
I-280 @ Hwy 101 San Francisco, CA

AS HAMAL was centering his bomb below the propane tanker the mid-morning sun hung above a misty Pacific horizon where it outlined the brooding San Bruno Mountains in a beautiful golden glow. The first rays from the sun had just peaked over their summit and began illuminating their craggy eastern flanks and flooding dazzling morning light onto the choppy waters of a majestic San Francisco Bay.

Like all busy weekday mornings, the dense traffic moved along Hwy-101 toward the metropolis of San Francisco at a hectic but consistent pace. Occasionally, a commuter's eyes would be struck by the sun's glinting reflection from the millions of windows below. Major Al-Doleh admired this view of the great port city as he led his commandos in a disciplined formation. Their goal: to destroy everything possible within the infidel's hedonistic capitol that lay sprawled before them.

He took the beauty of the scenery as a good omen for their success and also as proof that they had Allah's blessings. So far his commandos had made excellent time and were well within their planned time table. They had not encountered a single problem as they had travelled from Texas, across the American west, to the staging point outside Pleasanton. They had found the tankers and vans ready and waiting for them, just as the Kashmiri said they would. Now, barring some unforeseen circumstance they would soon be inside the heart of the city, with never being challenged at any point along their long journey from Iran.

Years ago, Al-Doleh had doubted when the Texan-jihadist had confidently boasted to General Nakisa that he would be able to get the entire Iranian strike force into America easily. The psychopath had stated then that it would be child's play to get the men, their weapons, and their explosives from Monterrey, across the border to his family's Texas ranch, in a single day. Now, after a mere four days from the border crossing checkpoint at Del Rio, Texas, the ease with which he and his men had gotten into and then travelled across America was beyond shocking to the terrorist commander. *Has it always been this easy?*

The years of confidence gained by using the cramped confines of the hidden compartments inside the box trailer to smuggle drugs and migrants into this country had proven him right in his boasting. It astounded Al-Doleh at how easily the Kashmiri and his bloodthirsty cartel friends could make their way repeatedly across the border with such impunity and how this infidel-jahilli society voluntarily, and with deliberation, laid their beating hearts out on a silver platter for predators like him and his men to feast upon.

After being provisioned with their weapons, explosives, ballistic vests, and communications gear at the Texas ranch, his only real distress, to date, had manifested when the unbalanced Kashmiri had murdered his parents. Allah would judge Al-Doleh for sparing the insane fool and not eliminating him then and there, and yet he did not regret his decision. For without the continued assistance the jihadist had given, the major and his men might not have gotten to this point successfully.

As agreed, Al-Doleh had kept his men away from the ranch house, on penalty of death. They were well-trained and committed to the mission but he had no idea what might ensue if they had seen the dead bodies. It was simply a distraction that he did not need to deal with. The Kashmiri had shown up the next day with the large yellow school bus that Al-Doleh and his men had then used as their transportation here to California. Al-Doleh chuckled at how easy it had been to travel over 1,700 miles in a stolen school bus, with prepaid credit cards to fuel and satellite phones to keep in constant contact with the Houston strike teams he had left back in Texas. *The insane bastard did well for me.*

The major's excitement grew as he contemplated how he was now mere minutes away from shepherding in the creation of the next great Persian Caliphate, to rule the entire Muslim world. Very soon the pedophile dominated Kingdom of Saud would be brought low and the Holy Cities and the Káaba would once again be the property of the true Islamic path – the Shia!

Throughout the morning, his convoy had moved from the staging point along I-680 under Pleasanton Ridge. It then progressed through the City of Milpitas and across the Southbay Freeway until it eventually turned onto Hwy-101, which now was carrying it toward the center of their target. During that trip Al-Doleh had earnestly watched across the wide bay toward Oakland. Unlike his men, or even his second-in-command, Lieutenant ud-Daulah, the major had been informed by General Nakisa that he had activated the other sleeper-cell jihadist which had been stationed here in California the past two years. Al-Doleh had never met the Iraqi-jihadist that Nakisa had instituted here, and all he did know was that that shahid was prepared to carry out a strike similar to his own mission, but within the city of Oakland. Nakisa had assured that the two simultaneous attacks would

255

decimate the entire bay area between the anvil of the attack on Oakland and the hammer of Al-Doleh's attack on San Francisco.

So the major had watched for any sign of that other attack but had so far seen nothing. Sleeper cells were notoriously unpredictable since they were so often sniffed out by the FBI before they could succeed, and if nothing happened he would not be surprised, especially since he had not been part of that plan.

Al-Doleh's most trusted man, Abbas, sat in the driver seat of the stolen school bus that had been home to Al-Doleh and his men for the past three days. The bus was the lead vehicle in the procession as they turned from Hwy-101 and merged into the traffic moving along the Southern Embarcadero Freeway. The group would soon separate into their individual strike teams to attack each of their pre-assigned targets inside the city. Al-Doleh looked back to monitor the procession following behind the bus and saw that it was perfectly spaced, single-file, rolling down the gentle slope of the hill, with each of the three tankers immediately followed by its own assigned three-man escort team in a van. Including himself, his small force of only seventeen men planned to successfully destroy an entire city.

Looking out confidently, he examined the traffic ahead and saw that it was getting more congested, and he was about to give another update to his men behind. But as he raised the little Motorola radio to his lips an odd movement caught his eye before he could speak, and he stared, slack-jawed, across the sparkling bay at the distant city of Oakland.

The tremendous fireball of the thermobaric explosion erupted skyward, rising in a plume of fire, smoke and debris as if some undiscovered and long dormant volcano was suddenly erupting and releasing its pent-up energy toward the heavens. The explosion was unnervingly silent, because of the distance, but was so massive that for more than a second Al-Doleh actually feared that the sleeper cell had possibly detonated a small nuclear weapon. The explosion quickly caught the attention of Abbas, who gave a surprised exclamation as the thunderclap bang from the explosion finally arrived from eight-and-a-half miles away, with enough volume to hurt their ears.

They both craned their eyes upward, following the rising mushroom cloud that extended like an ugly misshapen pillar above the distant city, until the massive dark cloud punctured the virgin blue sky like a spear above the East Bay hills. Al-Doleh gaped at the extent of destruction he was witnessing, and marveled at what his contemporary had accomplished. *Can I do better than that?*

He keyed the mike on the little radio and broadcast for his men to pay attention to the explosion and relayed to them what little knowledge he had of the mujahideen who had wrought the destruction there. They could all plainly see the success of that operation for themselves, and as Abbas howled his joy and bounced in jubilation, he paid no attention to the traffic ahead of the bus.

Several vehicles ahead were now slowing as more and more people, driving their busy morning commute to San Francisco, witnessed the catastrophe that was occurring across the beautiful bay. Al-Doleh jumped up and down while continuing to urge his men to do great deeds against the infidel, and be worthy of glory equal to that of the Oakland shahid. Then, suddenly, he saw the slowing traffic ahead.

He screamed into his radio, "Pay attention to the road! Pay attention to the road!"

Abbas immediately turned his attention back to the road ahead, where now an almost solid wall of traffic slowly crawled. He punched his foot down on the brake pedal and pulled hard on the steering wheel. The bus swerved to the right as he attempted to miss a slow-moving minivan filled with three children and their parents, all gawking at the far-off explosion. Straddling the aisle in the center of the bus, Al-Doleh braced himself in preparation for the collision to come. The forty-foot long yellow bus clipped the back of the minivan, shoving it into the side of a faster moving tractor-trailer in the left lane. The bang of the collision echoed throughout the interior of the bus as it rocked violently while Abbas worked to get it under control, cursing loudly.

The impact caused the major to fly off his feet, and land hard on a bench seat where he struck his head against one of the side windows. The truck and minivan collided before the trucker was able to swerve his rig away. The minivan was knocked into other vehicles as the rig turned hard, which caused its box-trailer to jackknife with its tires complaining loudly. As the rear of the trailer made a wide swing it crashed into the mass of other commuters on the busy highway. A cacophony erupted as mangled metal, shattered glass, and screams punctuated the collision of over two dozen vehicles.

As Abbas straightened the bus along the shoulder of the highway, Al-Doleh poked his head above the seat back; he stared, wide-eyed, at the tremendous pile-up of vehicles occurring in the far left lanes. He watched as the large truck flipped over and crushed even more vehicles at nearly forty-miles an hour. His glanced back and saw that his strike team vehicles and tankers were able to stay in line behind the bus and had completely avoided becoming involved in the wreckage caused by Abbas's inattention.

Al-Doleh gave a heavy sigh of relief as he saw the last van squeeze past the carnage and follow behind the convoy. Al-Doleh

257

turned and glared at Abbas, whose normally dark skin was a sickly ashen pale as he maintained a death grip on the steering wheel. The major pulled himself out of the child's bench seat and placing his mouth next to Abbas's ear; his right hand pulled a long-bladed knife which he pressed into the flesh of Abbas's neck.

He whispered in a cold voice, "Do not do that again! You stupid fool."

Abbas swallowed hard as he nodded his head slowly and wincing at the blade buried a half-inch into his neck.

The rapid hammering of the major's heart began to soften as he withdrew the blade and slapped it back into its scabbard. The bus continued descending toward the east until the far side of the Bay became difficult to see through the growing mass of buildings that now blocked their view. But the growing pillar of smoke and dust from the distant detonation was still easily visible in the morning sky as the Pacific trade winds began widening it into a foreboding pale above Oakland.

The freeway curved to their left and Abbas was forced to slow even more as he wound a path through the slower moving, and even stopped, traffic. They successfully wormed their way through, although he was forced to occasionally nudge a vehicle out of the caravan's way. The longer semi-tankers were forced to rudely shove and bump vehicles even more.

Abbas negotiated the traffic very attentively now, as numerous vehicles had pulled onto the shoulder of the road. Abbas waved his arms and screamed profanity at the gawking people who either stood next to or even on top of their cars, trying to see what had occurred across the Bay. The convoy followed the bus down the freeway off-ramp where they finally exited the choked traffic at 6th Street.

*****

(three minutes ago)

AS ABBAS approached his turn to merge onto the Southern Embarcadero Freeway, fourteen-year veteran San Francisco policewoman Marta Blackwood and her partner Shea Ogelby chatted with each other. They had spent the first hour of their shift lazily watching the busy arrangements of city work crews preparing Civic Center Plaza. The park was located across the street from city hall, and was to be used for a political rally in the afternoon.

Both officers liked working these security details for the many events held across from the Mayor's office. They always made sure to be the first to sign up on the overtime roster. Except for when things got too rowdy or turned flat-out violent, these events were typically pretty good entertainment. It made for a great way to watch some of the funniest and weirdest stuff imaginable, and not have to pay for admission.

Marta looked west at the beautiful sunrise and could see the street vendor, Maria Esperanza, setting up her taco stand on the southwest corner of Grove and Polk streets. It was a prime location, near the rotunda of City Hall, for the tourists and locals who might show up for the event. Marta admired how Maria always seemed to snag that spot before any of the other vendors who vied for the same hungry pedestrian traffic these rallies provided.

Marta had even once seen people in the middle of rioting, still busily buying Maria out of every bit of food she had, all the while dutifully jumping up and down on top of a new police cruiser for the media cameras. And during that entire maelstrom of lawlessness, Maria had coolly worked her business stand amid the yelling and chanting. Not once did the rioters turn their hostile attentions toward her little stand.

Marta loved the tamales and decided to get over to the stand as soon as she could break away from the intersection. She might even grab a couple more for dinner with her girlfriend, Peggy. Peggy also loved the tamales, and if Marta came home with a couple of those she might just get in on some of Peggy's royal loving for dessert.

Today's planned event was supposed to be a fairly small one and scheduled to end by early afternoon. A local environmental group, The Bay Area Energy Independence Coalition, hoped for a big crowd to show, but Lieutenant Miller was expecting only a couple hundred people to turn up for the same old speeches. The spiraling economy had even the greenies lackluster about these shows nowadays, and everything certainly appeared as though it should fit on the plaza grounds easily enough. The city had not even put up barricades to block the streets around City Hall since it appeared to be such a non-event. She even doubted that the mayor would show up for the few cameras present today. *This'll be a total yawner.*

The officers were assigned to their usual duty of patrolling the crowd while making small talk with the folks. They were exceptional at keeping a good gauge on the tempo of the event for the lieutenant. It also worked great for outgoing Marta who loved chatting up a storm with everyone they met. Whether it was the flashiest drag queen at a gay rights parade, or a group of skinhead neo-Nazi KKK members, Marta could get people to communicate openly with a down-to-earth, human manner. Shea called her the Oprah of the Beat, for the way she got just about everyone they contacted to spill their guts and talk freely. Presently, the angry bark of a car horn, off to her left, drew Marta's attention away from Maria's. She turned to see a frustrated man with his head tilted out his driver-side window, yelling and pumping an enraged middle finger at the driver of a large RV, who was trying to make an illegal turn from Polk onto Grove. A bewildered and overwhelmed seventy-something gentleman driving the large recreational vehicle, obviously a tourist, had made a wrong turn and had come bumper-to-bumper with an irate local. There had been no crash but their bumpers were mere inches from each other, with many more vehicles pressing in from behind so that they could not move.

"I think you should get this one, Marta. I didn't get enough beauty sleep to deal with this sort of thing this early. You mind, honey?" Shea bemoaned with a big wink.

Marta shrugged good-naturedly and sauntered over to the perplexed driver, who appeared about ready to have a heart attack.

"Hey, sweetie! Hey, Sweeetie!" she sang while she waved her arm and snapped her fingers above her head.

The elderly man looked up from his dashboard, and upon seeing the female officer walking toward his RV, relief washed across his stressed face. He quickly lowered his window and poked his head out.

"Oh, thank God you're here, oh, thank God," he exclaimed. "I really need some help – I, uh, I'm really lost."

With an easy tone to her voice, Marta melted the tension from the man in a second.

"Lost? Naw, sweetie, you know right where you're at and you even know what that means, sugar? Why, that means you're right here, and that means you're here with me, right? So that means you're right where you need to be, honey."

The gentleman sat back in his seat and gave a meek smile.

"I'm so sorry to cause you any trouble, ma'am. Shelly and I wanted to see City Hall but I've been driving around in circles and I can't find parking for this thing," he volunteered. "We left our son's home in Nevada yesterday and we just came over the Bay Bridge this morning, God it was beautiful, and since I got off the interstate I can't seem to…."

The man looked down at the stoic but polite expression on Marta's face as she waited patiently for him to finish telling her about his life, grandkids, retirement, and if his prostate was still okay. Just like every good person in such a situation, he was ready to divulge his entire life to her if she let him. He glanced at the long line of frustrated drivers he had blocked in and sheepishly asked, "Can you help me?"

Marta, pleased to see he could focus on the situation at hand, winked at both him and his nervous wife who sat behind him with her fingers clasp tightly in her lap. Both of them looked back at Marta hopefully.

"Aw, hon, and I was hoping you were going through all this trouble just to come down here and see me," she said with a glance to the front and back of the RV.

"Now, honey, you just sit here a couple seconds while I clear out a way for you to go, okay? Now, you do know I want you to stay right here and not go until I get back and tell you, right?"

"Yes, ma'am, I do," he said, feeling more secure than he had since he and his wife had entered the city over a half hour before.

The angry horn honked twice more and a long string of cars continued to build up behind the frustrated local man, who was hopelessly boxed in. The man looked up at Marta as she walked toward his car, and with an exaggerated frown he lowered his head between his shoulders and raised both hands in an overly-mocking gesture that said to Marta, 'Well? What now?'

Marta moved her five-foot, eight-inch high, two-hundred-ten pound frame in a calm and easy stride toward his passenger window, and lazily rolled her wrist, indicating for him to lower the glass as she bent forward to speak. The dull whine of the small electric motor lowering the window buzzed as she leaned further into the car.

With a pleasant look on her face and a genuinely concerned tone in a quiet voice she said, "Sir, the older gentleman in the RV will be moving out of your way momentarily. Can I please ask you to give me just a few moments of your day to wait here patiently while I get his big vehicle moved, so you can move on with your obviously busy schedule?"

The wind that had built-up behind the man's sails died off and his off-the-rack business suit deflated a bit as he replied, "Ah, yes, well – I guess so. I'm in a hurry and need to go – ah, please?" he ended up asking in a tone that was more flustered than angry, as her charm had deflated his anger.

"Yes, sir, once I get him backed up and you have room to proceed I will make sure you move along with your day first, and you, sir – have a good day, too, okay?"

"Ah, well, yes –thank you," he finished with a weak but genuine smile back at hers.

She strolled back to the RV and saw that Shea had already moved in and gotten some of the traffic behind it backed up enough

261

for it to move. There were a couple impatient horns that honked several cars back in each stalled line as Marta gave instructions to the elderly tourist.

"Sugar, you turn your wheel a little to the left now and back up until I say stop."

The old man backed the RV slowly as Marta walked alongside, giving him reassurance by gently waving him on. When he had moved away from the other man's car, with enough room to get by, she had him stop. The man in the business suit stayed where he was and waved for the RV to go by first while he held the traffic back. Marta gave him a grateful thumbs-up and turned to the RV driver while pointing down Goodlet.

"Now, sugar, you go straight down this road one block to the other side of the park, then turn left and drive two blocks to McAllister and then turn right. There'll be parking on your right side, okay?"

"Straight one block, left for two blocks, then right and parking on the right?" he asked while making the same motions with his right arm.

"You got it, sugar."

"You're a miracle. Many thanks, ma'am," he said, as he slowly drove away and tipped his head to the driver he had almost hit moments before.

Marta turned to the man in the car, who now slowly moved forward and she blew him a kiss as he passed. He grabbed the imaginary smooch from the air and placed it in his shirt pocket with a smile. Marta turned and sauntered back to the sidewalk and, with a wide grin, stood next to Shea. Traffic moved into the now-open lanes and found its way forward as the intersection began to clear.

Shea glanced over at the satisfied expression on her partner's face and said with reverence, "You're awesome, partner."

She gave Shea a sassy grin and a wink.

"Hell, I'm better than skinny-dippin' in the Bay with some Kansas City BBQ waiting, honey," she said and they both broke up laughing.

They were still laughing as a loud but distant bang rent the air, causing them to instinctively duck their heads. A dozen or so car alarms started to blare along the surrounding city blocks, while dozens of birds flew into the sky. The two women spun their heads around, looking with surprised concern as a deep, rumbling noise followed and a soft tremble moved through the ground under their feet. The strange occurrence even caused Maria, at her food cart, and many other pedestrians around to stop and wait quietly for what might follow.

"Earthquake?" Shea asked, turning to Marta.

"No, not with a sound like that. What the hell, Shea?"

"Oh, my dear God," came a quiet voice behind them.

Marta looked around and saw a small woman in a cute blue pantsuit which matched her eyeliner perfectly. The woman had covered her mouth with her hands and had an expression of deep fear set on her face.

"No, no, not again," she said through her fingers as she looked down Grove Street toward the strange noise.

"What's a matter, sweetie? It's just a little quake is all, huh? You're going to be fine," Marta assured the woman.

The woman shook her head.

"Sweetie, you okay?" Marta asked.

The woman looked into Marta's eyes.

"I was at Gramercy Park, in the East Village on 9/11. I know what the sound and feel of the Twin Towers coming down was like and I'm telling you, what just happened, that was no damned earthquake."

Without another word the woman made a quick turn on her two-inch pumps and walked back the way she had come, still holding her hands over her mouth.

Marta turned and looked suspiciously down Grove Street for several seconds.

"Shea, go get the car," she finally said quietly.

"What? Our assignment is this boondoggle here at the park, Marta," Shea replied in confusion.

Marta continued looking east past Shea and calmly said, "Go – get – the car, sugar."

Shea looked at her partner for a second and, seeing the seriousness in her face, turned and headed down the block to their squad car. Marta looked around at the folks who were now starting to move around again as if nothing was amiss. Meanwhile a strange and inarticulate fear began to creep into her soul. People gave one another the kind of sheepish and relieved grins that happened after the long-awaited 'Big One' earthquake failed to materialize once again. They then went back to what they were doing before the weird occurrence, but Marta felt none of the assurances that they did. She was suddenly becoming scared, but of what she did not know.

A few minutes later Shea pulled up next to the curb, leaning over the passenger seat as she called out the passenger window, "Marta, you need to hear this on the city band."

She turned up the volume on the police radio.

"....I can see some sort of cloud, way up into the air over the city. The fireball is gone now but there is one heck of a big cloud over there, central."

"Copy, 4 Adam 12. Stand by."

Beep...beep...beep

"All units be advised. Repeat, all units be advised. A possible mass-casualty event has occurred in the City of Oakland. I repeat. A possible mass-casualty event has occurred in the City of Oakland. Stand by for further instructions to follow."

Beep...beep...beep

Marta quickly climbed into the squad car as her heart sank in her chest.

"How the hell does something that happened all the way over in Oakland get felt all the way across the bay, over here?" Marta mumbled quietly to herself.

Shea, still confused about what her longtime squad-car partner was possibly thinking, replied tentatively, "Well, I don't know, Marta."

"Just go ahead and roll on down toward the bay, honey," Marta said in a disconnected tone.

"What? Marty, we can't leave here without the okay from Lieutenant Miller. We'll get our asses hung out to dry if we do. What are we going to do, drive to Oakland? That isn't even our city."

Marta turned to her lifelong friend and spoke with such seriousness that Shea was amazed.

"We got to move – right now. I feel it deep, Shea. I don't know what's going on, but something is telling me we got to go, hon. Now, I'm asking you to take me to the bay."

Shea stared at her partner and nodded. "I got your back, sister."

The squad car pulled away from the curb and headed down Grove Street toward downtown.

*****

THE POLISHED marble floor had just ended its little spate of movement and the barely noticeable rumbling noise had passed. Saul Goldman was relieved that the little tremor had gone unnoticed by most of the shoppers making their way through the brightly-lit corridors of the mall. He had noticed that several people, probably longtime California residents, had stopped their shopping and waited a few precious moments to make sure the tiny quake had ended, but most of the other bargain hunters went blissfully along their way without so much as a second of hesitation or showing the slightest awareness that the earth had moved under their feet.

They would've been haul'n butt for the exit if it hadn't stopped. Ever since the massive quake that hit Japan in the spring, Saul had feared that the 'Big One' was heading this way. But since it appeared to have not hit this morning, and with his metal hip starting to ache, he figured that his walking the halls for the day was pretty much done. So he turned for the nearest service-hall door and went fishing for his keys, way down in his pocket.

Most people, who had not worked inside a mall complex, never knew the veiled world behind the manicured facades of the big chain and box stores. Hidden away behind the service doors lay a labyrinthine maze of back halls and access corridors that weaved through each floor. They gave access to work elevators where the mall maintenance staff and security guards, like Saul made their way out of sight of the thousands of pedestrians who moved daily through the main corridors.

Mall security had turned out to be the perfect retirement job since Saul had left the Air Force five-years ago. He received decent medical insurance and the pay supplemented his and Edith's monthly income nicely. Ever since his hip replacement four-years ago he could not go for long on foot and usually spent the second half of his shift cruising around on his Segway. He knew it was a short trip through the service hall to the elevator, where in just minutes he would be delivered to the security office to pick up his electric steed.

Saul turned his key in the door handle and as the metal door swung open, he heard the familiar sound of numerous skateboard wheels rolling across tiled floors. He leaned back, craning his head over his shoulder and saw the culprits weaving their way through the moderate amount of walkers in the large hall. *Billy Gafney! You little turd, how many times do I have to ride your ass?* Saul popped out from the door's cubby hole and raised his hands just as he witnessed the teenager's eyes roll.

*****

THE EVIL procession of school bus, big rigs, and vans filled with homicidal intent continued to move efficiently block-by-block as it made its way down 6th Street. The other motorists here were apparently oblivious to the explosion across the bay and so they went about their daily routine in complete ignorance of the tragedy occurring there. Al-Doleh kept in constant contact with his strike teams via his radio but he had little concern since his men had memorized the routes to their individual targets. It was as if they had driven these streets ten thousand times before today, and the only thing different was the traffic.

Abbas slowed the school bus as he prepared to turn right onto Mission Street. Al-Doleh tightened the straps on his explosive vest and checked his ammunition pockets for what seemed like the fiftieth time. He no longer troubled himself with the last tanker in line, since Sergeant Diba's strike force van and tanker had already turned east onto Harrison Street. What fate was in store for them at their target at One Rincon Tower was now in their hands alone. Al-Doleh felt a wave of liberation flood through his body, causing him to feel as light as a feather. No longer did he have any responsibilities for their mission other than his own fate now, and with those shackles of duty and responsibility melting off his shoulders, it gave his spirit the greatest sense of freedom he has known in a very long time. From now on, he was little more than another gunman in the attack force, and no longer did he need to lead or direct much of anything.

The traffic on Mission Street was heavy and after travelling only a block, Abbas made his pre-planned stop just past a crosswalk, straddling the double-yellow center lines, blocking the normal flow of traffic. Almost immediately horns blared loudly their disapproval as commuters became snarled by the blockage. The tankers and their escort vans easily moved past the bus as confused and irritated motorists and curious pedestrians looked on. The tankers took the lead in the convoy procession and now proceeded toward the heart of the financial district, while the bus pulled into line behind them, rudely scraping several cars who tried nosing their way through the unexpected traffic jam. The move was carried out flawlessly, just as they had practiced so many times in the busy streets of Karaj.

Numerous horns blared and their drivers yelled profanity at the strange parade that now moved away down Mission Street, leaving behind several fender-bender victims in its wake. The disconcerted drivers stared in confusion at the unconcerned bus that pulled away and left them with scarred vehicles. Neither Al-Doleh nor any of his men saw the police car, a block away on 5th Street, turn on its red and blue strobe lights and accelerate toward the scene of the minor wrecks and traffic snarl that the officers there had just witnessed.

The two remaining tankers were now pointed directly at their intended targets. The tanker driver's only mission from here on was to ram their trucks as deep as possible inside the ground floor of their target buildings. After impact, if the driver was still alive and functioning, he would detonate the rig. But if the drivers were dead or incapacitated so that they could not detonate, both Al-Doleh and the

266

two remaining escorting strike teams had secondary detonators for the trucks' explosives. Nakisa's well-laid plan guaranteed that absolutely nothing had been left to chance as long as the tankers got to their targets.

General Nakisa's use of the gasoline tankers was intended to achieve the same eventual collapse of these buildings that the hijacked airplanes of 9/11 had achieved at the Twin Towers. But instead of beginning with a massive fire high up on the 100th floor or so, these fires would be started on the ground floor, and thereby trapping every person inside and eliminating any chance of escape from the ensuing inferno. This would guarantee the highest death-toll possible.

Abbas lagged behind the tankers as the rigs began their suicide run and Al-Doleh prepared to release the teams of gunmen in the vans from their primary job of escorting the tankers. He would allow them to break off and complete their secondary mission; to create havoc and panic throughout the city center by attacking the general population directly with their explosives and weapons. Nakisa had planned that the ensuing mayhem would compound the problems for all emergency responders throughout the downtown area and also trap the city's population the resulting crossfire.

The major gripped his radio tightly and broadcast his final orders to the tankers to proceed. He was immediately rewarded by seeing the dark smoke of diesel exhaust blow from their stacks as they accelerated. He then gave his orders that released the escort teams and immediately the vans peeled away from Mission Street, and turned north into the oncoming one-way traffic of 4th Street. There the startled drivers braked and swerved with horns blaring, as the maniac drivers in the vans wove their way through them.

During their final rush, the tankers accelerated to over fifty miles per hour as they reached 2nd Street and slammed their way through several cross-traffic vehicles in the intersection. Those vehicles were sent careening into pedestrians and other vehicles. Nothing stopped or even slowed them as screams came from people in every direction. The little walkie-talkie radio speakers inside the cabs of the tanker trucks came alive with the voices from the gunmen strike teams, advising that they had reached their target – the shopping mall of Westfield San Francisco Center.

Al-Doleh could hear the sound of gunfire in the background of the voices coming over his handheld radio, when suddenly he heard a police siren and spun to look behind the bus. A speeding black and white San Francisco Police squad car raced its way through traffic along Mission Street toward the rear of the bus. *We have finally attracted their attention!* The commandos were well prepared for this eventuality. Now he, the leader of the entire mission, would be the first to confront and eliminate the first law enforcement response from the city's front-line defenders. He barked orders at Abbas to continue down the street as he quickly made his way to the back of the bus.

The squad car rapidly approached the back of the bus and Al-Doleh observed the two cops inside: a middle-aged balding white man driving, with a younger Asian woman, maybe Chinese, talking on the radio handset. As Abbas drove the bus across 2nd Street it became apparent that the officers were uninterested in the bus, as the squad car moved to pass along the left side, the officers watched for oncoming traffic and never even looked up at the bus.

Al-Doleh raised his AK47 to his shoulder; the rifle bucked in his hands as he sent a stream of red-hot bullets at the squad car. The female cop must have seen movement inside the bus, for at the last moment she glanced up. The bullets punched through the glass in the bus's rear emergency door, shattering it into a million pieces with some peppering Al-Doleh's face, causing him to squint.

The Asian cop's head exploded as blood, bone, and brain matter sprayed the interior of the squad car. More bullets riddled the windshield in a continuous spray that made a dotted line of frosted holes across the windshield and hood. Al-Doleh pulled at his bucking rifle, and sent a fusillade of rounds directly at the driver. This caused the cop to swerve hard to the left and ram straight into the front grill of a parked FedEx van stopped along the curb.

The impact of the police car into the delivery truck sent the blue-shirted delivery man airborne, out the side door, vaulting him across the sidewalk, where he crashed through the window of a cafeteria. His body landed in a pile of shattered plates and utensils, as the torn flesh from his exposed arms, legs, and face poured out streams of blood onto the overturned meals of the patrons.

"Allahlu Akbar!" Abbas yelled loudly from the front of the bus, while pumping his fists up and down.

"Pay attention to your driving," said the major. He picked up his radio and yelled.

"Khoda hafez!"

He walked back and stood next to Abbas as they intently watched the first tanker barrel by the front of the Transbay Terminal, continuing to gain more terrible speed. Pedestrians were now stopped, watching the two barreling trucks. Many others thought they had just heard firecrackers farther up the street and gazed back toward the bus. As the sounds of crunching metal and blaring horns echoed between the buildings, the lead tanker crashed into slower moving cars and shoved them out of its way. People cried out in alarm while others turned and ran, and even more simply stood, stunned, and stared, paralyzed by shock and disbelief.

The lead tanker reached Fremont Street travelling at over sixty miles an hour as it plowed into a Jeep Wrangler waiting for the light to change. The impact sent the unsuspecting SUV rocketing into the air, spinning it with such force that the hardtop separated from the vehicle and sailed upward through a second floor window of the Millennium Tower. A second later, the front of the powerful Volvo semi-truck plowed through the large plate-glass windows of that building's lobby, plunging deeply into ground floor offices.

Terrified pedestrians scattered in all directions as the tanker completely disappeared inside, impaling the building's interior like a massive spear. The eighteen-wheeled projectile expended its energy by crashing through the furniture, drywall, and the people who inhabited the interior work spaces. Meanwhile the driver survived, battered and stunned, but still securely seat-belted behind the wheel.

Once the entire tractor and trailer disappeared inside the structure of the tall office building, pedestrians outside stared in shocked-horror at the gigantic hole made in the façade of the 645-feet high building. The stunned observers, many of whom had to dive for cover from the rampaging truck, had precious few seconds to climb to their feet before a terrible rising wail of agony came from the jagged tunnel. The numerous humans inside the wounded structure immediately began to cry pitifully for rescue.

Dozens of their fellow citizens rushed to clamber through the jagged opening in the gutted Millennium Tower, to begin the seeking out the wounded, just as the driver of a second guided-missile tanker was arriving at his own target. The 600-feet tall building, 50 Freemont Center, was located less than half a block up Mission Street. As the still quivering foundations of the Millennium Tower groaned from the impact, the second driver rammed his truck into the southwest corner of the Freemont Center at nearly seventy.

The impact sent chunks of cement blasting off the building as shocked witnesses, still staring in shock at the first building, spun to gape at the second. And immediately, just as the brutal realization dawned when the world watched as the second plane, United 175, plowed into 2 WTC, everyone along Mission and Freemont streets knew they were under intentional attack.

But the corner of the Freemont Center was far stouter than the glass façade of the Millennium Tower, and only the tractor could penetrate the building's interior. This left the jostling tanker outside the building, rocking while jackknifed and dripping fuel onto the sidewalk. The dead driver, impaled by rebar jutting from a crushed

269

cement stanchion, bled-out while still strapped securely into the driver seat of the demolished tractor. Many people outside ran away from the smoking truck, while others, quickly being joined by people pouring out of from neighboring buildings, ran to help the injured, and dozens more either called 911 or took photos with their cell phones.

Each gasoline tanker was filled with 10,000 gallons of fuel, and along each side of the fifty-foot long trailers sat hollow tubes normally used to hold fuel hoses for the loading and offloading of fuel at local service stations. These side tubes, however, were now filled with hundreds of pounds of RDX explosive; numerous detonators were rigged with wireless receivers as well as hardwired to an electrical line, secured to the side of the tanker and extending into the cab of the truck, where the ends of the wire attached to the detonator switchbox.

The driver of the first truck, well over a hundred feet inside the Millennium Tower, began feeling around his seat for the detonator. He smelled the strong stench of gasoline flowing all around him from the ruptured tanker. Light fixtures sparked as people both near and far yelled for help, and broken chunks of building crashed down here and there. His bleeding hand finally found the switchbox hanging near his leg. His fingers lifted the cover and he thumbed the lever over, thus completing the electrical circuit between the truck's battery and the detonators buried in the explosives. The tremendous blast that followed tore apart the trailer as if were made of tissue paper, at once both igniting and dispersing the fuel it contained.

The resulting pressure wave of the explosion ripped its way through the interior walls of the Millennium Tower as it forced its way to the exterior glass façade, all in under a thousandth of a second. The exterior walls blew outward, followed by a massive wave of flame that reached out every window of the bottom four floors of the structure. A nanosecond later, as the shattered glass sprayed across the streets and cut hundreds of people to ribbons, the pressure wave hit the windows of the neighboring buildings and caused their windows to burst inward, shredding the occupants as they stared outward.

Along with the pressure wave, there came a 1300 degree Fahrenheit blast of flame and heat that spewed from all four sides of the wounded structure.

What was left of the people and cars along Fremont and Mission were then engulfed and incinerated in searing flame. That heat and flame crossed the streets and slammed into the buildings on the other side. The conflagration then entered those buildings through the newly shattered windows and instantly created raging infernos within those buildings.

Thick, black smoke roiled out from the mortally wounded Millennium Tower and rose in dense clouds that quickly spread, filling the narrow skyscraper canyons on its way skyward.

Watching intently, Abbas and Al-Doleh stood in the bus, now stopped in the middle of the intersection of Mission Street and Anthony Street, two blocks from the burning Millennium Tower.

The major, admiring the results of his leadership, stood on the bottom step of the bus, where once countless Texas children had entered and exited on their way to and from their schools. Abbas was inside the bus, busily working at putting on his own explosive vest as he prepared to follow his leader on a rampage through the panicked streets of the burning and bleeding city. Now that the tankers had completed their missions, Abbas and the major were free to wreak havoc and destruction on the helpless people running in terror in the closeted and deadly streets of downtown San Francisco.

The approaching sirens of police cars and fire trucks echoed through the man-made spires of the city. As the defenders steadily drew closer, Al-Doleh welcomed their arrival. He and Abbas were prepared to deliver far more destruction upon those responders and the other kafirs who surrounded them. His ears also caught the distant sounds of gunfire and muffled explosions coming from the direction of the Westfield Mall and the northern financial district beyond.

But as this input came his eyes stayed glued to the second tanker. The fact that it had not exploded meant either the detonators had failed or the driver was out of commission.

He was mildly disappointed that the truck had not gotten inside its target as effectively as the first tanker had. Suddenly, his ears picked up the sounds of even more gunfire, but this time it was far off to his right, toward the third target that had been assigned to Sergeant Diba. Those sounds told him that the 641feet-tall structure of One Rincon Hill Tower, which rose above the western entrance to the Oakland Bay Bridge, was now under attack. The gunfire was accompanied by a powerful explosion that made nearby windows wobble inside their frames. Shards from several dozen of those windows came raining down upon people who lined the sidewalks. Those people not hit by the falling glass ran screaming into the streets.

Most of the pedestrians and drivers who had actually witnessed Al-Doleh's attack on the police squad car had already fled, leaving few who knew anything of the danger he and Abbas represented. As more people rapidly poured from the surrounding buildings, they swelled the crowds into the hundreds and further choked the streets. Some ran away after seeing the massive blast at the Millennium Tower, while others ran forward to help. But many more

271

just stood, paralyzed and gawking, filling the streets and sidewalks around the bus. Some vehicles tried to navigate through the mass, but the traffic rapidly snarled, and became an inescapable quagmire that became more compressed by the second. But still, that futility did not stop dozens of drivers from shouting and honking at anything and everything that prevented them from going where they wanted to go.

There were numerous distractions: blast and fire, distant explosions and gunfire, and streets filled with honking vehicles and thousands of gawking heads swiveling back and forth. Very few people took any notice of the strangely dressed man holding the rifle in the doorway of the out-of-state bus. Those few who did happen to notice Al-Doleh were quick to flee down the street, looking frightfully over their shoulders as they ran away. Al-Doleh's evil eyes watched them run and he chuckled at those few who tried to make their escape, vainly trying to drag others to follow. All the while the vast majority of the population simply stood and stared down the street, captivated by the massive fire raging two blocks away, with some turning to their equally bewildered pedestrian neighbor to ask useless questions. Their minds, oblivious to the threat close at hand, focused on the stunning sight down the street.

Upon hearing the explosion at One Rincon Hill, the major knew that his mission had been completed successfully. He knew those enormous fires would quickly spread to other buildings as the inferno gathered its strength. It would be especially successful if he and his men were able to effectively keep the police and firefighters at bay long enough to let the heat build to create a self-perpetuating conflagration within the closed confines of the metropolis. Fear of dying in that terrible fire would then press in upon the tens of thousands of people trapped inside the clogged streets and towering buildings. Between those flames and the weapons of his men, a massive wave of panic would then spread through the populace. Any effective firefighting equipment would be impossible to deploy through the city's choked avenues, and very soon millions of terrorized people would be in very real danger of burning to death.

He pulled from his vest a cell phone and punched in the number for the detonator waiting inside the last tanker, sitting little more than four-hundred feet away. He placed his thumb over the 'send' button; an instant later the fuel-gorged trailer erupted into a fireball that blew outward as much as it went upward along the side of the building. The heat was intense upon the major's face and he quickly ducked back inside the bus to shield himself, while the explosion sprayed burning fuel up and down Mission Street. The

Transbay Terminal was completely engulfed in a sheet of thick flame, like a gigantic wave crashing onto a beach.

The people within a hundred feet of the exploding tanker were instantly set alight; those farther away were thrown to the ground, their screams quickly cut short as their lungs were blistered and singed by the roasting heat. As the initial blast died away, leaving behind a raging inferno, several still-running human torches, arms flapping, ran short distances until collapsing into smoldering piles of charred flesh.

A Subaru Outback peeled-out from the edge of the flames, and drove manically onto the curb. It accelerated rapidly down the sidewalk, mowing down dozens of people as others jumped out of the panicked driver's way. Al-Doleh watched this with great amusement. Visible through the blackened windshield of the fleeing car, the father-driver tried to escape the flames while his horrified wife and children screamed. All the while one pedestrian after another slammed off the vehicle's grill and was sent flying into the air. Al-Doleh smiled at everything he was witnessing. *It has begun.*

The fear and dread inside the people hovering around the bus was a palpable force. Al-Doleh could almost feel the overwhelming terror that was radiating through the crowd. It was swiftly consuming the rational thoughts and stable emotions within the mass of people, as they tried to analyze the unexpected and shocking scenes of horror that were unfolding around them. The terrorist commander found the visual fascinating as he watched the thousands of individuals clump into groups, just like animal herds did before an approaching storm. *They are becoming the mindless and terrified sheep I need them to be!* He looked over his shoulder at Abbas, who stood ready with his rifle.

"Abbas, do you have anything to say to me before we begin the slaughter?"

"No."

"Very well," he said, lifting his own rifle and scanning the crowd.

Ahead of him, some boys stood gawking atop a wall. They appeared just like a string of targets set up at the training range at the Bahonar garrison back in Iran. He lifted his rifle and sent a long blast of bullets at them. As their bodies were punctured and fell, the remaining mass of stunned people scattered in all directions as they attempted to flee for their lives.

273

(three minutes ago)

AS MAJOR Al-Doleh gave the orders to the gunmen inside the vans to peel away and attack the Westfield Mall, Shea and Marta were just passing the Market Street entrance of the huge shopping complex. The officers had just cleared the intersection and were halfway down the next block as the two red vans emerged from 4th onto Market. The congested intersection was lost from view in Shea's rearview mirror, blocked by the vehicle and foot traffic behind her, as the vans screeched to a halt in the middle of the large five-way intersection comprised of Market, 4th, Ellis, and Stockton, at the entrance to the mall.

Six heavily-armed men burst from the vans and began firing at the astonished pedestrians and drivers who were trapped and then mowed down by the ensuing crossfire. Pandemonium filled the intersection as motorists attempted to dodge gunfire while ramming into other vehicles and crushing pedestrians. The bell of a trolley car sounded for a final time as it was struck broadside by a double-sectioned SFMTA bus, knocked from its rails as sparks flew from the overhead power lines. Passengers were ejected and sent flying across the road as the trolley tipped and crashed violently on its side.

One group of gunmen sprayed bullets at clumps of fleeing people while the other group charged the entrance to the mall and burst through its doors. In mere seconds, the intersection was largely clear of people, leaving only the severely injured and dead behind. The remaining gunmen started moving down Stockton Street, two hunting for victims, while the third drove their explosive- and ammunition-laden van behind them.

Meanwhile Marta and Shea knew nothing of the mayhem spreading through the city streets a mere two blocks behind them as they listened intently to their police radio. Shea turned left down 2nd Street, proceeding down the gentle slope, passing the brick tenement buildings of Jessie Street on their right as they approached Mission. Suddenly their eyes were drawn to the sight of the two speeding semi-tankers, barreling across 2nd on Mission, where the lead tanker bumped a Jetta out of its way, knocking it into another car.

"Where the hell? Did you see that?" Shea blurted.

"Let's move, Shea."

Marta felt relief at finally having something tangible to justify her demand that they leave their post at City Hall. She just picked up her police radio mike to report what they had just witnessed, when a slow-moving school bus below them suddenly had bullets erupt from its rear window, showering a white cloud of shattered glass onto the street.

The next thing that came to her stunned mind was the accompanying sound of automatic gunfire. They then watched as a FedEx truck was knocked onto the curb by a police car crashing into it at roughly thirty-miles an hour.

"Holy shit!" Shea exclaimed as she automatically hit the brakes and stopped in the middle of 2nd Street. "Did you see that? What the fuck was that?"

"I don't know!" Marta yelled.

Cars skidded to a stop behind them, almost smashing into the rear of their squad car as both women stared transfixed, locked in place, at the sudden and unbelievable carnage they had just witnessed.

Marta came to her senses first.

"Get us closer to the corner, but go slow. Those shots came from the back of that bus. Those were bullets that caused the crash, right? Tell me you saw that, too. Gawd, did I see that, Shea?"

"Yeah, yeah, you did – uh, I mean, yeah, I saw something come from the back of that bus. Oh, Jesus! What's happening?"

Shea slowly moved the squad car down the street while keeping a lookout for the bus.

Marta broadcast to central dispatch what they had just witnessed. Shea continued forward until she saw the rear of the school bus, with its shattered rear window. It was parked a short distance from 2nd on Mission Street.

"Holy shit! There it is! There it is!" she squealed, throwing the car into park.

Marta tossed the radio mike.

"Damn! Oh, shit! Get outta the car, Shea – get out! We need our gear outta the back, right now!"

Shea stared down at the wrecked police car.

"But we've got to see who is in that cruiser and get them some help. What do we do for them, Martie?" she frantically appealed.

A group of people came sprinting up toward their squad car, gesturing wildly.

"We can't do anything for them until we're suited up. This is real bad, Shea, and we need our gear on, right the fuck now!"

Marta did not wait for a reply as she jumped out and ran to the trunk.

Shea's staggered brain swam in a deep pool of fear and confusion. The police term for it was 'code-black' and she fought to comprehend and deal with the fast-developing and mind-boggling nightmare she found herself in. In a dreamlike state she nodded her head and exited the car, saying quietly, "Yeah, right – we need our gear."

A dozen people instantly surrounded their cruiser, all excited and confused. The loudest of the group was a fortyish woman in a brown pantsuit who stuck her frantic face just inches in front of Marta's, yelling while gesticulating toward the bus.

"Oh, God help us! Oh, please, God help us! There're two cops all-shot-up down there! You've got to help them! That wacko bastard inside that bus just shot 'em up and they're hurt, real bad!"

Several more people yelled similar things while they all hopped impatiently from one foot to the other. Their nervous movements and desperate facial expressions reminded Marta of the last-standing member of a dodge-ball team, tired of being pummeled, nervously waiting for the next speeding ball to come. The frantic people pranced around anxiously while waiting for Marta to reply.

Marta threw the palm of her hand up into the face of the loud woman and gave the 'talk to the hand' gesture as she turned to Shea.

"Honey, you get suited up right now, ya hear? I'm going to go check on the cops down there, okay?"

Without looking, Shea distractedly bobbed her head up and down as she continued, trance-like, through the motions of withdrawing her ballistic vest from the trunk of the car.

The loud woman stood, flummoxed and silent, as Marta left her and ran down the street toward the wrecked police car. She reached the crumpled front bumper and knelt down, looking over at the school bus. She saw movement inside but could not tell how many people were in it or what they were doing.

She turned her head back and was immediately horrified to see what was left of the destroyed face of Brenda Cho, a vivacious young officer who had joined the force only two years ago. The dead cop had half her face spread in dripping gore across the front seats and dash of the cruiser. Her partner, ten-year veteran of the force Steve Carson, was being pulled from the driver seat by civilians as he moaned pitifully from his own gunshot wounds. Blood poured from his mutilated right arm that had taken several rounds and hung by exposed tendons as loose, bone-infused hamburger. His left arm clutched at his chest as he gasped in pain.

A woman rudely grabbed Marta's arm and pointed frantically down Mission Street toward the school bus, but before the woman could speak, the massive explosion inside the Millennium Tower rocked the ground under their feet. Car alarms roared, people yelped and screamed as the roar of the blast and its pressure wave struck them a second later. Marta fell backward onto her butt, stunned, as she watched the devastating fireball exploding skyward from the building, beyond the parked bus. The woman who had clenched so tightly onto Marta's arm had also fallen, and knelt on bleeding knees, staring mouth-agape at the disaster occurring down the street.

A huge mass of panicked humanity came rushing around the bus as they fled from the explosion. In the periphery of Marta's vision she was sure she saw a man pointing to the bus and yelling at her, something about terrorist and rifles. *Yeah, buddy, I know.* Shea came running up and followed Marta's eyes down the street. Shea gasp when she saw the fire and smoke billowing into the sky.

"What the fuck is going on?" she exclaimed.

Marta felt a sense of horror at what she was witnessing and hearing all around her. But as her heart drummed fast under her breast, she also felt an all-encompassing sense of defeat wrap around her soul. The taste of bile invaded her mouth as a wave of nausea turned her stomach. Her ribs felt constricted and made her breathing feel extremely labored. She desperately wished that she could shuck the tight ballistic vest she wore. *I can't breathe in this thing.*

The woman again gripped Marta's arm and asked the policewoman in a despondent voice, "What's going on? What's happening? My God, this can't be happening again? Not again?"

Marta forced her eyes to obey her will and unlock their gaze from the firestorm down the street. They refocused on the woman's face and were confronted with an expression of pleading angst that hovered near hopelessness. The desolation and vulnerability reflected back at Marta was so profound that she was shocked by its depth. The pale of distress that had overcome the stylish and obviously successful businesswoman was both foreign and revolting to Marta's mind.

An emotional cord snapped deep inside and shook the foundations of Marta's being. The rising feelings of defeat and doom were brushed back by a surging wave of rage and antagonism toward those murderers who would dare to come to her city with such evil intent.

Marta's level-toned voice was firm as she replied to the frightened woman, "We are under attack – and it appears they intend to kill us all, honey."

The woman stared back in silence as she absorbed the impact of Marta's words. Marta stood and looked away from the woman and back down the street at the maelstrom of death that existed there.

She said, "You need to run along and find as much safety as you can. I think it's just gonna get a lot worse around here. Let's go, Shea."

Marta turned and walked quickly back to the patrol car with Shea by her side. Filled with disbelief, the woman's eyes followed them for several seconds. Then, like waking from a trance, she decided to follow the advice given and look after herself and seek out the safest and quickest way to get away from here, and get into the arms of her loved ones. She looked miserably over her shoulder at the burning building behind her and then started to run west down Mission, as fast as her feet could go.

Marta face was set in a grim mask as she glared over her shoulder at the school bus. She was sure that she saw at least two people moving around inside of it, near the front. She was equally certain that one occupant was holding a rifle. She could also see the growing throng of unsuspecting people that had stopped running away from the explosion and were once again gathering around the bus. They all stared off toward the burning building down the street, ignoring the deadly bus. Her heart told her that the same explosion which captivated those on-lookers would soon draw out many more thousands of people from the buildings all around them. *That's what the bastard's are waiting for.*

Marta calmly hooked Shea's arm, pulling her close until her mouth was little more than an inch from Shea's ear.

"Sweetie. You got to listen to me now. This is an attack. We're in a war zone. This is worse than New York on 9/11. There are hundreds of people dying down there, right now, and we got thousands more up here with us. And, right now, there are at least two real bad people in that bus right there."

"What about those cops? Are we just gonna leave them?"

"You remember Brenda Cho?"

Shea nodded.

"Well she's sitting in that car back there with her brains blown all over the place, honey. She's dead. Her partner's arm is shot to pieces and we're all alone. There is no help coming to him if we don't stop these killers right here, right now. Do you understand what I'm saying, sweetie?"

Shea slowly nodded.

"Now, honey, we got to get our stuff out of the car and get ready. You with me now, girl?" she pleaded, her face almost nose-to-nose with Shea's.

Tears rolled down Shea's cheeks and she looked into Marta's eyes and mouthed unspoken words until she finally gained her voice.

"I can't believe this is really happening, and here? Now? Us? Why, Martie?"

278

Marta could think of nothing to say that could be of any use and simply turned and began digging through the open trunk, grabbing her ballistic vest and one of the two AR15 rifles.

What Marta was doing was a new stage in the evolving mindset of law enforcement in the United States. After witnessing the North Hollywood bank robbery shootout, law enforcement had its eyes opened to the prospect of direct confrontation with adversaries armed with military capable weapons and ballistic protection. So, it was surmised, that if the cops were to survive and win such deadly encounters, they needed to be armed with training and weapons and tactics capable of meeting those threats. And even in the über-liberal world of the San Francisco Bay area, the cops had been issued those weapons as fast as the city could, without raising any political alarm bells. Now Marta and Shea busied themselves with donning the bulky and unfamiliar gear.

As they suited up, the multitude surrounding them swelled as people demanded they do a multitude of things: call for more help, go help this person or that person, call for fire trucks, call for SWAT teams, clear traffic, fight fires, give directions, but mostly, people just wanted to know what was going on. Both officers actively ignored the throng since there was absolutely nothing that they could do or say that would be anything other than a waste of time.

Meanwhile, the police radio was a constant procession of voices on every channel that reported shots fired here, large fires and explosions there, armed suspects going this way, as wounded civilians were evacuated that way. Every voice demanded any and all assistance possible as confusion reigned supreme and situational awareness was nonexistent. In a city of over 1.2 million people with a police force of more than 2,200 officers, it was clear to both Marta and Shea that they were utterly alone in what they had before them.

And bedlam was quickly engulfing the immediate situation surrounding them. As thousands poured onto the streets from the neighboring buildings, the crowds were expanding geometrically. They heard the sound of automatic gunfire coming from just a few blocks away, back toward Westfield Mall. This drew Marta to look up and she watched as the thousands of people around her tried to decide what to do about their lives and their safety. Thousands of heads turned on shoulders like weather vanes in a storm. Horns blared, metal and plastic crunched in a whole host of small fender-benders, and people yelled profanity as confusion ruled everywhere. To Marta it looked as if some gigantic foot had kicked a city-sized anthill as hundreds of confused and worried people moved one way, while hundreds more moved the other way, and even more hundreds stood motionless, bewildered, and genuinely afraid.

A clean-shaven man, smelling of expensive cologne, dressed in an equally expensive business suit, and holding a fine-leather briefcase with manicured hands stood several feet from Marta as the officers strapped on their gear and loaded their rifles. He repeatedly tried to gain Marta's attention by raising his hand and opening his mouth, as if to ask a question. And when she ignored him, he would simply lower his arm and close his mouth, but each time he took another baby-step closer and would then try again. This continued until he was little more than an arm's length from Marta's side. The last time, he reached out and touched her shoulder as she tried to zip her bulky tactical vest, but before he uttered a word she spun, shoving her nose toward his.

Marta's sweaty hair stuck to her flustered face but she spoke in a calm, overly-polite voice while resting her hand on her sidearm.

"You little pencil-dick shithead! You fucking leave *now* or I'm going to pull this gun out and blow your *goddamn balls* off!"

The white-collared pencil-dick recoiled as if he had been shot and his hands moved his briefcase to cover his groin. He turned on his heels and ran quickly away through the crowds of people, looking over his shoulder fearfully.

Shea's hands were sweaty and shook badly as she fumbled with her rifle until finally she lost her grip and it clattered onto the street.

"I'm so fucking scared, Martie!" she exclaimed as she knelt to pick it up.

"You're okay, hon, we're together and we're stayin' that…."

Suddenly a large explosion to the south, several blocks away toward One Ricon Hill, made them and the people around them turn and look. The powerful blast rumbled through the ground as windows rattled and cracked in buildings up and down the blocks around them. Several large panes of broken glass fell out of a third floor window above the wrecked police car and crashed down onto its hood, spraying glass over the people rendering aid to the wounded officer. Many people screamed and ran as more car alarms blared in all directions.

"Shit!" Marta exclaimed while staring off to where the blast came from.

"Jesus, Martie! Are they everywhere? Are they fucking bombing the entire city?"

Marta rested her hand on Shea's arm as she heard the faint but clear sounds of more gunfire coming from the area of the last explosion. The sounds of gunfire were also unmistakable from the financial district behind them, much closer now than the shots that had come from the Westfield Mall a short time ago. Dozens of distant sirens wailed from every direction as thousands of heads spun on twisting necks. The tension and apprehension in the crowd had now built to a fever pitch. *It's about to boil over into blind panic. They're all about to go mad with panic, good God, no.*

Marta raised her belt radio to her mouth as many yelling voices and alarms came out of its speaker. Heedless of whether her transmission would be heard, she keyed the mike.

"Central, Baker 345. Officers down – officers down at 2nd and Mission! I heard a large explosion and gunfire south of my location toward One Rincon Hill. I also hear more gunfire toward the Westfield Centre. I repeat, officers down – officers down at 2nd and Mission! Baker 345 is moving to contact possible shooters in a yellow school bus at 2nd and Mission!"

No acknowledgement came from her radio, just a stream of yelling voices.

"This is real fucking bad, Martie," Shea said while staring down the street.

"I know, Shea. The whole city is getting chewed up," Marta admitted as she shouldered her rifle. "You ready, sweetie? We're gonna do this thing, right now."

Shea swallowed hard as she summoned every ounce of courage she had and slowly nodded, hoisting her own rifle up to her shoulder. They took off together across the street as they moved shoulder-to-shoulder, their rifles pointing forward. They advanced toward the stone and cement cover offered by the large building at the corner of 2nd and Mission.

The two cops maneuvered their way as rapidly as possible through the throngs of pedestrians and drivers stuck in the congested street, while everyone stared at them with scared and questioning looks. As the two women, dressed for battle and carrying weapons moved forward, the people in the crowd saw the intensity on their faces and quickly opened a path, like water being split by the prow of a boat.

Two men followed just a few steps behind the two cops with their cell phones cameras held up, filming the two women as if they were paparazzi following two red-carpet starlets entering a dance club. The odd procession reached the corner of the building, where Shea stood while Marta knelt as they both peeked around the edge with their rifles leading the way. As Marta bent forward the thick leather of her

281

duty belt shoved into her gut and her ballistic vest pinched hard into her side, making her gasp and grimace.

They both had a clear view of the bus parked in the center of the intersection of Mission and Anthony. Through the large windows of the bus Marta saw the stationary outline of a man who appeared to be standing on the steps at the bus entrance. She also saw the top of another man's head who appearing to be doing something on the floor of the bus. The man on the steps held a rifle and stared off toward the raging fire down the street at the Millennium Tower.

Shea bent over, saying, "Martie, look at the semi crashed into the Freemont Center!"

Marta had no more than focused her eyes on the wrecked tanker when it abruptly disintegrated in a tremendous explosion and fireball. The blast tore at the façade of the building as a sheet of flame rose into the air. Large chunks of the building collapsed downward on top of the destroyed tanker. Those people not torn apart by the detonation tried to run but were quickly brought down by the flames encasing their bodies. The colossal fireball filled Mission Street for almost a block and flung burning fuel up and down the street as a vast black cloud of roiling dense smoke and flame lifted skyward.

Scorching wind blew through Marta's hair as she exclaimed, "Fuck me! How in the fuck are they doing all this shit?"

She glared back toward the bus and saw a cell phone bounce onto the asphalt below the bus.

"That motherfucker standing over there is blowing up *my city*! Well, *fuck him*!"

"Oh, Jesus, oh, Jesus, we're going to die!"

Marta's forty-two year old knees strained to push her and her gear up. She backed Shea against the cool stone wall and got to her face.

"We're not dying today, honey. We're going out there to stop that bastard over there. He's dying, not us! We've got to go put his ass down, okay?"

"Right," Shea said with a trembling voice. She regained her composure as the two women rested their foreheads against one another.

Marta caressed Shea's cheek with her palm and gave a gentle pat as they stared into each other's eyes.

"Let's go, hon."

The sound of shattering glass came from across the street as falling panes of broken windows crashed down. The officers lifted their rifles, and after Marta peeked around the corner and saw the two men still inside the bus, left the cover of the building and started toward the bus. One of the men who had been filming the scene with his cell phone had taken off after the explosion, but the other remained and now followed several steps behind the two officers.

Suddenly a loud burst of gunfire came from the other side of the bus and instantly the large mass of terrified people around them broke and ran in every direction possible, to take them away from the deadly bullets flying from the rifle barrels of Major Al-Doleh and Abbas.

The last shred of civilization in the minds of the population snapped asunder in the hail of hot-lead that flew through the air. Like a herd of panicked zebra breaking and fleeing from the charge of a pride of lions, people scattered and ran. Marta and Shea found it impossible to stay together as the wave of fleeing human bodies bolted this way and that, ducking and screaming. Any who fell were immediately trampled under the feet of those who stayed upright.

*****

A FORMER center linebacker for the Baltimore Colts, Bruce Gordon stood heartsick at the fifth floor window of the waiting room of Henderson Orthopedic Associates. He was stunned and silent, filled with shock and disbelief at what he had been witnessing. The last three minutes of his life had been spent watching the horror unfold below him on Mission Street.

He had arrived at the offices of his surgeon twenty-minutes earlier for a post-surgery follow up on his left knee; the same knee that had already been through eleven previous surgeries; the same knee that had been destroyed in a lousy third quarter three-yard run play, in a lousy pre-season game against the New Orleans Saints; the same knee that still felt like a sack of loose gravel when he walked.

In only his second season in the league, and his first season of being off the practice squad, with a real chance of becoming a first string starter he had his dreams of a glorious football career end after an offensive tackle fell backward onto his leg. That was the moment when Bruce's knee had been inverted to point the wrong way and his life's career choice had changed from pro-football player to that of a limping insurance salesman.

His personal life revolved around keeping in touch with his two daughters after his divorce, and also having to work hard every day to make sure the NFL still paid for his continuing medical expenses. Having just completed his twelfth surgery on it, he was standing at the waiting room window, watching absentmindedly the daily movement of people and cars below. Just a few minutes before,

283

he thought he felt a small earthquake nudge the building around him but no one else in the lobby appeared to take any notice. A few minutes later, mass murder began to play out on the streets below him.

He had watched the busy motorist and pedestrian traffic move around in its anonymous way through the metropolitan world, when suddenly his attention was drawn to the faint siren's wail and flashing red and blue lights of a police car rushing down Mission. It approached the rear of a flat-nosed school bus and made to pass when a glittering shower of broken glass blew out from the back of the bus and bullet holes printed ugly black and white dots into the metal hood and windshield of the speeding cop car. Bruce watched in stunned horror as the bus continued across the intersection and the police car crashed into a Fedex truck. Bruce had exclaimed loudly, drawing by his outburst all the other people in the room to the window. Once there they had all became front-row witnesses to what became an unrehearsed, real-time display of evil.

He excitedly told the story to his unbelieving fellow observers, of how the innocent-looking school bus, parked in broad daylight below them, was actually responsible for the wreckage of the police car. Some believed but most did not. They all watched the traffic snarl and clog around the bus and wrecked police car. Bruce felt like he was watching a movie set as suddenly two female cops appeared, with one running down the street to the cop car while the other got into the trunk of their squad car. He helplessly banged against the window and yelled at the running cop to beware of the bus, but he was only heard by the people standing with him.

His companions debated whether the man in the bus might be another wacko shooting-rampage-type guy, and if he was, what could happen next. Some pontificated about what they should do if the shooter barged into their building. Just as they started to make claims about whether they would fight or flee came the first massive explosion at the Millennium Tower, down the street to their right. Startled yelps were uttered from some as the building under their feet shook, unnerving the stoutest souls in the room. The room's large windows wobbled and quivered, and two actually cracked under the strain. The bystander quality of the scene below evaporated inside the room as each person instantly became participants in the activities.

One woman yelled loudly for everyone to look down at the tanker that was jammed into the side of the Freemont Center. Puzzled and horrified they all stared at the gasoline tanker; they craned their heads and pressed their faces against the glass, trying to see alongside the exterior wall of the building a little more of the fire, smoke, and massive damage done farther down the street. They buzzed with questions and quizzed each other about what could be happening.

A nurse ran behind the reception desk and dialed 911 as several other people quickly gathered up their belongings and left the room, fleeing down the hallway. Bruce and another nurse stayed glued to the window, riveted to the spectacle they were watching. Their heads swiveled to the left and right as they tried to absorb the large number of things happening all at once. Everything blurred and blended in his mind as Bruce turned his eyes from the bus, to the wrecked tanker, to the fireball, to the two female cops, then to the smoke down the street, then back to the wrecked police car, and then once again back to the bus when suddenly a second blast occurred, farther away but still powerful enough to send a tremor through the building. *Maybe that wasn't a small earthquake I felt earlier. My God, what's going on?*

"Was that another explosion?" the nurse asked.

"Uh, I think it was."

"Do you think there are big gas leaks in the city or what?"

Bruce looked at the woman and gave her honest question an incredulous look and then pointed a finger at the wrecked gasoline tanker sticking out of the Freemont Center.

"No, I think it's those."

"What? What do you mean – those? A crashed truck?"

Bruce gave another incredulous look at the uncomprehending woman.

"Just what the fuck do you think is in the trailer of that wrecked truck?"

Her eyes widened as the dim-bulb lit up in her brain.

"Oh! Oh, God, no! What, this is 9/11 all over again?"

Bruce looked down on the still unmoving and silent bus below them.

"No. I think this is far worse than 9/11."

"Did that one there just not explode or what? You think the bomb on it broke or something?"

"I don't know, lady, let's hope."

They looked over at the two female cops getting suited up in tactical gear at the back of the patrol car.

"They're going to get that stuff on and go after those guys in the bus, aren't they?" the nurse asked.

"I think so. I'm pretty sure they know those guys in the bus are the bad guys that shot up that other cop car."

"Yeah, you said that someone in that bus shot at those other cops. Why do you think, they are still in the bus? You think they got children as hostages in there?"

"God, I hope not."

The nurse turned to her co-worker who was trying to talk with a 911 operator.

"Sandy! Tell them there are some cops here that need help at Anthony and Mission!"

A look of exasperation was plastered on the nurse's face as she replied, "I'm on hold! Can you believe it? With all this going on and they put me on fucking hold!"

Bruce could see the top of a man's head leaning out the side door to the school bus and he watched as the man punched in numbers on a cell phone in his hands. The next second, the third powerful explosion shook the building as the tanker embedded into the Freemont Center exploded. Both nurses let out screams while they reached for the walls to stabilize themselves. The window in front of Bruce cracked in several long jagged lines as the force of the explosion rippled through the air outside.

Bruce yelled while holding onto the wall for support.

"Jesus Christ!"

Both nurses rushed over next to his six-foot-ten inch, two-hundred-ninety pound pot-bellied frame and looked down in horror at the terrible sight of the last explosion.

"What happened?" asked Sandy.

A blind, raging fury welled up in Bruce's chest that he had not felt since the day he stood staring at his television, teary-eyed, as he watched the Twin Towers fall in New York a decade ago.

Staring in shock at what he had just seen, he exclaimed, "I can't believe what I just saw! That son of a bitch down in that bus just detonated the tanker truck! I just fucking *saw him do it!*"

Sandy's mind tried and failed to take in the enormity of the scene below her. Her brain left the realm of conscience thought and only worked now to motivate her feet to take the rest of her body somewhere safer than where she was. She burst away from the window and ran away, down the hallway as fast as she could move.

Bruce and the other nurse watched her run. She looked up at Bruce and asked, "What can we do? How do we help?"

Bruce turned back to the window and pressed his cheek against the glass, leaving behind a smear from his tears. He first looked through the cracked glass toward the latest inferno, and then he looked back and saw the two officers were now hunkered down at the corner of the street, not far from the bus. He placed the palm of his hand against the window and pushed, trying to judge its strength.

Again the nurse asked, "We have to help – what can we do?"

Bruce looked around the room and pointed to the office.

"Go in there and bring me that computer monitor. Rip it out of the goddamn wall if you have to! Go now!"

The nurse ran to complete the order as Bruce turned and bent down to grab hold of the large coffee table sitting on the floor. He tried lifting but put too much weight on his bad knee, gave a groan of pain and released the table. He cursed while gripping his knee, then again lifted the table, ignoring the pain. He braced it under his arm while backing away from the window. Then, like a charging knight, he ran with the crude battering ram, hitting the center of the cracked window. The force of the impact made the glass give way and sent large sections of the broken pane falling to the street below.

The nurse came running with the computer monitor as he leaned out to see what was happening below them. Suddenly, a long stream of automatic gunfire mixed with a clamor of screaming people.

"Shit!" Bruce yelled.

*****

LOOKING VERY much the typical seventeen-year old California street skateboarder; Andrew Yarrow's skinny body nervously stood in his Vans shoes. His one hand held his heavily scarred Madrid longboard as he nervously chewed the fingernails of his other. His equally acne-blistered and scarred face stared, frightened and yet intensely curious, toward the raging Millennium Tower fire. His two younger brothers, Ash and Nicholas, stood close by atop a five-foot high concrete wall over a large sign that read *555 Mission Street*.

Minutes ago Ash had been on his cell phone, arguing with their mother who had urged the boys to get home and leave downtown. But the call had suddenly ended and now all he had was a 'no service' signal. He had no idea that three-quarters of the city's cellular service had just crashed and was no longer functioning. He just stubbornly kept hitting redial and listening for the ring to start again.

Ten-year old Nicholas looked scared and had a fierce grip on the tail of Ash's oversized Tony Hawk t-shirt, staring wide-eyed down the street. The death, mayhem, and gore-filled video games and horror flicks they always watched had not prepared his young mind for the impact caused from real death and destruction. Especially with it being this close.

"Is that other truck going to blow up, too, Andy?" his high-pitched voice trembled.

"I don't know, dude," Andrew said with the tips of his fingers still mashed against his teeth. "Pretty fuck'n wild, ain't it, bro?"

Earlier they had skipped school and came downtown to do some skateboarding at the mall and were headed to their usual panhandling place near Bamboo Alley, a hundred feet from where they stood. Then the first explosion had happened. Since then they had stayed in this spot, transfixed on that amazing sight of the fire even though they had just heard another explosion several blocks away.

"I'm scared. Where are the cops, Andy?" Nicholas pleaded.

"Don't know, dude. I guess they're com'n, like those guys who crashed back there," he said thumbing over his shoulder behind him.

"Where are the firemen, Andy?"

"Dude, I don't know where the cops or the fire guys are, Nicky. I think they're …."

He was interrupted by the last tanker exploding in a huge blast of flame and smoke several hundred yards away. The boys instinctively ducked and crossed their arms before their faces to protect against the gust of intense heat. The fiery wind threatened to topple the two younger brothers from their perch on the narrow, elevated wall. Squinting in shocked wonder at the latest event, Andrew finally decided that he better get his brothers away from here. Just as he turned to tell them to jump down he watched his world go straight to hell.

The cell phone in Ash's hand, which was pressed onto his ear, disintegrated into shrapnel as a 7.62mm bullet smashed through it. His hand and head turned into red goo. His body immediately collapsed as more bullets from Al-Doleh's rifle slammed into it. The mix of blood, bone, brains and Iphone flew from the headless teenager's limp body as it fell off the backside of the cement wall.

Nicholas was next to be struck by the terrible flow of deadly missiles as several bullets made vicious little holes in the front of his t-shirt. His tiny body crumpled under the impact but did not follow Ash's body over the far side of the wall. He wrapped his arms around his stomach as he folded forward and fell into Andrew's outstretched arms.

Gritty, sharp chunks of shattered cement splintered off the wall and hit Andrew in the face as he reached up and caught his little brother's falling corpse. People nearby who were not immediately struck by other bullets scattered, running, screaming, ducking, and dodging as the projectiles ricocheted off cars and buildings all around. Al-Doleh and Abbas fully emerged from the bus and continued spraying the crowd as they turned in separate directions.

As Andrew Yarrow sobbed pathetically while cradling the lifeless body of his youngest sibling, Marta and Shea were busy trying to stay on their feet. Frantic and terrified people were barging their way in all directions in attempts to flee. A middle-aged man, running madly in the opposite direction, plowed into Shea, separating her from Marta. Both Shea and the man went tumbling gracelessly to the street. Marta was knocked sideways but was able to stay on her feet. As the panicked flow of people continued, she hugged the wall of the building to stay out of their way.

Shea's small body was not strong enough to get the frantic, terrified man off her. He pawed violently at her and the street in his attempts to get back up. He was finally successful in getting his feet under him and his shoes dug into her stomach and chest as he pumped his legs madly. Shea was close to physical exhaustion and could do little but try to protect her face from his scrambling feet. *So this is what getting trampled to death feels like.*

As he got off she was able to turn onto her side and grab for her rifle which had been kicked several feet away. She got to her knees and saw that everyone between her and the bus had fled, leaving her alone in the street. She glanced around to locate Marta and saw her partner moving about fifty feet farther down the sidewalk, hugging the building and nearing the front of the bus. Continuous gunfire still came from the other side of the vehicle.

Shea turned in the direction of the gunfire and saw, under the bus, spent shell casings bouncing off the street at the feet of the man walking toward the rear as he fired. She also saw the feet and legs of fleeing people who were being mowed down along the far sidewalk. Shea scrambled to her feet as two women in dresses fell against the shattered glass of the building. Other lifeless heaps lay crumpled a few feet away as mortar and brick from the building were blasted into chunks and fell bouncing around the bodies.

Shouldering her rifle, Shea started across the street toward the fallen women. Suddenly a shower of glass rained through the broad-leafed Brisbane Box trees lining the sidewalk and landed like a thousand diamonds being spilled onto the heads of the fleeing people being shot at. The falling glass cut into the terrified people but also had the side-effect of stopping the man from shooting at them further, as he was forced to jump backward behind the bus to keep from being hit by the shards of broken glass.

As Shea advanced across the street, Marta drew closer to the front of the bus. Marta worried about her partner but knew she could not waste time helping her while one of the mad gunmen was near the front of the bus and continued shooting at citizens. She pushed her shoulder into the notch of the concrete wall and tried to make as small a profile as she could. She watched in horror as a man was trying to flee on his hands and knees down Anthony Street, just a few feet ahead of her. His scrambling form already had bullets holes in his legs and trailed blood on the pavement as he crawled frantically forward. A short rat-a-tat of gunfire from behind the hood of the bus sent bullets ripping into the back of the crawling man, who then collapsed face forward onto the pavement, dead.

Horrified, Marta blinked sweat out of her eyes as she stared over the top of her rifle barrel and braced for the gunman to clear the front of the bus. She intended to kill the man immediately, as soon as she could get a shot at him. Everything seemed to now move in slow-motion as the shooter's body emerged from the front of the bus. All of her peripheral vision disappeared and all of her vision centered on the murderer and the smoking rifle in his hands.

As Marta's finger began to press on the trigger, the man she was aiming at was highly pleased with himself. Al-Doleh came around the front of the bus with his rifle held at his waist; the last thing he expected to see was an armed foe. His eyes widened in surprise as he registered Marta, standing with her rifle pointed at his chest. Her AR15 jumped as 5.56mm bullets were sent into his thick vest, packed with explosives. He immediately fell backward while firing bullets of his own.

His suicide-vest was packed with more than explosives. It had numerous loaded ammunition magazines in pockets, as well as dozens of metal bolts embedded in it. Those bolts were to become shrapnel; he would kill his last victims by detonating himself. Even as Marta's well-placed rounds struck, they were stopped short of tearing into his flesh by those same bolts, making her bullets utterly useless. Al-Doleh hit the pavement, shocked but unharmed, and he immediately rolled several times to get back behind the bus as bullets from Marta's rifle punched gouges in the asphalt behind him. He rolled in tight next to the front tire and peeked around it to see what his attacker was doing.

Marta had been forced to duck her head when bits of glass and shattered concrete peppered her face as Al-Doleh's bullets struck the wall she leaned against. Even though he had rolled behind the bus she knew she had hit him with some of her fire. She pressed in tightly against the building and waited to see what would happen next.

Immediately Al-Doleh began firing at her from under the bus. She watched her blood splatter against the concrete as his bullets tore through the muscles of her thighs, and she collapsed to the sidewalk while shrieking in pain.

Meanwhile at the other end of the bus, Abbas stood flummoxed while watching his leader being attacked. He was stupefied that any response could happen so quickly.

Heavy 7.62mm bullets were deflected off the flat surface of the sidewalk and whizzed past Marta's ears at supersonic speed, making a *zzweet-zzweet* noise. She quickly rolled until she hit the side of a yellow Mazda parked along the curb which afforded her some small protection from the fusillade. Searing pain, torn flesh, and pouring blood were all she saw and felt as she tried to examine her wounded legs. A sick wave of nausea swept through her as she observed the wet red trail she had left smeared across the sidewalk, and she vomited

Firing on full-automatic, Al-Doleh was unable to send accurate fire at the woman cop even though she made the perfect target. He cursed at himself loudly as she rolled out of his sight behind the small car. As he twisted, trying to see from the other side of the tire, an object landed and disintegrated a few feet away. Painful, biting particles showered his body as he spun around and saw the mangled remains of a computer monitor on the surface of the street. Both he and Abbas were plastered with shards of glass and plastic from the demolished monitor. But it landed much closer to Abbas and the major watched as Abbas staggered toward the rear of the bus, with bits of the erupting electronic debris deeply cutting his face. Al-Doleh rapidly scanned the buildings above for where the unusual missile had originated.

Bruce Gordon leaned out the shattered window of the orthopedic office's waiting room. He shook his fist as he screamed, "*I'll get your fucking ass with the next one, you cocksucker*!"

Instantly bullets started plastering the wall and window frame around him as Al-Doleh sent a burst of gunfire toward him. That caused Bruce to duck quickly back inside the building. The nurse, who was running to the window with their next missile, fell to the floor, screaming as the bullets shattered ceiling lights above her head.

At the same moment, Shea had worked her way closer to the rear of the bus and now hugged close to the building below Bruce, slowly stepping over the dead bodies lying there. She was trying to get the shooter in sight but did not have the angle yet. Her fear had kept her from moving rapidly forward. The horrific sights she had been experiencing left her mentally stunned and slow, but what she saw next left her flabbergasted.

A skinny teenager in a sopping, blood-soaked shirt came running toward the back of the bus, a long skateboard held high above his head. An unseen shooter at the front of the bus continued to fire at something above her, causing more concrete and glass to shower down on top of her head as she stared, frozen and amazed, at the charging, weeping boy.

Al-Doleh had concentrated his sight and gunfire on the foolish Good Samaritan above them, to keep him from throwing more items down. He had taken no notice of Andrew Yarrow's hollow eyes and bloody, tear-streaked face as he ran at Abbas. The junior terrorist still staggered and held his bloodied face near the rear of the bus. Abbas began to lower his hands from his face as his mind registered nearby movement. This happened just a split-second before the high-arcing swing of Andrew's longboard came smashing down onto the bridge of his nose. His upper cleft and the entire nasal chamber instantly shattered and sent a spray of his blood into the air. The devastating blow immediately knocked Abbas to the pavement, barely conscious. Feebly he raised his arms to protect his face and head, while standing above him the scrawny, young Andrew Yarrow continued pummeling the terrorist amid his own guttural, hatred-filled screams.

Al-Doleh's attention was drawn to the sound of the youth's screams and he looked on, stupefied, to see his compatriot; a man heavily armed with a rifle and explosives. Trained to be a cold-blooded killer, he had proven himself on many battlefields, and was now being beaten to a pulp by a teenage kafir boy armed with a skateboard. Al-Doleh did not know whether to laugh or cry at the absurdity of what he was witnessing. He lowered the barrel of his rifle until it pointed at the boy and squeezed the trigger to eliminate the ridiculous threat. Nothing happened. His rifle had depleted his forty-round magazine and was now empty and useless. Cursing loudly once again, he ejected the spent magazine and fed another into the hungry and waiting weapon. He racked the slide and again leveled it at the boy.

Smash!

A computer tower, thrown by Bruce, struck the street a mere two feet from where Al-Doleh lay. Shards of plastic and electronics sprayed outward from the impact; large, jagged projectiles struck his face. His hands sprung up and sent his rifle clattering across the street. Al-Doleh screamed while writhing in agony next to the stolen Texas bus.

292

"I told you I'd get your fucking ass, you murdering son of a bitch!" Bruce yelled as the nurse jumped for joy beside him, clapping her hands and hollering excitedly.

Marta looked up at the yelling couple in the window far above her. *God's angels aren't more beautiful than them two.* She looked over and saw the terrorist now rolling on the pavement behind the bus and took the opportunity to move. Using every ounce of will she still had she made her damaged legs move attempted to stand.

Her slippery blood-covered hands pawed at the Mazda in an effort to pull herself up. It proved useless and she was forced to take her rifle and plant the barrel into a crack in the sidewalk, which she then used as a cane to push herself up. Intense pain shot through the ripped muscles of her legs as she finally was able to make it to her feet, and panted as she leaned against the car. *Where the fuck is Shea?* She lurched forward on her bleeding legs in a stumbling and awkward, using the rifle as an unorthodox crutch. With as much speed as she could muster she made her way toward the front of the bus. She struggled for breath as small whimpers escaped her lips.

At the other end of the bus Shea knelt next to the eighth body she had found and checked it for a pulse. *None.* All of them were dead, with bullet holes perforating their bodies, oozing blood. There were now no more to check and she finally moved for the rear of the bus, with nothing else to distract her from what she feared so much. She took a deep trembling breath and poked her rifle past the end of the bus.

Abbas was just feet away and rolled, vainly attempting to block the savage hits he was receiving from the longboard.

"Get back! Get back!" she yelled at Andrew.

The boy took no notice of her and kept swinging his skateboard over his head as if it were an ax and he was chopping wood.

"Kid, get back! I've got him – get back, okay?"

The fury that had consumed Andrew was spent and his thin body paused in its assault as a crushing, weary sadness inundated his core. He wobbled as he held his board high above his head and looked at Shea with flowing tears streaking his face.

"He killed my brothers," he said meekly.

"I got'im. He isn't going anywhere. He'll pay for that. Step back now, okay?"

As skinny as Andrew was, he appeared to physically diminish even more as all of the remaining fury and rage-fueled energy melted away, replaced with devastating wretchedness. His shoulders slumped as he turned and slowly stumbled back to the corpses of his brothers, huge sobs racking his body.

Shea stared at the bloodied Abbas, whose face was now a mangled mass of shattered bones and swollen flesh. The fingers of his right hand were bent in unnatural directions and his forearm was obviously smashed, bent in an ugly way between the elbow and wrist. His left arm lay limply at his side.

"Don't move! Don't move!" Shea yelled at him.

She retreated to the rear of the bus to keep cover behind the vehicle, her rifle pointed at Abbas. She looked over to see what the other shooter was doing and saw Marta standing over the other man in almost the same manner as she.

As Al-Doleh writhed in pain he could not see out his right eye due to a four-inch long strip of plastic protruding from it, deeply embedded in the soft tissue of that orb. A raging fury burned his heart. A few seconds earlier he had been at the emotional pinnacle of his life, when it became obvious that his attack upon this heathen city had been executed so flawlessly. The devastation he had orchestrated would undoubtedly produce massive damage and death on the kafir population. The moment he had trained for over the last three long years had finally arrived, and he had embarked on his last acts of slaughter and martyrdom when, unbelievably, his efforts had unraveled into failure.

Marta had stumbled and staggered her way to the front of the bus and now stood leaning against it. She raised her rifle up as she cleared the edge of the fender, the pain in her legs was excruciating and she was lightheaded and dizzy as she glared down her gun sights at the terrorist lying before her.

Al-Doleh was looking at the woman who now pointed a rifle at the motionless Abbas when he heard a scraping noise come from above him. He tilted his head back and saw that he was now gazing straight down the barrel of Marta's gun, not more than three feet from his face.

Shame filled him and he was both confused and amazed at how quickly they had been neutralized by, of all things, women! How had these feeble kafir bitches done this? They had somehow defeated the commander of the operation that was going to destroy this entire infidel city. Their sense of safety and security should be obliterated. They should be fleeing from him, like rabbits fleeing the hunter, as he rampaged through the city streets. But now, instead of glorious victory, he and Abbas lay bleeding and helpless, totally at the mercy of two kafir women!

Vile hatred beamed from his single intact eye as blood dribbled from the other. Marta yelled at him to raise his hands, but he just glared at her, and his right hand moved toward a small box taped to the front of his vest.

"Get your fucking hands up, you son of a bitch!" she screamed.

There would be no glorious or triumphant act of martyrdom in store for the IRGC Quds Force Major Al-Doleh. His personal defeat and humiliation were complete and his death would achieve nothing except to protect his pride. It would only keep him from being paraded, alive, before the world as a weakling fool who, at the apex of his moment, was brought down by a woman. That was something he could never allow to happen, and with his death he would surely bring about the death of this disgusting woman, who dared to command him to do anything. That was indeed meager reward but it was all he had left. His hand found the detonator affixed to his vest.

Marta screamed in vain at the murderer. She was fully aware that his refusal to comply was not because he did not understand what she was saying. As she saw the small box with wires coming out of the vest pocket, she lurched forward and pressed the barrel of her rifle hard against his forehead.

"Fuck you," she grimly whispered.

The next instant she pulled the trigger rapidly four times and Al-Doleh's head erupted into red mist and gore as the detonator fell out of his limp hand, lying unused on his chest.

With the terrorist's blood spread across her face, Marta glared down at the bloody mess where the terrorist's head used to be. She wearily looked over at Shea, who stood looking back at her with wide, surprised, eyes that were ignoring the terrorist at her own feet. Marta glanced down and saw the other terrorist pulling out a similar switch on his vest.

"They're wearing bombs, Shea! Kill hi…."

Abbas's suicide vest exploded with tremendous force, sending chunks of his body flying in all directions. Shea disappeared from Marta's view in a cloud of red gore and flame. The rear of the bus lifted off the asphalt along with large chunks of the street's surface. The concussion wave hit Marta like a freight train and lifted her into the air. She was flung backward several feet and landed hard onto Anthony Street, where the impact knocked the air out of her lungs.

A strange bubble of silence seemed to encapsulate her and all she heard was a low ringing in her ears as she fought for breath. Her vision was filled with the clear blue California sky where a flock of pigeons flew through the canyon-like corridors of buildings that towered above her. Breath finally entered her desperate lungs and she gasped eagerly for more. The tall structures that proudly reached upward, framing her view of the sky, began to spin as nausea rippled through her belly. She rested her head against the asphalt for some sense of stability but still she vomited a small amount of bile that ran thick and bloody down the sides of her cheeks.

A man with a nasty gash on his head stood nearby with his arms outstretched, holding his cell phone before him while filming her. The world around her spun violently again and then began to darken, as the void of oblivion swept the horror of her last ten minutes from her consciousness as everything went black.

*****

MARTA PASSED out as Shea's broken corpse lay bleeding, draining onto the cracked sidewalk below 555 Mission Street. At that moment, several blocks away at the Westfield Centre Mall, Saul Goldman's own blood poured from the numerous bullet holes that perforated his torso. He lay on the marble floor inside the mall commons and looked upward at the beautiful blue rotunda dome six stories above him.

The acrid smell of electrical fires and burning plastic drifted through the air of the mall. Ruined, blazing boutiques surrounded him and his toppled Segway lay several feet away. Next to it sprawled the corpse of the boy, Billy Gafney. All around them the marbled floor was littered with over a dozen more corpses of shoppers and store clerks who never had a chance of escaping the rampaging killers that had burst in. The killers had stormed the mall with guns and explosives, killing everyone they saw. A wailing infant screamed loudly in her stroller with the body of her dead mother sprawled in an awkward pile next to it, her dead eyes staring toward Saul.

Saul could still hear the rapid crack of gunfire in different directions, followed by the occasional explosion that would rock the building's interior and cause lights to flicker. Screams and cries got progressively further away as the mall's occupants continued fleeing the hunters who chased them.

Saul deeply regretted stopping the Gafney boy. He figured that maybe the boy would have stood a better chance if Saul had let him go. *Sorry, kid, don't hold it against me when I see ya next.* The rotunda blurred and darkened and Saul closed his eyes.

11:55am MST UTC -7
El Moro School
Trinidad, Colorado

COLORADO STATE Patrol Trooper Ralph Martinez and Officer Colby Owens were the only law enforcement personnel to not be killed or incapacitated by the explosions that had destroyed the grocery store. Their fellow first-responders had all been torn apart in the successive blasts from the caged BBQ propane cylinders after the bomb in the toolbox blew. Along with the cops, firemen, EMT's, and ambulance crews, dozens of citizens in the crowd had also been slaughtered or severely hurt.

Jim, Billy, and Lonnie had arrived just moments after the explosions ended and began helping Owens and Martinez by triaging the wounded as Jim requested that more resources respond to the scene. The process of ascertaining the living from the dead was underway when police dispatch reported that the school complex was being attacked by gunmen.

Aghast and sickened, the four cops instantaneously ran to their vehicles as Jim ordered Lonnie to stay and help with rescuing people from the carnage at the store. Before he got into the police cruiser he felt the firm grip of Lonnie's big right hand grab him by his shirt collar. The next thing he saw was Lonnie's face, inches from his.

"I'm going with you. I can help there more than here. Give me a gun and let me help you, Jim."

Without hesitation Jim replied, "My daughter's in that school, the same as Billy's kids – alright, we can use your help. C'mon, marine, let's roll!"

They peeled out of the area, forced to leave the wounded and dying scattered where they lay in the shattered ruins of the store's parking lot. They drove like wild men through streets crowded with confused and shocked townspeople who were responding to help. And those townspeople knew nothing yet of the ongoing butchery of their children that was occurring on the edge of town.

On the way to the school Jim had radioed for assistance but was told that all law enforcement across the state was ordered, by the Department of Homeland Security, not to respond. With one major attack after another, Oakland, San Francisco, and now the multiple attacks here in the community of Trinidad, DHS had no idea where the next attack might occur. So Trinidad, a small and isolated town, became expendable and DHS ordered a hold-and-see response. They had further ordered that all additional requests for help, anywhere, would be handled the same way until other necessary infrastructures could be secured. Power stations, government buildings, airports, hospitals, as well as the thousands of other schools filled with innocent children had to be protected across the entire country before they would release emergency units to assist neighboring jurisdictions.

The old El Moro School sat just outside town limits, overlooking it like a mansion on a hill. Upon arriving, the four officers were confronted by a screaming menagerie of fleeing kids and teachers. Some ran alone, as fast as their feet could carry them, while others moved slower, carrying their injured classmates. All of them were terrified, but many just stumbled around in a kind of dazed stupor, shell-shocked by the extreme violence they had just witnessed. Blood was everywhere and on most everyone.

As they jumped out of their police cruisers and began collecting their equipment and guns, George Van Horn, the forty-two year old grounds keeper and custodian came running up to them. His plaid shirt and denim bib overalls were covered in blood. Alongside him came a panting Wilbur Howlett, the wrestling coach and lead Phys Ed teacher. Neither of them was familiar with firearms, but both eagerly volunteered to go inside with the officers and help as best they could.

Still wet bloodstains glistened under the noonday sun, along with the shiny brass badge that was pinned to the teal blue shirt of Colorado State trooper Ralph Martinez. He racked the slide, chambering a round into his department-issued, military-surplus Korean War-era, M14 rifle. He then ran and joined the gathering of six other men who were waiting impatiently for him near the gym entrance. This group of shaken men were about to enter the El Moro school complex to hunt down and kill the terrorists who were inside and slaughtering the children there. As Martinez arrived Big Jim looked over his shoulder and could see thick black smoke coming from second floor windows. The old brick building that he had once attended from kindergarten, through to high school graduation, now had growing flames visible through many of those windows.

The school complex was shaped like a huge letter 'T' with the gymnasium located at the bottom leg of the shape. The middle-school classrooms sat above the gym while the elementary and high-school sections split off to either side at the top of the 'T.' The school stretched away from the men as they gathered together to make their plan of attack. Jim knelt down like a quarterback in a huddle as he started instructing the semicircle of men on their assignments.

Colby's blood splattered and cut face showed the wounds he had received from the explosions at the grocery store. A jagged and bloody cut ran from his left ear to his chin with clotted blood as its only bandage.

"Colby, you and Martinez take George and Mr. Howlett with you. Billy and I go with Lonnie, here, okay?"

Martinez and Colby gave curt nods of acknowledgement to the two brave civilians who would be entering with them.

"We're all going to enter together here at the gym and work our way as one group up through the middle school. Once we get to the other end we'll split up. You guys take the left side and clear the elementary school while we cut off to the right and clear out the high school and admin offices. You see the fuckers doing this shit – you kill them! No talking or debating. They fucking die, got it?"

"Hold up, Jim," Martinez interjected. "We don't know how many of the bastards are running around in there. We need to question them, if we can, and find out what the hell is going on and how many we're up against."

"Goddammit, Ben! My daughter is around here somewhere and all I know is that we've got to stop these killers and we don't have any time for questioning. We don't stop our search until the entire school is cleared. If there are more – we'll find out in due time. What the fuck are you going to do? Read'em their Miranda Warnings and start a twenty-hour interrogation to see if they have accomplices? Fuck, man, c'mon." Jim blustered.

"I hear what you're saying, Jim, but I…."

The blaring sound of multiple rifles opening up came from inside the school, followed by high-pitched squeals and screams that were instantly cut off.

"*Move – move!*" Jim yelled as they all ran for the gymnasium doors.

*****

ON THE far side of the school sat a sobbing Sally Goldberg, who also heard the same gunfire. She gently cradled the limp form of Ieesha Jefferson against her breast. The eight-year-old child gurgled because the hole punched into her little chest let blood invade her lungs. The jagged hole was due to shrapnel from the last hand grenade thrown into the room. Sally had taken a cellophane sheet from one of her office's many binders and tried covering the terrible gash with the airtight material. She was attempting to minimize the sucking of air through the wound that could thereby cause the complete collapse of the lung.

In this fashion Sally had worked at keeping the lung inflated and had been successful so far. But unfortunately there was nothing she could do for the excruciating pain the child was enduring, and she hesitated to move the child any more than she must. She feared that if she moved the child too much, the shrapnel's sharp edges, embedded deep inside the baby's body, would continue to slice at the organ. And she knew that the pain would not stop until the jagged metal was removed by a surgeon. Every time the child moaned or squirmed Sally cringed at the misery the girl was suffering.

When the attack began Sally had just gotten off the phone with the superintendent of the school district. They had been discussing what they were going to do with students since the news of the terrible terrorist attacks in Oakland and San Francisco was quickly spreading throughout the student body. They had decided to immediately close the school for the day, but notifying parents to pick up their children would take some time, and the superintendent was going to draft a press release to start the process. Sally had just sat her phone down and was turning up the volume on the television set in her office when Ieesha and her classmates arrived there.

Ieesha was one of only three African American children attending the school. The child's vivacious, warm personality made her one of the most popular kids in her age group. Her gregarious nature was also why she lay so grievously injured in Sally's arms. Ieesha was the class leader of Mrs. Hilkey's third-grade history class and was leading a class delegation with four other students to the school's administration office. There they were to request permission from Sally, the school principal, for their class to go on a field trip to one of Trinidad's local historical sites, the place where the famous wild-west figure and American scout, Kit Carson, was buried at a municipal park downtown.

Mrs. Hilkey stood beaming, delighted, behind the small student delegation, totally oblivious to the horrible news of the day's tragedy in California. Ieesha handed their official written request, written in blocky childish script, to Sally. At that moment the three killers had burst through the hall doors just outside the administration offices. The psychotic murderers screamed strange words while spraying hundreds of bullets at every adult and child caught in the open. The large glass dividers between the office and hall were shattered as bullets caught Sally's secretary, Pat Shroeder, and Mrs. Hilkey. They were both practically cut in two as everyone else either tried to run or crouch low to escape being shot. Screams erupted everywhere.

300

Moments later the odd looking pipe came bouncing into the office and in a devastating detonation that knocked Sally senseless, it sent shrapnel shredding through bodies, including Ieesha. Fire alarms rang and the sprinkler system discharged stale cold water as Sally lost consciousness and sank into blackness.

She lay dazed for some time, finally becoming alert to her surroundings and able to understand what was happening at her school. She then began searching through the bodies, only to find that Ieesha and she were the only ones still alive inside the offices. The rampaging killers were gone and Sally listened as the screams, gunfire, and explosions continued to propagate around her school.

Seconds ticked by like hours as no sounds of sirens came, but far-too-close gunfire would erupt again and again, occasional explosions would echo through the building, causing Sally to flinch each time it happened. She felt totally helpless as the distant screams and squeals from dying and fleeing children filled the campus grounds. The nightmare seemed to go on forever and Sally considered fleeing as well. But she could not get her feet to obey and leave her remaining students still trapped inside the school.

Eventually the sounds of scurrying feet came to her ears as two dozen terrified and whimpering elementary-age students came into the administration offices. They were led by a petrified middle-schooler. Sally had quickly crowded all of them into her little office, where many let loose with sobs and cried while she assessed their wounds and tried to comfort them as best she could.

As principal of the school it had been Sally's duty and responsibility to be prepared for this day. A day that every school administrator and teacher across the country has known, full-well, could occur at their school. Terrorists, the insane, murderers, violent whackos, psychopaths, lunatic parents, and estranged, marginalized, violent students were all possible attackers to a school. Any day a Columbine High School copycat-killer or some blood-thirsty terrorists could be out there, ready to commit a successful attack on another American school. Sally's greatest fear was an attack like what had occurred on the Russian school in Beslan. That depraved attack had ended with the terrorists murdering over four-hundred innocent adults and children. Now, Sally's greatest fear had come to her own school.

She remembered watching the live video of SWAT officers marching with raised rifles behind fire trucks outside Columbine High School. She remembered watching news footage of heavily-armed bank robbers, wearing body armor and spraying thousands of bullets at cops and civilians in North Hollywood. She remembered hearing the stories told at school symposiums by the first-responders and survivors

301

of other school shootings: the Amish school, Virginia Tech, Platte Canyon, Jonesboro, and so many more. Those stories were unnerving, horrific, and heartbreaking.

She knew deep down it could happen at her school, too, but what exactly could she do to stop it? The parents, the community, and the government knew all about those incidents as well. She had a limited budget, an open campus, no perimeter fence of razor-wire outside, no tanks or watchtowers, or soldiers patrolling with guns at the ready. Against bombs and guns, what was she supposed to do for the safety of her wards?

But Sally also knew it was she who was ultimately responsible for doing something to ensure her school was safe. She had failed, and now she was also responsible for every dead child, secretary, and teacher lying butchered throughout her school. She was responsible as each distant scream was cut short by gunfire. The weight of her failed responsibility felt like a sledge that hammered mercilessly down upon her vanquished spirit.

Ieesha inhaled a ragged breath as her small fingers reflexively squeezed Sally's arm. The warm flow of the child's blood, squeezing out under the cellophane and running over the back of Sally's hand, told the administrator that time was getting very short for her to act. Sally looked down at the girl's angelic face and confronted reality. A reality that showed that all the excuses and fawning platitudes to school safety by two-faced politicians and the wasted hyperbole from school administrators, school leaders, teachers, unions, parents, and the public meant absolutely nothing. The only thing that mattered right now was that she was going to save as many children as she possibly could.

The terrified children around her were all locked into an overwhelming vortex of terror and each burst of gunfire made them jump and squeal. They were not safe here in her office, and they would all be executed if the killers returned. She was the adult, the principal, their leader, and she must act. She had failed the dead, but she was going to do everything she could for the living.

To her right squatted the oldest student and the leader who had brought the children to Sally, thirteen-year-old Becky Aragon, the sister of the school's athletic hero, Tony Aragon.

"Becky," Sally whispered with no effect.

"Becky!" she said louder.

The teenager looked at her with wide, frightened eyes and pleaded in a weak and terrified voice, "Be quiet, they'll hear you. Don't let them hear you."

Sally lowered her voice to little more than a whisper.

"Becky, please help me. We have to get out of the building now. Those men *will* return and I need you and these children to be gone when they do. Please – help me!"

The girl's body shook with fear-induced tremors, as she looked around the room at all the dead bodies and refused to move. Sally realized pleading would not work and that she must lead by command. Standing, she looked through the shattered windows down the hall and saw the bodies of several children lying limp and motionless on the floor. Her eyes caught movement. A lone, wounded boy tried to pull himself along the floor toward them, leaving a glossy crimson trail of blood on the tiled floor.

Sally held Ieesha tightly and turned back to the children around her, and in a steady but firm voice she said, "Children. We are all leaving now. You will all follow me out of the door and we will go across the hall to those doors."

She pointed with her free hand to the school's main doors across the atrium. The very same doors the killers had burst into the school through.

"Now – everyone up!"

Only two rose from the floor while the rest remained crouched. Sally addressed Becky once again, this time noticing the tiny red spots of blood splatter on her face and clothes. Sally's heart broke at thinking of what this girl must have already been forced to deal with and yet, this child had still accomplished getting this many children to her principal's office in hopes of refuge. *I must give her a new mission to focus on.*

In a tone that was both harsh and pleading she said, "Becky, get up! I need you to help me lead them out. Now, get up!"

Becky hesitantly rose on shaking knees and stepped up to the principal as Sally held out Ieesha's limp body.

"Here! Take this girl and get her to medical attention as fast as you possibly can."

Becky hesitated and then took the child as Sally showed her how to hold the plastic over the wound.

"Make sure you try and keep this plastic with a tight seal on that wound, okay? Becky, listen to me, dear, I'm putting you in charge of these children," she said, while staring hard into the teenager's eyes and then turned to the others in the office.

"Children! All of you get up, now! You will all follow Becky. Now, let's go, get up!"

She quickly walked around the room, pushing them into a group near Becky and then she led the way toward the broken office

303

door, stepping over corpses the whole way. At the wrecked office door she looked left and right down the hall.

"Becky, once you're out those doors, you will take these kids to the football field and look for help. Girl, these children are now your responsibility – get them to their families. Understand?"

Becky slowly nodded.

"Okay, children, quietly now, let's go."

Sally led the way across the atrium to the doors.

The group shuffled along behind her like a strange inchworm-type creature as each child, crowding tightly against the one in front, tried to stay as close as possible and yet move as fast as they could. Arriving at the doors, Sally looked out across the grass and saw nothing moving. She pushed open the doors and waved the children outside. As they broke into the clear air their once-tight little group suddenly opened up as they all began sprinting as fast as they could, away from the school, giving out sobbing whimpers as they ran.

Sally watched them go, desperately wanting to follow. In seconds they were gone from her sight. She closed the door and turned, looking back down the hall. She took a deep breath, and with gritted teeth and a trembling body, she started walking along the wall. Slowly she made her way toward the young boy who was crawling along the floor of the hallway.

*****

JOHNNY GRIMES knelt behind Tony Aragon's mud-covered truck, gripping the rear bumper tightly while looking to his right and left. He had managed to get out of his third-hour science classroom as the gunmen came barging in, shooting. He had ran down the stairs and got out of the building without getting shot. The one bad guy he saw with a rifle was shooting the other way down the hallway toward the gym as Johnny ran frantically the other way.

Now outside, he did not know what he should do. He saw a lot of other kids running down the road toward town and he had thought about following them. But before he could, one of the murderers inside had fired out of a second floor window of the elementary school at some of the fleeing kids. Johnny had watched, horror-struck, as several of them fell and did not get back up. He did not want to be killed in the open that way. He desperately wanted protection, but above that, he wanted to be able to fight back. Right now he was hidden pretty well, and he also knew that Tony kept a rifle in his truck that the school officials knew nothing about. And Johnny was going to get his hands on that gun, fast.

Johnny briefly wondered where Tony was and if he was okay. He figured if anyone could find a way to get out of this alive, it would be Tony. After all, he was the best at everything. Johnny wished that he could be half the hero Tony was. He looked around at the school and saw dark smoke lifting into the sky on the far side of the gym where Tony had been in PE class. As his eyes scanned that end of the school he noticed the unmoving torso of a girl with long black hair, hanging halfway out a second floor window. The girl's hair flowed like a flag in the breeze and he recognized her. It was the beautiful Stephanie Cordova, one of the girls who had walked with him and Tony into the school that morning. Johnny cursed and punched his fist into the tailgate.

Hunkering down, he made his way around to the passenger door and tried to open it, but it was locked. He looked inside and saw that the driver door was also locked. He pulled off his t-shirt and wrapped it around his right hand and then slammed his fist against the door's window, breaking it with a single punch. He opened the door and pulled the truck's bench seat forward, revealing Tony's .22 caliber lever-action rifle lying behind the seat. It had been a Christmas present to Tony from his grandfather several years ago. Tony and Johnny often hunted small-game with it and also plinked at empty beer cans and bottles at kegger parties.

Johnny grabbed the rifle and a small box of ammunition out of the glove box. Dumping the bullets from the box into his pocket, he began to load the rifle. He inserted one cartridge after another into the gun as quickly as possible, but still dropped several cartridges on the ground as he fumbled with the small things. He had bent to pick one up when a noise stopped him and he froze. Off to his left a group of terrified younger students came running around a corner of the school, very near the administration offices. He immediately recognized the girl leading them as Tony's sister, Becky. Johnny was irresistibly pulled to her and he bolted away from the truck, the loaded rifle in his hand.

As he approached, a child running with Becky saw him, as well as the gun he carried. The boy screamed and veered away, running fast. This caused the others in the group to panic and they all ran, with high-pitched squeals, behind the first terrified child. Becky almost ran with them but then recognized Johnny, and a wave of relief flushed across her face as she turned and ran to him. They met and he pulled her under an ancient cottonwood tree that had sat in the school yard since before the school was built in 1903. Its gnarled bark had over a hundred years of notched messages of school-age love.

"Are you hurt?" Johnny asked upon seeing the blood on her face and shirt, and the wounded child in her arms.

"No, no, I'm okay. This girl is hurt, though."

"Have you seen Tony?"

"No. He should have been in gym at the start."

"I know, but I haven't seen him come out of the gym. I've been waiting at his truck and I...."

A long burst of gunfire punctuated by screams erupted from the other side of the school, causing Becky and Johnny to duck and hug each other. They pushed in close to the tree with Johnny placing his body to shield hers. They remained frozen for several seconds until Ieesha gave a moan, making Johnny lean back and look down at the wounded girl.

"I know her. Did she get shot?"

Becky pulled the girl to her bosom.

"She was in the principal's office when the killers came in there. I don't know how she got hurt, but Mrs. Goldberg made her my responsibility and I have to get her to an ambulance. She's bleeding so much! My God, Johnny! There were bombs and bullets and, and, oh so much screaming! I just ran and ran! I thought I was going to die! I'm so scared. Where's my brother?"

Tears ran down her face as quiet sobs came from her trembling lips. Johnny looked into her eyes and ran his trembling palm across her cheek.

"You're gonna be okay, I swear. You take this kid to get help. I'll go find Tony."

The desperation in her eyes calmed a little.

"I almost had a heart attack until I saw it was you with that rifle. Then I felt safe when I saw your face," she said with a warm smile.

Johnny blushed.

"You got to move. I'm going in there to look for Tony."

"No! I need your help with her. I know my brother and he'll be able to take care of himself."

Johnny shook his head.

"You just head toward town and you'll be fine. I thought I heard some sirens coming up over there a minute ago. God! Where are the fucking cops, huh? When we fucking need them, where in the hell are they? We're getting killed up here and there's none around! Shit!"

Their eyes searched the campus around them for an army of uniformed men, their sirens announcing loudly their arrival to save the day. But instead of a ghost cavalry appearing before their eyes, all they saw was the eerily silent grounds and a pillar of black smoke rising from the middle of town below them. The smell of smoke and death was thick upon the breeze.

Johnny turned to Becky.

"Listen, you get this girl out of here. I'm going in there. What did you see inside those doors you came out of?"

"We left Mrs. Goldberg in there. I don't know where she went."

"Okay – okay. You get out of here."

Johnny stood and helped Becky to her feet; before he let go of her hand he squeezed it and looked into her eyes.

"Tony is my best friend and I'm going in to see if he needs some help. But I love you, Becky – I always have. I want you to know that."

Becky smiled at him.

"If I don't get out of there – tell my parents that I had to go back, and tell them that I love them, okay?"

"I will. I love you, too, Johnny," Becky said as he gently pushed her to leave.

"Now, run, I'll cover you."

She turned and ran across the parking lot toward the football field. Johnny watched the school building as she ran away, and when she was gone he left the tree and made a quick sprint around the corner of the building, headed for the doors to the school.

Moments later he cautiously entered the atrium. He was taken aback, revolted to see the little dead bodies that littered the atrium and down each hallway. His ears strained to hear anything and he thought he caught the sound of movement down the hall to his left. He swallowed hard and raised the rifle to his shoulder as he began walking that way.

After crossing the atrium he looked down the hall where he saw his petite principal, Mrs. Goldberg, trying to pull a boy along the floor. It appeared to be a struggle for her small frame; her outstretched arms were tucked under his armpits and his feet dragged on the floor. Johnny sprinted down the hall, and as Sally heard him approach she gasped and recoiled, almost dropping the injured boy.

"It's okay, Mrs. Goldberg! It's me, John Grimes, ma'am."

Sally did not relax as her eyes darted back and forth.

"Sshh! Quiet! They're still here in the school! I've heard them," Sally said in an earnest whisper.

Johnny's mouth clamped shut and his feet immediately slowed. He brought the rifle back up to his shoulder and started looking down the hallway, past her and then back over his shoulder. He then looked down at the wounded child and recognized the semiconscious boy as 8th grader Andrew Mackey. The rotund boy was very large for his age. Johnny saw that he was shot at least twice. There was a terrible exit wound in his back and his left arm had severely torn muscles where it had almost been amputated from a gunshot wound. The gruesome appendage hung limply. He could see that Sally had covered it with a makeshift wrapping of clothing to try to stop the bleeding.

"What can I do to help?"

Sally breathed hard from the exertion of pulling the overweight boy.

"I need you to take over. He's just too big for me."

"But the rifle…?"

"Just give it to me. I can shoot. Give it to me," Sally ordered, waving her outstretched arm at him and trying to hold the hurt child with her other.

Johnny suddenly felt naked and vulnerable again as he doubtfully gave up the rifle and took over holding the wounded boy.

Sally gripped the gun, looking at it.

"Is this the safety?" she asked, pointing to a small lever.

"Yeah, you also need to keep that hammer back all the way so when you pull the trigger, it'll fire."

"Okay. Now, if I shoot, I need to rack this lever under here, right?"

"Yep."

"Good. Okay, I got it. Now I need you to help this boy so we can get him out of here," Sally ordered in a hushed voice.

Johnny stood pensively, holding the bleeding boy's shoulders, looking at his principal for further instructions. Sally began walking, headed for the atrium as Johnny's young and muscular frame easily carried the boy up the hallway with Sally beside him.

"Good, John, I'm very proud of you. Once we have him outside we'll take him to the football field where I can do more for him."

They continued back down the hall until they both heard the sound of movement behind them and Sally spun, pointing the rifle toward the noise. The tension on her face melted as she saw over two dozen kids moving along the corridor near the high school science department, heading her way. They were led by a teacher, Kimberly Thompson. Sally waved her arm vigorously above her head, eagerly motioning for the group to make their way down the hall. Some members of the group almost broke into a run, but after a terse word from Kim they immediately fell back into the orderly column.

308

Sally swelled with admiration and pride at the way her students worked in unison for Kim. Tony Aragon was at the front of the group, holding the metal front legs to a cafeteria chair while a 10th grader, Melvin Goddard, held the chair's backrest. In the chair sat unconscious teacher Judy Spencer-Hargrove, who had a large and bloody bandage wrapped around a gunshot wound to her chest. Melvin also had a large gash across his forehead that had bled badly and was now covered by a towel, wrapped around it like a turban.

Kim and two other students carried 30 lb. fire extinguishers in their hands as their only means of defense, but nonetheless they carried them with purpose and treated them as if they were real weapons. The group arrived scared and trembling but in good order. Johnny and Tony gave each other curt nods of welcome. Tony saw the rifle and immediately knew how the principal had gotten it.

"I saw Becky – she's okay and outside the school, taking a hurt girl and looking for help," Johnny said as a flood of relief mixed with gratitude washed across Tony's face.

"Good job, Kim. I'm so proud of you," Sally said to her teacher as her own eyes watered with respect at the display of leadership.

Kim nodded back.

"I've been collecting any students I find as we worked our way from my classroom. I was able to get all the students in my classroom out through the cafeteria after the attack started."

She looked around the atrium at the shattered main office and was dismayed to see all the dead children.

"It looks like you've been through hell here."

Sally choked back sobs as her eyes narrowed, and all she managed in response was to slowly nod her head. After a few seconds she regained her composure.

"I've been sending everyone to the football field. We need to get this group there. You take them and I will stay and keep searching for more children."

"No, I'm staying with you to help. Tony and Johnny can get these kids out there," Kim said firmly.

Sally gave her a small smile.

"Thanks."

Suddenly they heard noises down the hall from where Kim had come. An unmistakably evil voice of a man speaking in a strange language came to their ears, and the sounds quickly became louder and closer. The evil voice was followed by the sounds of laughter. Sally and Kim looked at the children around them, each showing a frantic and alarmed expression. Sally looked desperately at Tony and Johnny.

"You two – you take these kids to the football field and see to it that they get help. You have no other job to do other than that, you understand? Now go, all of you – go! I'll stop them here, go!"

Johnny did not hesitate as he took the chair from the hurt younger boy, Melvin. Tony and Johnny, with the wounded teacher, then led the group of kids toward the atrium as the evil voice and the accompanying vile laughter came closer. The wounded Melvin hit the bar on the doors, opening them for everyone behind. As the last child exited the building he gave a quick glance back at Kim and shot her a quick nod of unspoken admiration, and then turned and started running across the grass in quick pursuit of the group.

Sally and Kim turned from the door and began to retreat down the hallway. But the sounds of the killer's laughter made Sally slow and turn. She leveled the rifle back down the hall toward the approaching child-murderer.

"No more," Sally said grimly.

*****

LONNIE'S STIFF, sixty-three year old knees complained bitterly at all he was forcing them to do. He, along with Jim and Billy, had kept searching methodically through the school but had been unsuccessful so far. His stiff knees ached badly as he tried to keep up with the two younger, healthier men. The two sheriff deputies were counting on him to cover their backs and help them save these children who were being massacred. *I cannot fail them!*

He remembered that these types of physical challenges were far easier to do when he was the young eighteen-year old marine, perspiring rivers of sweat while he slogged through the jungles of the Que Son Valley. He also still clearly remembered the smells and emotions of those long-ago days when his booted feet tromped through the hell that Vietnam became during his three tours of duty there.

Lonnie was more than a little unnerved to be sweating so much more now, here in this school, than he had under the humid canopy of trees in Southeast Asia. He also knew that he could not chock it up to his fat belly or old age, either. He was now sweating out buckets of pure rage as the sight of the innocent babies who lay dead and wounded at his feet were tearing at his emotions. A blinding white-hot fury had built up and now engulfed his mind as he was forced to continue walking right past the injured, crying children who begged for help.

Their continuing searches had become one evil choice after another, as to their left and right were the agony-filled bodies of bleeding children. Most of them were just babies. If they stopped, more would be condemned to die somewhere else. Leaving these wounded and dying children behind them was both awful and haunting, but necessary. Lonnie watched as the horrendous reality came across the child's face as they stared with desperate, pleading eyes at the three big, strong men leaving them behind. There was no way they could possibly comprehend the reasons for their abandonment, lying there helpless, in pain, with their blood oozing out of their small mangled bodies. Tears streaked down their faces while they pathetically pleaded for help, only to watch miserably as the strong men moved away, leaving them behind to die, alone.

In this repellent manner the three men had carried grimly on down the halls, staying focused on the necessary task. They were not heartless men who ignored the agony and fear of the wounded. They were simply the only hope to stop the slaughter of the rest of the children still trapped inside the death school. Lonnie knew this. He understood this. He had seen death's many faces before, but he also knew something else – his essence would never be free and his psyche would be forever haunted by these awful but required choices. Pure wretchedness defined would be the burdensome branding that would be seared onto his soul for all eternity. He doubted that God would ever grant him the removal of this stench from his spirit.

Moreover, the pace of their search had gone maddeningly slow, as they were forced to search every room they came to. Each one could contain the terrorists inside, waiting, hiding in ambush, to sneak out and begin once again to start slaughtering more innocents. Occasionally they would find students and faculty hiding in those rooms. When they could, they would drag the nearby wounded from the hall into those rooms, to be with the others so that there was some possibility of aid. Many of the children wanted to flee and Jim was forced to order them to stay where they were. Especially since he did not know where the terrorists actually were. He told them it was safer to stay rather than accidently run into the killers again as they fled.

Lonnie could also see another great wretchedness for both Jim and Billy that they hid away from the others. Neither of the men had seen or heard any word about their own children. Children who were quite possibly lying dead somewhere inside the school complex, just like the other children they had been forced to walk past. And yet both men stayed focused upon their duty, knowing that to stop the murderers was the best way to save their own babies. Lonnie's soul bled pity for their terrible distress.

311

The lack of manpower to conduct a quick and thorough search made the task even more difficult to complete effectively. Since the original burst of gunfire when they entered they had heard only one burst echoing through the halls. There were no further indicators of where the killers were, and the students and teachers they had found all agreed that there were at least three killers prowling the campus. Lonnie was becoming concerned that they might not even still be at the school. Billy openly feared that they may have completed their attack here, possibly moving on to another target in the community.

Jim had spoken briefly to his father on the radio. Sheriff Griego was coordinating emergency responders to the school as those resources became available. Several deputies, city cops, state troopers, and deputized citizens were presently rushing toward the school to assist with the search and establish a perimeter around the area, but they were still minutes away. With the murderers still unaccounted for, the sheriff had to keep some manpower in reserve, since no one knew where to send the force that was being gathered. The terrorists had already shown that they were capable of attacking at multiple locations.

Lonnie leaned his shoulder against the end of a long string of student lockers and watched and listened for any sign of the evil men they were hunting. His hands held the AR15 given to him by Jim. The two deputies were currently inside the room behind him, checking it while he stayed tucked into the nook by the door. A large explosive had been used inside and there was the odor of the stale water that rained down from a broken sprinkler head. A small severed arm of an elementary-age student lay on the floor at Lonnie's feet, acting as a ghastly door stop that held the broken door ajar.

The ear-splitting and incessant screech from the building's fire alarm was maddening but he still heard the voices and cries of children off in the distance. For the past several seconds he thought he might have heard the deeper tone of grown men speaking. As he strained to understand what he thought he was hearing, his ears clearly heard a piercing yell echoing through the hall. That sound was immediately followed by the bark of multiple guns opening fire.

Without hesitation, Lonnie sprinted down the hall until he reached a stairwell and plunged down the steps as he charged toward the gunfire. His knees almost buckled on the landing as he dashed down the concrete steps, Billy and Jim just a few strides behind.

WHILE LONNIE stood contemplating the misery of the search, Kim ducked into a doorway, just before the murderers cleared the bend in the hallway. Upon entering the room she saw three kids huddled together in fear, hiding under a table at the back of the room. They squirmed and squealed when she burst into the room. Kim stopped and raised her finger in front of her mouth, indicating to them to be quiet. Alarm radiated from their faces as they realized that the killing monsters they were hiding from were coming back. They trembled but remained silent.

Sally Goldman never saw the children inside the room with Kim; she kept her eyes looking down the hallway, facing the approaching killers. She backed into the room's doorway with the Winchester leveled at her waist. She saw the first child-murderer come sauntering around the corner, smiling and chatting like he had been playing a win-the-stuffed-animal shooting game at an amusement park.

Instantly, an uncontrollable and blinding fury fueled by manic hate surged inside of Sally at the sight of the smirking child-killer. Her cognitive mind shut down and her primal lizard-brain gripped her nervous system, forcing her to react. The rifle rose to eye level, and as the small iron sights aligned with the small troll-like grinning man, Sally let loose a savage, penetrating scream as she began firing.

The first small bullet bypassed all the protection of Aziz's vest and punched into his shoulder. Pain registered through his revelry, and his smirk vanished as the second small bullet tore off a sizable piece of his right ear. That was quickly followed by another that zinged by, millimeters from his face. Crying out in pain, his arm reflexively released his rifle, letting it clatter to the floor, as he twisted and ducked back down the hall. Ajay also jumped back behind the bend in the hall, but slipped on the trail of wet blood left by the crawling Mackey boy, landed hard on his back, and bellowed loudly in pain as the embedded cactus in his body was viciously jarred by the impact.

Faruk, however, reacted quickly by extending his rifle around the bend, spraying bullets down the hall at Sally. His wild sweeping arcs of automatic gunfire forced Sally to duck behind the row of lockers that lined the wall. Bullets impacted the lockers by her and sent shards of metal ricocheting through the air. The children inside the classroom screamed and cried out as murderous havoc erupting outside the door to their miserable sanctuary. Surprised and dismayed by the squeals of children directly behind her, Sally turned in alarm to see Kim hunkered down by the three petrified children.

"Oh, dear God above, no!" she cried.

Faruk glanced anxiously down the hallway but could not see the unknown attacker. He turned to help a livid and cursing Ajay to his feet. Meanwhile Aziz was on his knees, outstretching his wounded arm in an attempt to grab his discarded rifle that lay several few feet away, exposed in the middle of the hallway. But his near-useless shoulder no longer functioned properly and he could not hold it elevated away from his body. So he used his arm like a lasso and flung it out, trying to grasp the rifle.

All three killers suspected that the first law enforcement officers had finally arrived to interrupt their play and were now waiting to shoot at them again if they showed themselves. The murderers had been exhaustively trained to confront the threat posed by local law enforcement and Aziz cursed himself for being caught off-guard and injured so easily. The amphetamines coursing through his veins gave him tremendous energy but made it hard to concentrate.

He stretched out and the bullet lodged in the socket of his shoulder screamed at him. Movement caught his eye and he almost ducked backward, but what he saw shocked him so much that he stayed exposed and motionless while his drug-addled brain computed the input. He saw an older woman, short in stature and wearing a green dress, her dark hair visible in a doorway down the hall. A rifle in her hands looked like it belonged in an American western movie rather than in a battle with him.

His eyes locked with Sally's as she raised the rifle and snapped a quick shot at him without aiming. The bullet zipped several feet away from him and he did not even flinch. The audacity of a pathetic woman with a relic weapon who dared to challenge him was an insult to his wounded pride. Aziz's amphetamine-reinforced anger turned to rage.

"Jendeh!" he screamed as he jumped to his feet and began stomping indignantly out into the hall. He picked up his rifle with his good arm and began to trudge bitterly down the hall toward Sally.

Sally watched Aziz retrieve his rifle and advance.

"Get out now!" she yelled over her shoulder at Kim.

Like a gunslinger from a 1960s television western, Sally stepped from the doorway and began firing at Aziz with the rifle held at her hip. She racked the lever action as fast as possible but none of her bullets landed on target. Her fear and frustration blinded her to the danger of being so exposed. Faruk poked his rifle out from around the bend and fired at her, but his aim was as poor as hers as he tried to

314

avoid hitting Aziz. The string of 7.62mm rounds flew mere inches from Sally and hammered into the tin lockers and cement walls all around her as she continued shooting at the onrushing Aziz.

Kim was astonished at the volume of gunfire outside the door and looked frantically around the room for any means of escape for her and the children. The only avenue available was an open doorway at the far end of the room that led to the science lab. Grabbing one child with her free hand and shoving the others with the fire extinguisher in her other hand, she pushed and dragged them toward the exit as fast as possible.

Unknowingly, Sally had fired her last cartridge and racked the lever again, but this time when she pulled the trigger, the hammer fell forward and only made a small metal *click* as the firing pin slammed down on an empty chamber.

"Shit!" she cursed.

Aziz was now less than ten feet away and she reflexively ducked back out of sight into the doorway. Flipping the rifle, she grabbed it by the blistering hot barrel and lifted it high above her head, ready to swing it down on the man's head when he came around the lockers. Kim saw this out of the corner of her eye and knew the people coming were too close to escape from. She shoved the children hard enough to send them sprawling to the floor with a yell. She turned from them and ran to the side of the door, out of sight next to Sally, and raised the fire extinguisher above her head.

Aziz neared the doorway entrance but he was not about to be ambushed again by the witch. He stopped just short, stuck the barrel around the corner and pulled the trigger, firing off a dozen bullets as he swept the gun left and right. Four slugs tore into Sally Goldberg's chest, lifting her off her feet. As her body fell backward Tony's rifle left her scorched hands and went skidding across the floor of the classroom. She landed just inside the door, gasping and dying as Aziz came past the lockers and smirked at her. Her vision waxed and blurred as she looked up at the vile man. He stepped forward and pointed the smoking barrel at her face.

Just before Sally died, her mind absorbed the sight of Kimberly Thompson savagely swinging her bright red, 30 lb. fire extinguisher around, smashing it into the killer's jaw. Sally, darkly contented, watched as Aziz's face crumpled under the impact. His shattered jaw dislocated from his skull, forced sideways, tearing through muscle and tendon underneath his skin, until it stopped halfway toward his left ear. His rifle fell useless to the floor as he collapsed to his knees, holding his destroyed face in his hands. He tried to scream through gurgling, bubbling blood that poured from his misshapen mouth. It was the last thing on earth that Sally Goldberg ever knew.

*****

BILLY, LONG and lanky, quickly caught up to Lonnie as they landed together at the bottom of the stairwell and rushed down the hall in the direction of the gunfire, Lonnie following and Jim trailing. They rounded the corner and saw two of the men they had been hunting about forty-feet-down the hall. Lonnie's cowboy boots skidded to a stop on the polished floor as he brought his rifle to his shoulder to fire.

"*Freeze*! *Don't move*!" Billy yelled instinctively as Lonnie and Jim cursed at the man's stupidity.

Before Lonnie could fire, Ajay took off running; Faruk spun around and sent a long burst of fire at Billy and Lonnie. Both men dove in different directions as the bullets whizzed by. Ajay disappeared from view as Faruk backed away, but continued firing. Exposed in the middle of the hall, Lonnie rolled back and forth, firing wildly back at the terrorist, as red-hot missiles ricocheted off the floor and walls around him.

Jim reached the corner as Billy stood, and the two joined Lonnie in the gun battle. The volume of fire they sent down the hall forced Faruk to duck out of sight. Lonnie took the opportunity to scamper from the middle of the hall just as Faruk leaned back out and sent another long string of bullets down the hall at where Lonnie had just been.

The sound of gunfire in the hall was almost deafening but Jim still heard the squeals of children farther away. Now that they found the child-killers he knew they must kill them or at least pin them down until more help arrived. Jim started to advance down the hall in pursuit of the killers, Billy and Lonnie at his side.

Ajay had thought that the vast pit of emptiness, that had fueled his hate throughout his life, would be filled with the misery and terror he was going to inflict on the world. But as he watched the life of one child after another get torn away by his hands, the pit had become more hollow and far colder than ever before. *Why can't I have what I want!* He now limped down the hall as the barrage of noise from the firefight behind him raged. He turned into the doorway Aziz had entered and was stunned to see Aziz lying in the doorway next to a small dead woman. Aziz moaned as crimson blood poured out of his severely disfigured face.

The cries of children broke Ajay's attention from the baffling sight at his feet and he looked over and saw a black woman, herding kids through a door at the other end of the room. As the roar of gunfire drew closer behind him he stepped over Aziz and the dead woman and followed after them.

Completely outgunned, Faruk desperately looked around for help and found he had been abandoned. He quickly backpedaled, thinking he was following Ajay. He kept his attention focused back down the hall and unknowingly passed the doorway where Aziz lay. Together Jim, Billy, and Lonnie came storming around the bend and into the straight hall, side by side. In a last-ditch effort to slow their advance, Faruk jerked a hand grenade off the front of his suicide-vest. Pulling the pin he hurled it down the hall.

"*Grenade*!" Lonnie yelled as he ran toward Faruk.

The bouncing canister of explosives and Lonnie passed in opposite directions as Lonnie began firing at the retreating terrorist. Jim saw the grenade and impulsively dove for the floor, curling into a fetal position against the wall as Billy ran backward as fast as his legs could move him.

The distance between Faruk and Lonnie closed rapidly as both men fired their rifles at one another. Some of Lonnie's bullets found their mark and stitched holes into Faruk's lower right hip and then across his belly. The murderer doubled-over but still kept firing. Two of his rounds struck along Lonnie's left side, causing him to spin around and sink to his knees. Faruk fell back onto his butt and then collapsed onto his back.

Meanwhile Jim's body had reacted to the threat of the grenade without him thinking. The numerous SWAT drills he had participated in over the years had taught his body to just react under stress. Now he instinctively tucked his ear into his shoulder to help lessen the effect on his hearing, while also opening his mouth wide to keep his ears from over-pressurizing. He tightened into a compact ball just as the grenade exploded a few feet away. The impact from the blast was extreme, lifting his large body and pounding it against the wall. The explosive's percussion wave also lifted Billy off his churning legs and threw him, flailing backward through the air. The deafening effect of the blast made Jim's ears hurt as he felt the hot needle-like jabs of shrapnel bite into his leg. Billy landed and tumbled head-over-heels until stopping in a motionless heap.

The explosion rocked but did not incapacitate Lonnie as he tried to point his rifle at the terrorist, who lay just a few feet away. The torn muscle in Lonnie's side and shoulder made the rifle hard to lift. His opponent could not rise due to the slugs that had torn into his guts, but he continued to spray bullets blindly at Lonnie, his rifle resting across his chest as he swept the barrel up and down. Bullets whizzed past Lonnie's head and he grunted as he felt another slug punch into his right thigh. The pain of the impact folded his leg under him, causing him to fall backward against the lockers in the hall.

Bullets impacted wildly all around Lonnie.

"Fuck this shit!" Lonnie yelled.

Ignoring the fusillade of bullets he calmly reset his rifle tightly in his shoulder and aimed carefully with the barrel resting on his knee. Bullets landed inches from his head as the sights aligned with the body of the terrorist and he softly squeezed off four well-aimed rounds. He was immediately rewarded with a guttural moan followed by a long wheeze of air that trailed off. Faruk's rifle fell silent across his motionless chest as his arms collapsed limply to the floor.

"Take that, ya fuck'n sack o' crap," Lonnie said with grim satisfaction.

Then, wincing and groaning, he began trying to stand but his wobbly and bleeding leg protested greatly.

Jim heard little other than a loud ringing in his ears as he stumbled toward his partner, praying that Billy was not dead. Then, all at once, his skinny friend sat up quickly, wide-eyed but disorientated as thin trails of blood ran down from his nostrils and ears. Jim slapped him on the cheek several times before Billy's eyes became fully awake and showed signs that he recognized Jim.

Slowly, with Jim's help, Billy was able to stand. The two men looked down the hall and saw Lonnie hobbling his way back toward them. A motionless dark mass lay in the distance behind him. The three men converged outside the doorway where Aziz and Sally Goldberg lay next to one another. They lifted their weapons to the ready and moved through the door.

The big lawman looked down at the familiar face of Sally Goldberg. A lifelong friend of the Griego family, she had assisted Jim's mother for over thirty-years with Salvation Army chores and bell-ringing duty every Christmas season, even though she was a devout Jew. Jim's eyes watered bitterly as he looked upon her corpse.

Lonnie tapped his shoulder and pointed down at Aziz.

"That one's still breath'n."

Aziz stared up at the big cop and moaned as Jim put the barrel of his rifle below the man's disfigured face and fired three quick shots into his upper chest, dispatching him to hell.

Back out in the hallway, Faruk heard the shots but was unconcerned by them. The last three rounds fired by the old American

318

had punched fatal holes into his chest and neck. The entire left side of his body was paralyzed as he felt life speedily ebbing away. He heard the sound of his own breath gurgling through the warm fluid flooding his throat as he started to drown in his own blood. Similar to the way a large open drain empties a vat of water, his strength was rapidly being replaced by emptiness. With a last effort he reached for the vest's detonator. Finding it, he closed his hand around it as the blankness of eternity enveloped him.

Near the science lab entrance Ajay waited in ambush, hunkered down by the door that the black woman and trio of children had fled through. The sounds of Aziz being dispatched made him jump, and pain shot through his swollen body. Unable to stay motionless any longer he shoved his rifle out and fired bullets into the room with Jim and Lonnie. They jumped backward as hot lead punched jagged holes into the concrete wall behind them. Just then, Faruk's vest detonated in a massive eruption that shook the building and ruptured more overhead sprinkler pipes, releasing gallons of water into the room.

Ajay was as astonished as the three rescuers by the sudden explosion and he used the opportunity to turn and run. As he reached the door to the science lab he once again saw Kim herding the children ahead of her. Ajay lumbered for the doorway, chasing after them in the loping gate of an ape, and crossed through the science room door in seconds. As he barged into the room he saw movement on his left and turned. A blond teenage girl was falling out of an open window onto the grass outside, with a red-headed boy waiting to follow her out of the window.

The boy's face perfectly reflected the dismay and terror he felt at seeing his nightmare come bursting into the room. Ajay opened fire, striking the boy with several rounds in the chest. The bullets easily penetrated through the boy's body, exiting his back and scattering blood across student backpacks filled with books. The open window's glass was shattered and sprinkled shards on the girl outside. The boy collapsed to the floor, where his freckled face twitched until it went blank with death.

Toward the front of the room a child screamed and Ajay spun to see the black woman pushing the children toward the teacher's desk. He lurched after her and caught them just as she pushed the three children under the desk. Kim began to turn and face her pursuer when Ajay slammed the butt of his rifle into her shoulder blades, causing her to crumple to the floor.

Ajay grabbed her long hair and tried shoving her and the children behind the desk. He followed her down and crushed his weight on top of them as Lonnie barged through the doorway in chase. Lonnie's immediately fired, just missing Ajay's head as he ducked. The grease boards hanging behind the desk bounced as the bullets punched holes through them, sending erasers, markers, and papers flying into the air.

Lonnie limped into the room, then stopped and knelt next to the dead youth Ajay had just murdered. The boy's body lay sprawled, his head resting on his outstretched arm, his dead eyes staring into oblivion. Jim and Billy arrived at the door behind him and Lonnie pointed toward the far desk.

"He's back there, tuck'd behind that desk!" he yelled.

The room was split into two rows of older black-ceramic topped science lab tables. Each one was equipped with small stainless steel sinks in the middle and little wooden racks of glass beakers. Metal stools surrounded each table and four decades of dried chewing gum was stuck under the countertops. Lonnie glanced up and saw a frantic blond girl, outside the shattered window, running across the grass for her life, racked with terrified sobs.

The blare of the fire alarm droned incessantly at a riotous decibel. Lonnie crouched, blinking water from the raining sprinklers out of his eyes as he reached down and felt for a pulse in the boy's neck. But the boy was indeed lifeless, with his blood trickling from his perforated chest. Lonnie guessed the child may have been thirteen years old.

"I'm sorry I wasn't here sooner," Lonnie whispered quietly.

Peering carefully around the corner of the table Lonnie saw backpacks, books and notepads strewn around the room from when the students had fled earlier. The bullet-riddled grease board showed that the teacher had been discussing the periodic table.

The embedded cactus barbs continued to burrow ever deeper into Ajay's back, thighs, and groin as he tried to stay crouched behind the desk. He screamed in frustration at his pursuers.

"I've brought the jihad to you and your children, you fucking kafir assholes! I am the deliverer of God's law to your miserable lives!" Ajay yelled as he jerked Kim backward by her hair.

The children squealed as she tried to keep hold of his hand, to keep him from pulling her hair out by the roots.

"Put your gun down and surrender, asshole! You're alone now, we've killed the others!" Jim yelled back.

"Come! Save them if you can, pig!"

Jim knelt behind the row of tables opposite from Lonnie while Billy stood in the doorway they had entered through. Jim could not see how many hostages were trapped behind the desk. He very much wanted to flank the murderer but the room's size would simply not allow that.

"You see anything, marine?" he asked Lonnie.

"A couple of kids back there. A woman, too, I think, could be a teacher or maybe a parent."

Jim looked back at Billy.

"Anything?"

"A black woman, she's a teacher. I think her name is Kim, maybe. I can see several kids, too. What do you want me to do?"

"You get a shot – you kill that fucker."

Billy only nodded.

The insidious and unending pain from the cactus bore into Ajay's mind and threatened to drive him berserk. The blaring alarm concealed any sound of movement from the men at the far end of the room. Ajay was forced to shift from one side of the desk to the other, trying to keep watch on them. But the black woman and kids he had pinned down kept getting in his way and caused him to expose himself far more than he dared to.

"Get in there, bitch!" he yelled while attempting to shove Kim farther under the desk, but there just was not enough room and it changed nothing.

"Fuck!" he screamed in aggravation.

He gave up on the futile effort and grabbed Kim by her arm. And with the manic strength possessed by the insane, he flung her backward against the wall beneath the grease board.

The older girl and boy under the desk shrieked as their protector suddenly disappeared, and the swollen red-faced monster bent inward, grabbing at them. Ajay pulled them from under the desk and flung them backward, one by one, leaving the smallest child under the desk – Maggie Griego.

Blood-fever and nausea swam in unison within Ajay's body, as the cactus barbs had caused his skin to swell, stretching it grotesquely, akin to a filled balloon. Sweat and blood were smeared across his face as his bloodshot eyes bulged above his bloated cheeks. Maggie stared up at the gruesome sight and saw the same ghastly face as that of the towering monster from her nightmare. She let out an ear-splitting cry of terror as the monster mercilessly grabbed her.

Kim's thin frame was not made for getting slammed around, and when she was thrown back against the wall she had tried to brace herself with her arm. That had turned out to be a big mistake, as her arm got pinned between the wall and her falling weight, snapping at the elbow and wrist. Incredible pain shot out of her elbow while numbness flooded her fingers.

With her good arm Kim pulled the two children to her and kept her eyes glued to the back of the yelling executioner of children who crouched behind the desk. Blood soaked his clothing around his right hip and neckline where his flesh had earlier been ripped apart by Toby's sharp teeth. She scanned the large vest that covered his torso and recognized what she believed to be hand grenades hanging from it. The strangely formed vest appeared to have several wires taped around it and it dawned on her that it was an explosive vest. *Suicide bomber! You fucking coward!*

Ajay's right arm curled tight around Maggie's neck while his left hand felt around his vest's front. The little girl's eyes bulged as his arm pinched her throat. Highly agitated, he bounced repeatedly to each side of the desk as he yelled at the men across the room. Suddenly, he shoved his rifle under the desk and grabbed a small box at his waist that was wrapped in duct tape.

He knows he's caught! We're all about to die! Kim knew she must act now to keep from being blown to bits. A raging fire of adrenalin-fueled desperation and fury fueled her veins with strength and power. *Die here? Like this? No!*

She looked at the two quivering children with her. One of them, Enrique Sanchez, was a student in her fourth period class, and the other was a familiar girl, maybe a fifth-grader, both pleadingly stared back at her. Kim's most-treasured quote ran through her brain. *It is better to die on your feet than live on your knees!* She made her choice and prepared to act.

Lonnie leaned out to see as much as he could of what was happening. He could not see the murderer he desperately wanted to kill, but he was able to see Kim and the two kids. He watched in admiration as she moved her dreadfully distorted and misshapen arm against the pain.

Kim wrapped her shattered arm around Enrique's waist, and as she curled it and lifted his weight she felt the jagged end of her broken ulna pierce the muscles of her forearm. The pain was agonizing but she endured and pulled the child to her bosom, clenching her teeth. She shed her two-inch heeled shoes and let her bare feet grip the tiled floor. Maneuvering her feet under her, she glared at the murderer for any sign that he might look back. Instead, he just yelled hate-filled slogans and ordered the rescuers to stay away.

Enrique was stiff as a board in her arm as she got her feet under her and knelt, her back against the wall. She pulled the girl in close to her body and gripped her waist. She did not know if she could lift the girl but she knew she would drag her if she had to.

"You hold onto me, child, and never let go, okay?" she whispered.

The girl nodded as she wrapped her trembling arms tightly around Kim's neck. Kim raised her head and looked along the wall between the windows and tables and saw at the far end of the room the water-soaked face of an elderly man with a matted white beard. He held a rifle in his hands and looked right at her. Hope entered her heart.

Lonnie's and Kim's eyes met and he saw the steely determination within her. He knew her decision had been made and all he could do was help in any way possible. Kim knew her only salvation was in reaching the man as fast as possible. Her face hardened as her body tensed like a coiled spring, ready to let go.

Lonnie pointed at her and then at his chest and Kim gave back a nod of understanding. She glanced back at Ajay who was still screaming at Jim, who was trying to get him to surrender. Maggie's little legs swung like a ragdoll as Ajay darted to the right and then left side of the desk. Fully engrossed with the rescuers, he dodged back to his left and Kim moved.

The weight of the two children was heavier than she expected and intense pain shot up her arm, but she did not release them. She winced as the eraser bench on the grease board scraped along her spine and she put all of her remaining power into her legs, propelling her and the children away from the wall. Lonnie stood up and trained the rifle at the teacher's desk, ready to give her cover. Then, as she made the third step in her lunge for freedom Kim's bare feet came down on shattered glass that gouged into her flesh and acted like marbles, shifting under her weight. They immediately went down, landing hard on the floor. Lonnie cursed as he watched them fall.

Drawn to the noise, Ajay turned to look. Lonnie saw the very top of Ajay's head and fired shots to keep him down. Kim's fractured arm floundered in a ghastly fashion in her attempts to pull herself and the children up. Ajay poked his face out from the side of the desk and just as Lonnie leveled his rifle sights on the swollen face it was again concealed behind Maggie's suspended body, which Ajay used as a tiny human shield. Outraged and appalled by the cowardly act, Lonnie's finger froze on the trigger, and he watched in shock as Ajay's rifle extended past Maggie and began spraying rounds across the room. Lonnie ducked behind the science table as bullets flew all around Kim and the two children.

Billy, in the doorframe, felt his heart almost stop in his chest at recognizing the child who screamed and dangled from Ajay's grip as his best friend's daughter. He dared not shoot for fear of hitting

323

Maggie, and he felt as though the shotgun he held was now utterly useless. His mind desperately sought for ideas to aid the flailing teacher and children in escaping.

Jim rose up to see what was going on and was stunned to glimpse his daughter hanging from Ajay's hand just as spraying bullets forced him to duck back down.

Slugs gouged holes in the wall above Kim's head, shredding text books as her bloodied feet tried to gain traction. The glass shards, glistening like ice, ground into the soft underside of her bare feet as she made agonizingly slow progress across the room. As her feet frantically churned she hugged the children to her bosom, attempting to shield them with the only protection available, her body.

Disregarding the fusillade of fire, Lonnie stood amid the hail of bullets and fired back, aiming above Maggie's head. Jim saw Lonnie firing toward his child and, blinded by fear, stood with arms outstretched and screamed.

"*Noooo!*"

Lonnie's fire forced Ajay to duck back behind the desk as Kim doggedly plowed on.

Abruptly Ajay's arm came over the top of the desk and Lonnie's eyes widened as he saw a grenade come tumbling through the air in pursuit of the fleeing teacher. Again, Lonnie reacted without delay and charged forward. The instant and unexpected feeling of relief that Kim felt upon seeing the elderly rescuer start forward instantaneously evaporated as she observed the anxiety displayed on his face. Her muscles put even more urgency into her effort to run as she could almost feel the claws of the devil sinking into her back. Lonnie reached out and grabbed at her blouse and jerked her and the children behind him, getting between them and the bouncing grenade. As he kicked at it, the tremendous discharge of its detonation, inches from his toes, slammed full-force into him, propelling his body backward into Kim.

That impact lifted Kim violently off the floor and launched her and the children into the air. She scarcely had time to twist her body between the children and back wall before colliding face-first into the dimpled layers of paint that coated the cinderblock. She collapsed motionless atop the two children.

Time moved in slow-motion for Jim after he saw Maggie in the terrorist's arms. His entire being was frozen in blinding terror; locked immobile by his anxiety he did nothing as he watched Lonnie react to the grenade. He stood staring, as inert as stone as he observed Lonnie's body absorb the blast from the grenade, and saw his extended leg disintegrate into flying chunks of pulverized meat and bone. Jim's peripheral vision perceived the compression wave propagate across the room, sending miscellaneous items from the tables flying.

Then mere moments after the devastating blast, Jim's nightmare sank into a deeper level of hell as Ajay rose up from behind the desk. In one hand he once again extended Maggie as a human shield before his swollen, bleeding face, while in his other he held his detonator high. Maggie's terrorized eyes locked on her father's familiar face and she hysterically extended her arms and screamed for him while pumping her legs vainly in the air. Despairing of any hope, Jim's now-useless .45 pointed at the floor as he realized what was about to happen.

Raining water drenched Ajay's face as he observed the horror-stricken display on the face of the cop. With hate-filled glee Ajay felt his last moments might finally give him every last drop of terror-filled ecstasy he had hoped this day would bring.

"*Stop*!" Jim screamed. "*Maaggiiee*!"

Ajay sucked in a deep breath.

"Allalu Ak….ahheee!"

The Remington 12 gauge shotgun bucked against Billy's shoulder as the 1 oz. hunk of lead flew across the room, slamming into Ajay's detonator-filled hand. Both flesh and electronics were annihilated and scattered into small pieces of metal, bone, plastic, and muscle. Ajay looked up, dismayed and furious, at the mangled stump and two sparking wires. He dropped the screaming Maggie, who hit the floor running and dashed forward to be rapidly swept up into her father's outstretched arms.

Ajay gripped the bloody remnant of his appendage and glared impotently across the room at the monster-rescuers who had just destroyed his personal fantasy of apocalypse. The big Hispanic cop now cradled the child while the skinny punk who had just blown off his hand pointed a shotgun at his face.

Wrathful loathing radiated off Ajay akin to steam as he hunched over, calculating what he could do. Amphetamines still coursed through his body, giving enough energy to fight, but he had no more weaponry with which he could strike out.

Jim smothered his daughter against his chest as she clung intensely to him. The miserable creature crouching at the front of the room resembled nothing human, appearing as some grotesquely bloated thing, seething with vile hate.

Their eyes locked and the tremendous depth of abhorrence and enmity that each imparted to the other was so forceful and concentrated that it almost scorched the air between them.

"Why? Why did you do this?" Jim barked.

325

Ajay's face unexpectedly softened from incomprehensible fury and odium into an expression of pure incredulity as he studied the big cop quizzically.

"Why not," he sneered back.

The loud crack of a gunshot cut the air as a small .223 bullet abruptly punched a tiny hole into the side of Ajay's head. It tore a path through his cranium until it excavated a jagged golf ball-sized hole out the back of his skull, taking with it chunks of his minced brain that flew out and splattered on far wall. His corpse collapsed into a twitching heap.

"Shut the fuck up," Lonnie muttered.

With trembling arms Lonnie sat his rifle gently down on his lap and stared down at the shredded stump that had once been his right leg. He could only see out of his right eye, as his left was just bloody mush.. Blood seeped from his shattered nose, saturating his thick moustache and beard.

Back in 1967, in the Que Son Valley, Lonnie had assumed that the Viet Cong had instructed him in everything he could ever learn about human barbarity as he walked the blood-soaked dirt of Bhin Son. He always considered their rampage through that village to be an epic display of cruelty. Today, however, had proven him wrong. His understanding of the depths possible inside man's savage brutality had been expanded greatly. He weakly looked over his shoulder and contemplated with deep reverence the brave woman who had struggled inside today's vortex of depravity and unflinchingly fought to save the innocent. He was profoundly gratified to see that both of the children she had sacrificed herself to save now sat, alive and sobbing, next to her unmoving body, which lay crumpled against the wall.

Billy ran up and kicked at Ajay's corpse to confirm he was dead.

"I wouldn't do that too hard, boy," Lonnie rumbled with a hoarse voice. "Your dumb white-bread ass might regret kick'n that vest, dipshit!"

Billy looked down at the suicide-vest and slowly backed away. Jim, with a clinging and weeping Maggie in his arms, walked over and stood above Lonnie. He scanned the old marine from top to bottom. Lonnie's broken, torn, and bleeding face tried to produce a smile, but its mangled features only achieved a ghastly sneer.

Jim glanced over at the two crying children on the floor by Kim.

"You saved those children. I can't thank you enough for standing with us in this hell."

326

Lonnie looked at Maggie in Jim's arms.

"We all did the job God put us here to do Jim, nuth'n more. You be a good papa to her. She'll need yer love more than ever after a day like this."

Billy walked up and stared down at Lonnie in admiration.

Jim said, "Billy, help me get him up and out of here so we...,"

"No," Lonnie interupted. "You get your girl and those other two babies outta of this hell hole."

He nodded to the motionless teacher and freckled boy.

"Me, the lady, and this other child will just stay here and rest awhile."

Jim nodded.

"Thank you, marine."

Lonnie gave another ghastly looking grin.

"Turns out, me not kill'n your ass this morn'n was a good thing, huh?"

Jim found nothing to say and just smiled warmly as sprinkling water hid his flowing tears.

Lonnie winced in pain and muttered, "Do me favor, will ya? Shut that damn alarm off – its giv'n me a split'n headache."

"As quick as I can, my friend."

Jim turned for the door as Billy nodded farewell. The deputy then bent down to pick up the two crying children from Kim's side, and then followed Jim out of the room. A few minutes later Jim and Billy encountered other teams of searchers who were also methodically gathering up those inside the school who still lived. The word quickly spread that the three terrorists were now dead, but the search continued late into the night.

Once outside, Jim found a local fireman; together they quickly discovered the control panel and shut off the fire alarm's breaker. As the persistent alarm finally fell silent Jim cradled his baby girl and looked back at the smoldering ruins of the school.

"I hope that was fast enough, Mr. Garcia."

Inside the classroom the alarms finally went silent and Lonnie was indeed thankful. As he lay bleeding, he faded in and out of consciousness, but his eyes never wavered from the dead psychopath who lay in a pile by the desk. Lonnie cared nothing about reasons or excuses. Fair, equal, good, or bad were concepts that meant nothing in the presence of pure evil. Lonnie did everything he could and he felt grim satisfaction that the evil that had torn at the soul of his community was now dead and defeated, at his feet.

The sprinklers slowly worked at cleansing the blood and gore from the walls of the old school he had long-ago attended. As he felt his last moments at hand he swung his good eye back to look upon the body of the woman. Then, even as his vision blurred and darkened he was positive he saw her move.

"Wish I coulda met ya when I was younger, honey, I like you," he said with his last breath.

*****

13:03pm EST UTC -5
Smith College
Northampton, MA

THE BRASS frame of the stately pedestal sign had a maple leaf design around its border. It was positioned atop a shiny brass pole on a wheeled base outside the closed doors to Wright Hall's Leo Weinstein Auditorium. The words inside the case read:

Competitive Visions
Lecturer: Professor William Frederick "Fred" Thompson, PhD
Author of The Tragic Statist

The four-hundred-seat gallery was half-full with mostly twenty-something's who attentively listened as he paced behind an ornate wooden lectern. He would periodically mark off some point in his scribbled outline, written on a pocket-sized notepad he carried in his hand. As he spoke he would absentmindedly rub the stem of his reading glasses against his lower lip while the heels of his well-worn brown loafers clacked against the floor of the stage.

Fred Thompson was a large man, dressed in a black polo shirt with more than a bit of paunch pushing against the fabric above the waistline of his relaxed grey slacks. The dark skin atop the high-domed, balding head was bracketed by a groomed salt-and-pepper band of hair that extended into large sideburns that braced his strong jaw. His large eyes were quick and piercing, betraying to the world both the intelligence within and the good-natured humor that dwelt close to the surface.

His tall body moved with the purposefulness of middle-age, with more than a hint of the fluidity of youth still present in his joints. The once-robust muscles of his arms and legs no longer pressed against his clothing, yelling their existence, but occasionally when he turned correctly, the ladies in the audience detected, quite clearly, that his tall frame was still solid and had not completely atrophied.

"….to paraphrase Stalin's classic utterance: one man's death is a tragedy; a million deaths are a statistic. We can see the poignant

328

reality of man's worth in this statement. We should all be familiar with examples like the 150 million-plus murdered people that socialism has given us. The 12 million people annihilated during the Holocaust. Or the one-hundred days of rampaging, machete-wielding, slaughter of 800,000 in Rwanda. Those cases speak volumes, but I would like to illustrate my point with what's much closer to home for me and you.

"Now I ask: how much attention did the horrendous murder of Jon Benet Ramsey get? How much of your time was taken up with this one death? Were you engrossed in the Casey Anthony trial that riveted our nation this summer?"

"Now consider the 2010 death toll in Iraq is slightly more than 6,000 for the good guys, bad guys, and civilians combined. In Afghanistan that toll measured little more than 10,000. Meanwhile, across our nation's southern border the Mexican government's official death toll for the cartel drug war for 2010 was over …."

The double-door entrance to the auditorium banged open, drawing everyone's attention. The audience watched Margaret Hudson from the administration office walk quickly to the stage, her heeled shoes clickity-clacking, and her puffy face appearing as though she had been crying.

"I'm so sorry to interrupt your lecture, Professor, but I must address the students immediately."

Fred noted the distress the woman was suffering weighed heavily on her.

"Absolutely, my dear lady. What has happened?"

"Everyone, please pay attention, I…."

"Is there a shooter on campus?" asked a nervous female voice in the back.

There were several gasps around the room as Mrs. Hudson waved away the question.

"No! No, now please listen! All of you, just listen," she said with emotion breaking in her voice.

She waited for silence as she gained her composure before continuing.

"There is a terrible tragedy going on in our country today. Terrorists have struck at numerous places across our nation and it appears to be far worse than 9/11."

Gasps and whispers spread around the room.

"Please turn on all of your phones and computers so you can see if anyone is trying to reach you. From what I have learned before I came here, there are at least two major assaults occurring in the cities of San Francisco and Oakland. There is also a report of a school in rural Colorado that has been attacked by several gunmen. Nothing that

329

I am aware of has happened anywhere on the east coast. But the college is not taking any chances. I must ask you to go to your dorm rooms immediately; for the time being we are placing the campus on lock-down. Please go to your dorms and watch the news for the latest updates. The school administration does not have any information more accurate than what you can find on the television news."

Students broke into talk that rose to a roar as they got up and made their way out of the auditorium. Mrs. Hudson turned to Fred, apologizing.

"I'm sorry I cut your lecture short but once we saw how bad the situation was becoming the Dean decided the school had to act."

"Forget any concerns you have about me, Margaret. I'm so thankful you came to let us know what's happening. But I must ask you – a school in Colorado was attacked by terrorists? Where? My daughter teaches third grade at a school in Colorado, do you know what school?"

"Oh, my goodness, there is *so* much news coming out, and all of it so fast. There have been so many different names I've heard – I'm not certain at all whether it is terrorists at the school or some nutcase. But it was in southern Colorado, I believe, in a small town called Trinidad – you know, like the Caribbean islands of Trinidad and Tob…."

Her voice trailed off as she saw Fred's face turn ashen and grim.

"Oh. Oh, my God. I'm sorry."

She put her hands over her mouth and stepped closer.

Fred's stomach tightened into a ball of angst as his face turned pallid. *No! Not Kimberly!*

Mrs. Hudson reached out and touched his shoulder.

"I haven't heard much about what is happening at that school. You know law enforcement is well prepared for these things nowadays. I pray your daughter is okay."

He nodded and gave her arm a gentle squeeze.

"I thank you. I should let you go about your business on this terrible day and I shall look to my own concerns. You run along now."

The tears that she had cried before her entry into the room returned and she left him standing, forlorn and alone as her clacking heels quickly made their way out of the room. Fred grabbed his cell phone, turned it on, and impatiently waited for it to boot up.

AS THE black Crown Victoria pulled off the I-35 exit ramp and headed toward the tiny community of Thorn Hill, its two occupants sat silent as the news continued to stream out of their car's radio. FBI agents David Parker and Lemi Turan were distracted from their current assignment as they intently listened to the news being aired over the public radio, while at the same time they waited impatiently to hear any new bulletins come from their FBI radio.

Parker hardly took notice of his surroundings as he drove them through the little city of New Braunfels, on their way from their San Antonio offices. They had received a request from the National Counterterrorism Center (NCTC) to go to the Easy Creek Ranch and question the people living there about their son. Before leaving, the two agents talked briefly about cancelling the interview. Parker had argued that they would have a lot going on back at their offices regarding the attacks and this interview with the Majumbar family was not a priority on a day like this. Turan was the senior agent and it came down to him making the decision and he felt they could complete this task and still stay up-to-date with the tragedy in California.

Parker was a guy who never liked being overruled by anyone but he knew his partner was right. It was his frustration and anger over the attacks that had him distracted from his duty. He was not sure why this guy from rural Texas had gotten so much attention from the NCTC but it was not his place to just disregard it out-of-hand. Besides, there was always the outside possibility this guy had information on the attacks today.

Parker slowed after he exited the freeway and Turan lowered his window to let the midday Texas air flood into the car. A strong smell of diesel smoke came from the school bus ahead of them but he tolerated the smell since he needed to have the fresh air in his lungs. The dry, cool air from the car's AC unit made his throat itch and caused him several coughing fits. As the warm air hit his lungs he began another coughing fit.

They pulled up to a stop behind the bus that now waited for a traffic light to turn green. To their left sat a Pit Stop gas station and as they waited, neither of the federal lawmen took any notice of the line of semi-trucks stopped facing them in the opposite lane, waiting for the same light to turn green.

Parker tapped on the steering wheel.

"Hey, partner, you going to be okay? I can pull in over there and you can run in and get some water or something," Parker said, thumbing toward the Pit Stop where a red passenger van sat idling alongside the roadway.

"Thanks, but no. I still got a little coffee in here." Turan chugged a swig of cold coffee from his plastic 7-11 mug.

"Alright, but you aren't going to impress anyone out at this ranch with you coughing up a lung."

"I've got it under control. I just want to get out there and get back so we can be available for what's going to fall out from this mess in California. Assignments are going to start flying like confetti tomorrow."

"Yeah, I hear that. The crap is really going to hit the fucking fan after this. How in the fuck do you think they all got in, Lemi? Somebody really screwed the fucking pooch on this one, just like 9/11, but fucking worse, man! I mean, what the fuck, Lemi? We get that fucker, bin Laden, this very summer and now we got an even worse attack this fast – Jesus! How does that shit work?"

"I thought we'd gotten on top of all this stuff, too, Dave. I don't know, but we've got to find out what the hell happened and plug that hole. This – this is a fucking disaster. It's 9/11 on steroids."

The traffic lights changed to green and the bus accelerated, leaving a large black cloud of exhaust billowing in the air. Parker accelerated through the dark cloud, while the lead gasoline tanker in the oncoming lane lurched forward into the intersection, headed for I-35 with two more following it.

"Yeah, it sure sounds bad. There's got to be someone like this spook friend of yours – what's his name? McDermott, right? Yeah, someone like this McDermott guy at the NCTC is who must've fucked this shit up. I mean, the bureau can't go around sticking our fingers in every hole in the dike there is. With these spooks not stopping these bastards before they get in here – it has to be a failure of the intelligence thing, not a law enforcement thing. Those assholes in the CIA, or NSA, or military intelligence need to get their empty heads out of their asses, you know? They got to kill these bastards before they get over here. Wipe'em the fuck out!"

The driver of the last gasoline tanker popped the clutch too fast and accelerated rapidly behind the truck ahead, forcing him to hit the brakes hard to keep from rear-ending the second tanker that was crossing the intersection. All eighteen wheels locked up as the air brakes barked under the strain and the tires screeched loudly. The noise caused Parker to look into the rear view mirror to see the cause of the commotion.

332

He watched ambivalently as the truck started rolling again, accelerating in a herky-jerky manner and following after the others. Two identical red passenger vans followed closely behind the last tanker. Watching them, his eyes were drawn to where he had seen another van stopped at the store. It was now gone and it took him a moment to locate it, travelling ahead of the three gasoline tankers. He shrugged and figured that all three vans must be travelling in a group and that their drivers were probably frustrated that they were stuck with the three semi-trucks splitting them up.

He turned and saw that the commotion has also attracted Turan's attention, as he was looking over his shoulder at the receding vehicles.

"Everyone has their problems, I guess," Parker muttered under his breath as they picked up speed down Old FM 306.

"What? Oh, yeah. Heck, I thought he was about to rear-end that other one. That is not what we need to deal with right now, you know?"

"Yeah, I hear that. Hey, tell me again, what did this McDermott guy say was such the big attraction to this Majjamber guy, anyway?".

"It's pronounced *Mah-jum-bar*. Listen, Dave, Harry is a good man and I've worked with him in setting up important undercover operation going on right now with another colleague of mine, who's doing a great job with Operation Cannonball. Hell, this whole fiasco today could be tied in with that operation for all I know."

Parker cocked his head to look at Turan. "I thought the *New York Times* blew the cover on that operation and that it had been cancelled?"

"You know those dumbasses at the Times never get it straight. The agency just buried the whole thing under several more layers of bureaucracy and kept going. It's a real deep undercover gig that even my friend wouldn't tell me about. Anyway, Harry is a desk-jockey but he does what he can," Turan asserted.

"Anyway, the old man, this Pushkar Majumbar, is a real solid guy. He immigrated to the United States back in the '60s and when asked, he did great work for the CIA in Afghanistan when Reagan still needed the mujahedeen to turn back the Soviets. Pushkar had two brothers, Subhash and Mayur, and the three of them really assisted in our cause there. From what Harry tells me, they were instrumental in smuggling men and materials across the Hindu Kush. But in the end they paid for that help in a harsh way. Pushkar watched his brother get Subhash killed by the Russians and he lost a leg in the same attack. I guess the guy never complained about his lot or what it cost his

333

family. He always expressed pride at serving his new home and country. But his kid, Ajay, turned out to be a mess and he's why we're going down there."

Turan paused and went through another spate of coughing. The cool of the morning was gone and for mid-September it was unusually hot, in the mid-90s, but he still left the window down.

"Harry says the son has a police record going back to his teens and is an ex-con who served a couple years. He has strong ties with a sicario enforcer for the Monterrey Cartel in Mexico. This associate, a Miguel Luis Sanchez, is wanted by Texas on two murder warrants on a double homicide seven years ago in Corpus Christi, but he stays in Mexico. That Sanchez dude is a real bloody son of a bitch. He has a penchant for beheadings and likes doing acid baths when he kills for the cartel. This Ajay guy and Sanchez were childhood friends and runabouts here in these parts in their teens and twenties. Sanchez eventually went south to disappear into the cartel while Ajay Majumbar served a stint in the state pen for running cocaine across the...."

Turan paused as something on the radio caught his attention.

The radio was tuned to 1200 WOAI out of San Antonio and played live audio feed from Fox News Radio with Shepard Smith talking to retired New York City Police Chief, Clarke O'Rourke.

"....as the men and women of the San Francisco police continue their heroic efforts of engaging in this fierce fight with the armed terrorists. The cops are spread thin throughout the financial and downtown districts and they're reportedly having problems getting organized. The streets are hopelessly clogged, fires seem to be everywhere, and tens of thousands of civilians are caught in the middle. It looks to me like getting law enforcement into a coordinated fighting force that can address these coordinated military-style attacks is extremely difficult, Clarke."

"They are unfortunately finding themselves in a situation that can only be described as a warzone. Shepard, America's law enforcement officers are the very best peacekeepers and criminal investigators on the planet, but they aren't properly equipped or trained to deal with this combination of tactics. They are structured to respond well to rampage-shooters with overwhelming numbers but today they are just too thinly dispersed to address all of these threats simultaneously. These terrorists have created a situation where every engagement is an underdog situation for law enforcement. Remember, these are peacekeepers not combat marines.

"American law enforcement has found itself in few situations even remotely similar to this, like the incident during the North Hollywood bank shootout in 1997, or maybe the Newhall Incident back in 1970, or even the LAPD's shootout with the SLA in '74. But Shep, none of those were anywhere near this scale. These coordinated attacks are going to push that city's law enforcement resources to their extreme limits. And with Oakland being decimated there will be no help coming from there."

"And what about the people caught between the cops and the terrorists? They can see across the bay and know what has happened over in Oakland. They've got to know that if law enforcement doesn't get this thing controlled, and fast, the same wholesale destruction is happening to their city, just slower. These police officers may be going up against pure hate and murder with nothing but their sidearms and their courage, but the civilians don't even have that! What can we expect to develop in this battle for the city, Chief O' Rourke?

"This is an attack modeled after the terrible attacks in Mumbai, India – but this – this scale is tenfold what happened there. Shepard, the San Francisco police are among the very best cops fielded anywhere in the country. And right now there are hundreds more law enforcement officers flooding to their assistance from all over the western states, but until they arrive and get deployed – Frisco is in a fight for her survival and she is alone for now. And with so many spread-out attacks across the country, every single community must secure its own interests and people before they can send re-enforcements. Even so, I cannot express to you just how proud I am of them and every single cop in California right now. I can tell you this, they are charging toward the sound of gunfire in that city as fast as they can and they're going to win!"

"Chief, we're hearing reports amid this chaos that up to a dozen separate armed groups of terrorists are roving the streets of the city, and we want to make clear that those numbers haven't been confirmed yet. But at least two groups of gunmen we know of are at this time terrorizing the downtown area. Most insidiously, these murderers have made themselves a form of barrier, between the citizens and the first responders. Obviously their intent is to prevent medical personnel from reaching the wounded and firefighters from stopping the fires in the buildings downtown. But they are also effectively 'caging in' the remaining civilian population inside downtown in an apparent attempt to maximize the death toll - very evil and diabolical!"

"Yes, I know. Law enforcement at least has weapons. But these other responders have nothing but water hoses and medical

335

supplies and, as we've seen, they've been slaughtered where they have gotten caught by the rampaging gunmen without police protection with them! Shepard, it is literally hell-on-earth in the bay area right now."

"That is not an overstatement, Chief. The whole city is in turmoil and death reigns supreme in the streets and schools of America today. It's a national tragedy."

"It is indeed a tragedy. Our national strategy has been predicated on stopping this type of attack from ever getting onto our soil. Now that it is actually here, the only way this will end, Shepard, is through the brave actions of individual cops, responders, and citizens taking it upon themselves to storm the bullets and hunt these killers and murderers down and stop their rampage of murder one by one! That is a terrible scenario but I'm afraid it is all we have left."

"It is surely one of the worst days in our nation's history. I have never seen video of anything worse; it's even far worse than the 9/11 attacks. The apparent wholesale devastation inside what was once Oakland is almost unbelievable. I know we have received confirmation that there is no radiation, and hopefully, therefore no nuclear device was used – but it's almost, well, biblical in its scale of destruction. And now these murderous attacks on the people of San Francisco, may God be with them now in this dark hour of trial and death, Chief."

"I pray God is with them and all of us in this desperate hour, Shepard."

"But, Clarke, do we know yet exactly what type of bombs these terrorists have used today? I mean, the absolute carnage in Oakland is far different than that occurring in San Francisco. Does this mean that the explosives they successfully used in Oakland have failed in San Fran, causing only fires?"

"I am not a bomb expert, Shepard, but my inclination would be to say no. These appear to be very different types of explosives used in the two cities. I'm watching all this happening as you are and I'm just flabbergasted and revolted at the comprehensive devastation from the blast in Oakland. I hate to speculate, but all I can guess at this early time is that maybe they were able to get some type of massive thermobaric device. Perhaps somehow there was something that got slipped into one of the port facilities on a ship. How they got that much catastrophic damage there – I, I don't really know what else could do that.

"But from what I've heard from my colleagues this morning, sketchy as it is at this point, it appears these horrendous fires spreading throughout San Francisco were definitely made by

336

individual truck bombs of some sort. Some of my colleagues have speculated that fuel trucks were simply rammed into these building and detonated. But with the dense smoke rising from the city center I haven't been able to get any direct view to see for myself. But let me make clear, if the terrorists did detonate the fuel at street level and thereby trapping every person inside those buildings – then we are going to have an extremely high death toll, indeed."

"It is cold-blooded mass-murder, Chief. Once again these murderers show us that the slaughter of innocent people is their only goal.

"I want to advise our audience that we're desperately working to get a live feed from a helicopter as fast as we can – and for our viewers, I must let you know that we've been advised that the feds may soon, very soon I am told, shut down the air space above the entire bay area. There is even talk that they may ground all air traffic nationwide just as they did after 9/11. So – we here at Fox News will keep you posted with the latest, and as soon as we can obtain video feed from the air above the fires, you have my word, you'll see it first and fastest right here."

"Shepard – Shepard, Can I break in, please?"

"Yes, Chief O'Rourke, go."

"I must put this out there right now for everyone within the sound of my voice. Every civilian or law enforcement officer throughout the nation must be on guard right now. We have two of our cities fighting for survival. Somehow the enemy has gotten inside our national defenses in force. We are naked to more attacks and if there are more terrorists out there – you brave citizens and cops, you are our only defense at the moment. Be hyper-vigilant for an enemy who may still be out there and about to strike where you are."

"That is a terrifying thought, Chief O'Rourke, and a very sad reality of this tragic day. Realistically, this could be only the first wave. With as much planning as these attacks obviously took to be this successful, that would strongly indicate to me that...."

"Yeah right, like there's anything going to happen in this dried-up town," Parker muttered cynically as he drove the car through the sparse traffic of the little town of Sattler.

This area of Texas was still dominated by farming and ranching and he briefly wondered how did a guy, from Kashmir of all places, end up in a cowboy, shit-kicker place like this. The Texas wind spun up thin wisps of dust as he turned the car off the main drag and headed north up River Road. Very quickly the low buildings of the rural town gave way to pinion trees and hay fields.

"....local media feed that we are now showing is an NBC affiliate of KNTV. Chief O' Rourke, I can clearly make out the figures of at least a hundred people who have made it onto the roof of that building, as the flames rage and climb upward...."

Parker punched the palm of his hand against the steering wheel and turned down the volume of the radio.

"I can't take this anymore! Tell me more about this guy we're heading to see. I got to get my mind right or I'm going to explode!"

Turan nodded his head sadly in agreement and then spoke.

"Harry says this guy supposedly found Allah while he was in the state penitentiary and then became enamored in the teachings of a radical Egyptian, Sayyid Qutb, who was also a big influence on Zawahiri and bin Laden. The Egyptians hung Qutb back in '66 but his ideas loom large in our war on terror, to this day.

"Anyway, this Majumbar guy turned to some hard-line Muslim beliefs but he never gave any indication of being militant or jihadist. Over the past couple of years he's been travelling to and from Pakistan and Kashmir quite a bit. While visiting his uncle in Kashmir, he made several stops in Lahore and Peshawar that evidently caught the attention of Indian secret-intelligence who then alerted Harry. They said he has had some pretty high-level contact with the same radical factions within the Pakistani ISI that was hiding bin Laden. So here we are."

"Sounds to me that this pal of yours at the NCTC should've gotten off his desk-jockey ass awhile back and started looked at this guy earlier."

Turan gave his partner an irritated glance.

"Back off, Dave, you know damn well these guys are a dime-a-dozen over there. This guy's been on our radar more for running dope than any religious militancy."

Parker stared down the road, frustrated, and gave a dismissive shrug.

"Anyway, several years ago this guy did the Hajj along with his parents and uncle. And before you ask, taking your family on a spiritual pilgrimage to Mecca for the Hajj is hardly a red flag, Dave. After that he went to live with his uncle who still lives in Kashmir and has some long-standing contacts with some real rough folks from his old days in the mujahedeen. Those connections were evidently enough to get Ajay in touch with the Lashkar-e-Tayyiba, a real nasty group that wants total Muslim domination of Kashmir and independence from India. The Indians believe it was this group that got him into talks with some rotten apples inside the ISI.

"Harry tells me that after this Ajay talked with an ISI agent, and almost overnight he disappeared from all surveillance; for the past two years Harry wasn't sure where he's been or what he's been doing. Then, last October, out of nowhere he pops back up on Harry's radar.

"He once ran a fairly lucrative trucking company until it started to wither and go bust after the family trip to Saudi Arabia. Back then the DEA had him identified as an intermittent runner of dope, but mostly a legit hauler who worked the roads from Austin to Monterrey, Mexico. Nobody at the DEA wanted to screw with the political points being scored with NAFTA back then. And since this Ajay didn't cause any waves with the federales down in Mexico, he was never targeted for arrest. But Harry says that he has suddenly started trucking again, and during the last four months he has been making quite a few cross-border trips."

"So if he's running dope again, why didn't your buddy just call the DEA to shut him down? Why contact us? America is start'n to see NAFTA for the screw-job it is, so why not shut this fucker down?" asked an irritated Parker.

"Well, I guess at first anyway, Harry thought it may just be an attempt to start the trucking company again. But after some checking, he can't seem to find where any of this guy's shipments have been going south of the border, nor to whom they're going up here. If he is hauling dope, Harry figures it's probably the same small stuff that he was doing before. But recently he has come to fear that it could become something bigger. Legit or not, Harry has enough concerns and red flags that he wants this guy checked out before he tries to smuggle in something real bad."

Parker shot his partner a look over his shoulder that was equal parts surprise and incredulity.

"What? If your friend has those kinds of concerns, why haven't we been out here sooner? Shit, Lemi, this guy could be involved with the crap hit'n us today, for God's sake."

"Maybe, Dave, maybe, but it's still pretty weak and this numb-nut isn't the only damn fish in the sea that Harry and all the rest of us are chasing around. It's this stupid defensive war, Dave; you damn-well know that.

"You see, Harry has a hunch, or maybe I should say, he has a fear about this guy's close connection to his childhood buddy, Sanchez, and his interest with the Pakistani ISI. We all know the cartels are being supplied with arms from that fat-ass Chavez down in Venezuela, as well as raiding the military arsenals down in Guatemala and Nicaragua. And with the Chavez regime getting so cozy with the Iranians, Harry fears the Iranians might try to recruit a guy like this Ajay Majumbar. If we get to him first, he could be a good mule for us. But if we don't move fast enough, he could funnel some Hezbollah sleeper-cells in here or maybe even worse. I mean, look at what's happening today."

Both men sat silent as the hot air coming in the window cooled momentarily as the car coasted across a well-manicured bridge above the Guadalupe River. The placid flow of water had a faint smell of mud and swampy humidity that came as a surprisingly welcome therapy for Turan's dry throat. But the heavy thoughts of the two men kept somber and silent reign inside the car as they moved along the county road.

Parker wound the car through pasture land filled with herds of horses and cattle that grazed lazily; the only animal concerns were getting fed, stinging bugs, and the afternoon heat.

The car's GPS announced they had arrived at their destination. The driveway had a simple metal gate marked with the correct address. Nailed to a rotting railroad tie was a rusted and fading sign that read *Easy Creek Ranch*. Lying below it, barely seen in a thick patch of dried out weeds, was a newer sign that read *AJ TRUCKING*.

Numerous curving trails made of dried dirt lay printed across the asphalt, showing dusty proof of recent and heavy vehicle traffic in and out of the property.

Parker slowly advanced the car down the drive with the tires crunching in the gravel. They both closely watched the ranch house as it became visible in a thick stand of cottonwood trees, bunched up along the bank of the river. Off to their right sat a large metal building that appeared to be the heart of the trucking business. The full-grown weeds and grass that surrounded the building were thick but trampled flat from the recent travel of many tires. A single old, rusted, and heavily scarred box trailer sat neglected next to the building; its rear doors hung ajar and swung in the lazy Texas breeze.

They saw no vehicles until they turned for the front of the ranch house. There sat an older green Toyota truck, quietly waiting to be useful again, parked outside the front door. Parker eased to a stop behind it, blocking it in.

"Seems quiet. You think maybe somebody's home?" he asked.

"I hope we didn't come all the way out here for nothing. Let's go knock."

The agents climbed out of the car and worked to straighten out the wrinkles in their slacks. They looked around, saw and heard nothing but arid wind rustling through the drying leaves of the cottonwood trees above them. Footpaths to the front door were well worn and the place had seen a lot of recent activity; nonetheless, it had a desolate feel that was devoid of any humanity, reminding Parker of a graveyard as he approached the front door.

The house appeared well-built, constructed with pride by skilled workman, but time had taken its inevitable toll, dimming the luster of a once-handsome building. It needed fresh paint and minor repair and had several years of fallen leaves and dry, thin tree branches clogging the nooks and crevasses of the warped and cracked cedar-shingle roof. Once lively and vibrant summer flowers sat dried and wilted in the many pots that lined the walk. Hanging above the dying plants was a small wind-chime that sounded rather weak and forlorn instead of welcoming. Parker could see the languid water of the small river meandering amid rocks, choked with the clog of autumn's leaves. A strange sadness rested over the place and he shivered as his mind produced an image that the morose residence was in fact mourning a loss. *People say they like the colors of autumn? I hate it.*

Agent Turan stepped onto the covered porch that creaked as he entered. Upon opening the screen door, he reached in and knocked lightly on the window of the old inner door. The thin, single-pane rattled in its frame as several black flies floated around his head, making the stifling air inside the porch sizzle.

His Turkish birthright had given Turan the ability to speak both Farsi and Turk fluently, and he could do a decent job of Arabic. Those skills made him a natural for initiating contacts with Muslim families like this Majumbar family. The fellowship of similar heritage and religion always enhanced a law enforcement officer's ability to connect with people. And since 9/11 his assets were in high demand for the bureau. He took a step back and shut the screen door as he waited for a response. He listened for any hint of movement inside but the only sounds that came to his ears were the faint buzzing of flies.

After several disappointing seconds of silence he motioned for Parker to check around the back of the house while he again rapped on the window. This time he also tried turning the knob and found the door was indeed locked. He bent inward and noticed that the view inside was much darker than he would have expected for such a sunny day. The old house had numerous windows and he guessed that the interior should be better lit. But instead it appeared dark and closed-in. His eyes made some adjustment to the dim light as he glanced around and noticed that many window shades and curtains were drawn shut. *I hope they're not on vacation.*

With a bit of irritation he swiped his hand through the air in front of his face to combat a small squadron of flies that swirled there. An uneasy feeling came from points unknown and settled in his gut. *Nothing on this shitty day feels right.* He squinted while trying to peer deeper into the interior. The home was obviously lived-in and even though it was going to be a very warm fall day, there did not appear to be any reasons for the closed window shades, unless they were on a trip, and that would mean he had wasted his time in coming here.

Parker finished his circumnavigation of the structure and came back, scratching at his thinning hair line.

"I can't see anything inside, Lemi. Everything's closed up tight all the way around. You get anything?"

"Nothing, it's like they left on holiday or something."

Parker scanned the property, eyes squinting against the harsh light. He shook his head and gave his partner a cock-eyed look of consternation.

"I found the weirdest damn thing in the backyard. Someone had a recent fire-pit going back there – and you know what was being burned up? Strange, someone has burned up a trophy-mounted cat back there. It looks like it was leopard or something, and the mounting work appeared to be of real good quality, but now it's destroyed."

"Huh? That is weird. I'll go back with you and check it out in a second."

Parker stared out at the parched grass bending in the prairie wind and shook his head slowly. If he did not know he was with his partner he could almost swear that there was not another human soul within a hundred miles. He felt desperately alone.

"This place gives me the creeps."

Turan nodded while waving at the irritating buzz around his ears again, then reached into his jacket and brought out a business card. He tried to stick it between the glass pane and sill but the thin card bent and he lost his grip on it, and watched, exasperated, as it fell to the floor.

"Dammit," he whispered as he reached down to pick it up.

Bent over, he grasped the card and observed faint boot prints in the dust of the porch floor. Curiosity piqued, he focused on a small smear of color in the dust at the bottom door jamb. The dried smear seemed to extend under the door. The stain had a burned reddish color that was tinged slightly yellow and brown, and the smudge gave the impression of someone's boot trailing paint or some other wet substance across the well-worn wood.

He scanned the other boot prints across the floor and could discern that there were many more smears in the numerous tracks. He

342

could also make out that they all showed the direction of the smears was going out the door, not in.

A chill went down the agent's spine as the constant sound of two dozen or so buzzing flies seemed to dramatically increase in volume inside his ears. Still kneeling, his eyes focused back to the seal around the door where he finally took notice of a dozen more flies crawling along the door's edges, trying vainly to seek out a way to get inside. His eyes widened and he stood up so rapidly that it caused a slight head rush and made Parker jump back in surprise. Turan leaned forward and pressed his face tightly against the glass pane in the door, shading his eyes with him palms.

Parker tensed at the sudden and unexpected actions of his partner and his hand instinctively grabbed hold of his sidearm on his hip.

"What the fuck, Lemi?"

Even with the help of his cupped hands shading his eyes, it still took a couple of seconds for his eyes to adjust enough to the interior gloom that he could finally distinguish individual shapes. Slowly the darkness retreated and the interior came into better view, so much so that he could make out dark swaths on the white tiled floor.

Tilting his face from left to right he concentrated on looking into the recesses of the dark room and was finally able to make out what he thought might be the hunched-over shape of a person, slumped in a chair at the kitchen table. At the same moment he saw Pushkar's body, the very faint but unmistakable smell of human putrefaction seeped out through the thin gap between the window pane and the door sill. The dawning crystallization of what drew the devoted interest of the flies flashed into his mind as coldness settled into the pit of his stomach.

"Holy shit," Turan exclaimed as he stepped back and shoved his foot against the old door.

The door nearly broke in two by the force of his kick and the old pane of glass shattered and sprayed across the floor. The broken door struck the interior wall, where it stopped and hung tilted from broken hinges.

Turan immediately disappeared inside the house as Parker drew his Sig Saur P226 and charged forward after his partner. As he reached the door a wave of sickeningly pungent stench blasted up his nostrils, causing an involuntary gag reflex in his throat and stopped him in his tracks just inside the door. His hand quickly covered his mouth against the vile odor while his will power and stomach muscles worked feverishly to keep him from vomiting at the revolting smell.

Accustomed to the bright daylight outside he could not make much of the dark shapes surrounding him as he thrust his firearm out in front. A short distance away he heard Turan moving around, but mostly his ears picked up the droning noise of thousands of buzzing black flies that swarmed around his head, making the same sound as that of an enormous hornets' nest that had been jostled.

Suddenly, harshly, light radiated violently into the room as Turan jerked open the kitchen sink curtains. The light caused Parker to squint as he raised his arm reflexively to his face. Through the dark cloud of flying insects the light allowed his eyes to take in the ghastly sight now revealed.

The extreme heat of the Texas summer was gone but the cooler autumn had not stopped the natural course of decay. The three-and-half days since Asha and Pushkar were murdered had wrought disastrous results on their corpses. Pushkar's body still sat in his dinner chair but had grown far larger as it swelled from the gases created from decomposition. The bloated belly pushed against the table's edge, causing his chair to tip slightly backward. His skin was stretched to near-bursting and was cracked in various places that ran with slimy dark fluid. The skin color had darkened to shades of black and purple and his swollen tongue was forced out through his lips. Light glistened off the moist fluid draining from his blackened eye sockets and nostrils.

He was covered in a roving mass of flies that busily looked for any opportunity to nest their eggs and feed. Parker forced his eyes to leave that grotesque sight and look around the room. He was taken aback even more when he saw the decapitated and rapidly desiccating corpse lying in a large pool of blackish liquid by the refrigerator. The many wounds to the body had drained its putrid fluids and not allowed it to bloat, and so it had already begun to dry out. Dried skin was stretched tight and had started to peel and crack, leaving the reddish purple sinew of dead muscle in plain view.

A bowling-ball sized lump sat on the kitchen counter above the mutilated body. It was completely enclosed in a mass of flies and their small white maggot larvae. He watched as the small rice-sized creatures that moved and strayed too close to the counter's edge would then fall into a large squirming pile on the floor. At first he could not identify what the object was until a revolting realization dawned: it was the severed head from the corpse lying below it.

He shuddered with disgust at the sight. He then noticed, appearing to be scrawled in dried blood across the refrigerator door, were the words *Allahlu Akbar* and the word *azadi* below them.

Parker had seen death many times but the shocking sight that was here, along with the horrid smell made his head swim and stomach churn. The walls seemed to constrict as the foul air no longer wanted to enter his lungs, and when he could no longer stand it, he turned and quickly dashed out the door into the clean air outside.

Lunging off the porch, he reared back, his face to the blazing sun as he took large gulps of the sweet, wholesome oxygen that had never felt more welcome. With slow steps Turan came walking out behind him, with one hand over his mouth as the other shielded his eyes against the bright sun.

"Jesus, Lem, that's a slaughter house in there," Parker said, still gasping for fresh air. "Do you think those are the people we were coming here to see?"

"I think so. I looked and there were no other bodies in the house that I could see, anyway, but I only did a quick look. It stinks like hell in there and I need some air."

"Stinks? That's an understatement."

Parker vigorously shook his head.

"I'm not sure that I've ever smelled one that bad before. I'll go back in with you if we need to double check."

Turan shook his head.

"No, I think we can wait until we get some local cops and a coroner out here before we do another look in that mess."

Turan's squinting eyes surveyed the ranch and it felt heavy with emptiness.

"There's nothing alive here," he muttered softly.

They walked to the car; Turan sat in the driver seat and started the engine. He reached over and turned the air conditioner vent full-blast and directed it to his face. Parker joined him in the small cleansing ritual, and as the cooled air washed the stink from his nostrils he pulled his cell phone out and began dialing their field office. Meanwhile Turan let the cool air wash over him as his partner relayed what they had found, and requested for the local cops to respond to the ranch.

The mental visions of what he had just seen in the east-Texas Muslim-American home refused to leave his mind. Lemi Turan was raised in a solid Turkish immigrant, middle-class American home in Pennsylvania that was much like this one. The thought of this type of carnage in a Muslim home, here in America, was abhorrent to all of his religious and cultural sensibilities. He had read the same words written in blood on the refrigerator door that Parker had. They were so reminiscent to the old black and white photographs that showed the

345

words *Helter Skelter* scrawled in dried blood at the sites of the Tate/LaBianca murders back in the '60s.

His gut told him the level of intense hate that had caused the deaths inside this home was something that had been twisting, forming, and molding itself into a hideous and grotesque thing for a very long time. He feared it may now be loose upon the world. He reached out and turned on the car radio while his partner gave out more information over the phone.

"....can now see that the fire that was started at the bottom of this structure has now engulfed the bottom fourteen floors as we continue to watch more and more people come streaming out onto roof. My God, this is terrible! For our television viewers, I know the footage coming to us from our San Francisco affiliate KTVU helicopter is shaky, but they are under a lot of stress right now and are trying to get as much recorded as they can. We apologize for losing the footage of that active gunfight between law enforcement and terrorists going on right now along I-80 near the Oakland Bay Bridge!"

"What is it that we appear to be watching now, Chief O'Rourke?"

"Shepard, I think the good fire chief you just spoke with has said it all. The gunmen are effectively keeping firefighters and emergency responders from getting to these blazing buildings, and if this one goes down it stands a good chance of toppling across I-80 and successfully shutting the Bay Bridge down for months, if not longer. The coordinated use of suicide trucks filled with so much fuel and these additional armed terrorists fighting to keep the first responders and firemen from getting to these blazing buildings is a coordinated attack plan."

"I agree. But as time passes I seem to be seeing the strategy that these attackers are using include more than just these truck bombs and gunmen. It's becoming apparent that the panic created in the citizenry and the congestion within the city appears to be an active part of that plan. A plan that has made the civilian population itself another layer – dare I say, a sort of human shield to help block the first responders from getting to those same people who need them so badly. Fire Chief Robertson, you are familiar with fighting fires in skyscrapers, how do these firefighters do battle in this situation? Do they stand any chance of stopping these murderers from bringing these buildings down like the Twin Towers?"

"This is a far worse situation than I could have ever imagined. For these men and women to be confronted with this is

346

nothing short of a nightmare. Shepard, it's just devastating. Listen, the Twin Towers came down, but not due to the direct structural damage done as a result of the planes hitting the buildings. What brought those magnificent buildings down was the heat of the fire created by the burning of the jet fuel that was carried onboard those planes. The inferno created by that jet fuel fire caused temperatures well in excess of 1,800 degrees. Those high temperatures then warped and weakened the steel sub-frame of the structure that then caused the only example of a total progressive collapse of a steel-framed structure in history. What I'm terribly afraid of now, Shepard, is a repeat of those two catastrophic collapses, that this will be repeated in the six buildings currently burning in San Francisco. Without the firefighters getting access to those buildings, I just simply see no way to stop that from happening."

"So what you're saying, Chief, is that this tactic is an effective way of bringing down an entire skyscraper without the use of a plane like on 9/11? Or the failed use of sheer explosive force like what happened at the first World Trade Center Bombing or the bombing of the A.P. Murrah Federal building in Oklahoma City?"

"That's exactly what I'm saying. Now Shepard, the fires at Ground Zero had the assistance from the initial impact of the planes blasting off the fireproofing material from the steel framing. That type of impact did not occur in these attacks today, but I can see that the threat of collapse is being exacerbated by the time delay in starting to quench these fires. I'm afraid we could see the real possibility of structural collapse here."

"I would like to interject just one other bit of terrible reality here as well."

"Go ahead, Clarke."

"For the people in those buildings a collapse may be – God damn me for saying this – a blessing, in a horrible way. Remember that almost all the people who died in the towers at Ground Zero were above the impacts of the planes. They were trapped and had no chance of escape. The poor people who are trapped in these buildings in California were above fires that started at ground level. If we can't get in there and put the fires out and the buildings don't collapse – all of those people will burn or be forced to jump!

"Oh, dear God, I hope – uh, my goodness – I – I'm very sorry, folks. This is extremely difficult for me right now.

"Uh, umm, Chief Robertson, how exactly does the mechanics of this fire lead to possible structural collapse?"

"Unfortunately it's pretty straight forward, Shepard. If the reports are correct on the size of the tankers, we're talking about an

average capacity between, say 9,000 to 10,000 gallons of fuel. Now the heat from that much burning fuel can get hot enough to both weaken the concrete casing of the substructure as well as start the actual melting and weakening of the steel reinforcement inside. Once the dead weight above that weakened steel gets to be more than it can handle, basic gravity takes over and the buildings will then come down."

"Damn their evil souls to hell. They have used our basic infrastructure system against us. Who would ever think anything suspicious or out of place with a gasoline tanker driving by? They are around us daily, delivering fuel to every gas station inside every city. I surmise that they just drove these tankers into San Francisco in a convoy of death, along with the armed suicide squads of gunmen as a sick form of protection. When they rammed the fuel inside the buildings and detonated it – whamo, you got…."

Parker closed his cell phone and said, "Mitchell is working on getting the Comal County Sheriff and the Texas Rangers headed this way. He'll also get a B.O.L.O. out for this Ajay Majumbar."

"Fine, I figure it'll take at least a half-hour before any of the locals show up."

"Yeah, what do you think we should do, look around?"

"I think we better. This is a real strange one, Dave. I've never seen this sort of a thing in a Muslim home before. If their son did this and not some other, uh, person – well, it's just that this sort of thing doesn't happen in a Muslim household."

"Well, excuse me, Agent Turan, but I didn't know that this sort of thing has become an everyday occurrence in Christian homes, either," Parker said indignantly.

"Hey, drop that crap, Dave. You know I didn't mean anything like that. It's just that the family thing is real important in the Muslim community. And this was a first generation immigrant home. This is weird. Harry didn't say anything about any domestic issues – and it just doesn't make any sense to me. With those words smeared on the refrigerator – this was real personal. It might very well be a murder-suicide between the husband and wife that doesn't involve the son. Let's go down to that garage and see what we got down there, okay?"

"Yeah, I think we better. Hey, you think we'll find the son swinging from the rafters down there?"

Turan shrugged and started to walk down the gravel driveway to the offices for AJ Trucking. He knew no one was around but he still drew his sidearm, leaving it hanging along his leg with Parker doing the same as he followed.

Recent activity was obvious from all the tire tracks in the dirt and compressed weeds in the area. Approaching the office door and looking inside the uncovered windows they could see that the desks inside had not been used for quite some time, as dust thickly coated everything. But he also took notice that the trash cans were all overflowing with empty soda cans and trash that had no dust on them. Parker tried the door and found it unlocked.

"We have no warrant yet, shall we?"

"Warrants? We ain't got no warrants. We don't need no warrants. I don't need to show you any stinking warrants," Turan quipped sarcastically in a terrible Alfonso Bedoya voice.

Turan's usual high-level of professional decorum had been ruined by the sight the bloated corpses and the terrorist strikes. Parker, surprised by the strange levity, gave a queasy grin in return, as he tried to let his partner's offhand remarks disappear from his memory quickly so he would not have to write them in his report later.

They entered and worked their way around the trash and furniture while only giving marginal interest to the miscellaneous and nondescript items strewn around the room. They found the rear door of the office unlocked and entered the large bay garage, where they were immediately struck by the stench from a clogged and overflowing toilet in a small side bathroom.

No equipment, vehicles or furniture other than chairs was inside the bay, but they pondered the piles of blankets and sleeping bags lying on the cement floor. A large stack of pizza boxes was in the far corner, along with dozens of empty soda cans and candy bar wrappers. Crumpled bags from McDonald's and Burger King were in a large pile of trash. Turan surmised that it would take several hundred meals to accomplish the pile of trash thrown into that corner of the shop.

`"Hey, Lemi, check this shit out. What the hell is all this about?" Parker asked as he pointed at another pile near the garage bay doors.

As Turan walked over and stood next to Parker he began to recognize things in the pile. Dozens of pre-molded plastic containers for cell phones and small civilian hand-held radios, rolls of wire and duct tape, and behind the main pile sat several open and empty cases of 7.62mm rifle ammunition.

"What the fuck, Lem, Was this guy outfitting an army of redneck Boy Scouts or what?"

349

Agent Turan stood perplexed, staring at the pile of stuff as his mind swam with the possibilities of what he was looking at. Suddenly, his memory shot back to seeing the three gasoline tankers driving away with the three matching red vans they had passed on their way here. *A convoy of death!* The veins in his forehead pounded and swelled as he turned and screamed to Parker.

"Damn! Dave, give me your fucking phone, right now!"

*****

14:35pm CST UTC -6
Rudd's Sand & Gravel Freeman Rd
Katy, TX

JESSE LOGAN-Jaramillo listened intently to the radio updates that were coming in fast and furious. All of the media outlets had cranked up their coverage to meet the magnitude of the disasters unfolding across the nation. He sat in the cab of his dump truck, completely dumbstruck at the amount of damage and death he heard being described. His mind was having trouble grasping the total extent of the calamity. *Please God, dear Jesus, see our country through this catastrophe.* He hated to listen, yet he yearned for as much information as he could possibly get.

The line of dump trucks ahead moved slowly forward across the weigh scale of the gravel pit. As each truck left the scale, Jesse eased his large blue Mack slowly along. He was lucky enough to keep his single-truck excavating and dirt hauling business going as the economy had tanked, killing off so many of the construction and excavation jobs that were his bread and butter. He survived on the small-bid contracts that were still available. Texas had fared better than most so far but things were still tough and money was tight all through the Houston area. It required that he fight tooth-n-nail with his competition for every bid he put out, but he was surviving and feeding his family okay.

Today, he was intending to haul road-base gravel to a Texas DOT project inside the city, but, with the news coming over the radio, all he wanted to do was pick up his family, hold his kids tight, and pray. The news anchors pontificated about the relevance of the attacks occurring during the month of September on the ten-year anniversary of 9/11. They already came up with the new catch phrase that Jesse figured was going to become the name for these attacks – 9/11 2.0! Jesse imagined that some dunce executive had dreamt up the lame name, but it seemed to be sticking with the talking-heads.

Currently he listened to KPRC 950 AM and the anchor sounded almost panicked by the casualty reports coming in.

"....I don't know how else to describe what I'm watching out of California. It's absolutely devastating, horrible, just....Oh, God! It's just unbelievable, folks. The entire bay area is awash in thick black smoke and it is like the usual fog you'd see – I don't know if you've ever been there, but it kind of looks like when a thick fog is down in the bay on a rainy morning, but this – this is black, dark, and very thick – and it's everywhere. Wait – wait a minute, Jamie, you have that connection ready to go? Yeah? Okay, folks, we are going to give you the most up-to-date information you can find anywhere on your AM dial. We are receiving a feed from – hang on. Uh, this is coming from KFBK 1530 FM out of Sacramento. A traffic reporter is flying over the bay area right now with a firsthand report.

"Okay, Yoshi, are you in the area yet?"

"Yes, Jack, we are flying over Piedmont Heights and coming into view of downtown Oakland as I speak. We're still a couple miles out and I am having difficulty seeing through the smoke billowing up from the city. Wait just a minute – Yes, we're at 8,500 feet and I can see down into the city now...."

"Folks, this is San Francisco KRON-4 news chopper with traffic reporter Yoshi Oshiro-Burns, who is currently flying over the devastation in the city center of Oakland with a live report – Yoshi, can you tell us what you see?"

"Jack, the destruction in the city center is unbelievable! It – it goes in an almost perfectly formed circle. I'd say it is....Bill, how big do you think? The circle of destruction is immense, Jack. The circle, Bill and I estimate at a mile in diameter, at least. And the area inside that circle is flattened, Jack. Just flat! It looks like old photos of the cities of Hiroshima and Nagasaki after the nuclear blasts at the end of WW II. There are some – some –....It is just horrible! There are some walls still standing here and there and many, many fires. The whole city is on fire!

"I grew up in the bay area as you know, Jack, and I know Oakland very well. The area near City Hall is where the blast epicenter appears to be and it radiates in a zone of destruction that extends all the way out from there to the port docks at the shipping terminals in the Oakland Inner Harbor, around Posey Tube and Wevster Street I can see – one, three, seven – yes, seven ships are in flames at the shipping terminal docks and there might be more, but the smoke is just so thick I can't see yet. There is a large circular wall of flame inside the city that runs along the edges of the blast zone. It

351

appears to be raging the worst toward the west and south. Numerous fires inside the blast zone, good God, it's all on fire down there!

"The section of I-880 west of downtown and other elevated roadways in that area have collapsed. I-980 through downtown is completely gone and chocked with debris. I can see where it is supposed to be but the roadway is gone and huge piles of burning debris litter the area all the way to I-880. The whole area is broken and ablaze. The blast wave appears to have been so extreme that the elevated sections of the highway itself appear to have been thrown as far as the bay.

"There doesn't seem to be that much burning or smoking debris inside the central blast zone, but downtown and uptown between Grand Avenue and Lakeside Park – there are hundreds of fires spread throughout and in uptown toward I-580 and the MacArthur Boulevard. Oh, dear God! Jack – it's just gone! The entire center of the city is just gone! I cannot imagine that anyone inside of that blast zone survived this. They're all dead. No one could live through that. Oh, my God! My city, my home – it's – it's gone...."

"Yoshi? Yoshi? I'm so sorry, folks, the situation is just as bad for us as it is for you and obviously our reporter, the very first reporter to fly above this terrible destruction. is having trouble and we will continue as soon as we can regain our connection to...."

"Dammit," Jesse cursed to himself in the cab of the truck, "How could it hap'n again?"

Jesse's fingers turned pale and his hands hurt from his tight grip on the steering wheel. The same sickening and helpless feeling he had while watching the Twin Towers fall swelled inside of his chest, as he seethed with anger and frustration. After 9/11 he had joined the Army, and survived two deadly deployments to Iraq before his first four-year enlistment was up. The Army used stop-loss to keep him around for a third deployment of watching his buddies get blown to pieces by IED explosions.

He had sweated out his fear and bravado with his fellow Task Force Ironhorse soldiers in the dusty streets of Mosul under the blistering Tigris Valley sun. Now, almost four years of civilian life later, four years of building a family and a future for himself back home in Texas, with two chunks of shrapnel stuck deep in his thigh. Four years after he left the battlefield, he now sat listening to his nation being attacked again. Jesse fumed – all the hard work and sacrifice he and his buddies gave for the protection of the country. *And it achieved absolutely fucking nothing!*

The last truck ahead of his pulled away from the scale and he inched forward until he was outside the window where Amanda was printing out his weight ticket. Her eyes were red and damp from crying and he could see the television behind her showing terrible scenes of destruction that his mind could barely believe. *An American city should never look like that!*

"Hey Manda, is that video of Oakland or San Francisco?"

Amanda looked over her shoulder at the scene then quickly turned away.

"That's Oakland, Jesse," she replied meekly as her slender little frame was racked by sobs. "It's horrible, Jesse. I can't stop crying."

"I'm all torn up inside, too, girl. You be strong, now, it'll work itself out okay," Jesse said without much confidence.

"Listen, I think my daddy is going to close the yard early 'cause of what's happen'n. Do you have more loads goin' out today?"

"I was goin' to deliver three trucks today for that D.O.T. project in North Houston, but if your pa is goin' to shut down I sure understand. I was thinkn' I'd just head home myself. You know, pick up the wife and kids and just go home. Just have us be together through this mess, you know."

"That'd probably be for the best, Jesse. I don't think there'll be much business the rest of this week. Here."

She handed him his scale receipt.

"You take care of yourself and the family, Jesse. I'll see you next time."

He looked down at the crying teenager and smiled.

"You stay strong, hon'. It'll be okay. America is strong and we'll make it through this. We're made of stuff they can't tear apart. There'll be pay back for this, big time!"

Amanda gave Jesse a long look that started to make him uncomfortable before she asked, "Jesse, I was just nine when the towers fell in New York. You did a couple tours over in Iraq, right?"

Jesse nodded.

"I grew up in school through all of the turmoil of the Bush years, and the whole country arguing during all that. What a mess. All the emotion and heart it took for the country, you soldiers, and us at home praying for you – to do everything we've done for the last ten-years. God, Jesse, can we go through all this again? How are we supposed to take this stuff every ten years or so? How do we survive that?"

Jesse was a proud soldier and loved his country, and the young girl's questions hit like a gut punch into every ounce of

353

patriotism he had. His heart sank deep into his chest and felt like it wanted to hide there, out of sight, unchallenged, weak. But deep down a spark of stubborn Texas grit chewed its way up his spine and he gave the girl a tender smile, but looked at her with hard eyes.

"I saw people blown to bits for daring to wear purple ink on their fingers, just to have the opportunity to vote. I stood hour after hour with Iraqi guards who wore face masks just so their families wouldn't be slaughtered because they had a job standing next to me. I saw strong, brave men and women doing tower'n acts of heroism just for a chance to be free. Amanda, sweetie, we're already free. We're strong, too. America's built outta fighters, honey! We'll make it through this."

"I hope so," she said as she wiped tears from her cheeks, perking up a tiny bit.

Jesse took the receipt from her hand and, with a confident wink he slowly pulled off the scale, giving her a thumbs-up. She watched as his truck disappeared from the pit. There were no other trucks to be seen and she thought about locking up and leaving, but instead she sat down, staring at the images coming across the small television screen and cried.

As Jesse pulled the loaded truck out of the pit he turned the volume up on his radio and pulled into traffic, kicking up dust as he accelerated.

*****

AN ELEVEN-year veteran of the Houston Police Department, Corporal Richard Trundle sat heartsick, listening to the same radio reports as Jesse. But unlike Jesse, he also had his police radio giving him more information, and right then, that additional information had him on edge.

A half-hour ago, a be-on-the-lookout (BOLO) report had been aired over the police network advising all law enforcement throughout Texas that the FBI was reporting their agents had seen a convoy of at least three gasoline tanker trucks with accompanying red vans near the New Braunfels area. The feds were saying it was a 'high probability' that those vehicles were another terrorist attack force connected to the attacks in California.

The worst part of the report, by far, was that the vehicles' current location was unknown and that they could be headed for any of the major targets in San Antonio, Austin, or Houston. *How in the hell do the feds see this and then lose them? What the fuck?*

Richard wished he could scoff at such a report but with the hell that was happening out in California, he knew it could happen here, too. DHS Secretary Napolitano had activated the National Response Plan, causing the hulking behemoth of the federal bureaucracy to shift gears and begin to move into action against the growing disaster. The DHS Regional Response Coordination Center in Atlanta was in command of Texas and the rest of the southern states. It was also busily issuing BOLOs and alerts while it also collected and coordinated data on the tons of reports of suspicious activity from first responders and citizens throughout the region. The most burdensome nationwide DHS directive issued so far, almost an hour ago, directed all law enforcement personnel nationwide to stop and detain every propane, gasoline or fuel tanker truck spotted anywhere across the entire nation.

The local DHS administration had already activated the Harris County Emergency Operations Center (EOC) to directly handle the greater Houston area and coordinate all of the services and information collected there. Meanwhile locating, contacting, stopping, and investigating every mobile tanker everywhere was an immense task and took every cop that was working the streets, running like crazy. Thankfully the chief of police had just also ordered out overtime crews that would soon be on their way to help.

Richard heard the tension in the voices of his fellow officers as they made one contact after another. He was damn sure some poor trucker was going to be contacted somewhere across the country by a hyper-reactive cop and get drilled if he got the slightest bit lippy.

If further attacks spread to this region of the country, emergency response in the metropolitan areas was now better prepared, but Richard still felt a nagging sense that they were just playing a game of catch-up. His personal marching orders, as part of that entire national response system, were clear and simple: he had been ordered to assist Texas DPS troopers in keeping an eye on traffic entering the metropolitan area around Houston, Sugar Land, and Baytown. No small feat, but his specific assignment was something he figured he could manage. He was responding toward the small suburb of Katy to assist in observing eastbound traffic on I-10 for anything suspicious and stop all tanker traffic heading into the metro area.

He and his wife lived in Bunker Hill Village, a suburban community on the eastern flank of the massive metropolitan area that encircled Houston. He had requested assignment to the Westside Division, which covered the village, and after several years of working downtown his request was eventually approved. Now he patrolled district-20 of that division and made it home for meals most every day.

He had just stopped by and hugged his wife when he received his orders. He could still smell her perfume on his collar.

He continued through traffic, headed north on Kirkwood Road on his way to the interstate and kept an eye on traffic heading south into the suburbs where his family waited. He craned his head around at every tanker truck he saw, but he could not stop and check them all. There was no time, and there were so many. Each one looked perfectly innocuous, and yet each one possibly held cargo that could be used for such a sinister and deadly purpose. *How the fuck do I protect against something that's everywhere?* Now that he was looking for them, he saw tanker trucks everywhere; big ones, short ones, propane, gasoline, water, septic, and each one possibly filled with explosives. *Shit!*

So far he had not seen a group of tankers nor any suspicious accompanying vans. Rushing through the traffic as fast as he could, he wanted to meet the troopers waiting out at Sealy, eight miles from the city, where he could finally do something useful and be kept busy. He wanted to get to work to help him focus and keep his mind from wandering away to the disaster in California. *This is a horrible day.*

His heart ached for the cops who were desperately attempting to deal with the horrible mess out in California and he had to make sure that nothing like that happened here. After 9/11 he had wasted almost six months of his rookie year chasing down every report of the Terrorist Boogeyman: a creature constantly seen around every corner of the countryside by frightened citizens and paranoid city bureaucrats who wanted nothing like 9/11 to happen on their watch. Then immediately, and without any facts, the boneheads in the media would gleefully report how either the authorities were actively chasing bad guy monsters, or were acting foolishly by going after ghosts with heavy hands. The story always changed to whichever one made for the better ratings fodder for that day.

He found himself dispatched to every suspicious-looking guy the community busybodies saw. When he finally contacted the poor bastard, it always seemed to turn out to be just some no-name dude who happened to be at the wrong place at the wrong time. Meanwhile in Washington, DC, the leaders in Congress shit their pants, pointed fingers in every direction but at themselves, and ended up doing nothing to actually stop it from happening again, and today the country was paying the price.

Richard wondered how many more hundreds of thousands of American troops were going to be ordered to trudge through more blood-soaked shithole countries around the globe after today. He ground his teeth and slammed his foot down on his squad car's accelerator just as the high-tone alarm blared out of his police radio speaker.

Beep...beep...beep

"Attention, all Westside and Northwest Division cars, attention, attention.

"Attention, all Westside and Northwest Division cars, attention.

"Harris County Emergency Operation Center is immediately ordering all Westside district-20 and all Northwest district-4 cars respond immediately to converge on the eastbound lanes of I-10 at the Hwy-90 Sam Houston Tollway interchange. I repeat, Harris County Emergency Operations Center directs all Westside Division district-20 and Northwest Division district-4 cars to immediately respond to I-10 eastbound lanes at the Sam Houston Tollway interchange.

"DPS is advising that troopers are currently in pursuit of three gasoline tanker trucks eastbound I-10 from Sealy. I repeat, DPS troopers are in pursuit of three gasoline tanker trucks that are refusing to stop, eastbound I-10 from Sealy. The three tractor trailers are refusing to stop for troopers and match the description of the suspected tanker convoy reported earlier by the FBI out of New Braunfels."

Richard flipped the switch on his cruiser's emergency equipment and his strobes flashed and siren wailed. Cars parted like the sea did before Moses as he rushed for the interstate. *It's really here. On my watch!* The dispatcher continued.

"Department of Public Safety Commander Bill Thompson is responding to be the on-scene commander. I repeat, Commander Bill Thompson is the designated on-scene commander."

"Shit!" Richard yelled as his heart sank.

*****

MAJOR AL-DOLEH's second-in-command, Lieutenant Ud-Daulah, looked into the rearview mirror, watching the flashing LED lights of the DPS vehicles chasing after his convoy of tankers. Ud-Daulah cursed himself for allowing his arrogant and selfish ego to be so stupid as to let his men convince him that they should stay at the trucking company and watch for news of Major Al-Doleh's strike in San Francisco.

357

At first, when the massive explosion occurred in Oakland, they were extremely happy, but also a little confused. Argument erupted as to whether one of Al-Doleh's teams could be responsible or whether it was another jihadist operation. In a few minutes, the news started broadcasting information about the assault on San Francisco. Shortly after that they saw that all three tankers had successfully attacked their targets. They celebrated the success of their compatriots and also the unknown shahid who had destroyed so much of Oakland.

Quickly Ud-Daulah quieted the cheering and boasting and challenged his enthusiastic men to accomplish the same success in their own assault on Houston. But after their departure from the ranch, he realized that they should have never delayed. He realized that this infidel nation was now on guard and would be looking for similar threats. *I was so foolish.*

Now staring at the pursuing cop cars he knew he had been correct. The rest of their attack would be a struggle, but nonetheless, it was a fight that he and his men had been trained to engage and win. *They think because they have found me that I am no longer the hunter. Ha!*

He analyzed the traffic that flowed along, unconcerned and ignorant down the smooth lanes of the Interstate ahead. The oblivious infidels took little or no notice of the speeding tankers charging up from behind, until they blew by. *They have not been warned. They are not ready for what I bring.*

His confidence and anticipation grew as he observed the skyscrapers of Houston protruding above the distant horizon, silhouetted against the overcast sky. Large car dealerships and hundreds of businesses lined the freeway, knowing nothing of Ud-Daulah's parade of death that rushed by at over ninety-miles an hour. The spacious six-lanes made it easy for him to negotiate the heavy tanker through traffic. Many hapless Iranians had been hurt or killed by his men practicing these maneuvers on the streets of Karaj and Bushehr. The skills obtained by those sacrifices were now paying off as he and the other two tanker drivers barreled toward their targets.

He barely took notice when the underpass of Westgreen Boulevard passed below his rig as he yelled into his small radio. He gave out orders to his escort strike teams, riding in their three vans. Two vans were presently stationed several miles ahead of the convoy while the third van trailed far behind, ready to take out the unsuspecting cops chasing him. Very soon he would release them to attack the kafirs and begin their own butchery of the defenders of Houston.

He and his men had been trained for every contingency, including this one, and they were about to utilize that capability to annihilate all obstacles that would possibly get in their way.

*****

RICHARD WAS only the second Houston Police car to arrive at the Sam Houston Tollway. He parked along the shoulder of I-10 as it paralleled the Katy Freeway Frontage Road. Continuous updates came across his radio as he retrieved his tactical vest from the trunk. The evil intent of the tankers had been confirmed, as they still refused to stop and still travelled together. The thought of the three gasoline-filled tankers speeding toward him at over one-hundred miles an hour was terrifying. There were still no reports on the whereabouts of any possible escort vans. The FBI had seen them but no one knew where they were, and that had Richard very worried. If those vans were lurking out there somewhere, they could pop out at any moment and wreak havoc. *This isn't cop work – this is soldier work! Shit!*

Commander Thompson was getting closer to the scene, and he had ordered that every car even remotely capable of reaching the pursuit head that way. Now seven DPS troopers, fourteen Harris County Sheriff deputies, and thirteen Houston Police officers were all screaming through city traffic to help their brother and sister cops defend the city.

But DHS coordinator Jack Wesley had broadcast word to the responding units to use extreme caution in determining the intent of the tankers. Since there were no more sightings of the vans, he wanted to make absolutely sure that some stupid, but innocent, truckers were not hurt by an overreaction. Thompson, a grizzled thirty-two year veteran of the Texas troopers was not about to acquiesce to the bureaucrat's wishes. Even over the police radio his graveled voice conveyed contempt at the queasiness that came from Wesley.

"I repeat, Commander, I do not authorize deadly force against the trucks for simply failing-to-yield at this time. Do you understand?"

"I damn well understand everything you're saying, Jack. Do you understand that if these are terrorists like those that hit California this morning, and we don't stop them – we'll have hell all over Houston tonight?"

"Commander Thompson, the Department of Homeland Security is in charge of this action. You are not authorized to allow

any use of deadly force on possible innocent citizens of this country who are travelling the roads of the State of Texas."

"Innocent? These trucks are refusing to stop for marked police cruisers with bright lights and loud sirens! Their intent is crystal-clear as far as I'm concerned. I will not allow Houston to be hit. I want them stopped and I want it done immediately! If they aren't terrorists – then they're too stupid to be alive after this morning! So, Jack, you go get the okay from your bosses if that's what you need. I will damn well make the decision for myself and my men, if you don't."

"Captain Thompson, you are under the command of the Department of Homeland Security! You will not take action without authorization! Do you understand?"

"Jack, I'm not going to argue with you any longer. I will not allow thousands of gallons of fuel to be blown up in the heart of this city! So you and the DHS can go fuck yourselves!"

Richard smiled grimly as Thompson explained reality to the foolish man who sat safe inside a bunker, hundreds of miles away. Richard thanked God that there were still leaders of men around with rank. They had not all been purged by the bureaucratic system, and Thompson was proving it.

"This is Texas Department of Public Safety Commander Bill Thompson speaking to all units responding to the Sam Houston Tollway – I am issuing this direct order. You will shut off all exit ramp access to the three tanker trucks currently being chased by my troopers. If any tanker attempts to exit I-10 onto off-ramps or roadways, I hereby authorize you to use all force necessary to stop them. That includes deadly force! If they don't comply immediately – kill the bastards'!"

"I repeat, if any of the tankers being followed by my troopers attempt to exit I-10 you will use deadly force. This order is given by my lawful authority from the Texas Department of Public Safety. If none of the tankers attempt to exit the interstate, then you will all get into standard pursuit formation and we will set up a termination point for the pursuit just west of the Washington Avenue underpass. I repeat, we're going to set up a termination point for the pursuit just west of the Washington Avenue underpass."

Richard immediately grabbed his radio mike and broadcast his confirmation of Commander Thompson's orders. He was immediately followed by dozens more officers.

*****

JESSE BARELY took notice of the monotonous traffic around him. They were all slowly making their way toward Houston. His attention, and that of his fellow commuters, was concentrated on their vehicle radios and the news, not driving. He had given up surfing the stations and finally settled on one. It had been so confusing, trying to listen to all of the differing reports from the various stations. The media sounded like they were in complete pandemonium, and so much conflicting information was coming in that nobody was able to confirm.

"....the sight from the roof where I am standing, here atop the Itel Building at 101 California Street, inside the financial district. I can see – just a few blocks to my south – the flames coming from another part of the financial district, south of Market Street. I must say that being here in the middle of this chaos – it is absolutely frightening!

"The smoke is so acrid I can barely breathe. It is so dense that my view of the lower portions of the Millennium Tower is completely blocked. But as you can see from our simulcast video, a large group of people, maybe two hundred now, have made it to that building's roof and now stand less than a half mile from me. I've already seen several of those desperate souls plunge over the side, only to disappear into that terrible smoke and fire. They're choosing to die that way rather than accept a fate of burning in the inferno maelstrom that is slowly and unstoppably making its way up the building toward them! Jim, it's – it's as horrible to see and to describe as…"

"But, Kyle, if the flames from the buildings on Mission Street continue spreading your way, you'll still have plenty of time to escape the building you're in, right?"

"Yes, I hope so, Jim. I want to stay – I feel obligated to stay – to document this tragedy for those desperate people. But the inferno of those fires – it is definitely spreading this way.

"The problem that I and those with me have is the same as everyone else in the city: everyone in this building is confronted with the choice between staying here inside the locked doors of our building, trying to keep away from the rampaging gunmen on the streets below, or trying to get away from the approaching fire and leave the modest sanctuary that this building offers. We have to brave the dangers of the streets or stay here and risk being caught by the fire!"

361

"I'm so sorry, Kyle. All of our prayers are with you and with everyone there in the city faced with those bleak prospects. Our prayers also go out to all the brave police and firefighters who are performing extreme acts of courage. Only with their sacrifice and success will any organized help reach the citizens. My word! I can't believe I'm talking about an American city!

"Kyle, please stay with me as I again relate to our listeners the sight of that amazing footage you forwarded to us. Uh, folks, I know you aren't able to see what's in this video feed that Kyle Morrison has sent us. Kyle, a print journalist with the San Francisco Chronicle, was able to capture this stunning webcam footage with his laptop, and what horrible video it is.

"Let me try to describe the scene to you. From his vantage point on the roof of the Itel Building, he was able to hold his laptop over the edge of the roof. The video shows a responding fire engine with a police car escort that was attempting to get through vehicle and pedestrian traffic below on Market Street. They were apparently working their way to the fires on Mission Street.

"As they approached a large intersection the video shows dozens of people moving around the street suddenly disperse as gunmen rush out, shooting at the fire engine and police. The fire engine wrecks and flips onto its side on Market as a policeman engages in a gunfight with the terrorists. Regrettably, the video shows the horrifying deaths of the policeman and several firefighters. Folks, the streets of San Francisco are a flat-out warzone right now.

"It tears at my heart to try and relate this news to you folks but this story has to get out. You've got to learn what the people of San Francisco are suffering through as I speak.

"Kyle – Kyle, I want to go back to…

"Wait just a moment, folks. Kyle – wait. I'm getting word that we have breaking news here. Please stand by.

"Ladies and gentlemen, we here at KPRC know how important the news from California is. We understand that a lot of you quite likely have loved ones in or near the area of those terrorist attacks occurring in Oakland and San Francisco. We all need and want as much information as possible. But we are making the decision to break away from the coverage of that disaster and go to news that is breaking, right now, here in the Houston area. Our news room staff has been continuously listening to the local police radio traffic and for the last fifteen minutes – it sounds like there…

"Listen, folks, we have breaking news. But before we deliver this news I must stress that everyone out there within the sound of my voice inside the greater Houston area must remain calm. I cannot *stress that enough! Please remain calm. We at KPRC radio and our television partners must stress that you do not panic at the following news we're going to broadcast.*

"We've been trying hard to get confirmation from the Department of Homeland Security Emergency Operations Center here in Houston as to whether what we are listening to over the police band radio is accurate, but they have not yet responded to our requests. What our management has decided to do is to send our KPRC and KRIV NewsCorp helicopter to the area of Interstate-10. They are to check on reports that local law enforcement authorities are engaged, at this very moment, with a convoy of possible terrorists driving gasoline-type tanker trucks toward the Houston area. The police band radio has broadcast that these tankers are driving eastbound on Interstate-10, headed toward downtown Houston and they are refusing to stop for the pursuing troopers.

"Our helicopter has just arrived above that area and we will be momentarily going to reporter Adam Jones for a live report. I repeat, we have reports from local police radio that there are several Texas troopers in pursuit of as many as three gasoline tanker trucks on Interstate-10. Ladies and gentlemen, I turn over this report to Adam Jones in our helicopter, who is observing what is occurring. Adam?"

"Yes, Jim, right now I am travelling above I-10 near the Sam Houston Tollway interchange. Things are happening very fast below me and I will attempt to get our listeners updated with what I'm seeing. KPRC and KRIV have been listening to local police radio traffic for quite some time. We surmise from what we have heard that local authorities were notified by agents of the Federal Bureau of Investigation who observed three gasoline tankers at or near New Braunfels. Those tankers are suspected to be linked to the terrorists who have attacked the San Francisco Bay area today.

"Law enforcement throughout Texas has been on the lookout for those tankers. Then, approximately fifteen-minutes ago, three tankers matching that description were sighted by DPS troopers driving eastbound on I-10 near Sealy. The troopers then attempted to stop the tankers but the trucks refused to stop and a high-speed pursuit of all three tankers has since ensued.

"A massive call for law enforcement assistance then went out to all local area agencies and I have personally seen that Houston Police, Harris County Sheriff, Texas troopers, and the Fort Bend County Sheriff have all responded to the call and have marked patrol cars below me along the I-10 eastbound lanes here at the interchange.

"I have also overheard orders broadcast over the police band that law enforcement has been authorized to use deadly force on the semi-trucks if they attempt to exit the interstate. I repeat, I have directly heard orders relayed over the police radio giving the officers below me the authority to use deadly force if the tanker trucks attempt to leave the interstate.

"Huh? Yes – yes – I see them, get us over there.

"Uh, ladies and gentlemen, I can now see the tankers coming! I see two – no, I see all three tanker trucks now – and I also see – yes, I see three DPS vehicles in pursuit behind the tankers…"

Stunned at what he was hearing, Jesse slowed the loaded Mack truck as he listened, coasting off the right lane and stopping the truck on the narrow shoulder of I-10. The Sam Houston interchange was only a few miles behind him. He pulled up so close to the cement divider that his tires rubbed against it, leaving black smears. His blood ran like ice in his veins as his heart pounded loudly in his chest and a cold sweat broke out on his brow.

"….like speeding torpedoes the tankers appear to be going far too fast to take the exit ramps here at this interchange. They are weaving between what traffic there is on the interstate. There is nowhere for them to go and no way to escape so I'm not sure what they expect to accomplish by continuing to refuse to stop for the troopers. It does appear to me that they are working in tandem. They follow each other's moves through traffic – almost with military-like precision. I see several cop cars lining the ramps and shoulders of the interchange as…

"Now, what the…? Oh, my G…

"Good Lord! Bill, did you get that? Tell me you got that!

"Ladies and gentlemen, a van – a red van – just raced up behind the three pursuing troopers and gunmen, uh -- they shot them! I mean, gunmen in the van started shooting at the troopers and they – I don't believe the troopers ever saw them and they were just wiped out. I saw a tremendous crash as one of the trooper's vehicles struck a line of cop cars along the shoulder. There's carnage everywhere! Uh, now that van is following the tankers and – and the gunmen are still shooting at the law enforcement officers set up along the interchange! Oh, my God!

"I – I…

"Stay with them – no, no! Stay with the tankers, Bill!

"Shit! Look there! Yes, I see it! Wait, there's another one over there, too!

"Yes, yes, stay with them. Jesus Christ! I can't believe what I'm seeing down there.

"The tankers are through the interchange! They're through! I – I...

"Folks, we are following the tankers as they continue toward Houston, but I don't know how to describe what I just saw. I estimate the trucks are now travelling at over seventy-five miles an hour. We are going to stay with them as they continue toward the city.

"Ladies and gentlemen, I've just witnessed the most terrible thing I have ever seen in my life! A red van, yes, a red van came up behind the Texas troopers who were chasing the tankers and at least two men in that van began shooting at the troopers. One trooper was taken out immediately while the other two tried to dodge the bullets, but very quickly they all crashed – one of them going directly into three or four cop cars waiting along the roadside.

"Now that van has accelerated and has gotten in front of the tankers and is now firing on any law enforcement they see. But – but then...

"That van was not alone. Two more red vans just showed up, seemingly out of nowhere. As the tankers drove through the overpasses, the two other vans came down the on-ramps and got behind the line of law enforcement vehicles taking up the chase. Gunmen in those vans then began shooting and the officers were caught between two sets of gunmen – and they were slaughtered. It was absolute devastation!

"Oh, my...

"The killers in the vans – oh, Jesus – they are right now shooting at not only law enforcement vehicles trying to pursue them, but they are also shooting at every civilian vehicle on the eastbound lanes of the interstate. It's horrible! They're shooting at everyone! They're causing massive crashes everywhere! These commuters have no idea what is coming from behind them and they are getting massacred!

"Stop! Get out of the...

"These poor drivers need to be warned. Jesus, no! It's a slaughter down there!

"It's clear to me that there's absolutely no possible way that any law enforcement can get anywhere near the tankers now! The entire interstate behind them is now clogged with dozens of massive vehicle crashes and pileups! There's nothing to stop them from..."

Jesse's skin glistened from a cold sweat that dripped from his forehead and nose. He slowly pulled the Texas flag bandana off his head and crumpled it up in his hand to wring out the sweat that soaked it. He ran his fingers through his curly hair. Raising his head he looked from left to right at all the familiar sights of his life. From birth Houston had been his home, and now a war that had been raging for centuries, a war that had pulled him across vast oceans to do battle in far-off desert sands had finally came here to his hometown.

He looked off to the south, across the concrete-lined banks of the White Oak Bayou, and saw the shaded green grass beneath tall cottonwood trees of Olivewood Cemetery. Its old grave markers rested tranquil in the shade, caressed by the soft Texas breeze. He and his wife had taken their three children to visit that cemetery just last year. He had wanted to show his girls the graves of their ancestors who were buried there, and how their family had deep ties to the long history of Texas. The old cemetery was the final resting place of many black slaves, and later the first black alderman and other notable black citizens of Houston. Jesse took great pride in being able to claim three blood relatives buried in that cemetery.

Jesse's familial lines had long roots that were sunk deep into the soil and spirit of south Texas. The Jaramillo blood in his veins represented at least one ancestor who had fought at the Battle of San Jacinto. The republic of Texas itself had been born amid the mesquite trees and arroyos with the sacrifice of blood, sweat and tears from Jesse's heritage.

Jesse took as much pride in being from Texas as he did in being an American. Staring at the city, his mind pictured it burning, with tall pillars of vile smoke rising high above the skyscrapers. He imagined his city looking wounded and violated like a dust- and smoke-covered Manhattan on 9/11. He envisioned the Angle of Death chuckling and gloating over the smoldering ruins while licking its lips as thousands more innocent people were killed. *No, not today! Never again!*

Right now, his wife was at work at the DMV downtown while his girls attended Sherman Elementary School, a short distance from their mother. His eyes stared lovingly at the tall gleaming buildings, massed into a tight cluster of spires, raising high into the sky above his family. A single tear rolled down his cheek as he reached up, took his rosary from the visor and bowed his head to pray.

He quickly crossed himself and then pulled the damp bandana back down on his head. He could not risk any sweat getting into his eyes to blur his vision. He draped the rosary around his neck. His one hand flipped the blinker lever on the steering column while his other shoved the gear-shifter into first. A faint column of black smoke escaped from the stack as he pulled off the shoulder, watching his mirror for traffic coming from behind.

A large section of road was clear behind him and he took the opportunity to enter the traffic lanes. His muscles pulled hard as he cranked at the steering wheel, and the heavily-loaded truck swung hard over, crossing all six lanes of the freeway until he completed a U-turn. He now accelerated along the center divider, facing west into eastbound traffic. He kept the truck hugged tightly against the divider to stay well inside the narrow emergency lane and out of the oncoming traffic lanes. His left leg and right hand worked in perfect rhythm as he shifted smoothly through the gears and swiftly picked up speed.

Jesse's eyes lowered to a photograph of his wife and three daughters that he kept taped to his dash, a sight he eyed for strength and clarity every day as he worked for their future prosperity. The loving, beautiful smiles beaming out, eternally frozen on the picture paper as they sat in the shaded park that was their favorite picnic place. They had stared happily into his camera that lovely day he remembered with so much happiness and joy. *I love you, babies. Daddy's going to see you're safe.*

He turned on his headlights and emergency flashers as his speed passed forty. A terrified trucker in a large cattle hauler blew his air horn as their mirrors passed within inches of one another. In the distance, not too far ahead, Jesse saw thin columns of black smoke rising above the freeway, apparently from the wrecks that the killers were leaving in their wake.

"....and as the remaining two Houston Police cars continue to battle heroically against the killers inside the last van, I'm still awestruck by the bravery of that officer, who must surely have died ramming into, and thereby taking out, the other two vans. His sacrifice has narrowed the gap that we are fighting against. These murderers obviously have no other intent than to crash these massive suicide bombs as deep into the city as they can.

"I hear more orders being issued over the police band and it sounds like they are trying to get city work crews organized and headed to the interstate ahead. It sounds like authorities are going to try to set up a crude road block made up of heavy equipment across the interstate closer to the city, but time is quickly running out. I just can't see how they can possibly get that equipment there in time to stop them. The last four miles of interstate are now filled with burning debris and the tankers are poised to go under the I-610 interchange as they continue to speed toward downtown. I..."

Ud-Daulah watched with grim satisfaction the traffic ahead as he maneuvered his rig, acting as the spearhead of the convoy. The other two tankers followed their leader's every move as he kept their path as straight as possible, slamming into other vehicles where necessary and knocking them out of the way. His men had gotten him close and he knew that nothing from behind could stop them now. His concentration was solely fixed on what lay ahead. Everything that these foolish kafirs had tried so far had failed to come close to stopping the convoy and its mission. As he maneuvered under the maze of suspended roadway, Houston was momentarily hidden from his view, but very soon he would have it in flames that would be visible to the entire world.

Meanwhile, a short distance away, glancing up, Jesse saw the news helicopter flying above the tangle of the I-610 interchange and knew things were about to go very fast, and he only had one chance at getting this thing ended successfully. Neither hesitation nor indecision could get in his way. *I have to do this right.*

The wide eastbound lanes of the freeway made a sweeping S-curve under the interchange and as two unsuspecting cars and a pickup truck came into view they saw the startling sight of Jesse's big blue Mack truck charging the wrong way at them. The shocked drivers, reminiscent of a school of fish, swerved in unison to their right, away from the speeding behemoth, completely unaware of the evil procession of charging tanker trucks in the curve right behind them.

In the lead tanker, Ud-Daulah saw the strange and unexpected swerve of the vehicles ahead of him and lifted his eyes to see what would have caused their movement. Amazement, then sudden despair as he instantly sighted the shining chrome grill and proud bulldog at the front of Jesse's 50,000 pound metal steed, now speeding toward him from less than a hundred feet away.

Like jousting knights they both quickly closed the dwindling distance between them. The Quds Force commander pulled at the wheel but the tanker's weight made the effort futile. Knowing it was too late, he tensed in terror as he realized his death was certain, and his dreams would die, too.

Each mammoth vehicle raced forward, colliding at over seventy-miles an hour as Jesse's and Ud-Daulah's eyes' met.

"Welcome to Texas," Jesse said as the vehicles struck.

The irresistible force met the immoveable object as 50,000 pounds of Detroit steel and Texas gravel plowed into the lead tanker. All four massive rigs crumpled into a mangled mass while 24,000 gallons of fuel was disgorged from all three ruptured tankers and dispersed into the air. It then erupted into a massive explosion that sent a gigantic fireball skyward, obliterating several concrete stanchions of the overpass. As the large columns collapsed, seven elevated sections of roadway fell into the enormous fire below.

Out of the explosion the ghastly apparition of a malevolent angel raised its sinister face above the Texas plain, high atop a thick, pitch-black column of smoke and fire. Its loathsome wings were made of roiling red and yellow clouds of searing flame and dense smoke that bowed menacingly forward. Tens of thousands of troubled eyes stared fearfully outward from their protected spires inside the vast city, shocked and frightened by the appalling sight.

The beastly shape slouched toward them with hateful, hungry intent as a large indignant flock of prairie crows circled like a crown of dark thorns around its head, squawking angrily at the chaotic disruption to their lives. Then vexed and completely defeated, the dreadful column was dismissed to memory as it was caught on the autumn breeze. Its awesome dark force was eventually scattered, impotently leaving a pall across the horizon.

Meanwhile, the funeral pyre of the newest martyred Son of Texas burned brightly, long into the dark night.

Book Three – THE EVENT

"It is possible to provide security against other ills, but as far as death is concerned, we men live in a city without walls."
Epicurus

*****

THE PLAINTIVE and incessant complaints of gulls drifted down from their hectic, circling flight above the fantail. Below them, the drifting container ship lounged quietly on the current. With its engines now silent, the only non-bird sounds came from its Iranian flag flapping lazily on the salty breeze and small white-capped breakers that lapped against the water line.

With large binoculars, Lieutenant Nadar ed-Din scanned the horizon and saw only two small fishing trawlers in the distance. Those boats matched the location of the blinking green contacts on the radar screens on the ship's bridge. The busy eastern seaboard shipping lanes had scant business on this momentous day and that pleased him. *We are free from any interference.*

As news of the successful strikes across America continued to stream out from the vessel's radio speakers, Din leaned forward and watched as his lead engineer and a technician completed their checks to the missile guidance and launch control systems. Din raised the satellite phone to his ear.

The two men on the other end of that call waited nervously for Din's order. Each man stood in the wheel house of his own merchant container ship, as all three vessels were now staged at differing points on the oceans of Earth. Lieutenant Ahmad Dulabi, aboard the MV Iran Tavastland, was three-hundred-fifty miles west of San Luis Obispo, California. The third commander, Lieutenant Hassan Bani-Sadr, was aboard the MV Iran Esharaghi, floating ninety-miles east-northeast of the rocky island of Minorca in the Mediterranean Sea.

Each ship had triumphantly delivered its Russian-supplied two-megaton warheads, installed within their Shahab-4 missiles. The Makeyev-designed MRBM launch platforms had been customized to fit inside the equally modified shipping containers during their

370

construction at the Bushehr terminal. During the ocean transport, nothing about those harmless looking containers hinted at the massive capabilities hidden inside. The ships appeared as just three more merchant vessels plying their trade upon the busy shipping lanes of the world. Once they had arrived at their current stations, the ship's crane had removed the welded tops to the containers and the missiles were raised and readied for launch. Each of the three nuclear-tipped missiles now sat, waiting, at an eighty-five degree angle. The heavy smell of oxidizer and grease floated in the air around the launchers.

As each ship had left Bushehr, the missile arming sequence had been initiated. That was an extremely dangerous thing to do, but had been necessary. The decision meant that the Islamic Republic would be protected against immediate and massive retaliation if the attack plans were compromised and the missiles discovered. If the ships were threatened with boarding from the military forces of either NATO or the United States, the ship's commander would detonate their weapon. This act would obliterate any evidence as well as kill some infidel scum. And since it was highly improbable that any intelligence service that might discover the operation would also be capable of identifying all three ships, it was almost guaranteed that one or more of the ships would be able reach their launch point unmolested, and any that were forced to detonate would act as an excellent distraction.

Din understood the necessity for the precaution, especially since it was one of the stipulations the Russians had demanded be in place. It was the ultimate precaution to ensure that they could never be associated with the attacks if the mission was a failure. Din felt it was unfortunate that without Russian and Chinese assistance, the entire operation would have never gotten this far, ending long ago. That irked Din mightily. *Very soon we will have no need of them.*

If they were discovered, President Ahmadinejad had prepared a cover speech, accusing the western powers of 'brutally' attacking 'innocent' merchant vessels. All nuclear explosions would be blamed on NATO and the Americans. Iran and her allies would accuse them of causing the explosions as a cover-up to make the Iranians appear guilty of attempting to obtain nuclear weapons. The western governments would know better but their domestic populations would fracture politically over the resulting confusion, and that should be enough political mayhem to halt any nuclear retaliation, especially with the Russians and Chinese running interference at the United Nations.

Din was confident that even if the entire flotilla were forced to sacrifice themselves before missile launch, and the mission were to

371

ultimately fail, the western populations would still be deeply alarmed and that would make it highly likely they would withdraw even further out of involvement and interest in the matters of Asia Minor and the Middle East.

Those populations would sink ever deeper into a mindset of severe vulnerability. This would cause ever greater isolationism and protectionism among their terrified masses. At the same time the other Muslim nations would be forced, by Iran's bold action and nuclear capabilities, to be ever more respectful and subservient to Persia's growing power and influence. The rise and spread of the next great Persian Caliphate would gain momentum and eventually expand toward the domination of all the Islamic nations. From Gibraltar to Malaysia, oil and other resources contained therein would fall under the control of the Persians. Then, isolated and unprotected by any western powers, Israel's demise would be assured.

The ships had left port innocuously, one by one, travelling the regular international shipping lanes. Din's flag ship, the Deyanat, had triumphantly sailed past two American and one British naval task forces, the USS Abraham Lincoln carrier group in the Indian Ocean and a USS Nassau led MARG in the Mediterranean. The last was the British HMS Illustrious carrier group, just three days ago during his transit of the Atlantic. Each time his men had yelled their victory cries after they successfully passed under the noses of the arrogant enemy fleets.

Din had marveled at how much brute strength his enemies had at their disposal, and yet, how poorly they used it. He well understood that all the force in the world was useless if the moral and political will was not there. If he had that power, even the atheistic Russians and Chinese would be on their knees praying to the Kaába. Nadar ed-Din was a man who had the strength of will necessary to use power like that very effectively. He looked forward to showing these complacent infidels, these timid and weak fools, the error of their ways. Soon, when they looked with tears upon the destruction that he had wrought upon their miserable lives, they would know deep inside their godless souls the extent of his great wisdom and their own pathetic weakness.

Taking in a large breath from the salty air he looked out with satisfaction. The long-awaited and momentous day was finally here. His racing heart drummed in his ears as his excitement rose. The culmination of his lifetime of planning, hard work, and sacrifice had finally paid off. He stood at the cusp of the world turning a page, and starting a new chapter in the book of world history. He would be that historic figure, the fulcrum that would turn that page, by taking his nation's nuclear sword and cutting out the beating heart from the arrogant west and feeding it down their screaming throats.

The great Salidin would not rank nearly as mighty as Nadar ed-Din in the future Shia-dominated world to come. He would be held in high esteem among all Muslims, maybe second only to the Prophet himself. No others would ever equal his accomplishments. The Supreme Leader had already commissioned a giant Masjid to be built in his honor on the flanks of the Alborz Mountains north of Tehran. Its construction would begin after his success today. Its gold-plated minarets would stand taller than the Milad Tower and be a place of solemn pilgrimage for every follower of Ali to worship in.

The engineer waved off the technician and looked up at Din, saying, "Done!"

Din smiled and brought his fist down on the handrail as the engineer climbed down from the launcher. Din turned to his men who stood at attention inside the wheel house, impatiently waiting for the launch. The moment had arrived. He lifted his fist into the air as he yelled the fire command into the phone as he pressed the fire switch

"Allahlu Akbar!"

The electrical circuit completed its route to the fuel igniter in one-one-thousandth of a second. The Shahab-4 rocket instantly streaked off the launcher, quickly reaching over 3,400 mph. It left behind a long white contrail of burned rocket fuel.

Din and his men bellowed with joy and jumped with excitement, praising Allah for their successful launch. Din yelled into the satellite phone, seeking confirmation from his fellow commanders that their launches had gone as well. For several seconds all he heard was a clamoring of voices, yelling joyously. The jubilation from his men softened as they watched him eagerly for news of their compatriots. Din loudly repeated his demands for launch confirmation. Finally, the other field commanders affirmed their success had matched his own.

The weighty consequence of the moment came crushing down on Din and his men, tears of joy and divine reverence poured down their faces. The will of heaven was done and nothing could stop the future, and the proud and arrogant would be laid low. They all dropped to their knees and began to fervently pray.

*****

THE FRIGATE, *D620 Forbin*, a French Horizon class warship, cruised leisurely at nine knots as it approached the last buoy marker at the harbor exit to the port of Toulon. The rosy, late-evening sky made the painted and picturesque hillside challis and villas on Mount Faron stand out brilliantly against the stone cliffs and olive trees. The old sixteenth-century stone fortifications of Fort Saint Louis overlooked a vast bay of sparkling blue waters. The small escort tug bobbed on the water next to the larger vessel, and standing in the doorway to his pilot house the harbor-master gave three short blasts on his air horn to salute and say farewell to his longtime friend. Gulls croaked and squawked their displeasure at the burst of rude noise as they trailed after the departing ship, hoping for cast-away scraps.

Captain Francis Ouelette waved goodbye to the older man and passed off piloting duties to the Officer of the Deck. He turned and strolled down the narrow halls into the darkened confines of the Combat Information Center (CIC). He believed, undoubtedly, that with the Americans being attacked so terribly today, that very soon his crew would be sent out to many more duty stations around the globe, and their training schedule must keep apace.

The French fleet had been downsizing their capitol ships for decades, but his ship was one of France's modern and sophisticated missile frigates, and even though it was smaller, the *Forbin* now completed duties that were once handled by the larger ships of the past.

They had recently returned home for refit and resupply after maritime security duties in Operation Enduring Freedom, in cooperation with the USS Eisenhower carrier group assigned to the Indian Ocean. Today the *Forbin* was leaving port for a high-speed engine r.p.m. test and the captain looked forward to cruising on the open sea on such an extraordinarily gorgeous Mediterranean evening.

Unlike her commander, the young naval officer Aspirant Camille Piercy sat unhappy and unenthusiastic in her chair inside the dimly lit CIC. She stared blankly at the two uninteresting screens in front of her. A green radar screen was to her right and a black sonar screen to her left. Beside her sat Sub-lieutenant Antoine Jouet, who, as her instructor, thumbed through the pages in the thick training manual, but he felt as sullen and miserable as she.

Her training assignments for the night would keep them both glued to the darkened room, staring at those screens for the next six hours. As one of the ships newly commissioned midshipmen, Camille was learning first-hand how each of the complex electronics within CIC operated, and she would be stuck there all night. The two young officers were going to miss the beauty of the early fall night as they were forced to endure the glum mechanical and electrical prison, its artificial air and cramped space feeling very much like a tomb. Then tomorrow they would be sleeping for their next night-shift while the blue waters shined below sunny skies. *Depressing.*

Captain Ouelette entered and quickly shut the door behind him to keep the brighter light from disturbing those inside. Making their unhappiness quickly evaporate from their faces, the two young officers greeted their commander warmly as he passed by. He had only taken two steps past them when all hell broke loose.

Dozens of blinking lights and buzzing alarms suddenly clamored to life while almost every computer screen came on and displayed rapidly changing words and numbers, causing Camille's heart to leap into her throat. The abruptly activated panels and electronics in front of her seemed to have a crazy sort of consciousness. She frantically watched it all in bewilderment, as if someone had rudely placed a smelly and crying baby in her lap. Her eyes quickly darted from left to right as she attempted to absorb the incoming data.

Jouet jumped in his seat, sending the training manual flying as he reached for the wall, to keep himself from tipping over onto his back.

"What did you do?" he screamed.

"Nothing, I did nothing! I don't know what's happening!" she screamed back excitedly. Her long blond ponytail swung wildly as she scanned the screens and panels.

As they tried to determine what had activated the alarms, the tactical officer and captain came running up behind them. Very quickly all four sets of eyes were drawn to the air defense radar screen. Shocked, silent, strangely curious, and becoming rapidly horrified they all stared at the impossible and unexplainable. A bright green blinking dot moved rapidly across the radar screen with accurate and terrifying readouts documenting its travel.

As the dot crossed the thin green line representing the French coastline, Jouet frantically adjusted the screen resolution to reveal a greater view of the surrounding European continent.

Captain Ouelette jerked at his tactical officer's shoulder.

"Man fire control! Get your ass to fire control, now!"

*****

SIMILAR TO Camille, Canadian Air Force Sergeant Greg Miller also sat amid a large bank of computer terminals. Every work day, for the past four months he had typed at those terminals while monotonously staring up at the twelve huge wall-mounted flat-screens that blanketed the far wall. His workstation was square in the middle

375

of the old NORAD Command Center that sat deep inside the hard granite rock of Cheyenne Mountain. Before today, he had thought that the most exciting thing he would ever do was cataloging Santa's holiday travels for the website in December.

The famously non-secret missile defense center for the entire North American continent was once holed-up inside these cavernous vaults under the eastern flanks of the majestic Colorado Rockies, due west of Colorado Springs. The NORAD complex had since moved to Peterson Air Force Base in 2006, but the facilities under the mountain were still manned as a back-up.

Unlike young Camille's radar screen that showed only one dot, the giant screens Greg stared at showed many more blinking lights, each one representing a single missile that was being methodically tracked by the multitude of military satellites, land-based radar stations, planes, and naval ships that fed information directly to the installation.

His screens showed a total of seventeen missiles in flight, three red ones and fourteen blue ones. There was one red dot that represented the same missile that Camille was watching fly above the European Alps. Then there was the red dot that had crossed the eastern coast of the United States and was now flying above the Appalachians, while the third red dot had crossed the west coast and now flew high over the Sierra Nevada range.

Meanwhile, across those same screens, Greg watched as eleven blue dots were converging toward, and very slowly catching up to, the two missile threats to North America, while three NATO blue dots converged toward the single missile above the Alps. Those blue dots represented air-to-air missiles launched to destroy the attacking weaponry.

The sudden and complex electronic game had existed for a mere thirty seconds, yet Greg was still trying to wrap his mind around what was happening. If not for the automatic responses that had been triggered inside the massive bank of super-computers that controlled allied missile-defense, there would be few, if any, speeding blue dots up on the screens. Greg was rapidly realizing that relying on human reaction speed for missile defense was a useless and pitiful endeavor.

Greg stared, transfixed, at the red blinking light that travelled over the California coastline and was now speeding high above the dry desert of central Nevada, directly above the lanes of scenic Highway 50. His eyes darted to the European map where another red dot was crossing over the city of Bern, Germany headed northeast. His gaze shifted to the last red dot as it cleared southern Maryland and was now a hundred miles above central West Virginia. A fast moving blue dot, from the missile defense arsenal around Washington, DC, had rapidly closed to within fifty miles of downing that threat.

Sergeant Miller pounded at the keys to his terminal as he attempted to extrapolate the location of origin for the incoming missiles. The atomic clocks that so precisely calibrated the digital time displayed on his screens read 16:38:41pm EST when the red dot over West Virginia stopped blinking forever, and every screen in front of Greg went dark.

*****

16:32pm EST UTC -5
Smith College
Northampton, MA

FRED THOMPSON stood at the back of the Wright Hall faculty lounge, before him several dozen students and faculty crowded in tightly next to one another. Everybody's attention was focused on watching two television sets at the front of the room.

The size, scope, and far-flung nature of the events had everyone in shock, and seriously taxed everyone's capacity to get a complete grasp on the information that streamed in. Several quick, bitter arguments had erupted over specifics. One person would claim to have heard something, another would dispute the information. But as the hard facts continued to trickle out and the extent of the devastation was confirmed, the initial shock and denial began to evolve into deep sorrow mixed with seething anger. Fred recognized another emotion being felt by most of the men and women in the room with him: fear. *They know their own lives are at risk in this war.*

The overwhelming scale of the attacks had shattered the multi-generational conception that, as American citizens on American soil, the United States was a safe and separate place from the devastating human-on-human barbarity that flourished in such large quantities elsewhere in the world. A couple of Americans killed by terrosists here and there, perhaps a few dozen, or maybe even on a terrible day, another 9/11 where some thousands died. Never could a Rwanda, Cambodia, or Bosnia happen here; not inside the United States of America.

As they all watched the on-going horror, there were not just a few thousand, but hundreds of thousands or more of their fellow Americans being effectively and rapidly slaughtered on American soil. And it was being done inside multiple major cities, all of which were supposedly well-prepared for this eventuality. A deep understanding spread through the little audience: they could each be the next victim

377

at virtually any moment the terrorists wanted to harm them, too, anywhere.

The people comprehended that all the fabled buildup of security, and the time, effort, money, and modification to their personal liberties that they had experienced since 9/11 had actually achieved only one thing, that they lived their lives in a delusional perception of safety based upon illusionary safeguards.

Moments ago the latest up-to-the-minute story told how another major attack had been thwarted in Houston. The attacks seemed to be rolling in one after another, with no apparent end in sight. Everyone felt that another major strike could come at any time, against anyone, anywhere across the nation. A tingle of trepidation flushed across Fred's skin and as he looked around him, he could see the apprehension in the eyes of most everyone in the room. More than once he saw a nervous glance out the window or a peering look over their shoulders, wondering if the next attack could be just outside the room. The media's talking heads were openly uttering words like martial law, and not just for California, but for the entire nation. The Terrorist Boogeyman was no longer just a cerebral threat to be intellectually debated, but it was an existential monster affecting everyone's personal welfare.

This new concern for personal security manifested itself in odd ways as each person yearned to become the most informed arbiter of their lives. This even showed in silly ways. It was no longer just an ideological debate to determine which news outlets gave out the best, the most informed, or the least-biased slants in their reporting. This debate morphed from being an ideologically-driven nuance into a bitter and personal dispute over one's personal safety.

A half-hour earlier an argument between two girls over which channel should be on the television had escalated into a hair-pulling, screaming, teeth-chipping, lip-splitting, eye-gouging girl-fight that left them both badly hurt and bleeding. After they were eventually separated, another student had retrieved a second television, and in minutes the technical geeks inside the room had the extra TV set up so that everyone could watch both television sets at the same time.

Presently, the screen on the right was set to CNN, where Wolf Blitzer and John King were working in tandem to shuffle through the mass of incoming reports and trying to disseminate information as quickly as it was received. The television on the left was set to Fox News, where Shepard Smith tried to orchestrate that network's reporting. Fred's ears absorbed every detail possible while desperately hoping for some news, any news, about the school in Colorado, and his daughter.

The terrible scenes of carnage in California worsened by the moment as more cameras were able to get into the areas of ruin. Every person in the room was glued to each word spoken, as the two channels strangely complimented each other in clarifying points of fact while showing similar but slightly differing angles of the disaster. Under the circumstances, feeling informed and up-to-date with information was the single cold comfort to those in the room.

Fred repeatedly glanced at his cell phone, hoping and praying that any second it would come alive with his daughter's voice, telling him she was safe, unharmed, and waiting for him. But he was sorely disappointed as minute by minute the phone continued its stubborn silence, deepening a dreadful fear creeping into his mind. He prayed that he would not be included in the ever-growing list of Americans who had lost their loved ones to cold-blooded murder today. He surmised that list was indeed rapidly expanding, arbitrary and pitiless.

The news from Colorado was understandably lower on the breaking-news food chain. If for no other reason, it was simply a matter of scale. The much larger catastrophes in California, and now in Texas, too, outweighed the school in sheer numbers of dead and injured. The bitterness of that jagged emotional pill was very hard to swallow. It was appallingly apparent to him that the rampage-shooting at schools around the world had obviously taken murdered children to a lower interest level for network executives, when compared to the scope of death occurring in California.

One meager consolation was that Kim's name was not been spoken as a confirmed death. What with Trinidad being eighty-miles from the nearest large city, with its own news crews, it would be awhile before they would get live coverage, so he kept what hope he could. So far there was nothing but amateur cell phone video of scenes from the school and the site of the IED explosions at a store downtown.

Fred knew Kim was very intelligent and a resourceful woman who would fight to the bitter last to survive. If there was even the slightest chance for survival, she would be alive.

A short time ago he bumped his morning flight out of Bradley International Airport to a seat on a flight leaving in only four hours. He hoped that the DHS did not ground all air traffic again, like what had happened on 9/11.

He had been invited to speak at the college by his good friend, Herbert Blunt, and minutes ago they had spoken on the phone. Herb was a professor of sociology here at the college and had been a close friend since the days they had attended boot camp together. Herb was currently busy assisting the administration in preparing to handle the fallout of the day's events on both the campus faculty and student body. Herb had tried to assure Fred that Kim would make it through.

"She's got powerful blood running through her veins. I tell you, Fred, there isn't a stronger person around than Kim. She'll make it okay."

"Thanks, Herb, you're the best."

"Hey, I'm just speaking the truth. Listen, I want to be with you right now, you know that, but I've got to stay up here for a bit. We're getting these lines to the phone banks open and I'm helping set up our campus grief counselors. But you come by and see me before you head to the airport, okay?"

"You bet, talk to you soon."

Presently, Fred watched as John King stood in the CNN Situation Room studio with Wolf Blitzer.

"....graphic parts of this footage have been edited by our producers here at CNN. But I must repeat my warning that this is very raw and violent video we are about to show you. If you feel that you or someone in your household should not see this video – please walk away from your television sets.

"This footage was obtained and then sent to us by a young man who used his cell phone camera to record it. This amazing and graphic video recording is of two very brave San Francisco policewomen. These courageous women were battling to save citizens from the terrorists attacking that city today. Additionally, this recording has captured how ordinary and unarmed citizens have entered the fight to survive and also protect their city. We at CNN feel this crude and graphic video must be broadcast to show every one of us just what kind of terrible ordeal our nation is experiencing. Roll the video."

The gathering in the faculty lounge stared, mesmerized, as the extremely shaky video from the small camera moved wildly on the television screen. The image was at once foreign, and yet familiar at the same time. The YouTube-feel of the video was reminiscent of footage from battlefields in distant countries like Sarajevo, Chechnya, Rwanda, Somalia, Syria, or Libya. But the detached feeling of watching some horrible event happening to faraway people was missing. Instead, a visceral and intensely personal recognition swept hearts and minds in the room: This occurrence was happening right here, on American soil, and the dead and injured were fellow Americans, friends, neighbors, or even family.

It showed the wreckage of the police car and Fedex truck at the corner of 2nd and Mission streets. Nearly a dozen citizens worked together to assist the horribly injured cop from the driver seat and render medical treatment to his grievous wounds. The gore of Officer Mary Lui's destroyed skull was pixilated, but was still plainly recognizable. Several people in the room groaned. Seconds later, the jumbled action on the scene got centered behind Marta and Shea as the videographer followed after them as they advanced toward the bus with rifles raised. Monotone explosions and screams came from the audio. The shaking camera became highly erratic as the gunfire erupted from the rifles of Major Al-Doleh and Abbas.

Pure pandemonium was visible as masses of terrified and frantic faces crossed the camera's lens. The cameraman was knocked to the pavement as screaming people fled the fusillade of bullets. Shea disappeared to the right as the cameraman got back to his feet and stayed with Marta as she lurched through the crowd and then hugged the wall, edging closer to the school bus. The massive fires at the Freemont Center and the Millennium Tower were visible in the distance.

Gunfire was closer now and the camera swung wildly in all directions, ending up on the pavement. The sound of the whimpering and cursing voice of the cameraman was loud as he crouched for protection. Bits of concrete blasted up from where bullets impacted mere inches away. The primitive terror in the man's voice was primal, and everyone in the room felt his terror as they sobbed and cursed.

The chaotic awfulness finally ended as the video steadied on a view of a wounded Marta, crawling across the sidewalk, a trail of blood following her. Marta's face grimaced in pain as she tried to staunch the gruesome, gaping wounds in her pulverized thigh. More bullets careened off the sidewalk next to her head, causing her to instinctively roll with her wounded leg flopping miserably.

Bizarre noises of yelling, screaming and gunfire mixed with an odd, crashing bang that was followed by the sound of shattered glass. The cameraman rose above the car and captured the sight of Bruce hanging out a window several floors up a building, shaking his fists and giving the finger while he screamed challenges to the terrorists behind the bus. Bullets impacted the building around him as powdered concrete, shattered glass, and debris erupted around the window and he disappeared back inside.

The video swung back to Marta's face, covered in sweat and matted hair, frozen in fear, anger, and determination as she attempted to stand, only to fall awkwardly face-first onto the concrete. She remained motionless as people in the room moved to the edges of their chairs, tilting toward the television. Her trembling arms pushed her body upward as a cry of agony escaped her mouth. Her shaking hands grasped her rifle, first raising it, and then planting it barrel down onto the concrete. With a herculean effort she gained her feet on swaying, wobbling legs and began to stagger forward as blood from her wounds soaked her clothes.

Many of the affluent girls and boys of the tier-one school sat glued to the action of the television sobbing, while others who sat next to them glared angrily with gritted teeth. A skinny girl in a jumpsuit, with her knees pressed up against her chest, repeatedly tapped her fist against her leg as tears streamed down her face. She softly mouthed the words – "go, go, go." The whole room began mouthing her mantra as they all watched the wounded officer staggering forward into the fight.

Marta reached the grill to the bus and leveled her rifle at the killer lying supine on the street before her. The camera, held over her shoulder, gave a view of Shea standing over another terrorist at the far end of the bus. The remains of a shattered computer and monitor were scattered across the street, while a bloody, dazed and forlorn boy stumbled down the sidewalk, holding a bloodied skateboard loosely from his thin fingers.

For Fred the most riveting sight contained in the video was the seething hostility emanating from the one good eye of the terrorist at Marta's feet. A feeling of deep enmity was emitted like a laser directly at everyone watching the video. As Marta ordered him to comply he produced his detonator switch, and several gasps were heard throughout the room as they all realized what they were witnessing. Marta pressed her rifle barrel into the flesh of his face and mass of reddish pixels did nothing to hide from the viewers what happened when the killer's head exploded.

Harsh, angry cheers of victory erupted from the crowd as justice was delivered to the evil creature. But those grimly triumphant emotions were brutally extinguished when the other officer did not dispatch her captive so quickly. His vest detonated, violently rocking the scene as the cameraman fell behind the bus. Numerous quick and erratic frames follow with grunting, stumbling, and cursing that eventually end with a view of Marta lying broken and bleeding in the street. Desolation invaded the room as they all stared at the haggard hero who lay helpless in the middle of Anthony Street. Marta's bloodied face looked directly at the audience as she fainted and went limp.

The frame stayed frozen on Marta for several seconds as the network let the impact of the video sink in. Then John King's voice, loaded with graveled emotion:

"That, my fellow Americans – that is what we are facing on this day of murder and death, brought to our shores by a cadre of vicious murderers. I understand that it was a graphic experience we just showed you, but all I can say is that we <u>had</u> to bring that footage to you. These brave citizens and those law enforcement officers who are fighting and dying as we speak deserve nothing less from us. We feel we must broadcast their fight to you so that you may all bear witness to what we, as a nation, are experiencing."

"Deeply harrowing and disturbing, John. That is very remarkable footage indeed."

"Yes, Wolf, and I want to let our audience know that as far as we know, that woman officer that you saw at the end of that footage was removed alive. We have reports that she was transported by citizens from that terrible location and taken to a hospital some distance away from the violence. We pray for her survival and her recovery from her horrific wounds."

"Yes, yes, John – we pray for her safety and quick recovery. I again apologize for the extremely graphic nature of that footage, ladies and gentlemen. But we felt that today's news is of such grave importance that we could not edit the gritty reality of the violence occurring. And wow, that was absolutely amazing footage sent in to CNN by that young man! His bravery in capturing that video is reminiscent of the combat cameramen of World War II. Incredible.

"Now, I want to cut away from that story and quickly move on to other breaking news we have just received here in the Situation Room. CNN is now confirming that the airspace above San Francisco has been closed to all civilian air traffic. The Department of Homeland Security has ordered an FAA ban on all non-military or government flights. That ban has been placed on a four-hundred nautical-mile radius around the San Francisco Bay area. Our local affiliates, who have helicopters in that area and who were broadcasting the video we have been showing you, have all been ordered to leave the area immediately. The only air travel the government will allow within the air space is military, medical rescue, and emergency management flights. John, what do you make of this?"

"Well, Wolf, like we were talking earlier, this has been expected for several hours now. I'm somewhat surprised it took this long to have the order come out of the Department of Homeland Security."

"Yes, John. We have also learned that by an extraordinary order from the president himself – the Department of Homeland Security has directed the Department of Defense to shut down the maritime shipping lanes and all marine traffic in and out of the San Francisco Bay. They have stationed two US Coast Guard ships – the cutters Boutwell and Sherman are assigned to patrol the entrances to all inner-harbor areas.

"Our understanding is that all ships currently inside the harbor have been ordered to stay docked and that any movement within the waters of the bay is to be done under the direction and supervision of the Coast Guard. The Department of Homeland Security operations center has also issued orders for the Coast Guard to commandeer and press into service all ships and other marine vessels, as well as their crews, to assist in the rescue efforts, and also the suppression of any further terrorists acts in both Oakland and San Francisco. You know, for me, the most notable thing concerning that order is the phrase – press into service. That makes me feel the shocking reality of this terrible day all the more keenly, John."

"I know, Wolf. It's hard to fathom the extent of the damage done to these two cities, and to the psyche of our nation, from these attacks. And let us not forget just how narrowly we avoided the same catastrophe in Houston. There, the fires still rage at the site of the collision on Interstate-10.

"As yet we still do not know the name of the patriot in that dump truck who finally stopped those tankers by sacrificing himself. Right now the death toll in Houston stands at a confirmed ninety-five people, mostly law enforcement and motorists along I-10, motorists who were arbitrarily executed by the terrorists as they made their suicidal dash for the city.

"As those poor civilians were being cut to pieces by the terrorists, the wreckage left behind formed a nearly impenetrable wall of burning obstacles that had made any pursuit of the tankers virtually impossible. I cannot begin to imagine the destruction and death that could have resulted in Houston if those tankers hadn't been stopped by that courageous truck driver."

"If I may interject, John, we have breaking news here in the Situation Room. CNN has received tentative numbers on the confirmed death toll in Oakland, and they are at a devastating testament to the hardship we are facing today. A total of 13,545 people confirmed dead so far. I tragically fear that those figures will rise dramatically as rescue personnel get farther into the heart of that city. I cannot help but to shudder at the sights they must be seeing as they continue making their way closer to where the epicenter of the devastating blast *occurred, and unfortunately, where many bodies may simply have been vaporized, forever lost."*

"A thought that was unimaginable to me when I awoke this morning, Wolf. The California Governor's office in Sacramento, where Governor Brown has instituted the State's command center, estimates the death toll from the daytime population of downtown Oakland may exceed 100,000. That also does not take into account the people still fighting for survival in San Francisco. There CNN has another confirmed death toll of 4,670 people."

"Wolf, we have reports that there are still at least three active terrorist cells of armed gunmen, one at the Westfield Centre Mall. That group is attempting to break out of a police cordon. There is another group of gunmen reported to be roaming the area near Post and Market Streets, deep in the financial district. And a third group that may soon be wiped out, near the collapse of the building near the Bay Bridge. We are also looking at the six buildings currently burning in downtown along Mission Street. I pray we do not see another complete collapse there like we saw at One Rincon Hill, an hour ago. The magnitude of this day's destruction is absolutely horrifying!"

"I have a hard time getting my mind around the numbers, too, John. It's horrible! I do want to let our viewers know – regarding those groups of gunmen still at large in San Francisco – there is some good news for the people of that stricken city. While the courageous policemen and firemen continue to bravely resist the terrorists they will soon be assisted by units from the United States Army base at the Presidio, in Monterey. The army has a school there called the – uh, the Defense Language Institute Foreign Language Center. It is where they teach soldiers to speak foreign languages. Luckily, there were three Alpha Detachments of Army Special Forces attending that school.

"Uh, this statement I have in my hands from the Department of Defense says that two of the Alpha teams were Companies B & C of the 10th Special Forces Group 1st Battalion, and the third Alpha team was Company B of the 19th Special Forces Group 3rd Battalion. All of those fine men have been flown by helicopter to a police command post in the downtown area. They have been sent to assist civilian law enforcement with neutralizing these terrorists."

"Thank God for small miracles, Wolf. I believe that this is the first time that active-duty military has been deployed in battle within our nation's borders since...."

Fred's head spun as his ears picked up the word Trinidad coming from the voice of Shepard Smith on the other television set.

"....Colorado is the scene of the fourth terrorist attack, so far, spreading mayhem and death across our nation today. We are expecting to have a video crew from our affiliate KXRM out of Colorado Springs, at the scene of the school massacre, any minute.

"It's very hard to say that any particular one of these attacks today is any worse than another, but I must admit – this one at the school in Colorado is the single most disturbing and tragic story I have ever delivered as a broadcaster in my twenty-five year career. Tragic, horrible, sad – there is not a single term I can think of that would ever be able to encompass the, the very wrongness of this attack on innocent school children. We have seen this type of tragedy in our schools before today, but this is so steeped in malevolence and pure evil that it surpasses all others. And I do not speak of just numbers of dead and injured. For me, this is a walk in the sorrow of hell itself.

"The antiterrorism experts have been warning us for many years, in the United States and elsewhere around the globe, that our schools were a highly-desired target for Al Qaida and other such terrorists. Well – today, the terrorists, apparently modeling this attack in Colorado after another school attack that occurred in 2004, a horrendous attack that happened in a small community in North Ossetia, Russia. We know the name of that small town of hard working, good salt-of-the-earth people – Beslan. Beslan is now a name synonymous with misery and sorrow. A school was once there. That school was also attacked by a group of terrorists who wanted to brutalize the innocence and destroy hope – all to make a vicious and cruel statement to the rest of us around the world. The same sort of butchery that the terrorists used on that sleepy town was today unleashed on another small, unsuspecting, and innocent community of good people – Trinidad, Colorado.

"The tale of two towns, separated by great distance – almost on opposite sides of the planet. They were separated by language, culture, and country – but now they are to be forever linked by tragedy, murder, and the loss of innocence life. We'll have that story for you as soon as our local affiliate's crew gets online – stay with us. Now we go back to giving you the latest we have on the atrocious situation in California.

"I want to start out our Fox News team coverage with Adam Housley reporting with fast breaking news from the California Emergency Management operations building that is located in an old and small air force base in a suburb of Sacramento. Adam – I understand the State's emergency operations center has released some new and starkly devastating news, at that."

The reporter stood in a packed parking lot where dozens of uniformed police chiefs, sheriffs, fire chiefs, and highway patrol commanders were deeply engrossed in discussions. Other emergency personnel, wearing fluorescent vests, milled about in the background outside the cobalt blue two-story building that represented the state-of-the-art in emergency management operation. Along with the many California law enforcement and emergency management personnel, there were also numerous military uniforms visible. The reporter appeared disheveled and slightly out of breath as he held his microphone and DHS papers.

"Shepard, as these bulletins keep rolling out from the California EOC I have a hard time grasping the magnitude of the news. You hear one piece of almost unbelievably horrible news, and then it is immediately followed up with an even worse piece of news. It is emotionally crushing to see and hear what the extent of the devastation is. This bulletin, released just moments ago by the EOC, gives us some confirmation on known infrastructure damage, numbers on confirmed dead and injured, and also on how the existing command structure is being organized and instituted for the cities of Oakland and San Francisco for the foreseeable future.

"It follows like this, Shepard – first of all, they are confirming what we ourselves have suspected from the video of the blast zone in Oakland. The epicenter of the blast, and evidently the target where the terrorists detonated their weapon of mass destruction, and yes, the EOC is now using the term weapon of mass destruction. That weapon was indeed detonated on or near Clay Street, next to the Federal Building.

"They are calling the weapon a fuel-air mixture – or thermobaric device, which used either a tanker truck of propane or natural gas as the main explosive material. The extent of the blast is most evident from the aerial footage we obtained before the air space was closed to non-military uses. But the EOC is confirming that the following landmarks have been completely leveled: A, the Federal Building, B, City Hall, C, the Oakland Convention Center, D, the Pacific Renaissance Plaza, E, Lincoln University, as well as all of City Center Plaza. They are also confirming that several sections of I-980, the Grove Shafter Freeway, have completely collapsed.

"Those specific areas are listed as complete losses that have been obliterated or have suffered complete structural collapse. The extensive damage that radiates out past that immediate epicenter extends out to include virtually everything inside a circumference

387

extending from Lowell Park, to Lake Merritt and then follows I-880 around to Grand Avenue.

"Inside of the epicenter, rescue crews have not been able to penetrate very far, as yet. When they do, the EOC states casualty totals are expected to spike dramatically. As for the numbers of people confirmed dead and injured at this time, the EOC has issued the following terrible figures: 14,739 confirmed dead, most of which have not been identified yet. The number of critically injured stands at 22,340 with a far larger but as yet undetermined number of lesser injured. All critically injured are being sent to Mcafee Coliseum where the entire parking lot and stadium structure are designated, temporarily at least, as the major medical care center for the Oakland disaster. The neighboring Oracle Arena is now designated the temporary morgue for that city."

"I'm afraid the end result of today's deadly attacks on our nation will be far worse than any estimation that can be made at this point, Adam. Tell us, what is the government out there saying about the future daily operations of the cities? What emergency structure have they decided on at this time?"

"Shep, the EOC and Governor Brown are officially declaring martial law throughout the state, effective immediately. They believe that the Oakland mayor and his staff, the city council and their staff, and most all department heads and almost all municipal employees have been killed inside the epicenter of the blast. This is believed to have occurred during a citywide meeting to discuss budget shortfalls. That large meeting was being held at City Hall and that building is a complete loss. The EOC is stating that the entire city administration and its infrastructure have been completely decimated. No physical administration or any staff there, whatsoever, still exists.

"The EOC has ordered that all Oakland City government responsibilities are to be organized and administered out of Sacramento for the foreseeable future. Right now the National Guard has been put in charge of security and infrastructure inside the entire bay area and is working in tandem with the governor's office. The guard will soon be in command of the entire state and all government entities until further notice.

"The administration of Mayor Edwin M. Lee is still intact and operating effectively out of San Francisco's City Hall at this time. But it is still under complete lockdown until the situation on the ground, with terrorist gunmen still at large inside the city's financial districts, is eliminated. But even they will still be under the overall direction of the military along with the rest of the state per that martial law decree.

"Accordingly, the main issue that must be addressed first in San Francisco is the containment and mitigation of the fires that are raging there. Those fires have now spread to between eight and twelve separate high-rise structures that are now fully engulfed. We are now forced to learn the extent of that fire from the military since our flight crews have been grounded. But there are multiple collapses that are considered to be imminent. Of course, the sites of the three building collapses that have occurred thus far have become secondary to the buildings with ongoing fires.

"The military is taking charge of all terrorist suppression, firefighting efforts, rescue efforts, and all other emergency management efforts inside the city. It appears, Shep, that the problems here will dwarf the challenges faced in New York after 9/11, and it is prompting the federal authorities to take charge statewide."

"What an unforgettably tragic day, thank you, Adam. I know that what you are reporting is hard for you, too, but we need to get this information out. Stay with me, Adam, as I bring into our discussion Mr. Welsh.

"Ladies and gentlemen, here in the studio I have Doug Welsh, former Emergency Management Coordinator for Prince William County in Virginia. Mr. Welsh, I am hearing from some experts who say they are very concerned about the propagation of the fires in the city center. They feel it is almost a foregone conclusion if, as is forecast, these southeasterly winds off the Pacific continue to increase. Tell me, has the EOC made any comments or statements to you regarding how they plan to stop or mitigate these fires before they face the possible loss of the entire downtown districts?"

"The people I know at the EOC have not made any such statements directly to me related to those concerns, Shepard. And to be quite frank, what I am getting in off-the-record comments from those people is that decisions that were unthinkable not very long ago, are quickly becoming realistic scenarios. As the evolution of this tragedy unfolds and the extent of destruction becomes apparent, the decisions these people may have to make are terrible.

"Seriously, Shepard, hearing the emotional stress in their voices, and knowing how these EOC operations run, I truly feel sorry for these old colleagues of mine. They must be getting punch-drunk. Not only are these people seeing the casualty figures first, but they must then carry on with decisions that affect so many people still living and desperately needing help. And I must say to the American people that these people at the EOC are being traumatized and brutalized in their own terrible way by those hard decisions.

"What I can tell you is this: they are very worried that those winds may indeed cause the loss of many more structures and precipitate what is known as a firestorm. A firestorm much like that glimpsed during the fire in the Oakland suburbs back in 1991. You may remember that fire engulfed almost four thousand homes and apartment buildings. These fires today, they are locked within the tight confines of a dense urban setting and could result in a biblical level of disaster!

"The discussions at the EOC are centered on ways to try and make effective fire breaks inside the city. This action would be similar to how it is done with fighting large forest fires – by flying in aerial water tankers and drenching the main streets around the burning structures that have already been deemed a loss."

"Deemed a loss? What exactly are you saying, Mr. Welsh?"

"I am not speaking for or defending the EOC in Sacramento, or the military either, Shepard. But I certainly believe the heat of these fires and the ongoing collapses of these buildings are on the verge of starting a conflagration within the confines of the city. Normal fire suppression methods simply cannot stop this. And just like the fire-bombed city of Dresden, we could see a huge portion of San Francisco destroyed in a resulting uncontrolled inferno."

"Historically, almost the entire city of San Francisco burned to the ground once before. That happened after the great quake of 1906. The city of that age was a mostly wooden city, this one is largely steel, concrete, and glass, so how can that possibly happen in this day and age?"

"All of those buildings are filled with flammable material and the extreme heat necessary to begin the inferno is already being supplied from the existing fires. If these winds pick up to the thirty-plus-knot speeds that are being forecast – I'm sorry, but it is basic physics from there if there are no effective firefighting efforts put in there."

"Good Lord."

"Shepard, there is the possibility that they might be able to create a containment around the fires by using the aerial tankers. By using large aerial water drops they may be able to isolate, slow or even completely halt the spread of the conflagration. But, unfortunately, the second they do start with that strategy they are by default writing off anyone on the ground who has not yet been evacuated. People could be hurt or killed by the falling water. But most sickeningly, those people caught inside those drops, on the ground or in the burning structures, are completely on their own."

"But, Doug, I – wait.

390

"Doug, Adam, stay with me, please, I will be returning to you two momentarily. But, right now I have been informed that we are finally receiving video from Trinidad, Colorado."

Fred felt a shock of anxiety shoot from his feet to the tip of head as goose bumps broke out all over his skin. His shoulders tensed dramatically.

"Ladies and gentlemen, I'm sorry, I know how important our current discussion is but we will now be transferring our news away from California to receive an update on the terrorist attack at the school in Colorado. I am now speaking with KXRM reporter Daniel Chavez. He is standing with Gloria Alvarez who is the Emergency Management Coordinator for Las Animas County. That is the county that Trinidad is the county seat of. They are both standing on the grounds of the very school that was the site of the assault earlier, the seventy-two year old El Moro School."

The screen suddenly showed two people, a nervous reporter and a squat, plump Hispanic woman whose eyes were puffy and swollen. Her hands unconsciously tugged and pulled at a wad of torn tissue paper that was scrunched into a ball in her fist. While she had been obviously traumatized and her sullen appearance evoked emotions of deep sadness, her back was held straight and rigid. Fred saw she was not defeated, deflated, or broken. Anger and defiance burned behind her sharp eyes as she waited, resolute, for questions.

The school's immaculately manicured lawn and tall rust-colored brick walls of the administration building were in the background. Barely noticeable whiffs of smoke escaped from several upper windows. Looking closely at the grass, Fred observed what he thought were reddish smears, each one marked with little pink surveyor flags that fluttered atop thin metal rods, planted like flowers across the grass. *Jesus, there are so many.* Yellow crime scene tape was dancing in the wind, tied and woven around trees, posts, and cars in an attempt to isolate the carnage from the non-carnage.

In the distance sat dozens of cop cars, fire trucks, and ambulances near a large crowd of people who stood staring and crying as cloth-draped gurneys were wheeled into waiting vehicles. Hands were held over mouths while tears flowed, and the local people surveyed the horror that had been wrought on their community. A group of nearly a dozen burly policemen, dressed in their SWAT gear, holding helmets and rifles were speaking with four state troopers wearing their wide brimmed Smokey Bear hats. One of the troopers, with an immaculately pressed uniform and a lot of shiny brass that glinted in the sun, looked toward the camera and began to walk quickly across the grass toward it.

Fred's eyes were drawn to the caravan of gurneys coming from the building in the background. Many had blood-stained sheets draped over small bodies. But then his attention was drawn to one that was being rapidly pushed by the others, with a female EMT holding aloft an IV bag. The wheels of the bed bounced and jostled the rider. A thin female arm fell dangling below the sheet. Fred's heart leapt into his throat; the skin of the arm was black. *Kimberly!*

"Daniel, can you and Mrs. Alvarez hear me okay?"

The reporter's head bounced like a bobble-head doll as he replied quickly.

"Yes, Shepard. We can..."

(16:38:41pm EST)

ALL AT once, dozens of overhead fluorescent light bulbs popped, showering shattered glass along with sparks down on top of the people below. The room went dark and the televisions blank and silent, with the only light coming in through small windows. Startled cries came from around the room and adjacent hallway as more light bulbs popped down the hall.

Many students jumped to their feet while covering their heads. Fearful voices asked, "Are they here? Are we being attacked?"

Tension built and a lone voice bellowed, "Run, get out!"

Instantaneously, the individual people gathered inside the room morphed into a frightened herd that broke for the doors. As people started to violently shoulder each other at the exits they succeeded only in making a human dam. Panic sank its talons deep into people's hearts as two girls got knocked to the floor and were about to be trampled under the stampede when suddenly, a deep and booming baritone voice burst like a flood from the back of the room.

"Knock it the fuck off! No one is attacking the school." Fred yelled with a sharp tone of irritation.

People froze in mid-flight, their eyes darting to and fro. A doubtful young male voice came from the far corner.

"How do you know?"

The whites of Fred's eyes glinted in the dim light as he turned toward the timid boy and spoke low and slow.

"Shut up. That was a large power surge – not an explosion. Someone from the faculty, get your ass out there and start checking breaker boxes."

Everyone stared wide-eyed, sheepish and silent at the large pragmatic man who had just ended their moment of blind panic. The faint whir of motor-driven fans slowing mingled with chuckles of chagrined embarrassment as the assembled group of students and faculty regained their composure. People helped the fallen girls who indignantly dusted themselves off and rubbed at sore hips and shoulders. The voices across the room quickly melded together into a quiet roar of questions and comments as they began to move and break apart, seeking out their lives again.

As the would-be mob changed back into thinking adults, Fred's emotions sank to his shoes in response to the disheartening loss of electrical power at such an important moment. *That was Kim! I know it.*

The lost opportunity to learn something about his daughter's fate was disheartening, but he did have some news. *There was an IV bag. I saw it! I know I saw it! She's alive!*

He raised his eyes and looked in vain at the two silent televisions, wishing they would suddenly spark back to life. Finally, after a few moments of disappointment he turned away, shaking his head.

"Damn," he muttered.

As he was about to leave the room a skinny girl who had been sitting cross-legged in a chair off to his right cursed at her laptop. Until the power was lost she had been busily typing, posting entries on blogs while watching the news come in. Now she tapped on the blank flat screen of her computer with a puzzled expression.

"What the hell is wrong with you?" she asked.

A pimple-faced teen stood near the window behind her as he held his cell phone up to the light, looking dejectedly at the dark screen with squinting eyes.

"Damn thing! First I lose my signal and now the damn battery, too?" he said to himself.

Several girls who stood next to a now-dark vending machine busily discussed their own non-working phones as they handed them around to one another.

A blond in a red track suit complained, "….was talking to my dad, you know, about my Uncle Ben. Like, who works in Berkley, right? Then, like, it all of the sudden, it just – like, you know – quit. I have no tones – like, what the hell, you know? I don't have a screen anymore. Like, what's going on?"

"I know. I don't get it. If the power goes out at the cellular tower, like it did here, it wouldn't shut down our phones, too, would it?" asked another girl.

A blond in blue shorts looked at her incredulously. "There's no way power in the phone could be affected by the tower going down. That's stupid, Angela! The government is doing something, I think. They don't want us to be able to know anything, you know, so we will still be in the dark about what's happening."

Something bad moved inside Fred's chest. Like water being absorbed by parched soil, a nauseous feeling of dread was absorbed into Fred's gut. His eyes roamed, taking notice of more people having perplexed expressions and reactions to more strangely dead and now useless electronic devices, all independent of the electrical grid.

He slowly, almost reluctantly, lifted his hand and looked at his Blackberry. Dark. He started pushing buttons but nothing responded to his commands. He stopped and pulled his tote case behind him into the hallway. The hall was moderately lit by sunlight coming from the glass doors at the entrance, and he quickly walked that direction. Once there, he pulled his laptop out of the carrier and attempted to turn it on. Nothing.

He noticed a very faint odor and lifted the computer up to his nose and caught the faint but unmistakable bitter-acrid smell of burned-out electrical components. The queasiness that was building in his belly now shot a sharp pang of fear surging through his body. His heart began stammering wildly with poignant anxiety. He glanced up at a passing male student wearing a digital sports watch.

"Excuse me, son, excuse me."

The young man stopped.

"Yeah?"

"What kind of a watch do you have?"

He gave Fred a quizzical expression and lifted his arm, glancing at his watch as if he did not remember.

"Uh – uh, a Casio G-Shock. Why?"

Fred nodded slowly as he looked down at his shoes and asked in a sullen and quiet voice.

"Can you tell me what time it is, please?"

The young man shrugged and raised his watch, squinted, brought the watch closer to his face, tilted it as he pushed one button after another, and then looked back at the watch.

Finally he exclaimed, "What the hell?" He looked at Fred suspiciously, asking, "Is this some sort of trick?"

Fred looked up with sad, depressed eyes at the irked young man.

"I take it you can't tell me what time it is?" he muttered glumly.

"This isn't a day to screw with somebody, mister. There are people dying today. What did you do to my watch? How did you stop it from working? What are you trying to pull?"

Fred slowly stood and the skinny young man quickly realized the black man was about seven inches taller and outweighed him by almost one hundred pounds. Suddenly nervous, he took two steps back. Meanwhile, Fred shoved away from the wall with his shoulder blades and stood looking down. He raised his own watch; it was a silver colored Mavado that had been a present from Kim on his fortieth birthday. The thin second-hand sat motionless and the tiny light failed to work when he depressed the button.

He gave a sad smirk.

"Funny, mine doesn't seem to work, either. That sucks, doesn't it?"

Intimidated but not backing away anymore, the young man asked, "Uh, really, dude? What did you do to my watch?"

Without asking Fred reached forward and firmly grasped the stranger's arm and brought his watch up to examine it. The man squirmed but felt the strength in Fred's grip and did not try to pull away. Fred examined the non-functioning watch and then released the arm, which the young man retracted immediately.

"I didn't do anything to you or your watch. I just wanted to know the time," Fred said without enthusiasm, as he turned and walked away.

Leaving his travel case and useless laptop sitting on the floor, he pushed through the doors and stepped out into the bright sunlight. Thoroughly depressed and miserable, he slowly started walking across the campus. The flummoxed young man continued staring at Fred's departing back as he tried to figure what the joke had been and how the strange man had done it.

Fred's mind swam in a pool of anguish. *An EMP! God, no!* Moments ago he could not have fathomed that the day's bitter news of multiple attacks across the nation, chocked-full with the slaughter of thousands of children and innocent people could get worse. But his mind quickly realized that it had just gotten far worse, by an order of magnitude.

Kimberly is alive, I have to believe in that. Her strength and tenacity had somehow helped her survive the murderous attack on the school. *But she's injured. How bad?*

There was simply no way for him to know how badly she had been injured, and now, if an EMP strike on America had actually occurred, what medical attention would she get? *What medical attention would anyone get?* He knew she had all of the qualities necessary to survive if given any chance at all. *But injured and alone?* Soon there could be a lot of desperate and hungry people all around her, and he did not know how she could survive then, especially if she were severely wounded.

She had the natural beauty, quick wit and spirited perseverance of her mother, Eva. Fred and Kim had lost Eva only a year ago, after a long and bitter five-year battle with thyroid cancer. Fred had been blessed to have married such a good woman.

Eva was a person who could stand waist-deep in the fiery lake of hell and stare unflinching into the face of the devil, intimidating the dark prince himself with her strength of spirit. Eva had taught him how true dignity looked and had been the solid rock upon which he had leaned at the very time the cancer had eaten her alive from within. Fred knew his Kimberly had those same qualities in abundance, and he prayed that her strength of mind and body would be enough until he could get to her side.

He had hoped to be in Colorado this evening, holding Kim before midnight. But it was now apparent that everything in the world had lost all guarantees and that he might not see the face of his beautiful girl for many days, weeks, or possibly even months. *What if she dies before I get there?* The sudden and unwanted thought of her lying dead in a morgue somewhere appeared, a rotting corpse left unattended on an abandoned autopsy table. *No! I cannot think that! I can never think that again!* Despair filled his heart as a splitting migraine seemed to drill a hole through his head. He squinted at the bright sun while rubbing at his temples and praying his rental car still worked.

*****

16:23pm EST UTC -5
34,225 ft above Pittsburgh
United Flight 346
Baltimore to Kansas City

JIMMY MADISON loved the idea of flying. He just wanted it to be done like superheroes did it, no planes, just flying. For him, the reality of actual flight through the sky inside a plane, well, that just sucked. The part he disliked most was the utter boredom. Sitting in one place for an extended period of time was, like for all young boys, mentally excruciating. But the daydream of flying in the sky without a plane, that was far different. And to let his mind wander away to that realm of make-believe, a place he dearly loved to go, was the only way to get through these long flights. Sitting at the window and watching the puffy white clouds outside made it easier for him to pretend he was one of his comic book heroes, flying off to his next great adventure.

In his imagination he could be Superman, bravely flying to the rescue all the people being hurt in Oakland and San Francisco. There he could smash the bad men with fists of steel and quench the fires with icy breath. His fertile mind allowed him to live in a world where he did great deeds, stopping the bad and saving the good. But he had spent very little of the last hour imagining himself as a hero. Forgetting about the boring flight today had been very easy to do, but it did not involve Superman.

His mother Iris sat in the middle seat next to him, listening to Journey, her favorite hair-band, on her IPod. She had learned well from past flights that if Jimmy got stuck in a middle seat, or even worse, in the aisle seat, he hated life for the duration of the flight. And quite simply, that would mean Iris would also hate life for the duration of the flight. So he always got the window seat and she planted her IPod buds in her ears and drifted away within herself, cramped between her son and whatever stranger was sitting in the aisle seat. That allowed Jimmy to sit quietly, contentedly daydreaming out the window for hours, and not being a pain in her ass.

She was very relieved that he was not fidgeting today. It had already been a very long and sad day that she wanted to have gone. The terror attacks were just terrible. She could not even try to wrap her mind around what was happening out in California. The two-day trip to her sister's place in Baltimore for her oldest niece Angela's sixteenth-birthday party had gone well enough. But with the news of the terror attacks Iris knew things were going to go downhill pretty quick, so she wanted this flight, and this depressing day, over and done with.

When they had boarded the plane she only knew of the attacks in California. But since they had taken off the pilot had informed them about another attack in Texas, and that there was breaking word of another one that had possibly happened at some school in Colorado. *What the hell is happening to this world?*

Iris worried that if they did not hurry up and get home the FAA may order all flights grounded and then God only knew where they would land. She and Jimmy would more than likely get stuck in some crowded airport somewhere, trying vainly for days to get themselves home. *What a huge pain in the ass that would be.*

All she wanted was to have this plane land on time. Then she could pick up the scattered pieces of her life before any new bullcrap screwed with her and her son. With Jimmy's dad down in Arizona with his 'other family,' Iris had been a single mother from day one. She had to do everything herself and some days, like today, she felt like she could not keep up.

She started to mentally run through the laundry list of things she needed to do once they landed back in Kansas City. First, get their luggage and then make their way through late-afternoon traffic. Second, stop at the kennel and pick up Ben and Max from their stay at the doggie hotel. Those two retrievers were going to be wound-up and excited at seeing Jimmy, and they would be like trying to corral a hurricane when they got them to the car. *Well, I'll just have to cram Jimmy in the back seat with them, and kid, you'd better not give me a hard time about it.* Third, she had to heat up some dinner for everyone so they could finally get settled down. Even if it was a ready-to-make meal from the freezer it was still going to take time that she just did not have enough of. Lastly, she still had to unload the bags and start laundry so her brown outfit would be ready for work in the morning for the meeting about the Robertson contract.

As Iris checked-off her life in the order she had planned it, Jimmy sat quietly next to his mom and was deeply engrossed in his own thoughts. But unlike his mother, his thoughts were less stressful and more enjoyable. Unknown to his mother, he was not daydreaming of heroes or action figures doing great deeds. He did not even have the slightest interest in the stack of comic books that she had bought for him at the airport bookstore; they sat ignored on his lap. He had barely even looked at the covers yet, all of them with badass-looking super villains and heroes in various fighting poses.

His eyes stared unseeing into the puffy expanse of clouds and sky that stretched to the horizon. His mind had forgotten about what was happening in California, as terrible and immediate as that was. His thoughts had been irresistibly pulled away from that disaster and were centered on one all-encompassing thought that did not allow room for anything else; Laila Bhatt.

Last week he had hated the thought of going to his cousin's birthday party. An agonizing thing that only girls could have fun at, but there was something even worse. And that was the fact that Angela was, according to his best friend Tommy, a snotty bitch. She no more wanted to see him than he wanted to see her.

Angela's mother Auntie Teresa had gotten divorced from Uncle Burt a couple years ago and had moved with Angela to Baltimore just last year. Burt had worked as a manager at a Target store back in Kansas City and Jimmy heard his mom and aunt talking once about how he had 'diddled' some clerk at the store. Jimmy did not know what diddled meant but it was evidently a pretty bad thing to do, because every time Auntie Teresa mentioned it she cried a lot and cussed even more.

When Auntie Teresa had moved away Jimmy had been ecstatic that he would not have to put up with the snotty Angela anymore, but it had upset his mother a bunch. So when they got invited to the party, she had dragged him unhappily along. Once there, all he wanted to do was to find a hole somewhere and hide until it was time for them to leave.

All that had instantly changed when he saw Angela's new best friend standing in the living room. The golden morning light was shining across her silky dark hair and smooth skin. Time stopped and his whole world turned into a focused tunnel that led straight into her large brown eyes. It was a magical feeling, like a vampire was sucking out his blood and then filling him up with tingling bugs in his belly. The feeling was new and really weird but Jimmy liked it a lot! Jimmy had melted inside, all the way from his stomach and out through his eyeballs, like when Kryptonite sucked the strength from Superman's muscles.

Jimmy could even remember the small little specks of dust slowly floating, like super-tiny elfish fairies, through the shafts of sunlight as they danced in the air before Laila's beautiful eyes. Dumbfounded, he had not moved until his mom poked him, hard, in the back.

He could tell that his presence at the party irritated Angela to no end, but he no longer cared about her or what she thought. He clung near Laila as all of the presents were torn open and the cake and ice cream were served. While talking with her he had learned that her dad owned a Copy-Copy store and he giggled when she had told him that her nickname for him was Apu, after the Qwiki-Mart owner on the Simpsons. They had done a lot of giggling together and Jimmy was in heaven as he heard angels singing in her laughter.

They had all ended up in Angela's room, playing a game Jimmy had not played before, Truth-or-Dare, and when Angela dared Laila to kiss Jimmy, he was positive Angela was planning to use the moment to embarrass him. But instead of being embarrassed, he had experienced the single greatest moment in the history of the world.

His mind relived the moment over and over. They sat facing each other as Laila's large eyes looked nervously to Angela and then back at Jimmy. His heart raced a million miles an hour. A furious buzzing of tingling butterflies swirled inside of his tummy as the smooth surface of her chocolate skin came close. Her face bent inward and the smells of pink lemonade and birthday cake were mixed on her breath. They exhaled together as their lips met and the sweetness of her mouth was sweeter than anything he could have imagined.

As their lips touched there was an expanding aura of electric power that had radiated across his skin. It blossomed into a pool of warm energy that undulated through his mind like ripples on a pool of water. The waves of intense joy mixed with a new and powerful feeling deep inside. A surging energy swelled in his groin as his penis became painfully rigid and shoved against his restrictive pants. His entire body seemed to be enveloped in armor of exquisite sensation.

He raised his arms to her shoulders and pulled her even closer. The other boys and girls watched them, stunned into silence at the new and amazing sight that they had only seen their parents and people on TV do before. The all-consuming moment allowed Jimmy and Laila to have everyone in the room vanish as they shared each other's kiss.

Then, the total dweeb Angela had to ruin the moment by rudely pulling them apart, staring in shocked surprise at Laila. Angela, her fun being ruined, barked orders for everyone at the party to vacate her room immediately. Jimmy and Laila burst out laughing as their hands found each other's and they trotted outside. The rest of the afternoon he and Laila had been inseparable. They exchanged phone numbers and email addresses. They made many promises and pledges, in between the times they spent finding new places to kiss all around the house and yard.

The first thing he would do when he got home would be to send her a request to be Facebook friends and he knew that tomorrow he would be listening to her lovely voice and staring at her beautiful face on Skype. She said her dad would have to meet and talk with him before he would allow them to talk too much, but she promised she would help him keep her daddy happy.

So while he looked quietly out the window he kept thinking of that first kiss as the soft cool air from the overhead vent blew in his face. He looked off into the distance at two other jet planes coursing through the sky like him. His mind drifted off into make-believe. He imagined that the plane was still flying through the sky, but back to Baltimore, not Kansas City.

Jimmy's imagination flew him back to Laila, leaving behind the real Boeing 'Triple Seven.' It sliced through the thin cold air of the stratosphere, producing a long fluffy contrail that extended for miles. The three-hundred-two lives aboard the plane were in the skilled hands of the pilot, Captain Ronald Watkins. He was a twenty-seven-year veteran of the commercial airline business who was as solid and competent a pilot as United could hope to employ.

His record of service was without blemish or drama, just a good work ethic and commitment to no-nonsense flight deck management. He did this on a reliable and repetitive schedule of performance, and today was no exception to that history. The autopilot was on, guiding the plane through a moderate headwind but they were still timed to arrive above Kansas City in a little over fifty-seven minutes.

Watkins was finding it difficult to relax with his second cup of coffee, as he was forced to listen to the lead flight-attendant, Helen Rickers. She was telling his co-pilot, Rick Mason, how her son was intending to join the Marines instead of attending her alma mater at Northwestern University.

"I don't know what to do about it, Rick," Helen said as exacerbation and melodrama oozed from her pores. "I mean, God knows, what if he goes off to some place like Iraq and gets hurt, or worse? I'd just die! I want him to be educated, not….the other way, you know?"

"Listen, Helen, I was in the United States Air Force and learned to fly there. That ended with me getting this career and making a good life for Alice, the kids, and myself. Now, the marines, they wouldn't be my first choice, I admit. But obviously Ted thinks they're great. I'm sure he'll be fine and I guarantee that it'll help make a man out of him."

Helen's eyes rolled.

"I know the military has a lot to offer, especially in this horrible job market. But I want him here and not traipsing through the streets of some Taliban or Al Qaida country. What if he gets sucked into some dumb action in Syria or some other Arab mess that this doofus in the White House gets us into? I want my country safe and protected from these bastards, too, don't get me wrong, but I don't want my son sacrificed in these wars. If those people want freedom, let them earn it like we did. And now, with these new attacks going on today, it's sure to get him riled up to go off and be a damn hero. But you know what'll really happen next – he'll be in some godforsaken hell-hole, somewhere around the globe, fighting for his life."

"Oh, Helen, come now. We've kicked butt all over the planet since 9/11 and chances are real good that he can become very involved in a deployment somewhere and still not get anywhere near harm's way. He'll come home okay. Anyway, after today, you've got to understand that he can get killed, right here in the United States, by these jihadist murderers just as fast as he can die overseas, fighting in uniform."

"Easy for you to say, Rick, your boys are still in elementary school. It'll be years before they're Teddy's age. He says he wants to make a difference in the world and help out. Help out? In a world full of these killers, how in the hell does he help out? You know what he really means by that, just as well as I do. He's acting like a pure macho jock and he'll find himself in one of these shit-hole places and there'll be a bomb somewhere waiting and God –I can't even think of it!"

"Whoa, slow down there, Mrs. Rickers. I suggest you just take a deep breath and step back from such emotional nonsense," Captain Watkins said.

"My flight deck is not the place for this conversation anyway. Maybe you two should move this back there if you want to continue," he said, thumbing over his shoulder toward the door to the cockpit.

"But I must say, it is you who's out of line, Mrs. Rickers. I believe you are judging your son unfairly and being far too emotional about it. I don't think that you're even thinking straight, let alone helping your son to make the best decision for his future."

Caught off-guard by the captain interceding in the debate Helen calmed down and gave a sigh.

"I don't know, maybe you're right, sir. I want to make the best decision for my son and I guess panicking about his safety won't do that."

Helen knew she was a high-maintenance woman but backing down was not her style, so taking the opportunity to get the captain involved, she prodded.

"Captain, if I may ask, you're also a naval pilot, too, right? What would you say if a son of yours wanted to do what mine wants to do?"

Captain Watkins was not at all enthusiastic about conversing with any emotional women, especially ones like Helen. He had always preferred women who were stoic, intelligent, and emotionally stable. But it sounded like her son was about to make some big choices. With today's escalation in the War on Terror, somewhere and somehow, the boy was going to be in the thick of it. And there was still quite a bit of the flight left and what he had to say would not take too long.

"Okay, I'll give you my thoughts, if you really would like to know what I think. But I don't want any drama or grief from you over it, okay? You ask for my opinion and that's all I'm offering."

"Yes, sir, understood."

"I was in the military but now I'm retired. I was a reservist in the Navy for over twenty years and I always enjoyed the challenge of taking off and landing on an aircraft carrier. I left that behind five

402

years ago and now only fly civilian aircraft. As far as your son and your wishes regarding his choices, I would say first that you need to come to grips with one big reality – your son is now eighteen. That makes him a grown man, and being an adult, he can do as he damn well chooses and you just have to learn to live with it. And, quite frankly, that means butt-out if you cannot be supportive of his decisions. Thinking of him in any other light only clouds the issue for you. He's now a man, to rise or fall on his own choices, and you should learn to look at him and his decisions though that prism."

"Well now, sir, I…."

"I'm not done, Mrs. Rickers. You asked for my thoughts and I'm giving them as you requested. Please have the courtesy to listen for that which you have asked before interjecting yourself," he replied sternly.

"Sorry."

"This world isn't a Disneyland adventure without real consequences. You know that well, like most people do. But often when life is hard and unforgiving, people can forget why the consequences occur. There are no frivolous guarantees for anyone and to pretend otherwise is purely a waste of time. You're correct in pointing out that Captain Mason's children are in elementary school, but we've heard today that just such a school was attacked by terrorists. Children, little more than babies, were mercilessly slaughtered today on our American soil. So, with due respect to reality, being a child in America is no safer than being a warrior in Iraq.

"I don't wish to insult you, Mrs. Rickers. I say that with all sincerity. But there are two rules to life that I believe are basic truths. Evil exists and must be fought wherever it forms. The other truth is that very bad things can happen to good people for absolutely no legitimate moral reason. Life is not a game of chance, but it is unforgiving and promises the living nothing.

"Furthermore, I do have two daughters who are a couple years older than your boy. It might surprise you to know that they are both in the armed forces and deployed overseas."

He paused. Few people knew this much about him, but he was in it now so he continued.

"My oldest, Beverly, is aboard the USS Abraham Lincoln sailing in the Mediterranean and flies the SARS helicopter. That's Sea Air Rescue helicopter, and she's a darn good pilot in her own right. She's also a medic, and is working on achieving her master's degree from Colorado State University. She is also a fantastic single mother of two wonderful boys, both of whom are probably right now playing in my backyard with my wife."

He continued on but more slowly, "Their daddy, Bill Sampson, was a big man with a strong chin and hard eyes. But when I watched him look at his sons he would turn into the softest teddy bear, full of love and tenderness."

Watkin's eyes turned glassy and he set his chin hard to keep from showing too much emotion. The whole flight-deck crew stared in amazement, learning things about the man they never thought they would.

"He was killed in action, leading his platoon in battle in Fallujah, Iraq back in '05. It tore my Beverly and our whole family's hearts out. He was a brave man, a good man, a good husband to my girl, a good Marine. He left behind two great boys who I hope live up to be men like their father. If that eventually leads them to be marines, well, I'll be there to salute them with pride at their graduation from boot camp.

"Beverly serves our country for many reasons. For herself, her career, her national pride, and for her memory of that fine man who loved her, and who died protecting her and those boys. As her father I couldn't be prouder. I work to support her choices every day.

"My youngest, Stephanie, is deployed with the Army's 66th Military Police Company and has seen multiple combat deployments in Afghanistan. In 2007, an IED left a scar on her neck outside Jalalabad, and her actions that day earned her the Bronze Star. She is engaged to be married later this year.

"Your son wants to offer service to his country? I can't think of a better choice a young person like him can possibly make in this life than that. Without the men and women like him, we would have fallen a long time ago. It's up to those of us left here at home who must do our part to make the most of their hard work and sacrifices."

After a few moments Helen regained her composure. "Captain Watkins, I really appreciate your point of view."

(16:38:41pm EST)

THE SMALL current of air that had been blowing on Jimmy's face fizzled to nothing. The faint sound of music coming from his mother's IPod stopped, and the cabin lights went dark. But the oddest thing that gained Jimmy's attention was when the constant vibration and hum from the jet engines instantly quit, leaving behind an eerie silence that lasted for about two seconds. Then people reacted.

"What the devil?" Iris asked as she vainly fiddled with the dark and silent IPod.

There were soft gasps from some people while other passengers exclaimed in mild surprise. Jimmy began to stand and look down the cabin, causing his comic books to fall to the floor. But as he moved he felt an unnerving, slightly-forward tilt to the floor that made him immediately recoil back into his seat. The timing coincided so perfectly, it was as if his small movement had caused the tilting. It slowly but steadily increased as he hurriedly fastened his seatbelt.

An ever-rising volume of voices came, building inside the cabin. But Jimmy's ears detected something else that he found to be even more distressing than the tilting – those voices were the only sounds inside the cabin.

He was astonished to recognize the dramatic lack of sounds. There were no mechanical sounds, no electronic sounds, nothing but human voices and movement as the sound of wind passed outside the window.

Helen Rickers came running up the tilting isle and yelled loudly, *"Everyone put on your seatbelts! Put them on!"*

Immediately, frightened screams broke out as people in the filled cabin began wrestling around with their seatbelts, cursing and yelling, and reaching for loved ones.

An elderly man across the aisle asked, "What's happened? What's going on?"

Helen ignored the man as she worked to hold onto an aisle seat and yelled again, *"Put your seatbelts on! We've lost power! Put on...."*

A woman farther back in the plane had lost her footing and grip. She tumbled down the aisle, banging into seats until she reached Helen. Crashing together they disappeared down the aisle as a bouncing ball of arms and legs.

As Jimmy watched, fearful, he braced himself into his own seat by putting his feet against the seatback in front of him as the plane became pointed nearly vertical and started to spin slowly. His mother had vainly worked at trying to tighten her own seatbelt that she now hung from. But once she saw what Jimmy had done, she followed his example and planted her feet onto the backrest that was now below her.

Purses, plastic cups, diaper bags, and hundreds of other miscellaneous items came falling by their heads. Screams came from all around as more men and women, who had not gotten their seatbelts strapped on, also fell past them, slamming with heavy thuds in the first-class section below.

Iris grabbed frantically at Jimmy. "Hold onto me, baby!" she pleaded.

He grasped her tightly and turned to look out the window. He glanced to where he had seen the other jets a few moments before, but now there was nothing. The contrails were still there but there were no longer any shiny objects at their front. Then, below the contrails, his eyes caught sight of two tiny objects, glinting in the sunlight as they spun. Staring at them he suddenly realized that the other planes were just like his – plummeting out of the sky.

The airliner began to shudder and vibrate as it plunged through thermal layers in its rapid descent. The seatbelt bit sharply into his side and he winced in pain as he was rudely jostled. He looked up at his mother as she openly wept and gripped his hand so hard it hurt. The plane was accelerating rapidly and the noise from air outside no longer whistled, but roared. The screams and cries from passengers had mostly disappeared and now the cabin was strangely quiet with only faint mummers, speedy praying, and wretched sobs heard over the roar of the passing air outside. Loved ones as well as complete strangers embraced one another in final acts of companionship.

Jimmy's young age did not keep him from understanding his impending death, and with the calmness and sincerity of a much older person, he looked into his mother's eyes.

"I love you," he said warmly.

He squeezed her hand softly and then turned back to his window. The ground was much closer now, spinning below him outside the window. There was no Superman out there saving the day from evil, just clouds and ground. His eyes searched for the other planes but he could not spot them. He closed his eyes.

Once again his lips felt the rose-pedal softness and sweet moistness of her lips. The flavors of raspberries, chocolate cake, and vanilla ice cream crossed his tongue. He opened his eyes and all he saw were the deep brown orbs of Laila Bhatt as she kissed him.

*****

16:33pm EST UTC -5
Marine One en route from Andrews AFB
Washington DC

PRESIDENT BARACK Obama's Sikorsky VH-60N Whitehawk travelled at 183 m.p.h. at an elevation of 700 ft. above the Potomac River as it shifted its position within the formation of four other identical VH-60N helicopters. This standard procedure of rotation helped conceal the exact whereabouts of the president from any possible attackers on the ground, and today the precision of the pilots was razor-sharp.

The National Incident Command was currently being orchestrated out of NORAD at Peterson Air Force Base, until President Obama could assume command after he arrived at the underground bunker of the White House. Just minutes earlier he had disembarked from Air Force One at Andrews Air Force Base, along with Vice President Biden and DHS Secretary Napolitano. They had been flying across the Atlantic, headed to a conference with British Prime Minister David Cameron, when the terror attacks had begun. The president had immediately ordered a return to Washington, DC after hearing the first reports of destruction in Oakland.

At present, the commander-in-chief sat staring out the cabin window. A Marine sergeant entered and braced himself with an outstretched hand against the cushioned wall of the aircraft as he approached. The president looked up grimly at the sheet of paper in the sergeant's hand.

"Sir, I have the latest numbers from San Francisco."

President Obama gave a resigned sigh and looked at the carpet.

"Go ahead."

"Sir, the governor's office is confirming that casualty estimates are accurate for the metropolitan area. The main variable on those numbers is how many people are still caught inside the fire's perimeter. The governor also wishes to confirm for you that the fourth building collapse did occur, this one at the Millennium Tower, and that it was just broadcast by several national media outlets."

The president grimaced and slammed his fist down on his knee as he turned to glare at Napolitano.

"Dammit, Jan, I want that airspace shut down, right now! I told you that we need to be able to direct those images towards something constructive! This is too big and out of our control. I need to manage the message that goes out to the country and the world, now!"

"I'm working on it, Barack. I'm doing the best I can. The airspace was shut down but that news crew flew in anyway. I can't have them shot down, right?"

President Obama glared at the floor bitterly.

"Goddamn these terrorist bastards to hell," he said through clenched teeth, "Doing this while I'm in office, I'll make them...." his voice trailed off to silence.

While still looking at the floor he asked, "What's the latest from Oakland, sergeant?"

The marine hesitated before replying.

Obama looked up at the soldier and saw the man's eyes were watering. He reached out and lightly patted the marine's crisply pressed pants.

"Please go ahead, sergeant."

With a trembling lower lip the marine said, "My – my apologies sir. I – I have family in Oakland."

A wave of grief swept over Barack's usually stoic face as he quickly stood and clasped hands with the sergeant.

"I pray they are safe, young man."

They stood hand-in-hand for several seconds until the man was able to regain his composure.

"Now, I'm sorry, but please continue with your report, young man."

Gaining his voice, the man gave a terse nod.

"General Reynolds confirms that there was only a single device used and that it produced thermobaric properties. Some remaining parts of a propane tanker have been discovered at the blast's epicenter. That tanker has been confirmed to be the origin of the explosion. Federal agents are beginning their investigation of a local gas company and are searching their employee records."

"The general is still compiling casualty figures and, unfortunately, he believes that the current estimates of between 60,000 to 80,000 fatalities in the inner blast zone to be light. It has been discovered that two scheduled public events and an economic conference were taking place in the city center and the numbers of people in attendance is only a speculation at this time. He states that the martial law order has been delivered and that the air space has been shut down. His communication teams are making rapid progress on effectively controlling media access and what they will be reporting."

"So what progress is he having on the search-and-rescue operations?" Vice President Biden asked.

"General Reynolds says they have recovered 28,455 fatalities and are moving over 140,000 ambulatory and non-ambulatory casualties to the triage facilities at McAfee Coliseum. Those numbers are rising rapidly as he is able to get the resources to penetrate and search further into the blast zone. Unfortunately, the fires are very extensive and heavy equipment such as large dozers and track-hoes are needed to get through the blast debris, and the numbers they have are still quite limited for the size of the task."

The sergeant turned back to the Commander in Chief.

"Sir, Governor Brown is making a second formal request that it be you who must make the decision to write-off the two sectors of Lakeside and Gold Coast so that the resources they have on-hand can be concentrated toward the city center. He still argues that, due to the national consequences of these attacks, he doesn't feel it is his responsibility to make those types of decisions."

Biden flung his arms up in disgust.

"Moonbeam! That fucker! He's the man on the ground. He and Reynolds are the two people with eyes on the ball and hands in the soup!"

He turned angrily to Obama.

"You know damn-well, Barack, he's just looking at putting that albatross of dead people around your neck instead of taking it on himself!"

The President of the United States slowly shook his head as he stared out the oval window.

"Joe, this whole day and everything happening on it will be an albatross, forever hanging around my neck – and yours," he finished with a weary stare at his ashen-faced VP.

Biden's exasperated look deflated as he looked down at his shoes and returned to his seat. President Obama rested his forehead against his forearm as he stared out the window at the approaching Washington Mall.

"What about Houston? And what about that school in Colorado?" he asked.

"Houston's numbers are pretty solid at three-hundred-twenty fatalities and seventy-five injured. All evidence, at this time, confirms that there are no further terrorist cells in the area. And when that citizen stopped the attackers like he did, the damage was limited to what had already been done. The FBI agents at the farm in Sattler are still finding more evidence that indicates that this family was indeed the facilitators for the strikes on both Houston and San Francisco. They have also found evidence of another attack planned for the capitol center in Denver. Local authorities in Denver have been notified and are now on high alert and have locked down the area. Governor Hickenlooper and his family have been collected and are being taken to a secure facility. But both the school in Trinidad and the attack on Oakland are not mentioned in any documents they have found as yet at the ranch in Texas.

"The preliminary numbers for the school and the explosion inside the town are at two-hundred-five fatalities, most of which are children and faculty at the school. There are another forty-three known injured."

Obama's eyes remained closed as the marine's voice faded away.

After a couple of seconds he said, "Sergeant, get Governor Brown on the line for me."

"Yes, sir."

The military officer turned and walked up the buffeting cabin.

Vice President Biden looked at Obama with incredulity while rubbing his temple.

"Goddamn, Barack! You know that bastard is going let you swing…"

(16:38:41pm EST)

THE ELECTRONICS of the fleet of presidential helicopters, like the planes in the Air Force One fleet, had been engineered to be resistant to the effects of an electromagnetic pulse since the days of the Cold War. But being resistant to a thing is not a guarantee of being protected from a thing. The jet-turbine engine in the helicopter carrying President Obama cut in and out, sputtering, as some circuits failed and others remained alive and active, while lights dimmed then brightened. Bright sparks from numerous circuits and a few lights exploded and popped around the cabin and cockpit, making Secretary Napolitano scream. The helicopter lurched hard from the loss of full power as the pilot fought to save the wounded machine. All people were sent flying around the cabin as the aircraft swung hard around. President Obama reached for something to hold onto but his hand only caught air as he pitched backward, his legs catching the cushioned chair he had been sitting in earlier. His feet went high as his head went low and struck the carpeted floor, making an audible snap as his fractured neck cut through his spine, killing him instantly.

Biden, Napolitano, and the sergeant flew into the cabin walls, each other, and the bolted-down furniture as the floundering helicopter quickly decelerated and began to pitch downward. The tail rotor failed and the pilot attempted to auto-rotate the craft to the manicured south lawn of the White House. It struck the ground sideways at eighty-miles an hour.

Two of the other helicopters remained airborne, barely being affected by the EMP, while the fourth helicopter that had been trailing the others nose-dived immediately into the Potomac River.

The helicopter carrying the dead President of the United States pitched, flipped and rolled several times across the grass, debris flying everywhere, until the torn machine finally came to rest in a

410

smoldering pile of wreckage forty-feet from the iconic building that once housed the most powerful man in the world.

*****

THE EVENING sun had set behind the forest canopy, but a soft, purple-pink glow still hung delicately above the rustling leaves. Standing with the handle bars to his bicycle in his hands, Ansel Prideaux's fifty-nine year old eyes gleamed at the sight of the restored 1967 Grunostraat Citroën van that sat in the otherwise deserted parking lot.

The beautiful restoration job had the chrome bumpers shining and the body was covered in a new coat of glossy red paint that made the old-workhorse look fantastic. Ansel fondly remembered driving one just like it when he was a much younger man, making deliveries of milk, bread, and produce to the people living throughout the greater Lorraine Provence. His van had been blue, but he liked the red on this one.

He stood in the visitor parking lot at the aged Ouvrage Galgenberg memorial site, curious as to who had parked the vehicle here. Glancing around at the weathered concrete formations and rusted steel turrets, he wondered where the vehicle's owner could be. The military formations at this site had once housed, at the ready, his nation's 137mm howitzers and 7.5mm MAC 34 machine guns in defense against attack from Hitler's Nazi Germany.

But nowadays the useless monument to military failure sat quiet and lonely in the forest, blackened by moss and covered in bird droppings. It was getting very late and Ansel had never seen tourists strolling around the place this late in the evening before. He strongly suspected that the restored Frenchman's working van was probably a conveyance for lovers on this clear night.

Earlier, his heart had been heavy with the terrible news from America. *Soon they'll be rampaging around the world again!* So he decided upon an evening bike ride to separate himself from the sadness of the day, and to his delight and surprise, his journey had produced this great find. So, with a childish sense of glee and curiosity he snuck up to the vehicle and ran his hands along the smooth paint, admiring the metal work and custom paint job that made the curved body and boxy front look so first-rate.

411

Leaning his bike against his leg, he cupped his eyes and pressed his face against the glass. He was rewarded with a clear view of a beautifully restored interior that was as immaculate as the exterior. Ansel admired the man who had taken the time to rebuild a vehicle with such care and love, a thing that was not to be found that commonly in the throwaway society of modern France. His eyes danced happily from one item to another as he scanned the interior, until he saw the four large crates, strangely out of place, sitting in the back compartment.

*****

MAJOR XU Leung, from the Chinese Ministry of State Security, stood with his four civilian-clad commando companions in the cool autumn under the oak, chestnut, and birch trees. Their riotous fall color was now dimmed and had turned uniform shades of grey in the deepening dark. The fiercely loyal and obedient soldiers were handpicked by Xu from the ranks of MSS Sixth Bureau. As yet he had withheld all information on their mission objectives, and they now waited, piddling away the time by walking about the crumbling and rusted chunks of the old Maginot Line. But as the day turned to night they had started to eye their commander more often with curious interest.

Xu felt that this sad and withered monument to France's incompetent and pathetic attempt to keep a dynamic Hitler at bay with a strategy of static defense, was a very fitting lesson for his men to absorb. Only he knew that they waited on the edge of a great destiny today, but he knew they would soon understand. If successful, their motherland of Zhonghua would bring low every other rival around the world by using a dynamic strategy over their enemy's modern version of static defense. Xu well understood why the Chinese had produced the most renowned strategist in human history, Sun Tsu. Today, the world would begin to understand that fact anew.

The 80s pop music floated on the air, mixing with the voices of a few songbirds as they fluttered among the trees, preparing for their nightly slumber. The small IPod and speakers had been operating reliably for the past half hour, playing one song after another. There had been no indication to the men that Xu was using the device as anything other than some music player. That was another part of their commander's odd behavior for the day, but he had given no indication that the music would not continue for hours more.

412

WITHOUT WARNING, the device ceased to play and fell silent. The men turned and looked with mild curiosity at the device and then at their leader.

Xu's eyes were instantly drawn to the device as well, but in contrast to his men's nonchalant manner, his heart stammered, his eyes widened, and his face tensed in anticipation. The mild reaction from the men quickly dissipated as they rapidly gathered from their leader's tense deportment that something momentous must have occurred.

Xu quickly checked his wristwatch, then undid the clasp and tossed the useless device to the ground. He pulled his cell phone from his pocket, examined it, and then tossed it to the ground like so much garbage. He scanned the confused and curious faces of his commandos and could not resist breaking into a long, deep-throated laugh as they stood watching in stunned amazement as their usually stoic leader appeared to act completely insane.

Drawn through the trees by the sounds of the hearty laughter, Ansel pushed his bike toward it, like mice following the Pied Piper of Hamelin. Through an opening in the brush, he walked into a manicured glade where he saw the five athletic Asian men standing, one of which was laughing merrily. The four younger men spun like cats and eyed the interloper suspiciously, causing Ansel to step backward. Xu finally gained control of his merriment and leveled a roguish glance at the interloping Frenchman.

The oddity of the wonderfully restored van, to be followed by a giggling Chinaman in the forest, surrounded by four serious looking men doing great imitations of Japanese ninjas, was all more than Ansel could comprehend as he addressed them.

"Is that your Citroën back there? It's beautiful."

The top graduate from the 1994 class at Tsinghua University, Xu was an exceptional student who fluently spoke eight languages and enjoyed French second only to his native Mandarin.

"Yes, you like it?" he asked.

Ansel's face brightened, and with a large smile he replied, "Yes, yes! It is marvelous work you did. I drove one many years ago. I love those old vans."

"Do you still have one?" Xu asked.

Ansel shook his head while smiling.

"No, I have an Audi now."

Xu gave him a disappointed look.

"Too bad, your family would be better served with the van."

A good-natured but quizzically incredulous look crossed Ansel's face.

"That's crazy! An old van cannot beat an Audi, my friend."

Xu's face lost the softness of humor and he responded coldly, "You are wrong. Do you have the time?"

Ansel's brow wrinkled at the change he sensed in the Chinaman. He apprehensively glanced down at his wrist watch and was surprised to see that his dependable Timex was blank. He pushed several buttons but got nothing for the effort. He raised a puzzled face back to the man and found himself looking down the barrel of a pistol.

The sharp crack of the slug fired into Ansel's brain gave a faint ringing echo throughout the forest of the Moselle Valley. The upkeep of the pristine grounds effectively hid from the everyday view of the casual passers-by the sad reality that this soil had seen tremendous bloodshed, barbarity, and miserable death throughout the preceding centuries. Neanderthal, Cro-Magnon, Romans, Gauls, Spaniards, Moors, Mongols, and many others known and unknown had killed and died on this ground. But today, no living soul other than Xu knew that the tiny blast signaled the beginning of another massive bloodletting. And Xu also knew that the coming bloodbath would soon send many more souls along a path to follow Ansel Prideaux's ethereal spirit into the afterlife.

The commandos quickly followed their commander's long strides past the dead man's body, as Xu made his way back to their waiting vehicle. They continued to wait patiently for him to explain their orders as they emptied the contents of the lead-lined, Faraday Cage-insulated crates from the back of the Citroën. Their watches and phones were as useless as Xu's and were quickly discarded, and just as quickly replaced with the working watches, communications gear, radio detonators, and computers that had been perfectly protected from the EMP blast by the Faraday cages.

The very same EMP blast that had signaled to Xu that his moment in history had arrived was actually caused by a nuclear blast in the upper stratosphere, high over Germany. That blast had also signaled the instantaneous and permanent crippling of the electronic grids and virtually all of the electronic devices across a vast landscape that stretched from the United Kingdom to the Ural Mountains, and Scandinavia to the Mediterranean Sea.

The extensively-trained cadre quickly strapped on their tactical vests and deployed their silenced QSZ-92 pistols and Type-05 submachine guns, both of which fired 5.8x21 mm cartridges. Each man was armed with over a thousand rounds of ammunition, along with dozens of hand grenades. Two men also produced a pair of QLB-

06 grenade launchers that they strapped to their backs. Once equipped and ready they sat uneasy and cramped in the back of the old van and watched as Xu affixed the terminal wires back to the vehicle's battery. He then went to the driver seat and started the vehicle without difficulty.

In minutes he was driving down the quaint gravel road, heading away from the old monument. Once he cleared the tree line, facing into the west, he pointed across the cut wheat fields where several dozen cows lazily munched their cud in the night breeze.

His men followed his pointing finger across those fields and looked past the tranquil lapping waters of Mirgenbach Lake. Above the far bank rose thick clouds of steam that drifted up into the star-choked sky. That steam came from the top of the four large concrete cooling stacks, poking high into the air above the Cattenom Nuclear Power Station.

"That is first of three power plants we will destroy, and we only have two days," Xu stated cryptically.

Book Four – PIGS IN ZEN

*****

Dressed very dapper in his tailored grey Dormeuil suit, Professor Herbert Blunt hurried past students and colleagues in a brisk walk that was almost a trot. His polished Mephisto Gaetan oxfords clacked across the tiled floor. He descended as quickly as possible down the crowded squared staircase to the atrium of Ford Hall. His neatly manicured hands brushed back wayward locks from his brow, which was now furrowed into an unusual look of consternation and worry.

His thirty-year academic career had been resurrected in recent years at Smith, where he was expecting to earn tenure in the coming year. He liked to think that his professional resurrection was at least partly due to his skills at teaching and counseling students as dean of the senior class. But realistically he had to admit to himself that it was mainly due to him keeping his philandering urges under control. Even so, he still loved the look and feel of the young ladies, and he enjoyed how their eyes watched him, the best-dressed and well-heeled man on campus.

Unfortunately, that was not the impression he made to all the young ladies at the moment. Instead of looking the confident, testosterone-filled professor, he now appeared rather more like a gambler dodging a bookie to whom he owed a lot of money.

He launched off the bottom step and quickly crossed the atrium. He reached the broad glass doors that lead out into the bright light of the sunny Massachusetts's afternoon. He shoved through the doors with such force he surprised a young woman who stood just outside of the swinging doors. Startled, she sent her laptop flying high into the air.

Stopping in midstride beside the hapless girl, they watched as the computer clattered across the concrete walkway and broke into pieces. Helplessness washed over her face as she started to collect the useless bits. Herb quickly joined her.

"You jerk!" she snapped, exasperated. "I had my midterm papers on there and now they're all gone."

"I'm so sorry, young lady, my deepest apologies. Today has been a truly terrible day and I was in such a hurry that, I'm sorry, I didn't see you."

As they knelt alongside one another, the mildly sweet masculine smell of his cologne caught the brunette's attention. She glanced over, her anger melting, and positively assessed his strong jaw, green eyes, and athletic features. His eyes met hers and appraised her interest, and he flashed a soft smile. Bowing her head demurely, her soft skin blushed, turning the color of a blooming pink rose. She bit her lower lip and nervously ran her fingers along her face, brushing aside the long straight hair that hung carelessly across her cheeks. Composing herself, she looked back up, meeting and holding his piercing eyes with her own.

"Again, my dear young lady, I beg your forgiveness. My haste has caused this catastrophe. For you....?" his voice gently lingered as he waited for her response.

"Jane – Jane Pendergast." she finally blurted. "I'm taking biology this semester!"

Embarrassed by her awkward and unrefined response she turned away, biting her lip.

Herb reached out and cupped her chin and brought her eyes back to his.

Smiling, he said, "I'm quite sure you'll excel in your courses, my dear."

His eyes roamed easily over her well-tanned form. Her large breasts were inviting, even as they were held tightly within the confining embrace of her sports bra, tucked under a loose fitting tank top. Unashamed, his soft gaze followed the hourglass curvature of her slender waist that expanded into firm hips encased in thin cotton shorts. Long legs flowed like silk down to her freshly painted toe nails and flip-flop sandals.

Her eyes made their own canvas of his body until they were interrupted by a glint from his wrist that drew her gaze.

"That really looks like a nice watch. Is it real?" she asked, tactlessly.

He glanced down at the white gold Rolex Cosmograph, and for nearly the hundredth time in the past half hour he looked again at the slender second-hand that sat motionless under the crystal face. The intoxication from the young woman's beauty evaporated, along any lustful thoughts. Akin to a cold shower, reality jolted his brain back to the situation at hand. He looked up at her delicate features and large brown eyes, looking innocently back at him, and made a quick assessment of her future over the forthcoming winter months.

"Where is your family, my dear?"

"Excuse me?" she replied with a puzzled look.

"Your family – where is your family? Where are you from?"

"Uh, Florida – Pensacola, actually."

He easily took her hand into his and unclasped the Rolex from his wrist. He cupped it in her palm and gently closed her fingers around it.

"My lovely young girl, you must do me this favor. Take this as an offering of mine, in payment for my carelessness. Will you accept?"

"Uh?" she managed to say while glancing down at the obviously expensive watch. She slowly shook her head.

"Uh, I really appreciate the thought, but that old laptop isn't worth all this, really. Besides, for some reason the damn thing wasn't working anymore."

He smiled knowingly and pointed to the watch.

"It is a real Rolex, I assure you. It is covered in white gold. I'm afraid after today it doesn't work any better now than your computer does, my darling. But it may be worth something for you to trade in the months ahead. Please take it," he said, closing her fingers around it. "I would be crushed if you refused me this."

He finished by again flashing his brilliant white teeth in his most earnest smile.

Her fine skin blushed again as she shyly replied, "Uh, sure. But why would I trade it?"

His face hardened and he simply shrugged in response, especially since anything else would just be a useless waste of time. He nodded to her and stood, then turning away from the intoxicating woman he quickly made his exit as he headed toward the parking lot, where he hoped to find his longtime friend and mentor.

Fred was the emotional hard-ass and dear friend who had helped him reestablish his life and career after his extravagant philandering episodes back at USC San Diego. Herb's extremely poor judgment back then had cost him his twenty-two year marriage, the custody of his twin kids, and his tenure at USC.

Herb made his way along Green Street, his eyes focusing on the back of a rented Dodge Caravan with its rear hatch open. There Fred sat on the rear bumper with his head in his hands.

"Fred! Fred!" Herb yelled.

He jogged across the street between two cars stopped in the middle of the road. Their drivers were bent under their open hoods, examining the engines, trying to determine why their vehicles were no longer functioning.

Fred's bloodshot eyes had a remote and distraught look. He moved to meet Herb in the street, where they embraced in a bear hug as Fred openly wept. The befuddled motorists looked up from their vehicles and stared with puzzlement at the two grown men, one crying, as they embraced.

After about a minute passed they pushed away from each other until each held the other by the shoulders. Herb looked earnestly at his teary-eyed friend.

"Did you ever get word from Kimberly before the event?"

Fred slowly lowered his head, shaking it sadly.

"No."

He looked back up at his friend.

"Just before everything blew, there was…Herb, there was a live news report that had just started when it happened. I saw her, Herb! She was on an ambulance gurney and I know it was her. They were holding an IV bag up and running for an ambulance! I know that's what I saw," he finished with a quiet sob; he was about to start to cry again but clenched his fists tight to keep from losing control of his emotions again.

"I believe you. That girl's a fighter. She'll make it just fine."

"I know, and I hope so. I just don't know how bad she's hurt. And now with all this – this mess…."

Fred waved his arm in the air.

"What the hell, Herb? An EMP? Shit! What kind of medical help is she going to have? Who'll take care of her this winter? It's – it's mid-September and snow is right around the corner."

His shoulders sank and Herb saw something in the big man that he never would have believed possible. Fred looked defeated. Herb gripped Fred's shoulders, gave him a mild shake and lowered his head to get Fred to look in his eyes.

Once their eyes locked he said, "You know goddamn well that girl will make it! Don't ever give up on that thought! It's what you have to stay with now, no matter what happens. Grab that thought and *never* let it go!"

Leaning into Herb until their foreheads touched, Fred steadied himself. He had helped Herb out of hundreds of bars, stumbling drunk, bleating and crying at the loss of his marriage and career. Now it was Fred who gained strength and support from his resurrected friend, who now buoyed his depressed soul at a moment of weakness.

419

Quietly Herb whispered, "You pull yourself together. We've got to figure out what to do from here. If this time it's my turn to kick your ass out of self-pity, yeah, that's right, self-pity – that's what I'll do. You're going to look pretty damn stupid with my oxfords sticking out of your ass! Despair won't get you any closer to your baby girl. You know that better than me. Now reach in, grab your nutsack and pull yourself out of that wasteful depression bullcrap."

The barely perceptible humor crossed Fred's face as a final tear rolled down his cheek.

"You better keep holding me up, Herb. If I grab that sack I'll need both hands."

Both men burst out laughing as equal measures of satisfaction and relief swept over Herb's face.

"That's better," he said.

They stepped to the minivan and sat beside one another on the rear bumper. Fred stared quietly at the pavement until he noticed the missing watch from his Herb's wrist.

"What happened there? That overpriced gewgaw of yours gave up the ghost, huh? I would've thought your vanity would keep even a non-functioning Rolex on that wrist."

"Ah, yes, have no fear of me ever losing my vanity. The one true vice I'll go before Jesus with – my vanity. No, I met a beauty who may need it sooner than I. I gave it to her in payment of a debt."

"You're an incorrigible Valentino. The day the whole world falls apart on us, and you're still stuck on the girls. I hope the debt didn't have to do with another unacknowledged child of yours."

"No, no, it was nothing quite so tawdry. But with things looking as they do, I believed it would be of better service to her than me."

"A true gentleman, just as I always feared. Eva knew there was something honorable way down in the depths of your being. And now it finally shows up and proved her right. On the day the world goes to hell you turn out to be a hopeless romantic."

"And here I thought that confidence in my brutish manliness would be undying."

Herb smiled while remembering Fred's wife, whom he loved as much as his friend.

"Eva always could see through to the heart of anything and anyone. Jesus, I miss her," Herb said wistfully. Fred's eyes drifted away to memories of his own as he gently patted Herb's knee.

The two sat quietly for quite some time, deep in their thoughts until Herb finally spoke, "So, Fred, you do agree with me that this event was an EMP of some magnitude?"

Fred's eyes came back to the present as he slowly raised his arm and pointed down the street.

"Take a look at the corner power pole, there – down at the intersection, the one with the three transformers."

Herb followed Fred's pointed finger, and at first saw nothing unusual about the wooden pole until his eyes focused on the grey, circular transformers bolted near the top. Their normal light grey color was now blackened, and thin, dark trails of smoke rose from them. One had a small but jagged hole in its side from where it had exploded inside.

"Shit! Those things got fried," Herb said.

Fred nodded his head as he thumbed over his shoulder back toward Wright Hall.

"I went behind that building and found the building transformer back by the dumpster. It was just as burned-out as those on the pole. I can only surmise that the whole grid must be devastated."

"Holy cow, an EMP strike really did happen! Remarkable."

"That's not the word I'd use, Herb."

Herb's amazement faded as his face turned glum.

"But you're right, it couldn't possibly be anything else. Everything is gone. Everything connected to the grid, along with personal electronics like watches, computers, phones, and vehicles. And it's that last one, the vehicles that worry me the most, Herb. Even the parked vehicles, that were shut down and not running – and they still got knocked out. At least mine is, as well as two others I know of for sure. While I've been sitting out here I watched a couple other people come out and try to start some vehicles down the street and they got nothing. You can still see them down there, with the hoods up. That's one powerful and devastating EMP.

Fred paused, shaking his head.

"That is a far worse result than anything disclosed in the unclassified report from Bill Graham's EMP commission. That indicates to me that the effects are going to be very wide-spread. There's nothing else I can imagine that could cause this. The only question I can think of asking right now is, was it nature that did it or was it man who caused it?"

Herb looked to the sun, squinting.

"Well, from what my scientific analysis with my eyes can determine, we still have an atmosphere with air to breath and the sun still hangs in the sky, so I believe that rules out a supernova, at least in our solar system. And I would hope that we would have had plenty of warning if a massive flare was coming our way from our own sun. If

I'm wrong, and if the ozone is fried, then we'll start to roast with the nasty effects of radiation in less than a few hours."

"Cute, Herb, you're really an asshole, you know?"

"Yep, I'm proud of it, too," Herb said, smirking without real humor.

Fred ignored him.

"With everything else that has happened today it weighs far too heavy on the scales for man to be the cause. If it's the death of the ozone, we'll all be dead soon enough anyhow."

"So, then, who is the villain in our investigation?"

"Well, forget about the North Koreans. That creep in charge over there, Wong Dong Illness or whatever his name is. He's mafioso, a thug. Insane, narcissistic, and imbalanced he may be, but suicidal he is not. He's also not a religious man. No true believer in anything but his power and the protection of his little realm and dynasty. He's not a direct player in this.

"Now, it could always be the Russians or Chinese, as they've got the means and know-how, but it's such a bold stroke. I have a hard time imagining them doing this without a lot of saber rattling beforehand, especially the Chinese – it's just not the Confucian way.

"So Fred, are you going to try and tell me that the dead goatherder, bin Laden, got a hold of nukes, and now after he's been feeding the fishes all summer, somehow his minions got the nukes here? That's crazy."

"Don't be naïve, Herb. I believe that you take too lightly how easy it is for big fish to use surrogates. You really think a group of devoted martyr wannabes can't be effectively used by those with the real capability? The only thing needed for that to become a reality is the motivation of those with the capability, my friend.

"Realistically, I believe there're two groups that are possibly both capable and willing to try it. The Iranians and Syrians, or even a group like Al Qaida or Al Shabab is not completely out of the realm of possibility. Although a ragtag terrorist cell that is capable of zapping our asses back to the 1600s isn't going to do it without the direct support and supervision of someone much bigger and badder."

"We've been told over and over that none of those groups have any nuclear capability yet. Hell, Fred, I thought their missiles weren't even capable of reaching us, with or without nukes," Herb interjected.

"Herb, since when do you get your strategic information from MSNBC? Look around you. You see aliens? Is some malevolent monster rampaging around? This is real, and it's right now.

"I can only guess that the bullshit about their capabilities was either wrong or we simply weren't told. The government may have determined that they needed to keep it from the public eye, all in the interests of national security or some such shit. You know how gun-shy our intelligence community was after the Hussein weapons-of-mass-destruction fiasco! They never saw the end of the Cold War; they totally missed Pakistan nuking up, and both of those debacles happened right under their noses. So imagine, even if they had a pretty good idea that someone else had finally gotten nukes, I would guess that they would be very reluctant to say anything to the American public without real hard facts to back them up. That's one thing we can always count on. Bureaucrats have always been better at covering their asses than uncovering the truth."

Fred paused as he wagged his finger next to his head.

"You know? If we already knew Iran had nukes – it could really explain why we've known they are the terrorism kingpins of the planet, and yet we have done nothing to them directly, but fought them through proxy by loitering around in mud and blood of Afghanistan and Iraq, hmm."

Fred stared at his shoes for a couple of seconds as he pondered his thoughts. Then he shrugged and moved on.

"Pandering and political correctness isn't going to change this. Obviously somebody had the capability, and we were all sitting here, like stupid ducks on a pond waiting to get blasted, and the honchos in Washington, DC didn't stop it from happening!"

Fred punched his luggage in frustration.

"Listen, Herb, you know as well as I do what's going on. Dr. Graham's commission reported about the threat publicly back in 2008. Today is no fucking surprise! Is it a shock? Yes. Is it a disaster? Yes! As it turns out, it's probably the destruction of our entire country and our way of life if it covers most of the continent. But there is no fucking surprise in this, Herb. It must've been orchestrated to happen along with the other attacks of earlier today."

Fred clamped his lips shut and sat fuming.

"Easy, partner, I agree with you. I wasn't trying to be facetious with you when I asked who could be responsible. I just meant that I find it difficult to believe that simple terrorists could pull off something this big, is all. It stands to reason that it's going to be the same bastards who are responsible for the earlier attacks, but like all conspiracies, people talk, information leaks. Obviously, someone's been planning and working a long time on this. How could we have missed something that big, and for so long?"

"That's something I just don't know," Fred said shaking his head. "Whoever it was, they had a hard-on for us a very long time and they were real damn smart about it. And, you know? Now that I think about it, as odd as it may sound, the only bastards I can imagine pulling this off would be the ChiComs."

"The Chinese? Why would they want to kill the golden goose? We've been funding their infrastructure creation and building their military into a first-rate modern force with our tax money for years. With us gone, their money will dry up and not be back again anytime soon."

Fred looked at his friend.

"Well, isn't that the idea? Look at what the results are from an EMP strike on us, especially if it is an attack that we cannot determine who was responsible. The United States won't be able to recover from something like this for years and years, and all the while our military capability will degrade every day. They would damn well understand the conflicts that are coming in our future world where there will be far more than seven billion people on this planet. All those mouths wanting food and water, and needing resources and energy to support and maintain large, diverse, and needy populations. With us knocked out of their way by an EMP for a decade or longer, just who the hell on earth is going to stop them from taking whatever they want, any time they want it? Absolutely nobody."

Fred looked around at the wandering groups of flummoxed people. A block away, three female students were pushing a new Audi Quatro down the street.

"It's a total game changer today, Herb."

"These poor kids around here are in for a real shock. Hell, I'm in total shock myself. Good Lord, we're totally fucked."

Herb slapped his palms down on his knees as they both stared at the roaming groups of students who were taking stock and questioning one another about what was happening.

"I'm in shock, too. The difference between us and those kids, Herb, is that we know how bad this might be and where we go from here. These post-hippie soccer babies, and their soccer moms and dads probably don't have the slightest clue how miserable their world is about to get. The question I dearly wish I had the answer to is just how much of the nation has been damaged by this EMP?"

An icy cold shiver shot up Herb's spine as he contemplated the year ahead of them, but he still looked at Fred, hopefully.

"We can only hope that it's a partial strike. If we have substantial sections of our territory that is unaffected by the pulse, then maybe we'll still have considerable infrastructure intact. If that is the case, we can build out from there. Reconstruct the grid. If we don't have some infrastructure still in place out there – well, if we don't it simply means that it will be nothing but shit sandwiches to eat for a very long damn time! Fred, everybody hates shit sandwiches."

"I hear that, partner. But you know the rule on how to eat one. Get as many people eat'n it with you as you can. That way, each person's portion is as small as possible."

"Yes, sir."

Herb grimly nodded at the old combat joke and thought back to when he first met Fred in boot camp. They were young, lean, and healthy back then, filled to the top with piss-n-vinegar and a good dose of arrogance. Now Herb felt the slow creep of arthritis in his left knee every morning. *This is the biggest shit sandwich in history.*

Unexpectedly, both men were shaken from their thoughts as their eyes were drawn to an old 1960s VW Beetle that came puttering down Green Street, passing by the confused and frustrated motorists of the newer but non-functioning vehicles.

Herb's fingers caressed his bad knee as he asked, "How bad do you think it is? What does your situational awareness tell you, Fred? I mean, we're in agreement that an EMP has gotten us. There's no way for me to argue against that, but could it be localized? You know, we just don't have much information yet. Are you going to wait a day or two for the authorities to come out with a prognosis?"

Fred slowly bobbed his head as he pondered how to answer the questions.

"I've been calculating those odds ever since my head accepted the idea of the EMP. I don't like any of the options I've came up with so far, either. I figure things are real bad."

"Fred, you've always been my personal hero. You saved my ass on the battlefield and you saved my ass from the bottle and my own stupidity. I trust your judgment more than my own, mainly because you've always lived every day in the real world. You and Eva never lived in the world of how-we-want-it-to-be that so many others do, which includes me far too often. If it is bad, I need to be prepared, too. Help me get my mind right. Tell me how bad you think it really is?"

"All right," Fred said nodding to Herb. He stood and turned to his luggage and began sorting through his belongings as he started reciting his thoughts.

"Listen, if I'm wrong, that'll be a great thing, and in a couple of days we can get around to rebuilding our lives. But if I'm right, we've got very little time to get as far ahead of the curve as we can. Winter is just weeks away. You just said this morning that the first hard frost of the year happened here only two days ago. That means there'll be snow and freezing temperatures in a few weeks, maybe a month at the outside.

"So, we know what's coming, now let's focus on our situation today. Firstly, we know we are the victims of a major military strike upon the United States from an enemy that had the capability to implement a successful EMP attack on, at a minimum, the northeastern seaboard, as well as orchestrate multiple and major attacks around the country in California, Colorado, and Texas before the EMP. That tells me that whoever did it risked everything to see it done. It means that if they're good enough to be that successful in everything we've seen today, then I reason that they were successful enough with the EMP to pretty much guarantee that we wouldn't dare strike back. Whether that is because of our resulting weakness after the EMP or they simply covered their tracks well enough that we do not know for sure who is responsible. Either way, you and I are out-n-out fucked!

"Herb, basic physics is what it is, and it simply can't be argued with. An EMP strong enough to kill electronics in these stationary cars was strong enough to effectively fry some important part that disabled the entire vehicle. The computer, or the ignition, or God knows what else could get zapped, but that damage was accomplished when the vehicles were not even in operation. That speaks clearly to the fact that the pulse was extremely powerful or that our modern electronics were far more susceptible to EMP damage than was made public. Either way it's bad, and it just keeps getting far worse from there. Let's say that even if there were only one EMP, say over the east coast only, an EMP that powerful would make the effected range of the blast reach far to the west. The effects could possibly extend all the way out to California, depending on the elevation of the detonation. That means that the vast majority of vehicles across the effected range are now down and out.

"At this moment, with us being without any reliable communication, we've got absolutely no idea how far it actually goes and reliable communications is one thing we won't have any time soon. Not until some home-grown ham radio operators get their gear up and running on portable generators, and who knows how long that'll be. Why, hell, that might not be until spring or summer of next year in a worst case scenario. So, without reliable eyes and ears telling us the situation across the whole country, we are left with the only other option for situational awareness we have – what does our own eyes, ears, and brains tell us from the immediate empirical evidence available?

426

"What I'm seeing tells me this: we've seen with our own eyes that nothing but a single older car is the only working vehicle we've seen around here, for at least the past hour, and even parked cars have been neutralized. Well, from what I've seen and heard, it tells me that we don't have a power grid, either. There will be no heating supply system, no food delivery system, no medical system, and no medical supplies once local supplies have dried up. We have no emergency services anywhere, no firefighting capabilities, no law enforcement, and no ambulances. It tells me the railroad system, commercial air travel, and any form of public mass transit is now non-existent. Obviously, some motor vehicles are working and many more will get up and operating as mechanics swap out some spare electronics, but all that takes time, way too much time.

"Herb, look at the time of day it is. We're at the beginning of rush hour on the east coast. Say that the effects of the EMP are spread as far as the mid-west. That means that, from Maine to Florida, and out to Ohio, all the freeways, highways and inner city streets are now choked with millions of non-functioning vehicles whose electronics were destroyed in some manner by the EMP. Each one of those vehicles had at least one or more commuters making their way home.

"And even if you are in a vehicle that still operates, you'll be stuck, surrounded by those that don't. Right now I can see clearly in my mind's eye, millions of families spread miles apart from one another; husbands without wives, wives without husbands, and kids of all ages without their parents. Very few of the people will be at or near their homes, with most of them at work or school or somewhere along their commutes to and from. They'll all be stuck, on foot, with millions of other people, with a cold night coming and miles separating them from their loved ones. I see panic and death for thousands in just the first twenty-four hours."

Tortured by his own vision, Fred stopped and hung his head while he composed himself. Herb's mind reeled at the magnitude of the pending disaster Fred was describing for people all across the country.

Fred, his voice now heavily-graveled with emotion, continued through the progression of his analysis.

"Fire discipline will become a major community problem with cold weather and a long winter coming. There will be freezing people and, at least in the short term, no firefighting capabilities of any size larger than a bucket brigade. That's a recipe for disaster in these large cities that will be clogged with so many desperately cold people."

427

Fred stopped and shook his head. His mind blocked out the larger picture and focused on his own concerns.

"Getting away from here and reaching Colorado and my daughter is all I can focus on. It has to be my only priority – I simply cannot stay and help you here, I'm sorry. Even if I find an operating vehicle, the roads between here and Colorado will be heavily choked with abandoned vehicles. I can siphon fuel anywhere but I may get to a place I can't get by or around. Plus, I'm sure to run into desperate people who'll want that vehicle. If I'm outnumbered too badly I won't be able to…. I just can't risk that. Anyway, there won't be any plows clearing the snow-covered roads. If I get caught on the plains in a blizzard – well, hell, that'll be like the Donner party but with only me to eat."

Fred shook his head, considering his possibilities.

"No. I don't think I can risk a vehicle. Maybe I'll snag a bicycle. Between that and walking I should be able to make decent time. Maybe after a couple of days I'll see that things aren't that bad and go for a four-wheel-drive vehicle somewhere."

Herb stared at Fred dubiously.

"I don't think that's your best option for travelling from here to Colorado. You aren't a young man anymore and a bike is still awful slow going. You know, I might have a better idea for you, but first, what about supplies, food and shelter?"

Fred patted the paunch of his belly pressing against his shirt.

"I'm not young but I bet pedaling a bike from here to Colorado will work off this excess baggage. But supplies? Heck, with the desperate need everyone around us is going to be in, the only problem I'm going to have is getting into the stores and stealing something while there are still supplies to be had."

Herb nodded agreement as they stood quietly, thinking to themselves until Fred asked, "What are you going to do? You would be very welcome. I know Kim would love to have you around and I sure wouldn't mind keeping my friends close if things have gone as bad as I think."

A flock of buntings swooped and circled overhead as the two men watched the campus grounds coming more alive with groups of young people and faculty, spilling from the surrounding buildings to debate and question what was going on.

Herb shook his head as he replied.

"Jessica is still doing post-graduate work in Oslo. Boy, am I worried about her. At least she wasn't caught up in this disaster. Hopefully she stays put until we get back on our feet over here. Brian,

428

he has the law firm down in Boston. No, thanks for the invite, but I'll stay close to my family here."

A second later he reassessed his comments.

"Uh, Fred, I – I didn't mean that I am going to leave you hanging. I just want to stay close to my son. He may hate me as much as his mother, but he's still my son."

Fred gave his friend an irritated look.

"Hell, I'm the ass. I should've thought of that before asking. You damn well better stay with him. Things will get bad around here and you'll need each other. I'll be fine. I just got to make good time."

Herb looked around as he added, "I also feel responsible for these kids. Most of them will probably try to reach their homes, but a lot will be stuck here."

Fred nodded agreement.

"The next week will determine what the greater part of people here at the college and inside the nearby communities are going to try to do. It'll take days for the majority to really grasp their situation. You'll need to watch for nutcases losing it and trying to hurt others – there'll be one or two. Suicides will spike, then settle down and become fairly steady throughout the winter. Don't let hopelessness get ingrained in whatever group you end up with."

"Right, we'll have a hell of a lot of work to get done and I'll keep them busy. I think I can keep people motivated. Those that give up – well, they'll just have to be left to Darwin's rules. I cannot drag those along that just give up."

"Yep, I'm afraid you're right," Fred replied glumly as he kept digging through his luggage.

From between the folded legs of a pair of pants Fred pulled out a silver pistol stuck in a tan holster. Setting it aside with the things he would be taking, he went back to rummaging through his travel bag.

"Are you still carrying around that old Smith and Wesson? I would've thought you'd have upgraded to a Glock or something by now."

"The 4506? I like the weight in my hand. The Glocks are just too light for me. Plus, the punch of the .45 is a sentimental favorite of mine. Do you have a peashooter or something up there in your office or do you have to go all the way home to Worcester to get some protection?"

"Mama Blunt did not send her little boy into this world with the brains of a squirrel. I got a Glock up in my bag in the office. For years now it's usually gone with me everywhere. I typically keep it on me in case of some asshole trying to pull a Virginia Tech here. But

429

today, I got caught with my pants down. How characteristic, the day I would like to have it with me and I go and leave it somewhere else! Kimberly carried too, right?"

"Yep, I only hope she was able to reach hers in time and was not caught off guard as well."

"Me, too."

Fred flipped his tote bag over and examined it skeptically.

"Herb, do you have a backpack or something handy in your office? I can't cross a thousand miles of country pulling this worthless thing the whole way."

"No, I don't, but on a college campus I can solve your carrying issue pretty quick. You stay here. Get what you want out and have it ready. I'll be right back."

Without a further word Herb headed off. Fred watched him leave and weave his way through students on his way toward some dorm houses along Green Street. As he disappeared in the crowds Fred turned and continued organizing his effects.

*****

FIFTEEN-MINUTES later Herb came strolling back, a sleeping bag tucked under one arm and a backpack dangling from his hand. On his head sat a wide-brimmed Stetson cowboy hat. Fred, sitting on the bumper again, stared at his friend's cocky grin.

Herb stopped a few feet before him and asked, "Well, buckaroo, how's your cowboy skills?"

With a sideways grin Fred replied, "I don't think I'm much of a cowboy, Herb. It's never been my style, I'm afraid. And looking at you in that suit and hat combo I can see it's not your style, either."

Herb shrugged good-naturedly.

"Well, if your doomsday scenario is real, I believe you will become a real cowboy, real fast. Let's face it, you don't have the physical capability to go traipsing across the post-apocalyptic human wilderness like you're Davie Crockett, and I can't see your fat butt pedaling across thousands of miles like Lance Armstrong, right? So, I got a proposal for you."

Fred's grin grew wider.

"I was thinking, you need locomotion that can get you safely across 1,600 miles of country with clogged-up roads, jammed metropolitan hubs, past caravans of refugees, and still be able to handle all different weather conditions you may be faced with. A tall order, but one that I think I have right here on campus and readily at your disposal," Herb said confidently.

430

"Okay, so when did Smith College get an Abram's tank and unlimited fuel? What's your surprise, cowboy?" Fred asked doubtfully.

"Well, now, tanks aren't my specialty. But I've got a sweetie here on the faculty that I share some time with now and again when her husband is away to Europe on business, and she is big into horses. She turned me onto riding and every once in a while we go out and trot around. The horses are actually a lot of fun. Anyhow, if you think you can master the art of riding a beast like the buffalo soldiers from your family tree, then I think we've got a solution to your quandary."

Fred considered the idea for a moment.

"Uh, sure, I hadn't really thought about that, but you know that's not a bad idea. I'm willing to give it a shot, but where do I find one here around Northampton?"

"Well, now, I have a solution. The campus has more than a dozen, right over there on the far side of the creek. They're down the road this way, at the equestrian center," he said pointing down the street.

"At the stables they've got tack, rope, and just about everything you could possibly need to gear up with. While I was gone I did a quick check of my car and found it as dead as this rental of yours, and I still haven't seen another one moving. So I'm going down there to the barn to commandeer one of the quarter horses for myself, as my personal mode of transportation, at least for the time being. You come along and we'll select a couple for you to take. You can take two for you and another as a present to Kimberly, from her Uncle Herbie. Whaddaya say?"

Honored and humbled, Fred just smiled. He positively assessed his friend's good looks. Grey hair was beginning to show and crow's feet had started to infiltrate around the eyes, but he was still the man who had introduced Fred to Eva, was his best man at the wedding, and was also godfather to Kimberly. A single tear rolled down Fred's cheek as he reached out and grabbed his friend in a tight hug.

Minutes later Fred's belongings were stuffed in the backpack and the two made their way east down Green Street, passing the picturesque Paradise Pond, whose calm waters divided the main campus from the athletic fields. The landscaping of the campus created an idyllic northeastern landscape of smooth, glassy water, thick vegetation, and quaint century-old brick buildings and houses with large stands of maple trees that spread out in all directions.

Autumn colors had begun to appear among the dense canopy of trees and brush that lined the beautifully manicured lawns and ran along the water's edge, covering both banks. Athletic fields, reminiscent of pasture fields stretched into the distance across the stream. They paused halfway across the old bridge to admire the pristine view and spent a few moments together in silence.

The melodic but somber sounds of flutes and stringed instruments floated through the air, emanating from students who were still practicing inside the open windows of nearby Sage Hall. Below them the soft flush of dancing water flowing over rocks and the cheerful chirps and clacks of many happy songbirds blended with the music. A young lady sat below them next to the stream's bank, watching the waterfall, her books and notepads scattered around her as she still worked on her studies. The crystal clear water slowly wound its way through the Eden-like setting on its way to the Atlantic, and there were no obvious warnings present of the calamity both men knew was coming this way.

Herb broke the quiet of their thoughts and asked, as he watched the unconcerned and unknowing girl below them, "How long before they realize what's happened?"

Fred grimaced as he considered the question.

"Sadly, maybe forty-eight hours or so before the full weight of the situation begins to set in, and then the hording will start. Most violence should be modest, at least as long as food is easy to acquire. But the shit will hit the fan in no more than a week. When people start looking down the barrel of the on-coming winter, everything goes south real fast after that. You really need to take charge and get things well organized long before that."

"I know. I will."

Fred started to recite a laundry list of ideas as they resumed walking.

"Water is plentiful and handy. Food gets scarce quickly, stock dry goods, and keep pets, zoo animals, and any other available livestock in mind for your food supply when things get bad later. Hunger may be the single biggest driving force you will be confronted with this winter. Locate and centralize all food and medicine. Especially medicine! That'll become a huge resource in a new barter-driven economy – medicine. Check medicine cabinets in every abandoned house, stockpile everything you can get your hands on. Of course, collect any arms and ammunition you can get a hold of. You'll dearly need it at some point and at some time this winter. You've got to move fast. You have to get any and all supplies that you can find – quickly, before the gravity of the situation sinks in. The loss of central control and accountability will embolden junkies and opportunists to seek out medicines and drugs very quickly, maybe even tonight. Get to your pharmacies tonight. Do not be afraid to use force to protect what you'll need."

Herb scratched at his chin as he interjected, "You and I are in some sort of 'golden hour' of foreknowledge. You're saying I need to take advantage of it before the rest of society here crumbles, when they suddenly realize that they have taken the greatest technological step backward in the history of the world?"

"That's exactly what I'm saying. These folks are going to get it figured out. Many will do so very quickly, and when they decide to act, it will be motivated by desperation – they may be dangerous. Don't underestimate other people, be wary. The ones who take the longest to get their minds around this reality will be the farthest behind in preparedness and will be the first to become helpless. They will either die off or become slaves to others, or both."

All of a sudden, they stopped their conversation and together stared at the restored 1960s Volkswagen Bug as it drove by once again. The convertible puttered by as the two men stared at it like it was some miracle of science never seen before.

Herb spoke up, "It's only been, what, two or three hours? I'm already looking at that car like I want to carjack it. By the end of the week people will do exactly that."

"I'm afraid you're right, especially if the effects on vehicles we've seen here is widespread. If you can harvest a couple of vehicles that old, you'll have a good chance of having some reliable transportation. There is plenty of fuel around as every one of these cars around here probably has a half-tank or more in it. I recommend some 4x4s with the winter coming."

"Yeah, that makes sense. Most or all of the older vehicles, like that one, shouldn't have been severely affected by the EMP. I've seen quite a few up here in the northeast that are restored, running around on weekends," Herb said while taking note in his memory of when and where he had seen those vehicles.

"Keep in mind older commercial vehicles, too, like dump trucks, or maybe even some types of construction equipment. Those have fewer electronics in them. But they usually run on diesel, not gasoline, so you'll have to segregate your fuel supplies," Fred added.

Herbert nodded as he mentally made his list of things to get done and things to look for.

"Just remember from your own sociology class, Herb. Most people are looking for leadership and will quickly accept it if you're firm but level-headed. But those who want to go off from the group, for whatever reasons, must not be allowed to take away from your group's supplies. Compassion must, and I do mean must, stay with those who cluster with you and accept your leadership and who are also fully willing to participate in the necessary labors. Everyone else, well, sadly, they must be forced to fend for themselves and you're probably going to be required to be ruthless about it on some occasions."

Herb grimly nodded.

"You're going to be on your own out there and that means you'll be scavenging as well. Are you up to being on the receiving end of someone like me out there, down the road, a couple weeks from now, telling you to pound sand and not giving any handouts to your requests? That sounds like you may be headed into a pretty brutal situation of your own, my friend."

"I know. It's going to be a real challenge, to be honest with you. I really don't know how I will make it yet. I guess I'll have to play it by ear. How many cities do I have between here and the plains, each one full of desperate, hungry people? Eva was far stronger than I am. But I have to make it. I have to try. Kimberly is all I have, Herb. If I have to, I'll break down the gates of hell and castrate the Devil with a dull knife in order to see my girl again."

"I have no doubts," Herb said confidently.

Looking up at the afternoon sky he turned his head left and right.

"Fred, I just realized – no planes! No contrails anywhere at all. There are almost always planes flying out of Bradley International, down south of here. Now there are none."

Fred looked up with a resigned sadness.

"Yeah, I've been looking since I first stepped outside. Odds were stacked pretty high against any of them that were flying at the time of the EMP."

Realization crystallized on Herb's face.

"God almighty, how many people did we lose just in the air today?" Herb asked in a shaking voice. "I'd guess – what? Maybe two to four-thousand flights in the air at any given time on a weekday. Each plane with an average of two-hundred people on board, Good Lord – we've already lost thousands in the air today!"

Silent, Fred soberly scanned the sky for a few seconds longer before he hung his head and started walking again.

"I'd better get moving. Where are these horses?"

"Follow me," Herb said despondently as he led the way.

The tall brick smokestack from the college's now-quiet power plant laid a slab of afternoon shade across the two lanes of Hwy. 66 as the evening sun met with the horizon. Two electric company technicians stood scratching their heads and talking near the main building with the hood of their service truck up.

Herb and Fred followed the road as it wound another two-hundred yards to some large red barns used by the intercollegiate equestrian team. They quickly crossed the gravel parking lot, Herb leading the way into the darkened barn that was lined with large stalls along both walls. Fred saw the dim shapes of women grooming and feeding horses. As they walked toward the ladies Fred felt the eyes of the large animals inside the stalls watching him as he walked by. The air was heavy with the earthy smells of their humid breath, hay, and horse manure, but the background odor was of disinfectant.

"Hi, Ashley. Are you handling the power outage alright?" Herb asked.

"Uh, hi, Professor. Yeah, we're trying to get the evening feeding done while we stumble around here in the dark. What brings you down here?"

"Oh, I was bringing my friend here to see the horses before it got too dark."

"Well, it's not really a good day for a tour, Professor. Have you heard when the power will be back on? It's getting so dark in here we're having trouble finding stuff and we still got some medications to give out."

Herb and Fred looked at one another before Herb turned back to the earnest looking woman and said, "Ashley, I'm afraid the power won't be back on for a very long time. The sad truth is that these conditions will be a long-term problem we will be forced to deal with."

The two women with Ashley stopped what they were doing to listen, while the perplexed expression on Ashley's face morphed into fear.

"You're not joking, are you? What's happened? Have the terrorists attacked around here, too? Are there terrorists around Northampton – or Boston?"

"What's going on?" a blond fiftyish woman asked. "What is it you're saying?"

Herb raised his hands, palms out.

"Ladies, please don't get upset. I know of absolutely no terrorists anywhere near us. Furthermore, the power isn't out because of any gunmen around here, nor is it out because of some usual power outage. I – oh, how do I say this…."

Fred saw the consternation that was barely held in check by the women. The day had been terrible, the heartache and distress of the day's attacks had taken its toll on them as well as everyone else. Now

435

it was dark and they were deeply confused. Fred pitied them. *They need to know.*

He stepped forward and asked, "Herb, may I speak?"

"Uh, yes, please do."

Fred addressed the women, "Ladies, we weren't expecting anyone to be here. So the professor is having a difficult time explaining what we are doing. Let me first assure you that we do not believe that any terrorist-type attacks, such as what happened earlier in California, has happened anywhere near here. We also do not believe that attacks like those are responsible for the power being out. But…."

The fixation of the three sets of eyes was intense as they stared at him; their fear was real and very near the surface, their minds desperate for any credible news as to what was happening.

"….but, I am very certain, actually I am positive and have no doubts whatsoever about what our situation is. I believe that the power is out due to a very different form of attack upon our nation. I believe that attack was in the form of a massive electromagnetic pulse that has shorted out the electrical grid and virtually all electronic devices. I believe that it has probably, at a minimum, affected a huge swath of the east coast of the United States."

The two men stared at the women and waited for a response to Fred's pronouncement. But the women just stared back at them in silence. After several seconds, the first response came from the older blond; with an exasperated look she flung her hands skyward.

"What kind of sick joke are you two trying to pull?" she angrily challenged. "After a day like today, you come down here to scare us with some stupid science-fiction prank? What the hell is wrong with you?"

With a flat, unemotional stare Fred responded, "As you are fully aware, the power outlets and lights aren't functioning. If you haven't checked, you'll find that your phones and other electronic devices will not operate either."

Ashley nodded as she looked from the blond to Fred, "We tried calling our families, but none of our phones would work. I – I figured it must've been something to do with the power outage."

"It does, but probably not in any way you think. The patterns that you're used to, with the power coming back on after workmen fix whatever the problem is, are gone. The simple fact is that the power is not coming back for a very long time."

The older blond woman looked at Fred as though he was selling snake oil as she asked, "What do you mean? The power won't be back until tomorrow or later?"

Fred shook his head.

"No, ma'am. I mean the power won't be back for months or longer. I mean that we will have no electricity or working electronics of any kind for months, possibly even longer. No cars, no trains, no heat, no power, no emergency services. I mean that there will be no phones, no computers, little or no medical care, no food or water distribution, and no organized, working, or effective government services for weeks or months. That's what I'm saying," Fred stated calmly.

The blond cocked her head back indignantly while staring at him.

"Hhmmppht!" she said, wagging a finger at Fred. "Why, you're trying to scare us! This is just another power loss, like any other, and it will end like the others. What kind of sick practical joke are trying to pull?"

Fred waited until she paused for breath and then said bluntly, "You are wrong. I am not trying to scare you. I am not playing any joke on you. I am very serious and I am just trying to tell you the truth. Listen, I believe that our country, at least here in the northeast, has been attacked by a special type of military weapon. It probably was connected to the terrorist attacks earlier. I have no way of knowing how much of the entire country is affected, but I suspect it could be all or most of it."

Ashley interrupted, "What do you mean, *special weapon*?"

Fred addressed her question while staring into her eyes.

"This special weapon I refer to is called an EMP. It was probably a standard nuclear warhead of some magnitude. But instead of being used to hit a city or blowing up near the ground, this one would be detonated above the Earth's atmosphere over our heads. That explosion in space would then send a wave of very intense energy downward onto the planet. The interaction of that energy wave and the planet's magnetic field would cause an extremely powerful electromagnetic pulse to be generated, which would then sweep downward. That tremendous amount of electromagnetic energy then overpowered the surge protection in any electronic device, electronic system, or electrical grid that it came into contact with, instantly shorting it out and making it inoperable. That would include the national electrical grid and all of the millions of pieces of electronic equipment: watches, phones, computer, cars, and so on."

The three women stared quietly at Fred, like he was mildly insane and held a fresh, steaming turd in his hand.

"Do you ladies understand the consequences of this type of attack?" he finally asked.

The older blond stepped forward, her head leaning sideways and her finger pointing at Fred.

"You know, I think you're a real asshole. Coming down here on a day like today, scaring these girls and trying to scare me. Why, if you weren't so big I'd slap your face, you jerk!" she asserted with bravado while poking at Fred's chest. She then turned to Herb with undisguised anger and spoke venomously, "And you! You think your pretty face and over-the-top sex drive will protect you from losing tenure over this? Huh! Tomorrow, when the power is back on and I'm sitting with the college president and dean, I'll have your goddamn job over this. Mark my words, you fucking asshole!"

She spun around and addressed the other two women.

"Ash, Rose – I'm leaving for home. The horses are fed and the meds can wait until tomorrow. I'm not going to stay here and listen to the horrible crap that these two are spewing. Are you coming with me?"

Ashley and Rose looked at one another before Ashley finally said, "Rose, honey, go ahead home with Megan. I'll stay and close up shop for the night. I'll see you both in the morning, okay?"

Rose nodded and started down the hall; Megan turned and asked while thumbing over her shoulder at Fred and Herb.

"Are going to be okay with these two jerks?"

"Yeah, I'll be fine, go ahead."

Satisfied, Megan directed the young redhead down the gloomy hallway between the stalls and out the barn's door. Ashley turned back to the men waiting patiently and eyed them both closely for several seconds before speaking.

"I don't get suckered easily and I'm a good judge of people," she said, looking hard at Herb. "Professor, you're a good man, and I can tell you weren't joking with us and I trust you."

She then turned and addressed Fred, "You I don't know, but I'm positive you're serious in what you're saying. I'm also a science major and I understand what you are talking about and it makes perfect sense with what I've seen today. I also know that if you are right – the implications are really severe."

As Herb smiled at the thoughtful young woman, Fred replied solemnly, "Yes, my dear, very, very severe. We can only hope at this point that a small portion of the country is affected, but I'm not going to base my decisions on that chance."

Ashley tilted her head down and began to speak to herself as if she was alone.

"Both mine and Rose's cars wouldn't start. My Blackberry, watch, IPad, and laptop are all useless. The power's out and several

438

lights blew. I haven't heard any sirens or horns at all and I haven't seen but two cars drive by here for over an hour. People everywhere are walking around on foot…."

She lifted her head and looked at Fred.

"I think I may know why you came down here."

Herb interjected with a smile, "Smart girl."

Even in the dimming light Fred could see her blush.

"My friend here, Fred Thompson, is an author I invited to the school to speak today. His vehicle is also inoperable and he has a personal emergency. His daughter is a teacher at the school that was attacked earlier today in Colorado. He needs to leave immediately to get to her as quickly as possible. Now, I fully appreciate that you may not like what we're going to do, but I hope you realize we don't have much of a choice."

Ashley squared her shoulders to Herb and replied with confidence, "Let me give this the old college try, Professor. The power is quite possibly out everywhere within several hundred miles of here. Every single electronic device is no longer functioning, which means no communication, no services, no emergency aid, and no transportation. If all that proves to be correct – then what we're looking at, at least temporarily, is America has moved backward to a technological level on par with the 1700s, right?" she asked while staring at Fred, who nodded agreement.

"But, wait, my car battery still has power. The headlights came on and stuff. It just won't start up. So that means that it can be fixed, right? We can still have electricity, and equipment will work again, at least after they are all fixed, right? So we're still just talking about a temporary thing."

Herb gave a sad grimace.

"Yes, you are right, Ashley. Unfortunately, there are two big problems with fixing anything – time and volume."

"Now, wait a minute. It's a big problem, but we have auto part stores, factories, roads, and infrastructure. It'll take work, but it can be done. It's just…."

"And it will be done, young lady," Fred said in agreement. "But we're still talking about how much needs to be done and how much time we've got before the unmet daily needs of a society as large as ours has a truly devastating effect. Look at the ingredients of your hopes; we have parts and equipment, stores of food and medicine, and we have a completely built and existing infrastructure for a modern society of over three-hundred fifty million people – and I'm sorry, it all means absolutely nothing both in the short and long

439

terms. As a matter of fact, that all becomes a substantial liability for each of us."

"I don't get it. How can all that capability be a liability?" Ashley protested.

"Well, unfortunately it's very simple and direct," Herb said. "Our society runs at a very fundamental level – on electricity. Currently, though, we have none or what we do have is extremely limited and must, by necessity, be conserved for highest-priority uses. Picture this, Ashley: we have the occasional ice storm come through these parts of the northeast. You've lived through them up here so you know the effects. The ice builds up on wires, poles, and tree limbs until it physically damages a significant portion of the electrical grid's delivery system, right? Then it takes days or even weeks for those electrical lines and poles to be repaired and replaced, just to get a ready-and-waiting source of electricity from a local power plant restored to its consumers.

"Consider that, and then work out how long the repair time will probably be if that damage is as extensive as we believe it to be. At present we have thousands upon tens-of-thousands of pole transformers, electrical dispersion-hub transformers, and probably thousands of miles of electrical conduit that is fried, melted, or otherwise destroyed by the surge through the system. If you put that on the scale of a nationwide affect, not just a regional affect – that'll take literally years and years to repair completely.

"In addition to that, the big oil-immersed distribution step-up transformers that you see sitting in rows outside of power plants and the numerous step-down transformers sitting in clusters at the thousands of power distribution sub-station hubs – those pieces of machinery aren't even manufactured here in America anymore. They're made in Europe, China, and India and it takes almost a year to construct just one of the big ones. Couple that problem with the fact that all the power plants, distribution sub-stations, and electrical grid control and management all work via computer control.

"With thousands of miles of melted transmission lines, tens-of-thousands of blown transformers, and virtually all computer control for the entire grid's electrical production and distribution being fried – Ashley, just how long does it take for our nation to get the very first kilowatt of electricity to this barn, the school, your home, or the nearest hospital? That terrible situation I just described is only about power distribution. It doesn't even begin to encompass the loss of every single bit of electromagnetically saved and stored bit of data. All of the information that was once housed on every computer, database, and server across the nation, in every sector of business, government, and even in every private household within the affected area is now gone, forever. Yes, I can see your apprehension. Imagine – as of now, every single kilobyte of data has been wiped clean and erased from existence from all of those devices. Inconceivable amounts of information and stored records used for every imaginable purpose in our society have now been erased by the EMP surge.

"So, you see, most if not all of the nation is going to be without electricity of any kind for a very protracted time and the information that was once stored electronically is now gone – forever. Mull over for a few seconds all the stuff – everything in our lives, personal and professional, that need electricity to operate. Like your kitchen, your entire house, traffic lights, hospital equipment, manufacturing plants, food distribution centers, and city water supply pumps. And I'm talking about the big pump stations that supply water for entire cities, not just a single house or a neighborhood water pump, and, I mean, do you begin to understand the scope? Everything we need in order to have our modern society work, it all runs on electricity and now that power and the capability to make that power is gone, and it will be gone for a very long time."

Herb paused with his hands trembling as his own mind tried to grasp what he was saying.

Fred interjected, "And, my dear, that is unfortunately just the beginning of the bad news. Believe me, I fully appreciate the magnitude of the situation we are trying to have you comprehend. If you think it is hard for you to grasp now – just think of the three-hundred-plus million other Americans trying to grasp the situation they are now finding themselves in, right along with you and me. It isn't just electrical power generation and distribution. You see, the whole economy and therefore our entire daily societal structure is now non-existent and will be immediately replaced by a have and have-nots system. And you know I'm not talking about money – that is worthless for even making decent fires now.

"I'm talking about those people who have heat, fuel, food, medicine, and supplies of every type and those who have none or little of those very necessary things. Americans are the most generous people in the world, but we are now weeks away from another cold winter and soon we will be talking about freezing and starvation deaths for possibly millions of our countrymen and their families!"

Fred paused, shaking his head as his own mind fought to stay logical, and he tried to keep focused and not sink into despair. He quashed the emotion welling inside and continued.

"Regrettably, that type of stress will be the cause of much evil. Then you're still talking about the necessary repairs before we

441

can get a national electrical grid back. It will take even longer for electronic components and equipment to be repaired or replaced across the wide expanse of our nation, once we have some form of manufacturing back up and running.

"Like Herb said – it's all a matter of time and volume. It is just too great a disaster for a quick fix or repair. Look at the disaster of the Japanese earthquake and tsunami this spring and how they have only been able to get back to the current level of modified normalcy after seven months – how many good and decent souls have they lost to just one localized natural disaster? We here in America are now looking at the entire defeat and destruction of our society, and the utter collapse of our governmental structure, and the resulting deaths of hundreds of thousands or even millions of our countrymen over the coming year. The old, the infirmed, diabetics, asthmatics, people on dialysis or treatment for cancer, heart disease, or other serious ailments, the aged in senior homes, the helpless insane as well as the convicted criminals who are now locked inside their institutions of confinement – all of those groups of our countrymen and women will most likely all be dead very soon. Those that are healthy and free will then be forced to compete with the other healthy to try to survive whatever Mother Nature sends at us during this coming winter, before we can even hope, as a nation, to even begin the first baby steps of rebuilding in the coming spring."

Ashley stood silent and stunned. The magnitude of the situation shattered the barriers inside her mind as she strenuously worked to rapidly compute the vast data of possibilities that flooded into her consciousness. The faces of her family and friends from all across the country danced through her thoughts at a blistering pace as the effects of a post-EMP America streamed by her inner vision. Apocalyptic movies were her only reference and somehow they seemed puny and insignificant to what her heart said was coming. Somewhere, stuck between terror and revulsion, her mind jumped up and down while screaming its wish to stay securely within the safety of denial and the calmness that came with disowning the truth. The mental and emotional turmoil roiled inside her at hurricane strength and continued until her body could no longer take the building strain. She spun quickly, vomiting onto a loose pile of hay on the floor.

She spit chunks of half-digested food and bile-coated liquid vomit, and then wiped her dripping mouth as she looked up, horrified.

"Oh, God, my parents!" she exclaimed, "Oh, my God, my dad's diabetic. What do I do?" she whimpered.

Fred's eyes softened at the young woman who just had her whole world turned upside down. A deep sadness weighed on his heart as he thought of the millions more people who would, over the next few days and weeks, come to their own individual levels of crushing comprehension.

"Are they close by?" he asked.

Ashley nodded as she wiped at her face.

"Then I'm sure there is a pharmacy between here and there, right? We will just need to appropriate a good supply of insulin, but I don't really know how to help you with the refrigeration of the supply so it doesn't spoil."

Several feet away a mop clattered to the floor, making Ashley, Fred, and Herb all jump in fright. Rose, the short redhead who they believed had left with Megan, now stood shaking and looking sheepishly down the darkening hallway at them. Her attempts at giving a calm demeanor were betrayed by the fear in her eyes as she nervously nibbled at a fingernail.

Without taking the finger from her teeth she mumbled, "Wow, I thought it was something real bad. What do we do?" she asked with searching eyes.

"I thought you'd left with Meg?" Ashley asked.

"Megan just wanted to show how tough she is. Once we got outside she broke down and went off crying. I figured I'd come back in and listen. This is real bad. What are the cops saying? What is the faculty saying? Do they agree with you two?" she asked the men.

"We haven't seen any cops. And anyhow, they would be on foot and unable to contact their communication centers. As far as the faculty goes, I haven't worried about that, since they will all be here all night with us anyhow. My priority is to look after my friend here and see him on his way," Herb replied.

Ashley looked at the items that Fred was holding.

"So, you're here to take a horse, right?"

Fred did not answer but just sat the rolled sleeping bag and backpack down on the floor, walked over to a stall door and looked in at the older thoroughbred mare that stared back at him. Her huge brown eyes appraised him as she sniffed the strange smells coming from this stranger at her stall door.

"Young lady, my daughter is in Colorado. I can't fly or drive there and I don't trust trying to get there with a vehicle. I'm a little old to walk that far and Herb and I agree that my butt wouldn't make it that far riding a bike. So I'm here to take two or three of your horses to use as my transportation. My sincere hope is that you will cooperate with me."

"That's stealing," Rose asserted defensively.

443

"Yes, yes, it is," Fred replied in an even tone. "I can assure you that if I can return them in the future I will, but I can make you no guarantees."

Rose grabbed for Ashley's arm, protesting. "Ash, we can't let him take...."

"Slow down, Rose," Ashley said, rested her hand on top of Rose's hand and looked at Fred.

"Okay, I'm with you, mister. My family lives about fifteen miles southwest of here toward Westhampton. That is in the direction you say you want to go. If what you're saying turns out to be true – I should have all the confirmation I need by tomorrow night. I'll help you get the type of horses you'll need for a trip like that, and then I'll ride with you to my parent's house. You can help me get my dad's medications and stay the night with us. If you're lying to me I'll cut your balls off and then I'll come back and do the same with you, Professor." she said, pointing to Herb's crotch.

"Ash, no, we may need those animals," Rose pleaded.

"You get to the dorm, Rose. I'll be back to help take care of the horses whether what they say is true or not. If they're lying, I'll bring the horses back and if they're telling the truth, this man will need them more than us, I hope."

Fred nodded to Ashley.

"I can only offer you my sincerest thanks, young lady."

"Come on, we got a lot of work to do and we're losing daylight fast," she said as she turned and waved for them to follow.

Fred grabbed his items, and with Herb in step beside him, they followed after the intelligent woman who now had so many more cares and worries than she had just five minutes ago.

*****

13:55pm PST
Beale Air Force Base
Yuba City, California

THE PEOPLE inside were silent. Uttering a word would feel like a sacrilegious act, a violation of decorum that, if done, would have some unknown but presumably drastic consequences for the person who committed the breach. Tension, everybody felt it, sharp and taut. This was new territory, a line never before crossed, a hallowed ground that bordered on the divine with its weighty measures and consequences. Each soul lived with the knowledge that they walked on a tightrope of dawning history. A page had been turned and nothing

444

could bring back the Camelot that was. Humpty Dumpty was broken and no one had any illusions about a fix.

So the only noise heard inside the US Army MRAP Cougar was the deep purr of the big Caterpillar C-7 engine and the soft rumble from the tires as they rolled down the smooth pavement of Hwy-65 nearing its destination of Beale AFB. The massively armored vehicle was in the fourth position of the twelve-vehicle convoy, and nobody who watched the procession pass by had any idea that those few vehicles contained all that was left of the Executive Branch of government for the United States of America.

Large fields of corn, beans, and cabbage passed by as the convoy navigated around stalled cars on the road leading to Yuba City. There were tens of thousands of people caught by the west coast EMP while in the process of their afternoon commutes. As the convoy roared by, those commuters either stood next to their now-useless cars, trying vainly to get them working again or had given up and had started the long slog to their distance homes and families. The huge columns of newly-made Golden State refugees was growing even larger and at a rapid pace as individual realization migrated from the few, to become the broad consensus of the many: the problem with their vehicles was something far worse than they knew.

As the mass of humanity acquainted their legs with long distance foot travel, many stopped and stared, perplexed at the line of vehicles going by. The sight of the military between Yuba City and Sacramento was common for the locals as the army and air force often used the roads between the many military bases in the area. But after today's bitter attacks across the nation, and now with their cars and electronics no longer functioning; this convoy appeared different than what they were used to. With manned machine guns and spinning weapons turrets it looked downright menacing as it seemed prepared and ready to do battle on the streets of Kandahar or Baghdad. For the men and women who paid their taxes for the hardware moving by it definitely felt far more worrisome than reassuring.

As the convoy neared the base, an older Subaru Outback sat in the middle of the lane with its hood up. The convoy commander, USAF Major Rick Bellevue, stared out the passenger window at the very dark-skinned family standing next the car. A migrant worker stood alongside his woman who held a baby wrapped in a Powerpuff Girls blanket, while the man rested a hand atop his young son's head, the boy tightly hugging his father's thigh. The man locked his questioning eyes with the major's as the column of vehicles kicked up dust and continued on.

445

Their strong Mesoamerican-Indian features identified them as from Central America, maybe from Guatemala or Honduras. They had come to work the lush fields of California's farming region. Their inquiring, fearful looks were accentuated by a knowing that they were no longer in a place of opportunity, but somewhere that had an ominous and unknown future.

Bellevue had seen the same looks from people who had lined the streets as he patrolled Baghdad and Ar Ramadi during his two combat tours in Iraq. He never imagined that he would ever see the same desperation in the eyes of people here in California. It was more than unnerving; it was very frightening and shook him to his core.

He desperately wished that he knew how his own family was and if they were stranded somewhere miles from home like these families were. His convoy had passed many such families since he had picked up the indispensible cargo from Mathers. That cargo had to arrive at Beale and all other considerations were secondary, and his personal concerns would have to wait.

Knowing how bad thing were and having a good idea how bad things would soon become, he was sorely tempted to just steal the Cougar and go AWOL, heading straight to his family to ensure their safety. But that would mean desertion, and a direct dereliction of his sworn oath of service to his country, a betrayal of every duty he held important as a man and as a soldier. It also meant that he would probably be quickly caught and summarily executed for desertion during wartime. But the past half hour had been the greatest trial of his entire life. Even so, his personal honor and patriotism did nothing to keep his mind from seeing the faces of his children and wife in the faces of the people he drove by.

Very few people outside the convoy knew that President Obama and Vice President Biden were both dead. Or that nationwide martial law had been declared by the Vice Chairman of the Joint Chief's in NORAD where General Cartwright had established USNORTHCOM as the global headquarters for not only all US, Canadian, and NATO military forces but also the center of civil governance for the United States until a new president could be sworn in. Major Bellevue knew one more very chilling piece of information: the military forces of both America and Canada were now at Defcon-1 status and a complete worldwide nuclear strike could happen at any moment. The obliteration of several billion human beings could happen with the flick of a single switch.

Little more than an arm's length away from the major sat the Democrat Whip for the House of Representatives, Beth Gossett, who silently contemplated her future while she restlessly and continuously manipulated her now-useless IPhone 4 in her hands. She was amazed at the opportunities that had come her way from the odd chances of today's catastrophe. *Lucky seven come eleven. Mama needs a new pair of shoes.*

She looked down at the device, half-hoping it would suddenly work, while the darker half of her soul prayed it was indeed still dead and powerless. A bony finger pressed on the power button as she closed her eyes and prayed to the gods of chance. Opening her eyes she looked down to see the results. *Nothing!* She suppressed a smile as her big eyes danced around the vehicle's interior. She felt a spark of excitement shoot through her, feelings of trepidation mixed with a jolt of sexual arousal. Nothing this exciting had happened to her body in years and she relished its return.

Her large eyes stopped roving as they landed on her Chief of Staff, Bill Langley, who sat across from her, staring at his toes and fidgeting even more than usual. On either side of him sat two military police, holding their rifles. Beth glanced up and her eyes met the stern gaze of the sergeant. She held his eyes and saw the knowing in them, that he had been watching and analyzing her. An emotion flashed through his eyes quickly that soon faded away, almost imperceptible. *Was that curious or disgusted?* Due to his military efficiency in completely and immediately removing any emotion from his face she could not tell what he was thinking, as he quickly directed his eyes down at his desert-tan combat boots.

She canvassed her memory for his first name but only drew a blank. She read the blocky black-stitched letters on his chest, GAVNEY. His large muscular frame and jutting, square-jawed face showed no more outward emotion, but the master sergeant's body language told the congresswoman everything she needed to know; it made her anxious and even a little scared.

Fright was normally an unknown station for Beth to inhabit. Power, position, and prestige were the usual grounds she walked and maneuvered upon. A life-long politician and power broker, before today she had fully intended to be only the second female Speaker of the House in history. She had a pedigree that oozed strength, not fear, and she was very comfortable in the realm of decree and mandate. Fear was, well, an uncomfortable reality for her to realize on such an auspicious day as this.

She had gotten to her political heights by being able to read people accurately and quickly. She was proud of her talent to correctly size-up everyone she ever met with little more than a glance. Foes, friends, idiots, or geniuses were all measured properly in mere seconds by her piercing eyes and intellect. For her, making decisions to work

447

with, outflank, or fight and destroy people was an easy and instantaneous reaction throughout her daily life. While other power brokers hemmed and hawed on possibility and nuance, she acted.

At the pinnacle of her career as House Minority Whip she was just two steps away from being in the most powerful political position in the entire legislature, the speaker. And that glorious position was just another two steps away from the most coveted position of power on the planet: the presidency. Many loved Beth and far more hated her, but either way none of them could ever deny that she was one cold, hard, tough bitch who could slit your throat with a grin on her face. Both allies and enemies took her very seriously, and very few came away from an encounter with her unscathed, whether they were friend or foe.

The master sergeant sat and simmered under her continuous gaze. As he bristled she was able to clearly see that he hated her. *Is that what Caligula saw in the praetorian?* She made a mental note: in the world-after-the-event politics that were to come, she would need to keep her attention fixed on spotting people like him as she walked the dark corridors of her future glory. *The rules for political power are returning to some very old ones, and I'm ready for that.*

When the neocons had successfully removed her mentor from the speakership, Beth had chafed under the clueless-boob Boehner becoming speaker. He had so much fun when he had proudly proclaimed that he would only fly commercial aircraft. Now the orange-skinned imbecile's flight from his district in Ohio to Washington, DC was missing, and presumed down somewhere in West Virginia. *Ha! How did that decision taste, Johnny, just before you ate the ground?*

With Barack and ol' Joe both killed on Marine One, it meant the Presidency would have passed to that human orange peel from Ohio. Beth would have been beside herself with fury with that result. But now with his jet missing and Boehner presumably dead, the nation still needed a person in the wide-open vacancy for the Presidency, and fast. Time was critical and decisions needed to be made. With so much damage being done across the breadth and width of the country, waiting to discover if indeed Boehner was alive or dead was simply not a luxury that could be afforded in this extreme emergency. Immediate action was necessary.

That meant that the next in the chain of succession went to the Secretary of State, Hillary Clinton. And guess where she had been this morning? At a conference in Los Angles with the Taiwanese Ambassador, just down the coast when the attacks had begun. *Luck is the byproduct of preparedness!*

Clinton had been rushed in a military helicopter to the CalEMA headquarters at the old Mathers Air Force Base, where Beth was assisting Governor Brown in organizing the response efforts to the attacks in the Bay. It was less than an hour after Hillary had arrived when the event had occurred. Shortly thereafter confirmation had come in that Marine One had gone down. After that it was just a few more anxious minutes of waiting before they were notified of the recovery of Obama and Biden's burned and mangled bodies. As the seconds ticked by, Beth's grand meeting with destiny came closer and closer. The surviving members of the Joint Chiefs had taken immediate over-lordship of the national and international government and military responses.

The First Lady and her daughters had been collected from the White House and were with the bodies of the president and vice president, en route for safekeeping on the USS Guam docked at Norfolk Naval Station in Virginia. Meanwhile, the military had started a frantic and desperate search to find Boehner and get him sworn in as president.

Beth's juices flowed hard by that point, but they quickly went into maximum-overdrive when news came into CalEMA that Boehner's plane was also missing. So until it was confirmed that Boehner was alive, Hillary was the heir apparent and was now on her way to be sworn into the Presidency. And she would need an appointed vice president for the immediate future, and that meant the selection for Hillary was limited to a choice of either Governor Jerry 'Moonbeam' Brown or Beth Gossett!

Every brain in the vehicle ran laser-sharp. Furtive notice was given to every noise and movement, but mouths remained silent as they contemplated their futures. The nation needed leadership and that was now embodied in Hillary who happened to be sitting in the right chair at the right time, and so was Beth. The corner of her mouth turned up slightly before she stopped it from becoming a full-blown grin. Beth knew that in a matter of hours Boehner could turn up alive and so what? The positions of president and vice president would already be filled and no one would ever take it away. She would make damn sure of that!

Beth remembered the look on Hillary's face when selecting her as the interim vice president. It had been a look similar to what the master sergeant had given her. Beth did not care. Like and dislike had nothing to do with politics, and circumstances made for strange bedfellows. All Beth needed was to stay with the pantsuited bitch while her star remained in ascension. Beth would wait for an opportunity to arrive, and would then climb into the high chair herself! *The ides of March will get here soon, you old cunt!*

Beth Gossett's thoughts strayed to her husband and family. She has no idea where they were. They had not been found before she left with the convoy. She had no idea if they were alive or dead. What she did know was that they would not see her inauguration today. She was about to become the Vice President of the United States of America, the second most important day in her life, and they would not see it.

*****

MEANWHILE, as the convoy rolled through the gates to the military base, Hillary Clinton was also thinking of the Presidency, and just what she would be required to do once she finally had the job she had always wanted. A very short time ago she had stared at the seemingly never-ending line of stalled vehicles clogging the highway on her way here and wondered if that was what every road across the nation must look like at this moment *What the hell am I supposed to do with a non-functioning country?*

She had vaguely paid attention during the Senate's closed-session briefings on the effects of an EMP attack. She, like everyone else in the briefing, had merely scoffed at the idea of such a thing ever occurring. She knew what the intelligence reports said about who could, and, more importantly, who would be willing to carry out such an attack. The steps necessary for a successful strike to happen were many, and so tenuous for terrorists to accomplish; it had seemed so laughable at the time.

Now, though, the surreal sight of the thousands of stranded motorists plodding the long miles of I-80, with the dark haze of smoke from fires in the Bay Area that hung in the air, it was like some post-apocalyptic movie set or something straight out of a child's nightmare. Hillary felt like a helpless Alice who had fallen through some terrible rabbit hole of her own. *Is this even real?* She pinched her arm and could feel the realness of her pain.

Her political instincts told her to stop and reassure those people, but Major Bellevue quickly ixnayed the idea as it would clog the convoy's path with people, and he also had warned that the reaction from the crowd could be unpredictable, possibly even dangerous. So she had been forced to leave them to their fates for the time being. Her priority was to get to the base, get officially sworn in, and then she would have the power required to start the hard work that lay ahead. Since her idealistic days at Wellesley and Yale she had dreamt of the day she might become president. But to receive that largess on a day like today was a jagged pill itself. She felt the heavy weight that came with the highest office already pressing down hard upon her shoulders. *If the whole nation so affected – can I handle this?*

Hillary's eyes focused outward and she noticed that there were no longer any vehicles or people along the road. The base commander, Colonel Tung Ho Dang, had already organized his resources and mobilized his personnel into action. Dang, a studious man who had fled the pogroms of the Viet Cong after the fall of Hanoi as an orphaned Vietnamese boat kid, had worked up to being a colonel in the US Air Force. His diligence, fast thinking and competence made assimilating into American military culture easy for the workaholic. That diligence had already gotten every street on the base cleared while all base personnel had been collected and accounted for.

The convoy turned off the main drag, Doolittle Drive, onto Grumman Avenue headed for the airstrip. For the first time since coming onto the military base Hillary saw people on foot; many people walking toward the airstrip tarmac. Some stopped and stared, squinting as they tried to see who was inside the vehicles that roared by, while others simply sobbed and kept walking.

The vehicles pulled onto the mile-long tarmac, parking in front of a finely manicured lawn where Colonel Dang stood with a dozen other military officers. In a flash he covered the distance to the Cougar, opening the door for soon-to-be-President Clinton.

"Madam Secretary, welcome to Beale."

"Thank you. You are the base commander?"

"Yes, ma'am, Colonel Tung Ho Dang."

Hillary cocked her head to the side.

"I'm sorry?"

Well-versed in this, Dang did not miss a beat.

"It's a Vietnamese name, Madam Secretary. Please, just call me Dang."

Hillary nodded.

"Do you have reliable communications with NORAD yet?" she asked as Congresswoman Gossett quickly walked up to them.

"Yes, ma'am. I've conveyed to them that you have arrived. They've dispatched one of the two still-operational 747s of the presidential fleet to retrieve you for immediate delivery to Cheyenne Mountain."

"Yes, fine. Uh, we received confirmation while coming here that Speaker Boehner's plane has gone down but that he had not been located yet. Has that changed?"

451

"No, ma'am. That information is still all we have. I have been able to consult with General Cartwright at USNORTHCOM, and we are all in complete agreement that you're swearing-in must be completed immediately. Due to the extreme nature of the threat and grave situation our entire nation is in, the vacancy in civilian command and control must be filled straight away to ensure continuity of government during our response to this attack," the colonel explained.

"I have also been instructed to assure you that if any issues arise from bypassing Speaker Boehner's succession, if he is found alive, they are wholly subsidiary to the needs of the nation at this hour. We all swear our full support to you in that matter, ma'am."

Hillary reached out and placed her palm against the Colonel's breast.

"I thank you. No word on General Dempsey or any of the other members of the Joint Chiefs?"

"No, ma'am, no word at this time. All members, except for the Vice Chairman and Chief of Naval Ops, are feared lost over the Atlantic as no survivors have yet been found in the wreckage. At least that is how it stood as of fifteen minutes ago, when I spoke with General Cartwright and Admiral Roughead. That is why we were forced to keep your delivery here via land travel. We could not risk losing you to another EMP strike.

"With so many legislators, agency heads, and military staff being on flights after being recalled to Washington or their duty stations after this morning's ground attacks, I am deeply afraid, ma'am, that we have had a great many of our nation's leaders wiped out today. Right from the get-go, it appears as though we are headed into this war with the fourth string being all we have left. Uh, uh, I meant no offense, Madam Secretary."

"None taken, Colonel," Hillary replied. "Believe me, this is indeed an overwhelming situation and I fully appreciate your candor."

Beth Gossett leveled a cold stare at the colonel as he nodded acceptance to Hillary and continued.

"We have also received confirmation that the EMP strike over Europe is as devastating as, or even more so, than the two that detonated over our two coasts. Blanket coverage of EMP effects appears to be virtually complete across all of Western Europe, Britain, and with severe effects extending far into the Caucuses. To put it simply, Madam Secretary, practically all NATO forces and their countries appear to be a complete wash. USNORTHCOM has also just received disturbing news from Russia and China that you must be briefed on as soon as possible."

Hillary shook her head in disbelief.

452

"Dear Lord. I, I must ask – what about Italy?"

"Uh – Italy? I, uh, have nothing specific on the situation there in Italy. May I inquire as to…"

"Chelsea. My daughter Chelsea is there. I need you to find out about Italy immediately."

The colonel's head bobbed rapidly.

"Yes, ma'am. I will get that to General Cartwright immediately."

Beth Gossett rested her hand on Hillary's shoulder and gave a squeeze of reassurance. With cold eyes she watched the colonel give orders to a lieutenant, who then took off running for a nearby building.

Hillary looked around at the people gathering at a nearby monument of a SR-71 Blackbird airplane. The display was surrounded by a small grass park where people were assembling.

"What exactly do you have planned, Colonel?"

The colonel gestured for her to accompany him as he turned and led her toward the corner of the small park.

"Yes, well – I have some technicians attempting to get some recording devices up and running but they're having quite a lot of difficulty. But in the meantime I have ordered all military and civilian personnel on this base, those not otherwise occupied with other duties, to report to our U2 Park here. I thought it would be appropriate to have them as witnesses to your swearing-in, Madam Secretary. Given that there are so few functioning recording devices, I believed that it would be beneficial if we had as many eyes on this occurrence as absolutely possible."

Hillary nodded her affirmation and touched his arm.

"Thank you again, Colonel Dang, very thoughtful and wise"

Suddenly she felt her knees wobble and was forced to stop walking. The entire delegation around her stumbled awkwardly to keep from crashing into one another. Her eyes watered and her lower lip trembled slightly as she covered her mouth with her hand. Repeatedly she swallowed hard while working hard at choking back the emotions that were very near the surface. Almost two thousand sets of eyes were rigidly transfixed on her and as she surveyed the crowd she could see the strain on each face. Many people saw her trepidation and averted their eyes while she collected herself, but Beth's eyes stayed glued, watching her very closely. After several seconds she was able to regain her composure. A single tear had made a wet path down her cheek that she hurriedly wiped away as she cleared her throat. She turned to the colonel.

"It's such a terrible day for us, isn't it?"

The muscles of Dang's rigid jaw flexed several times before he was able to reply.

"It is the worst day in the history of all mankind, Madam Secretary."

He gently placed his hand on her shoulder and led her across the lawn. A speaker's podium had been placed near the monument. Nearby sat a young airman hunched over a folding table that had been erected several feet from the podium. He was busily testing one green circuit board after another, a dozen digital cameras waiting to be tested on the table in front of him. He ignored the approaching group while he sifted through a bewildering pile of electrical wires, circuit boards, and fuses.

He held in his right hand a soldering iron that got its power from a small portable generator, while his left hand held a set of black and red probes like chopsticks. The probes had been taken from a digital multimeter that was now lying useless on the ground. The probes wires had been cut and soldered onto the back of a small round needle voltmeter gauge that appeared to have been taken from the dashboard of a vehicle. A small motorcycle battery sat on the grass, supplying power to the crudely-rigged piece of testing equipment.

On the cement behind the airman's feet was a considerable pile of shattered plastic pieces of what had once been very expensive electronic equipment and circuit boards. Just as Clinton and her entourage stopped at the table the airman cursed and took the circuit board he was testing and threw it onto the pile.

"Fucking worthless shit!"

"Airman! This is not the time for that," Colonel Dang barked.

The airman leveled tired, frustrated eyes at his commander as he slowly stood and came to attention.

"Sir."

The colonel looked around at the jumbled mess of now worthless electronic devices strewn around and his demeanor softened.

"At ease, airman, I appreciate your hard work. Have you had any success at all?"

"I'm sorry, sir, no. The computers in every camera are useless. Every board I test is fried. Even the spare boards I took from IT are destroyed. The static charge from the pulse fried them all, too. It's hopeless, sir," he said in frustration. "Sgt. Jones was able to retrieve this old tape recorder here along with several rolls of audio tape from the air tower storage. We've tested them and although the recordings are very scratchy, it does record audio."

The airman pointed to an ancient-looking reel-to-reel audio recorder that sat at the edge of the table. Beth Gossett stepped forward

454

with an incredulous expression on her face as she addressed the colonel.

"You can't seriously expect Mrs. Clinton to be sworn-in as President of the United States of America, and have it recorded for posterity by this old piece of junk!"

The silent gathering of military officers stood looking at her stone-faced as her eyes searched their faces for some hint of cooperation or concession. Completely unsatisfied with their reactions, she spoke over her shoulder to the airman at the table.

"Young man, this is completely unacceptable. This woman is about to become the very first female president of this country and I simply won't accept that this is the only device capable of recording this event. You must go find something more suitable."

Before the colonel could speak the young airman's built-up frustration poured out in an angry voice.

"That device – ma'am, believe it or not, IS now the state-of-the-art in electronic instrumentation in a significant portion of America today. There are no other devices to record with here on base. Sgt. Jones should be back momentarily with his old Olympus 35mm camera that he's getting from his locker."

He paused as Beth turned and looked at him with a cold expression on her face. Far from being intimidated by her glare, and having decided that good judgment was a waste of time, the airman lost the rest of his military etiquette and spoke in a voice that was heavy-laced with sarcasm.

"Of course, ma'am, I do have another option in recording devices for you – why, I believe that I can produce a nice slab of rock and a fucking chisel to immortalize the whole swearing-in ceremony in fucking stone! Is that what you'd like, lady?"

Before Beth could utter a sound Hillary stepped forward and rested her hand on her shoulder and said, "Thank you, young man. Your hard work is deeply appreciated by me and all of us."

Beth and the airman both bit their tongues and nodded, looking at the ground. Colonel Dang stepped forward.

"Madam Secretary, it is time, please follow me."

He led her to the podium where a military chaplain stood. The gathered crowd waited below a flagpole as the billowing American flag snapped in the wind above their heads. Beth followed closely behind.

The chaplain turned to the crowd and spoke into the podium microphone. His voice came out of several speakers that ran off of power supplied by the portable generator as he addressed Hillary.

"Madam Secretary, we were able to find the exact wording for the swearing-in from an encyclopedia at the Lincoln Public Library. I can begin on your word."

Hillary Clinton turned and faced the crowd as she stood next to the chaplain. Crowds of peering faces had been a common sight throughout her life, but as she scanned the expressions of anxiety, grief, and fear, she now felt more out of place than at any time in her adult life. She covered her mouth, coughing to clear her throat, and then raised her right hand as she placed her left on top of a bible in the chaplain's outstretched hands. She opened her mouth to speak and the horizon began to quiver and melt as words in her throat stopped like they were caught in a vice. Again her knees buckled under her and she took one quick step backward to keep from collapsing as Colonel Dang sprang forward to give her support. She abruptly raised a stern hand to stop him and he retreated. Her eyes blinked and the faces of the crowd blurred as the swelling wetness in her eyes filled all but the center of her vision.

Her eyes locked on the face of a small child, maybe three-years old and being held up on the shoulder of his father who was several people deep into the crowd. The boy's large brown eyes were piercing and stared directly back into hers. His little hands rested lightly below his father's ears, the little fingers absentmindedly massaging the starched and pressed collar of the man's uniform. In one small hand the child clenched a tiny wooden stick with a small American flag stapled to it. His think curly hair was matted and pressed and misshapen from play and sleep.

The morose weight on her spirit eased, and her heart began to lift. The short distance between her and the child melted away and all evil thoughts were erased from Hillary's mind as everyone around them disappeared from view. Her essence felt encapsulated within the warm eyes of the child and she watched in fascination as his expression slowly changed; his pudgy angelic innocence was enhanced a million-fold as his expression broke into a wide smile of pure connection and joy. Happiness beamed from him as his little gleaming teeth sparkled under the California sun. He instinctively raised and extended his arms to a soul he recognized as a mother like his own, as he pleaded without words to be hugged, all the while bouncing and laughing impatiently on his father's shoulders.

The emotional dam burst and tears gushed down her face, leaving mascara streaks painted on her cheeks.

With a trembling voice she addressed the father of the boy, "I – I have no family here with me. I'm – alone. Wou – would you and your son please stand by me?"

456

Mostly stunned silence reigned as people slowly parted for the man and child to approach the podium. Hillary smiled through her tears as they reached her. Excited, the boy squirmed with joy as the burly arms of his father lifted him from his shoulders and released him into her waiting arms. The child gave a happy squeal and waved his chubby arms.

"His name is Tyrone, ma'am. Tyrone Watson."

She cuddled the child in one arm and ran her fingers through his hair. They smiled at one another for several seconds until she finally extended her hand out and took hold of the father's hand.

Then turning to the chaplain, she said, "I'm ready."

The chaplain looked questioningly at her then at the child.

"Uh, Madam Secretary – uh, I need you to raise your right hand," he said, holding out the bible before him.

"Yes, yes, of course."

After handing the child back to his father, she took the bible with both hands, raised it up to her lips and kissed it gently. Slowly and reverently she returned it to the chaplain and kept her left hand resting on it as she raised her right. The chaplain then read from the open encyclopedia sitting on the podium.

"Please repeat after me – I, Hillary Diane Rodham Clinton."

"I, Hillary Diane Rodham Clinton…."

*****

AFTER THE final words were spoken and the attending military officers had signed as witnesses to the affidavit, the crowd stood staring at the first female President of the United States of America. Tyrone was back in her arms, bouncing on her hip as she played with him by nibbling on his fingers, all the while he laughed and giggled in high-pitched screams of joy. She kissed his forehead, hugged him tightly and turned to the father.

"Thank you again for sharing Tyrone with me. I needed him to help get my head on straight."

"Yes, Madam President. It was an honor for us," the young officer said humbly.

Hillary took in a deep breath and scanned the assembled crowd. The classic Clinton look of confidence, eager for a political speech, glinted in her eyes. She motioned toward the crowd to gather closer. As the reel-to-reel spun, she began to speak into the podium's microphone as Tyrone playfully pulled at her blouse.

"My fellow Americans, the human animal's capacity for acts of evil is only surpassed by its capacity to do acts of good. Good and evil, they are two sides of the same coin. A coin minted by the hands of God in heaven; a coin that He then tossed upon the waters of our human soul. Those rippling waters within us have made their way through time and space to create our true nature."

"I tell you now that our true nature is to find a glorious and triumphant end. An end that will prove worthy of the efforts God put into our shaping. God's glory is not achieved cheaply, and our ultimate triumph can only be reached through the brutal furnace of evil's mighty forge. The tempest of that fire is the heat, the hammer, and the anvil upon which our very souls will be tempered, shaped, and forged to carry-on our grand purposes."

"The furnace of our forging has scorched our souls with a terrible tempest of tragedy on this day of sorrows and tears. Evil is not a wicked happenstance that God uses in any trivial manner. The depths of our future understanding of this terrible day shall write chapters into the book of life we will live to produce."

"Hard work, hard choices, and hard acts are now before us and we strive to meet these heinous acts with the resiliency that marks the great strengths of our human condition. Our nation and our form of governance is the last, best hope, for peaceful coexistence for all peoples on this world and we will engage our destiny; well-met I say, on the fields of love and pain that are to come."

"And when the days of pain are hard-pressed upon our hearts, we will rise to the dire challenges of our calling and find the strength and ability to master our fear and shape our triumphant future!"

"My fellow Americans, our day of pain is ending and our challenging work awaits us. Stand with me and we will meet the days ahead and be victorious!"

Wild cheers erupted all around her.

*****

18:30pm EST
Smith College Equestrian Center
Northampton, Massachusetts

WITHOUT WORKING clocks or watches Herb could only guess at how long it must have taken for Ashley to round up her chosen horses and outfit them with tack and gear as they all stumbled around in the pitch black. His intuition said it was around two hours but he felt tired enough to believe it was five. Luckily Fred turned out to be a quick study with her riding instructions and now he and Ashley sat atop two horses and looked down at Herb as he held a flashlight.

Two more horses, tied with leads, were ready to follow behind when they left.

Herb looked up at his longtime friend and offered his hand. Fred took it and gave a warm squeeze in the darkness. Patchy clouds, millions of stars, and a crescent moon hung in brilliant display across the sky over their heads. They finally broke off their handshake and Herb stepped back.

"You've been the best pal. I'll miss you. You take care of Kimberly and tell her that Uncle Herbie loves her dearly."

"She knows that very well, my friend, but I'll be happy to deliver your words. I hope we meet again soon. Take care and be safe. You have responsibilities here with these girls – I know you'll excel at seeing them through this. Remember now; medicine, food, arms – that's your priorities. Goodbye, Herb – Semper Fi."

"Goodbye and Semper Fi."

Ashley and Fred prodded their horses and quickly disappeared into the dark. Very soon all Herb could hear was the receding sound of the horse's hooves making their *clop-clop-clop* on the pavement of the deserted roadway. Herb stood, looking up at the unusually crisp view of the multitude of stars shining in the sky. He could not remember a single time in his life when he had seen so many stars and he was awed by their stunning beauty.

He remained until even his imagination could no longer hear the faint sound of horses any longer. He then reluctantly turned and slowly led his own horse toward the campus. With little help from the pale quarter moon he was finally able to find his way to the campus where eventually he and the other members of the faculty got themselves and their students organized by flashlights and torches. In the morning they began the hard work of preparing for a terrible winter ahead.

Over the hard months that followed, Herb wondered about Fred and his journey. Soon deep snowfalls came and covered Massachusetts with frigid cold and the biting winds of nor'easters. Sickness brought its bounty while hunger gnawed mercilessly at empty bellies. As unbearable as the winter became and as desperation showed its haggard face daily, Herb still thought of his friend every day. He hoped beyond hope that Fred had made it to Colorado and Kim, but he never learned the truth.

18:30pm MST
Air Force One 33,000ft
above Ogden, UT

FOUR HOURS after being sworn in Hillary sat in the deep cushions of a chair inside the conference room aboard one of the remaining planes of the Air Force One fleet. The appointed vice president, Beth Gossett, sat to her right while her appointed Chief of Staff, Bill Langley, sat fidgeting in his chair to her left. The 747 flew within a protective formation of twenty FA-18 Super Hornet fighters on its way to Peterson Air Force Base on the outskirts of Colorado Springs, Colorado.

Visible on the wall-mounted flat screen were the jumpy, pixilated images of Defense Secretary Leon Panetta on the right and Vice Chairman of the Joint Chiefs General James Cartwright on the left. Much of Panetta's salt-and-pepper hair was hidden under a large bandage taped to the side of his head, a small red stain visible near his left temple. His monotone scratchy voice came through the speakers as though it came from a 1930s RCA turntable.

"….and so in their mutual statement the Russians and Chinese have confirmed to us that any retaliatory strike from us against Iran would result in strong, but unspecified military reprisal from them against us and our disabled NATO allies throughout Europe and the Middle East. Their statement was clearly prepared beforehand and I can only assume they were, at the very least, advising the Iranians on these attacks well before today. I certainly see no way that both of them were not directly involved in the planning and execution of these attacks."

"So, the Russians, Chinese, and Iranians scored a trifecta against us? I agree with you, Leon, I simply do not see how they could not be in collusion with one another after this communiqué. Do you see it differently, Jim?" asked Hillary.

General Cartwright had a better satellite signal that allowed for his voice to come in much clearer.

"I have no proof of that, Madam President. From the data from intelligence we still have at the NSA and Pentagon, it appears as though this was an Iranian operation from beginning to end. So far, the joint investigation by the FBI and CIA has provided scant evidence that the Russians or Chinese directly assisted or participated in the EMP event. But that being said, I cannot imagine that the yield of the warheads used was made by Iranian development alone, it's impossible. It is therefore strongly indicative that they were, at a minimum, supplied with the warheads by the Russians from the deterrent munitions that Putin had deployed there in 2004."

"As far as the earlier terror attacks, they were apparently orchestrated through this American-born Kashmiri-jihadist; all statements from the terrorists that we've captured alive, and the identity papers recovered from the bodies of the dead, all point toward them being members of the Iranian IRGC Quds Force and that they gained access via this jihadist byway of his connection with the Mexican cartels. There is no evidence I have seen that shows Russia or China had a hand in that part of the coordinated operation against us.

"Clearly, the Iranian's want it to be very obvious to us, and the entire world, that they are directly responsible for all of the attacks against us and Europe. Their public proclamations are strident as to how they are the sole actor against us today. Putting all of these factors together, it says to me that the Russians and Chinese were fully informed on all of the attacks against us and have been in collusion with the Iranians for several years. But in order to evade being tied to anything that we might have uncovered before today, they kept the Iranian's well out in front. Unfortunately we didn't see anything beforehand and now with us knocked out so severely they can swoop in and take their share of the spoils with no repercussions.

"We've got no indications, as yet, that any other Islamic country participated in the endeavor. But I can already confirm that the nations of Syria, Lebanon, Pakistan, Kuwait, Qatar, and the UAE have all publicly declared fidelity and obedience to the establishment of a Persian Caliphate. I suspect that by the end of the week most every Islamic nation in Asia Minor and Africa will have sworn allegiance to that Caliphate as well, and our allies in Iraq and Jordan are going to be squeezed hard not to abandon us," Cartwright finished.

"So Iran is willing to risk all retaliations from us and NATO? And now the entire Islamic world is willing to join in on the receiving end of our wrath? That makes no sense to me, Leon."

"No, ma'am, I don't believe that's what Jim and I are saying. Our belief is that Iran is putting itself forward as the sole antagonist in these attacks so that they will become the, well, the masters of the entire Islamic world. They're not backing away from this an inch. In a nutshell, ma'am, they know that they have handed us our asses on a silver platter and they want the entire world to know it! They did this with at least tacit approval from the Russians and Chinese, who are both willing to run cover for them. I think it's clear that the Iranians intend this to put them as the top-dog in the Islamic world. Thereby allowing them to be able to dictate to whom, how much, and at what

461

price the entire Middle East's oil supplies are to be rationed out globally into the foreseeable future," Panetta asserted.

Cartwright interjected, "And regarding NATO, Madam President, Brussels is still off-line and we've been unable to make contact with EUCOM at Stuttgart or many of our other ground forces on the continent. Tactical air defense is getting established by the 3rd Air Force at Ramstein but with our satellite losses we are still blind to a second EMP strike in Europe. Together, with the French and British, we are assembling some NATO naval capabilities in concert with our 6th Fleet as quickly as we can. But no coordinated effort or coordinated command-and-control structure exists at this point outside of our ties to the British fleet. In effect, the entire European continent is now the proverbial fish swimming in the barrel, and our middle and eastern European friends are even far more defenseless than the western arena."

Hillary slammed her fist down on the table and the pen that Bill Langley was tumbling under his fingers went flying to the floor. Beth gave her long-time advisor a sharp look while resting her hand on Hillary's sleeve.

Hillary barked at the screen, "If the Russians and Chinese think they can take this as their opportunity for strategic benefit then they are sadly mistaken! I will not be intimidated. I will not allow this direct assault on the homeland to go unanswered. The retaliation I order will…."

"Ma'am, please," interrupted General Cartwright. "Please be more cautious about what pronouncements you make about what we will and won't do at this time."

Beth bolted to her feet and jammed a boney finger toward the screen.

"How dare you talk to the president in that tone, General? These are extraordinary times but decorum will be maintained and your words are out of line!"

"Extraordinary times? Decorum?" the general asked wearily. "Listen to me, and listen very closely, Mrs. Gossett. With General Dempsey lost to us when his jet went down in the Atlantic, I am now the highest ranking commander of the United States military. A global military who, I might add, is now staring down the barrel of nuclear Armageddon with China and Russia. I have acquiesced to Secretary Panetta's demand that civilian control of the government will be maintained – even, as you say, in these *extraordinary times*!"

The general paused and even in the highly pixilated image they saw him loosening the tie under his starched collar before he spoke again.

"I intend to keep that decision in effect and I will allow President Clinton's word, as the civilian commander-n-chief, to be the final decision on most matters but not those regarding the military. I will not allow – pardon my French – fucking amateurs like you two to endanger what's left of our military or our nation at this point in this crisis! I hope I made myself clear on that because I will NOT repeat myself!"

Vice President Gossett's face turned crimson with rage as her thin body trembled while trying to keep herself under control. The veins of her neck pulsated as she closed her fists. Hillary tapped her forearm.

"Beth, please sit down," she said calmly as she gave a barely perceptible wink. Beth sat down in a huff and glared at the general's image. *Your days are numbered, big man.*

Panetta remained silent as the general continued, "I will run down some simple facts you must consider before we respond in any willy-nilly fashion. We and NATO are hampered by a minimum – a minimum, I say, 70% reduction in our civilian and military satellites after the three EMP strikes. An exact number will not be ascertained until we've completed our reboot attempts. Radar shows the space station is intact but there are no indications that the crew survived and therefore they cannot help with global communications. To put it simply, our entire global military capability to communicate, to see and hear, or to attack and defend our forces or our home soil has been virtually wiped out. We are deaf and blind; defenseless before two very powerful enemies who have made it very clear that they will retaliate in defense of the Iranians. We simply cannot, I repeat, we cannot risk a bold response at this time," he asserted.

"I concur," interjected Panetta.

Cartwright continued on, "Even if we were to strike out with everything we've got at our disposal, we could make a devastating attack, yes. But its effectiveness would be very limited compared to what we could do this morning. We would also be left absolutely defenseless here and around the globe to any and all counterstrikes. And I won't allow the consideration of a focused attack upon the Iranians to be done without our forces and homeland having the ability to defend against retaliation from the Chinese and Russians. Simply put, any large military response against anyone at all at this time is nothing but an act of suicide."

With tightly clenched fists, Hillary stretched her arms out on the polished table as she absorbed what the general had just stated. After a few moments she spoke in a purposefully level tone.

"I appreciate your input, General, and I am looking forward to a face-to-face briefing from you when we arrive at Cheyenne Mountain. Your concerns are duly noted, and for the time being, I concur with your assessment of our limitation and capabilities."

She gave a sigh.

"We cannot afford to be our own worst enemy right now. As you so eloquently point out, since you are the senior military commander, I expect you to expedite every effort to re-establish and expand our military defense capabilities and to mitigate our liabilities and limitations against the threats posed by China and Russia. I will work closely with you on that, but I will have many taxing duties on the domestic front, and between getting resources and food delivered, and the rebuilding of our domestic infrastructure, those are going to be my immediate priorities. So, for the time being, I will postpone our immediate considerations for retaliation."

Hillary stared hard at the general's image on the screen.

"But, General, I will do so only temporarily. Do you concur?"

"No one wants a day of payback more than I do, Madam President. I assure you that I will do everything possible to have a working plan on your desk, ASAP."

Hillary gave a stern nod as Beth voiced her approval.

"Yes, Hillary, we will rebuild the country. Right now we need to consolidate our resources and take stock of our losses. Retaliation, against anyone at this time, seems to me to come from a place of anger and would be ill-timed."

Hillary spun and leveled a cold gaze at her vice president.

"I don't know where my daughter is! There are thousands of Americans dead and many more will die soon. Anger, Beth, it is consuming me, and mark my words, I will let it out someday, someday very soon."

Beth stayed stone-faced as her and Bill Langley's eyes met.

Panetta spoke up.

"As I said earlier, Madam President, we are extremely lucky to still have a working electrical grid throughout some of the central Midwest. It seems that our nation's fly-over country was our saving grace today."

"It appears the effects of the Atlantic EMP reach out in an arc from the Florida Keys in the south, then stretching west into middle Kansas, and finish with a sweep back north through Ontario, Quebec and into Labrador. It will take time to determine the extent of damage in that large of an area but roughly two-thirds of our population now sits under that impacted zone. At the same time the effects of the

Pacific EMP stretch from Mexico City to British Columbia but appear to have done little damage east of the Rocky Mountains. The swath of territory that still has some working form of electrical grid now stretches from Texas to Manitoba. With that area being mostly operational, it must be the core that brings the rest of the country back to its feet."

"Gentlemen, for the time being I will operate the office of the presidency from NORAD. Leon, I want all surviving members of the Congress, the Supreme Court, and all Cabinet members to be delivered to Denver where we will establish the institutions of Federal authority until Washington, DC is functional again," Hillary ordered.

"Yes, ma'am," was the responses from both Panetta and Cartwright.

Then Hillary was silent for several seconds before she addressed Panetta's image, dancing on the flickering screen, and asked, "Leon, have you been able to locate my daughter? Where is Chelsea?"

The defense secretary paused before answering.

"We have been unable to contact any high-ranking members of the Italian government, and it is a distinct possibility that much of their Cabinet, including the Prime Minister, were lost when the Airbus went down in Milan. The entire peninsula appears to have been affected by the European EMP and the area of Naples is – Madam President, I…."

"Tell me."

"An F-18 over-flight from Sigonella Air Station got visuals of the metropolitan area. Those pilots reported that obvious signs of pandemonium and widespread rioting were rampant inside the city. We've received no word yet on the status of your daughter or her husband, I'm sorry. Our detachment of air-base security forces should be landing in the area of the La Stanze Del Vicere Hotel within the hour and we hope to have your daughter collected soon thereafter, if she is there. I will immediately inform you of any developments."

"Find my daughter, Leon. Whatever it takes, she *is* a priority, understood?"

"Yes, ma'am, I understand very well."

Hillary slowly took a drink from a glass of water from the table; crushed ice tinkled as she leaned back in her chair in silence.

"Ma'am, we do have significant naval forces in New York harbor helping local authorities there. I was just about to order a search team to begin looking for your husband and…."

"Secretary Panetta, I did not ask you to send anyone to look for Mr. Clinton."

465

"Uh, I thought that it would…."

"You thought wrong. Your priorities are my daughter. You will not make any additional efforts to find or collect Mr. Clinton in New York City. Let me make this very clear to you gentlemen, Mr. Clinton is not a priority. Is that clear?"

"Uh – yes, ma'am, it is."

*****

September 21, 0001 A.G.E. 11:23am EST
New World Order Day – 1
Fort Tyron Park Manhattan, NY

MICHAEL STRUGGLED to push the shopping cart as it bounced herky-jerky over the cobblestone path below the beautiful brick and stone buildings of The Cloisters. To him, the elegantly designed Romanesque-gothic masonry abutments of the Metropolitan Museum of Art always appeared out of place and way too hoity-toity to be located right next to his neighborhood of Inwood.

Dressed in a ratty tank-top that was three sizes too big, a grungy pair of faded blue Bermuda shorts and dollar store flip-flops, Michael's clothes were heavily soiled, making it obvious to anyone he passed that he probably had not washed them in months, if ever. The caked-on grime plastered to his fingers, along with his pungently sour body odor indicated to those same people that he most definitely had not taken a bath or even spot-washed himself in just as many months. In addition to the odors of poor hygiene there was a tart bitter-rot that radiated out from the many dank layers of drug-induced sweats, as well as the blisters and puss-oozing scabs that covered his arms and legs along with his regular grunge. The mix of wreaking odors clung to the air around him, making everyone within arm's distance gag, but with even a mild breeze his stank was easily carried, strong and potent, downwind fifty feet or more.

With his oily hair and ponytail dangling behind his lanky, emaciated and meth-abused form, he looked like a grimy version of a male Olive Oil. A glance from any movie director would instantly typecast him as a survivor from Auschwitz in a World War II movie. A part he would be especially esthetic for, due to the way his ribs created such a ghastly accordion effect along his upper torso. His spring-tight jaw muscles pulsated incessantly as he ground his teeth hard against one another. He had done this for so long that his cheeks were now swollen knots that jutted outward like a squirrel with a mouthful of nuts. The perpetual grinding had also worn down his rotted teeth to a thin brown line atop infected and bleeding gums.

Sunken eye-sockets encircled hollow, emotionless eyes that still conveyed a desperate need. His awkward stiff-legged walk, caused from the brain damage bestowed upon him at birth by his drug-addicted mother, gave him a stutter-stepping gate that made him appear zombie-like to the local kids around Inwood. Even in his drug-addled brain he was able to understand how he looked to them, but he still hated their moniker for him: The Cannibal.

Tweaking badly, he desperately needed a fix of the crystal dragon, and knew he had very little time before the cramps and convulsions were going to tear him a new asshole. He quickened his pace as he shoved the loaded shopping cart, making a beeline across the grass and leaving the frustrating cobblestones. But the tree roots and thick grass were no better and he nearly fell head-long against the trunk of an aged and gnarled honeylocust tree. Cursing and sweating profusely he strained his wiry muscles to keep the cart upright and moving.

Emerging from the shade of the tree canopy of the park, he made his way across the sidewalk onto the weirdly deserted Riverside Drive, headed for his basement apartment located in the alley off Payson Avenue. Quickly passing by the Dyckman Street subway portal he kept the cart rolling down the oddly quiet asphalt street. The East Village vibe that the once working-class neighborhood had developed over the past decade was now absent. The normally hectic rush of traffic was gone, creating the feeling of a ghost town across the city and Upper Manhattan.

The people who were actually out walking the streets quickly parted as they let Michael go by without any interruption from them. A creature of revulsion to be shunned, not challenged. Michael cared nothing for what they thought; he only cared about the crystal dragon.

There was nothing in the world that Michael hated more than withdrawal. It was nothing less than hell-on-earth and he could tell it was getting close. The itch had already started and it always freaked him out when he felt that it. It was a mistake to call it an itch, but he knew of no other way to describe it. It did not feel like a bug bite, dandruff, or a rash of the skin. No, his meth-itch was far deeper, and went down under the skin and inside the bone itself. The feeling made his mind envision a billion little metal spiders, with tiny pointy metal legs stomping away with their spiky legs into the center of his bones. And right now it felt like they were just having a small party, but he knew they would soon be doing a mosh-pit inside of his skeleton.

Once, two years ago, he watched his bro, Kevin, take a shard of beer bottle and peel the skin from his face trying to get at that itch. The last thing he ever saw of Kevin was an EMT trying to keep a thin oxygen hose lying across his bloody skull that had no ears or nose as they shoved him into an ambulance. Kevin had looked over with lidless eyes and gave Michael the thumbs up. What a fucking party that was!

But the last time Michael had gotten the itch this bad he had damn near torn away all of his flesh from his chest and stomach with nothing but his fingernails. Of course it had gotten infected and he had almost died. But the sweet meth had brought him through the itch and healed his skin. Those mutilated scars, like burn scars, lay bumpy and rough under the thin fabric of his tank top as he rubbed his palm over his chest, feeling the itch building deep inside once again.

Life for Micheal O'Leary was tough enough without the lousy terrorists messing with him getting the crystal. Earlier he had heard people saying the power was out all over the city, and not just throughout Inwood and Upper Manhattan. *The entire City of New York, that's pure bullshit*. He knew that there was just no fucking way that Bloomberg would allow New York to not have power! Maybe Inwood, Washington Heights, and the South Bronx would be without power for a bit, but never the whole city. It was all just another lie from the fucking Man.

Normally, Michael scored his shit off a fat 'rican named Pancho who worked the northern subway terminal at Broadway and 8th. That Pancho was a sadist 'banger that had throw-up tagged all over Broadway. His crew, the 34th Precinct Thugs, claimed this territory as their own and sliced several rival mules every year to keep it that way. Even though he was real a sick fuck, Pancho had always been Michael's best bet for a good score of crystal, but now with the subway shut down by the power outage, the dude was nowhere to be found and Michael had quickly ran out of his supply.

Michael did not understand what everyone was saying; talking shit about the end of the world, and that the fuckhead terrorists had pulled off the Big One yesterday. *The big one, what big one?* Sure some cars had broken down, the subway was out, and there were no lights and shit, but it did not seem like all that big a deal. All Michael cared about was his fix and that was what mattered. But yeah, he was still pissed off at the terrorists, too; they were fucking with his supply and that shit did not cut it.

This morning he felt the withdrawals start to kick his ass and knew he needed to score real fast. Michael figured with no cops, no cars, and nothing moving around it would mean that the alarms at Zuckerman's Pharmacy over on Elwood Street would not be working, either. He knew the opportunity would not last, for despite what the idiots in the neighborhood were saying, the power would return. So he tromped right over and with a little help from a brick, got inside and helped himself to a heaping load of first-rate, quality shit. He snagged Sudafed and Ephedrine by the case and grabbed every bit of codeine and morphine he could find. He collected every slammer he could fit in the cart, along with a ton of wadding, alcohol, ammonia, and a shitload of batteries. He was set for months of free cooking. Soon the candy-laced euphoria of the blissful glass would take him away to paradise.

Although there were far fewer people than usual out and about, the crowds were steadily growing as the morning grew older, and it looked to Michael like the whole neighborhood was getting ready to throw a block party. Usually everyone was in transit from one place to another but this morning it was like everyone was just looking for something to do. No one had any television to watch, no cars, no buses, and no subway. The situation had people on edge, both nervous and irritated. He heard some people talking about how even the water was no longer running out of their faucets. *Does that mean there are no shitters, too?* With no cops around to quiet things down, he figured a riot might happen soon.

As the contagious leper known as The Cannibal moved in their midst, he gave a ghastly grin that revolted all who saw it. *I'm 'bout to Bake'em, Lite'em, and Smoke'em!*

Meanwhile, high above him, old man Mancuso leaned on his railing and stared down at the addict trundling his way along the street below. A lifelong local and retired teamster, Mancuso hated the filthy creature that he had been watching for years with disgust, spreading filth everywhere in Mancuso's neighborhood. Looking down from his second floor fire escape landing, Mancuso had the expression of looking at a pile of cockroaches swarming on top of a fresh steaming pile of crap as he yelled.

"Yo, Mikey! What the fuck is yor ass duing wit dat shit in dat cart?"

Michael cringed at the familiar voice and looked at the man with the fat gut and hairy chest, holding a beer. Distracted, Michael did not see the large crack in the asphalt street and caught the front of his worn flip-flops in the jagged scar in the street's surface. He stumbled and took several flailing and awkwardly giant steps forward. If he had not had the cart for support he would have sprawled face first.

His toes throbbed as he stood, glaring up at the laughing fat man while stopped in the middle of the usually busy street, now quiet with several abandoned cars. He looked down at the fresh gash across the top of several toes which were bleeding badly. The yellow toenail from his big toe was torn backward, now stuck upward in an ugly fashion.

Furious, he forgot for a couple seconds the itch building inside as he craned his head back and yelled, "Mind ya own fuck'n bidness, yah!"

With his laughing finally dying down, Mancuso asked, "You rob a joint wit da power gone, ya piece a shit? Rosco will be look'n for yer ass in no time, shit-for-brains."

Michael lifted his arms up in a big shrug and glanced around.

"You see any o' dem fuck'n cheesedicks run'n da fuck 'round here, ya old fuck? It's my fuck'n birfday!" he said triumphantly.

"Fuck'n Rosco will catch up ta yer ass, ya slimy tweeker! Did ya hurt anyone when ya ripped off dat load a shit?" Mancuso yelled.

He rested his folded arms on the railing. A longneck beer bottle dangled from his fingers; lifting the bottle to his lips he took a long pull.

Michael gave a sincere look of indignation at the accusation that he could actually hurt someone. Michael was an unashamed thief and burglar, and addict, but he would never hurt a soul but himself. No fucking way!

"I didn't hurt no one!" he yelled indignantly. "Now mind ya own fuk'n bidness, ya fat bast'rd."

The widowed ironworker was down to his last two beers of his six-pack and was not looking forward to running out of booze on a day when there is no stinking power. He mildly wondered which place Michael had robbed but he did not really care all that much. All he wanted was some more beer. Shrugging, he raised his beer and drank the last half in one long swig and brought the glass bottle down with a bang onto the metal railing.

Mancuso looked down at the wasted human being and remembered watching this kid through the years grow up around Inwood. He saw the end spelled out for this piece-of-shit before he was even born. His mother, a whore of the first order, was getting banged a couple dozen times a day for chump change before he ever popped out of her swag. When the little shit was still in diapers he would squall hour after hour while his whore-mother turned tricks.

When her disease-infested ass moved out of Mancuso's tenement, the ironworker had been one happy son of a bitch. But she did not take her shit-covered mongrel son with her. Mancuso had heard a while later that she had turned up dead in a tenement over on Sherman Avenue. *Good fuck'n riddance!* He considered the bastard kid just one more piece of city vermin that should have died with her.

"Ya mutha was a stink'n whore and I fuck'd 'er good when I want'd it! Ya might be my fuck'n rugrat! Wadda tink a dat, ya little fuck!"

Michael had fended for himself, all alone on these streets since he was eight years old. The only clear memories he had of his mother was the sound of her dry humping in the next room, and the feel of a hard slap across his face when he got in her way. The day he had walked into the apartment and saw her lifeless, maggot-covered eyes staring at the ceiling, he'd been filled with relief, not sadness.

Through the years that followed his daily survival had depended upon selling anything he had, including his ass to the sick perverts that wanted to use his boy-body to get their jollies. There was nothing Michael was not willing to sell or do to get his junk and the occasional meal. Insulting his mother had the same emotional impact as telling him the sky was blue.

"C'mon, tell me, ya ol' fat shitbag – waddya say when she gave ya the fuck'n clap, asshole? Did it rot yer puny ol' one-eye into a pimple? Now go fuck yerself, ya ol' fuck!"

Michael jammed both his fists into the air, boney middle fingers stuck high. Then, ignoring the stream of curses that came down from the fat man he went back to pushing his cart down the street.

Mancuso balled up his fists and gave a one finger salute to Michael's back. Then he reached down and grabbed an empty beer can from the grating at his feet, crushed it and threw it at Michael's head. It missed its target by more than a dozen feet and went skittering harmlessly down the street. Mancuso fumed as he watched the skinny freak limp his way down the street. *I'll catch yer little prick ass later, shitbag.*

He grabbed his last beer and felt it was getting warmer. He hated warm beer. Over the years he had seen black-outs and brownouts time and again along with the other weird shit that happens in the city. But today he felt like something new and very bad had happened. Maybe, if things did not get going again soon, he could run down to the small Cambodian-ran store on the corner and stock up on some more booze and beer. With the way things felt he figured he would need a fresh supply to handle it all. The problem was, if the power was out, their beer would probably be warm, too. *Shit!* He popped the top on the last longneck. *Fuck it, down the hatch.*

Meanwhile Michael quickly forgot about the old man's empty words as he went flip-flopping down his alley with nothing but the crystal dragon on his mind. His bleeding toe still throbbed but it was just background static to his business at hand. The building had changed a lot over the years and this back-alley apartment was one of

471

the last few crap-holes left where someone like Michael could still live in the quickly moving-upscale evolution that was happening throughout Inwood.

He was relieved to finally be approaching his apartment door while he nervously kept a watch out for anyone who might see his big score; the last thing he needed now was to be ripped off. He dashed for the door and pulled the cart inside as fast as he could. It snagged on the frame and as he pulled and jerked it inside, items got spilled to the floor. He did not have time to waste as the itch was getting real bad and he figured that he would do a fast 'shake-and-bake' job.

He shoved piles of filthy clothes and trash aside, which sent swarms of flies buzzing into the air and cockroaches scurried for the corners. Working frantically he pulled supplies from the cart and began to set up his cook. Cracked fingernails dug into his skin, leaving red marks and scratches as he rubbed desperately at the crawling need. He fumbled with one item after another, cursing when he dropped something. With an old lighter he started the flame to his propane hot plate and spun the dial to high.

The itch went from bad to worse as he left claw marks on his chest and face. Michael's jaw twitched madly as he crushed a handful of pills into a coffee filter and mixed them into an old Mountain Dew bottle along with hastily poured ammonia. He continually swirled the mixture while trying to peel lithium strips from batteries. Everything became increasingly difficult as the vapors from the mixture and his withdrawals combined, making his vision blur and head swim.

He stumbled and dropped the bottle onto the counter. His vision left him and he blindly rubbed at his eyes as his head swam and his stomach cramped violently. He bent over, dry-heaving and panting for breath until his senses returned. Once his head cleared enough, he took to completing the lithium strips and dropping them into the mixture in the bottle. *The dragon! The dragon!* He swirled the concoction while vapors poured out. He soon stood tottering, eyes closed, in a trance-like state as he swirled the bottle and dug at the itch in his chest.

Suddenly, instinctively, some alarm bell deep inside Michael's head went off, telling him the smell was not quite right. He tried to move but more cramps racked his body. *No!* He propped himself rigid against the wall as he tried to stay on his feet. The bottle fell from his hands and the convulsions of withdrawal began to sweep into his muscles. *Too late.* His guts erupted in agony as if he was being eating alive from within. The hallucination monsters began eating his flesh, as the metal spiders began their stomping dance inside his bones, and Michael's mind collapsed into the misery of hell.

Blackness covered his eyes as his tense body writhed with pain. He pitched face-first onto the floor where his nose hit first, shattering and spraying blood. His twitching body lay among the filth of the apartment as a white mist rose above the counter where the meth continued cooking.

The expanding vapor reached the red-hot burner flames, and with a sudden flash and a small blast, the contents of the container exploded in a fireball around the small room, lighting it and Michael on fire.

*****

MANCUSO STILL leaned on the railing and sipped his last beer as the morning sun warmed the street below. The number of people who were pouring onto the streets had continued to swell. They had broken into groups of dozens and hundreds, some groups were yelling, and others were watching. The usual community pot-stirrers were busy rousing their followers into a slow simmer that could turn into a mob-led frenzy very quickly.

The pot-stirrers yelled about blame. They yelled about who to blame for the power outage, who to blame for trash services not being done, who to blame for no cops, who to blame for no subway, and who to blame for no cold beer. As they yelled about who was to blame they always picked the malevolent Someone to blame. A Someone who was never identified very well. Most said the Someone was the system, others said the Someone was the City, or maybe it was the Man, but it always seemed the government, in its myriad of forms, was the Someone. That Someone, the pot-stirrers yelled, was letting them all down and they needed to organize, they needed to march. They would make things fair, and they would protest until their needs and wants were met with due satisfaction and in a timely manner by contrite and friendly servants of the people!

As the pot-stirrers preached about the Someone, the watchers were fewer in number but they had a strong core group that was tightly bound together. They were the brains and muscle of the neighborhood. They were the ones who did all the necessary things that the followers and their pot-stirrers never wasted anytime worrying about. The watchers were vested in the community; residents with a stake in things here who had a lot to lose if the followers of the pot-stirrers got wound up too far. No cops were driving around and the watchers saw they were on their own.

Inwood was a rough-and-tumble, tough-as-nails neighborhood, but over the past decade it had begun to get a new and

473

unusual feel; it was becoming gentrified. Mancuso knew the feel of the old neighborhood was changing, but the nuts-and-bolts, blue-collar roots to this piece of Upper Manhattan were far removed from the glitz of Lower Manhattan. He knew it would be an awfully hard shell for the artsy-fartsy crowd to break. After all, this part of the Big Apple was one tough-ass town.

Mancuso slugged down the last of his warming beer and slung the empty bottle back inside his apartment window. He had decided that it was going to be a long wait before the power came back on, so for the time being he figured it would be better if he just stayed here and watched the crowd awhile before venturing down into the street. *Things are shitty down there.* He had a mild buzz going and he was enjoying the show below, especially since his TV shows were as gone as the power was.

He raised his head and noticed some dark smoke rising up from an alleyway a couple blocks away. He was pretty sure it came from the same area where the pipsqueak tweeker had his hovel.

*****

September 23, 0001 A.G.E. 23:10pm EST
New World Order Day – 3
Hudson Valley near Middletown, NY

FRED HELD the reigns loosely in his one hand while he gently stroked the cheek of Saul with the other. The steady and intelligent four-year old quarter horse stallion had matured quickly under the tutelage of the girls at Smith College. He exuded confidence, strength, and controlled energy; the other two horses deferred to him in all things. Saul raised his head and sniffed the air as some curious odor drifted by. His dark-chestnut color and jet-black mane made him hard to see in the starlight. He had quickly become Fred's favorite out of the three that Ashley had given him.

As a matter of fact, his admiration for that young woman's wise choices grew daily. Pixy, a bay colored three-year old thoroughbred mare, had a bouncing gate that made her the most uncomfortable to ride, but she was fleet of hoof, strong, and had energy to spare. He felt positive that she could outrun just about anything he would come across in a post-electronic world. She stood hobbled, off in the dark behind the third horse Ashley had acquired, a strong seven-year old roan-colored quarter horse gelding named Bill. He was a sure-footed working animal that could haul inexperienced riders or gear equally without complaint. True to their natures, Pixy had her ears up, searching through the many tiny night sounds while Bill lazily munched on grass.

Saul's humid breath left a hint of fog on Fred's glasses as they stood cheek-to-cheek, bonding in the night air. Fred looked east through the gap in the thick stand of white cedar and sugar-maple trees where he had set up their camp for the night. He guessed the hilltop was close to two-hundred feet higher than the valley floor and it gave him a commanding view in all directions. Normally from here he imagined that he could see the lights of several cities and homes in the area below, but now after the EMP event there was nothing but blackness stretching out in all directions. The only artificial light he saw anywhere was from a single set of headlights about ten miles to the south that slowly marked the passage of people making their way through the night toward destinations unknown along I-84.

The sun had set hours ago and the half moon was still a couple hours from rising, so the only light came from the thick band of the Milky Way. Fred envisioned an ancient Cro-Magnon ancestor standing at the entrance to a Neolithic cave looking up at those same stars on a night as dark as this. Travelling without modern electronics, and by horseback, gave him a feeling of kinship with that ancestor.

But one thing that had gained Fred's attention would have deeply puzzled his Neolithic relative as much as it did Fred. A strange glow now rose above the eastern horizon that certainly was not supposed to be there. He debated with himself for almost an hour, as the light of sunset had faded, as to whether the glow was a creation of his imagination or whether it was something real. But as the dark of night deepened he dropped all pretext of internal debate as it became evident that the strange glow was an actual light, far in the distance but definitely there. Now hours later, the light was a plainly visible yellowish-orange radiance that had a deeper crimson at the edges. It spread over more than eight degrees of the horizon to the southeast.

Fred studied it with binoculars but achieved little more knowledge. His 'procurement' process had evolved as things became available over the past two days and included many useful items, two of those being a compass and map that he had obtained from what was left at a looted Sports Authority store. While there, he also picked up a handheld GPS but after he powered it up, it would not, or it could not, acquire any satellite signals, so he tossed it for the compass.

Together the map and compass now told him in what direction the glow originated and the only thing he needed to guess at to pinpoint the location was distance. Navigation was never his forte, but mathematics were and he came to the sad conclusion that a very large area near or inside New York City was experiencing something terrible.

The light was the wrong color for anything other than fire, and to produce that large of a glow at this distance could only mean that some horrible conflagration was occurring there. *The center falls and refuses to hold.*

The first two days of travelling had gone well enough, but other things he had discovered were far worse than his deepest fears when he began the journey. Ashley was a pleasant enough companion the first night as they both emotionally came to grips with the reality of the new world order. Together, they had liberated all the supplies and weapons that Fred figured they would each need. They had also liberated as much insulin as they could find along with a portable generator to keep the refrigerator at her parent's house operating for quite a long time. He believed that would give her family as good a chance as possible for her father to fight his diabetes until the world of modern medicine could recover and produce more.

The kindness of strangers still existed and most people he met after he had left Ashley's home had just waved-off his prognostications of electromagnetic-pulse doom and gloom. Fred refused to argue the case and just gratefully accepted their acts of kindness and sharing. He knew that time would soon bring reality crashing down upon their understanding.

The threads of civilization were still intact and today he had witnessed the first signs of people beginning to pull together in preparation for a winter where they would have no electricity. He saw no signs of panic as yet, but he knew that pressure would build quickly. The typical targets of basic looting had already been cleaned out; discount stores, grocery stores, furniture stores, and even electronic stores had been looted but very few buildings had been burned down yet.

It was not until mid-afternoon, as he rode past the smoldering ruins of a looted Radio Shack, when things turned very, very bad. The evil that existed along with man no longer had the restrictions of society to hold it in check. God had loosed his horsemen upon America and Fred had found some of their first work.

A hundred yards behind the smoldering pile of ash and metal framing, off below a large red oak tree Fred had seen a group of crows squawking and complaining as they jumped and danced around something in the tall grass. Fred still did not know what actually drew him to go investigate the unremarkable sight, but he knew it was a decision that would haunt him every day for the rest of his life.

The black birds lifted into flight as he had approached them and he judged from the large amount of blood he found on the trampled grass below the tree that it was obvious that something terrible had happened there. Torn clothing and footprints in the dirt also instructed him that the cause for the blood was not an act of wild animals, but something evil and cruel that had been done by the hands of men. His rifle at the ready, he had investigated further into the trees until he came upon what he was searching for.

The boy was perhaps seven or eight and his father was in his thirties, their burned and eviscerated corpses dangled from wire nooses. The jagged cuts on their faces extended into a sickening smile that went all the way to their ears.

Dozens of feasting crows and magpies bitterly complained as Fred cut down and buried their bodies. His blood ran ice cold during the task with the father, but handling the tiny, rigid body of the boy had made his blood boiling hot. Standing over the graves he had vowed that he would extinguish the life from the monsters responsible, and Fred was a man of his word. The rest of the day he followed the trail of the evil men, by their tracks numbered three. From the freshness of the trail he knew he was getting close. Hopefully tomorrow he would dispense justice.

Less than seventy-two hours ago Fred was a retired widower who wrote books and did the occasional lecture. But now he stared at the distant glow and his heart was heavy with the sad reality of his new world. The die-off had begun and it would not stop for a long and horrific time. He still had not seen a single plane or helicopter in the sky and that dreadful sign spoke volumes to just how bad the EMP was in affecting a major swath of the eastern United States and Canada. It meant that no military flights were yet occurring anywhere across the vast area that was visible above his head. With the northeast being the most densely packed area of human habitation in the country he had hoped that there would have been at least a few military aircraft flying by now. *Nope. Not even one.*

Every once in a while he had seen older cars and trucks moving, but too many people still acted like it was a holiday outing instead of a quick race to get enough tools and supplies to survive the coming winter. The delusion blanket that covered society's eyes with false hope was threadbare on the fringes and fraying toward the middle. But it held together just enough to blind most people from the reality of their plight. The mental chasm from what they had known to the stark reality of their lives now was still far too wide for most people to bridge.

Staring at the dreadful glow his mind tried to grasp the scenario; around nine-million people trapped in the greater New York City area by the greatest rush-hour traffic jam ever created. No effective way into or out of the city except by foot or bike. No way to get emergency vehicles anywhere effectively due to the clogged streets. A fire now raged that was big enough and bright enough for Fred to see its glow from over a hundred miles away. A fire that had enough heat and burnable material to easily become a self-perpetuating conflagration until it finished consuming all of that material. A fire raging through a city whose entire water supply operated off huge electrical pumps that no longer functioned, and not enough fire trucks to obtain and disperse water from the rivers, and nowhere for people to flee except toward the wide harbor or East River. *Yep, the die-off's begun.*

Saul, sensing his master's anxiety, snorted and nuzzled Fred's face as the animal's large shoulder twitched and jumped. Fred leaned against the big animal for support and comfort. His back and butt were saddle-sore but he knew they would soon get used to the riding. He dearly wanted to sleep, but with his thoughts on the glowing horizon, and on the deadly hunt that would start at daylight, any restful solace in the embrace of sleep was impossible.

Millions of people trapped in canyons of burning skyscrapers and brownstones; a world without electricity. A father and child slaughtered by a roving band of vile sadists and no authorities to go to for help. With justice delivered to the guilty only by happenstance, when those people who are both willing and capable pass by. *Oh, what a world. What a world.*

Fred tottered on the edge of despair as he gently stroked the beast's flanks and watched the glow until morning light was close. His thoughts dwelt on his Kimberly as he tried to focus on what it would take to reach his daughter.

GLOSSARY

8-ball: 1/8 ounce methamphetamine $250 +

A.G.E.: After Global Event. The universal calendar designation imposed globally for year-numbering after the end of the Common Era (CE) for the purposes of this novel.

Allah: Arabic word for God

Apostate: Arabic word for traitor

Asman-Rayan: Persian: Sky Kings

Aspirant: French Naval rank - midshipmen

Ayatollah: This is the third highest ranking in the four tier system of Shia Islam's hierarchy of scholars. From this group of several dozen men the Grand Ayatollah (marja-al-taqlid) or Supreme Leader is selected.

Azadi: Persian and Kashmiri word meaning liberty, freedom, or succession.

Aztlán: The legendary land of the pre-history Mesoamerican tribes. Often used in the Chicano movement to refer to restored ancestral land from within the United States and Mexico.

Bisht: A formal Muslim male robe worn by religious leaders and high-level government officials.

BLEVE: Boiling Liquid Expanding Vapor Explosion

Brahman: A high caste on the subcontinent that is descended from the priestly class.

Cabron: Mexican slang term for billy goat

Caliph: Arabic word meaning Head of State

Caliphate: Arabic word referring to a system of governance under sharia law and Islamic faith.

CCRM: Chicano Civil Rights Movement

Chishti Order: A religious order that is a part of the Sufi version of worship in the Islamic faith.

Coffeepot: A slang street term used to refer to a method of methamphetamine manufacture that uses a coffee pot, usually in a motel room. Used during the Nazi-method of meth production.

COIN   US military acronym meaning counterinsurgency doctrine

CPLA: Chinese People's Liberation Army

Crank: Slang term for crystal methamphetamine

Dáwah: Arabic word meaning making an invitation. Often used to describe preaching.

Dhimmi: Arabic word referring to indigenous non-Muslim populations who surrendered to Muslim domination.

Dhuhr: Arabic word for the second of the five daily prayers of the Islamic faith.

Dom: Sanskrit word for outcast. Often used as an insult and used to describe the lowest caste in Indian culture.

EMP: Electromagnetic pulse

EUCOM: US military European command based at Stuttgart, Germany

Fajr: Arabic word for the first of the five daily prayers of the Islamic faith.

Faraday cage: A shielded enclosure that stops external electric fields from affecting the interior.

Fedayeen: Arabic word meaning self-sacrificer and often used to describe Muslim volunteers who fight in holy war.

FFG: French guided missile frigate

Fitna: Arabic connotative word often referring to disunion, division, or disagreement within Islam. Used to name past civil wars within the Islamic faith.

Fitra: Arabic word that when used in a mystical sense connotes the divine oneness of man with God achieved by Abraham and Muhammad.

Fiqh: Arabic term for all Islamic jurisprudence

Ghutra: A Muslim male head scarf affixed with a (typically black) head band.

Glass: Slang term for crystal methamphetamine

GMT: Greenwich Mean Time

Gujjar: An ancient and large ethnic group of the subcontinent. Mainly worshipers of Islam or Hinduism.

Haadi: Arabic word meaning quiet or shut up.

Hadith: Arabic word meaning narrative. Refers to a collection of works from the Companions of Muhammad that are used to assist in understanding the Quran and matters of jurisprudence. Sunni and Shia sects have differing hadith collections.

Hadji: Common word used by US military personnel to refer to Muslim civilians. Reference originates from Johnny Qwest cartoon character Hadji Singh (non-Muslim).

Haqqani: Insurgent group of up to 12,000 fighters allied with but independent of the Taliban. Headquartered in North Waziristan and led by Jalaluddin Haqqani.

Hijab: Head scarf worn by Muslim women.

Hajj: Arabic word that refers to the pilgrimage to Mecca, one of the Five Pillars (religious duties) of every Muslim.

Halal: Arabic word meaning lawful. Refers to things, actions, or food that is permissible under Sharia law.

Haraam: Arabic word meaning forbidden.

Hawala: An informal banking system for money transfers and loans in the Islamic culture.

Hijra: Arabic word that refers to the migration of Muhammad and the Jama'ah from Mecca to Medina before the establishment of the Caliphate.

Idtirar: See taqiyya

IED: Improvised Explosive Device

Imam: Arabic word for a leadership position.

IRGC: Islamic Revolutionary Guard Corps. A large segment of the Iranian military structure that has land, sea, and air paramilitary capabilities, which also controls the Basij militia; with an estimated 5-11 million members.

IRISL: Islamic Republic of Iran Shipping Lines

ISI: Inter-Services Intelligence. The Pakistani government intelligence agency which is considered to be a world class organization.

Jahili: A concept in Islam of people who are outside the guidance of God. Refers often to non-Muslim peoples.

Jamáah: Arabic word refers to the people of the tradition and community of Muhammad.

Jamarat: Arabic word referring to the stone pillars, and since 2004, stone walls in the town of Mina, Saudi Arabia where Muslims conduct a ritual of throwing rocks at these symbolic devils as part of the Hajj.

Jendeh: Farsi vulgar slang word for whore.

Jihad: Arabic word meaning struggle. There is a great amount of debate over the exact meaning and usage of the word. Common religious usage refers to three types of struggle; struggle in holy war, struggle to maintain Islamic faith, and struggle to improve Muslim society.

Káaba: Arabic word meaning cube. Refers to the large cube structure that houses the Black Stone in the center of the Masjid al-Haram, the most sacred site in Islam.

Kharijite: Arabic for those who went out. A seditious sect who rebelled against the fourth and final Rightly Guided Caliph Sayyidna Ali. Modern Kharijite ideology espouses the killing of Muslims and innocent non-Muslims as religiously justified acts of terrorism.

Keer: Farsi vulgar slang word for penis.

MARG: Marine Amphibious Ready Group

Madhi: The prophesied messiah or redeemer of the Islamic faith.

Madrasah: Arabic word meaning school.

Masjid: Arabic word meaning place of prostration. English word is mosque.

MRBM: Medium Range Ballistic Missile

Mujahideen: Arabic word meaning struggler. Typically refers to freedom fighters that battle in a cause for the Islamic faith.

Mujtahid: This is the second tier in the four-tier system of ranking within Shia Islam's hierarchy of scholars, just below that of ayatollah.

Mutawas: Arabic word for the Saudi Arabian government's morality police.

Mullah: This is the first tier in the four-tier system of Shia Islam's hierarchy of scholars.

NORAD: North American Aerospace Defense Command

Pahari: An ethnic group that populates the mountainous areas of Himalayas. They include high and low caste. Some are Hindu and others Muslim.

Pinche: Mexican slang term for sexual intercourse.

Polleros: A human smuggler. Also referred to as a coyote in English or a coyotaje in Spanish.

Qibla: Arabic word refers to the direction Muslims pray to the Kaába in Mecca, Saudi Arabia.

Quds Force: A strong force (2,000-50000) within the IRGC that is responsible for exporting the Iranian Islamic revolution to extraterritorial locations around the globe. They have close ties to Hezbollah.

Quran: Arabic word meaning the recitation. The verbal message of Allah given to Muhammad by the angel Gabriel. The Arabic verbal text is considered by Muslims to be the final revelation of God.

URNG-MAIZ: Unidad Revolucionaria Nacional Guatemalteca or the Guatemala National Revolutionary Unity. An umbrella organization that included several anti-government groups during the near forty years of Guatemalan civil war.

Rajput: A high caste on the subcontinent that is descended from warrior groups of India.

Rashidun: The four Caliphs of the Rashidun Caliphate following the death of Muhammad.

red-P: A method of refining methamphetamine from ephedrine or pseudoephedrine that uses red phosphorous.

Sahaba: Arabic word that refers to the Companions of Muhammad. These people are the primary source for collections of works that make up the hadith.

Shahada: Arabic word that refers to the Islamic Creed which is the declaration of belief in Islam and the oneness of Allah.

Salafi: Arabic word meaning ancestor that refers to the first three generations of Muslims who are venerated as proof of how Islam should be practiced by everyone.

Salat-al-Istikhara: Islamic prayer for guidance.

SCO: Shanghai Cooperation Organization.

Shahid: Arabic word meaning witness. Religious usage refers to martyrs and is an honorific for those who die fulfilling a religious commandment or in holy war.

Shake and bake: A method of producing methamphetamine quickly.

Sharia: Arabic word meaning path. It refers to God's Law and encompasses but is not limited to the Quran, hadith, and sunnah. It regulates parts of the Fiqh- Islamic jurisprudence, which includes but is not limited to; economics, politics, criminal law, sexuality, hygiene, diet, prayer, fasting, etc.

Sharmut: Arabic vulgar slang for whore.

Shaylah: Female head scarf.

Shia: The second largest branch of the Islamic faith.

Shilpkar   Hindi word used generically to describe a lower caste in Indian culture.

Sirah: An Arabic term that refers to being on a journey. A person's sirah is their path or journey from birth to death and all the events and sayings that occurred in it.

Slammer: Slang term for syringe.

SSG: Pakistani Special Service Group-A commando division of the Pakistan Army.

Sufi: A large branch of the Islamic faith that has influences from Christian, Hindu, and Buddhist faiths.

Sunnah: Arabic word meaning usual habit or custom. A collection of some living habits and sayings of Muhammad.

Sunni: The largest branch of the Islamic faith, accounting for nearly 90% of all Muslims.

Tagging: Graffiti

Taqiyya: Arabic word describing a practice of Shia jurisprudence whereby a Muslim is held blameless before Allah when concealing, hiding, lying, or presenting false oaths about being a Muslim or things about other Muslims during times of persecution or danger.

TCAF: Tactical Conflict Assessment Framework - US military system of diagnosing tactically the causes of conflict in areas of operation.

Teenager: 1/16 ounce methamphetamine $110 - $200.

Thobe: An informal Muslim male robe that covers from the neck to the ankles.

Throw-up: A highly stylized form of graffiti that usually uses more than one color of spray paint.

Tweeker: Slang term for Meth amphetamine addict.

Ummah: Arabic word meaning Muslim nation or community.

US NORTHCOM: United States Northern Command.

UTC: Coordinated Universal Time - A time standard based on International Atomic Time (TAI) and used to technically list global time zones.

Zhonghua: A central concept that encompasses a united China that transcends ethnic divisions.